GREAT
SHORT
STORIES
OF THE
ENGLISH-SPEAKING
WORLD

GREAT SHORT STORIES OF THE ENGLISH-SPEAKING WORLD

*Selected
by the Editors
of
The Reader's
Digest*

With an introduction by Rumer Godden

VOLUME ONE

The Reader's Digest Association
London, Sydney, Cape Town

First published 1977 by
The Reader's Digest Association Limited
25 Berkeley Square, London W1X 6AB

Reprinted 1981

The stories in this volume
appear at their original length except
for minor editing in a few instances, and
for the following, which have been condensed:
The Yellow Wall Paper, Hook,
Bartleby the Scrivener

"Christmas Is a Sad Season for the Poor"
by John Cheever, copyright 1949
The New Yorker Magazine, Inc.
Additional acknowledgments to copyright holders
appear on pages 605 through 607

Filmset by Typesetting Services Ltd., Glasgow and Edinburgh

Printed in Singapore by Tien Wah Press (Pte) Limited,
977 Bukit Timah Road, Singapore 2158.

CONTENTS

INTRODUCTION
BY RUMER GODDEN

A SHORT STORY can come to a writer in an hour; it can take six months; seldom indeed the first—that is vouchsafed to perhaps one writer in a thousand, once in his or her lifetime, a story of such inspiration that it seems almost as if it dictated itself. Usually, the writing takes a long, long time because, contrary to what most people think, the writing of short stories, even if that particular form suits a particular writer so well that he seems chosen for it, is still, as Roald Dahl says, "damnably difficult work"; more difficult than a novel, far more difficult than a biography, only a little less difficult than writing a book for small children or, most difficult of all, a poem.

One should not, of course, attempt a short story without being a born writer. The comparatively mundane ability to toil, have the patience to write a sentence or paragraph over and over again, to verify and clarify, to wrestle with words, may be enough for a biographer or other recorders of "fact"; but it is not enough for a short story writer. He or she needs a stronger impulse than that; he or she has to have an initial inspiration.

That necessary "impulse" or inspiration is usually only a seed—something seen, heard, read or even experienced that, for some reason, does not pass away as most such things do, but lodges in the mind and becomes fertile. Why one thing and not another should set this process off, nobody can tell, least of all the writer; it is part of the mystery of being any kind of artist. For me it is often a title. Once, for instance, it was the title of a picture, "Lily and the Sparrows". (The picture itself was completely non-evocative.)

These "seeds" are what writers are perpetually looking for, which is why all writers are arch-scavengers. Once found or picked up or planted, as with nature, such a seed has to be cultivated and it is here that the difficulty, and the discipline, of the short story begins.

Of course, many short stories are not stories in the strict sense; they are often, rather, "studies" without plot or shape, simply an evocation of a moment or fragment of life, like *The Man Who Saw the Flood*, by Richard Wright; others are built on an experience or happening that is never explained so that the reader has to search for the meaning, as in Eudora Welty's *The Key*, a story of extraordinary depth. Other stories in this collection are stories in the fullest sense of the word, having a plot that has a beginning, a crisis and an end which is sometimes clearly inevitable, sometimes artfully concealed until almost the last sentence, like a sting in the tail. O. Henry was a master of this, but it can be found here not only in his *The Furnished Room* but, for instance, in Aldous Huxley's *The Gioconda Smile* and, with really superb surprise, Edith Wharton's *Roman Fever*; but, no matter what kind of story, the difficulties of writing it are the same.

In a short story, because of its very shortness, there can be nothing that is not necessary to the whole, none of the lengthy descriptions, the digressions and discussions so dear to the novelist. This discipline, of itself, makes for simplicity; a simple style that brings a clarity often revealing more than is actually told; in H. E. Bates's *The Young Man From Kalgoorlie*, a brief tragic story, there is not an unnecessary word, and as in crystal gazing, one seems to see the past and future of the characters as clearly as their present.

Writing a short story is, indeed, almost as much a work of elimination as of creation. This does not make a story thin; it is in fact, a distillation and anything distilled is potent; it takes some four pounds of lavender spikes to make one ounce of lavender essence yet one drop of that essence has a scent stronger than a whole lavender hedge.

Kipling gave this advice: "Take of Indian ink as much as suffices and a camel-hair brush . . . read your final draft and consider faithfully every paragraph, sentence and word, blacking out where requisite. Let it lie by to drain as long as possible. At the end of that time re-read it and you should find it will bear a second shortening. Finally read it aloud alone . . . maybe a shade more brushwork will . . . impose itself . . . I have had tales by me for three or five years which have shortened themselves almost yearly." I am sure *The Elephant's Child* will still be read with delight a thousand years from now.

The thing that strikes most in this Collection, is the astonishing variety; no two stories, though sometimes from the same setting, are alike. Perhaps writers should keep away from other writers; influence is insidious and imitation can only be second best.

Particularly dangerous as an influence are writers like Katherine Mansfield; what she does seems so easy that the best of her stories seem just to "happen", are so entirely natural, that it would seem that anyone with a gift for words could be excused for thinking they could write them. In *The Garden Party* the plot is little more than its seed, which can be traced in her Journal, to a description of her parents' house in New Zealand next door to which lived "a family of half-castes who appeared to have planted their garden with empty jam tins and old saucepans and black iron kettles without lids".

Years later, from this entry, came the story of the garden party held in the big house, though disaster had struck over the hedge; then Laura, the young girl, is ordered to take some of the "party" left-overs to the widow in the hovels. That is all, yet that golden afternoon and its bitter contrast vibrates on and on in a way that is unique.

Not all the stories in this Collection are of this calibre—that would not be possible—but none has a "dead kernel". The lucky reader will find his favourites too: maybe the irony of "Saki" (I had forgotten how deadly he is against Aunts, how he must have suffered), maybe the wit of Graham Greene (*When Greek meets Greek* is a truly funny story), or maybe the gentleness of Elizabeth Jonsson (*The Silver Sky* is as elusive and simple as the Kalahari people she writes of, and exquisite). From Africa as well comes the power of Nadine Gordimer, while from Australia, there is the deeply moving, yet matter-of-fact *Jellicoe* by R. S. Porteous—but they are too many to name; in fact, here lies a fascinating task—out of this great anthology, make your own.

Rye, Sussex.
1977

THE YOUNG MAN FROM KALGOORLIE

H. E. BATES

I

H E LIVED WITH his parents on a sheep-farm two hundred miles north-east of Kalgoorlie. The house was in the old style; a simple white wooden cabin to which a few extensions had been added by successive generations. On the low hills east of the farm there were a few eucalyptus trees; his mother grew pink and mauve asters under the house windows in summer; and in spring the wattle was in blossom everywhere, like lemon foam. All of his life had been lived there, and the war itself was a year old before he knew that it had even begun.

On the bomber station, surrounded by flat grey English hills cropped mostly by sugar-beet and potatoes and steeped in wintertime in thick windless fogs that kept the aircraft grounded for days at a time, he used to tell me how it had come to happen that he did not know the war had started. It seemed that he used to go down to Kalgoorlie only once, perhaps twice, a year. I do not know what sort of place Kalgoorlie is, but it seemed that he did there, on that one visit or so, all the things that anyone can do on a visit to almost any town in the world. He used to take a room for a week at a hotel, get up at what he thought was a late hour every morning—about eight o'clock—and spend most of the day looking at shops, eating, and then looking at shops again. In the evenings he used to take in a cinema, eat another meal, have a couple of glasses of beer in the hotel lounge, and then go to bed. He confessed that it wasn't very exciting and often he was relieved to get back into the Ford and drive steadily back to the sheep-farm and the familiar horizon of eucalyptus trees, which after the streets of Kalgoorlie did not seem a bad prospect at all. The truth was that he did not know anyone in Kalgoorlie except an aunt, his mother's sister, who was very deaf and used a patent electrical acoustic device which always seemed to go wrong whenever he was there and which he had once spent more than a day trying to repair. He was very quiet and he did not easily get mixed up with people; he was never drunk and more than half the time he was worried that his father was making a mess of things at home.

It was this which was really the cause of his not knowing about the war. His father was an unimaginative and rather careless man to whom sheep were simply sheep and grass simply grass and who had kept sheep on the same two thousand acres, within sight of the same eucalyptus trees, for thirty years, and expected to go on keeping them there for the rest of his life. He did not understand that two years of bad luck had anything to do with his having kept sheep in the same way, on the same grass, for so long. It was the son who discovered that. He began to see that the native grasses were played out, and in their place he decided to make sowings of Italian ryegrass and subterranean clover; and soon he was able to change the flocks from one kind of grass to another and then on to a third, and soon he could see an improvement in the health of every breed they had.

After that he was virtually in charge of the farm. His parents, who had always thought him a wonderful person, now thought him more wonderful still. When neighbours came—and this too was not often, since the nearest farm was another thirty miles up country—they talked of nothing but Albert's achievement. The sheep had improved in health, the yield of wool had increased, and even the mutton, they argued, tasted sweeter now, more like the meat of thirty years ago. "Got a proper old-fashioned flavour," his mother said.

It was about a year after these experiments of his—none of them very original, since he had simply read up the whole subject in an agricultural paper—that war broke out. It seemed, as he afterwards found out, that his mother first heard of it on an early morning news bulletin on the radio. She was scared and she called his father. The son himself was out on the farm, riding round on horseback taking a look at the sheep before breakfast. When he came in to breakfast he switched on the radio, but nothing happened. He opened up the radio and took a look at it. All the valves were warm, but the detector valve and another were not operating. It seemed a little odd but he did not take much notice of it. All he could do was to write to Kalgoorlie for the spare valves, and he did so in a letter which he wrote after dinner that day. It was three miles to the post-box and if there were any letters to be posted his mother took them down in the afternoon. His mother took this letter that afternoon and tore it up in little pieces.

That must have happened, he discovered, to every letter he wrote to the Kalgoorlie radio shop in the next twelve months. No valves ever came and gradually, since it was summer and sheep-shearing time and the busiest season of the year, the family got used to being without the radio. His father and mother said they even preferred it. All the time he had no idea of the things they were doing in order to keep the war from him. The incoming post arrived once a week and if there were any letters for him his mother steamed them open, read them and then put the dangerous ones away in a drawer upstairs. The newspapers stopped coming, and when he remarked on it his father said he was tired of wasting good money on papers that were anyway nearly a week old before they came. If there were visitors his mother managed to meet them before they reached the house. In October the sheep-shearing contractors came and his father, ordinarily a rather careful man, gave every man an extra pound to keep his mouth shut. All through that summer and the following winter his mother looked very ill, but it was not until later that he knew the reason of it—the strain of intercepting the letters, of constantly guarded conversation, of warning neighbours and callers, of making excuses and even of lying to him, day after day, for almost a year.

The time came when he decided to go to Kalgoorlie. He always went there about the same time of the year, in late August, before the busy season started. His parents must have anticipated and dreaded that moment, and his father did an amazing thing. In the third week of

August, early one morning, he put two tablespoonfuls of salt in a cup of hot tea and drank it, making himself very sick. By the time Albert came in to breakfast his father was back in bed, very yellow in the face, and his mother was crying because he had been taken suddenly ill. It was the strangest piece of deception of all and it might have succeeded if his father had not overdone things. He decided to remain in bed for a second week, making himself sick every third or fourth day, knowing that once September had come Albert would never leave. But Albert was worried. He did not like the recurrent sickness which now affected his father and he began to fear some sort of internal trouble.

"I'm going to Kalgoorlie whether you like it or not," he said, "to get a doctor."

II

IT WAS ON the bomber station, when he had become a pilot, that he used to tell me of that first day in Kalgoorlie, one of the most remarkable in his life. When he left the farm his mother seemed very upset, and began crying. He felt that she was worried about his father; he was increasingly worried too and promised to be back within three days. Then he drove down to Kalgoorlie alone: perhaps the only man in Australia who did not know that the war was a year old.

He arrived at Kalgoorlie about four o'clock in the afternoon and the town seemed much the same as ever. He drove straight to the hotel he always stayed at, booked himself a room and went upstairs to wash and change. About five o'clock he came down again and went into the hotel lounge for a cup of tea. Except for a word or two with the cashier and lift-boy he did not speak to a soul. He finished his tea and then decided to go to the downstairs saloon, as he always did, to get himself a haircut. There were several people waiting in the saloon, but he decided to wait too. He sat down and picked up a paper.

He must have gone on staring at that paper, not really reading it, for about ten minutes. It was late August and the Nazis were bombing London. He did not understand any of it; who was fighting or what were the causes of it. He simply took in, from the headlines, the story of the great sky battles, the bombing, the murder and destruction, as if they were part of a ghastly fantasy. For the moment he did not feel angry or sick or outraged because he had been deceived. He got up and went out into the street. What he felt, he told me, was very much as if you were suddenly to discover that you had been living in a house where, without knowing it, there was a carrier of smallpox. For months you have lived an ordinary tranquil life, unsuspecting and un-afraid, and then suddenly you made the awful discovery that every fragment of your life, from the dust on your shoes to the air you breathed, was contaminated and that you had been living in danger. Because you knew nothing you were not afraid; but the moment you knew anything all the fears and terrors you had not felt in the past were precipitated into a single terrible moment of realization.

He also felt a fool. He walked up and down the street. As he passed shops, read placards, saw men in service uniform, fragmentary parts of his life during the past year became joined together, making sense: the broken radio, his unanswered letters, the newspapers, his mother's nervousness and the fact, above all, that they had not wanted him to come to Kalgoorlie. Slowly he understood all this. He tried to look on it as the simple cunning of country people. He was still too confused to be angry. But what he still did not understand, and what he had to find out about soon, was the war. He did not even know how long it had been going on. He stopped on a street corner and bought another newspaper. The day before, he read, eighty-seven aircraft had been shot down over England. His hands were trembling as he read it, but it did not tell him the things he wanted to know. And he realized suddenly, as he stood there trembling in the hot sunshine, so amazed that he was still without feeling, that there was no means of knowing these things. He certainly could not know by asking. He imagined for a moment the effect of asking anyone, in the street, or the hotel, or back in the barber's saloon, a simple question like "Can you tell me when the war began?" He felt greatly oppressed by a sense of ridicule and bewilder-ment, by the fear that now, any time he opened his mouth, he was likely to make a ghastly fool of himself.

He walked about for an hour or more, pretending to look at shops, before it occurred to him what to do. Then it came to him quite suddenly that he would go and see the only other person he knew, who, like himself, could be cut off from the world of reality: the deaf aunt who lived in Kalgoorlie.

So he spent most of that evening in the old-fashioned parlour of her house, drinking tea, eating custard tarts, lightly brown with veins of nutmeg, and talking as steadily as he could into the electrical acoustic device fitted to the bodice of her dress. From such remarks as "Things look pretty tough in England. Let's see, how long exactly has it been going on now?" he learned most of the elementary things he wanted to know. But there were still things he could not ask simply because he had no knowledge of them. He could not ask about France or Poland or Holland or Norway. All that he really understood clearly was that England and Germany were at war; that England was being bombed every day by great forces of aircraft; that soon, perhaps, she would be invaded. The simplicity and limitation of his knowledge was in a way, as he said, a good thing. For as he ate the last of the old lady's custard tarts and drank the last cup of tea and said good night to her he changed from being the man who knew least about the war in all Australia to the man who had perhaps the clearest, simplest, and most vivid conception of it in the whole continent. Forty years back his father and mother had emigrated from Lincolnshire to Kalgoorlie. Young, newly wed, and with about eighty pounds apart from their passage money, they started a new life. Now the roots of their existence, and so in a way the roots of his own existence, were being threatened with annihilation. This was the clear, simple, terrible thing he understood in such a clear, simple, terrible way.

When he got back to his hotel he drafted a telegram to his parents, telling them, as well as he could, that he understood. Then in the morning he went round to the nearest recruiting centre. I have not so far described what he was like. He was rather tall, fair, and brown in the face; his eyes were a cool blue and his lips thin, determined, and rather tight. He was just twenty-two and he had no way of holding back his anger.

"I want to be a pilot," he said.

"All right," they said. "Good. But you can't be a pilot all of a sudden, just like that."

"No?" he said. "No? We'll bloody soon see."

HE ADJUSTED HIMSELF as time went on but he carried some of his first angry, clear, terrible conceptions of things across the sea: across the Pacific to Vancouver, across the Atlantic to England. He was never angry with his parents and they in turn ceased being afraid about him. He used to describe to me how he went home on his first leave. From being stupidly affectionate in one way about him they became stupidly affectionate in quite another. They had not wanted him to go; now because he had gone, they behaved as if they had everything to do with sending him and nothing to do with keeping him away. They had arranged a party and he said it was the largest gathering of folks anyone had ever seen on the farm. They invited everyone for thirty miles around and one or two people from fifty miles away. They killed several spring lambs and about fifteen fowls and tea was brewing all day long. At night they sang hymns and old songs in the drawing-room round the piano, and they slept in round beds on the floor. In the end he was almost glad to get away.

He promised to write to them often, and he promised also to keep a diary. He always did write and he always kept the diary. He sailed for Vancouver early in the year and by the spring he was flying Ansons and by the summer he was in England. It was an uncertain and rather treacherous summer and the harvest was wet and late in the corn country where we were. The potato fields were blighted, so that they looked as if spattered by drops of coffee on the dark rainy autumn days, and for long periods low cloud kept the aircraft down. Gradually the harvest fields were cleaned and the potatoes sacked and carted away, and in place of them you could see pale golden cones of sugar-beet piled in the fields and by the roadsides. I mention the weather because it was almost the only thing about England that troubled him. He longed for the hot dry air of the Australian summer and he used to tell me, as we gazed over the wet flat country, of the days when he had flown over Victoria in a Moth in his shirt sleeves and had looked down on the white beaches shining all along the coast in the sun.

The weather troubled him because his anger was still there. He felt that it frustrated him. He could never forget the day in Kalgoorlie when he had first read of the bombing and the mass murder in England and the very headlines of the paper had seemed like an awful dream. He felt that so much of his life had still to be brought up to date. Something had to be vindicated. Yet you could never tell that he was angry. It was easier to tell that he was sometimes afraid: not that he was afraid of dying or being hurt, but of some material thing like mishandling a kite. As he graduated from Moths to Ansons, to Blenheims, and Wellingtons, and finally to Stirlings he felt each time that he would never be big enough for the change to the bigger aircraft, yet it was always because of that fear that he was big enough.

Late that autumn he became captain of a Stirling and about the same time he got to know a girl. Two or three evenings a week, if there were no operations, we used to go down into the town and drink a few glasses of beer at a pub called The Grenadier, and one evening this girl came in. She was very dark and rather sophisticated, with very red lips, and she never wore her coat in the ordinary way but simply had it slung on her shoulders, with the sleeves empty and dangling. "This is Olivia," he said. For some reason I never knew her other name; we most often called her Albert's popsie, but after that, every night we were in The Grenadier, she would come in and soon, after talking for a time, they would go off somewhere alone together. The weather was very bad at that time and he saw her quite often. And then for a few nights it cleared and one night, before going over to Bremen, he asked if I would keep his date with her and make his apologies and explain.

He had arranged to see her at seven o'clock and I made a bad impression by being late. She was irritable because I was late and because, above all, I was the wrong person.

"Don't be angry," I said. "I'm very sorry."

"I'm not angry," she said. "Don't think it. I'm just worried."

"You needn't be worried," I said.

"Why not? Aren't you worried? You're his friend."

"No, I'm not worried," I said. "I'm not worried because I know what sort of pilot he is."

"Oh! you do, do you? Well, what sort of pilot is he?" she said. "He never tells me. He never talks about it at all."

"They never do," I said.

"Sometimes I think I'll never know what sort of person he is at all. Never!"

I felt there was little I could say to her. She was angry because I was the wrong person and because she was frustrated. I bought her several drinks. For a time she was quieter and then once more she got excited.

"One night he'll get shot down and about all I'll know of him is that his name was Albert!"

"Take it easy," I said. "In the first place he won't get shot down."

"No? How are you so sure?"

"Because he's the sort that shoots other people down first."

"Are you trying to be funny?" she said.

"No," I said; and for a few minutes I tried to tell her why it was not funny and why I had spoken that way. I tried quite hard but I do not think she understood. I realized that she knew nothing of all that had happened in Kalgoorlie; the blank year, the awful discovery about England, the bewilderment and the anger. I tried to make her see that there is a type that thinks of nothing but the idea that he may be shot at; and that there is another type, of which he was one, which thinks of nothing but shooting first. "He's glad to go. He wants to go. It's what he lives for," I said. "Don't you see?"

No sooner had I said it than I realized that it was the stupidest thing in the world to say. It was herself, not flying, that she wanted him to live for. She did not understand, and it would have sounded very silly if I had tried to tell her, that he was engaged on something like a mission of vengeance, that because of all that had happened in Kalgoorlie, and especially that one day in Kalgoorlie, he felt that he had something damnable and cruel and hideous to wipe out from his conception of what was a decent life on earth. Every time he went up something was vindicated. Nor did she understand, and again it might have sounded foolish too, that it was the living and positive clarity of the whole idea that was really his preservation. All I could say was, "He's the sort that goes on coming back and coming back until they're fed up with him and make him an instructor."

Nevertheless, that night, her fears were almost justified. The flak over Bremen was very hostile and it seemed that he had to take a lot of hasty evasive action before he could get clear away along the coast.

They had brought him down even then to about 2,000 feet. The search-lights were very thick too and it was like daylight in the aircraft much of the time. But as if he couldn't possibly miss the opportunity, he came down to 300 feet, roaring over the searchlight batteries as his gunners attacked them. They flew for about forty miles in this way, until finally something hit the outer starboard engine and holed the starboard wing. After that they were in a very bad way and got home, as he said, later than originally proposed.

I do not think he told her about this. It went down into his log and some of it may have gone down into the diary he had promised faith-fully to keep for his people back on the farm. He was satisfied that he had blown out about twenty searchlights and that was all. Something else was vindicated. Two days later he had another go. In quite a short daylight attack along the Dutch coast he got into an argument with a flak ship. He was in a very positive mood and he decided to go down to attack. As he was coming in, his rear-gunner sighted a formation of Messerschmitts coming up astern, and two minutes later they attacked him. He must have engaged them for about fifteen minutes. He had always hated Messerschmitts and to be attacked by them made him very angry indeed. At the end of the engagement he had shot down two of them and had crippled a third, but they in turn had holed the aircraft in fifteen places. Nevertheless he went down just to carry out his in-struction of giving the flak ship a goodbye kiss. She had ceased firing and he went in almost to low level and just missed her with his last two bombs by the stern. As he was coming home his outer port engine gave up, but he tootled in just before darkness, quite happy. "A piece o' cake," he said.

I know that he did not tell her about this either, and I could see that she had some excuse for thinking him undemonstrative and perhaps unheroic. For the next two days there was thick fog and rime frost in the early morning that covered the wings of the Stirlings with dusty silver. He was impatient because of the fog and we played many games of cribbage in the mess on the second day, while the crews were stand-ing down.

On the third day he came back from briefing with a very satisfied look on his face. "A little visit to Mr. Salmon and Mr. Gluckstein at

Brest," he said. He had been flying just a year. He had done twenty trips, all af them with the same meaning. It was a bright calm day, without cloud, quite warm in the winter sun. There were pools of water here and there on the runways and looking through the glasses I could see little brushy silver tails spurting up from the wheels of the aircraft as they taxied away.

When I looked into the air, again through the glasses, I saw two aircraft circling round, waiting to formate before setting course. One of them was smoking a little from the outer port engine. The smoking seemed to increase a little and then became black. Suddenly it seemed as if the whole engine burst silently and softly into crimson flower. I kept looking through the glasses, transfixed, but suddenly the aircraft went away behind the hangars as it came down.

That evening I waited until it was quite dark before going into the town. I went into the bar of The Grenadier and the girl was standing by the bar talking to the barmaid. She was drinking a port while waiting for him to come. "Hullo," she said. Her voice was cold and I knew that she was disappointed.

"Hullo. Could you come outside a moment?" I said.

She finished her port and came outside and we stood in the street, in the darkness. Some people went by, shining a torch on the dirty road, and in the light I could see the sleeves of her coat hanging loose, as if she had no arms. I waited until the people had gone by, and then, not knowing how to say it, I told her what had happened. "It wasn't very heroic," I said. "It was damnable luck. Just damnable luck, that's all."

I was very afraid she would cry.

She stood still and quite silent. I felt that I had to do something to comfort her and I made as if to take hold of her arm, but I only caught the sleeve, which was dead and empty. I felt suddenly far away from her and as if we had known two different people: almost as if she had not known him at all. "I'll take you to have a drink," I said.

"No."

"You'll feel better."

"Why did it have to happen?" she said suddenly, raising her voice. "Why did it have to happen?"

"It's the way it often does happen," I said.

"Yes, it's the way it often does happen!" she said. "Is that all you care? Is that all anyone cares? It's the way it happens!" I did not speak. For a moment I was not thinking of her. I was thinking of a young man in a barber's saloon in Kalgoorlie, about to make the shocking disdiscovery that the world was at war and that he did not know it. "Yes, it's the way it happens!" she said. I could not see her face in the darkness, but her voice was very bitter now. "In a week nobody will ever know he flew. He's just one of thousands who go up and never come back. I never knew him. Nobody ever knew him. In a week nobody will know him from anyone else. Nobody will even remember him."

For a moment I did not answer. Now I was not thinking of him. I was thinking of the two people who had so bravely and stupidly kept the war from him and then had so bravely and proudly let him go. I was thinking of the farm with the sheep and the eucalyptus trees, the pink and mauve asters and the yellow spring wattle flaming in the sun. I was thinking of the thousands of farms like it, peopled by thousands of people like them: the simple, decent, kindly, immemorial people all over the earth.

"No," I said to her. "There will be many who will remember him."

THE MAGIC SHOP

H. G. WELLS

I HAD SEEN the Magic Shop from afar several times. I had passed it once or twice, a shop window of alluring little objects, magic balls, magic hens, wonderful cones, ventriloquist dolls, the material of the basket trick, packs of cards that *looked* all right, and all that sort of thing, but never had I thought of going in until one day, almost without warning, Gip hauled me by my finger right up to the window, and so conducted himself that there was nothing for it but to take him in. I had not thought the place was there, to tell the truth—a modest-sized frontage in Regent Street, between the picture shop and the place where the chicks run about just out of patent incubators—but there it was sure enough. I had fancied it was down nearer the Circus, or round the corner in Oxford Street, or even in Holborn; always over the way and a little inaccessible it had been, with something of the mirage in its position; but here it was now quite indisputably, and the fat end of Gip's pointing finger made a noise upon the glass.

"If I was rich," said Gip, dabbing a finger at the Disappearing Egg, "I'd buy myself that. And that"—which was The Crying Baby, Very Human—"and that," which was a mystery, and called, so a neat card asserted, "Buy One and Astonish Your Friends."

"Anything," said Gip, "will disappear under one of those cones. I have read about it in a book."

"And there, dadda, is the Vanishing Halfpenny—only they've put it this way up so's we can't see how it's done."

Gip, dear boy, inherits his mother's breeding, and he did not propose to enter the shop or worry in any way; only, you know, quite unconsciously he lugged my finger doorward, and he made his interest clear.

"That," he said, and pointed to the Magic Bottle.

"If you had that?" I said; at which promising inquiry he looked up with a sudden radiance.

"I could show it to Jessie," he said, thoughtful as ever of others.

"It's less than a hundred days to your birthday, Gibbles," I said, and laid my hand on the door-handle.

Gip made no answer, but his grip tightened on my finger, and so we came into the shop.

It was no common shop this; it was a magic shop, and all the prancing precedence Gip would have taken in the matter of mere toys was wanting. He left the burthen of the conversation to me.

It was a little, narrow shop, not very well lit, and the door-bell pinged again with a plaintive note as we closed it behind us. For a moment or so we were alone and could glance about us. There was a tiger in *papier-maché* on the glass case that covered the low counter—a grave, kind-eyed tiger that waggled his head in a methodical manner; there were several crystal spheres, a china hand holding magic cards, a stock of magic fish-bowls in various sizes, and an immodest magic hat that shamelessly displayed its springs. On the floor were magic mirrors; one to draw you out long and thin, one to swell your head and vanish your legs, and one to make you short and fat like a draught; and while we were laughing at these the shopman, as I suppose, came in.

At any rate, there he was behind the counter—a curious, sallow, dark man, with one ear larger than the other and a chin like the toecap of a boot.

"What can we have the pleasure?" he said, spreading his long, magic fingers on the glass case; and so with a start we were aware of him.

"I want," I said, "to buy my little boy a few simple tricks."

"Legerdemain?" he asked. "Mechanical? Domestic?"

"Anything amusing?" said I.

"Um!" said the shopman, and scratched his head for a moment as if thinking. Then, quite distinctly, he drew from his head a glass ball. "Something in this way?" he said, and held it out.

The action was unexpected. I had seen the trick done at entertainments endless times before—it's part of the common stock of conjurors —but I had not expected it here. "That's good," I said, with a laugh.

"Isn't it?" said the shopman.

Gip stretched out his disengaged hand to take this object and found merely a blank palm.

"It's in your pocket," said the shopman, and there it was!

"How much will that be?" I asked.

"We make no charge for glass balls," said the shopman, politely. "We get them"—he picked one out of his elbow as he spoke—"free." He produced another from the back of his neck, and laid it beside its predecessor on the counter. Gip regarded his glass ball sagely, then directed a look of inquiry at the two on the counter, and finally brought his round-eyed scrutiny to the shopman, who smiled. "You may have those too," said the shopman, "and, if you *don't* mind, one from my mouth. *So!*"

Gip counselled me mutely for a moment, and then in a profound silence put away the four balls, resumed my reassuring finger, and nerved himself for the next event.

"We get all our smaller tricks in that way," the shopman remarked.

I laughed in the manner of one who subscribes to a jest. "Instead of going to the wholesale shop," I said. "Of course, it's cheaper."

"In a way," the shopman said. "Though we pay in the end. But not so heavily—as people suppose. . . . Our larger tricks, and our daily provisions and all the other things we want, we get out of that hat. . . . And you know, sir, if you'll excuse my saying it, there *isn't* a wholesale shop, not for Genuine Magic goods, sir. I don't know if you noticed our inscription—The Genuine Magic Shop." He drew a business card from his cheek and handed it to me. "Genuine," he said, with his finger on the word, and added, "There is absolutely no deception, sir."

He seemed to be carrying out the joke pretty thoroughly, I thought.

He turned to Gip with a smile of remarkable affability. "You, you know, are the Right Sort of Boy."

I was surprised at his knowing that, because, in the interests of discipline, we keep it rather a secret even at home; but Gip received it in unflinching silence, keeping a steadfast eye on him.

"It's only the Right Sort of Boy gets through that doorway."

And, as if by way of illustration, there came a rattling at the door, and a squeaking little voice could be faintly heard. "Nyar! I *warn* 'a go in there, dadda, I WARN 'a go in there. Ny-a-a-ah!" and then the accents of a down-trodden parent, urging consolations and propitiations. "It's locked, Edward," he said.

"But it isn't," said I.

"It is, sir," said the shopman, "always—for that sort of child," and as he spoke we had a glimpse of the other youngster, a little, white face, pallid from sweet-eating and over-sapid food, and distorted by evil passions, a ruthless little egotist, pawing at the enchanted pane. "It's no good, sir," said the shopman, as I moved, with my natural helpfulness, doorward, and presently the spoilt child was carried off howling.

"How do you manage that?" I said, breathing a little more freely.

"Magic!" said the shopman, with a careless wave of the hand, and behold! sparks of coloured fire flew out of his fingers and vanished into the shadows of the shop.

"You were saying," he said, addressing himself to Gip, "before you came in, that you would like one of our 'Buy One and Astonish your Friends' boxes?"

Gip, after a gallant effort, said "Yes."

"It's in your pocket."

And leaning over the counter—he really had an extraordinarily long body—this amazing person produced the article in the customary conjurer's manner.

"Paper," he said, and took a sheet out of the empty hat with the springs; "string," and behold his mouth was a string-box, from which he drew an unending thread, which when he had tied his parcel he bit off—and, it seemed to me, swallowed the ball of string. And then he lit a candle at the nose of one of the ventriloquist's dummies, stuck one of his fingers (which had become sealing-wax red) into the flame, and so sealed the parcel. Then there was the Disappearing Egg, he remarked, and produced one from within my coat-breast and packed it, and also The Crying Baby, Very Human. I handed each parcel to Gip as it was ready, and he clasped them to his chest.

He said very little, but his eyes were eloquent; the clutch of his arms was eloquent. He was the playground of unspeakable emotions. These, you know, were *real* Magics.

Then, with a start, I discovered something moving about in my hat—something soft and jumpy. I whipped it off, and a ruffled pigeon—no doubt a confederate—dropped out and ran on the counter, and went, I fancy, into a cardboard box behind the *papier-maché* tiger.

"Tut, tut!" said the shopman, dexterously relieving me of my head-dress; "careless bird, and—as I live—nesting!"

He shook my hat, and shook out into his extended hand two or three eggs, a large marble, a watch, about half a dozen of the inevitable glass balls, and then crumpled, crinkled paper, more and more and more, talking all the time of the way in which people neglect to brush their hats *inside* as well as out, politely, of course, but with a certain personal application. "All sorts of things accumulate, sir. . . . Not *you*, of course, in particular . . . Nearly every customer. . . . Astonishing what they carry about with them. . . ." The crumpled paper rose and billowed on the counter more and more and more, until he was nearly hidden, from us, until he was altogether hidden, and still his voice went on and on. "We none of us know what the fair semblance of a human being may conceal, sir. Are we all then no better than brushed exteriors, whited sepulchres—"

His voice stopped—exactly like when you hit a neighbour's gramophone with a well-aimed-brick, the same instant silence, and the rustle of the paper stopped, and everything was still. . . .

"Have you done with my hat?" I said, after an interval.

There was no answer.

I stared at Gip, and Gip stared at me, and there were our distortions in the magic mirrors, looking very rum, and grave, and quiet. . . .

"I think we'll go now," I said. "Will you tell me how much all this comes to? . . .

"I say," I said, on a rather louder note, "I want the bill; and my hat, please."

It might have been a sniff from behind the paper pile. . . .

"Let's look behind the counter, Gip," I said. "He's making fun of us."

I led Gip round the head-wagging tiger, and what do you think there was behind the counter? No one at all! Only my hat on the floor, and a common conjurer's lop-eared white rabbit lost in meditation, and looking as stupid and crumpled as only a conjurer's rabbit can do. I resumed my hat, and the rabbit lolloped a lollop or so out of my way.

"Dadda!" said Gip, in a guilty whisper.

"What is it, Gip?" said I.

"I do like this shop, dadda."

"So should I," I said to myself, "if the counter wouldn't suddenly extend itself to shut one off from the door." But I didn't call Gip's attention to that. "Pussy!" he said, with a hand out to the rabbit as it came lolloping past us; "Pussy, do Gip a magic!" and his eyes followed it as it squeezed through a door I had certainly not remarked a moment before. Then this door opened wider, and the man with one ear larger than the other appeared again. He was smiling still, but his eye met mine with something between amusement and defiance. "You'd like to see our show-room, sir," he said, with an innocent suavity. Gip tugged my finger forward. I glanced at the counter and met the shopman's eye again. I was beginning to think the magic just a little too genuine. "We haven't *very* much time," I said. But somehow we were inside the showroom before I could finish that.

"All goods of the same quality," said the shopman, rubbing his flexible hands together, "and that is the Best. Nothing in the place that isn't genuine Magic, and warranted thoroughly rum. Excuse me, sir!"

I felt him pull at something that clung to my coat sleeve, and then I saw he held a little, wriggling red demon by the tail—the little creature bit and fought and tried to get at his hand—and in a moment he tossed it carelessly behind a counter. No doubt the thing was only an image of twisted india-rubber, but for the moment—! And his gesture was exactly that of a man who handles some petty biting bit of vermin. I glanced at Gip, but Gip was looking at a magic rocking-horse. I was glad he hadn't seen the thing. "I say," I said, in an undertone, and indicating Gip, and the red demon with my eyes, "you haven't many things like *that* about, have you?"

"None of ours! Probably brought it with you," said the shopman—also in an undertone, and with a more dazzling smile than ever. "Astonishing what people *will* carry about with them unawares!" And then to Gip, "Do you see anything you fancy here?"

There were many things that Gip fancied there.

He turned to this astonishing tradesman with mingled confidence and respect. "Is that a Magic Sword?" he said.

"A Magic Toy Sword. It neither bends, breaks, nor cuts the fingers. It renders the bearer invincible in battle against any one under eighteen. Half-a-crown to seven and sixpence, according to size. These panoplies on cards are for juvenile knights-errant and very useful —shield of safety, sandals of swiftness, helmet of invisibility."

"Oh, daddy!" gasped Gip.

I tried to find out what they cost, but the shopman did not heed me. He had got Gip now; he had got him away from my finger; he had embarked upon the exposition of all his confounded stock, and nothing was going to stop him. Presently I saw with a qualm of distrust and something very like jealousy that Gip had hold of this person's finger as usually he has hold of mine. No doubt the fellow was interesting, I thought, and had an interestingly faked lot of stuff, really *good* faked stuff, still . . . .

I wandered after them, saying very little, but keeping an eye on this prestidigital fellow. After all, Gip was enjoying it. And no doubt when the time came to go we should be able to go quite easily.

It was a long, rambling place, that show-room, a gallery broken up by stands and stalls and pillars, with archways leading off to other departments, in which the queerest-looking assistants loafed and stared at one, and with perplexing mirrors and curtains. So perplexing, indeed, were these that I was presently unable to make out the door by which we had come.

The shopman showed Gip magic trains that ran without steam or clockwork, just as you set the signals, and then some very, very valuable boxes of soldiers that all came alive directly you took off the lid and said—. I myself haven't a very quick ear and it was a tongue-twisting sound, but Gip—he has his mother's ear—got it in no time. "Bravo!" said the shopman, putting the men back into the box unceremoniously and handing it to Gip. "Now," said the shopman, and in a moment Gip had made them all alive again.

"You'll take that box?" asked the shopman.

"We'll take that box," said I, "unless you charge its full value. In which case it would need a Trust Magnate—"

"Dear heart! *No!*" and the shopman swept the little men back again, shut the lid, waved the box in the air, and there it was, in brown paper, tied up and—*with Gip's full name and address on the paper!*

The shopman laughed at my amazement.

"This is the genuine magic," he said. "The real thing."

"It's a little too genuine for my taste," I said again.

After that he fell to showing Gip tricks, odd tricks, and still odder the way they were done. He explained them, he turned them inside out, and there was the dear little chap nodding his busy bit of a head in the sagest manner.

I did not attend as well as I might. "Hey, presto!" said the Magic Shopman, and then would come the clear small "Hey, presto!" of the boy. But I was distracted by other things. It was being borne in upon me just how tremendously rum this place was; it was, so to speak, inundated by a sense of rumness. There was something a little rum about the fixtures even, about the ceiling, about the floor, about the casually distributed chairs. I had a queer feeling that whenever I wasn't looking at them straight they went askew, and moved about, and played a noiseless puss-in-the-corner behind my back. And the cornice had a serpentine design with masks—masks altogether too expensive for proper plaster.

Then abruptly my attention was caught by one of the odd-looking assistants. He was some way off and evidently unaware of my presence —I saw a sort of three-quarter length of him over a pile of toys and through an arch—and, you know, he was leaning against a pillar in an idle sort of way doing the most horrid things with his features! The particular horrid thing he did was with his nose. He did it just as though he was idle and wanted to amuse himself. First of all it was a short, blobby nose, and then suddenly he shot it out like a telescope, and then out it flew and became thinner and thinner until it was like a long, red, flexible whip. Like a thing in a nightmare it was! He flourished it about and flung it forth as a fly-fisher flings his line.

My instant thought was that Gip mustn't see him. I turned about, and there was Gip quite preoccupied with the shopman, and thinking no evil. They were whispering together and looking at me. Gip was standing on a little stool, and the shopman was holding a sort of big drum in his hand.

"Hide and seek, dadda!" cried Gip. "You're He!"

And before I could do anything to prevent it, the shopman had clapped the big drum over him.

I saw what was up directly. "Take that off," I cried, "this instant! You'll frighten the boy. Take it off!"

The shopman with the unequal ears did so without a word, and held the big cylinder towards me to show its emptiness. And the little stool was vacant! In that instant my boy had utterly disappeared! . . .

You know, perhaps, that sinister something that comes like a hand out of the unseen and grips your heart about. You know it takes your common self away and leaves you tense and deliberate, neither slow nor hasty, neither angry nor afraid. So it was with me.

I came up to this grinning shopman and kicked his stool aside.

"Stop this folly!" I said. "Where is my boy?"

"You see," he said, still displaying the drum's interior, "there is no deception—"

I put out my hand to grip him, and he eluded me by a dexterous movement. I snatched again, and he turned from me and pushed open a door to escape. "Stop!" I said, and he laughed, receding. I leapt after him—into utter darkness.

Thud!

"Lor' bless my 'eart! I didn't see you coming, sir!"

I was in Regent Street, and I had collided with a decent-looking working man; and a yard away, perhaps, and looking a little perplexed with himself, was Gip. There was some sort of apology, and then Gip had turned and come to me with a bright little smile, as though for a moment he had missed me.

And he was carrying four parcels in his arm!

He secured immediate possession of my finger.

For the second I was rather at a loss. I stared round to see the door of the magic shop, and, behold, it was not there! There was no door, no shop, nothing, only the common pilaster between the shop where they sell pictures and the window with the chicks! . . .

I did the only thing possible in that mental tumult; I walked straight to the kerbstone and held up my umbrella for a cab.

"'Ansoms," said Gip, in a note of culminating exultation.

I helped him in, recalled my address with an effort, and got in also. Something unusual proclaimed itself in my tail-coat pocket, and I felt and discovered a glass ball. With a petulant expression I flung it into the street.

Gip said nothing.

For a space neither of us spoke.

"Dadda!" said Gip, at last, "that *was* a proper shop!"

I came round with that to the problem of just how the whole thing had seemed to him. He looked completely undamaged—so far, good; he was neither scared nor unhinged, he was simply tremendously satisfied with the afternoon's entertainment, and there in his arms were the four parcels.

Confound it! what could be in them?

"Um!" I said. "Little boys can't go to shops like that every day."

He received this with his usual stoicism, and for a moment I was sorry I was his father and not his mother, and so couldn't suddenly there, *coram publico*, in our hansom, kiss him. After all, I thought, the thing wasn't so very bad.

But it was only when we opened the parcels that I really began to be reassured. Three of them contained boxes of soldiers, quite ordinary lead soldiers, but of so good a quality as to make Gip altogether forget that originally these parcels had been Magic Tricks of the only genuine sort, and the fourth contained a kitten, a little living white kitten, in excellent health and appetite and temper.

I saw this unpacking with a sort of provisional relief. I hung about in the nursery for quite an unconscionable time. . . .

That happened six months ago. And now I am beginning to believe it is all right. The kitten had only the magic natural to all kittens, and the soldiers seem as steady a company as any colonel could desire. And Gip—?

The intelligent parent will understand that I have to go cautiously with Gip.

But I went so far as this one day. I said, "How would you like your soldiers to come alive, Gip, and march about by themselves?"

"Mine do," said Gip. "I just have to say a word I know before I open the lid."

"Then they march about alone?"

"Oh, *quite*, dadda. I shouldn't like them if they didn't do that."

I displayed no unbecoming surprise, and since then I have taken occasion to drop in upon him once or twice, unannounced, when the soldiers were about, but so far I have never discovered them performing in anything like a magical manner. . . .

It is so difficult to tell.

There's also a question of finance. I have an incurable habit of paying bills. I have been up and down Regent Street several times, looking for that shop. I am inclined to think, indeed, that in that matter honour is satisfied, and that, since Gip's name and address are known to them, I may very well leave it to these people, whoever they may be, to send in their bill in their own time.

THE ROCKPILE

JAMES BALDWIN

James Baldwin

ACROSS THE STREET from their house, in an empty lot between two houses, stood the rockpile. It was a strange place to find a mass of natural rock jutting out of the ground; and someone, probably Aunt Florence, had once told them that the rock was there and could not be taken away because without it the subway cars underground would fly apart, killing all the people. This, touching on some natural mystery concerning the surface and the center of the earth, was far too intriguing an explanation to be challenged, and it invested the rockpile, moreover, with such mysterious importance that Roy felt it to be his right, not to say his duty, to play there.

Other boys were to be seen there each afternoon after school and all day Saturday and Sunday. They fought on the rockpile. Surefooted, dangerous, and reckless, they rushed each other and grappled on the heights, sometimes disappearing down the other side in a confusion of dust and screams and upended, flying feet. "It's a wonder they don't kill themselves," their mother said, watching sometimes from the fire escape. "You children stay away from there, you hear me?" Though she said "children," she was looking at Roy, where he sat beside John on the fire escape. "The good Lord knows," she continued, "I don't want you to come home bleeding like a hog every day the Lord sends." Roy shifted impatiently, and continued to stare at the street, as though in this gazing he might somehow acquire wings. John said nothing. He had not really been spoken to: he was afraid of the rockpile and of the boys who played there.

Each Saturday morning John and Roy sat on the fire escape and watched the forbidden street below. Sometimes their mother sat in the room behind them, sewing, or dressing their younger sister, or nursing the baby, Paul. The sun fell across them and across the fire escape with a high, benevolent indifference; below them, men and women, and boys and girls, sinners all, loitered; sometimes one of the church members passed and saw them and waved. Then, for the moment that they waved decorously back, they were intimidated. They watched the saint, man or woman, until he or she had disappeared from sight. The passage of one of the redeemed made them consider, however vacantly, the wickedness of the street, their own latent wickedness in sitting where they sat; and made them think of their father, who came home early on Saturdays and who would soon be turning this corner and entering the dark hall below them.

But until he came to end their freedom, they sat, watching and longing above the street. At the end of the street nearest their house was the bridge which spanned the Harlem River and led to a city called the Bronx, which was where Aunt Florence lived. Nevertheless, when they saw her coming, she did not come from the bridge, but from the opposite end of the street. This, weakly, to their minds, she explained by saying that she had taken the subway, not wishing to walk, and that, besides, she did not live in *that* section of the Bronx. Knowing that the Bronx was across the river, they did not believe this story ever, but, adopting toward her their father's attitude, assumed that she had just left some sinful place which she dared not name, as, for example, a movie palace.

In the summertime boys swam in the river, diving off the wooden dock, or wading in from the garbage-heavy bank. Once a boy, whose name was Richard, drowned in the river. His mother had not known where he was; she had even come to their house, to ask if he was there. Then, in the evening, at six o'clock, they had heard from the street a woman screaming and wailing; and they ran to the windows and looked out. Down the street came the woman, Richard's mother, screaming, her face raised to the sky and tears running down her face. A woman walked beside her, trying to make her quiet and trying to hold her up. Behind them walked a man, Richard's father, with Richard's body in his arms. There were two white policemen walking in the gutter, who did not seem to know what should be done. Richard's father and Richard were wet, and Richard's body lay across his father's arms like a cotton baby. The woman's screaming filled the street; cars slowed down and the people in the cars stared; people opened their windows and looked out and came rushing out of doors to stand in the gutter, watching. Then the small procession disappeared within the house which stood beside the rockpile. Then, *"Lord, Lord, Lord!"* cried Elizabeth, their mother, and slammed the window down.

One Saturday, an hour before his father would be coming home, Roy was wounded on the rockpile and brought screaming upstairs. He and John had been sitting on the fire escape and their mother had gone into the kitchen to sip tea with Sister McCandless. By and by Roy became bored and sat beside John in restless silence; and John began drawing into his schoolbook a newspaper advertisement which featured a new electric locomotive. Some friends of Roy passed beneath the fire escape and called him. Roy began to fidget, yelling down to them through the bars. Then a silence fell. John looked up. Roy stood looking at him.

"I'm going downstairs," he said.

"You better stay where you is, boy. You know Mama don't want you going downstairs."

"I be right *back*. She won't even know I'm gone, less you run and tell her."

"I ain't *got* to tell her. What's going to stop her from coming in here and looking out the window?"

"She's talking," Roy said. He started into the house.

"But Daddy's going to be home soon!"

"I be back before *that*. What you all the time got to be so *scared* for?" He was already in the house and he now turned, leaning on the windowsill, to swear impatiently, "I be back in *five* minutes."

John watched him sourly as he carefully unlocked the door and disappeared. In a moment he saw him on the sidewalk with his friends. He did not dare to go and tell his mother that Roy had left the fire escape, because he had practically promised not to. He started to shout, *Remember, you said five minutes!* but one of Roy's friends was looking up at the fire escape. John looked down at his schoolbook; he became engrossed again in the problem of the locomotive.

When he looked up again he did not know how much time had passed, but now there was a gang fight on the rockpile. Dozens of boys fought each other in the harsh sun: clambering up the rocks and battling hand to hand, scuffed shoes sliding on the slippery rock; filling the bright air with curses and jubilant cries. They filled the air, too, with flying weapons: stones, sticks, tin cans, garbage, whatever could be picked up and thrown.

John watched in a kind of absent amazement—until he remembered that Roy was still downstairs, and that he was one of the boys on the rockpile. Then he was afraid; he could not see his brother among the figures in the sun; and he stood up, leaning over the fire-escape railing. Then Roy appeared from the other side of the rocks; John saw that his shirt was torn; he was laughing. He moved until he stood at the very top of the rockpile.

Then something, an empty tin can, flew out of the air and hit him on the forehead, just above the eye. Immediately, one side of Roy's face ran with blood; he fell and rolled on his face down the rocks. Then for a moment there was no movement at all, no sound; the sun, arrested, lay on the street and the sidewalk and the arrested boys. Then someone screamed or shouted; boys began to run away, down the street, toward the bridge. The figure on the ground, having caught its breath and felt its own blood, began to shout. John cried, "Mama! Mama!" and ran inside.

"Don't fret, don't fret," panted Sister McCandless as they rushed down the dark, narrow, swaying stairs, "don't fret. Ain't a boy been born don't get his knocks every now and again. *Lord!*" They hurried into the sun.

A man had picked Roy up and now walked slowly toward them. One or two boys sat silent on their stoops; at either end of the street there was a group of boys watching. "He ain't hurt bad," the man said. "Wouldn't be making this kind of noise if he was hurt real bad."

Elizabeth, trembling, reached out to take Roy, but Sister McCandless, bigger, calmer, took him from the man and threw him over her shoulder as she once might have handled a sack of cotton. "God bless you," she said to the man, "God bless you, son." Roy was still screaming. Elizabeth stood behind Sister McCandless to stare at his bloody face.

"It's just a flesh wound," the man kept saying, "just broke the skin, that's all." They were moving across the sidewalk, toward the house. John, not now afraid of the staring boys, looked toward the corner to see if his father was yet in sight.

Upstairs, they hushed Roy's crying. They bathed the blood away, to find, just above the left eyebrow, the jagged, superficial scar.

"Lord, have mercy," murmured Elizabeth, "another inch and it would've been his eye." And she looked with apprehension toward the clock. "Ain't it the truth," said Sister McCandless, busy with bandages and iodine.

"When did he go downstairs?" his mother asked at last.

Sister McCandless now sat fanning herself in the easy chair, at the head of the sofa where Roy lay, bound and silent. She paused for a moment to look sharply at John. John stood near the window, holding the newspaper advertisement and the drawing he had done.

"We was sitting on the fire escape," he said. "Some boys he knew called him."

"When?"

"He said he'd be back in five minutes."

"Why didn't you tell me he was downstairs?"

He looked at his hands, clasping his notebook, and did not answer.

"Boy," said Sister McCandless, "you hear your mother a-talking to you?"

He looked at his mother. He repeated:

"He said he'd be back in five minutes."

"He said he'd be back in five minutes," said Sister McCandless with scorn; "don't look to me like that's no right answer. You's the man of the house, you supposed to look after your baby brothers and sisters—you ain't supposed to let them run off and get half killed. But I expect," she added, rising from the chair, dropping the cardboard fan, "your Daddy'll make you tell the truth. Your Ma's way too soft with you."

He did not look at her, but at the fan where it lay in the dark red, depressed seat where she had been. The fan advertised a pomade for the hair and showed a brown woman and her baby, both with glistening hair, smiling happily at each other.

"Honey," said Sister McCandless, "I got to be moving along. Maybe I drop in later tonight. I don't reckon you going to be at Tarry Service tonight?" Tarry Service was the prayer meeting held every Saturday night at church to strengthen believers and prepare the church for the coming of the Holy Ghost on Sunday.

"I don't reckon," said Elizabeth. She stood up; she and Sister McCandless kissed each other on the cheek. "But you be sure to remember me in your prayers."

"I surely will do that." She paused, with her hand on the doorknob, and looked down at Roy and laughed. "Poor little man," she said, "reckon he'll be content to sit on the fire escape *now*."

Elizabeth laughed with her. "It sure ought to be a lesson to him. You don't reckon," she asked nervously, still smiling, "he going to keep that scar, do you?"

"Lord, no," said Sister McCandless, "ain't nothing but a scratch. I declare, Sister Grimes, you worse than a child. Another couple of weeks and you won't be able to *see* no scar. No, you go on about your housework, honey, and thank the Lord it weren't no worse." She opened the door; they heard the sound of feet on the stairs. "I expect that's the Reverend," said Sister McCandless placidly. "I *bet* he going to raise cain."

"Maybe it's Florence," Elizabeth said. "Sometimes she get here about this time." They stood in the doorway, staring, while the steps reached the landing below and began again climbing to their floor. "No," said Elizabeth then, "that ain't her walk. That's Gabriel."

"Well, I'll just go on," said Sister McCandless, "and kind of prepare his mind." She pressed Elizabeth's hand as she spoke and started into the hall, leaving the door behind her slightly ajar. Elizabeth turned slowly back into the room. Roy did not open his eyes, or move; but she knew that he was not sleeping; he wished to delay until the last possible moment any contact with his father. John put his newspaper and his notebook on the table and stood, leaning on the table, staring at her.

"It wasn't my fault," he said. "I couldn't stop him from going downstairs."

"No," she said, "you ain't got nothing to worry about. You just tell your Daddy the truth."

He looked directly at her, and she turned to the window, staring into the street. What was Sister McCandless saying? Then from her bedroom she heard Delilah's thin wail and she turned, frowning, looking toward the bedroom and toward the still open door. She knew that John was watching her. Delilah continued to wail; she thought, angrily, *Now that girl's getting too big for that*, but she feared that Delilah would awaken Paul and she hurried into the bedroom. She tried to soothe Delilah back to sleep. Then she heard the front door open and close—too loud; Delilah raised her voice; with an exasperated sigh Elizabeth picked the child up. Her child and Gabriel's, her children and Gabriel's: Roy, Delilah, Paul. Only John was nameless and a stranger, living, unalterable testimony to his mother's days in sin.

"What happened?" Gabriel demanded. He stood, enormous, in the center of the room, his black lunch box dangling from his hand, staring at the sofa where Roy lay.

John stood just before him, it seemed to her astonished vision just below him, beneath his fist, his heavy shoe. The child stared at the man in fascination and terror—when a girl down home she had seen rabbits stand so paralyzed before the barking dog. She hurried past Gabriel to the sofa, feeling the weight of Delilah in her arms like the weight of a shield, and stood over Roy, saying:

"Now, ain't a thing to get upset about, Gabriel. This boy sneaked downstairs while I had my back turned and got hisself hurt a little. He's all right now."

Roy, as though in confirmation, now opened his eyes and looked gravely at his father. Gabriel dropped his lunch box with a clatter and knelt by the sofa.

"How you feel, son? Tell your Daddy what happened?"

Roy opened his mouth to speak and then, relapsing into panic, began to cry. His father held him by the shoulder.

"You don't want to cry. You's Daddy's little man. Tell your Daddy what happened."

"He went downstairs," said Elizabeth, "where he didn't have no business to be, and got to fighting with them bad boys playing on that rockpile. That's what happened and it's a mercy it weren't nothing worse."

He looked up at her. "Can't you let this boy answer me for hisself?"

Ignoring this, she went on, more gently: "He got cut on the forehead, but it ain't nothing to worry about."

"You call a doctor? How you know it ain't nothing to worry about?"

"Is you got money to be throwing away on doctors? No, I ain't called no doctor. Ain't nothing wrong with my eyes that I can't tell whether he's hurt bad or not. He got a fright more'n anything else, and you ought to pray God it teaches him a lesson."

"You got a lot to say *now*," he said, "but I'll have *me* something to say in a minute. I'll be wanting to know when all this happened, what you was doing with your eyes *then*." He turned back to Roy, who had lain quietly sobbing, eyes wide open and body held rigid; and who now, at his father's touch, remembered the height, the sharp, sliding rock beneath his feet, the sun, the explosion of the sun, his plunge into darkness and his salty blood; and recoiled, beginning to scream, as his father touched his forehead. "Hold still, hold still," crooned his father, shaking, "hold still. Don't cry. Daddy ain't going to hurt you, he just wants to see this bandage, see what they've done to his little man." But Roy continued to scream and would not be still and Gabriel dared not lift the bandage for fear of hurting him more. And he looked at Elizabeth in fury: "Can't you put that child down and help me with this boy? John, take your baby sister from your mother—don't look like neither of you got good sense."

John took Delilah and sat down with her in the easy chair. His mother bent over Roy and held him still, while his father, carefully— but still Roy screamed—lifted the bandage and stared at the wound. Roy's sobs began to lessen. Gabriel readjusted the bandage. "You see," said Elizabeth, finally, "he ain't nowhere near dead."

"It sure ain't your fault that he ain't dead." He and Elizabeth considered each other for a moment in silence. "He came mighty close to losing an eye. Course, his eyes ain't as big as your'n, so I reckon you don't think it matters so much." At this her face hardened; he smiled. "Lord, have mercy," he said, "you think you ever going to learn to do right? Where was you when all this happened? Who let him go downstairs?"

"Ain't nobody let him go downstairs, he just went. He got a head just like his father, it got to be broken before it'll bow. I was in the kitchen."

"Where was Johnnie?"

"He was in here."

"Where?"

"He was on the fire escape."

"Didn't he know Roy was downstairs?"

"I reckon."

"What you mean, you reckon? He ain't got your big eyes for nothing, does he?" He looked over at John. "Boy, you see your brother go downstairs?"

"Gabriel, ain't no sense in trying to blame Johnnie. You know right well if you have trouble making Roy behave, he ain't going to listen to his brother. He don't hardly listen to me."

"How come you didn't tell your mother Roy was downstairs?"

John said nothing, staring at the blanket which covered Delilah.

"Boy, you hear me? You want me to take a strap to you?"

"No, you ain't," she said. "You ain't going to take no strap to this boy, not today you ain't. Ain't a soul to blame for Roy's lying up there now but you—you because you done spoiled him so that he thinks he can do just anything and get away with it. I'm here to tell you that ain't no way to raise no child. You don't pray to the Lord to help you do better than you been doing, you going to live to shed bitter tears that the Lord didn't take his soul today." And she was trembling. She moved, unseeing, toward John and took Delilah from his arms. She looked back at Gabriel, who had risen, who stood near the sofa, staring at her. And she found in his face not fury alone, which would not have surprised her; but hatred so deep as to become insupportable in its lack of personality.

His eyes were struck alive, unmoving, blind with malevolence—she felt, like the pull of the earth at her feet, his longing to witness her perdition. Again, as though it might be propitiation, she moved the child in her arms. And at this his eyes changed, he looked at Elizabeth, the mother of his children, the helpmeet given by the Lord. Then her eyes clouded; she moved to leave the room; her foot struck the lunch box lying on the floor.

"John," she said, "pick up your father's lunch box like a good boy."

She heard, behind her, his scrambling movement as he left the easy chair, the scrape and jangle of the lunch box as he picked it up, bending his dark head near the toe of his father's heavy shoe.

THE BLACK MAMBA
ERNEST GLANVILLE

Ernest Glanville

WE WERE talking about snakes at the little roadside *winkle*—a composite shop, where you could buy moist black sugar, tinned butter, imported; tinned milk, also imported; cotton, prints, boots, "square face", tobacco, dates, nails, gunpowder, cans, ribbons, tallow candles, and the *Family Herald*.

We always did talk about snakes when other topics failed, and no one had been fishing for some time, and the big pumpkin season had passed.

"Man," said Lanky John, the ostrich farmer, "I killed a snake, a ringhals, yesterday morning back of the kraal, and in the evening when I went by there was a live ringhals coiled round the dead one."

"There's a lot of love among snakes," said Abe Pike, who had swapped a bushbuck hide for a pound of coffee and a roll of tobacco. "They don't talk much, but they think a lot, and you can't plumb the feelings of silent folk; they're that deep."

"Ever been in love, Uncle?" asked Lanky John, popping a big lump of black sugar into his mouth.

"I guess it won't take more'n a foot measure to get to the bottom of your feelings, tho' you are long enough to be a telegraft pole," snorted Uncle Abe.

"Snakes haven't got any brain," said Lanky John, after an awkward pause.

"No more has a whip-stick," said the old man, with a contemptuous glance at Lanky's long, thin limbs.

"That's true," replied John, with a wink at us; "though I've heard of a snake that glued on to a whip-stick all for love of you, Uncle."

"Snakes," said Abe, "knows when to speak and when to keep shut, which is more than some folk can do. If you come unexpected on a snake in a path, and he sees your foot coming down on him, he lets you know he's about, and that foot of yours is jest fixed in the air. Well, suppose that snake is not in the path, but jest stretched out 'longside, he don't call out. For why? 'Cos he knows it's safer for him and for you that he should keep quiet. I tell you there's not a man here who hasn't time and again passed in the dark within a few inches of a snake."

A listener, who was seated in a dark corner, moved out into the sunshine.

"Did I ever tell you that yarn about the black mamba?"

"You never did, old man, so shove along."

"You may thank your stars there's no mambas down in this country, for of all critturs that crawl, or fly, or walk, there's not one for nateral cussedness and steady hate to come up to a black mamba. Why! thunder! if there was a mamba in these parts, and he'd a grudge against me, I'd move off a hundred miles to where my sister 'Liza lives."

"A hundred miles! That's a good step."

"Maybe it wouldn't be fur enough neither. You wait! Ten years ago I was riding goods to the Diamond Fields, and after one trip I was starting back with the empty wagon, there being no produce to load up with, when a chap came up and offered three guineas for his passage. Well, a man's wagon is his home, and you don't want to give a fellow the run of your tent for a month without knowing something about him. So I jes looked him all over—saw that his boots were worn out, and that he kep' looking over his shoulder, when he climbed into the wagon and drew the blanket over him—though the sun was fierce enough to light your pipe. He gave me sich a look when he went in that

I had not the heart to drag him out, and off I trekked. He didn't join me at the fire that night, and when I climbed in, thinking he was asleep, he was shiverin' as though he had the ague. Well, I gave him a glass of Cango and went to sleep. At sunrise I trekked again, and bymby I see him draw the canvas aside and look back over the veld, which was as flat as the palm of my hand. Thinks I, he's expecting the police, but I let him be, and at dinner he came out, looking as skeered as a monkey with a candle. First he took a walk round the wagon, then he shaded his eyes as he glanced over the veld, then he took a bite and a look, then a sip and a look.

" 'What are you looking for?' says I.

"He let the beaker fall out of his hands and turned white.

" 'Have you seen it?' he whispered, with a sort of choke.

" 'Seen what?' I said.

" 'I don't feel well,' he answered, with a twitch for a smile, and climbed back into the wagon.

"I tell you his looks made me feel queer, and I slept that night under the wagon. Well, I made a long skoff the next day, crossed the Modder River, and no sooner'd we get across than the river came down with a rush, brimming full with a boiling yeller flood right up to the lip of the steep banks. That coon spent the whole day on the bank watching the other side, and fixing his eyes on every tree and branch that went sailing down.

" 'It's a grand flood,' he said, rubbing his hands together; ''twould sweep a whale away like a piece of straw.'

" 'Yes, and a policeman too, eh?' said I, looking at him hard.

"He noticed the meaning in my words, and a human smile broke over his face, chasing away the worried look that seemed carved into it. 'Policeman,' he said. 'I've no cause to fear a policeman, or any man. Good God!' he cried, catching me by the arm, 'what's that?'

" 'Where?' said I, fit to jump out of my skin for the terror in his face.

"He stood there with his eyes glaring at the water, and a shaking finger pointing into the very heart of the yeller flood. There stood out the root of a tree, and clinging to the root the coils of a snake, with his gleaming head moving like a branch. Jest a moment it showed, then the water swirled over it again.

" 'Let go of my arm,' I said, for his fingers were biting into me, and the look of him made me afeard, so that I talked gruffly.

" 'Did you see it?' he said, and then he jest collapsed like a bundle of clothes. I had a good mind to leave him there, but, instead, I histed him onto my shoulders, and poured enough Cango into him to make him forget his name. He wasn't fit to stand until a couple of days after, and then wha' jer think he did? Cut up his clothes into shreds and laughed fit to kill himself when I found him at it. Of course, I thought he was clean daft, but he weren't, and for the first time, with my old corduroys on him, he sat by the camp fire, sipping his coffee, and talking—talking mainly about snakes and bloodhounds, and things that made my backbone whang like a broken fiddle-string. He frightened himself, too, so that when he saw the long *achter-oss* sjambok quivering on the ground where the driver had thrown it, his jaw got rigid, and moved up and down without any words coming from his mouth. Then, with a sort of sob, he snatched up the axe, and I'm blowed if he didn't cut that sjambok into a thousand bits. It was a good sjambok, too, made of rhinoceros hide, as thick as your wrist at the butt and going off to a point, and when I told the idiot what he'd done, he jes went off into another unnateral fit of wild laughter, after which he paid me a guinea and went to bed. Putting this, that, and the other together, with the Cango brandy, I guessed my man had got snakes in his head, and I kept the demijohn under lock. That calmed him down, and he was all right until we came to the Orange River, where we had to camp while the water went down. About fifty wagons were there waiting to cross, and there was quite a stir with all the fellows moving about visiting. When we had outspanned, I joined a group to hear about the state of the roads, the condition of the veld for grazing, and all them things that transport riders talk about, when one chap asked if I had heard the news. 'What news?' says I. 'About that snake,' says he; 'he was seen at the Riet River drift last week.' 'Yes,' says another, 'and two days before he was at Aliwal North.' 'I heard from the mail coach driver,' says a third, 'that the snake overtook his coach, stopped the horses, and took a steady look at all the passengers, after which he went across the veld, leaving 'em all frozen with terror. It was twenty feet long, and its eyes were like black diamonds.'

"Of course, I wasn't swallering that, but when I told my traveller the sweat gathered in big drops on his forehead, and the old hunted look came into his face. 'You don't believe this silly yarn?' says I, placing my hand on his shoulder. 'Believe it, man!' he said. 'Good heavens! that snake is after me.' 'After you,' says I. 'Yes,' says he, making an effort to swallow something. 'It has chased me up and down over a thousand miles for two months.' 'Nonsense!' I said; 'you're nervous and fanciful.' 'Listen,' he said. 'Two months ago I was hunting in the Zulu country, and one day, ten miles away from my camp, I shot a mamba. I took the body back with me to skin it; but when the two blacks I had with me saw it, they cried out to me to take it away, or the mamba's mate would come in the night. I left them sleeping by the fire, and the next morning they were still sleeping—ay, they were sleeping the last sleep, for the mamba had been in the night.

" 'As I looked at them, with the blood in me like water, I heard a heavy breathing, and saw my horse on the ground, his eyes glazed and his nostrils fighting for breath, while resting on his body, was the awful head of a mamba, his eyes fixed on mine, and his forked tongue darting in and out. I fired at him with the rifle barrel, but clean missed in my flurry; then I ran until my courage came back. I found that I had left the powder behind and slowly turned back. I had not gone a hundred paces when I met him on my track, slipping like a black streak through the grass, and I thought of nothing then but escape. After a time I met a party of Zulus, but when I asked for their assistance, they fled with loud cries of alarm, and at a Zulu kraal, where I stopped to ask for thick milk, they drove me out when they learnt why it was I fled. That night as I slept that snake coiled by my side.'

" 'What!'

" 'Yes; he could have struck me then, but he preferred to have full vengeance. I woke at the flicker of his tongue on my cheek, thinking it was a fly—a fly! good Lord! and my hand fell upon his cold, sinewy folds, and his head was resting on my shoulder. Ever since he has been after me, with a deadly hate that is slowly driving me mad. Sometimes he disappears, but I never escape from the glint of his unwinking eyes, and one day he will strike, unless—unless—'

" 'Well?' said I, looking at his drawn face.

" 'Unless,' he said, 'I forestall him.'

" 'No, my lad,' said I, 'for that would be a sin, and when you are stronger this dream of yours will go.'

"He looked so fallen in, so weak, all of a sudden, that I took him for a walk to the river, and the rush of the waters seemed to comfort him. He sat on a big boulder looking across, and the whiteness presently went from his cheeks.

" 'I've got an idea,' he said, 'if I could reach the other side I'd be all right again.'

"We sat there in a sort of dream for an hour or two, when I happened to look round, and right there on the flat on the ground was stretched out the biggest and ugliest snake I ever saw, black as night, with a great vicious diamond-shaped head, and a pair of eyes that glowed all colours. He looked as if he'd travelled; his scales, instead of being glossy, were dull with scratches here and there, and his skin had a sort of bagginess as if he hadn't eaten for weeks. As soon as he saw me turn he raised his head about five feet from the ground, and from his eyes there shot a look that jest kept me fixed like a stone. Then that poor young feller on the stone began to speak again, in a soft way, of the river and its journey to the sea.

" 'I wish,' he said, 'I could look on the sea again.' Then I heard him move, and I knew he was looking into the eyes of his enemy, for that snake began to sway his head to and fro, to and fro, while his tail went twisting in and out, sending his body nearer and nearer. Suddenly there was a shriek, and a splash, and the snake went by me—streamed over the rock into the water, and when I leapt to my feet with a yell that startled the whole camp, I saw an arm thrust above the yeller flood, and above the arm the bend of the black snake, his head turned down looking into the water, and a coil of his body around the elbow. Ole Abe Pike has swound away once, and that was the time. Yes; there was his black body gleaming with the water on it, and his head turned towards the face of the enemy—that poor chap he had follered over three countries for one thousand miles—one thousand English miles."

"That a true story, Uncle Abe?"

"Ain't I told it? That's why I gave up transport riding. I darsn't go near the Orange River again."

THE PIONEER HEP-CAT

JOHN O'HARA

[signature: John O'Hara]

EVERY TIME I come here you all seem to want to hear some more about Red Watson. I declare, if I ever thought there would have been such a demand for stories about Red Watson I would have sat down and written a book about him. I've told you story after story about people that I thought were much more interesting than Reds. Big people. People that made something of themselves instead of a man that nobody ever heard of outside of two or three counties in Pennsylvania, and even here the name Red Watson never meant a thing to people generally considered worthwhile. You young people nowadays, I'd much rather tell you about a mine boy, a young lad that worked in a breaker but was rescued from that and went away to a seminary and became a cardinal. We had one young fellow in this town that most of you don't even know he was born here, but he was. I'm talking about General Henry T. Corrigan. Lieutenant General Corrigan was born right here in this town and sold papers here till his family moved away. I used to play ball with Henny Corrigan, out at the old Fourteenth Street schoolyard. He caught, and I played shortstop on a team we used to have, called the Athletics. I guess *some* of you would be able to guess where we got that name. Those of you that can't guess, we didn't get the name from Kansas City, if that's any hint. And I might mention that a few years ago, when I was attending the newspaper editors' convention in New York City, the principal speaker was none other than Lieutenant General Henry T. Corrigan, all decorated with a chestful of ribbons and surrounded by famous editors and publishers from all over the country, all wanting to ask him questions about the

Strategic Air Command. And there I was, not a very important person I must admit, but when it came my turn to meet the general he looked at me and then he looked at my name on the convention badge we were all wearing and he burst into a big smile. "Winky Breslin!" he said. That was my nickname when I was young. "Winky, you old son of a gun," and with that he took me by the arm and the two of us went over and sat down and you'd be surprised how many local people he remembered, some now dead and gone, but quite a few still living. Some of them the parents and grandparents of you here today. I ran a little story about it at the time, but I guess not many of you saw it. In any case, that's the kind of man I'd rather talk about, but every time I'm asked to speak at one of your Press Club suppers your representative either asks me outright or gives me a strong hint to the effect that the person you'd like me to talk about is Red Watson. I don't understand it.

I'd understand it a lot better if Reds were still alive, and some rock-and-roll idol. But he passed away before you even had swing, let alone rock-and-roll. And it isn't as if there were any of his old records floating around. Reds never made a record in his life. I don't say he wouldn't have been good, or popular. He would have been. If they'd ever heard of him outside of this section of the country, he might have been, well, not as popular as Gene Austin, or the early Crosby. He had a totally different style. As I've told you before, or your predecessors, there's nobody around today to compare him with. The styles of singing have changed so much from when Reds was around. Beginning I'd say with Rudy Vallee and then on to Russ Columbo and Bing, the crooners came in. All toned down as far as the volume was concerned, and running ahead of or behind the beat. Not Reds. When Red Watson let go, he belted out a song in a way that you'd think was going to break every window in the place. And on the beat. Perfectly on the beat. And he was a tenor. The singers nowadays, if you can classify them at all, you'd have to call them baritones. But Reds was a tenor, a high tenor.

I was thinking the other evening, I happened to be watching a show on TV and one of your Tommy Sandses or Bobby Darins came on and those squealing girls, that I suspect are paid, began screeching. And I thought to myself, Red Watson hit a higher note than any of those bobby-soxers, but when he did it it was music. Yes, it was. That's the sad part about it that there aren't any records around to prove it.

When I was the age of some of you, or a little older, the name bands used to come through this region, playing the parks in the summer and the ballrooms in the winter. I notice you don't get many big bands anymore. In fact, I'm told there aren't any, to speak of. But when I was a young fellow there wasn't a name band in the country that didn't play here and all around here. And over and over again. It won't mean anything to you, but I can remember one night when Paul Whiteman, with a thirty-five-piece band, was playing a one-nighter and only two miles away was Vincent Lopez, with *his* big band. How to compare it nowadays, it would be like—I don't know the names of the bands anymore. Ray Conniff and Neal Hefti, I guess. But I can tell you this much, one of the singers with Whiteman was a young practically unknown singer with a trio, named Bing Crosby. And if memory serves, the famous Bix Beiderbecke was also with Whiteman around that time. Those of you that collect records will recognize the name Bix Beiderbecke. First name, Leon. Played cornet. Also piano. You have a musician today, Bushkin, he plays piano and horn, but Bushkin was never idolized the way Bix was. They even wrote a novel about him, and if I'm not mistaken, it was turned into a New York play.

Well, what I don't understand is your interest in Red Watson, because Reds died around the time I've been speaking of. He was popular *before* Whiteman and Lopez started playing the parks and the ballrooms in this section. The big band then was the Sirens. The Scranton Sirens. Of course you've heard about the Sirens. Both Dorseys played with the Sirens. We had that in our paper when Tommy and Jimmy passed on there a little while ago, and I got a lot of letters from some of your mothers and fathers and I guess your grandparents, that still loved the Scranton Sirens. But with all due credit to the Dorsey boys, the real attraction was Red Watson. Mind you, it was a fine band. None better in the whole United States, because I heard them all. All the big ones of that day. Fletcher Henderson. Earl Fuller. The Barbary Coast. Art Hickman. Oh, my, just saying the names takes me back. Ted Weems. The Original Dixieland. Goldkette. Paul Biese. The Coon-Sanders Kansas City Nighthawks. Jack Chapman. I can remember more than once driving all the way to Atlantic City in a friend of mine's flivver, just to hear a band at the Steel Pier, and then *driving back the same night* so I'd be at work in the morning. That was a long trip then. It's still a long trip, but when we made it—I guess there isn't one of you here that would know how to vulcanize an inner tube. I can see you don't even know what I'm talking about. In those days you could go in any five-and-ten and buy an ignition key for your Ford, and it had a square hole cut in the key to turn on the tank for your headlights. No, you don't register. I might as well be talking about whipsockets.

You must bear in mind, when I graduated from this school, in other words the same age as some of you within sound of my voice, jazz was such a new thing that they weren't even sure how to spell it. Some spelled it j, a, s, s, and I've seen Victrola records with Jass Band instead of Jazz Band printed on the label. But I'll tell you one thing. If you ever heard Red Watson sing "Jazz Me" you knew it was spelled with two z's. To be quite frank with you, I'm always hesitant about coming here and speaking about Red Watson, because as the—I hope—respectable editor of a family newspaper, I don't consider Reds a proper subject for a talk before a group of young high school students. If I weren't so convinced that you know as much about some things as I do, I'd have to decline your invitations. Or at least I'd choose another subject. But then I always say to myself, "These young people today, they know a lot more than I did when I was their age, about certain things, and maybe I can sneak over a moral lesson somehow or other." And I can. You see, boys and girls, or young ladies and gentlemen, Red Watson was an example of great talent wasted. He had a God-given voice, completely untrained, but I was told that he was given many offers to go away and take singing lessons. He came from a little town outside of Scranton and several rich people up there wanted to pay for his vocal training, but he'd have no part of it.

The story was—and those of you that were here two years ago must excuse me for repeating it—but according to the story that I always heard, and I could never summon up the courage to ask Reds to verify it—Reds was a breaker boy, too. Like that cardinal. But when he was about thirteen years old, working in the breaker, his arm got caught in the conveyor and was so badly mangled that they had to amputate above the elbow. Thirteen, maybe fourteen years old. You can imagine what dreadful torture he must have gone through. The accident itself, and then the amputation which left him with a stump about, well, he used to fold up his left sleeve and pin it with a safety pin just under the shoulder. He was an orphan, living with relatives, and after he got out of the hospital he tried selling papers, but that wasn't as easy as you might think. A paper route was just about impossible to get, and selling papers on street corners was just as hard. You had to fight for the busy corners, and Reds only had one arm. So he used to get a few papers and go around to the saloons and try to sell them there, but somehow or other they found out that he could sing, and he began to make as much money singing for nickels and dimes, and pennies, as he could selling papers. At the age of fourteen he was known in all the saloons, and sometimes the miners used to get him liquored up, even though he was hardly more than a child. They'd give him whiskey and get him singing, and he told me himself that by the time he was sixteen years of age, he could drink beer all night long without getting intoxicated. Whiskey was another matter, but beer he could drink till the cows came home, and it wouldn't affect him. That much of the story is true, because Reds told me himself.

This part I can't vouch for, but you can take it for whatever you think it's worth. I've never been able to make up my mind one way or the other whether it's just imagination on someone's part, or based on the truth, and I never asked Reds. But according to the story that a lot of people believed, when Reds wanted to hit his high note, he'd think back on the time he lost his arm and the pain would come back to him and he'd scream. I don't know. It wasn't the kind of question I could ever ask Reds, although I got to know him pretty well. But I remember hearing a story about Caruso, too. He was supposed to be the greatest tenor that ever lived, and they say he hit his highest note when he was in pain from an abscess in his lung. Who knows? I have a hard time believing it, but I think Caruso died of an abscessed lung, or the effects of it, so there may be some connection between the pain and the high note. I know that Red Watson's stump always bothered him, and he became a heavy drinker to take his mind off the pain. But he wouldn't see a doctor. Oh, no. He said another operation—well, not to be squeamish about it, the stump was so short that there was hardly anything left of the arm, and where would they go after that? He said to me once that he wasn't like most people, because he knew exactly how long he had to live. He said he didn't have to measure it in years, like most people, but in a few inches of bone.

People ask me what Reds was like, because when I was a young fellow, I confess that it wasn't only my duty as a reporter that took me into the various places where alcoholic beverages were for sale. And I guess I was one of the pioneer hep-cats, although they didn't use that expression, and in fact I'm told by the modern generation that you don't even say hep anymore. Hip? Or is that passé, too? Well, anyway, I know that the musicians used to call us alligators, because we'd stand in front of a band with our mouths open like alligators, so if you ever heard the expression, "Greetings, 'Gate," that's where it came from. The alligators. And I was one back in the early Twenties, just after the first World War. When we wanted to hear a good jazz band, an orchestra that didn't play waltzes all night, we had to go to the public dances on Saturday nights at the Armory, and whenever I hear you young people being called juvenile delinquents, I have to remind myself that there was plenty of it when I was about your age. Those dances at the Armory, I think the admission was fifty cents for ladies and seventy-five for gents. It may have been less. Fifty for gents and twenty-five for ladies. We had a name for those dances. We called them rock fights. In fact, we didn't even bother to call them by the full name, rock fights. We used to say, "Are you going out to the rocky tonight?" And out of that grew another nickname, the quarry. We used to speak of the rock fights as the quarry. In front of our parents we could say, "I'll see you at the quarry," and our fathers and mothers would think we were talking about going for a swim in the quarry dam. Oh, we were just as wild as you think you are, or almost.

You know, I don't often get to see TV in the daytime, but last year when I was laid up with arthritis I watched you kids, or young people of your generation, dancing on an afternoon program. And one great difference between you and us, *you* don't seem to be having a good time. You hardly even smile at each other. It wasn't that way in my youth. Good Lord, everybody was laughing and jumping around,

55

racing all over the floor when they played a one-step. Now you just glare at your partner and she spins around and you pull her towards you. You don't have any fun. Incidentally, I don't think you dance very well, either, but that's a matter of opinion. I remember a fast tune called "Taxi!" When they played that, you moved fast or you got out of the way. That was good exercise, and fun. There'd always be a few fellows pretty well liquored up and they'd take a spill, but that was part of the fun. And there was always at least one fistfight at the rockies. At least one. You see, most of the girls at those dances, they were high school age, but they weren't going to school. They had working permits and a lot of them worked in the silk mill, the box factories, and some of them were servant girls. You hear the expression, going steady, and you think it's new. Well, it isn't. Girls and boys went steady then, and what that meant was that a girl would go to a rock fight and pay her own way in, dance with as many fellows as she wanted to, but she always went home with the boy she was going steady with, and if she tried to go home with somebody else, there'd be a fistfight. That's really where those dances got the name, rock fights. They didn't throw rocks, and they wouldn't have called them rocks anyway. They called them goonies. A gooney was a piece of stone that boys would throw at each other on the way home from school. In some sections of town the boys used to in the winter take a gooney and wrap it up in snow. A snowball with a gooney in it could inflict a lot of damage. See this scar here in back of my ear? That was a gooney wrapped in snow. I never knew who or what hit me at the time, but a bunch of boys from Third Street school were waiting for us boys from Fourteenth Street one afternoon, and I was one of the casualties. My poor mother when they brought me home!

Well, you're very patient with me, and I don't know why it is that the mere mention of Red Watson opens up the floodgates of reminiscence, only it's more about me than about Reds. I started to answer the question, What was he like? Well, in spite of his name being Watson, he had a real Irish face, no doubt about it. He wasn't a very big fellow. In fact, he was on the short side. But he looked a lot older than his real age. When I first knew him he was only about twenty years of age, but he looked easily thirty. Face was almost purple from drink and he was already starting to get bald. He was usually smiling and he was *always* smiling when he got up to sing. He'd flirt with all the girls around the bandstand that gathered around when he took his place to sing. He was a cake-eater. That was slang for fellows that dressed a certain way. They were also called sharpies. A sharpie, or a cake-eater, wore a suit that was padded at the shoulders and tight at the waist, then flared out. It had exaggerated peaked lapels that went all the way up to the shoulders, hence the name sharpie. The coat was buttoned at the waist with link buttons, sometimes three pairs of link buttons. The cuffs flared out and they were divided. The trousers were very wide at the bottom, and if you were really sharp, they were laced at the sides, like Spanish bullfighters'. The sharpies wore either tiny bow ties, on an elastic, or very narrow four-in-hands. And they wore low-cut vests so that the whole shirtfront was exposed. Tiny little collars. Hair was plastered down with Vaseline, and the cake-eaters wore sideburns. And that was the way Reds dressed, with one sleeve pinned up to his shoulder. You boys and girls are even too young to remember the zoot suit of twenty years ago, which was different from the cake-eater's outfit, but if Reds had lived in a later era, he'd have worn a zoot suit. I think.

As to his personality, he had two. One when he was singing, and the other when he wasn't. When he wasn't singing he wasn't a very remarkable young fellow. Good-natured as a rule, although quick-tempered at times. He liked the girls, and they certainly liked him, not because of his looks, you can be sure of that. And not only because of his singing. He had a car, a yellow Marmon roadster it was, and I went on a couple of rides with him after we became friendly, and we'd drive to Reading and Philadelphia, places where they didn't know him at all, and we'd stop someplace to get a sandwich. If they had a waitress that was halfway good-looking, Reds would start to kid her a little, and always end up with a date. Sometimes he had no intention of keeping the date, but he just had to convince himself that he was irresistible. And he usually was. In fact, too much so. I guess I knew him two or three years before he happened to mention that he was married when he was eighteen and had a baby daughter. He supported his wife and child, but he wasn't a good husband or father by any stretch of the imagination. I could understand his not getting along with his wife, but I've never been able to understand why he didn't seem to take the slightest interest in his daughter. But that was a closed subject, and I decided it was none of my business. In my opinion Reds was one of those people that seem to have a talent for certain things, such as music, writing, art, but they're deficient in the common-ordinary, everyday things that you don't hear so much about, but they're an accomplishment nevertheless. I mean the simple, ordinary things like the sacrifices that some of your mothers and fathers make for you boys and girls, that you may not even know of unless you stop to think about it. Forty boys and girls in this room. How many of you girls had a new dress this year? Don't raise your hands, because my next question is, How many of you girls got a new dress this year because your mother got one for you instead of for herself? And you boys. How many of you have cars—and don't *you* raise your hands, either. Because some of you must know, if you stop to think, that you wouldn't have a car if your fathers didn't decide to spend that money on you instead of on themselves. This isn't a lecture. I'm not at all sure what it is except an informal talk by a newspaper editor to some young people that are interested in the field of journalism. And you don't especially want me to talk about the newspaper business. But in fairness to you, if I'm invited to talk about a colorful character whose example I wouldn't want you to follow, in fairness to you I have to call your attention to the fact that you all have fathers and mothers that do set a good example in love and kindness, and patience and understanding. My conscience won't let me talk about Red Watson, and glamorize him, unless I point out to you that Reds only lived to be twenty-five years of age, and as far as I know—and I knew him pretty well—he never did anything for anybody but himself. With that understanding, I'll continue talking about him. But I had to make that clear. He never did anything for anybody but himself, and he died—well, I'll save that till later, inasmuch as half the members of your Press Club probably are hearing about Reds for the first time. The seniors and juniors were here when I spoke two years ago, but the sophomores and freshmen weren't.

So to continue about his two personalities. The one, he was fun to be with, but I only saw him on his visits to town, maybe four times a year.

I don't know how he'd have been as a steady diet. Selfish, and no respect for girls whatsoever, and as I said before, he seemed good-natured, but he had a quick temper, too. I guess if I had to be completely frank about it, I was flattered because he wanted me for a friend. I was just a young fellow starting out in the newspaper business, and I used to enjoy it when some of our local prizefighters and celebrities would call me by my nickname. And in that little world, Red Watson was as big a celebrity as Kid Lefty Williams or Young Packy Corbett, two fighters we had at the time, both since passed on. Made me feel big, even though I had some misgivings about Reds.

But I'll tell you this, you always forgot what he was like when he got up to sing. I mean the things about him that I didn't go along with. It'd come his turn to sing a number and he'd go behind the piano and take a swig out of a pint bottle of whiskey, and a couple of fast drags on his cigarette, and then he'd go to the middle of the bandstand and stand there grinning at the people gathering around while the orchestra played a full chorus. And then he'd close his eyes and put his head back and start singing. It didn't make any difference what the number was. It might be a sort of risqué song like "Jazz Me" or it might be a ballad. But the dancing would stop and everybody would stand still, as close to the bandstand as they could get, and you'd look at their faces and they were hypnotized. They'd be moving in time to the rhythm, but not dancing, and it was almost as though he were singing for them. Not only to them, but for them. I can remember thinking of him as a misplaced choirboy, and the crowd around him some of the toughest characters in the county. The girls just as tough as the young fellows. They'd all stop chewing gum while he was singing, and even when he happened to be singing a dirty song, they'd smile, but they didn't laugh. And if it was a ballad, he could make them cry. There's a high note in "Poor Butterfly"—"but if he don't come *back*"—that *always* made them cry. Then he'd finish his song and open his eyes and smile at them while they yelled and applauded, and he'd wink at them, and they'd start dancing again. One chorus. No encores, one song every half an hour. That was his agreement. He was paid fifty dollars a night with the band. But then after the dance was over we'd all meet at some saloon and after he had enough to drink you couldn't stop him. He'd get up on the bar and sing whatever you asked him, till the joint closed. The next night it'd be the same thing in some other town, six nights a week.

How he kept it up as long as he did, I don't know. He slept all day, but when he had his breakfast, at seven o'clock in the evening, that was often the only meal he ate all day. By eight o'clock he was hitting the bottle, and usually at half past eight, sometimes nine, he'd be with the band, ready to sing his first number. Naturally he couldn't keep that up, and he began failing to show up with the band. The first few times that happened, he got away with it, but then the crowds were disappointed and the managers of the dance halls were afraid to advertise that he was coming. Then the band broke up and for about a year I didn't see Reds at all. I heard he was forming his own band, Red Watson's Syncopators. And he was leading the band, himself. But that didn't last long. Two or three months of that was all he could stand. And all the musicians could stand. He'd order special arrangements, but then he wouldn't pay for them, and he got in trouble with the union about paying his musicians, and the first thing he knew he was put on the unfair list. After that he just disappeared, and whenever I'd ask about him from people around Wilkes-Barre and Scranton they had conflicting reports, probably all true. I heard he'd opened a speakeasy in Wilkes-Barre and someone else told me he was in prison for non-support of his wife and child. The last time I saw him I was in Scranton, covering a United Mine Workers meeting, and I asked around and finally tracked him down. I asked him how things were, and not knowing I knew anything about him, he put on a great show. He said he'd got rid of the yellow Marmon and was buying a Wills-Sainte Clare. That was an expensive car. He had offers to go in vaudeville, et cetera, et cetera. And he wouldn't let me pay the check. We were in a speakeasy where his credit must have been good, because he told the bartender to put it on his tab and the bartender made a face, but said okay, Reds. I had a feeling that the bartender would have much preferred my cash. So I said to Reds, approaching the subject in a roundabout way, I said I was glad things were better. And he asked me what I meant by better, and I said I'd heard he'd a little trouble. Well, such vituperation! Such invective! And all directed at me. I was a cheap newspaper reporter that never made more than thirty dollars a week in my life, which was true, but I was also a snooping so-and-so, probably sent there by his wife's lawyer to find out all I could. He took a beer bottle off the bar and smashed the neck off it. That was a weapon known as a Glasgie Slasher, and he held it up to my face and said I deserved to have my eyes gouged out, snooping around and asking questions. I didn't dare move, for fear I'd get that thing in my face. And then, I guess because I hadn't made any move, he dropped the broken bottle in the gutter in front of the bar, and ran out.

I was given a drink by the bartender, and I needed it after that experience.

"He'll murder somebody yet," the bartender said. "He's suspicious of everybody." I asked the bartender how Reds live, and the man told me. I don't have to go into that here, but Reds was about as low as a man can get to make a living. Any real man would rather dig ditches, but Reds only had one arm and all he ever did was sing. Anyway, he had a place to live and a little cash. And then the bartender, a nice fellow, asked me how well I'd known Reds. Had Reds ever told me that he didn't measure his life by years, but inches of bone? And I said yes, he'd said that to me some years back. And the bartender said, "Well, he's heard the bad news. No more inches, and no more years. Months, and more likely weeks." Then he said he just hoped Reds got through the next couple of months without killing somebody.

Well, he did, boys and girls. The next I heard of Reds was a few weeks later at the office, the city editor handed me a little squib that came in over the UP wire. Patrick Watson, known throughout the coal region as Red Watson, the popular tenor, was found dead on the bandstand of the Alhambra dance hall in Scranton. It was summer, the wrong time of the year for a dance at the Alhambra. So I got Scranton on the phone and checked. Yes, they found Reds at the Alhambra. Nobody else in the place, which was closed for the summer, and the watchman had no idea what Reds had gone there for. There was nothing worth stealing.

But you and I know why he went there, don't we? Yes, I think as I look at you, you know.

Thank you.

THE TELL-TALE HEART

EDGAR ALLAN POE

TRUE!—NERVOUS—very, very dreadfully nervous I had been and am; but why *will* you say that I am mad? The disease had sharpened my senses—not destroyed—not dulled them. Above all was the sense of hearing acute. I heard all things in the heaven and in the earth. I heard many things in hell. How, then, am I mad? Hearken! and observe how healthily—how calmly I can tell you the whole story.

It is impossible to say how first the idea entered my brain; but once conceived, it haunted me day and night. Object there was none. Passion there was none. I loved the old man. He had never wronged me. He had never given me insult. For his gold I had no desire. I think it was his eye! Yes, it was this! One of his eyes resembled that of a vulture—a pale blue eye, with a film over it. Whenever it fell upon me, my blood ran cold; and so by degrees—very gradually—I made up my mind to take the life of the old man, and thus rid myself of the eye forever.

Now this is the point. You fancy me mad. Madmen know nothing. But you should have seen *me*. You should have seen how wisely I proceeded—with what caution—with what foresight—with what dissimulation I went to work! I was never kinder to the old man than during the whole week before I killed him. And every night, about midnight, I turned the latch of his door and opened it—oh, so gently! And then, when I had made an opening sufficient for my head, I put in a dark lantern, all closed, closed, so that no light shone out, and then I thrust in my head. Oh, you would have laughed to see how cunningly I thrust it in! I moved it slowly—very, very slowly, so that I might not disturb the old man's sleep. It took me an hour to place my whole head within the opening so far that I could see him as he lay upon his bed. Ha! Would a madman have been so wise as this? And then, when my head was well in the room, I undid the lantern cautiously—oh, so cautiously—cautiously (for the hinges creaked)—I undid it just so much that a single thin ray fell upon the vulture eye. And this I did for seven long nights—every night just at midnight—but I found the eye always closed; and so it was impossible to do the work; for it was not the old man who vexed me, but his Evil Eye. And every morning, when the day broke, I went boldly into the chamber, and spoke courageously to him, calling him by name in a hearty tone, and inquiring how he had passed the night. So you see he would have been a very profound old man, indeed, to suspect that every night, just at twelve, I looked in upon him while he slept.

Upon the eighth night I was more than usually cautious in opening the door. A watch's minute hand moves more quickly than did mine. Never before that night had I *felt* the extent of my own powers—of my sagacity. I could scarcely contain my feelings of triumph. To think that there I was, opening the door, little by little, and he not even to dream of my secret deeds or thoughts. I fairly chuckled at the idea; and perhaps he heard me; for he moved on the bed suddenly, as if startled. Now you may think that I drew back—but no. His room was as black as pitch with the thick darkness (for the shutters were close fastened, through fear of robbers), and so I knew that he could not see the opening of the door, and I kept pushing it on steadily, steadily.

I had my head in, and was about to open the lantern, when my thumb slipped upon the tin fastening, and the old man sprang up in the bed, crying out, "Who's there?"

I kept quite still and said nothing. For a whole hour I did not move a muscle, and in the meantime I did not hear him lie down. He was still sitting up in the bed listening—just as I have done, night after night, hearkening to the deathwatches in the wall.

Presently I heard a slight groan, and I knew it was the groan of mortal terror. It was not a groan of pain or of grief—oh, no!—it was the low stifled sound that arises from the bottom of the soul when overcharged with awe. I knew the sound well. Many a night, just at midnight, when all the world slept, it has welled up from my own bosom, deepening, with its dreadful echo, the terrors that distracted me. I say I knew it well. I knew what the old man felt, and pitied him, although I chuckled at heart. I knew that he had been lying awake ever since the first slight noise, when he had turned in the bed. His fears had been ever since growing upon him. He had been trying to fancy them causeless, but could not. He had been saying to himself, "It is nothing but the wind in the chimney—it is only a mouse crossing the floor," or "it is merely a cricket which has made a single chirp." Yes, he has been trying to comfort himself with these suppositions; but he had found all in vain. *All in vain;* because Death, in approaching him, had stalked with his black shadow before him, and enveloped the victim. And it was the mournful influence of the unperceived shadow that caused him to feel—although he neither saw nor heard—to *feel* the presence of my head within the room.

When I had waited a long time, very patiently, without hearing him lie down, I resolved to open a little—a very, very little crevice in the lantern. So I opened it—you cannot imagine how stealthily, stealthily—until, at length, a single dim ray, like the thread of the spider, shot from out the crevice and full upon the vulture eye.

It was open—wide, wide open—and I grew furious as I gazed upon it. I saw it with perfect distinctness—all a dull blue, with a hideous veil over it that chilled the very marrow in my bones; but I could see nothing else of the old man's face or person: for I had directed the ray as if by instinct, precisely upon the damned spot.

And now have I not told you that what you mistake for madness is but overacuteness of the senses? Now, I say, there came to my ears a low, dull, quick sound, such as a watch makes when enveloped in cotton. I knew *that* sound well too. It was the beating of the old man's heart. It increased my fury, as the beating of a drum stimulates the soldier into courage.

But even yet I refrained and kept still. I scarcely breathed. I held the lantern motionless. I tried how steadily I could maintain the ray upon the eye. Meantime the hellish tattoo of the heart increased. It grew quicker and quicker, and louder and louder every instant. The old man's terror *must* have been extreme! It grew louder, I say, louder every moment! Do you mark me well? I have told you that I am nervous—so I am. And now at the dead hour of the night, amid the dreadful silence of that old house, so strange a noise as this excited me to uncontrollable terror. Yet, for some minutes longer I refrained and stood still. But the beating grew louder, louder! I thought the heart must burst. And now a new anxiety seized me—the sound would be heard by a neighbor! The old man's hour had come! With a loud yell, I threw open the lantern and leaped into the room. He shrieked once—once only. In an instant I dragged him to the floor, and pulled the heavy bed over him. I then smiled gaily, to find the deed so far done. But, for many minutes, the heart beat on with a muffled sound. This, however, did not vex me; it would not be heard through the wall. At length it ceased. The old man was dead. I removed the bed and examined the corpse. Yes, he was stone, stone dead. I placed my hand upon the heart and held it there many minutes. There was no pulsation. He was stone dead. His eye would trouble me no more.

If still you think me mad, you will think so no longer when I describe the wise precautions I took for the concealment of the body. The night waned, and I worked hastily, but in silence. First of all I dismembered the corpse. I cut off the head and the arms and the legs.

I then took up three planks from the flooring of the chamber, and deposited all between the scantlings. I then replaced the boards so cleverly, so cunningly, that no human eye—not even *his*—could have detected anything wrong. There was nothing to wash out—no stain of any kind—no blood spot whatever. I had been too wary for that. A tub had caught all—ha! ha!

When I had made an end of these labors, it was four o'clock—still dark as midnight. As the bell sounded the hour, there came a knocking at the street door. I went down to open it with a light heart—for what had I *now* to fear? There entered three men, who introduced themselves, with perfect suavity, as officers of the police. A shriek had been heard by a neighbor during the night; suspicion of foul play had been aroused; information had been lodged at the police office, and they (the officers) had been deputed to search the premises.

I smiled—for *what* had I to fear? I bade the gentlemen welcome. The shriek, I said, was my own in a dream. The old man, I mentioned, was absent in the country. I took my visitors all over the house. I bade them search—search *well*. I led them, at length, to *his* chamber. I showed them his treasures, secure, undisturbed. In the enthusiasm of my confidence, I brought chairs into the room, and desired them *here* to rest from their fatigues, while I myself, in the wild audacity of my perfect triumph, placed my own seat upon the very spot beneath which reposed the corpse of the victim.

The officers were satisfied. My *manner* had convinced them. I was singularly at ease. They sat, and while I answered cheerily, they chatted familiar things. But, ere long, I felt myself getting pale and wished them gone. My head ached, and I fancied a ringing in my ears; but still they sat and still chatted. The ringing became more distinct—it continued and became more distinct. I talked more freely to get rid of the feeling, but it continued and gained definitiveness—until, at length, I found that the noise was *not* within my ears.

No doubt I now grew *very* pale—but I talked more fluently, and with a heightened voice. Yet the sound increased—and what could I do? It was *a low, dull, quick sound—much such a sound as a watch makes when enveloped in cotton.* I gasped for breath—and yet the officers heard it not. I talked more quickly—more vehemently; but the noise steadily increased. I arose and argued about trifles, in a high key and with violent gesticulations, but the noise steadily increased. Why *would* they not be gone? I paced the floor to and fro with heavy strides, as if excited to fury by the observation of the men—but the noise steadily increased. O God! What *could* I do? I foamed—I raved—I swore! I swung the chair upon which I had been sitting, and grated it upon the boards, but the noise arose over all and continually increased. It grew louder— louder—*louder!* And still the men chatted pleasantly, and smiled. Was it possible they heard not? Almighty God!—no, no! They heard!—they suspected!—they *knew!*—they were making a mockery of my horror! This I thought, and this I think. But anything was better than this agony! Anything was more tolerable than this derision! I could bear those hypocritical smiles no longer! I felt that I must scream or die!— and now—again!—hark! louder! louder! louder! *louder!*—

"Villains!" I shrieked, "dissemble no more! I admit the deed!—tear up the planks!—here, here!—it is the beating of his hideous heart!"

WINTER NIGHT

KAY BOYLE

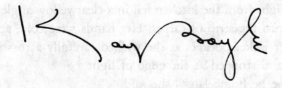

THERE IS A time of apprehension which begins with the beginning of darkness, and to which only the speech of love can lend security. It is there, in abeyance, at the end of every day, not urgent enough to be given the name of fear but rather of concern for how the hours are to be reprieved from fear, and those who have forgotten how it was when they were children can remember nothing of this. It may begin around five o'clock on a winter afternoon when the light outside is dying in the windows. At that hour the New York apartment in which Felicia lived was filled with shadows, and the little girl would wait alone in the living room, looking out at the winter-stripped trees that stood black in the park against the isolated ovals of unclean snow. Now it was January, and the day had been a cold one; the water of the artificial lake was frozen fast, but because of the cold and the coming darkness, the skaters had ceased to move across its surface. The street that lay between the park and the apartment house was wide, and the two-way streams of cars and buses, some with their headlamps already shining, advanced and halted, halted and poured swiftly on to the tempo of the traffic signals' altering lights. The time of apprehension had set in, and Felicia, who was seven, stood at the window in the evening and waited before she asked the question. When the signals below would change from red to green again, or when the double-decker bus would turn the corner below, she would ask it. The words of it were already there, tentative in her mouth, when the answer came from the far end of the hall.

"Your mother," said the voice among the sound of kitchen things, "she telephoned up before you came in from nursery school. She won't be back in time for supper. I was to tell you a sitter was coming in from the sitting parents' place."

Felicia turned back from the window into the obscurity of the living room, and she looked toward the open door, and into the hall beyond it where the light from the kitchen fell in a clear yellow angle across the wall and onto the strip of carpet. Her hands were cold, and she put them in her jacket pockets as she walked carefully across the living-room rug and stopped at the edge of light.

"Will she be home late?" she said.

For a moment there was the sound of water running in the kitchen, a long way away, and then the sound of the water ceased, and the high, Southern voice went on:

"She'll come home when she gets ready to come home. That's all I have to say. If she wants to spend two dollars and fifty cents and ten cents' carfare on top of that three or four nights out of the week for a sitting parent to come in here and sit, it's her own business. It certainly ain't nothing to do with you or me. She makes her money, just like the rest of us does. She works all day down there in the office, or whatever it is, just like the rest of us works, and she's entitled to spend her money like she wants to spend it. There's no law in the world against buying your own freedom. Your mother and me, we're just buying our own freedom, that's all we're doing. And we're not doing nobody no harm."

"Do you know who she's having supper with?" said Felicia from the edge of dark. There was one more step to take, and then she would be standing in the light that fell on the strip of carpet, but she did not take the step.

"Do I know who she's having supper with?" the voice cried out in what might have been derision, and there was the sound of dishes striking the metal ribs of the drainboard by the sink. "Maybe it's Mr. Van Johnson, or Mr. Frank Sinatra, or maybe it's just the Duke of Wincers for the evening. All I know is you're having soft-boiled egg and spinach and applesauce for supper, and you're going to have it quick now because the time is getting away."

The voice from the kitchen had no name. It was as variable as the faces and figures of the women who came and sat in the evenings.

Month by month the voice in the kitchen altered to another voice, and the sitting parents were no more than lonely aunts of an evening or two who sometimes returned and sometimes did not to this apartment in which they had sat before. Nobody stayed anywhere very long anymore, Felicia's mother told her. It was part of the time in which you lived, and part of the life of the city, but when the fathers came back, all this would be miraculously changed. Perhaps you would live in a house again, a small one, with fir trees on either side of the short brick walk, and Father would drive up every night from the station just after darkness set in. When Felicia thought of this, she stepped quickly into the clear angle of light, and she left the dark of the living room behind her and ran softly down the hall.

The drop-leaf table stood in the kitchen between the refrigerator and the sink, and Felicia sat down at the place that was set. The voice at the sink was speaking still, and while Felicia ate it did not cease to speak until the bell of the front door rang abruptly. The girl walked around the table and went down the hall, wiping her dark palms in her apron, and, from the drop-leaf table, Felicia watched her step from the angle of light into darkness and open the door.

"You put in an early appearance," the girl said, and the woman who had rung the bell came into the hall. The door closed behind her, and the girl showed her into the living room, and lit the lamp on the bookcase, and the shadows were suddenly bleached away. But when the girl turned, the woman turned from the living room too and followed her, humbly and in silence, to the threshold of the kitchen. "Sometimes they keep me standing around waiting after it's time for me to be getting on home, the sitting parents do," the girl said, and she picked up the last two dishes from the table and put them in the sink. The woman who stood in the doorway was a small woman, and when she undid the white silk scarf from around her head, Felicia saw that her hair was black. She wore it parted in the middle, and it had not been cut, but was drawn back loosely into a knot behind her head. She had very clean white gloves on, and her face was pale, and there was a look of sorrow in her soft black eyes. "Sometimes I have to stand out there in the hall with my hat and coat on, waiting for the sitting parents to turn up," the girl said, and, as she turned on the water in the sink, the contempt she had for them hung on the kitchen air. "But you're ahead of time," she said, and she held the dishes, first one and then the other, under the flow of steaming water.

The woman in the doorway wore a neat black coat, not a new-looking coat, and it had no fur on it, but it had a smooth velvet collar and velvet lapels. She did not move, or smile, and she gave no sign that she had heard the girl speaking above the sound of water at the sink. She simply stood looking at Felicia, who sat at the table with the milk in her glass not finished yet.

"Are you the child?" she said at last, and her voice was low, and the pronunciation of the words a little strange.

"Yes, this here's Felicia," the girl said, and the dark hands dried the dishes and put them away. "You drink up your milk quick now, Felicia, so's I can rinse your glass."

"I will wash the glass," said the woman. "I would like to wash the glass for her," and Felicia sat looking across the table at the face in the doorway that was filled with such unspoken grief. "I will wash the glass for her and clean off the table," the woman was saying quietly. "When the child is finished, she will show me where her night things are."

"The others, they wouldn't do anything like that," the girl said, and she hung the dishcloth over the rack. "They wouldn't put their hand to housework, the sitting parents. That's where they got the name for them," she said.

Whenever the front door closed behind the girl in the evening, it would usually be that the sitting parent who was there would take up a book of fairy stories and read aloud for a while to Felicia; or else would settle herself in the big chair in the living room and begin to tell the words of a story in drowsiness to her, while Felicia took off her clothes in the bedroom, and folded them, and put her pajamas on, and brushed her teeth, and did her hair. But this time, that was not the way it happened. Instead, the woman sat down on the other chair at the kitchen table, and she began at once to speak, not of good fairies or bad, or of animals endowed with human speech, but to speak quietly, in spite of the eagerness behind her words, of a thing that seemed of singular importance to her.

"It is strange that I should have been sent here tonight," she said, her eyes moving slowly from feature to feature of Felicia's face, "for you look like a child that I knew once, and this is the anniversary of that child."

"Did she have hair like mine?" Felicia asked quickly, and she did not keep her eyes fixed on the unfinished glass of milk in shyness anymore.

"Yes, she did. She had hair like yours," said the woman, and her glance paused for a moment on the locks which fell straight and thick on the shoulders of Felicia's dress. It may have been that she thought to stretch out her hand and touch the ends of Felicia's hair, for her fingers stirred as they lay clasped together on the table, and then they relapsed into passivity again. "But it is not the hair alone, it is the delicacy of your face, too, and your eyes the same, filled with the same spring lilac color," the woman said, pronouncing the words carefully. "She had little coats of golden fur on her arms and legs," she said, "and when we were closed up there, the lot of us in the cold, I used to make her laugh when I told her that the fur that was so pretty, like a little fawn's skin on her arms, would always help to keep her warm."

"And did it keep her warm?" asked Felicia, and she gave a little jerk of laughter as she looked down at her own legs hanging under the table, with the bare calves thin and covered with a down of hair.

"It did not keep her warm enough," the woman said, and now the mask of grief had come back upon her face. "So we used to take everything we could spare from ourselves, and we would sew them into cloaks and other garments for her and for the other children. . . ."

"Was it a school?" said Felicia when the woman's voice had ceased to speak.

"No," said the woman softly, "it was not a school, but still there were a lot of children there. It was a camp—that was the name the place had; it was a camp. It was a place where they put people until they could decide what was to be done with them." She sat with her hands clasped, silent a moment, looking at Felicia. "That little dress you have on," she said, not saying the words to anybody, scarcely saying them aloud. "Oh, she would have liked that little dress, the little buttons shaped like hearts, and the white collar—"

"I have four school dresses," Felicia said. "I'll show them to you. How many dresses did she have?"

"Well, there, you see, there in the camp," said the woman, "she did not have any dresses except the little skirt and the pullover. That was all she had. She had brought just a handkerchief of her belongings with her, like everybody else—just enough for three days away from home was what they told us, so she did not have enough to last the winter. But she had her ballet slippers," the woman said, and her clasped fingers did not move. "She had brought them because she thought during her three days away from home she would have the time to practice her ballet."

"I've been to the ballet," Felicia said suddenly, and she said it so eagerly that she stuttered a little as the words came out of her mouth. She slipped down from the chair and went around the table to where the woman sat. She took one of the woman's hands away from the other that held it fast, and she pulled her toward the door. "Come into the living room and I'll do a pirouette for you," she said, and then she stopped speaking, her eyes halted on the woman's face. "Did she—did the little girl—could she do a pirouette very well?" she said.

"Yes, she could. At first she could," said the woman, and Felicia felt uneasy now at the sound of sorrow in her words. "But after that she was hungry. She was hungry all winter," she said in a low voice. "We were all hungry, but the children were the hungriest. Even now," she said, and her voice went suddenly savage, "when I see milk like that, clean, fresh milk standing in a glass, I want to cry out loud, I want to beat my hands on the table, because it did not have to be . . ." She had drawn her fingers abruptly away from Felicia now, and Felicia stood before her, cast off, forlorn, alone again in the time of apprehension. "That was three years ago," the woman was saying, and one hand was lifted, as in weariness, to shade her face. "It was somewhere else, it was in another country," she said, and behind her hand her eyes were turned upon the substance of a world in which Felicia had played no part.

"Did—did the little girl cry when she was hungry?" Felicia asked, and the woman shook her head.

"Sometimes she cried," she said, "but not very much. She was very quiet. One night when she heard the other children crying, she said to me, 'You know, they are not crying because they want something to eat. They are crying because their mothers have gone away.'"

"Did the mothers have to go out to supper?" Felicia asked, and she watched the woman's face for the answer.

"No," said the woman. She stood up from her chair, and now that she put her hand on the little girl's shoulder, Felicia was taken into the sphere of love and intimacy again. "Shall we go into the other room, and you will do your pirouette for me?" the woman said, and they went from the kitchen and down the strip of carpet on which the clear light fell. In the front room, they paused hand in hand in the glow of the shaded lamp, and the woman looked about her, at the books, the low tables with the magazines and ashtrays on them, the vase of roses on the piano, looking with dark, scarcely seeing eyes at these things that had no reality at all. It was only when she saw the little white clock on the mantelpiece that she gave any sign, and then she said quickly: "What time does your mother put you to bed?"

Felicia waited a moment, and in the interval of waiting the woman lifted one hand and, as if in reverence, touched Felicia's hair.

"What time did the little girl you knew in the other place go to bed?" Felicia asked.

"Ah, God, I do not know, I do not remember," the woman said.

"Was she your little girl?" said Felicia softly, stubbornly.

"No," said the woman. "She was not mine. At least, at first she was not mine. She had a mother, a real mother, but the mother had to go away."

"Did she come back late?" asked Felicia.

"No, ah, no, she could not come back, she never came back," the woman said, and now she turned, her arm around Felicia's shoulders, and she sat down in the low soft chair. "Why am I saying all this to you, why am I doing it?" she cried out in grief, and she held Felicia close against her. "I had thought to speak of the anniversary to you, and that was all, and now I am saying these other things to you. Three years ago today, exactly, the little girl became my little girl because her mother went away. That is all there is to it. There is nothing more."

Felicia waited another moment, held close against the woman, and listening to the swift, strong heartbeats in the woman's breast.

"But the mother," she said then in the small, persistent voice, "did she take a taxi when she went?"

"This is the way it used to happen," said the woman, speaking in hopelessness and bitterness in the softly lighted room. "Every week they used to come into the place where we were and they would read a list of names out. Sometimes it would be the names of children they would read out, and then a little later they would have to go away. And sometimes it would be the grown people's names, the names of the mothers or big sisters, or other women's names. The men were not with us. The fathers were somewhere else, in another place."

"Yes," Felicia said. "I know."

"We had been there only a little while, maybe ten days or maybe not so long," the woman went on, holding Felicia against her still, "when they read the name of the little girl's mother out, and that afternoon they took her away."

"What did the little girl do?" Felicia said.

"She wanted to think up the best way of getting out so that she could go find her mother," said the woman, "but she could not think of anything good enough until the third or fourth day. And then she tied her ballet slippers up in the handkerchief again, and she went up to the guard standing at the door." The woman's voice was gentle, controlled now. "She asked the guard please to open the door so that she could go out. 'This is Thursday,' she said, 'and every Tuesday and Thursday I have my ballet lessons. If I miss a ballet lesson, they do not count the money off, so my mother would be just paying for nothing, and she cannot afford to pay for nothing. I missed my ballet lesson on Tuesday,' she said to the guard, 'and I must not miss it again today.'"

Felicia lifted her head from the woman's shoulder, and she shook her hair back and looked in question and wonder at the woman's face.

"And did the man let her go?" she said.

"No, he did not. He could not do that," said the woman. "He was a soldier and he had to do what he was told. So every evening after her mother went, I used to brush the little girl's hair for her," the woman went on saying. "And while I brushed it, I used to tell her the stories of the ballets. Sometimes I would begin with *Narcissus*," the woman said, and she parted Felicia's locks with her fingers, "so if you will go and get your brush now, I will tell it while I brush your hair."

"Oh, yes," said Felicia, and she made two whirls as she went quickly to the bedroom. On the way back, she stopped and held on to the piano with the fingers of one hand while she went up on her toes. "Did you see me? Did you see me standing on my toes?" she called to the woman, and the woman sat smiling in love and contentment at her.

"Yes, wonderful, really wonderful," she said. "I am sure I have never seen anyone do it so well." Felicia came spinning toward her, whirling in pirouette after pirouette, and she flung herself down in the chair close to her, with her thin bones pressed against the woman's soft, wide hip. The woman took the silver-backed, monogrammed brush and the tortoiseshell comb in her hands, and now she began to brush Felicia's hair. "We did not have any soap at all and not very much water to wash in, so I never could fix her as nicely and prettily as I wanted to," she said, and the brush stroked regularly, carefully down, caressing the shape of Felicia's head.

"If there wasn't very much water, then how did she do her teeth?" Felicia said.

"She did not do her teeth," said the woman, and she drew the comb through Felicia's hair. "There were not any toothbrushes or toothpaste, or anything like that."

Felicia waited a moment, constructing the unfamiliar scene of it in silence, and then she asked the tentative question.

"Do I have to do my teeth tonight?" she said.

"No," said the woman, and she was thinking of something else, "you do not have to do your teeth."

"If I am your little girl tonight, can I pretend there isn't enough water to wash?" said Felicia.

"Yes," said the woman, "you can pretend that if you like. You do not have to wash," she said, and the comb passed lightly through Felicia's hair.

"Will you tell me the story of the ballet?" said Felicia, and the rhythm of the brushing was like the soft, slow rocking of sleep.

"Yes," said the woman. "In the first one, the place is a forest glade with little pale birches growing in it, and they have green veils over their faces and green veils drifting from their fingers, because it is the springtime. There is the music of a flute," said the woman's voice softly, softly, "and creatures of the wood are dancing—"

"But the mother," Felicia said as suddenly as if she had been awaked from sleep. "What did the little girl's mother say when she didn't do her teeth and didn't wash at night?"

"The mother was not there, you remember," said the woman, and the brush moved steadily in her hand. "But she did send one little letter back. Sometimes the people who went away were able to do that. The mother wrote it in a train, standing up in a car that had no seats," she said, and she might have been telling the story of the ballet still, for her voice was gentle and the brush did not falter on Felicia's hair. "There were perhaps a great many other people standing up in the train with her, perhaps all trying to write their little letters on the bits of paper they had managed to hide on them, or that they had found in forgotten corners as they traveled. When they had written their letters, then they must try to slip them out through the boards of the car in which they journeyed, standing up," said the woman, "and these letters fell down on the tracks under the train, or they were blown into the fields or onto the country roads, and if it was a kind person who picked them up, he would seal them in envelopes and send them to where they were addressed to go. So a letter came back like this from the little girl's mother," the woman said, and the brush followed the comb, the comb the brush in steady pursuit through Felicia's hair. "It said good-by to the little girl, and it said please to take care of her. It said: 'Whoever reads this letter in the camp, please take good care of my little girl for me, and please have her tonsils looked at by a doctor if this is possible to do.' "

"And then," said Felicia softly, persistently, "what happened to the little girl?"

"I do not know. I cannot say," the woman said. But now the brush and comb had ceased to move, and in the silence Felicia turned her thin, small body on the chair, and she and the woman suddenly put their arms around each other. "They must all be asleep now, all of them," the woman said, and in the silence that fell on them again, they held each other closer. "They must be quietly asleep somewhere, and not crying all night because they are hungry and because they are cold. For three years I have been saying, 'They must all be asleep, and the cold and the hunger and the seasons or night or day or nothing matters to them. . . .' "

IT WAS AFTER MIDNIGHT WHEN Felicia's mother put her key in the lock of the front door, and pushed it open, and stepped into the hallway. She walked quickly to the living room, and just across the threshold she slipped the three blue fox skins from her shoulders and dropped them, with her little velvet bag, upon the chair. The room was quiet, so quiet that she could hear the sound of breathing in it, and no one spoke to her in greeting as she crossed toward the bedroom door. And then, as startling as a slap across her delicately tinted face, she saw the woman lying sleeping on the divan, and Felicia, in her school dress still, asleep within the woman's arms.

JELLICOE
R. S. PORTEOUS

HIS NAME was Godfrey Vernon Smithers and he stood five feet four inches in his boots. If he had straightened his shoulders he might have increased his height to five feet five, but it always seemed too much of an effort to him to stand up straight.

Apparently shaving was also too much of an effort, for his jaw was usually covered with a greyish-brown stubble. He neither rolled his sleeves up nor buttoned them at the wrists. They hung flapping over his knuckles in a manner that could have intensely annoyed most men. His age must have been about fifty and he, or rather his wife, kept a small grocery shop.

Mrs. Smithers was a large aggressive woman who ruled Godfrey with a firm hand. There was also a tribe of young Smitherses, noisy, dirty and apparently ruled by no one.

Apart from his unshaven chin and flapping sleeves the only thing you noticed about Mr. Smithers was his umbrella. Except on the finest of days he never went down the street without it. He never swung it like a walking-stick and he seldom opened it. He hooked his left thumb into the waist-band of his trousers and hung the umbrella on his wrist. Unkind people said he used it solely as a weapon of defence—to protect himself against the onslaughts of Mrs. Smithers.

The last thing you would have called Mr. Smithers was a hero. You might have called him a waster or even a worm, but a hero—never.

Before Mrs. Smithers married him he had been a sailor and, what is more, an officer. Only in a very humble way, it is true. For a few months he had been mate of a small lighter carrying sugar along a fifty-mile stretch of the coast. He was given the job because the first (and only) mate had been taken to hospital badly injured, and the company could not put their hands on another man with the necessary qualifications. As soon as the mate recovered Godfrey Smithers went back to the fo'c'sle.

He held a ticket, too—a master's "mud" ticket—allowing him to take a vessel anywhere along the Queensland coast within sight of land. Up to the time of his marriage no one had seemed inclined to trust him with the responsibilities of command, and Mrs. Smithers had quickly put an end to any ambitions he may have had in that direction. She took possession of his savings and bought the grocery shop. Another seaman had thankfully "swallowed the anchor".

With the outbreak of war in the Pacific a gradual change came over Godfrey Smithers. His sleeves still flapped untidily round his wrists, and he still carried his umbrella hung over his arm. He didn't shave any more frequently, but he seemed brighter in some indefinite way. It was even said that he stood up to Mrs. Smithers when she attacked him one morning. But that is only hearsay.

As Australia's peril grew greater the change became more marked. On several occasions he was seen to straighten his back and attempt to throw out his narrow chest.

And then one morning he was gone. He left a note to Mrs. Smithers in which he handed over the shop and (presumably) the entire Smithers tribe to her. He was going back to sea, he said, "where good men are urgently needed". Mrs. Smithers made the appropriate remarks to the neighbours about "good men".

What authorities Godfrey Smithers interviewed and what rebuffs he suffered he alone knows, but he eventually turned up in Darwin. He came up on one of the coastal boats to take over his first command—an ancient lighter with no engines in her. When she had to be moved the services of a tug were necessary.

But Godfrey was in command of her and he had a crew of two. There was only one change in him when he arrived in Darwin. He still walked with a stoop; his shirt-sleeves still flapped about his wrists; but his face was different. He had solved the shaving problem by growing a beard— a real beard, neatly trimmed in true naval fashion. He stepped ashore carrying a battered old suitcase in his right hand, and over the crook of his left arm hung the umbrella.

In a few weeks his manner underwent a change. He issued orders with an air of authority. Certainly no one took him seriously, but that didn't seem to worry him.

It was the tug master who gave him the name that stuck to him wherever he went, right up until the day he died. The tug was having some difficulty in berthing the old lighter in a tight corner one hot afternoon. Godfrey was pacing the deck in true nautical style, evidently not at all pleased at the way things were going.

"Go astern," he ordered the tug master.

That was quite all right with the tug master. He was about to go astern in any case. He'd just gathered sternway when Godfrey held up his hand.

"Stop 'er," he ordered, "Now come slow ahead and hard a'starb'd."

The tug master put his head out of the wheelhouse.

"Listen!" he bellowed. "Who do you think you are? Jellicoe?"

In two weeks the whole of Darwin waterfront was calling him Jellicoe. But it didn't worry Godfrey. In fact, he seemed rather proud of the name. When the lighter was alongside the wharf he would step ashore for his evening walk. On the edge of the wharf he would pause for a moment to survey his command.

"Bill," he would say, unshipping his umbrella and pointing aft with it, "tighten up that after spring."

And Bill would grin, and say, "Righto, Jellicoe. I'll fix 'er in a minute."

Then came the great Darwin raid. Bombs rained down on the water-front and ship after ship was struck. Anchored well off-shore, Jellicoe and his ancient lighter seemed far too insignificant a target. But apparently nothing was too small for the raiders that day. One of the last bombs to fall struck the lighter squarely amidships and in thirty seconds Jellicoe had lost his first command. Jellicoe himself was blown clean overboard and was the sole survivor.

He struggled ashore, apparently little the worse for his experience, and in half an hour was giving orders to the men engaged in rescue work along the shattered waterfront. But his umbrella had gone down with the ship and Jellicoe didn't seem to be the same man without it.

The next time I saw him was in Townsville. He was just the same stooped, untidy little Jellicoe as ever, but from his left wrist hung a brand-new umbrella.

Evidently, as there was nothing left in Darwin for him to command he had pestered the authorities until they shipped him round to Towns-ville. Here, after heaven only knows what persistence, he was given his second command.

She was an old lighter of about three hundred tons gross register, powered with Diesel engines, and about the ugliest, unhandiest craft afloat. Originally intended for lightering cargo on short runs, she had a designed speed of eight knots. She may have reached eight on her trials, but she certainly never did at any time thereafter. Her speed fell away till at last she could make only four knots with everything in her favour. She was so unhandy on her helm that she needed the whole bay to come round in. Masters left her one after another until no one would take her over and she was tied up and left to rust herself away in peace. Even in her prime she was hideous. She was flush decked—straight as a ruled line from stem to stern with no flare of bows or graceful curve of line. Dead amidships her living quarters stood four-square and barren. On top of this structure, as if erected as an afterthought, was a tiny bridge, and a wooden wheelhouse that even had a gable roof.

Directly aft of the wheelhouse was the funnel—a tall, skinny, rakish affair that looked more like the chimney from the galley stove than a ship's funnel. Right aft someone had absent-mindedly dumped another square house. When Jellicoe assumed command she was in the hands of a gang of dockside workers. Gear, old and new, littered her decks. Great patches of fresh red lead showed everywhere, and the sound of chipping-hammers made speech impossible. Dented and buckled plates showed where each successive master had left his mark on her as he tried vainly to put her alongside in a seamanlike manner.

But to Jellicoe she was a thing of beauty. No master of a crack Atlantic liner was ever more proud of his command. This was his ship— a ship that could move under her own power. He climbed to the bridge and stood admiring her. He went back on to the wharf and admired her afresh from there. No master was ever more anxious to get his ship to sea than Jellicoe. Once at sea his powers would be unlimited. He could ring "Full Ahead" and feel the engines throbbing as they obeyed his command. A word from him and she would swing obediently round. He was Captain Smithers now.

During the next few weeks they made a number of improvements in the old *Wordina*. They even put armour-plating around her absurd little wheelhouse, but they could not improve her looks. To Jellicoe it seemed as if they would never finish, but at last the great day came when he was ordered to report to Navy office for his sailing orders. Hooking his umbrella over his arm, he hurried off up town.

"Being in all respects ready for sea you are to depart from this port at 1500 hours today and, subject to safe navigation, proceed to Milne Bay via the inner route and the North-east Channel. At Milne Bay you will report to the naval control officer for further instructions. Signed R. T. Hague, Lieut.-Com., R.A.N."

For some time Jellicoe sat reading and rereading the orders. Milne Bay! New Guinea! He, Godfrey Vernon Smithers, was going to take a ship all the way to Milne Bay! Going abroad! What would Mrs. Smithers and the kids think if they only knew? He puffed out his puny chest with pride. Never for a moment did he doubt his ability to get his ship there. He'd get her there if it took him six months to do it.

They gave him a pilot to take the old *Wordina* out. Jellicoe would gladly have dispensed with his services, for he was yearning to assume sole command.

The pilot had heard all about the *Wordina* and was giving her plenty of room. He thanked his stars it was a calm day with only the lightest of breezes blowing. Jellicoe answered his few conversational remarks absently and could hardly disguise his pleasure when at last the pilot lowered himself into the waiting pilot launch. He leaned over the wing of the tiny bridge, waved a hand in half-salute to the pilot and strode to the engine-room telegraph. With feelings of intense pride and happiness and not the slightest misgiving for the future he rang "Full Ahead".

"Hard a'port," he said to the helmsman in his deepest voice. "Steady 'er on north by west." And the M.V. *Wordina* gathered headway and proceeded according to Navy orders.

Throughout the whole night Jellicoe stayed on the bridge, and in the whole Pacific Ocean there was no happier man. The breeze being from dead astern, the old *Wordina* was making her full four knots.

Back in port the pilot was having a drink with Lieut.-Com. Hague.

"Think he'll ever get there?" the pilot asked.

The naval man shrugged his shoulders.

"I doubt it," he answered. "Still, we've got to do the best we can with poor material these days. There's one good thing. If he hits anything he won't hit it too hard at the speed he's doing. Here's to him anyhow."

But Jellicoe did not hit anything. He took a long time over the voyage. When he got up among the reefs he took no chances. Sunset always found him with his anchor down in the lee of some island. Sometimes when the wind blew fresh from the nor'ard he made only twelve miles in the day. Once, with a heavy northerly buster blowing and a short, steep head-sea running, he weighed anchor at 6 a.m. and proceeded; at 3 p.m. he was only two miles from his previous night's anchorage, and, very wisely, he returned and waited two days for the wind to drop.

He arrived in Milne Bay long after the authorities had given him up for lost. In that busy port he settled down to a humdrum routine of lightering from the big ships to the various jetties around the bay. The only difference between this job and his Darwin job was that he was now independent of tugs and their abusive skippers. Sometimes he would be idle for days at a time while the old *Wordina* swung to her anchor. Whenever this happened Jellicoe would become restless. After the second day he would take his umbrella and go ashore to interview the supply officer. In this rainy climate the umbrella was proving of real value, and the whole waterfront had become used to the sight of the bearded little man, umbrella held high over his head, picking his way along the muddy road.

"Nothing for you today, Jellicoe," the supply officer would say. "Go back and take it easy. We'll let you know when we want you."

But Jellicoe didn't want to take it easy. Milne Bay had long ago become commonplace to him, and he was longing to go farther afield. To him it didn't seem right that a fine vessel like the *Wordina* should be wasting her time performing lightering jobs around this bay.

It was during one of his visits to the supply officer that he overheard an interesting bit of conversation. As usual, Jellicoe was standing just inside the doorway unobtrusively waiting for someone to notice him. The supply officer was talking to an irate colonel, and Jellicoe could plainly hear the conversation.

"I know it's urgent, sir," the supply officer was saying, "but I don't see how we can handle it. The barges are overloaded with rations and ammo as it is, and this stuff is so bulky. I'm short of shipping space, always short, and you can't expect me to manufacture ships out of nothing, can you, sir?"

At this point Jellicoe edged himself forward.

"Wot about the *Wordina,* sir?" he asked. "Why couldn't she take it?"

The supply officer waved an impatient hand. "Go away Jellicoe," he said. "Can't you see I'm busy?"

"But, captain," Jellicoe went on, "if it's heavy gear you want taken up the *Wordina* could do the job. She's doin' nothing, and—"

"Who *is* this man?" the colonel broke in.

"Oh, he's skipper of an old lighter we're using here in the bay, sir," the supply officer answered.

"Well, why can't he do the job?" the colonel asked.

The supply officer tapped his pad irritably with his pencil.

"It's impossible, sir," he said. "The old tub only does four knots at the best. If she got caught outside a port in daylight she'd be sunk by the first Jap bomber that came over."

"I'm sure she could do it, sir," Jellicoe put in pleadingly.

"Nonsense!" the supply officer snapped. "Clear out, Jellicoe, and leave us alone."

Jellicoe was sitting disconsolately in a patch of shade under the bridge when a launch came alongside.

"Hi, Jellicoe," the launchman hailed him. "You're wanted up at the transport office right away. You'd better come with me."

Pausing only to pick up his umbrella, Jellicoe clambered aboard the launch.

The colonel was still there when he reached the office, and seated opposite him was a young naval officer. On the table between them a chart was spread.

"Come over here, Jellicoe," the naval man said, "and have a look at this chart."

He pointed to a spot on the chart and explained the situation carefully.

"That's the job, Jellicoe," he finished up. "Do you reckon you could do it?"

Jellicoe shifted his umbrella to a safer position and drew himself up to his full five feet five.

"Easy sir," he said. His tone seemed to imply that where the British Navy could go he and the *Wordina* would follow.

"It won't be easy," the naval man said. "Get that idea right out of your head. You can't just go barging along in daylight or you'll mighty soon get sunk. Tojo's been pretty busy up there lately, so you'll have to make port and hide in the daytime and do your travelling by night. You can't mistake the place you're going to. Even at night it's easy to pick up, but for goodness sake don't try to get in there in daylight. The Japs hold a ridge overlooking the bay, and you'll cop hell if they spot you. If you anchor close inshore when you get there you'll be out of sight and fairly safe. Do you still want to take it on?"

"Yes, sir," Jellicoe answered. "I'll do it."

The following night the *Wordina*, loaded deeper than she had ever been in her long life, steamed slowly out of the bay. Up on her bridge stood Jellicoe, once more supremely happy.

Following Navy instructions, he reversed his usual order and slept by day and travelled by night. It didn't take him long to realize that the naval officer had been right. The job was *not* easy. Three times Jellicoe was lost, utterly and completely lost, but somehow sunrise on the third morning saw him dropping anchor in a place he was looking for. He would spend the day there and that night he would complete the last leg of his journey. He'd carefully worked the times out. By getting under way at 7 p.m. he would reach his destination by 3 a.m.—say 3.30 at the latest. Owing to her heavy load and deep draught the *Wordina* had barely been averaging three knots this trip.

At 7 p.m. he weighed anchor and proceeded. The night was calm and clear, but at ten o'clock a light off-shore breeze sprang up. By midnight it had hauled dead ahead, and was blowing hard. Until nearly three o'clock it continued, and in those three hours it is doubtful if the old *Wordina* altered her position. As far as Jellicoe could see she was just going up and down in the one spot.

No thought of turning back entered Jellicoe's head, although he must have known that it was now impossible to reach his destination before daylight. At 3 a.m. the breeze died away and the *Wordina* once more forged ahead. The sun was rising when she swung in towards the bay. As the naval officer had said, there was no mistaking the small bay with the razor-backed ridge dropping steeply into the sea and the little island just off the cape.

"Port about two points," Jellicoe ordered. "Steer straight for that strip of beach."

In spite of the fact that he had been up all night he had never felt better. He'd done it! The Navy bloke had said it wouldn't be easy, and the supply officer had as good as said he couldn't do it, and here he was. He, Godfrey Vernon Smithers, Master of the M.V. *Wordina*, had completed another hazardous voyage.

He was about to slip aft and cadge a cup of tea from the cook—for with all his newly-gained assurance he'd never been able to bring himself to order the cook to bring a cup of tea to the bridge—when he heard a long, faint whine. A few seconds later there was a crash, and a small fountain of water shot up away out on the starboard bow. Five seconds later there was another, a little closer this time, but still a long way off.

By the time Jellicoe realized he was being fired on there were quite a few fountains going up. A battery of Japanese guns on the far ridge was firing at him. The range was extreme, and the shooting poor. By turning round and steaming out to sea Jellicoe could have been out of range in ten minutes.

To get in under the safety of the razor-backed ridge was a full twenty minutes' steaming for the old *Wordina*, but Jellicoe never wavered. Straight for the little strip of beach that the naval officer had so carefully described the old *Wordina* held on. In ten minutes she was well within range of the guns, and the shooting was improving each minute. Great fountains of water were bursting up all around her. Fragments of metal were flying through the air with a sound like the buzzing of angry hornets. The crew had very wisely sought whatever cover was available, and Jellicoe was alone on the bridge. In the tiny armour-plated wheelhouse just behind him a badly scared helmsman was doing his best to keep his attention fixed on the strip of beach ahead.

Jellicoe must have been scared, too. No man could be otherwise in those conditions, but he was still very much the master of his vessel. Once, when a well-aimed shell landed close alongside and exploded with an ear-splitting crash, the helmsman let the ship swing off her course.

Jellicoe moistened his lips with his tongue, and in a queer high-pitched voice snarled, "Don't let 'er 'ead swing to starb'd like that! Watch your steerin' and keep 'er straight for that there beach."

To the watchers on the shore there was something both absurd and magnificent in the spectacle of this lumbering, ugly old caricature of a ship steaming at snail's pace straight through a hail of shellfire. They forgot her absurd looks in their admiration for the man who commanded her.

And as for Jellicoe—the real Jellicoe on the bridge of his giant flagship in the height of the battle of Jutland could not have had a more quiet, noble dignity than this queer little man standing all alone on his unprotected bridge. Scared he must have been, for his hands were shaking under his untidily flapping shirt-sleeves, but he did not crouch or seek the protection of the wheelhouse. He stood erect, drawn up to his full five feet five.

One shell struck right aft and the galley was no more. One carried the crazy funnel overside and then, when they were almost under the protecting ridge, one struck just for'ard of the bridge. It killed Jellicoe instantly, tore half the tiny bridge away and knocked the helmsman unconscious.

But the old *Wordina* held on. As if she owed a debt to the little man who had idolized her, she carried straight on for the last few hundred yards and ran her nose gently up on the shelving sandy beach. The *Wordina*, with Captain Godfrey Vernon Smithers still on the remains of her shattered bridge, had delivered her cargo "according to Navy instructions".

They buried Jellicoe in the little military cemetery up on the hillside. I expect he would have liked to be buried at sea; but also he would have liked his wife and his family to hear the final words of the chaplain as they filled in his grave.

"There, in the company of brave men," said the chaplain over the remains of Jellicoe, "lies a hero."

THE LADY OR THE TIGER?
Frank Stockton

Frank R. Stockton

IN THE VERY olden time, there lived a semi-barbaric king, whose ideas though somewhat polished and sharpened by the progressiveness of distant Latin neighbors, were still large, florid, and untrammeled as became the half of him which was barbaric. He was a man of exuberant fancy and, withal, of an authority so irresistible that, at his will, he turned his varied fancies into facts. He was greatly given to self-communing, and when he and himself agreed upon anything, the thing was done. When every member of his domestic and political systems moved smoothly in its appointed course, his nature was bland and genial; but whenever there was a little hitch, and some of his orbs got out of their orbits, he was blander and more genial still, for nothing pleased him so much as to make the crooked straight and crush down uneven places.

Among the borrowed notions by which his barbarism had become semified was that of the public arena, in which, by exhibitions of manly and beastly valor, the minds of his subjects were refined and cultured.

But even here the exuberant and barbaric fancy asserted itself. The arena of the king was built, not to give the people an opportunity of hearing the rhapsodies of dying gladiators, nor to enable them to view the inevitable conclusion of a conflict between religious opinions and hungry jaws, but for purposes far better adapted to widen and develop the mental energies of the people. This vast amphitheater, with its encircling galleries, its mysterious vaults, and its unseen passages, was an agent of poetic justice, in which crime was punished, or virtue rewarded, by the decrees of an impartial and incorruptible chance.

When a subject was accused of a crime of sufficient importance to interest the king, public notice was given that on an appointed day the fate of the accused person would be decided in the king's arena—a structure which well deserved its name; for, although its form and plan were borrowed from afar, its purpose emanated solely from the brain of this man who, every barleycorn a king, knew no tradition to which he owed more allegiance than pleased his fancy, and who engrafted on every adopted form of human thought and action the rich growth of his barbaric idealism.

When all the people had assembled in the galleries, and the king, surrounded by his court, sat high up on his throne of royal state on one side of the arena, he gave a signal, a door beneath him opened, and the accused subject stepped out into the amphitheater. Directly opposite him, on the other side of the enclosed space, were two doors, exactly alike and side by side. It was the duty and the privilege of the person on trial to walk directly to these doors and open one of them. He could open either door he pleased. He was subject to no guidance or influence but that of the aforementioned impartial and incorruptible chance. If he opened the one, there came out of it a hungry tiger, the fiercest and most cruel that could be procured, which immediately sprang upon him and tore him to pieces, as a punishment for his guilt. The moment that the case of the criminal was thus decided, doleful iron bells were clanged, great wails went up from the hired mourners posted on the outer rim of the arena, and the vast audience, with bowed heads and downcast hearts, wended slowly their homeward way, mourning greatly that one so young and fair, or so old and respected, should have merited so dire a fate.

But if the accused person opened the other door, there came forth from it a lady, the most suitable to his years and station that his Majesty could select among his fair subjects; and to this lady he was immediately married, as a reward of his innocence. It mattered not that he might already possess a wife and family or that his affections might be engaged upon an object of his own selection. The king allowed no such subordinate arrangements to interfere with his great scheme of retribution and reward. The exercises, as in the other instance, took place immediately, and in the arena. Another door opened beneath the king, and a priest, followed by a band of choristers and dancing maidens blowing joyous airs on golden horns and treading an epithalamic measure, advanced to where the pair stood side by side, and the wedding was promptly and cheerily solemnized. Then the gay brass bells rang forth their merry peals, the people shouted glad hurrahs, and the innocent man, preceded by children strewing flowers on his path, led his bride to his home.

This was the king's semi-barbaric method of administering justice. Its perfect fairness was obvious. The criminal could not know out of which door would come the lady. He opened either he pleased, without having the slightest idea whether, in the next instant, he was to be devoured or married. On some occasions the tiger came out of one door, and on some out of the other. The decisions of this tribunal were not only fair—they were positively determinate. The accused person was instantly punished if he found himself guilty, and if innocent he was rewarded on the spot, whether he liked it or not. There was no escape from the judgments of the king's arena.

The institution was a very popular one. When the people gathered together on one of the great trial days, they never knew whether they were to witness a bloody slaughter or a hilarious wedding. This element of uncertainty lent an interest to the occasion which it could not otherwise have attained. Thus the masses were entertained and pleased, and the thinking part of the community could bring no charge of unfairness against this plan; for did not the accused person have the whole matter in his own hands?

This semi-barbaric king had a daughter as blooming as his most florid fancies and with a soul as fervent and imperious as his own. As is usual in such cases, she was the apple of his eye, and was loved by him above all humanity. Among his courtiers was a young man of that fineness of blood and lowness of station common to the conventional heroes of romance who love royal maidens. This royal maiden was well satisfied with her lover, for he was handsome and brave to a degree unsurpassed in all this kingdom, and she loved him with an ardor that had enough of barbarism in it to make it exceedingly warm and strong. This love affair moved on happily for many months, until, one day, the king happened to discover its existence. He did not hesitate nor waver in regard to his duty in the premises. The youth was immediately cast into prison, and a day was appointed for his trial in the king's arena. This, of course, was an especially important occasion, and his Majesty, as well as all the people, was greatly interested in the workings and development of this trial. Never before had such a case occurred—never before had a subject dared to love the daughter of a king. In after years such things became commonplace enough, but then they were, in no slight degree, novel and startling.

The tiger cages of the kingdom were searched for the most savage and relentless beasts, from which the fiercest monster might be selected for the arena, and the ranks of maiden youth and beauty throughout the land were carefully surveyed by competent judges, in order that the young man might have a fitting bride in case fate did not determine for him a different destiny. Of course, everybody knew that the deed with which the accused was charged had been done. He had loved the princess, and neither he, she, nor any one else thought of denying the fact. But the king would not think of allowing any fact of this kind to interfere with the workings of the tribunal, in which he took such great delight and satisfaction. No matter how the affair turned out, the youth would be disposed of, and the king would take an aesthetic pleasure in watching the course of events which would determine whether or not the young man had done wrong in allowing himself to love the princess.

The appointed day arrived. From far and near the people gathered and thronged the great galleries of the arena, while crowds, unable to gain admittance, massed themselves against its outside walls. The king and his court were in their places, opposite the twin doors—those fateful portals, so terrible in their similarity!

All was ready. The signal was given. A door beneath the royal party opened, and the lover of the princess walked into the arena. Tall, beautiful, fair, his appearance was greeted with a low hum of admiration and anxiety. Half the audience had not known so grand a youth had lived among them. No wonder the princess loved him! What a terrible thing for him to be there!

As the youth advanced into the arena, he turned, as the custom was, to bow to the king. But he did not think at all of that royal personage; his eyes were fixed upon the princess, who sat to the right of her father. Had it not been for the moiety of barbarism in her nature, it is probable that lady would not have been there. But her intense and fervid soul would not allow her to be absent on an occasion in which she was so terribly interested. From the moment that the decree had gone forth that her lover should decide his fate in the king's arena, she had thought of nothing, night or day, but this great event and the various subjects connected with it. Possessed of more power, influence, and force of character than any one who had ever before been interested in such a case, she had done what no other person had done—she had possessed herself of the secret of the doors. She knew in which of the two rooms behind those doors stood the cage of the tiger, with its open front, and in which waited the lady. Through these thick doors, heavily curtained with skins on the inside, it was impossible that any noise or suggestion should come from within to the person who should approach to raise the latch of one of them. But gold, and the power of a woman's will, had brought the secret to the princess.

Not only did she know in which room stood the lady, ready to emerge, all blushing and radiant, should her door be opened, but she knew who the lady was. It was one of the fairest and loveliest of the damsels of the court who had been selected as the reward of the accused youth, should he be proved innocent of the crime of aspiring to one so far above him; and the princess hated her. Often had she seen, or imagined that she had seen, this fair creature throwing glances of admiration upon the person of her lover, and sometimes she thought these glances were perceived and even returned. Now and then she had seen them talking together. It was but for a moment or two, but much can be said in a brief space. It may have been on most unimportant topics, but how could she know that? The girl was lovely, but she had dared to raise her eyes to the loved one of the princess, and, with all the intensity of the savage blood transmitted to her through long lines of wholly barbaric ancestors, she hated the woman who blushed and trembled behind that silent door.

When her lover turned and looked at her, and his eye met hers as she sat there paler and whiter than any one in the vast ocean of anxious faces about her, he saw, by the power of quick perception which is given to those whose souls are one, that she knew behind which door crouched the tiger, and behind which stood the lady. He had expected her to know it. He understood her nature, and his soul was assured that she would never rest until she had made plain to herself this thing, hidden to all other lookers-on, even to the king. The only hope for the youth in which there was any element of certainty was based upon the success of the princess in discovering this mystery, and the moment he looked upon her, he saw she had succeeded.

Then it was that his quick and anxious glance asked the question, "Which?" It was as plain to her as if he shouted it from where he stood. There was not an instant to be lost. The question was asked in a flash; it must be answered in another.

Her right arm lay on the cushioned parapet before her. She raised her hand and made a slight, quick movement toward the right. No one but her lover saw her. Every eye but his was fixed on the man in the arena.

He turned, and with a firm and rapid step he walked across the empty space.

Every heart stopped beating, every breath was held, every eye was fixed immovably upon that man. Without the slightest hesitation, he went to the door on the right and opened it.

Now, the point of the story is this: Did the tiger come out of that door, or did the lady? The more we reflect upon this question, the harder it is to answer. It involves a study of the human heart which leads us through devious mazes of passion out of which it is difficult to find our way. Think of it, fair reader, not as if the decision of the question depended upon yourself, but upon that hot-blooded semi-barbaric princess, her soul at a white heat beneath the combined fires of despair and jealousy. She had lost him, but who should have him?

How often, in her waking hours and in her dreams, had she started in wild horror and covered her face with her hands as she thought of her lover opening the door on the other side of which waited the cruel fangs of the tiger!

But how much oftener had she seen him at the other door! How in her grievous reveries had she gnashed her teeth and torn her hair when she saw his start of rapturous delight as he opened the door of the lady! How her soul had burned in agony when she had seen him rush to meet that woman, with her flushing cheek and sparkling eye of triumph; when she had seen him lead her forth, his whole frame kindled with the joy of recovered life; when she had heard the glad shouts from the multitude and the wild ringing of the happy bells; when she had seen the priest, with his joyous followers, advance to the couple and make them man and wife before her very eyes; and when she had seen them walk away together upon their path of flowers, followed by the tremendous shouts of the hilarious multitude, in which her one despairing shriek was lost and drowned!

Would it not be better for him to die at once and go to wait for her in the blessed regions of semi-barbaric futurity?

And yet, that awful tiger, those shrieks, that blood!

Her decision had been indicated in an instant, but it had been made after days and nights of anguished deliberation. She had known she would be asked, she had decided what she would answer, and, without the slightest hesitation, she had moved her hand to the right.

The question of her decision is one not to be lightly considered, and it is not for me to presume to set up myself as the person able to answer it. So I leave it with all of you: Which came out of the opened door—the lady or the tiger?

THE KEY

EUDORA WELTY

Eudora Welty

It was quiet in the waiting room of the remote little station, except for the night sounds of insects. You could hear their embroidering movements in the weeds outside, which somehow gave the effect of some tenuous voice in the night, telling a story. Or you could listen to the fat thudding of the light bugs and the hoarse rushing of their big wings against the wooden ceiling. Some of the bugs were clinging heavily to the yellow globe, like idiot bees to a senseless smell.

Under this prickly light two rows of people sat in silence, their faces stung, their bodies twisted and quietly uncomfortable, expectantly so, in ones and twos, not quite asleep. No one seemed impatient, although the train was late. A little girl lay flung back in her mother's lap as though sleep had struck her with a blow.

Ellie and Albert Morgan were sitting on a bench like the others waiting for the train and had nothing to say to each other. Their names were ever so neatly and rather largely printed on a big reddish tan suitcase strapped crookedly shut, because of a missing buckle, so that it hung apart finally like a stupid pair of lips. "Albert Morgan, Ellie Morgan, Yellow Leaf, Mississippi." They must have been driven into town in a wagon, for they and the suitcase were all touched here and there with a fine yellow dust, like finger marks.

Ellie Morgan was a large woman with a face as pink and crowded as an old-fashioned rose. She must have been about forty years old. One of those black satchel purses hung over her straight, strong wrist. It must have been her savings which were making possible this trip. And to what place? You wondered, for she sat there as tense and solid as a cube, as if to endure some nameless apprehension rising and overflowing within her at the thought of travel. Her face worked and broke into strained, hardening lines, as if there had been a death—that too explicit evidence of agony in the desire to communicate.

Albert made a slower and softer impression. He sat motionless beside Ellie, holding his hat in his lap with both hands—a hat you were sure he had never worn. He looked homemade, as though his wife had self-consciously knitted or somehow contrived a husband when she sat alone at night. He had a shock of very fine sunburned yellow hair. He was too shy for this world, you could see. His hands were like cardboard, he held his hat so still; and yet how softly his eyes fell upon its crown, moving dreamily and yet with dread over its brown surface! He was smaller than his wife. His suit was brown, too, and he wore it neatly and carefully, as though he were murmuring, "Don't look—no need to look—I am effaced." But you have seen that expression too in silent children, who will tell you what they dreamed the night before in sudden, almost hilarious, bursts of confidence.

Every now and then, as though he perceived some minute thing, a sudden alert, tantalized look would creep over the little man's face, and he would gaze slowly around him, quite slyly. Then he would bow his head again; the expression would vanish; some inner refreshment had been denied him. Behind his head was a wall poster, dirty with time, showing an old-fashioned locomotive about to crash into an open touring car filled with women in veils. No one in the station was frightened by the familiar poster, any more than they were aroused by the little man whose rising and drooping head it framed. Yet for a moment he might seem to you to be sitting there quite filled with hope.

Among the others in the station was a strong-looking young man, alone, hatless, red-haired, who was standing by the wall while the rest sat on benches. He had a small key in his hand and was turning it over and over in his fingers, nervously passing it from one hand to the other, tossing it gently into the air and catching it again.

He stood and stared in distraction at the other people; so intent and so wide was his gaze that anyone who glanced after him seemed rocked like a small boat in the wake of a large one. There was an excess of energy about him that separated him from everyone else, but in the motion of his hands there was, instead of the craving for communication, something of reticence, even of secrecy, as the key rose and fell. You guessed that he was a stranger in town; he might have been a criminal or a gambler, but his eyes were widened with gentleness. His look, which traveled without stopping for long anywhere, was a hurried focusing of a very tender and explicit regard.

The color of his hair seemed to jump and move, like the flicker of a match struck in a wind. The ceiling lights were not steady but seemed to pulsate like a living and transient force, and made the young man in his preoccupation appear to tremble in the midst of his size and strength, and to fail to impress his exact outline upon the yellow walls. He was like a salamander in the fire. "Take care," you wanted to say to him, and yet also, "Come here." Nervously, and quite apart in his distraction, he continued to stand tossing the key back and forth from one hand to the other. Suddenly it became a gesture of abandonment: one hand stayed passive in the air, then seized too late: the key fell to the floor.

EVERYONE, EXCEPT Albert and Ellie Morgan, looked up for a moment. On the floor the key had made a fierce metallic sound like a challenge, a sound of seriousness. It almost made people jump. It was regarded as an insult, a very personal question, in the quiet peaceful room where the insects were tapping at the ceiling and each person was allowed to sit among his possessions and wait for an unquestioned departure. Little walls of reproach went up about them all.

A flicker of amusement touched the young man's face as he observed the startled but controlled and obstinately blank faces which turned toward him for a moment and then away. He walked over to pick up his key.

But it had glanced and slid across the floor, and now it lay in the dust at Albert Morgan's feet.

Albert Morgan was indeed picking up the key. Across from him, the young man saw him examine it, quite slowly, with wonder written all over his face and hands, as if it had fallen from the sky. Had he failed to hear the clatter? There was something wrong with Albert. . . .

As if by decision, the young man did not terminate this wonder by claiming his key. He stood back, a peculiar flash of interest or of something more inscrutable, like resignation, in his lowered eyes.

The little man had probably been staring at the floor, thinking. And suddenly in the dark surface the small sliding key had appeared. You could see memory seize his face, twist it and hold it. What innocent, strange thing might it have brought back to life—a fish he had once spied just below the top of the water in a sunny lake in the country when he was a child? This was just as unexpected, shocking, and somehow meaningful to him.

Albert sat there holding the key in his wide-open hand. How intensified, magnified, really vain all attempt at expression becomes in the afflicted! It was with an almost incandescent delight that he felt the unguessed temperature and weight of the key. Then he turned to his wife. His lips were actually trembling.

And still the young man waited, as if the strange joy of the little man took precedence with him over whatever need he had for the key. With sudden electrification he saw Ellie slip the handle of her satchel purse from her wrist and with her fingers begin to talk to her husband.

The others in the station had seen Ellie too; shallow pity washed over the waiting room like a dirty wave foaming and creeping over a public beach. In quick mumblings from bench to bench people said to each other, "Deaf and dumb!" How ignorant they were of all that the young man was seeing! Although he had no way of knowing the words Ellie said, he seemed troubled enough at the mistake the little man must have made, at his misplaced wonder and joy.

Albert was replying to his wife. On his hands he said to her, "I found it. Now it belongs to me. It is something important! Important! It means something. From now on we will get along better, have more understanding. . . . Maybe when we reach Niagara Falls we will even fall in love, the way other people have done. Maybe our marriage was really for love, after all, not for the other reason—both of us being afflicted in the same way, unable to speak, lonely because of that. Now you can stop being ashamed of me, for being so cautious and slow all my life, for taking my own time. . . . You can take hope. Because it was I who found the key. Remember that—I found it." He laughed all at once, quite silently.

Everyone stared at his impassioned little speech as it came from his fingers. They were embarrassed, vaguely aware of some crisis and vaguely affronted, but unable to interfere; it was as though they were the deaf-mutes and he the speaker. When he laughed, a few people laughed unconsciously with him, in relief, and turned away. But the young man remained still and intent, waiting at his little distance.

"This key came here very mysteriously—it is bound to mean something," the husband went on to say. He held the key up just before her eyes. "You are always praying; you believe in miracles; well, now, here is the answer. It came to me."

His wife looked self-consciously around the room and replied on her fingers, "You are always talking nonsense. Be quiet."

But she was secretly pleased, and when she saw him slowly look down in his old manner, she reached over, as if to retract what she had said, and laid her hand on his, touching the key for herself, softness making her worn hand limp. From then on they never looked around them, never saw anything except each other. They were so intent, so very solemn, wanting to have their symbols perfectly understood!

"You must see it is a symbol," he began again, his fingers clumsy and blurring in his excitement. "It is a symbol of something—something that we deserve, and that is happiness. We will find happiness in Niagara Falls."

And then, as if he were all at once shy even of her, he turned slightly away from her and slid the key into his pocket. They sat staring down at the suitcase, their hands fallen in their laps.

The young man slowly turned away from them and wandered back to the wall, where he took out a cigarette and lighted it.

Outside, the night pressed around the station like a pure stone, in which the little room might be transfixed and, for the preservation of this moment of hope, its future killed, an insect in amber. The short little train drew in, stopped, and rolled away, almost noiselessly.

Then inside, people were gone or turned in sleep or walking about, all changed from the way they had been. But the deaf-mutes and the loitering young man were still in their places.

The man was still smoking. He was dressed like a young doctor or some such person in the town, and yet he did not seem of the town. He looked very strong and active; but there was a startling quality, a willingness to be forever distracted, even disturbed, in the very reassurance of his body, some alertness which made his strength fluid and dissipated instead of withheld and greedily beautiful. His youth by now did not seem an important thing about him; it was a medium for his activity, no doubt, but as he stood there frowning and smoking you felt some apprehension that he would never express whatever might be the desire of his life in being young and strong, in standing apart in compassion, in making any intuitive present or sacrifice, or in any way of action at all—not because there was too much in the world demanding his strength, but because he was too deeply aware.

You felt a shock in glancing up at him, and when you looked away from the whole yellow room and closed your eyes, his intensity, as well as that of the room, seemed to have impressed the imagination with a shadow of itself, a blackness together with the light, the negative beside the positive. You felt as though some exact, skillful contact had been made between the surfaces of your hearts to make you aware, in some pattern, of his joy and his despair. You could feel the fullness and the emptiness of this stranger's life.

The railroad man came in swinging a lantern which he stopped suddenly in its arc. Looking uncomfortable, and then rather angry, he approached the deaf-mutes and shot his arm out in a series of violent gestures and shrugs.

Albert and Ellie Morgan were dreadfully shocked. The woman looked resigned for a moment to hopelessness. But the little man—you were startled by a look of bravado on his face.

In the station the red-haired man was speaking aloud—but to himself. "They missed their train!"

As if in quick apology, the trainman set his lantern down beside Albert's foot, and hurried away.

And as if completing a circle, the red-haired man walked over too and stood silently near the deaf-mutes. With a reproachful look at him the woman reached up and took off her hat.

THEY BEGAN AGAIN, TALKING rapidly back and forth, almost as one person. The old routine of their feeling was upon them once more. Perhaps, you thought, staring at their similarity—her hair was yellow, too—they were children together—cousins even, afflicted in the same way, sent off from home to the state institute. . . .

It was the feeling of conspiracy. They were in counterplot against the plot of those things that pressed down upon them from outside their knowledge and their ways of making themselves understood. It was obvious that it gave the wife her greatest pleasure. But you wondered, seeing Albert, whom talking seemed rather to dishevel, whether it had not continued to be a rough and violent game which Ellie, as the older and stronger, had taught him to play with her.

"What do you think he wants?" she asked Albert, nodding at the red-haired man, who smiled faintly. And how her eyes shone! Who would ever know how deep her suspicion of the whole outside world lay in her heart, how far it had pushed her!

"What does he want?" Albert was replying quickly. "The key!"

Of course! And how fine it had been to sit there with the key hidden from the strangers and also from his wife, who had not seen where he had put it. He stole up with his hand and secretly felt the key, which must have lain in some pocket nearly against his heart. He nodded gently. The key had come there, under his eyes on the floor in the station, all of a sudden, but yet not quite unexpected. That is the way things happen to you always. But Ellie did not comprehend this.

Now she sat there as quiet as could be. It was not only hopelessness about the trip. She, too, undoubtedly felt something privately about that key, apart from what she had said or what he had told her. He had almost shared it with her—you realized that. He frowned and smiled almost at the same time. There was something—something he could almost remember but not quite—which would let him keep the key always to himself. He knew that, and he would remember it later, when he was alone.

"Never fear, Ellie," he said, a still little smile lifting his lip. "I've got it safe in a pocket. No one can find it, and there's no hole for it to fall through."

She nodded, but she was always doubting, always anxious. You could look at her troubled hands. How terrible it was, how strange, that Albert loved the key more than he loved Ellie! He did not mind missing the train. It showed in every line, every motion of his body. The key was closer—closer. The whole story began to illuminate them now, as if the lantern flame had been turned up. Ellie's anxious, hovering body could wrap him softly as a cradle, but the secret meaning, that powerful sign, that reassurance he so hopefully sought, so assuredly deserved—that had never come. There was something lacking in Ellie.

Had Ellie, with her suspicions of everything, come to know even things like this, in her way? How empty and nervous her red scrubbed hands were, how desperate to speak! Yes, she must regard it as unhappiness lying between them, as more than emptiness. She must worry about it, talk about it. You could imagine her stopping her churning to come out to his chair on the porch, to tell him that she did love him and would take care of him always, talking with the spotted sour milk dripping from her fingers. Just try to tell her that talking is useless, that care is not needed . . . And sooner or later he would always reply, say something, agree, and she would go away again. . . .

And Albert, with his face so capable of amazement, made you suspect the funny thing about talking to Ellie. Until you do, declared his round brown eyes, you can be peaceful and content that everything takes care of itself. As long as you let it alone everything goes peacefully, like an uneventful day on the farm—chores attended to, woman working in the house, you in the field, crop growing as well as can be expected, the cow giving, and the sky like a coverlet over it all— so that you're as full of yourself as a colt, in need of nothing, and nothing needing you. But when you pick up your hands and start to talk, if you don't watch carefully, this security will run away and leave you. You say something, make an observation, just to answer your wife's worryings, and everything is jolted, disturbed, laid open like the ground behind a plow, with you running along after it.

But happiness, Albert knew, is something that appears to you suddenly, that is meant for you, a thing which you reach for and pick up and hide at your breast, a shiny thing that reminds you of something alive and leaping.

Ellie sat there quiet as a mouse. She had unclasped her purse and taken out a little card with a picture of Niagara Falls on it.

"Hide it from the man," she said. She did suspect him! The red-haired man had drawn closer. He bent and saw that it was a picture of Niagara Falls.

"Do you see the little rail?" Albert began in tenderness. And Ellie loved to watch him tell her about it; she clasped her hands and began to smile and show her crooked tooth; she looked young: it was the way she had looked as a child.

"That is what the teacher pointed to with her wand on the magic-lantern slide—the little rail. You stand right here. You lean up hard against the rail. Then you can hear Niagara Falls."

"How do you hear it?" begged Ellie, nodding.

"You hear it with your whole self. You listen with your arms and your legs and your whole body. You'll never forget what hearing is, after that."

He must have told her hundreds of times in his obedience, yet she smiled with gratitude, and stared deep, deep into the tinted picture of the waterfall.

Presently she said, "By now, we'd have been there, if we hadn't missed the train."

She did not even have any idea that it was miles and days away. She looked at the red-haired man then, her eyes all puckered up, and he looked away at last.

He had seen the dust on her throat and a needle stuck in her collar where she'd forgotten it, with a thread running through the eye—the final details. Her hands were tight and wrinkled with pressure. She swung her foot a little below her skirt, in the new Mary Jane slipper with the hard toe.

Albert turned away too. It was then, you thought, that he became quite frightened to think that if they hadn't missed the train they would be hearing, at that very moment, Niagara Falls. Perhaps they would be standing there together, pressed against the little rail, pressed against each other, with their lives being poured through them, changing. . . . And how did he know what that would be like? He bent his head and tried not to look at his wife. He could say nothing. He glanced up once at the stranger, with almost a pleading look, as if to say, "Won't you come with us?"

"To work so many years, and then to miss the train," Ellie said.

You saw by her face that she was undauntedly wondering, unsatisfied, waiting for the future.

And you knew how she would sit and brood over this as over their conversations together, about every misunderstanding, every discussion, sometimes even about some agreement between them that had been all settled—even about the secret and proper separation that lies between a man and a woman, the thing that makes them what they are in themselves, their secret life, their memory of the past, their childhood, their dreams. This to Ellie was unhappiness.

They had told her when she was a little girl how people who have just been married have the custom of going to Niagara Falls on a wedding trip, to start their happiness; and that came to be where she put her hope, all of it. So she saved money. She worked harder than he did, you could observe, comparing their hands, good and bad years, more than was good for a woman. Year after year she had put her hope ahead of her.

And he—somehow he had never thought that this time would come, that they might really go on the journey. He was never looking so far and so deep as Ellie—into the future, into the changing and mixing of their lives together when they should arrive at last at Niagara Falls. To him it was always something postponed, like the paying off of the mortgage.

But sitting here in the station, with the suitcase all packed and at his feet, he had begun to realize that this journey might, for a fact, take place. The key had materialized to show him the enormity of this venture. And after his first shock and pride he had simply reserved the key; he had hidden it in his pocket.

She looked unblinking into the light of the lantern on the floor. Her face looked strong and terrifying, all lighted and very near to his. But there was no joy there. You knew that she was very brave.

Albert seemed to shrink, to retreat. . . . His trembling hand went once more beneath his coat and touched the pocket where the key was lying, waiting. Would he ever remember that elusive thing about it or be sure what it might really be a symbol of? . . . His eyes, in their quick manner of filming over, grew dreamy. Perhaps he had even decided that it was a symbol not of happiness with Ellie, but of something else—something which he could have alone, for only himself, in peace, something strange and unlooked for which would come to him. . . .

The red-haired man took a second key from his pocket, and in one direct motion placed it in Ellie's red palm. It was a key with a large triangular pasteboard tag on which was clearly printed STAR HOTEL, ROOM 2.

He did not wait to see any more, but went out abruptly into the night. He stood still for a moment and reached for a cigarette. As he held the match close he gazed straight ahead, and in his eyes, all at once wild and searching, there was certainly, besides the simple compassion in his regard, a look both restless and weary, very much used to the comic. You could see that he despised and saw the uselessness of the thing he had done.

THE ACCIDENT
MAVIS GALLANT

Mavis Gallant

I

I WAS TIRED and did not always understand what they were asking me. I borrowed a pencil and wrote:

PETER HIGGINS
CALGARY 1935 – ITALY 1956

But there was room for more on the stone, and the English clergyman in this Italian town who was doing all he could for me said, "Is there nothing else, child?" Hadn't Pete been my husband, somebody's son? That was what he was asking. It seemed enough. Pete had renounced us, left us behind. His life-span might matter, if anyone cared, but I must have sensed even then that no one would ever ask me what he had been like. His father once asked me to write down what I remembered. He wanted to compose a memorial booklet and distribute it at Christmas, but then his wife died, too, and he became prudent about recollections. Even if I had wanted to, I couldn't have told much—just one or two things about the way Pete died. His mother had some information about him, and I had some, but never enough to describe a life. She had the complete knowledge that puts parents at a loss, finally: she knew all about him except his opinion of her and how he was with me. They were never equals. She was a grown person with part of a life lived and the habit of secrets before he was conscious of her. She said, later, that she and Pete had been friends. How can you be someone's friend if you have had twenty years' authority over him and he has never had one second's authority over you?

He didn't look like his mother. He looked like me. In Italy, on our wedding trip, we were often taken for brother and sister. Our height, our glasses, our soft myopic stares, our assurance, our sloppy comfortable clothes made us seem to the Italians related and somehow unplaceable. Only a North American could have guessed what our families were, what our education amounted to, and where we had got the money to spend on travelling. Most of the time we were just pie-faces, like the tourists in ads—though we were not as clean as those couples, and not quite as grown-up. We didn't seem to be married: the honeymoon in hotels, in strange beds, the meals we shared in cheap, bright little restaurants prolonged the clandestine quality of love before. It was still a game, but now we had infinite time. I became bold, and I dismissed the universe: "It was a rotten little experiment," I said, "and we were given up long ago." I had been brought up by a forcible, pessimistic, widowed mother, and to be able to say aloud "we were given up" shows how far I had come. Pete's assurance was natural, but mine was fragile, and recent, and had grown out of love. Travelling from another direction, he was much more interested in his parents than in God. There was a glorious treason in all our conversations now. Pete wondered about his parents, but I felt safer belittling Creation. My mother had let me know about the strength of the righteous; I still thought the skies would fall if I said too much.

What struck me about these secret exchanges was how we judged our parents from a distance now, as if they were people we had known on a visit. The idea that he and I could be natural siblings crossed my mind. What if I, or Pete, or both, had been adopted? We had been raised in different parts of Canada, but we were only children, and neither of us resembled our supposed parents. Watching him, trapping him almost in mannerisms I could claim, I saw my habit of sprawling, of spreading maps and newspapers on the ground. He had a vast appetite for bread and pastries and sweet desserts. He was easily drunk and easily sick. Yes, we were alike. We talked in hotel rooms, while we drank the drink of the place, the *grappa* or wine or whatever we were given, prone across the bed, the bottle and glasses and the ashtray on the floor. We agreed to live openly, without secrets, though neither of us knew what a secret was. I admired him as I could never have admired myself. I remembered how my mother, the keeper of the castle until now, had said that one day—one treeless, sunless day—real life would overtake me, and then I would realize how spoiled and silly I had always been.

The longest time he and I spent together in one place was three days, in a village up behind the Ligurian coast. I thought that the only success of my life, my sole achievement, would be this marriage. In a dream he came to me with the plans for a house. I saw the white lines on the blue paper, and he showed me the sunny Italian-style loggia that would be built. "It is not quite what we want," he said, "but better than anything we have now." "But we can't afford it, we haven't got the capital," I cried, and I panicked, and woke: woke safe, in a room of which the details were dawn, window, sky, first birds of morning, and Pete still sleeping, still in the dark.

II

THE LAST Italian town of our journey was nothing—just a black beach with sand like soot, and houses shut and dormant because it was the middle of the afternoon. We had come here from our village only to change trains. We were on our way to Nice, then Paris, then home. We left our luggage at the station, with a porter looking after it, and we drifted through empty, baking streets, using up the rest of a roll of film. By now we must have had hundreds of pictures of each other in market squares, next to oleanders, cut in two by broomstick shade, or backed up, squinting, against scaly noonday shutters. Peter now chose to photograph a hotel with a cat on the step, a policeman, and a souvenir stand, as if he had never seen such things in Canada— as if they were monuments. I never once heard him say anything was ugly or dull; for if it was, what were we doing with it? We were often stared at, for we were out of our own background and did not fit into the new. That day, I was eyed more than he was. I was watched by men talking in dark doorways, leaning against the façades of in-hospitable shops. I was travelling in shorts and a shirt and rope-soled shoes. I know now that this costume was resented, but I don't know why. There was nothing indecent about my clothes. They were very like Pete's.

He may not have noticed the men. He was always on the lookout for something to photograph, or something to do, and sometimes he missed people's faces. On the steep street that led back to the railway station, he took a careful picture of a bakery, and he bought crescent-shaped bread with a soft, pale crust, and ate it there, on the street. He wasn't hungry; it was a question of using time. Now the closed shutters broke out in the afternoon, and girls appeared—girls with thick hair, smelling of jasmine and honeysuckle. They strolled hand in hand, in light stockings and clean white shoes. Their dresses—blue, lemon, the palest peach—bloomed over rustling petticoats. At home I'd have called them cheap, and made a face at their cheap perfume, but here, in their own place, they were enravishing, and I thought Pete would look at them and at me and compare; but all he remarked was "How do they stand those clothes on a day like this?" So real life, the grey noon with no limits, had not yet begun. I distrusted real life, for I knew nothing about it. It was the middle-aged world without feeling, where no one was loved.

Bored with his bread, he tossed it away and laid his hands on a white

Lambretta propped against the curb. He pulled it upright, examining it. He committed two crimes in a second: wasted bread and touched an adored mechanical object belonging to someone else. I knew these were crimes later, when it was no use knowing, no good to either of us. The steering of the Lambretta was locked. He saw a bicycle then, belonging, he thought, to an old man who was sitting in a kitchen chair out on the pavement. "This all right with you?" Pete pointed to the bike, then himself, then down the hill. With a swoop of his hand he tried to show he would come straight back. His pantomime also meant that there was still time before we had to be on the train, that up at the station there was nothing to do, that eating bread, taking pictures of shops, riding a bike downhill and walking it back were all doing, using up your life; yes, it was a matter of living.

The idling old man Peter had spoken to bared his gums. Pete must have taken this for a smile. Later, the old man, who was not the owner of the bike or of anything except the fat sick dog at his feet, said he had cried "Thief!" but I never heard him. Pete tossed me his camera and I saw him glide, then rush away, past the girls who smelled of jasmine, past the bakery, down to the corner, where a policeman in white, under a parasol, spread out one arm and flexed the other and blew hard on a whistle. Peter was standing, as if he were trying to coast to a stop. I saw things meaningless now—for instance that the sun was sifted through leaves. There were trees we hadn't noticed. Under the leaves he seemed under water. A black car, a submarine with Belgian plates, parked at an angle, stirred to life. I saw sunlight deflected from six points on the paint. My view became discomposed, as if the sea were suddenly black and opaque and had splashed up over the policeman and the road, and I screamed, "He's going to open the door!" Everyone said later that I was mistaken, for why would the Belgian have started the motor, pulled out, and *then* flung open the door? He had stopped near a change office perhaps; he had forgotten his sunglasses, or a receipt. He started, stopped abruptly, hurled back the door. I saw that, and then I saw him driving away. No one had taken his number.

Strangers made Pete kneel and then stand, and they dusted the bicycle. They forced him to walk—where? Nobody wanted him. Into a pharmacy, finally. In a parrot's voice he said to the policeman, "Don't touch my elbow." The pharmacist said, "He can't stay here," for Pete was vomiting, but weakly—a weak coughing, like an infant's. I was in a crowd of about twenty people, a spectator with two cameras round my neck. In kind somebody's living-room, Pete was placed on a couch with a cushion under his head and another under his dangling arm. The toothless old man turned up now, panting, with his waddling dog, and cried that we had a common thief there before us, and everyone listened and marvelled until the old man spat on the carpet and was turned out.

When I timidly touched Pete, trying to wipe his face with a crumpled Kleenex (all I had), he thought I was one of the strangers. His mouth was a purple colour, as if he had been in icy water. His eyes looked at me, but he was not looking out.

"Ambulance," said a doctor who had been fetched by the policeman. He spoke loudly and slowly, dealing with idiots.

"Yes," I heard, in English. "We must have an ambulance."

Everyone now inspected me. I was, plainly, responsible for something. For walking around the streets in shorts? Wasting bread? Conscious of my sweaty hair, my bare legs, my lack of Italian—my nakedness—I began explaining the true error of the day: "The train has gone, and all our things are on it. Our luggage. We've been staying up in that village—oh, what's the name of it, now? Where they make the white wine. I can't remember, no, I can't remember where we've been. I could find it, I could take you there; I've just forgotten what it's called. We were down here waiting for the train. To Nice. We had lots of time. The porter took our things and said he'd put them on the train for us. He said the train would wait here, at the border, that it waited a long time. He was supposed to meet us at the place where you show your ticket. I guess for an extra tip. The train must have gone now. My purse is in the duffel-bag up at the the. . . . I'll look in my husband's wallet. Of course that is my husband! Our passports must be on the train, too. Our traveller's checks are in our luggage, his and mine. We were just walking round taking pictures instead of sitting up there in the station. Anyway, there was no place to sit—only the bar, and it was smelly and dark."

No one believed a word of this, of course. Would you give your clothes, your passport, your traveller's checks to a porter? A man you had never seen in your life before? A bandit disguised as a porter, with a stolen cap on his head?

"You could not have taken that train without showing your passport," a careful foreign voice objected.

"What are you two, anyway?" said the man from the change office. His was a tough, old-fashioned movie-American accent. He was puffy-eyed and small, but he seemed superior to us, as he wore an impeccable shirt. Pete, on the sofa, looked as if he had been poisoned, or stepped on. "What are you?" the man from the change office said again. "Students? Americans? No? What, then? Swedes?"

I saw what the doctor had been trying to screen from me: a statue's marble eye.

The tourist who spoke the careful foreign English said, "Be careful of the pillows."

"What? What?" screamed the put-upon person who owned them.

"Blood is coming out of his ears," said the tourist, halting between words. "That is a bad sign." He seemed to search his memory for a better English word. "An *unfortunate* sign," he said, and put his hand over his mouth.

III

PETE'S FATHER and mother flew from Calgary when they had my cable. They made flawless arrangements by telephone, and knew exactly what to bring. They had a sunny room looking on to rusty palms and a strip of beach about a mile from where the accident had been. I sat against one of the windows and told them what I thought I remembered. I looked at the white walls, the white satin bedspreads, at Mrs. Higgins's spotless dressing case, and finally down at my hands.

His parents had not understood, until now, that ten days had gone by since Pete's death.

"What have you been doing, dear, all alone?" said Mrs. Higgins, gently.

"Just waiting, after I cabled you." They seemed to be expecting more. "I've been to the movies," I said.

From this room we could hear the shrieks of children playing on the sand. "Are they orphans?" asked Mrs. Higgins, for they were little girls, dressed alike, with soft pink sun hats covering their heads.

"It seems to be a kind of summer camp," I said. "I was wondering about them, too."

"It would make an attractive picture," said Pete's mother, after a pause. "The blue sea, and the nuns, and all those bright hats. It would look nice in a dining-room."

They were too sick to reproach me. My excuse for not having told them sooner was that I hadn't been thinking, and they didn't ask me for it. I could only repeat what seemed important now. "I don't want to go back home just yet" was an example. I was already in the future, which must have hurt them. "I have a girl friend in the Embassy in Paris. I can stay with her." I scarcely moved my lips. They had to strain to hear. I held still, looking down at my fingers. I was very brown, sun streaks in my hair, more graceful than at my wedding, where I knew they had found me maladroit—a great lump of a Camp Fire Girl. That was how I had seen myself in my father-in-law's eyes. Extremes of shock had brought me near some ideal they had of prettiness. I appeared now much more the kind of girl they'd have wanted as Pete's wife.

So they had come for nothing. They were not to see him, or bury him, or fetch home his bride. All I had to show them was a still unlabelled grave.

When I dared look at them, I saw their way of being was not Pete's. Neither had his soft selective stare. Mr. Higgins's eyes were a fanatic blue. He was thin and sunburned and unused to nonsense. Summer and winter he travelled with his wife in climates that were bad for her skin. She had the fair, papery colouring that requires constant vigilance. All this I knew because of Pete.

They saw his grave at the best time of day, in the late afternoon, with the light at a slant. The cemetery was in a valley between two plaster towns. A flash of the sea was visible, a corner of ultramarine. They saw a stone wall covered with roses, pink and white and near-white, open, without secrets. The hiss of traffic on the road came to us, softer than rain; then true rain came down, and we ran to our waiting taxi through a summer storm. Later they saw the station where Pete had left our luggage but never come back. Like Pete—as Pete had intended to—they were travelling to Nice. Under a glass shelter before the station I paused and said, "That was where it happened, down there." I pointed with my white glove. I was not as elegant as Mrs. Higgins, but I was not a source of embarrassment. I wore gloves, stockings, shoes.

The steep street under rain was black as oil. Everything was reflected upside down. The neon signs of the change office and the pharmacy swam deeply in the pavement.

"I'd like to thank the people who were so kind," said Mrs. Higgins. "Is there time? Shirley, I suppose you got their names?"

"Nobody was kind," I said.

"Shirley! We've met the doctor, and the minister, but you said there was a policeman, and a Dutch gentleman, and a lady—you were in this lady's living-room."

"They were all there, but no one was kind."

"The bike's paid for?" asked Mr. Higgins suddenly.

"Yes. I paid. And I paid for having the sofa cushions cleaned."

What sofa cushions? What was I talking about? They seemed petrified, under the glass shelter, out of the rain. They could not take their eyes away from the place I had said was *there*. They never blamed me, never a word or a hidden meaning. I had explained, more than once, how the porter that day had not put our bags on the train after all but had stood waiting at the customs barrier, wondering what had become of us. I told them how I had found everything intact— passports and checks and maps and sweaters and shoes. . . . They could not grasp the importance of it. They knew that Pete had chosen me, and gone away with me, and they never saw him again. An unreliable guide had taken them to a foreign graveyard and told them, without evidence, that now he was there.

"I still don't see how anyone could have thought Pete was stealing," said his mother. "What would Pete have wanted with someone's old bike?"

THEY WERE flying home from Nice. They loathed Italy now, and they had a special aversion to the sunny room where I had described

Pete's death. We three sat in the restaurant at the airport, and they spoke quietly, considerately, because the people at the table next to ours were listening to a football match on a portable radio.

I closed my hand into a fist and let it rest on the table. I imagined myself at home, saying to my mother, "All right, real life has begun. What's your next prophecy?"

I was not flying with them. I was seeing them off. Mrs. Higgins sat poised and prepared in her linen coat, with her large handbag, and her cosmetics and airsickness tablets in her dressing case, and her diamond maple leaf so she wouldn't be mistaken for an American, and her passport ready to be shown to anyone. Pale gloves lay folded over the clasp of the dressing case. "You'll want to go to your own people, I know," she said. "But you have a home with us. You mustn't forget it." She paused. I said nothing, and so she continued, "What are you going to do, dear? I mean, after you have visited your friend. You mustn't be lonely."

I muttered whatever seemed sensible. "I'll have to get a job. I've never had one and I don't know anything much. I can't even type—not properly." Again they gave me this queer impression of expecting something more. What did they want? "Pete said it was no good learning anything if you couldn't type. He said it was the only useful thing he could do."

In the eyes of his parents was the same wound. I had told them something about him they hadn't known.

"Well, I understand," said his mother, presently. "At least, I think I do."

They imagine I want to be near the grave, I supposed. They think that's why I'm staying on the same side of the world. Peter and I had been waiting for a train; now I had taken it without him. I was waiting again. Even if I were to visit the cemetery every day, he would never speak. His last words had not been for me but to a policeman. He would have said something to me, surely, if everyone hadn't been in such a hurry to get him out of the way. His mind was quenched, and his body out of sight. "You don't love with your soul," I had cried to the old clergyman at the funeral—an offensive remark, judging from the look on his face as he turned it aside. Now I was careful. The destination of a soul was of no interest. The death of a voice—now, that was real. The Dutchman suddenly covering his mouth was horror, and a broken elbow was true pain. But I was careful; I kept this to myself.

"You're our daughter now," Pete's father said. "I don't think I want you to have to worry about a job. Not yet." Mr. Higgins happened to know my family's exact status. My father had not left us well off, and my mother had given everything she owned to a sect that did not believe in blood transfusions. She expected the end of the world, and would not eat an egg unless she had first met the hen. That was Mr. Higgins's view.

"Shirley must work if that's what she wants to do," Mrs. Higgins said softly.

"I do want to!" I imagined myself, that day, in a river of people pouring into subways.

"I'm fixing something up for you, just the same," said Mr. Higgins hurriedly, as if he would not be interrupted by women.

Mrs. Higgins allowed her pale forehead to wrinkle, under her beige veil. Was it not better to struggle and to work, she asked. Wasn't that real life? Would it not keep Shirley busy, take her mind off her loss, her disappointment, her tragedy, if you like (though "tragedy" was not an acceptable way of looking at fate), if she had to think about her daily bread?

"The allowance I'm going to make her won't stop her from working," he said. "I was going to set something up for the kids anyway."

She seemed to approve; she had questioned him only out of some prudent system of ethics.

He said to me, "I always have to remember I could go any minute, just like that. I've got a heart." He tapped it—tapped his light suit. "Meantime you better start with this." He gave me the envelope that had been close to his heart until now. He seemed diffident, made ashamed by money, and by death, but it was he and not his wife who had asked if there was a hope that Pete had left a child. No, I had told him. I had wondered, too, but now I was sure. "Then Shirley is all we've got left," he said to his wife, and I thought they seemed bankrupt, having nothing but me.

"If that's a check on a bank at home, it might take too long to clear," said his wife. "After all Shirley's been through, she needs a fair-sized sum right away."

"She's had that, Betty," said Mr. Higgins, smiling.

I had lived this: three round a table, the smiling parents. Pete had said, "They smile, they go on talking. You wonder what goes on."

"How you manage everything you do without a secretary with you all the time I just don't know," said his wife, all at once admiring him.

"You've been saying that for twenty-two years," he said.

"Twenty-three, now."

With this the conversation came to an end and they sat staring, puzzled, not overcome by life but suddenly lost to it, out of touch. The photograph Pete carried of his mother, that was in his wallet when he died, had been taken before her marriage, with a felt hat all to one side, and an organdie collar, and Ginger Rogers hair. It was easier to imagine Mr. Higgins young—a young Gary Cooper. My father-in-law's blue gaze rested on me now. Never in a million years would he have picked me as a daughter-in-law. I knew that; I understood. Pete was part of him, and Pete, with all the girls he had to choose from, had chosen me. When Mr. Higgins met my mother at the wedding, he thanked God, and was overheard being thankful, that the wedding was not in Calgary. Remembering my mother that day, with her glasses on her nose and a strange borrowed hat on her head, and recalling Mr. Higgins's face, I thought of words that would keep me from laughing. I found, at random, "threesome", "smother", "gambling", "habeas corpus", "sibling" . . .

"How is your mother, Shirley?" said Mrs. Higgins.

"I had a letter. . . . She's working with a pendulum now."

"A pendulum?"

"Yes. A weight on a string, sort of it makes a diagnosis—whether you've got something wrong with your stomach, if it's an ulcer, or what. She can use it to tell when you're pregnant and if the baby will be a girl or a boy. It depends whether it swings north-south or east-west."

"Can the pendulum tell who the father is?" said Mr. Higgins.

"They are useful for people who are afraid of doctors," said Mrs. Higgins, and she fingered her neat gloves, and smiled to herself. "Someone who won't hear the truth from a doctor will listen to any story from a woman with a pendulum or a piece of crystal."

"Or a stone that changes colour," I said. "My mother had one of those. When our spaniel had mastoids it turned violet."

She glanced at me then, and caught in her breath, but her husband, by a certain amount of angry fidgeting, made us change the subject. That was the one moment she and I were close to each other—something to do with quirky female humour.

MR. HIGGINS did not die of a heart attack, as he had confidently expected, but a few months after this Mrs. Higgins said to her maid in the kitchen, "I've got a terrible pain in my head. I'd better lie down." Pete's father wrote, "She knew what the matter was, but she never said. Typical." I inherited a legacy and some jewellery from her, and wondered why. I had been careless about writing. I could not write the kind of letters she seemed to want. How could I write to someone I hardly knew about someone else who did not exist? Mr. Higgins married the widow of one of his closest friends—a woman six years older than he. They travelled to Europe for their wedding trip. I had a temporary job as an interpreter in a department store. When my father-in-law saw me in a neat suit, with his name, HIGGINS, fastened to my jacket, he seemed to approve. He was the only person then who did not say that I was wasting my life and my youth and ought to go home. The new Mrs. Higgins asked to be taken to an English-speaking hairdresser, and there, under the roaring dryer, she yelled that Mr. Higgins may not have been Pete's father. Perhaps he had been, perhaps he hadn't, but one thing he was, and that was a saint. She came out from under the helmet and said in a normal voice, "Martin doesn't know I dye my hair." I wondered if he had always wanted this short, fox-coloured woman. The new marriage might for years have been in the maquis of his mind, and of Mrs. Higgins's life. She may have known it as she sat in the airport that day, smiling to herself, touching her unstained gloves. Mr. Higgins had drawn up a new way of life, like a clean will with everyone he loved cut out. I was trying to draw up a will, too, but I was patient, waiting, waiting for someone to tell me what to write. He spoke of Pete conventionally, in a sentimental way that forbade any feeling. Talking that way was easier for both of us. We were both responsible for something—for surviving, perhaps. Once he turned to me and said defiantly, "Well, she and Pete are together now, aren't they? And didn't they leave us here?"

O FAT WHITE WOMAN
WILLIAM TREVOR

William Trevor.

R ELAXING IN THE garden of her husband's boarding-school, Mrs. Digby-Hunter could not help thinking that it was good to be alive. On the short grass of the lawn, tucked out of sight beneath her deck-chair, was a small box of Terry's All Gold Chocolates, and on her lap, open at page eight, lay a paper-backed novel by her second-favourite writer of historical fiction. In the garden there was the pleasant sound of insects, and occasionally the buzzing of bees. No sound came from the house: the boys, beneath the alert tutelage of her husband and Mr. Kelly, were obediently labouring, the maids, Dympna and Barbara, were, Mrs. Digby-Hunter hoped, washing themselves.

Not for the moment in the mood for reading, she surveyed the large, tidy garden that was her husband's pride, even though he never had a moment to work in it. Against high, stone walls forsythia grew, and honeysuckle and little pear-trees, and beneath them in rich, herbaceous borders the garden flowers of summer blossomed now in colourful variety. Four beech-trees shaded patches of the lawn and roses grew, and geraniums, in round beds symmetrically arranged. On either side of an archway in the wall ahead of Mrs. Digby-Hunter were two yew-trees and beyond the archway, in a wilder part, she could see the blooms of rhododendrons. She could see as well, near one of the yew-trees, the bent figure of Sergeant Wall, an ex-policeman employed on a part-time basis by her husband. He was weeding, his movements slow in the heat of that June afternoon, a stained white hat on his hairless head. It was pleasant to sit in the shade of a beech-tree watching someone else working, having worked oneself all morning in a steamy kitchen. Although she always considered herself an easy-going woman, she had been very angry that morning because one of the girls had quite clearly omitted to make use of the deodorant she was at such pains to supply them with. She had accused each in turn and had got nowhere whatsoever, which didn't entirely surprise her. Dympna was just fifteen and Barbara only a month or two older; hardly the age at which to expect responsibility and truthfulness. Yet it was her duty to train them as it was her husband's duty to train the boys. "You'll strip wash, both of you," she'd commanded snappishly in the end, "immediately you've done the lunch dishes. From top to toe, please, every inch of you." They had both, naturally, turned sulky.

Mrs. Digby-Hunter, wearing that day a blue cotton dress with a pattern of pinkish lupins on it, was fifty-one. She had married her husband twenty-nine years ago, at a time when he'd been at the beginning of a career in the army. Her father, well-to-do and stern, had given her away and she'd been quite happy about his gesture, for love had then possessed her fully. Determined at all costs to make a success of her marriage and to come up to scratch as a wife, she had pursued a policy of agreeableness: she smiled instead of making a fuss, in her easy-going way she accepted what there was to accept, placing her faith in her husband as she believed a good wife should. In her own opinion she was not a clever person, but at least she could offer loyalty and devotion, instead of nagging and arguing. In a bedroom of a Welsh hotel she had disguised, on her wedding night, her puzzled disappointment when her husband had abruptly left her side, having lain there for only a matter of minutes.

Thus a pattern began in their marriage, and as a result of it Mrs. Digby-Hunter had never borne children although she had, gradually and at an increasing rate, put on weight. At first she had minded about this and had attempted to diet. She had deprived herself of what she most enjoyed until it occurred to her that caring in this way was making her bad-tempered and miserable: it didn't suit her, all the worrying about calories and extra ounces. She weighed now, although she didn't know it, thirteen stone.

Her husband was leaner, a tall man with bony fingers and smooth black hair and eyes that stared at other people's eyes as if to imply shrewdness. He had a gaunt face and on it a well-kept though not extensive moustache. Shortly after their marriage he had abandoned his career in the army because, he said, he could see no future in it. Mrs. Digby-Hunter was surprised but assumed that what was apparent to her husband was not apparent to her. She smiled and did not argue.

After the army her husband became involved with a firm that manufactured a new type of all-purpose, metal step-ladder. He explained to her the mechanism of this article, but it was complicated and she failed to understand: she smiled and nodded, murmuring that the ladder was indeed an ingenious one. Her husband, briskly businesslike in a herring-bone suit, became a director of the step-ladder company on the day before the company ran into financial difficulties and was obliged to cease all production.

"Your father could help," he murmured, having imparted to her the unfortunate news, but her father, when invited to save the step-ladder firm, closed his eyes in boredom.

"I'm sorry," she said, rather miserably, feeling she had failed to come up to scratch as a wife. He said it didn't matter, and a few days later he told her he'd become a vending-machine operator. He would have an area, he said, in which he would daily visit schools and swimming-pools, laundrettes, factories, offices, wherever the company's vending machines were sited. He would examine the machines to see that they were in good trim and would fill them full of powdered coffee and powdered milk and a form of tea, and minerals and biscuits and chocolate.

She thought the work odd for an ex-army officer, but she did not say so. Instead, she listened while he told her that there was an expanding market for vending machines, and that in the end they would make a considerable amount of money. His voice went on, quoting percentages and conversion rates. She was knitting him a blue pullover at the time. He held his arms up while she fitted it about his chest; she nodded while he spoke.

Then her father died and left her a sum of money.

"We could buy a country house," her husband said, "and open it up as a smart little hotel." She agreed that that would be nice. She felt that perhaps neither of them was qualified to run an hotel, but it didn't seem worth making a fuss about that, especially since her husband had, without qualifications, joined a step-ladder firm and then, equally un-skilled, had gone into the vending-machine business. In fact, their abilities as hoteliers were never put to the test because all of a sudden her husband had a better idea. Idling one evening in a saloon bar, he dropped into conversation with a man who was in a state of depression because his son appeared to be a dunce.

"If I was starting again," said the man, "I'd go into the cramming business. My God, you could coin it." The man talked on, speaking of parents like himself who couldn't hold their heads up because their children's poor performances in the Common Entrance examination de-prived them of an association with one of the great public schools of England. The next day Mrs. Digby-Hunter's husband scrutinised bound volumes of the Common Entrance examination papers.

"A small boarding-school," he later said to her, "for temporarily backward boys; we might do quite nicely." Mrs. Digby-Hunter, who did not immediately take to the notion of being surrounded day and night by temporarily backward boys, said that the idea sounded an interesting one. "There's a place for sale in Gloucestershire," her husband said.

The school, begun as a small one, remained so because, as her husband explained, any school of this nature must be small. The turn-over in boys was rapid, and it soon became part of the educational policy of Milton Grange to accept not more than twenty boys at any one time, the wisdom of which was reflected in results that parents and headmasters agreed were remarkable: the sons who had idled at the back of their preparatory school classrooms passed into the great public schools of England, and their parents paid the high fees of Milton Grange most gratefully.

At Milton Grange, part ivy-clad, turreted and baronial, Mrs. Digby-

Hunter was happy. She did not understand the ins and outs of the Common Entrance examination, for her province was the kitchen and the dormitories, but certainly life at Milton Grange as the headmaster's wife was much more like it than occupying half the ground floor of a semi-detached villa in Croydon, as the wife of a vending-machine operator. "Christ, what a time we're having with that boy for Harrow," her husband would say, and she would make a sighing noise to match the annoyance he felt, and smile to cheer him up. It was extraordinary what he had achieved with the dullards he took on, and she now and again wondered if one day he might even receive a small recognition, an OBE maybe. As for her, Milton Grange was recognition enough: an apt reward, she felt, for her marital agreeableness, for not being a nuisance, and coming up to scratch as a wife.

Just occasionally Mrs. Digby-Hunter wondered what life would have been like if she'd married someone else. She wondered what it would have been like to have had children of her own and to have engaged in the activity that caused, eventually, children to be born. She imagined, once a year or so as she lay alone in her room in the darkness, what it would be like to share a double bed night after night. She imagined a faceless man, a pale naked body beside hers, hands caressing her flesh. She imagined, occasionally, being married to a clergyman she'd known as a girl, a man who had once embraced her with intense passion, suddenly, after a dance in a church hall. She had experienced the pressure of his body against hers and she could recall still the smell of his clothes and the dampness of his mouth.

But Milton Grange was where she belonged now: she had chosen a man and married him and had ended up, for better or worse, in a turreted house in Gloucestershire. There was give and take in marriage, as always she had known, and where she was concerned there was everything to be thankful for. Once a year, on the last Saturday in July, the gardens of the school were given over to a Conservative fete, and more regularly she and her husband drove to other country houses, for dinner or cocktails. A local Boy Scout group once asked her to present trophies at a sports because she was her husband's wife, and he was well regarded. She had enjoyed the occasion and had bought new clothes specially for it.

In winter she put down bulbs, and in spring she watched the birds collecting twigs and straw for nests. She loved the gardens and often repeated to the maids in the kitchen that one was "nearer God's Heart in a garden than anywhere else on earth". It was a beautiful sentiment, she said, and very true.

On that June afternoon, while Mrs. Digby-Hunter dropped into a doze beneath the beech-trees and Sergeant Wall removed the weeds from a herbaceous border, the bearded Mr. Kelly walked between two rows of desks in a bare attic room. Six boys bent over the desks, writing speedily. In the room next door six other boys wrote also. They would not be idling, Mr. Kelly knew, any more than the boys in the room across the corridor would be idling.

"*Amavero, amaveris, amaverit,*" he said softly, his haired lips close to the ear of a boy called Timpson. "*Amaverimus,* Timpson, *amaveritis, amaverint.*" A thumb and forefinger of Mr. Kelly's seized and turned the flesh on the back of Timpson's neck. "*Amaveritis,*" he said again, "*amerverint.*" While the flesh was twisted this way and that and while Timpson moaned in the quiet manner that Mr. Kelly preferred, Dympna and Barbara surveyed the sleeping form of Mrs. Digby-Hunter in the garden. They had not washed themselves. They stood in the bedroom they shared, gazing through an open, diamond-paned window, smoking two Embassy tipped cigarettes. "White fat slug," said Barbara. "Look at her."

They looked a moment longer. Sergeant Wall in the far distance pushed himself from his knees onto his feet. "He's coming in for his tea," said Barbara. She held cigarette smoke in her mouth and then released it in short puffs. "She can't think," said Dympna. "She's incapable of mental activity." "She's a dead white slug," said Barbara.

They cupped their cigarettes in their hands for the journey down the back stairs to the kitchen. They both were thinking that the kettle would be boiling on the Aga: it would be pleasant to sit in the cool, big kitchen drinking tea with old Sergeant Wall, who gossiped about the village he lived in. It was Dympna's turn to make his sandwich, turkey paste left over from yesterday, the easy-to-spread margarine that Mrs. Digby-Hunter said was better for you than butter. "Dead white slug," repeated Barbara, laughing on the stairs. "Was she human once?"

Sergeant Wall passed by the sleeping Mrs. Digby-Hunter and heard, just perceptibly, a soft snoring coming from her partially open mouth. She was tired, he thought; heat made women tired, he'd often heard. He removed his hat and wiped an accumulation of sweat from the crown of his head. He moved towards the house for his tea.

In his study Digby-Hunter sat with one boy, Marshalsea, listening while Marshalsea repeated recently acquired information about triangles.

"Then DEF," said Marshalsea, "must be equal in all respects to—"

"Why?" inquired Digby-Hunter.

His voice was dry and slightly high. His bony hands, on the desk between himself and Marshalsea, had minute fingernails.

"Because DEF—"

"Because the triangle DEF, Marshalsea."

"Because the triangle DEF—"

"Yes, Marshalsea?"

"Because the triangle DEF has the two angles at the base and two sides equal to the two angles at the base and two sides of the triangle ABC—"

"You're talking bloody nonsense," said Digby-Hunter quietly. "Think about it, boy."

He rose from his position behind his desk and crossed the room to the window. He moved quietly, a man with a slight stoop because of his height, a man who went well with the room he occupied, with shelves of text books, and an empty mantelpiece, and bare, pale walls. It was simple sense, as he often pointed out to parents, that in rooms where teaching took place there should be no diversions for the roving eyes of students.

Glancing from the window, Digby-Hunter observed his wife in her deck-chair beneath the beeches. He reflected that in their seventeen years at Milton Grange she had become expert at making shepherd's pie. Her bridge, on the other hand, had not improved and she still made tiresome remarks to parents. Once, briefly, he had loved her, a love that had begun to die in the bedroom of a Welsh hotel, on the night of their wedding day. Her nakedness, which he had daily imagined in lush anticipation, had strangely repelled him. "I'm sorry," he'd murmured, and had slipped into the other twin bed, knowing then that this side of marriage was something he was not going to be able to manage. She had not said anything, and between them the matter had never been mentioned again.

It was extraordinary, he thought now, watching her in the garden, that she should lie in a deck-chair like that, unfastidiously asleep. Once at a dinner-party she had described a dream she'd had, and afterwards, in the car on the way back to Milton Grange, he'd had to tell her that no one had been interested in her dream. People had quietly sighed, he'd had to say, because that was the truth.

There was a knock on the door and Digby-Hunter moved from the window and called out peremptorily. A youth with spectacles and long, uncared-for hair entered the sombre room. He was thin, with a slight, thin mouth and a fragile nose; his eyes, magnified behind the tortoise-shell-rimmed discs, were palely nondescript, the colour of water in which vegetables have been boiled. His lengthy hair was lustreless.

"Wraggett," said Digby-Hunter at once, as though challenging the youth to disclaim this title.

"Sir," replied Wraggett.

"Why are you moving your head about like that?" Digby-Hunter demanded.

He turned to the other boy. "Well?" he said.

"If the two angles at the base of DEF," said Marshalsea, "are equal to the two angles at the base of—"

"Open the book," said Digby-Hunter. "Learn it."

He left the window and returned to his desk, He sat down. "What d'you want, Wraggett?" he said.

"I think I'd better go to bed, sir."

"Bed? What's the matter with you?"

"There's a pain in my neck, sir. At the back, sir. I can't seem to see properly."

Digby-Hunter regarded Wraggett with irritation and dislike. He made a noise with his lips. He stared at Wraggett. He said:

"So you have lost your sight, Wraggett?"

"No, sir."

"Why the damn hell are you bellyaching, then?"

"I keep seeing double, sir. I feel a bit sick, sir."

"Are you malingering, Wraggett?"

"No, sir."

"Then why are you saying you can't see?"

"Sir—"

"If you're not malingering, get on with the work you've been set, boy. The French verb to drink, the future conditional tense?"

"*Je boive*—"

"You're a cretin," shouted Digby-Hunter. "Get out of here at once."

"I've a pain, sir—"

"Take your pain out with you, for God's sake. Get down to some honest work, Wraggett. Marshalsea?"

"If the two angles at the base of DEF," said Marshalsea, "are equal to the two angles at the base of ABC it means that the sides opposite the angles—"

His voice ceased abruptly. He closed his eyes. He felt the small fingers of Digby-Hunter briefly on his scalp before they grasped a clump of hair.

"Open your eyes," said Digby-Hunter.

Marshalsea did so and saw pleasure in Digby-Hunter's face.

"You haven't listened," said Digby-Hunter. His left hand pulled the hair, causing the boy to rise from his seat. His right hand moved slowly and then suddenly shot out, completing its journey, striking at Marshalsea's jaw-bone. Digby-Hunter always used the side of his hand, Mr. Kelly the ball of the thumb.

"Take two triangles, ABC and DEF," said Digby-Hunter. Again the edge of his right hand struck Marshalsea's face and then, clenched into a fist, the hand struck repeatedly at Marshalsea's stomach.

"Take two triangles," whispered Marshalsea, "ABC and DEF."

"In which the angle ABC equals the angle DEF."

"In which the angle ABC equals the angle DEF."

In her sleep Mrs. Digby-Hunter heard a voice. She opened her eyes and saw a figure that might have been part of a dream. She closed her eyes again.

"Mrs. Digby-Hunter."

A boy whose name escaped her stood looking down at her. There were so many boys coming and going here for a term of two, then passing on: this one was thin and tall, with spectacles. He had an unhealthy look, she thought, and then she remembered his mother, who had an unhealthy look also, a Mrs. Wraggett.

"Mrs. Digby-Hunter, I have a pain at the back of my neck."

She blinked, looking at the boy. They'd do anything, her husband often said, in order to escape their studies, and although she sometimes felt sorry for them she quite understood that their studies must be completed since that was the reason for their presence at Milton Grange. Still, the amount of work they had to do and their excessively long hours, half-past eight until seven at night, caused her just occasionally to consider that she herself had been lucky to escape such pressures in her childhood. Every afternoon, immediately after lunch, all the boys set out with Mr. Kelly for a brisk walk, which was meant to be, in her husband's parlance, twenty minutes of freshening up. There was naturally no time for games.

"Mrs. Digby-Hunter."

The boy's head was moving about in an eccentric manner. She tried to remember if she had noticed it doing that before, and decided she hadn't. She'd have certainly noticed, for the movement made her dizzy. She reached beneath the deck-chair for the box of All Gold. She smiled at the boy. She said:

"Would you like a chocolate, Wraggett?"

"I feel sick, Mrs. Digby-Hunter. I keep seeing double. I can't seem to keep my head steady."

"You'd better tell the headmaster, old chap."

He wasn't a boy she'd ever cared for, any more than she'd ever cared for his mother. There were quite long hairs on his mother's face and often her breath was odorous. Mrs. Digby-Hunter smiled at the boy again, trying to make up for being unable to like either himself or his mother. Again she pushed the box of chocolates at him, nudging a coconut caramel out of its rectangular bed. She always left the coconut caramels and the blackcurrant boats: the boy was more than welcome to them.

"I've told the headmaster, Mrs. Digby-Hunter."

"Have you been studying too hard?"

"No, Mrs. Digby-Hunter."

She withdrew her offer of chocolates, wondering how long he'd stand there waggling his head in the sunshine. He'd get into trouble if the loitering went on too long. She could say that she'd made him remain with her in order to hear further details about his pain, but there was naturally a limit to the amount of time he could hope to waste. She said:

"I think, you know, you should buzz along now, Wraggett—"

"Mrs. Digby-Hunter—"

"There's a rule, you know: the headmaster must be informed when a boy is feeling under the weather. The headmaster comes to his own conclusions about who's malingering and who's not. When I was in charge of that side of things, Wraggett, the boys used to pull the wool over my eyes like nobody's business. Well, I didn't blame them, I'd have done the same myself. But the headmaster took another point of view. With a school like Milton Grange, every single second has a value of its own. Naturally, time can't be wasted."

"They pull the hair out of your head," Wraggett cried, his voice suddenly shrill. "They hit you in a special way, so that it doesn't bruise you. They drive their fists into your stomach."

"I think you should return to your classroom—"

"They enjoy it," shouted Wraggett.

"Go along now, old chap."

"Your husband half murdered me, Mrs. Digby-Hunter."

"Now that simply isn't true, Wraggett."

"Mr. Kelly hit Malcolmson in the groin. With a ruler. He poked the end of the ruler—"

"Be quiet, Wraggett."

"Mrs. Digby-Hunter—"

"Go along now, Wraggett." She spoke for the first time sharply, but when the boy began to move she changed her mind about her command and called him back. He and all the other boys, she explained with less sharpness in her voice, were at Milton Grange for a purpose. They came because they had idled at their preparatory schools, playing noughts and crosses in the back row of a classroom, giggling and disturbing everyone. They came to Milton Grange so that, after the skilled teaching of the headmaster and Mr. Kelly, they might succeed at an examination that would lead them to one of England's great public schools. Corporal punishment was part of the curriculum at Milton Grange, and all parents were apprised of that fact. If boys continued to idle as they idled in the past they would suffer corporal punishment so that, beneath its influence, they might reconsider their behaviour. "You understand Wraggett?" said Mrs. Digby-Hunter in the end.

Wraggett went away, and Mrs. Digby-Hunter felt pleased. The little speech she had made to him was one she had heard her husband making on other occasions. "We rap the occasional knuckle," he said to prospective parents. "Quite simply, we stand no nonsense."

She was glad that it had come so easily to her to quote her husband, once again to come up to scratch as a wife. Boys who were malingering must naturally receive the occasional rap on the knuckles and her husband, over seventeen years, had proved that his ways were best. She remembered one time a woman coming and taking her son away on the grounds that the pace was too strenuous for him. As it happened, she had opened the door in answer to the woman's summons and had heard the woman say she'd had a letter from her son and thought it better that he should be taken away. It turned out that the child had written hysterically. He had said that Milton Grange was run by lunatics and criminals. Mrs. Digby-Hunter, hearing that, had smiled and had quietly inquired if she herself resembled either a lunatic or a criminal. The woman shook her head, but the boy, who had been placed in Milton Grange so that he might pass on to the King's School in Canterbury, was taken away. "To stagnate," her husband had predicted and she, knitting another pullover for him, had without much difficulty agreed. Mrs. Digby-Hunter selected a raspberry and honey cream. She returned the chocolate-box to the grass beneath her deck-chair and closed her eyes.

"WHAT'S THE MATTER, son?" inquired Sergeant Wall on his way back to his weeding.

Wraggett said he had a pain at the back of his neck. He couldn't keep his head still, he said; he kept seeing double; he felt sick in the stomach. "God almightly," said Sergeant Wall. He led the boy back to the kitchen, which was the only interior part of Milton Grange that he knew. "Here," he said to the two maids, who were still sitting at the kitchen table, drinking tea, "Here," said Sergeant Wall, "have a look at this." Wraggett sat down and took off his spectacles. As though seeking to control its wobbling motion, he attempted to shake his head, but the effort, so Barbara and Dympna afterwards said, appeared to be too much for him. His shoulders slipped forward, the side of his face struck the scrubbed surface of the kitchen table, and when the three of them settled him back on his chair in order to give him water in a cup they discovered that he was dead.

When Mrs. Digby-Hunter entered the kitchen half an hour later she blinked her eyes several times because the glaring sunshine had affected them. "Prick the sausages," she automatically commanded, for today being a Tuesday it would be sausages for tea, a fact of which both Barbara and Dympna would, as always, have to be reminded. She was then aware that something was the matter.

She blinked again. The kitchen contained people other than Barbara and Dympna. Mr. Kelly, a man who rarely addressed her, was standing by the Aga, Sergeant Wall was endeavouring to comfort Barbara, who was noisily weeping.

"What's the matter, Barbara?" inquired Mrs. Digby-Hunter, and she noticed as she spoke that Mr. Kelly turned more of his back to her. There was a smell of tobacco smoke in the air: Dympna, to Mrs. Digby-Hunter's astonishment, was smoking a cigarette.

"There's been a tragedy, Mrs. Digby-Hunter," said Sergeant Wall. "Young Wraggett."

"What's the matter with Wraggett?"

"He's dead," said Dympna. She released smoke through her nose, staring hard at Mrs. Digby-Hunter. Barbara, who had looked up on hearing Mrs. Digby-Hunter's voice, sobbed more quietly, gazing also, through tears, at Mrs. Digby-Hunter.

"Dead?" As she spoke, her husband entered the kitchen. He addressed Mr. Kelly, who turned to face him. He said he had put the body of Wraggett on a bed in a bedroom that was never used. There was no doubt about it, he said, the boy was dead.

"Dead?" said Mrs. Digby-Hunter again. "*Dead?*"

Mr. Kelly was mumbling by the Aga, asking her husband where Wraggett's parents lived. Barbara was wiping the tears from her face with a handkerchief. Beside her, Sergeant Wall, upright and serious, stood like a statue. "In Worcestershire," Mrs. Digby-Hunter's husband said. "A village called Pine." She was aware that the two maids were still looking at her. She wanted to tell Dympna to stop smoking at once, but the words wouldn't come from her. She was asleep in the garden, she thought: Wraggett had come and stood by her chair, she had offered him a chocolate, now she was dreaming that he was dead, it was all ridiculous. Her husband's voice was quiet, still talking about the village called Pine and about Wraggett's mother and father.

Mr. Kelly asked a question that she couldn't hear: her husband replied that he didn't think they were that kind of people. He had sent for the school doctor, he told Mr. Kelly, since the cause of death had naturally to be ascertained as soon as possible.

"A heart attack," said Mr. Kelly.

"Dead?" said Mrs. Digby-Hunter for the fourth time.

Dympna held towards Barbara her packet of cigarettes. Barbara accepted one, and the eyes of the two girls ceased their observation of her face. Dympna struck a match. Wraggett had been all right earlier, Mr. Kelly said. Her husband's lips were pursed in a way that was familiar to her; there was anxiety in his eyes.

The kitchen was flagged, large grey flags that made it cool in summer and which sometimes sweated in damp weather. The boys' crockery, of hardened primrose-coloured plastic, was piled on a dresser that almost reached the ceiling. Through huge, barred windows Mrs. Digby-Hunter could see shrubs and a brick wall and an expanse of gravel. Everything was familiar and yet seemed not to be. "So sudden," her husband said. "So wretchedly out of the blue." He added that after the doctor had given the cause of death he himself would motor over to the village in Worcestershire and break the awful news to the parents.

SHE MOVED and felt again the eyes of the maids following her. She would sack them, she thought, when all this was over. She filled a kettle at the sink, running water into it from the hot tap. Mr. Kelly remained where he was standing when she approached the Aga, appearing to be unaware that he was in her way. Her husband moved. She wanted to say that soon, at least, there'd be a cup of tea; but again the words failed to come from her. She heard Sergeant Wall asking her husband if there was anything he could do, and then her husband's voice said that he'd like Sergeant Wall to remain in the house until the doctor arrived so that he could repeat to the doctor what Wraggett had said about suddenly feeling unwell. Mr. Kelly spoke again muttering to her husband that Wraggett in any case would never have passed into Lancing. "I shouldn't mention that," her husband said.

She sat down to wait for the kettle to boil, and Sergeant Wall and the girls sat down also on chairs near to where they were standing, between the two windows. Her husband spoke in a low voice to Mr. Kelly, instructing him, it seemed: she couldn't hear the words he spoke. And then, without warning, Barbara cried out loudly. She threw her burning cigarette on the floor and jumped up from her chair. Tears were on her face, her teeth were widely revealed, though not in a smile. "You're a fat white slug," she shouted at Mrs. Digby-Hunter.

Sergeant Wall again attempted to quieten the girl, but her fingernails scratched at his face and her fingers gripped and tore at the beard of Mr. Kelly, who had come to Sergeant Wall's aid. Dympna did not move from her chair. She was looking at Mrs. Digby-Hunter, smoking quietly, as though nothing at all was happening.

"It'll be in the newspapers," shouted Barbara.

She was taken from the kitchen, and the Digby-Hunters could hear her sobbing in the passage and on the back stairs. "She'll sell the story," said Dympna.

Digby-Hunter looked at her. He attempted to smile at her, to suggest by his smile that he had a fondness for her. "What story?" he said.

"The way the boys are beaten up."

"Now look here, Dympna, you know nothing whatsoever about it. The boys at Milton Grange are here for a special purpose. They undergo special education—"

"You killed one, Mr. Digby-Hunter." Still puffing at her cigarette, Dympna left the kitchen, and Mrs. Digby-Hunter spoke.

"My God," she said

"They're upset by death," said her husband tetchily. "Naturally enough. They'll both calm down."

But Mr. Kelly, hearing those remarks as he returned to the kitchen, said that it was the end of Milton Grange. The girls would definitely pass on their falsehoods to a newspaper. They were telling Sergeant Wall now, he said. They were reminding him of lies they had apparently told him before, and of which he had taken no notice.

"What in the name of heaven," Digby-Hunter angrily asked his wife, "did you have to go engaging creatures like that for?"

They hated her, she thought: two girls who day by day had worked beside her in the kitchen, to whom she had taught useful skills. A boy had come and stood beside her in the sunshine and she had offered him a chocolate. He had complained of a pain, and she had pointed out that he must make his complaint to the headmaster, since that was the rule. She had explained as well that corporal punishment was part of the curriculum at Milton Grange. The boy was dead. The girls who hated her would drag her husband's boarding-school through the mud.

She heard the voice of Sergeant Wall saying that the girls, one of them hysterical but calming down, the other insolent, were out to make trouble. He'd tried to reason with them, but they hadn't even listened.

The girls had been in Milton Grange for two and a half months. She remembered the day they had arrived together, carrying cardboard suit-cases. They'd come before that to be interviewed, and she'd walked them round the house, explaining about the school. She remembered saying in passing that once a year, at the end of every July, a Conservative fête was held, traditionally now, in the gardens. They hadn't seemed much interested.

"I've built this place up," she heard her husband say. "Month by month, year by year. It was a chicken farm when I bought it, Kelly, and now I suppose it'll be a chicken farm again."

She left the kitchen and walked along the kitchen passage and up the uncarpeted back stairs.

She knocked on the door of their room. They both called out together, saying she should come in. They were both packing their belongings into their cardboard suitcases, smoking fresh cigarettes. Barbara appeared to have recovered.

She tried to explain to them. No one knew yet, she said, why Wraggett had died. He'd had a heart attack most probably, like Mr. Kelly said. It was a terrible thing to have happened.

The girls continued to pack, not listening to her. They folded garments or pressed them, unfolded, into their suitcases.

"My husband's built the place up. Month by month, year by year, for seventeen years he has built it up."

"The boys are waiting for their tea," said Dympna. "Mrs. Digby-Hunter, you'd better prick the sausages."

"Forget our wages," said Barbara, and laughed in a way that was not hysterical.

"My husband—"

"Your husband," said Dympna, "derives sexual pleasure from inflicting pain on children. So does Kelly. They are queer men."

"Your husband," said Barbara, "will be jailed. He'll go to prison with a sack over his head so that he won't have to see the disgust on people's faces. Isn't that true, Mrs. Digby-Hunter?"

"My husband—"

"Filth," said Dympna.

She sat down on the edge of a bed and watched the two girls packing. She imagined the dead body in the bedroom that was never used, and then she imagined Sergeant Wall and Mr. Kelly and her husband in the kitchen, waiting for the school doctor to arrive, knowing that it didn't much matter what cause he offered for the death if these two girls were allowed to have their way.

"Why do you hate me?" she asked, quite calmly.

Neither replied. They went on packing and while they packed she talked, in desperation. She tried to speak the truth about Milton Grange, as she saw the truth, but they kept interrupting her. The bruises didn't show on the boys because the bruises were inflicted in an expert way, but sometimes hair was actually pulled out of the boys' scalps, small bunches of hair, she must have noticed that. She had noticed no such thing. "Corporal punishment," she began to say, but Barbara held out to her hairs that had been wrenched from the head of a boy called Bridle. She had found them in a wastepaper basket; Bridle had said they were his and had shown her the place they'd come from. She returned the hairs to a plastic bag that once had contained stockings. The hairs would be photographed, Barbara said, they would appear on the front page of a Sunday newspaper. They'd be side by side, added Barbara, with the ex-headmaster, his head hidden beneath a sack, and Mr. Kelly skulking behind his beard. Milton Grange, turreted baronial, part ivy-clad, would be examined by Sunday readers as a torture chamber. And in the garden, beneath the beech-trees, a man would photograph the deck-chair where a woman had slept while violence and death occurred. She and her husband might one day appear in a waxworks, and Mr. Kelly, too; a man who, like her husband, derived sexual pleasure from inflicting pain on children.

"You are doing this for profit," she protested, trying to smile, to win them from the error of their ways.

"Yes," they said together, and then confessed, sharing the conversation, that they had often considered telephoning a Sunday newspaper to say they had a story to tell. They had kept the hairs in the plastic bag because they'd had that in mind; in every detail they knew what they were going to say.

"You're making money out of—"

"Yes," said Dympna. "You've kept us short, Mrs. Digby-Hunter."

She saw their hatred of her in their faces and heard it in both their voices; like a vapour, it hung about the room.

"Why do you hate me?" she asked again.

They laughed, not answering, as though an answer wasn't necessary.

She remembered, although just now she didn't wish to, the clergyman who had kissed her with passion after a dance in a church hall, the dampness of his lips, his body pressed into hers. The smell of his clothes came back to her, across thirty years, seeming familiar because it had come before. She might have borne his children in some rectory somewhere. Would they have hated her then?

Underclothes, dresses, lipsticks, Woolworth's jewellery, unframed photographs of male singing stars were jumbled together in the two cardboard suitcases. The girls moved about the room, picking up their belongings while Mrs. Digby-Hunter, in greater misery than she had ever before experienced, watched them from the edge of the bed. How could human creatures be so cruel? How could they speak to her about being a figure in a waxworks tableau when she had done nothing at all? How could they so callously propose to tell lies to a newspaper about her husband and Mr. Kelly when the boy who had so tragically died was still warm with the memory of life?

She watched them, two girls so young that they were not yet fully developed. They talked about her. In this room, night after night, they had wondered about her, and in the end had hated her. Had they said in their nightly gossiping that since the day of her marriage she had lived like a statue with another statue?

It was all her fault, she suddenly thought: Milton Grange would be a chicken farm again, her husband would be examined by a psychiatrist in a prison, she would live in a single room. It was all her fault. In twenty-nine years it had taken violence and death to make sense of facts that were as terrible.

The girls were saying they'd catch a bus on the main road. Without looking at her or addressing her again they left the bedroom they had shared. She heard their footsteps on the back stairs, and Dympna's voice asking Barbara if she was all right now and Barbara saying she was. A white slug, the girl had called her, a fat white slug.

She did not leave the room. She remained sitting on the edge of the bed, unable to think. Her husband's face appeared in her mind, with its well-kept moustache and shrewd-seeming dark eyes, a face in the bedroom of a Welsh hotel on the night of her wedding day. She saw herself weeping, as she had not wept then. In a confused way she saw herself on that occasion and on others, protesting, shaking her head, not smiling.

"I'm leaving the army for a step-ladder firm," he said to her, and she struck his face with her hands, tormented by the absurdity of what he said. She cried out in anger that she had married an army officer, not a step-ladder salesman who was after her father's money. She wept again when ridiculously he told her that he intended to spend his days filling machines full of powdered coffee. He had failed her, she shrilled at him, that night in the Welsh hotel and he had failed her ever since. In front of boys, she accused him of ill-treating those who had been placed in his care. If ever it happened again, she threatened, the police would be sent for. She turned to the boys and ordered them to run about the gardens for a while. It was ludicrous that they should be cooped up while the sun shone, it was ludicrous that they should strive so painfully simply to pass an examination into some school or other. She banged a desk with her hand after the boys had gone, she spat out words at him: they'd all be in the Sunday papers, she said, if he wasn't careful, and she added that she herself would leave Milton Grange for ever unless he pursued a gentler course with the boys, unless he at once dismissed the ill-mannered Mr. Kelly, who was clearly a sinister man.

In the room that had been the maids' room Mrs. Digby-Hunter wept as her mind went back through the years of her marriage and then, still weeping, she left the room and descended the back stairs to the kitchen. To her husband she said that it was all her fault, she said she was sorry. She had knitted and put down bulbs, she said, and in the end a boy had died. Two girls had hated her because in her easy-going way she had held her peace, not wanting to know. Loyalty and devotion, said Mrs. Digby-Hunter, and now a boy was dead, and her husband with a sack over his head would be taken from Milton Grange and later would have sessions with a prison psychiatrist. It was all her fault. She would say so to the reporters when they came. She would explain and take the blame, she would come up to scratch as a wife.

Her husband and Sergeant Wall and Mr. Kelly looked at Mrs. Digby-Hunter. She stood in the centre of the kitchen, one hand on the table, a stout woman in a blue and pink dress, weeping. The tragedy had temporarily unhinged her, Sergeant Wall thought, and Mr. Kelly in irritation thought that if she could see herself she'd go somewhere else, and her husband thought that it was typical of her to be tiresomely stupid at a time like this.

She went on talking: you couldn't blame them for hating her, she said, for she might have prevented death and hadn't bothered herself. In a bedroom in Wales she should have wept, she said, or packed a suitcase and gone away. Her voice continued in the kitchen, the words poured from it, repetitiously and in a hurry. The three men sighed and looked away, all of them thinking the same thing now, that she made no sense at all, with her talk about putting down bulbs and coming up to scratch.

THE SHORT HAPPY LIFE OF FRANCIS MACOMBER

ERNEST HEMINGWAY

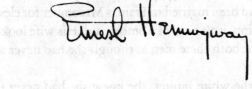

IT WAS now lunch time and they were all sitting under the double green fly of the dining tent pretending that nothing had happened.

"Will you have lime juice or lemon squash?" Macomber asked.

"I'll have a gimlet," Robert Wilson told him.

"I'll have a gimlet too. I need something," Macomber's wife said.

"I suppose it's the thing to do," Macomber agreed. "Tell him to make three gimlets."

The mess boy had started them already, lifting the bottles out of the canvas cooling bags that sweated wet in the wind that blew through the trees that shaded the tents.

"What had I ought to give them?" Macomber asked.

"A quid would be plenty," Wilson told him. "You don't want to spoil them."

"Will the headman distribute it?"

"Absolutely."

Francis Macomber had, half an hour before, been carried to his tent from the edge of the camp in triumph on the arms and shoulders of the cook, the personal boys, the skinner and the porters. The gun-bearers had taken no part in the demonstration. When the native boys put him down at the door of his tent, he had shaken all their hands, received their congratulations, and then gone into the tent and sat on the bed until his wife came in. She did not speak to him when she came in and he left the tent at once to wash his face and hands in the portable wash basin outside and go over to the dining tent to sit in a comfortable canvas chair in the breeze and the shade.

"You've got your lion," Robert Wilson said to him, "and a damned fine one too."

Mrs. Macomber looked at Wilson quickly. She was an extremely handsome and well-kept woman of the beauty and social position which had, five years before, commanded five thousand dollars as the price of endorsing, with photographs, a beauty product which she had never used. She had been married to Francis Macomber for eleven years.

"He is a good lion, isn't he?" Macomber said. His wife looked at him now. She looked at both these men as though she had never seen them before.

One, Wilson, the white hunter, she knew she had never truly seen before. He was about middle height with sandy hair, a stubby mustache, a very red face and extremely cold blue eyes with faint white wrinkles at the corners that grooved merrily when he smiled. He smiled at her now and she looked away from his face at the way his shoulders sloped in the loose tunic he wore with the four big cartridges held in loops where the left breast pocket should have been, at his big brown hands, his old slacks, his very dirty boots and back to his red face again. She noticed where the baked red of his face stopped in a white line that marked the circle left by his Stetson hat that hung now from one of the pegs of the tent pole.

"Well, here's to the lion," Robert Wilson said. He smiled at her again and, not smiling, she looked curiously at her husband.

Francis Macomber was very tall, very well built if you did not mind that length of bone, dark, his hair cropped like an oarsman, rather thin-lipped, and was considered handsome. He was dressed in the same sort of safari clothes that Wilson wore except that his were new, he was thirty-five years old, kept himself very fit, was good at court games, had a number of big-game fishing records, and had just shown himself, very publicly, to be a coward.

"Here's to the lion," he said. "I can't ever thank you for what you did."

Margaret, his wife, looked away from him and back to Wilson.

"Let's not talk about the lion," she said.

Wilson looked over at her without smiling and now she smiled at him.

"It's been a very strange day," she said. "Hadn't you ought to put your hat on even under the canvas at noon? You told me that, you know."

"Might put it on," said Wilson.

"You know you have a very red face, Mr. Wilson," she told him and smiled again.

"Drink," said Wilson.

"I don't think so," she said. "Francis drinks a great deal, but his face is never red."

"It's red today," Macomber tried a joke.

"No," said Margaret. "It's mine that's red today. But Mr. Wilson's is always red."

"Must be racial," said Wilson. "I say, you wouldn't like to drop my beauty as a topic, would you?"

"I've just started on it."

"Let's chuck it," said Wilson.

"Conversation is going to be so difficult," Margaret said.

"Don't be silly, Margot," her husband said.

"No difficulty," Wilson said. "Got a damn fine lion."

Margot looked at them both and they both saw that she was going to cry. Wilson had seen it coming for a long time and he dreaded it. Macomber was past dreading it.

"I wish it hadn't happened. Oh, I wish it hadn't happened," she said and started for her tent. She made no noise of crying but they could see that her shoulders were shaking under the rose-colored, sun-proofed shirt she wore.

"Women upset," said Wilson to the tall man. "Amounts to nothing. Strain on the nerves and one thing'n another."

"No," said Macomber. "I suppose that I rate that for the rest of my life now."

"Nonsense. Let's have a spot of the giant killer," said Wilson. "Forget the whole thing. Nothing to it anyway."

"We might try," said Macomber. "I won't forget what you did for me though."

"Nothing," said Wilson. "All nonsense."

So they sat there in the shade where the camp was pitched under some wide-topped acacia trees with a boulder-strewn cliff behind them, and a stretch of grass that ran to the bank of a boulder-filled stream in front with forest beyond it, and drank their just-cool lime drinks and avoided one another's eyes while the boys set the table for lunch. Wilson could tell that the boys all knew about it now and when he saw Macomber's personal boy looking curiously at his master while he was putting dishes on the table he snapped at him in Swahili. The boy turned away with his face blank.

"What were you telling him?" Macomber asked.

"Nothing. Told him to look alive or I'd see he got about fifteen of the best."

"What's that? Lashes?"

"It's quite illegal," Wilson said. "You're supposed to fine them."

"Do you still have them whipped?"

"Oh, yes. They could raise a row if they chose to complain. But they don't. They prefer it to the fines."

"How strange!" said Macomber.

"Not strange, really," Wilson said. "Which would you rather do? Take a good birching or lose your pay?"

Then he felt embarrassed at asking it and before Macomber could answer he went on, "We all take a beating every day, you know, one way or another."

This was no better. Good God, he thought. I am a diplomat, aren't I?

"Yes, we take a beating," said Macomber, still not looking at him. "I'm awfully sorry about that lion business. It doesn't have to go any further, does it? I mean no one will hear about it, will they?"

"You mean will I tell it at the Mathaiga Club?" Wilson looked at him now coldly. He had not expected this. So he's a bloody four-letter man as well as a bloody coward, he thought. I rather liked him too until today. But how is one to know about an American?

"No," said Wilson. "I'm a professional hunter. We never talk about our clients. You can be quite easy on that. It's supposed to be bad form to ask us not to talk though."

He had decided now that to break would be much easier. He would eat, then, by himself and could read a book with his meals. They would eat by themselves. He would see them through the safari on a very formal basis—what was it the French called it? Distinguished consideration—and it would be a damn sight easier than having to go through this emotional trash. He'd insult him and make a good clean break. Then he could read a book with his meals and he'd still be drinking their whisky. That was the phrase for it when a safari went bad. You ran into another white hunter and you asked, "How is everything going?" and he answered, "Oh, I'm still drinking their whisky," and you knew everything had gone to pot.

"I'm sorry," Macomber said and looked at him with his American face that would stay adolescent until it became middle-aged, and Wilson noted his crew-cropped hair, fine eyes only faintly shifty, good nose, thin lips and handsome jaw. "I'm sorry I didn't realize that. There are lots of things I don't know."

So what could he do, Wilson thought. He was all ready to break it off quickly and neatly and here the beggar was apologizing after he had just insulted him. He made one more attempt. "Don't worry about me talking," he said. "I have a living to make. You know in Africa no woman ever misses her lion and no white man ever bolts."

"I bolted like a rabbit," Macomber said.

Now what in hell were you going to do about a man who talked like that, Wilson wondered.

Wilson looked at Macomber with his flat, blue, machine-gunner's eyes and the other smiled back at him. He had a pleasant smile if you did not notice how his eyes showed when he was hurt.

"Maybe I can fix it up on buffalo," he said. "We're after them next, aren't we?"

"In the morning if you like," Wilson told him. Perhaps he had been wrong. This was certainly the way to take it. You most certainly could not tell a damned thing about an American. He was all for Macomber again. If you could forget the morning. But, of course, you couldn't. The morning had been about as bad as they come.

"Here comes the Memsahib," he said. She was walking over from her tent looking refreshed and cheerful and quite lovely. She had a very perfect oval face, so perfect that you expected her to be stupid. But she wasn't stupid, Wilson thought, no, not stupid.

"How is the beautiful red-faced Mr. Wilson? Are you feeling better, Francis, my pearl?"

"Oh, much," said Macomber.

"I've dropped the whole thing," she said, sitting down at the table. "What importance is there to whether Francis is any good at killing lions? That's not his trade. That's Mr. Wilson's trade. Mr. Wilson is really very impressive killing anything. You do kill anything, don't you?"

"Oh, anything," said Wilson. "Simply anything." They are, he thought, the hardest in the world; the hardest, the cruelest, the most predatory and the most attractive and their men have softened or gone to pieces nervously as they have hardened. Or is it that they pick men they can handle? They can't know that much at the age they marry, he thought. He was grateful that he had gone through his education on American women before now because this was a very attractive one.

"We're going after buff in the morning," he told her.

"I'm coming," she said.

"No, you're not."

"Oh, yes, I am. Mayn't I, Francis?"

"Why not stay in camp?"

"Not for anything," she said. "I wouldn't miss something like today for anything."

When she left, Wilson was thinking, when she went off to cry, she seemed a hell of a fine woman. She seemed to understand, to realize, to be hurt for him and for herself and to know how things really stood. She is away for twenty minutes and now she is back, simply enamelled in that American female cruelty. They are the damnedest women. Really the damnedest.

"We'll put on another show for you tomorrow," Francis Macomber said.

"You're not coming," Wilson said.

"You're very mistaken," she told him. "And I want *so* to see you perform again. You were lovely this morning. That is if blowing things' heads off is lovely."

"Here's the lunch," said Wilson. "You're very merry, aren't you?"

"Why not? I didn't come out here to be dull."

"Well, it hasn't been dull," Wilson said. He could see the boulders in the river and the high bank beyond with the trees and he remembered the morning.

"Oh, no," she said. "It's been charming. And tomorrow. You don't know how I look forward to tomorrow."

"That's eland he's offering you," Wilson said.

"They're the big cowy things that jump like hares, aren't they?"

"I suppose that describes them," Wilson said.

"It's very good meat," Macomber said.

"Did you shoot it, Francis?" she asked.

"Yes."

"They're not dangerous, are they?"

"Only if they fall on you," Wilson told her.

"I'm so glad."

"Why not let up on the bitchery just a little, Margot," Macomber said, cutting the eland steak and putting some mashed potato, gravy and carrot on the down-turned fork that tined through the piece of meat.

"I suppose I could," she said, "since you put it so prettily."

"Tonight we'll have champagne for the lion," Wilson said. "It's a bit too hot at noon."

"Oh, the lion," Margot said. "I'd forgotten the lion!"

So, Robert Wilson thought to himself, she *is* giving him a ride, isn't she? Or do you suppose that's her idea of putting up a good show? How should a woman act when she discovers her husband is a bloody coward? She's damned cruel but they're all cruel. They govern, of course, and to govern one has to be cruel sometimes. Still, I've seen enough of their damn terrorism.

"Have some more eland," he said to her politely.

That afternoon, late, Wilson and Macomber went out in the motor car with the native driver and the two gun-bearers. Mrs. Macomber stayed in the camp. It was too hot to go out, she said, and she was going with them in the early morning.

As they drove off Wilson saw her standing under the big tree, looking pretty rather than beautiful in her faintly rosy khaki, her dark hair drawn back off her forehead and gathered in a knot low on her neck, her face as fresh, he thought, as though she were in England. She waved to them as the car went off through the swale of high grass and curved around through the trees into the small hills of orchard bush.

In the orchard bush they found a herd of impala, and leaving the car they stalked one old ram with long, wide-spread horns and Macomber killed it with a very creditable shot that knocked the buck down at a good two hundred yards and sent the herd off bounding wildly and leaping over one another's backs in long, leg-drawn-up leaps as unbelievable and as floating as those one makes sometimes in dreams.

"That was a good shot," Wilson said. "They're a small target."

"Is it a worth-while head?" Macomber asked.

"It's excellent," Wilson told him. "You shoot like that and you'll have no trouble."

"Do you think we'll find buffalo tomorrow?"

"There's a good chance of it. They feed out early in the morning and with luck we may catch them in the open."

"I'd like to clear away that lion business," Macomber said. "It's not very pleasant to have your wife see you do something like that."

I should think it would be even more unpleasant to do it, Wilson thought, wife or no wife, or to talk about it having done it. But he said, "I wouldn't think about that any more. Any one could be upset by his first lion. That's all over."

But that night after dinner and a whisky and soda by the fire before going to bed, as Francis Macomber lay on his cot with the mosquito bar over him and listened to the night noises it was not all over. It was neither all over nor was it beginning. It was there exactly as it happened with some parts of it indelibly emphasized and he was miserably ashamed at it. But more than shame he felt cold, hollow fear in him. The fear was still there like a cold slimy hollow in all the emptiness where once his confidence had been and it made him feel sick. It was still there with him now.

It had started the night before when he had wakened and heard the lion roaring somewhere up along the river. It was a deep sound and at the end there were sort of coughing grunts that made him seem just outside the tent, and when Francis Macomber woke in the night to hear it he was afraid. He could hear his wife breathing quietly, asleep. There was no one to tell he was afraid, nor to be afraid with him, and, lying alone, he did not know the Somali proverb that says a brave man is always frightened three times by a lion; when he first sees his track, when he first hears him roar and when he first confronts him. Then while they were eating breakfast by lantern light out in the dining tent, before the sun was up, the lion roared again and Francis thought he was just at the edge of camp.

"Sounds like an old-timer," Robert Wilson said, looking up from his kippers and coffee. "Listen to him cough."

"Is he very close?"

"A mile or so up the stream."

"Will we see him?"

"We'll have a look."

"Does his roaring carry that far? It sounds as though he were right in camp."

"Carries a hell of a long way," said Robert Wilson. "It's strange the way it carries. Hope he's a shootable cat. The boys said there was a very big one about here."

"If I get a shot, where should I hit him," Macomber asked, "to stop him?"

"In the shoulders," Wilson said. "In the neck if you can make it. Shoot for bone. Break him down."

"I hope I can place it properly," Macomber said.

"You shoot very well," Wilson told him. "Take your time. Make sure of him. The first one in is the one that counts."

"What range will it be?"

"Can't tell. Lion has something to say about that. Don't shoot unless it's close enough so you can make sure."

"At under a hundred yards?" Macomber asked.

Wilson looked at him quickly.

"Hundred's about right. Might have to take him a bit under. Shouldn't chance a shot at much over that. A hundred's a decent range. You can hit him whenever you want at that. Here comes the Memsahib."

"Good morning," she said. "Are we going after that lion?"

"As soon as you deal with your breakfast," Wilson said. "How are you feeling?"

"Marvellous," she said. "I'm very excited."

"I'll just go and see that everything is ready." Wilson went off. As he left the lion roared again.

"Noisy beggar," Wilson said. "We'll put a stop to that."

"What's the matter, Francis?" his wife asked him.

"Nothing," Macomber said.

"Yes, there is," she said. "What are you upset about?"

"Nothing," he said.

"Tell me." She looked at him. "Don't you feel well?"

"It's that damned roaring," he said. "It's been going on all night, you know."

"Why didn't you wake me?" she said. "I'd love to have heard it."

"I've got to kill the damned thing," Macomber said, miserably.

"Well, that's what you're out here for, isn't it?"

"Yes. But I'm nervous. Hearing the thing roar gets on my nerves."

"Well then, as Wilson said, kill him and stop his roaring."

"Yes, darling," said Francis Macomber. "It sounds easy, doesn't it?"

"You're not afraid, are you?"

"Of course not. But I'm nervous from hearing him roar all night."

"You'll kill him marvellously," she said. "I know you will. I'm awfully anxious to see it."

"Finish your breakfast and we'll be starting."

"It's not light yet," she said. "This is a ridiculous hour."

Just then the lion roared in a deep-chested moaning, suddenly guttural, ascending vibration that seemed to shake the air and ended in a sigh and a heavy, deep-chested grunt.

"He sounds almost here," Macomber's wife said.

"My God," said Macomber. "I hate that damned noise."

"It's very impressive."

"Impressive. It's frightful."

Robert Wilson came up then carrying his short, ugly, shockingly big-bored .505 Gibbs and grinning.

"Come on," he said. "Your gun-bearer has your Springfield and the big gun. Everything's in the car. Have you solids?"

"Yes."

"I'm ready," Mrs. Macomber said.

"Must make him stop that racket," Wilson said. "You get in front. The Memsahib can sit back here with me."

They climbed into the motor car and, in the gray first daylight, moved off up the river through the trees. Macomber opened the breech of his rifle and saw he had metal-cased bullets, shut the bolt and put the rifle on safety. He saw his hand was trembling. He felt in his pocket for more cartridges and moved his fingers over the cartridges in the loops of his tunic front. He turned back to where Wilson sat in the rear seat of the doorless, box-bodied motor car beside his wife, them both grinning with excitement, and Wilson leaned forward and whispered,

"See the birds dropping. Means the old boy has left his kill."

On the far bank of the stream Macomber could see, above the trees, vultures circling and plummeting down.

"Chances are he'll come to drink along here," Wilson whispered. "Before he goes to lay up. Keep an eye out."

They were driving slowly along the high bank of the stream which here cut deeply to its boulder-filled bed, and they wound in and out through big trees as they drove. Macomber was watching the opposite bank when he felt Wilson take hold of his arm. The car stopped.

"There he is," he heard the whisper. "Ahead and to the right. Get out and take him. He's a marvellous lion."

Macomber saw the lion now. He was standing almost broadside, his great head up and turned toward them. The early morning breeze that blew toward them was just stirring his dark mane, and the lion looked huge, silhouetted on the rise of bank in the gray morning light, his shoulders heavy, his barrel of a body bulking smoothly.

"How far is he?" asked Macomber, raising his rifle.

"About seventy-five. Get out and take him."

"Why not shoot from where I am?"

"You don't shoot them from cars," he heard Wilson saying in his ear. "Get out. He's not going to stay there all day."

Macomber stepped out of the curved opening at the side of the front seat, onto the step and down onto the ground. The lion still stood looking majestically and coolly toward this object that his eyes only

147

showed in silhouette, bulking like some super-rhino. There was no man smell carried toward him and he watched the object, moving his great head a little from side to side. Then watching the object, not afraid, but hesitating before going down the bank to drink with such a thing opposite him, he saw a man figure detach itself from it and he turned his heavy head and swung away toward the cover of the trees as he heard a cracking crash and felt the slam of a .30-06 220-grain solid bullet that bit his flank and ripped in sudden hot scalding nausea through his stomach. He trotted, heavy, big-footed, swinging wounded, full-bellied, through the trees toward the tall grass and cover, and the crash came again to go past him ripping the air apart. Then it crashed again and he felt the blow as it hit his lower ribs and ripped on through, blood sudden hot and frothy in his mouth, and he galloped toward the high grass where he could crouch and not be seen and make them bring the crashing thing close enough so he could make a rush and get the man that held it.

Macomber had not thought how the lion felt as he got out of the car. He only knew his hands were shaking and as he walked away from the car it was almost impossible for him to make his legs move. They were stiff in the thighs, but he could feel the muscles fluttering. He raised the rifle, sighted on the junction of the lion's head and shoulders and pulled the trigger. Nothing happened though he pulled until he thought his finger would break. Then he knew he had the safety on and as he lowered the rifle to move the safety over he moved another frozen pace forward, and the lion seeing his silhouette now clear of the silhouette of the car, turned and started off at a trot, and, as Macomber fired, he heard a whunk that meant that the bullet was home; but the lion kept on going. Macomber shot again and every one saw the bullet throw a spout of dirt beyond the trotting lion. He shot again, remembering to lower his aim, and they all heard the bullet hit, and the lion went into a gallop and was in the tall grass before he had the bolt pushed forward.

Macomber stood there feeling sick at his stomach, his hands that held the Springfield still cocked, shaking, and his wife and Robert Wilson were standing by him. Beside him too were the two gun-bearers chattering in Wakamba.

"I hit him," Macomber said. "I hit him twice."

"You gut-shot him and you hit him somewhere forward," Wilson said without enthusiasm. The gun-bearers looked very grave. They were silent now.

"You may have killed him," Wilson went on. "We'll have to wait a while before we go in to find out."

"What do you mean?"

"Let him get sick before we follow him up."

"Oh," said Macomber.

"He's a hell of a fine lion," Wilson said cheerfully. "He's gotten into a bad place though."

"Why is it bad?"

"Can't see him until you're on him."

"Oh," said Macomber.

"Come on," said Wilson. "The Memsahib can stay here in the car. We'll go to have a look at the blood spoor."

"Stay here, Margot," Macomber said to his wife. His mouth was very dry and it was hard for him to talk.

"Why?" she asked.

"Wilson says to."

"We're going to have a look," Wilson said. "You stay here. You can see even better from here."

"All right."

Wilson spoke in Swahili to the driver. He nodded and said, "Yes, Bwana."

Then they went down the steep bank and across the stream, climbing over and around the boulders and up the other bank, pulling up by some projecting roots, and along it until they found where the lion had been trotting when Macomber first shot. There was dark blood on the short grass that the gun-bearers pointed out with grass stems, and that ran away behind the river bank trees.

"What do we do?" asked Macomber.

"Not much choice," said Wilson. "We can't bring the car over. Bank's too steep. We'll let him stiffen up a bit and then you and I'll go in and have a look for him."

"Can't we set the grass on fire?" Macomber asked.

"Too green."

"Can't we send beaters?"

Wilson looked at him appraisingly. "Of course we can," he said. "But it's just a touch murderous. You see, we know the lion's wounded. You can drive an unwounded lion—he'll move on ahead of a noise—but a wounded lion's going to charge. You can't see him until you're right on him. He'll make himself perfectly flat in cover you wouldn't think would hide a hare. You can't very well send boys in there to that sort of a show. Somebody bound to get mauled."

"What about the gun-bearers?"

"Oh, they'll go with us. It's their *shauri*. You see, they signed on for it. They don't look too happy though, do they?"

"I don't want to go in there," said Macomber. It was out before he knew he'd said it.

"Neither do I," said Wilson very cheerily. "Really no choice though." Then, as an afterthought, he glanced at Macomber and saw suddenly how he was trembling and the pitiful look on his face.

"You don't have to go in, of course," he said. "That's what I'm hired for, you know. That's why I'm so expensive."

"You mean you'd go in by yourself? Why not leave him there?"

Robert Wilson, whose entire occupation had been with the lion and the problem he presented, and who had not been thinking about Macomber except to note that he was rather windy, suddenly felt as though he had opened the wrong door in a hotel and seen something shameful.

"What do you mean?"

"Why not just leave him?"

"You mean pretend to ourselves he hasn't been hit?"

"No. Just drop it."

"It isn't done."

"Why not?"

"For one thing, he's certain to be suffering. For another, some one else might run onto him."

"I see."

"But you don't have to have anything to do with it."

"I'd like to," Macomber said. "I'm just scared, you know."

"I'll go ahead when we go in," Wilson said, "with Kongoni tracking. You keep behind me and a little to one side. Chances are we'll hear him growl. If we see him we'll both shoot. Don't worry about anything. I'll keep you backed up. As a matter of fact, you know, perhaps you'd better not go. It might be much better. Why don't you go over and join the Memsahib while I just get it over with?"

"No, I want to go."

"All right," said Wilson. "But don't go in if you don't want to. This is my *shauri* now, you know."

"I want to go," said Macomber.

They sat under a tree and smoked.

"Want to go back and speak to the Memsahib while we're waiting?" Wilson asked.

"No."

"I'll just step back and tell her to be patient."

"Good," said Macomber. He sat there, sweating under his arms, his mouth dry, his stomach hollow feeling, wanting to find courage to tell Wilson to go on and finish off the lion without him. He could not know that Wilson was furious because he had not noticed the state he was in earlier and sent him back to his wife. While he sat there Wilson came up. "I have your big gun," he said. "Take it. We've given him time, I think. Come on."

Macomber took the big gun and Wilson said:

"Keep behind me and about five yards to the right and do exactly as I tell you." Then he spoke in Swahili to the two gun-bearers who looked the picture of gloom.

"Let's go," he said.

"Could I have a drink of water?" Macomber asked. Wilson spoke to the older gun-bearer, who wore a canteen on his belt, and the man unbuckled it, unscrewed the top and handed it to Macomber, who took it noticing how heavy it seemed and how hairy and shoddy the felt covering was in his hand. He raised it to drink and looked ahead at the high grass with the flat-topped trees behind it. A breeze was blowing toward them and the grass rippled gently in the wind. He looked at the gun-bearer and he could see the gun-bearer was suffering too with fear.

Thirty-five yards into the grass the big lion lay flattened out along

151

the ground. His ears were back and his only movement was a slight twitching up and down of his long, black-tufted tail. He had turned at bay as soon as he had reached this cover and he was sick with the wound through his full belly, and weakening with the wound through his lungs that brought a thin foamy red to his mouth each time he breathed. His flanks were wet and hot and flies were on the little openings the solid bullets had made in his tawny hide, and his big yellow eyes, narrowed with hate, looked straight ahead, only blinking when the pain came as he breathed, and his claws dug in the soft baked earth. All of him, pain, sickness, hatred and all of his remaining strength, was tightening into an absolute concentration for a rush. He could hear the men talking and he waited, gathering all of himself into this preparation for a charge as soon as the men would come into the grass. As he heard their voices his tail stiffened to twitch up and down, and, as they came into the edge of the grass, he made a coughing grunt and charged.

Kongoni, the old gun-bearer, in the lead watching the blood spoor, Wilson watching the grass for any movement, his big gun ready, the second gun-bearer looking ahead and listening, Macomber close to Wilson, his rifle cocked, they had just moved into the grass when Macomber heard the blood-choked coughing grunt, and saw the swishing rush in the grass. The next thing he knew he was running; running wildly, in panic in the open, running toward the stream.

He heard the *ca-ra-wong!* of Wilson's big rifle, and again in a second crashing *carawong!* and turning saw the lion, horrible-looking now, with half his head seeming to be gone, crawling toward Wilson in the edge of the tall grass while the red-faced man worked the bolt on the short ugly rifle and aimed carefully as another blasting *carawong!* came from the muzzle, and the crawling, heavy, yellow bulk of the lion stiffened and the huge, mutilated head slid forward and Macomber, standing by himself in the clearing where he had run, holding a loaded rifle, while two black men and a white man looked back at him in contempt, knew the lion was dead. He came toward Wilson, his tallness all seeming a naked reproach, and Wilson looked at him and said:

"Want to take pictures?"

"No," he said.

That was all any one had said until they reached the motor car. Then Wilson had said:

"Hell of a fine lion. Boys will skin him out. We might as well stay here in the shade."

Macomber's wife had not looked at him nor he at her and he had sat by her in the back seat with Wilson sitting in the front seat. Once he had reached over and taken his wife's hand without looking at her and she had removed her hand from his. Looking across the stream to where the gun-bearers were skinning out the lion he could see that she had been able to see the whole thing. While they sat there his wife had reached forward and put her hand on Wilson's shoulder. He turned and she had leaned forward over the low seat and kissed him on the mouth.

"Oh, I say," said Wilson, going redder than his natural baked color.

"Mr. Robert Wilson," she said. "The beautiful red-faced Mr. Robert Wilson."

Then she sat down beside Macomber again and looked away across the stream to where the lion lay, with uplifted, white-muscled, tendon-marked naked forearms, and white bloating belly, as the black men fleshed away the skin. Finally the gun-bearers brought the skin over, wet and heavy, and climbed in behind with it, rolling it up before they got in, and the motor car started. No one had said anything more until they were back in camp.

That was the story of the lion. Macomber did not know how the lion had felt before he started his rush, nor during it when the unbelievable smash of the .505 with a muzzle velocity of two tons had hit him in the mouth, nor what kept him coming after that, when the second ripping crash had smashed his hind quarters and he had come crawling on toward the crashing, blasting thing that had destroyed him. Wilson knew something about it and only expressed it by saying, "Damned fine lion," but Macomber did not know how Wilson felt about things either. He did not know how his wife felt except that she was through with him.

His wife had been through with him before but it never lasted. He was very wealthy, and would be much wealthier, and he knew she would not leave him ever now. That was one of the few things that he really knew. He knew about that, about motor cycles—that was earliest—about motor cars, about duck-shooting, about fishing, trout, salmon and big-sea, about sex in books, many books, too many books, about all court games, about dogs, not much about horses, about hanging on to his money, about most of the other things his world dealt in, and about his wife not leaving him. His wife had been a great beauty and she was still a great beauty in Africa, but she was not a great enough beauty any more at home to be able to leave him and better herself and she knew it and he knew it. She had missed the chance to leave him and he knew it. If he had been better with women she would probably have started to worry about him getting another new, beautiful wife; but she knew too much about him to worry about him either. Also, he had always had a great tolerance which seemed the nicest thing about him if it were not the most sinister.

All in all they were known as a comparatively happily married couple, one of those whose disruption is often rumored but never occurs, and as the society columnist put it, they were adding more than a spice of *adventure* to their much envied and ever-enduring *Romance* by a *Safari* in what was known as *Darkest Africa* until the Martin Johnsons lighted it on so many silver screens where they were pursuing *Old Simba* the lion, the buffalo, *Tembo* the elephant and as well collecting specimens for the Museum of Natural History. This same columnist had reported them *on the verge* at least three times in the past and they had been. But they always made it up. They had a sound basis of union. Margot was too beautiful for Macomber to divorce her and Macomber had too much money for Margot ever to leave him.

It was now about three o'clock in the morning and Francis Macomber, who had been asleep a little while after he had stopped thinking about the lion, wakened and then slept again, woke suddenly, frightened in a dream of the bloody-headed lion standing over him, and listening while his heart pounded, he realized that his wife was not in the other cot in the tent. He lay awake with that knowledge for two hours.

At the end of that time his wife came into the tent, lifted her mosquito bar and crawled cozily into bed.

"Where have you been?" Macomber asked in the darkness.

"Hello," she said. "Are you awake?"

"Where have you been?"

"I just went out to get a breath of air."

"You did, like hell."

"What do you want me to say, darling?"

"Where have you been?"

"Out to get a breath of air."

"That's a new name for it. You *are* a bitch."

"Well, you're a coward."

"All right," he said. "What of it?"

"Nothing as far as I'm concerned. But please let's not talk, darling, because I'm very sleepy."

"You think that I'll take anything."

"I know you will, sweet."

"Well, I won't."

"Please, darling, let's not talk. I'm so very sleepy."

"There wasn't going to be any of that. You promised there wouldn't be."

"Well, there is now," she said sweetly.

"You said if we made this trip that there would be none of that. You promised."

"Yes, darling. That's the way I meant it to be. But the trip was spoiled yesterday. We don't have to talk about it, do we?"

"You don't wait long when you have an advantage, do you?"

"Please let's not talk. I'm so sleepy, darling."

"I'm going to talk."

"Don't mind me then, because I'm going to sleep." And she did.

At breakfast they were all three at the table before daylight and Francis Macomber found that, of all the many men that he had hated, he hated Robert Wilson the most.

"Sleep well?" Wilson asked in his throaty voice, filling a pipe.

"Did you?"

"Topping," the white hunter told him.

You bastard, thought Macomber, you insolent bastard.

So she woke him when she came in, Wilson thought, looking at them both with his flat, cold eyes. Well, why doesn't he keep his wife where she belongs? What does he think I am, a bloody plaster saint? Let him keep her where she belongs. It's his own fault.

"Do you think we'll find buffalo?" Margot asked, pushing away a dish of apricots.

"Chance of it," Wilson said and smiled at her. "Why don't you stay in camp?"

"Not for anything," she told him.

"Why not order her to stay in camp?" Wilson said to Macomber.

"You order her," said Macomber coldly.

"Let's not have any ordering, nor," turning to Macomber, "any silliness, Francis," Margot said quite pleasantly.

"Are you ready to start?" Macomber asked.

"Any time," Wilson told him. "Do you want the Memsahib to go?"

"Does it make any difference whether I do or not?"

The hell with it, thought Robert Wilson. The utter complete hell with it. So this is what it's going to be like. Well, this is what it's going to be like, then.

"Makes no difference," he said.

"You're sure you wouldn't like to stay in camp with her yourself and let me go out and hunt the buffalo?" Macomber asked.

"Can't do that," said Wilson. "Wouldn't talk rot if I were you."

"I'm not talking rot. I'm disgusted."

"Bad word, disgusted."

"Francis, will you please try to speak sensibly?" his wife said.

"I speak too damned sensibly," Macomber said. "Did you ever eat such filthy food?"

"Something wrong with the food?" asked Wilson quietly.

"No more than with everything else."

"I'd pull yourself together, laddybuck," Wilson said very quietly. "There's a boy waits at table that understands a little English."

"The hell with him."

Wilson stood up and puffing on his pipe strolled away, speaking a few words in Swahili to one of the gun-bearers who was standing waiting for him. Macomber and his wife sat on at the table. He was staring at his coffee cup.

"If you make a scene I'll leave you, darling," Margot said quietly.

"No, you won't."

"You can try it and see."

"You won't leave me."

"No," she said. "I won't leave you and you'll behave yourself."

"Behave myself? That's a way to talk. Behave myself."

"Yes. Behave yourself."

"Why don't *you* try behaving?"

"I've tried it so long. So very long."

"I hate that red-faced swine," Macomber said. "I loathe the sight of him."

"He's really *very* nice."

"Oh, *shut up*," Macomber almost shouted. Just then the car came up and stopped in front of the dining tent and the driver and the two gunbearers got out. Wilson walked over and looked at the husband and wife sitting there at the table.

"Going shooting?" he asked.

"Yes," said Macomber, standing up. "Yes."

"Better bring a woolly. It will be cool in the car," Wilson said.

"I'll get my leather jacket," Margot said.

"The boy has it," Wilson told her. He climbed into the front with the driver and Francis Macomber and his wife sat, not speaking, in the back seat.

Hope the silly beggar doesn't take a notion to blow the back of my head off, Wilson thought to himself. Women *are* a nuisance on safari.

The car was grinding down to cross the river at a pebbly ford in the gray daylight and then climbed, angling up the steep bank, where Wilson had ordered a way shovelled out the day before so they could reach the parklike wooded rolling country on the far side.

It was a good morning, Wilson thought. There was a heavy dew and as the wheels went through the grass and low bushes he could smell the odor of the crushed fronds. It was an odor like verbena and he liked this early morning smell of the dew, the crushed bracken and the look of the tree trunks showing black through the early morning mist, as the car made its way through the untracked, parklike country. He had put the two in the back seat out of his mind now and was thinking about buffalo. The buffalo that he was after stayed in the daytime in a thick swamp where it was impossible to get a shot, but in the night they fed out into an open stretch of country and if he could come between them and their swamp with the car, Macomber would have a good chance at them in the open. He did not want to hunt buff with Macomber in thick cover. He did not want to hunt buff or anything else with Macomber at all, but he was a professional hunter and he had hunted with some rare ones in his time. If they got buff today there would only be rhino to come and the poor man would have gone through his dangerous game and things might pick up. He'd have nothing more to do with the woman and Macomber would get over that too. He must have gone through plenty of that before by the look of things. Poor beggar. He must have a way of getting over it. Well, it was the poor sod's own bloody fault.

He, Robert Wilson, carried a double size cot on safari to accommodate any windfalls he might receive. He had hunted for a certain clientele, the international, fast, sporting set, where the women did not feel they were getting their money's worth unless they had shared that cot with the white hunter. He despised them when he was away from them although he liked some of them well enough at the time, but he made his living by them; and their standards were his standards as long as they were hiring him.

They were his standards in all except the shooting. He had his own standards about the killing and they could live up to them or get some one else to hunt them. He knew, too, that they all respected him for this. This Macomber was an odd one though. Damned if he wasn't. Now the wife. Well, the wife. Yes, the wife. Hm, the wife. Well he'd dropped all that. He looked around at them. Macomber sat grim and furious. Margot smiled at him. She looked younger today, more innocent and fresher and not so professionally beautiful. What's in her heart God knows, Wilson thought. She hadn't talked much last night. At that it was a pleasure to see her.

The motor car climbed up a slight rise and went on through the trees and then out into a grassy prairie-like opening and kept in the shelter of the trees along the edge, the driver going slowly and Wilson looking carefully out across the prairie and all along its far side. He stopped the car and studied the opening with his field glasses. Then he motioned to the driver to go on and the car moved slowly along, the driver avoiding wart-hog holes and driving around the mud castles ants had built. Then, looking across the opening, Wilson suddenly turned and said, "By God, there they are!"

And looking where he pointed, while the car jumped forward and Wilson spoke in rapid Swahili to the driver, Macomber saw three huge, black animals looking almost cylindrical in their long heaviness, like big black tank cars, moving at a gallop across the far edge of the open prairie. They moved at a stiff-necked, stiff-bodied gallop and he could see the upswept wide black horns on their heads as they galloped heads out; the heads not moving.

"They're three old bulls," Wilson said. "We'll cut them off before they get to the swamp."

The car was going a wild forty-five miles an hour across the open and as Macomber watched, the buffalo got bigger and bigger until he could see the gray, hairless, scabby look of one huge bull and how his neck was a part of his shoulders and the shiny black of his horns as he galloped a little behind the others that were strung out in that steady plunging gait; and then, the car swaying as though it had just jumped a road, they drew up close and he could see the plunging hugeness of the bull, and the dust in his sparsely haired hide, the wide boss of horn and his outstretched, wide-nostrilled muzzle, and he was raising his rifle when Wilson shouted, "Not from the car, you fool!" and he had no fear, only hatred of Wilson, while the brakes clamped on and the car skidded, plowing sideways to an almost stop and Wilson was out on one side and he on the other, stumbling as his feet hit the still speeding-by of the earth, and then he was shooting at the bull as he moved away, hearing the bullets whunk into him, emptying his rifle at him as he moved steadily away, finally remembering to get his shots forward into the shoulder, and as he fumbled to re-load, he saw the bull was down. Down on his knees, his big head tossing, and seeing the other two still galloping he shot at the leader and hit him. He shot again and missed and he heard the *carawonging* roar as Wilson shot and saw the leading bull slide forward onto his nose.

"Get that other," Wilson said. "Now you're shooting!"

But the other bull was moving steadily at the same gallop and he missed, throwing a spout of dirt, and Wilson missed and the dust rose in a cloud and Wilson shouted, "Come on. He's too far!" and grabbed his arm and they were in the car again, Macomber and Wilson hanging on the sides and rocketing swayingly over the uneven ground, drawing up on the steady, plunging, heavy-necked, straight-moving gallop of the bull.

They were behind him and Macomber was filling his rifle, dropping shells onto the ground, jamming it, clearing the jam, then they were almost up with the bull when Wilson yelled "Stop," and the car skidded so that it almost swung over and Macomber fell forward onto his feet, slammed his bolt forward and fired as far forward as he could aim into the galloping, rounded black back, aimed and shot again, then again, then again, and the bullets, all of them hitting, had no effect on the buffalo that he could see. Then Wilson shot, the roar deafening him, and he could see the bull stagger. Macomber shot again, aiming carefully, and down he came, onto his knees.

"All right," Wilson said. "Nice work. That's the three."

Macomber felt a drunken elation.

"How many times did you shoot?" he asked.

"Just three," Wilson said. "You killed the first bull. The biggest one. I helped you finish the other two. Afraid they might have got into cover. You had them killed. I was just mopping up a little. You shot damn well."

"Let's go to the car," said Macomber. "I want a drink."

"Got to finish off that buff first," Wilson told him. The buffalo was on his knees and he jerked his head furiously and bellowed in pig-eyed, roaring rage as they came toward him.

"Watch he doesn't get up," Wilson said. Then, "Get a little broadside and take him in the neck just behind the ear."

Macomber aimed carefully at the center of the huge, jerking, rage-driven neck and shot. At the shot the head dropped forward.

"That does it," said Wilson. "Got the spine. They're a hell of a looking thing, aren't they?"

"Let's get the drink," said Macomber. In his life he had never felt so good.

In the car Macomber's wife sat very white faced. "You were marvellous, darling," she said to Macomber. "What a ride."

"Was it rough?" Wilson asked.

"It was frightful. I've never been more frightened in my life."

"Let's all have a drink," Macomber said.

"By all means," said Wilson. "Give it to the Memsahib." She drank the neat whisky from the flask and shuddered a little when she swallowed. She handed the flask to Macomber who handed it to Wilson.

"It was frightfully exciting," she said. "It's given me a dreadful headache. I didn't know you were allowed to shoot them from the cars though."

"No one shot from cars," said Wilson coldly.

"I mean chase them from cars."

"Wouldn't ordinarily," Wilson said. "Seemed sporting enough to me though while we were doing it. Taking more chance driving that way across the plain full of holes and one thing and another than hunting on foot. Buffalo could have charged us each time we shot if he liked. Gave him every chance. Wouldn't mention it to any one though. It's illegal if that's what you mean."

"It seemed very unfair to me," Margot said, "chasing those big helpless things in a motor car."

"Did it?" said Wilson.

"What would happen if they heard about it in Nairobi?"

"I'd lose my licence for one thing. Other unpleasantnesses," Wilson said, taking a drink from the flask. "I'd be out of business."

"Really?"

"Yes, really."

"Well," said Macomber, and he smiled for the first time all day. "Now she has something on you."

"You have such a pretty way of putting things, Francis," Margot Macomber said. Wilson looked at them both. If a four-letter man marries a five-letter woman, he was thinking, what number of letters would their children be? What he said was, "We lost a gun-bearer. Did you notice it?"

"My God, no," Macomber said.

"Here he comes," Wilson said. "He's all right. He must have fallen off when we left the first bull."

Approaching them was the middle-aged gun-bearer, limping along in his knitted cap, khaki tunic, shorts and rubber sandals, gloomy-faced and disgusted-looking. As he came up he called out to Wilson in Swahili and they all saw the change in the white hunter's face.

"What does he say?" asked Margot.

"He says the first bull got up and went into the bush," Wilson said with no expression in his voice.

"Oh," said Macomber blankly.

"Then it's going to be just like the lion," said Margot, full of anticipation.

"It's not going to be a damned bit like the lion," Wilson told her. "Did you want another drink, Macomber?"

"Thanks, yes," Macomber said. He expected the feeling he had had about the lion to come back but it did not. For the first time in his life he really felt wholly without fear. Instead of fear he had a feeling of definite elation.

"We'll go and have a look at the second bull," Wilson said. "I'll tell the driver to put the car in the shade."

"What are you going to do?" asked Margaret Macomber.

"Take a look at the buff," Wilson said.

"I'll come."

"Come along."

The three of them walked over to where the second buffalo bulked blackly in the open, head forward on the grass, the massive horns swung wide.

"He's a very good head," Wilson said. "That's close to a fifty-inch spread."

Macomber was looking at him with delight.

"He's hateful-looking," said Margot. "Can't we go into the shade?"

"Of course," Wilson said. "Look," he said to Macomber, and pointed. "See that patch of bush?"

"Yes."

"That's where the first bull went in. The gun-bearer said when he fell off the bull was down. He was watching us helling along and the other two buff galloping. When he looked up there was the bull up and looking at him. Gun-bearer ran like hell and the bull went off slowly into that bush."

"Can we go in after him now?" asked Macomber eagerly.

Wilson looked at him appraisingly. Damned if this isn't a strange one, he thought. Yesterday he's scared sick and today he's a ruddy fire eater.

"No, we'll give him a while."

"Let's please go into the shade," Margot said. Her face was white and she looked ill.

They made their way to the car where it stood under a single, wide-spreading tree and all climbed in.

"Chances are he's dead in there," Wilson remarked. "After a little we'll have a look."

Macomber felt a wild unreasonable happiness that he had never known before.

"By God, that was a chase," he said. "I've never felt any such feeling. Wasn't it marvellous, Margot?"

"I hated it."

"Why?"

"I hated it," she said bitterly. "I loathed it."

"You know I don't think I'd ever be afraid of anything again," Macomber said to Wilson. "Something happened in me after we first saw the buff and started after him. Like a dam bursting. It was pure excitement."

"Cleans out your liver," said Wilson. "Damn funny things happen to people."

Macomber's face was shining. "You know something did happen to me," he said. "I feel absolutely different."

His wife said nothing and eyed him strangely. She was sitting far back in the seat and Macomber was sitting forward talking to Wilson who turned sideways talking over the back of the front seat.

"You know, I'd like to try another lion," Macomber said. "I'm really not afraid of them now. After all, what can they do to you?"

"That's it," said Wilson. "Worst one can do is kill you. How does it go? Shakespeare. Damned good. See if I can remember. Oh, damned good. Used to quote it to myself at one time. Let's see. 'By my troth, I care not; a man can die but once; we owe God a death and let it go which way it will he that dies this year is quit for the next.' Damned fine, eh?"

He was very embarrassed, having brought out this thing he had lived by, but he had seen men come of age before and it always moved him. It was not a matter of their twenty-first birthday.

It had taken a strange chance of hunting, a sudden precipitation into action without opportunity for worrying beforehand, to bring this about with Macomber, but regardless of how it had happened it had most certainly happened. Look at the beggar now, Wilson thought. It's that some of them stay little boys so long, Wilson thought. Sometimes all their lives. Their figures stay boyish when they're fifty. The great American boy-men. Damned strange people. But he liked this Macomber now. Damned strange fellow. Probably meant the end of cuckoldry too. Well, that would be a damned good thing. Damned good thing. Beggar had probably been afraid all his life. Don't know what started it. But over now. Hadn't had time to be afraid with the buff. That and being angry too. Motor car too. Motor cars made it familiar. Be a damn fire eater now. He'd seen it in the war work the same way. More of a change than any loss of virginity. Fear gone like an operation. Something else grew in its place. Main thing a man had. Made him into a man. Women knew it too. No bloody fear.

From the far corner of the seat Margaret Macomber looked at the two of them. There was no change in Wilson. She saw Wilson as she had seen him the day before when she had first realized what his great talent was. But she saw the change in Francis Macomber now.

"Do you have that feeling of happiness about what's going to happen?" Macomber asked, still exploring his new wealth.

"You're not supposed to mention it," Wilson said, looking in the other's face. "Much more fashionable to say you're scared. Mind you, you'll be scared too, plenty of times."

"But you *have* a feeling of happiness about action to come?"

"Yes," said Wilson. "There's that. Doesn't do to talk too much about all this. Talk the whole thing away. No pleasure in anything if you mouth it up too much."

"You're both talking rot," said Margot. "Just because you've chased some helpless animals in a motor car you talk like heroes."

"Sorry," said Wilson. "I have been gassing too much." She's worried about it already, he thought.

"If you don't know what we're talking about why not keep out of it?" Macomber asked his wife.

"You've gotten awfully brave, awfully suddenly," his wife said contemptuously, but her contempt was not secure. She was very afraid of something.

Macomber laughed, a very natural hearty laugh. "You know I *have*," he said. "I really have."

"Isn't it sort of late?" Margot said bitterly. Because she had done the best she could for many years back and the way they were together now was no one person's fault.

"Not for me," said Macomber.

Margot said nothing but sat back in the corner of the seat.

"Do you think we've given him time enough?" Macomber asked Wilson cheerfully.

"We might have a look," Wilson said. "Have you any solids left?"

"The gun-bearer has some."

Wilson called in Swahili and the older gun-bearer, who was skinning out one of the heads, straightened up, pulled a box of solids out of his pocket and brought them over to Macomber, who filled his magazine and put the remaining shells in his pocket.

"You might as well shoot the Springfield," Wilson said. "You're used to it. We'll leave the Mannlicher in the car with the Memsahib. Your gun-bearer can carry your heavy gun. I've this damned cannon. Now let me tell you about them." He had saved this until the last because he did not want to worry Macomber. "When a buff comes he comes with his head high and thrust straight out. The boss of the horns covers any sort of a brain shot. The only shot is straight into the nose. The only other shot is into his chest or, if you're to one side, into the neck or the shoulders. After they've been hit once they take a hell of a lot of killing. Don't try anything fancy. Take the easiest shot there is. They've finished skinning out that head now. Should we get started?"

He called to the gun-bearers, who came up wiping their hands, and the older one got into the back.

"I'll only take Kongoni," Wilson said. "The other can watch to keep the birds away."

As the car moved slowly across the open space toward the island of brushy trees that ran in a tongue of foliage along a dry water course that cut the open swale, Macomber felt his heart pounding and his mouth was dry again, but it was excitement, not fear.

"Here's where he went in," Wilson said. Then to the gun-bearer in Swahili, "Take the blood spoor."

The car was parallel to the patch of bush. Macomber, Wilson and the gun-bearer got down. Macomber, looking back, saw his wife, with the rifle by her side, looking at him. He waved to her and she did not wave back.

The brush was very thick ahead and the ground was dry. The middle-aged gun-bearer was sweating heavily and Wilson had his hat down over his eyes and his red neck showed just ahead of Macomber. Suddenly the gun-bearer said something in Swahili to Wilson and ran forward.

"He's dead in there," Wilson said. "Good work," and he turned to grip Macomber's hand and as they shook hands, grinning at each other, the gun-bearer shouted wildly and they saw him coming out of the bush sideways, fast as a crab, and the bull coming, nose out, mouth tight closed, blood dripping, massive head straight out, coming in a charge, his little pig eyes bloodshot as he looked at them. Wilson, who was ahead, was kneeling shooting, and Macomber, as he fired, unhearing his shot in the roaring of Wilson's gun, saw fragments like slate burst from the huge boss of the horns, and the head jerked, he shot again at the wide nostrils and saw the horns jolt again and fragments fly, and he did not see Wilson now and, aiming carefully, shot again with the buffalo's huge bulk almost on him and his rifle almost level with the on-coming head, nose out, and he could see the little wicked eyes and the head started to lower and he felt a sudden white-hot, blinding flash explode inside his head and that was all he ever felt.

Wilson had ducked to one side to get in a shoulder shot. Macomber had stood solid and shot for the nose, shooting a touch high each time and hitting the heavy horns, splintering and chipping them like hitting a slate roof, and Mrs. Macomber, in the car, had shot at the buffalo with the 6.5 Mannlicher as it seemed about to gore Macomber and had hit her husband about two inches up and a little to one side of the base of his skull.

Francis Macomber lay now, face down, not two yards from where the buffalo lay on his side and his wife knelt over him with Wilson beside her.

"I wouldn't turn him over," Wilson said.

The woman was crying hysterically.

"I'd get back in the car," Wilson said. "Where's the rifle?"

She shook her head, her face contorted. The gun-bearer picked up the rifle.

"Leave it as it is," said Wilson. Then, "Go get Abdulla so that he may witness the manner of the accident."

He knelt down, took a handkerchief from his pocket, and spread it over Francis Macomber's crew-cropped head where it lay. The blood sank into the dry, loose earth.

Wilson stood up and saw the buffalo on his side, his legs out, his thinly-haired belly crawling with ticks. Hell of a good bull, his brain registered automatically. A good fifty inches, or better. Better. He called to the driver and told him to spread a blanket over the body and stay by it. Then he walked over to the motor car where the woman sat crying in the corner.

"That was a pretty thing to do," he said in a toneless voice. "He *would* have left you too."

"Stop it," she said.

"Of course it's an accident," he said. "I know that."

"Stop it," she said.

"Don't worry," he said. "There will be a certain amount of unpleasantness but I will have some photographs taken that will be very useful at the inquest. There's the testimony of the gun-bearers and the driver too. You're perfectly all right."

"Stop it," she said.

"There's a hell of a lot to be done," he said. "And I'll have to send a truck off to the lake to wireless for a plane to take the three of us into

Nairobi. Why didn't you poison him? That's what they do in England."

"Stop it. Stop it. Stop it," the woman cried.

Wilson looked at her with his flat blue eyes.

"I'm through now," he said. "I was a little angry. I'd begun to like your husband."

"Oh, please stop it," she said. "Please, please stop it."

"That's better," Wilson said. "Please is much better. Now I'll stop."

A MOTHER
JAMES JOYCE

James Joyce [signature]

Mr. Holohan, assistant secretary of the *Eire Abu Society*, had been walking up and down Dublin for nearly a month, with his hands and pockets full of dirty pieces of paper, arranging about the series of concerts. He had a game leg, and for this his friends called him Hoppy Holohan. He walked up and down constantly, stood by the hour at street corners arguing the point, and made notes; but in the end it was Mrs. Kearney who arranged everything.

Miss Devlin had become Mrs. Kearney out of spite. She had been educated in a high-class convent, where she had learned French and music. As she was naturally pale and unbending in manner she made few friends at school. When she came to the age of marriage she was sent out to many houses, where her playing and ivory manners were much admired. She sat amid the chilly circle of her accomplishments, waiting for some suitor to brave it and offer her a brilliant life. But the young men whom she met were ordinary and she gave them no encouragement, trying to console her romantic desires by eating a great deal of Turkish Delight in secret. However, when she drew near the limit and her friends began to loosen their tongues about her, she silenced them by marrying Mr. Kearney, who was a bootmaker on Ormond Quay.

He was much older than she. His conversation, which was serious, took place at intervals in his great brown beard. After the first year of married life, Mrs. Kearney perceived that such a man would wear better than a romantic person, but she never put her own romantic ideas away. He was sober, thrifty, and pious; he went to the altar every first Friday, sometimes with her, oftener by himself. But she never weakened in her religion and was a good wife to him. At some party in a strange house when she lifted her eyebrow ever so slightly he stood up to take his leave and, when his cough troubled him, she put the eiderdown quilt over his feet and made a strong rum punch. For his part, he was a model father. By paying a small sum every week into a society, he ensured for both his daughters a dowry of one hundred pounds each when they came to the age of twenty-four. He sent the older daughter, Kathleen, to a good convent, where she learned French and music, and afterwards paid her fees at the Academy. Every year in the month of July Mrs. Kearney found occasion to say to some friend:

"My good man is packing us off to Skerries for a few weeks."

If it was not Skerries it was Howth or Greystones.

When the Irish Revival began to be appreciable Mrs. Kearney determined to take advantage of her daughter's name and brought an Irish teacher to the house. Kathleen and her sister sent Irish picture postcards to their friends and these friends sent back other Irish picture postcards. On special Sundays, when Mr. Kearney went with his family to the pro-cathedral, a little crowd of people would assemble after mass at the corner of Cathedral Street. They were all friends of the Kearneys —musical friends or Nationalist friends, and, when they had played every little counter of gossip, they shook hands with one another all together, laughing at the crossing of so many hands, and said goodbye to one another in Irish. Soon the name of Miss Kathleen Kearney began to be heard often on people's lips. People said that she was very clever at music and a very nice girl and, moreover, that she was a believer in the language movement. Mrs. Kearney was well content at this. Therefore she was not surprised when one day Mr. Holohan came to her and proposed that her daughter should be the accompanist at a series of four grand concerts which his Society was going to give in the Antient Concert Rooms. She brought him into the drawing-room, made him sit down and brought out the decanter and the silver biscuit-barrel. She entered heart and soul into the details of the enterprise, advised and dissuaded: and finally a contract was drawn up by which Kathleen was to receive eight guineas for her services as accompanist at the four grand concerts.

As Mr. Holohan was a novice in such delicate matters as the wording of bills and the disposing of items for a programme, Mrs. Kearney helped him. She had tact. She knew what *artistes* should go into capitals and what *artistes* should go into small type. She knew that the first tenor would not like to come on after Mr. Meade's comic turn. To keep the audience continually diverted she slipped the doubtful items in between the old favourites. Mr. Holohan called to see her every day to have her advice on some point. She was invariably friendly and advising—homely, in fact. She pushed the decanter towards him, saying:

"Now, help yourself, Mr. Holohan!"

And while he was helping himself she said:

"Don't be afraid! Don't be afraid of it!"

Everything went on smoothly. Mrs. Kearney bought some lovely blush-pink charmeuse in Brown Thomas's to let into the front of Kathleen's dress. It cost a pretty penny; but there are occasions when a little expense is justifiable. She took a dozen of two-shilling tickets for the final concert and sent them to those friends who could not be trusted to come otherwise. She forgot nothing, and, thanks to her, everything that was to be done was done.

The concerts were to be on Wednesday, Thursday, Friday, and Saturday. When Mrs. Kearney arrived with her daughter at the Antient Concert Rooms on Wednesday night she did not like the look of things. A few young men, wearing bright blue badges in their coats, stood idle in the vestibule; none of them wore evening dress. She passed by with her daughter and a quick glance through the open door of the hall showed her the cause of the stewards' idleness. At first she wondered had she mistaken the hour. No, it was twenty minutes to eight.

In the dressing-room behind the stage she was introduced to the secretary of the Society, Mr. Fitzpatrick. She smiled and shook his hand. He was a little man, with a white, vacant face. She noticed that he wore his soft brown hat carelessly on the side of his head and that his accent was flat. He held a programme in his hand, and, while he was talking to her, he chewed one end of it into a moist pulp. He seemed to bear disappointments lightly. Mr. Holohan came into the dressing-room every few minutes with reports from the box-office. The *artistes* talked among themselves nervously, glanced from time to time at the mirror and rolled and unrolled their music. When it was nearly half past eight, the few people in the hall began to express their desire to be entertained. Mr. Fitzpatrick came in, smiled vacantly at the room, and said:

"Well, now, ladies and gentlemen. I suppose we'd better open the ball."

Mrs. Kearney rewarded his very flat final syllable with a quick stare of contempt, and then said to her daughter encouragingly:

"Are you ready, dear?"

When she had an opportunity, she called Mr. Holohan aside and asked him to tell her what it meant. Mr. Holohan did not know what it meant. He said that the committee had made a mistake in arranging for four concerts: four were too many.

"And the *artistes!*" said Mrs. Kearney, "Of course they are doing their best, but really they are not good."

Mr. Holohan admitted that the *artistes* were no good, but the committee, he said, had decided to let the first three concerts go as they pleased and reserve all the talent for the Saturday night. Mrs. Kearney said nothing, but, as the mediocre items followed one another on the platform and the few people in the hall grew fewer and fewer, she began to regret that she had put herself to any expense for such a concert. There was something she didn't like in the look of things, and Mr. Fitzpatrick's vacant smile irritated her very much. However, she said nothing and waited to see how it would end. The concert expired shortly before ten, and everyone went home quickly.

The concert on Thursday night was better attended, but Mrs. Kearney saw at once that the house was filled with paper. The audience behaved indecorously, as if the concert were an informal dress rehearsal. Mr. Fitzpatrick seemed to enjoy himself; he was quite unconscious that Mrs. Kearney was taking angry note of his conduct. He stood at the edge of the screen, from time to time jutting out his head and exchanging a laugh with two friends in the corner of the balcony. In the course of the evening, Mrs. Kearney learned that the Friday concert was to be abandoned and that the committee was going to move heaven and earth to secure a bumper house on Saturday night. When she heard this, she sought out Mr. Holohan. She buttonholed him as he was limping out quickly with a glass of lemonade for a young lady and asked him was it true. Yes, it was true.

"But, of course, that doesn't alter the contract," she said. "The contract was for four concerts."

Mr. Holohan seemed to be in a hurry; he advised her to speak to Mr. Fitzpatrick. Mrs. Kearney was now beginning to be alarmed. She called Mr. Fitzpatrick away from his screen and told him that her daughter had signed for four concerts and that, of course, according to the terms of the contract, she should receive the sum originally stipulated for, whether the Society gave the four concerts or not. Mr. Fitzpatrick, who did not catch the point at issue very quickly, seemed unable to resolve the difficulty and said that he would bring the matter before the committee. Mrs. Kearney's anger began to flutter in her cheek and she had all she could do to keep from asking:

"And who is the *Cometty*, pray?"

But she knew that it would not be ladylike to do that: so she was silent.

Little boys were sent out into the principal streets of Dublin early on Friday morning with bundles of handbills. Special puffs appeared in all the evening papers, reminding the music-loving public of the treat which was in store for it on the following evening. Mrs. Kearney was somewhat reassured, but she thought well to tell her husband part of her suspicions. He listened carefully and said that perhaps it would be better if he went with her on Saturday night. She agreed. She respected her husband in the same way as she respected the General Post Office, as something large, secure, and fixed; and though she knew the small number of his talents she appreciated his abstract value as a male. She was glad that he had suggested coming with her. She thought her plans over.

The night of the grand concert came. Mrs. Kearney, with her husband and daughter, arrived at the Antient Concert Rooms three-quarters of an hour before the time at which the concert was to begin. By ill luck it was a rainy evening. Mrs. Kearney placed her daughter's clothes and music in charge of her husband and went all over the building looking for Mr. Holohan or Mr. Fitzpatrick. She could find neither. She asked the stewards was any member of the committee in the hall and, after a great deal of trouble, a steward brought out a little woman named Miss Beirne, to whom Mrs. Kearney explained that she wanted to see one of the secretaries. Miss Beirne expected them any minute and asked could she do anything. Mrs. Kearney looked searchingly at the oldish face which was screwed into an expression of trustfulness and enthusiasm and answered:

"No, thank you!"

The little woman hoped they would have a good house. She looked out at the rain until the melancholy of the wet street effaced all the trustfulness and enthusiasm from her twisted features. Then she gave a little sigh and said:

"Ah, well! We did our best, the dear knows."

Mrs. Kearney had to go back to the dressing-room.

The *artistes* were arriving. The bass and the second tenor had already come. The bass, Mr. Duggan, was a slender young man with a scattered black moustache. He was the son of a hall porter in an office in the city and, as a boy, he had sung prolonged bass notes in the resounding hall. From this humble state he had raised himself until he had become a first-rate *artiste*. He had appeared in grand opera. One night, when an operatic *artiste* had fallen ill, he had undertaken the part of the king in the opera of *Maritana* at the Queen's Theatre. He sang his music with great feeling and volume and was warmly welcomed by the gallery; but, unfortunately, he marred the good impression by wiping his nose in his gloved hand once or twice out of thoughtlessness. He was unassuming and spoke little. He said *yous* so softly that it passed unnoticed and he never drank anything stronger than milk, for his voice's sake. Mr. Bell, the second tenor, was a fair-haired little man who competed every year for prizes at the *Feis Ceoil*. On his fourth trial he had been awarded a bronze medal. He was extremely nervous and extremely jealous of other tenors and he covered his nervous jealousy with an ebullient friendliness. It was his humour to have people know what an ordeal a concert was to him. Therefore when he saw Mr. Duggan he went over to him and asked:

"Are you in it too?"

"Yes," said Mr. Duggan.

Mr. Bell laughed at his fellow-sufferer, held out his hand and said: "Shake!"

Mrs. Kearney passed by these two young men and went to the edge of the screen to view the house. The seats were being filled up rapidly and a pleasant noise circulated in the auditorium. She came back and spoke to her husband privately. Their conversation was evidently about Kathleen, for they both glanced at her often as she stood chatting to one of her Nationalist friends, Miss Healy, the contralto. An unknown solitary woman with a pale face walked through the room. The women followed with keen eyes the faded blue dress which was stretched upon a meagre body. Someone said that she was Madam Glynn, the soprano.

"I wonder where did they dig her up," said Kathleen to Miss Healy. "I'm sure I never heard of her."

Miss Healy had to smile. Mr. Holohan limped into the dressing-room at that moment and the two young ladies asked him who was the unknown woman. Mr. Holohan said that she was Madam Glynn from London. Madam Glynn took her stand in a corner of the room, holding a roll of music stiffly before her and from time to time changing the direction of her startled gaze. The shadow took her faded dress into shelter but fell revengefully into the little cup behind her collar-bone. The noise of the hall became more audible. The first tenor and the baritone arrived together. They were both well dressed, stout, and complacent, and they brought a breath of opulence among the company.

Mrs. Kearney brought her daughter over to them, and talked to them amiably. She wanted to be on good terms with them but, while she strove to be polite, her eyes followed Mr. Holohan in his limping and devious courses. As soon as she could she excused herself and went out after him.

"Mr. Holohan, I want to speak to you for a moment," she said.

They went down to a discreet part of the corridor. Mrs. Kearney asked him when was her daughter going to be paid. Mr. Holohan said that Mr. Fitzpatrick had charge of that. Mrs. Kearney said that she didn't know anything about Mr. Fitzpatrick. Her daughter had signed a contract for eight guineas and she would have to be paid. Mr. Holohan said that it wasn't his business.

"Why isn't it your business?" asked Mrs. Kearney. "Didn't you yourself bring her the contract? Anyway, if it's not your business, it's my business, and I mean to see to it."

"You'd better speak to Mr. Fitzpatrick," said Mr. Holohan distinctly.

"I don't know anything about Mr. Fitzpatrick," repeated Mrs. Kearney. "I have my contract, and I intend to see that it is carried out."

When she came back to the dressing-room her cheeks were slightly suffused. The room was lively. Two men in outdoor dress had taken possession of the fireplace and were chatting familiarly with Miss Healy and the baritone. They were the *Freeman* man and Mr. O'Madden Burke. The *Freeman* man had come in to say that he could not wait for the concert as he had to report the lecture which an American priest was giving in the Mansion House. He said they were to leave the report for him at the *Freeman* office and he would see that it went in. He was a grey-haired man with a plausible voice and careful manners. He held an extinguished cigar in his hand and the aroma of cigar smoke floated near him. He had not intended to stay a moment, because concerts and *artistes* bored him considerably, but he remained leaning against the mantelpiece. Miss Healy stood in front of him, talking and laughing. He was old enough to suspect one reason for her politeness, but young enough in spirit to turn the moment to account. The warmth, fragrance, and colour of her body appealed to his senses. He was pleasantly conscious that the bosom which he saw rise and fall slowly beneath him rose and fell at that moment for him, that the laughter and fragrance and wilful glances were his tribute. When he could stay no longer he took leave of her regretfully.

"O'Madden Burke will write the notice," he explained to Mr. Holohan, "and I'll see it in."

"Thank you very much, Mr. Hendrick," said Mr. Holohan. "You'll see it in, I know. Now, won't you have a little something before you go?"

"I don't mind," said Mr. Hendrick.

The two men went along some tortuous passages and up a dark staircase and came to a secluded room where one of the stewards was uncorking bottles for a few gentlemen. One of these gentlemen was Mr. O'Madden Burke, who had found out the room by instinct. He was a suave, elderly man who balanced his imposing body, when at rest, upon a large silk umbrella. His magniloquent western name was the moral umbrella upon which he balanced the fine problem of his finances. He was widely respected.

While Mr. Holohan was entertaining the *Freeman* man Mrs. Kearney was speaking so animatedly to her husband that he had to ask her to lower her voice. The conversation of the others in the dressing-room had become strained. Mr. Bell, the first item, stood ready with his music but the accompanist made no sign. Evidently something was wrong. Mr. Kearney looked straight before him, stroking his beard, while Mrs. Kearney spoke into Kathleen's ear with subdued emphasis. From the hall came sounds of encouragement, clapping and stamping of feet. The first tenor and the baritone and Miss Healy stood together, waiting tranquilly, but Mr. Bell's nerves were greatly agitated because he was afraid the audience would think that he had come late.

Mr. Holohan and Mr. O'Madden Burke came into the room. In a moment Mr. Holohan perceived the hush. He went over to Mrs. Kearney and spoke with her earnestly. While they were speaking the noise in the hall grew louder. Mr. Holohan became very red and excited. He spoke volubly, but Mrs. Kearney said curtly at intervals:

"She won't go on. She must get her eight guineas."

Mr. Holohan pointed desperately towards the hall where the audience was clapping and stamping. He appealed to Mr. Kearney and to Kathleen. But Mr. Kearney continued to stroke his beard and Kathleen looked down, moving the point of her new shoe: it was not her fault. Mrs. Kearney repeated:

"She won't go on without her money."

After a swift struggle of tongues Mr. Holohan hobbled out in haste. The room was silent. When the strain of the silence had become somewhat painful Miss Healy said to the baritone:

"Have you seen Mrs. Pat Campbell this week?"

The baritone had not seen her but he had been told that she was very fine. The conversation went no further. The first tenor bent his head and began to count the links of the gold chain which was extended across his waist, smiling and humming random notes to observe the effect on the frontal sinus. From time to time everyone glanced at Mrs. Kearney.

The noise in the auditorium had risen to a clamour when Mr. Fitzpatrick burst into the room, followed by Mr. Holohan, who was panting. The clapping and stamping in the hall were punctuated by whistling. Mr. Fitzpatrick held a few banknotes in his hand. He counted out four into Mrs. Kearney's hand and said she would get the other half at the interval. Mrs. Kearney said:

"This is four shillings short."

But Kathleen gathered in her skirt and said:

"*Now, Mr. Bell,*" to the first item, who was shaking like an aspen. The singer and the accompanist went out together. The noise in the hall died away. There was a pause of a few seconds, and then the piano was heard.

The first part of the concert was very successful except for Madam Glynn's item. The poor lady sang *Killarney* in a bodiless gasping voice, with all the old-fashioned mannerisms of intonation and pronunciation which she believed lent elegance to her singing. She looked as if she had been resurrected from an old stage-wardrobe and the cheaper parts of the hall made fun of her high wailing notes. The first tenor and the contralto, however, brought down the house. Kathleen played a selection of Irish airs which was generously applauded. The first part closed with a stirring patriotic recitation delivered by a young lady who arranged amateur theatricals. It was deservedly applauded, and, when it was ended, the men went out for the interval, content.

All this time the dressing-room was a hive of excitement. In one corner were Mr. Holohan, Mr. Fitzpatrick, Miss Beirne, two of the stewards, the baritone, the bass, and Mr. O'Madden Burke. Mr. O'Madden Burke said it was the most scandalous exhibition he had ever witnessed. Miss Kathleen Kearney's musical career was ended in Dublin after that, he said. The baritone was asked what did he think of Mrs. Kearney's conduct. He did not like to say anything. He had been paid his money and wished to be at peace with men. However, he said that Mrs. Kearney might have taken the *artistes* into consideration. The stewards and the secretaries debated hotly as to what should be done when the interval came.

"I agree with Miss Beirne," said Mr. O'Madden Burke. "Pay her nothing."

In another corner of the room were Mrs. Kearney and her husband, Mr. Bell, Miss Healy, and the young lady who had to recite the patriotic piece. Mrs. Kearney said that the committee had treated her scandalously. She had spared neither trouble nor expense and this was how she was repaid.

They thought they had only a girl to deal with and that, therefore, they could ride roughshod over her. But she would show them their mistake. They wouldn't have dared to have treated her like that if she had been a man. But she would see that her daughter got her rights: she wouldn't be fooled. If they didn't pay her to the last farthing she would make Dublin ring. Of course she was sorry for the sake of the *artistes*. But what else could she do? She appealed to the second tenor, who said he thought she had not been well treated. Then she appealed to Miss Healy. Miss Healy wanted to join the other group, but she did not like to do so because she was a great friend of Kathleen's and the Kearneys had often invited her to their house.

As soon as the first part was ended Mr. Fitzpatrick and Mr. Holohan went over to Mrs. Kearney and told her that the other four guineas would be paid after the committee meeting on the following Tuesday and that, in case her daughter did not play for the second part, the committee would consider the contract broken and would pay nothing.

"I haven't seen any committee," said Mrs. Kearney angrily. "My daughter has her contract. She will get four pounds eight into her hand or a foot she won't put on that platform."

"I'm surprised at you, Mrs. Kearney," said Mr. Holohan. "I never thought you would treat us this way."

"And what way did you treat me?" asked Mrs. Kearney.

Her face was inundated with an angry colour and she looked as if she would attack someone with her hands.

"I'm asking for my rights," she said.

"You might have some sense of decency," said Mr. Holohan.

"Might I, indeed? . . . And when I ask when my daughter is going to be paid I can't get a civil answer."

She tossed her head and assumed a haughty voice:

"You must speak to the secretary. It's not my business. I'm a great fellow fol-the-diddle-I-do."

"I thought you were a lady," said Mr. Holohan, walking away from her abruptly.

After that Mrs. Kearney's conduct was condemned on all hands: everyone approved of what the committee had done. She stood at the door, haggard with rage, arguing with her husband and daughter, gesticulating with them. She waited until it was time for the second part to begin in the hope that the secretaries would approach her. But Miss Healy had kindly consented to play one or two accompaniments. Mrs. Kearney had to stand aside to allow the baritone and his accompanist to pass up to the platform. She stood still for an instant like an angry stone image and, when the first notes of the song struck her ear, she caught up her daughter's cloak and said to her husband:

"Get a cab!"

He went out at once. Mrs. Kearney wrapped the cloak round her daughter and followed him. As she passed through the doorway she stopped and glared into Mr. Holohan's face.

"I'm not done with you yet," she said.

"But I'm done with you," said Mr. Holohan.

Kathleen followed her mother meekly. Mr. Holohan began to pace up and down the room in order to cool himself, for he felt his skin on fire.

"That's a nice lady!" he said. "O, she's a nice lady!"

"You did the proper thing, Holohan," said Mr. O'Madden Burke, poised upon his umbrella in approval.

THE HAUNTED BOY

CARSON McCULLERS

Carson Mc Cullers

Hugh looked for his mother at the corner, but she was not in the yard. Sometimes she would be out fooling with the border of spring flowers—the candytuft, the sweet william, the lobelias (she had taught him the names)—but today the green front lawn with the borders of many-colored flowers was empty under the frail sunshine of the mid-April afternoon. Hugh raced up the sidewalk, and John followed him. They finished the front steps with two bounds, and the door slammed after them.

"Mama!" Hugh called.

It was then, in the unanswering silence as they stood in the empty, wax-floored hall, that Hugh felt there was something wrong. There was no fire in the grate of the sitting room, and since he was used to the flicker of firelight during the cold months, the room on this first warm day seemed strangely naked and cheerless. Hugh shivered. He was glad John was there. The sun shone on a red piece in the flowered rug. Red-bright, red-dark, red-dead—Hugh sickened with a sudden chill remembrance of "the other time." The red darkened to a dizzy black.

"What's the matter, Brown?" John asked. "You look so white."

Hugh shook himself and put his hand to his forehead. "Nothing. Let's go back to the kitchen."

"I can't stay but just a minute," John said. "I'm obligated to sell those tickets. I have to eat and run."

The kitchen, with the fresh checked towels and clean pans, was now the best room in the house. And on the enameled table there was a lemon pie that she had made. Assured by the everyday kitchen and the

180

pie, Hugh stepped back into the hall and raised his face again to call upstairs.

"Mother! Oh, Mama!"

Again there was no answer.

"My mother made this pie," he said. Quickly he found a knife and cut into the pie—to dispel the gathering sense of dread.

"Think you ought to cut it, Brown?"

"Sure thing, Laney."

They called each other by their last names this spring, unless they happened to forget. To Hugh it seemed sporty and grown and somehow grand. Hugh liked John better than any other boy at school. John was two years older than Hugh, and compared to him the other boys seemed like a silly crowd of punks. John was the best student in the sophomore class, brainy but not the least bit a teacher's pet, and he was the best athlete too. Hugh was a freshman and didn't have so many friends that first year of high school—he had somehow cut himself off, because he was so afraid.

"Mama always has me something nice for after school." Hugh put a big piece of pie on a saucer for John—for Laney.

"This pie is certainly super."

"The crust is made of crunched-up graham crackers instead of regular pie dough," Hugh said, "because pie dough is a lot of trouble. We think this graham-cracker pastry is just as good. Naturally, my mother can make regular pie dough if she wants to."

Hugh could not keep still; he walked up and down the kitchen, eating the pie wedge he carried on the palm of his hand. His brown hair was mussed with nervous rakings, and his gentle gold-brown eyes were haunted with pained perplexity. John, who remained seated at the table, sensed Hugh's uneasiness and wrapped one gangling leg around the other.

"I'm really obligated to sell those Glee Club tickets."

"Don't go. You have the whole afternoon." He was afraid of the empty house. He needed John, he needed someone; most of all he needed to hear his mother's voice and know she was in the house with him. "Maybe Mama is taking a bath," he said. "I'll holler again."

The answer to his third call too was silence.

181

"I guess your mother must have gone to the movie or gone shopping or something."

"No," Hugh said. "She would have left a note. She always does when she's gone when I come home from school."

"We haven't looked for a note," John said. "Maybe she left it under the doormat or somewhere in the living room."

Hugh was inconsolable. "No. She would have left it right under this pie. She knows I always run first to the kitchen."

"Maybe she had a phone call or thought of something she suddenly wanted to do."

"She *might* have," he said. "I remember she said to Daddy that one of these days she was going to buy herself some new clothes." This flash of hope did not survive its expression. He pushed his hair back and started from the room. "I guess I'd better go upstairs. I ought to go upstairs while you are here." He stood with his arm around the newel-post; the smell of varnished stairs, the sight of the closed white bathroom door at the top revived again "the other time." He clung to the newel-post, and his feet would not move to climb the stairs. The red turned again to whirling, sick dark. Hugh sat down. *Stick your head between your legs,* he ordered, remembering scout first aid.

"Hugh," John called. "Hugh!"

The dizziness clearing, Hugh accepted a fresh chagrin—Laney was calling him by his ordinary first name; he thought he was a sissy about his mother, unworthy of being called by his last name in the grand, sporty way they used before. The dizziness cleared when he returned to the kitchen.

"Brown," said John, and the chagrin disappeared. "Does this establishment have anything pertaining to a cow? A white, fluid liquid. In French they call it *lait.* Here we call it plain old milk."

The stupidity of shock lightened. "Oh. Laney, I am a dope! Please excuse me. I clean forgot." Hugh fetched the milk from the refrigerator and found two glasses. "I didn't think. My mind was on something else."

"I know," John said. After a moment he asked in a calm voice, looking steadily at Hugh's eyes: "Why are you so worried about your mother? Is she sick, Hugh?"

Hugh knew now that the first name was not a slight; it was because John was talking too serious to be sporty. He liked John better than any friend he had ever had. He felt more natural sitting across the kitchen table from John, somehow safer. As he looked into John's gray, peaceful eyes, the balm of affection soothed the dread.

John asked again, still steadily: "Hugh, is your mother sick?"

Hugh could have answered no other boy. He had talked with no one about his mother, except his father, and even those intimacies had been rare, oblique. They could approach the subject only when they were occupied with something else, doing carpentry work or the two times they hunted in the woods together—or when they were cooking supper or washing dishes.

"She's not exactly sick," he said, "but Daddy and I have been worried about her. At least, we used to be worried for a while."

John asked: "Is it a kind of heart trouble?"

Hugh's voice was strained. "Did you hear about that fight I had with that slob Clem Roberts? I scraped his slob face on the gravel walk and nearly killed him sure enough. He's still got scars or at least he did have a bandage on for two days. I had to stay in school every afternoon for a week. But I nearly killed him. I would have if Mr. Paxton hadn't come along and dragged me off."

"I heard about it."

"You know why I wanted to kill him?"

For a moment John's eyes flickered away.

Hugh tensed himself; his raw boy hands clutched the table edge; he took a deep, hoarse breath. "That slob was telling everybody that my mother was in Milledgeville. He was spreading it around that my mother was crazy."

"The dirty bastard."

Hugh said in a clear, defeated voice: "My mother *was* in Milledgeville. But that doesn't mean that she was crazy," he added quickly. "In that big state hospital there are buildings for people who are crazy, and there are other buildings for people who are just sick. Mama was sick for a while. Daddy and me discussed it and decided that the hospital in Milledgeville was the place where there were the best doctors and she would get the best care. But she was the furtherest from crazy than anybody in the world. You know Mama, John." He said again: "I ought to go upstairs."

John said: "I have always thought that your mother is one of the nicest ladies in this town."

"You see, Mama had a peculiar thing happen, and afterward she was blue."

Confession, the first deep-rooted words, opened the festered secrecy of the boy's heart, and he continued more rapidly, urgent and finding unforeseen relief. "Last year my mother thought she was going to have a little baby. She talked it over with Daddy and me," he said proudly. "We wanted a girl. I was going to choose the name. We were so tickled. I hunted up all my old toys—my electric train and the tracks. . . . I was going to name her Crystal—how does that name strike you for a girl? It reminds me of something bright and dainty."

"Was the little baby born dead?"

Even with John, Hugh's ears turned hot; his cold hands touched them. "No, it was what they call a tumor. That's what happened to my mother. They had to operate at the hospital here." He was embarrassed and his voice was very low. "Then she had something called change of life." The words were terrible to Hugh. "And afterward she was blue. Daddy said it was a shock to her nervous system. It's something that happens to ladies; she was just blue and run-down."

Although there was no red, no red in the kitchen anywhere, Hugh was approaching "the other time."

"One day, she just sort of gave up—one day last fall." Hugh's eyes were wide open and glaring: again he climbed the stairs and opened the bathroom door—he put his hand to his eyes to shut out the memory. "She tried to—hurt herself. I found her when I came in from school."

John reached out and carefully stroked Hugh's sweatered arm.

"Don't worry. A lot of people have to go to hospitals because they are run-down and blue. Could happen to anybody."

"We had to put her in the hospital—the best hospital." The recollection of those long, long months was stained with a dull loneliness, as cruel in its lasting unappeasement as "the other time"— how long had it lasted? In the hospital Mama could walk around and she always had on shoes.

John said carefully: "This pie is certainly super."

"My mother is a super cook. She cooks things like meat pie and salmon loaf—as well as steaks and hot dogs."

"I hate to eat and run," John said.

Hugh was so frightened of being left alone that he felt the alarm in his own loud heart.

"Don't go," he urged. "Let's talk for a little while."

"Talk about what?"

Hugh could not tell him. Not even John Laney. He could tell no one of the empty house and the horror of the time before. "Do you ever cry?" he asked John. "I don't."

"I do sometimes," John admitted.

"I wish I had known you better when Mother was away. Daddy and me used to go hunting nearly every Saturday. We *lived* on quail and dove. I bet you would have liked that." He added in a lower tone: "On Sunday we went to the hospital."

John said: "It's kind of a delicate proposition selling those tickets. A lot of people don't enjoy the high school Glee Club operettas. Unless they know someone in it personally, they'd rather stay home with a good TV show. A lot of people buy tickets on the basis of being public-spirited."

"We're going to get a television set real soon."

"I couldn't exist without television," John said.

Hugh's voice was apologetic. "Daddy wants to clean up the hospital bills first, because as everybody knows sickness is a very expensive proposition. Then we'll get TV."

John lifted his milk glass. "Skoal," he said. "That's a Swedish word you say before you drink. A good-luck word."

"You know so many foreign words and languages."

"Not so many," John said truthfully. "Just 'kaput' and 'adios' and 'skoal' and stuff we learn in French class. That's not much."

"That's *beaucoup*," said Hugh, and he felt witty and pleased with himself.

Suddenly the stored tension burst into physical activity. Hugh grabbed the basketball out on the porch and rushed into the backyard. He dribbled the ball several times and aimed at the goal his father had put up on his last birthday. When he missed he bounced the ball to John, who had come after him.

It was good to be outdoors and the relief of natural play brought Hugh the first line of a poem. "My heart is like a basketball." Usually when a poem came to him he would lie sprawled on the living-room floor, studying to hunt rhymes, his tongue working on the side of his mouth. His mother would call him Shelley-Poe when she stepped over him, and sometimes she would put her foot lightly on his behind. His mother always liked his poems; today the second line came quickly, like magic. He said it out loud to John: " 'My heart is like a basketball, bounding with glee down the hall.' How do you like that for the start of a poem?"

"Sounds kind of crazy to me," John said. Then he corrected himself hastily. "I mean it sounds—odd. Odd, I meant."

Hugh realized why John changed the word, and the elation of play and poems left him instantly. He caught the ball and stood with it cradled in his arms. The afternoon was golden and the wisteria vine on the porch was in full, unshattered bloom. The wisteria was like lavender waterfalls. The fresh breeze smelled of sun-warmed flowers. The sunlit sky was blue and cloudless. It was the first warm day of spring.

"I have to shove off," John said.

"No!" Hugh's voice was desperate. "Don't you want another piece of pie? I never heard of anybody eating just one piece of pie."

He steered John into the house and this time he called only out of habit because he always called on coming in. "Mother!" He was cold after the bright, sunny outdoors. He was cold not only because of the weather but because he was so scared.

"My mother has been home a month and every afternoon she's always here when I come home from school. Always, always."

They stood in the kitchen looking at the lemon pie. And to Hugh the cut pie looked somehow—odd. As they stood motionless in the kitchen the silence was creepy and odd too.

"Doesn't this house seem quiet to you?"

"It's because you don't have television. We put on our TV at seven o'clock and it stays on all day and night until we go to bed. Whether anybody's in the living room or not. There're plays and skits and gags going on continually."

"We have a radio, of course, and a vic."

"But that's not the company of a good TV. You won't know when your mother is in the house or not when you get TV."

Hugh didn't answer. Their footsteps sounded hollow in the hall. He felt sick as he stood on the first step with his arm around the newel-post. "If you could just come upstairs for a minute—"

John's voice was suddenly impatient and loud. "How many times have I told you I'm obligated to sell those tickets. You have to be public-spirited about things like glee clubs."

"Just for a second—I have something important to show you upstairs."

John did not ask what it was and Hugh sought desperately to name something important enough to get John upstairs. He said finally: "I'm assembling a hi-fi machine. You have to know a lot about electronics—my father is helping me."

But even when he spoke he knew John did not for a second believe the lie. Who would buy a hi-fi when they didn't have television? He hated John, as you hate people you have to need so badly. He had to say something more and he straightened his shoulders.

"I just want you to know how much I value your friendship. During these past months I had somehow cut myself off from people."

"That's okay, Brown. You oughtn't to be so sensitive because your mother was—where she was."

John had his hand on the door and Hugh was trembling. "I thought if you could come up for just a minute—"

John looked at him with anxious, puzzled eyes. Then he asked slowly: "Is there something you are scared of upstairs?"

Hugh wanted to tell him everything. But he could not tell what his mother had done that September afternoon. It was too terrible and—odd. It was like something a *patient* would do, and not like his mother at all. Although his eyes were wild with terror and his body trembled he said: "I'm not scared."

"Well, so long. I'm sorry I have to go—but to be obligated is to be obligated."

John closed the front door and he was alone in the empty house. Nothing could save him now. Even if a whole crowd of boys were listening to TV in the living room, laughing at funny gags and jokes, it would still not help him. He had to go upstairs and find her. He sought courage from the last thing John had said, and repeated the words aloud: "To be obligated is to be obligated." But the words did not give him any of John's thoughtlessness and courage; they were creepy and strange in the silence.

He turned slowly to go upstairs. His heart was not like a basketball but like a fast, jazz drum, beating faster and faster as he climbed the stairs. His feet dragged as though he waded through knee-deep water and he held on to the banisters. The house looked odd, crazy. As he looked down at the ground-floor table with the vase of fresh spring flowers that too looked somehow peculiar. There was a mirror on the second floor and his own face startled him, so crazy did it seem to him. The initial of his high school sweater was backward and wrong in the reflection and his mouth was open like an asylum idiot. He shut his mouth and he looked better. Still the objects he saw—the table downstairs, the sofa upstairs—looked somehow cracked or jarred because of the dread in him, although they were the familiar things of every day. He fastened his eyes on the closed door at the right of the stairs and the fast, jazz drum beat faster.

He opened the bathroom door and for a moment the dread that had haunted him all that afternoon made him see again the room as he had seen it "the other time." His mother lay on the floor and there was blood everywhere. His mother lay there dead and there was blood everywhere, on her slashed wrist, and a pool of blood had trickled to the bathtub and lay dammed there.

Hugh touched the doorframe and steadied himself. Then the room settled and he realized this was not "the other time." The April sunlight brightened the clean white tiles. There was only bathroom brightness and the sunny window. He went to the bedroom and saw the empty bed with the rose-colored spread. The lady things were on the dresser. The room was as it always looked and nothing had happened . . . nothing had happened and he flung himself on the quilted rose bed and cried from relief and a strained, bleak tiredness that had lasted so long. The sobs jerked his whole body and quieted his jazz, fast heart.

Hugh had not cried all those months. He had not cried at "the other time," when he found his mother alone in that empty house with blood everywhere. He had not cried but he made a scout mistake. He had first lifted his mother's heavy, bloody body before he tried to bandage her. He had not cried when he called his father. He had not cried those few days when they were deciding what to do. He hadn't even cried when the doctor suggested Milledgeville, or when he and his father took her to the hospital in the car—although his father cried on the way home. He had not cried at the meals they made—steak every night for a whole month, so that they felt steak was running out of their eyes, their ears; then they had switched to hot dogs, and ate them until hot dogs ran out of their ears, their eyes. They got in ruts of food and were messy about the kitchen, so that it was never nice except the Saturday the cleaning woman came. He did not cry those lonesome afternoons after he had the fight with Clem Roberts and felt the other boys were thinking queer things of his mother. He stayed at home in the messy kitchen, eating Fig Newtons or chocolate bars. Or he went to see a neighbor's television—Miss Richards, an old maid who saw old-maid shows. He had not cried when his father drank too much, so that it took his appetite and Hugh had to eat alone. He had not even cried on those long, waiting Sundays when they went to Milledgeville and he twice saw a lady on a porch without any shoes on and talking to herself. A lady who was a patient and who struck at him with a horror he could not name. He did not cry when at first his mother would say: *Don't punish me by making me stay here. Let me go home.* He had not cried at the terrible words that haunted him—"change of life"—"crazy"—"Milledgeville"—he could not cry all during those long months strained with dullness and want and dread.

He still sobbed on the rose bedspread, which was soft and cool against his wet cheeks. He was sobbing so loud that he did not hear the front door open, did not even hear his mother call or the footsteps on the stairs. He still sobbed when his mother touched him and burrowed his face hard in the spread. He even stiffened his legs and kicked his feet.

"Why, Loveyboy," his mother said, calling him a long-ago child name. "What's happened?"

He sobbed even louder, although his mother tried to turn his face to her. He wanted her to worry. He did not turn around until she had finally left the bed, and then he looked at her. She had on a different dress—blue silk it looked like in the pale spring light.

"Darling, what's happened?"

The terror of the afternoon was over, but he could not tell it to his mother. He could not tell her what he had feared, or explain the horror of things that were never there at all—but had once been there.

"Why did you do it?"

"The first warm day I just suddenly decided to buy myself some new clothes."

But he was not talking about clothes; he was thinking about "the other time" and the grudge that had started when he saw the blood and horror and felt *why did she do this to me.* He thought of the grudge against the mother he loved the most in the world. All those last, sad months the anger had bounced against the love with guilt between.

"I bought two dresses and two petticoats. How do you like them?"

"I hate them!" Hugh said angrily. "Your slip is showing."

She turned around twice and the petticoat showed terribly. "It's supposed to show, goofy. It's the style."

"I still don't like it."

"I ate a sandwich at the tearoom with two cups of cocoa and then went to Mendel's. There were so many pretty things I couldn't seem to get away. I bought these two dresses and look, Hugh! The shoes!"

His mother went to the bed and switched on the light so he could see. The shoes were flat-heeled and *blue*—with diamond sparkles on the toes. He did not know how to criticize. "They look more like evening shoes than things you wear on the street."

"I have never owned any colored shoes before. I couldn't resist them."

His mother sort of danced over toward the window, making the petticoat twirl under the new dress. Hugh had stopped crying now, but he was still angry. "I don't like it because it makes you look like you're trying to seem young, and I bet you are forty years old."

His mother stopped dancing and stood still at the window. Her face was suddenly quiet and sad. "I'll be forty-three years old in June."

He had hurt her and suddenly the anger vanished and there was only love. "Mama, I shouldn't have said that."

"I realized when I was shopping that I hadn't been in a store for more than a year. Imagine!"

Hugh could not stand the sad quietness and the mother he loved so much. He could not stand his love or his mother's prettiness. He wiped the tears on the sleeve of his sweater and got up from the bed. "I have never seen you so pretty, or a dress and slip so pretty." He crouched down before his mother and touched the bright shoes. "The shoes are really super."

"I thought the minute I laid eyes on them that you would like them." She pulled Hugh up and kissed him on the cheek. "Now I've got lipstick on you."

Hugh quoted a witty remark he had heard before as he scrubbed off the lipstick. "It only shows I'm popular."

"Hugh, why were you crying when I came in? Did something at school upset you?"

"It was only that when I came in and found you gone and no note or anything—"

"I forgot all about a note."

"And all afternoon I felt— John Laney came in but he had to go sell Glee Club tickets. All afternoon I felt—"

"What? What was the matter?"

But he could not tell the mother he loved about the terror and the cause. He said at last: "All afternoon I felt—odd."

AFTERWARD WHEN his father came home he called Hugh to come out into the backyard with him. His father had a worried look—as though he spied a valuable tool Hugh had left outside. But there was no tool and the basketball was put back in its place on the back porch.

"Son," his father said, "there's something I want to tell you."

"Yes, sir?"

"Your mother said that you had been crying this afternoon." His father did not wait for him to explain. "I just want us to have a close understanding with each other. Is there anything about school—or girls—or something that puzzles you? Why were you crying?"

Hugh looked back at the afternoon and already it was far away, distant as a peculiar view seen at the wrong end of a telescope.

"I don't know," he said. "I guess maybe I was somehow nervous."

His father put his arm around his shoulders. "Nobody can be nervous before they are sixteen years old. You have a long way to go."

"I know."

"I have never seen your mother look so well. She looks so gay and pretty, better than she's looked in years. Don't you realize that?"

"The slip—the petticoat is supposed to show. It's a new style."

"Soon it will be summer," his father said. "And we'll go on picnics—the three of us." The words brought an instant vision of glare on the yellow creek and the summer-leaved, adventurous woods. His father added: "I came out here to tell you something else."

"Yes, sir?"

"I just want you to know that I realize how fine you were all that bad time. How fine, how damn fine."

His father was using a swear word as if he were talking to a grown man. His father was not a person to hand out compliments—always he was strict with report cards and tools left around. His father never praised him or used grown words or anything. Hugh felt his face grow hot and he touched it with his cold hands.

"I just wanted to tell you that, son." He shook Hugh by the shoulder. "You'll be taller than your old man in a year or so." Quickly his father went into the house, leaving Hugh to the sweet and unaccustomed aftermath of praise.

Hugh stood in the darkening yard after the sunset colors faded in the west and the wisteria was dark purple. The kitchen light was on and he saw his mother fixing dinner. He knew that something was finished; the terror was far from him now, also the anger that had bounced with love, the dread and guilt. Although he felt he would never cry again—or at least not until he was sixteen—in the brightness of his tears glistened the safe, lighted kitchen, now that he was no longer a haunted boy, now that he was glad somehow, and not afraid.

THE MOST DANGEROUS GAME

RICHARD CONNELL

Richard Connell

"OFF THERE TO the right—somewhere—is a large island," said Whitney. "It's rather a mystery—"

"What island is it?" Rainsford asked.

"The old charts called it Ship-Trap Island," Whitney replied. "A suggestive name, isn't it? Sailors have a curious dread of the place. I don't know why. Some superstition—"

"Can't see it," remarked Rainsford, trying to peer through the dank tropical night that pressed its thick warm blackness in upon the yacht.

"You've good eyes," said Whitney, "and I've seen you pick off a moose moving in the brown fall bush at four hundred yards, but even you can't see four miles or so through a moonless Caribbean night."

"Nor four yards," admitted Rainsford. "Ugh! It's like moist black velvet."

"It will be light enough in Rio," promised Whitney. "We should make it in a few days. I hope the jaguar guns have come from Purdey's. We should have some good hunting up the Amazon. Great sport, hunting."

"The best sport in the world," agreed Rainsford.

"For the hunter," amended Whitney. "Not for the jaguar."

"Don't talk rot, Whitney. You're a big-game hunter, not a philosopher. Who cares how a jaguar feels?"

"Perhaps the jaguar does."

"Bah! They've no understanding."

"Even so, I rather think they understand one thing—fear. The fear of pain and the fear of death."

"Nonsense." Rainsford laughed. "This hot weather is making you soft, Whitney. Be a realist. The world is made up of two classes—the hunters and the huntees. Luckily you and I are hunters. Do you think we have passed that island yet?"

"I can't tell in the dark. I hope so."

"Why?"

"The place has a reputation—a bad one."

"Cannibals?"

"Hardly. Even cannibals wouldn't live in such a godforsaken place. But it's gotten into sailor lore, somehow. Didn't you notice that the crew's nerves seemed a bit jumpy today?"

"They were a bit strange, now you mention it. Even Captain Neilson."

"Yes, even that tough-minded old Swede, who'd go up to the devil himself and ask him for a light. Those fishy blue eyes held a look I never saw there before. All I could get out of him was, 'This place has an evil name among seafaring men, sir.' Then he said gravely, 'Don't you feel anything?' Now you mustn't laugh, but I did feel a sort of chill, and there wasn't a breeze. What I felt was a—a mental chill, a dread."

"Pure imagination," said Rainsford. "One superstitious sailor can taint a whole ship's company with his fear."

"Maybe. Sometimes I think sailors have an extra sense which tells them when they are in danger. Anyhow I'm glad we are getting out of this zone. Well, I'll turn in now, Rainsford."

"I'm not sleepy. I'm going to smoke another pipe on the afterdeck."

There was no sound in the night as Rainsford sat there but the muffled throb of the yacht's engine and the swish and ripple of the propeller.

Rainsford, reclining in a steamer chair, puffed at his favorite briar. The sensuous drowsiness of the night was on him. "It's so dark," he thought, "that I could sleep without closing my eyes; the night would be my eyelids—"

An abrupt sound startled him. Off to the right he heard it, and his ears, expert in such matters, could not be mistaken. Again he heard the sound, and again. Somewhere, off in the blackness, someone had fired a gun three times.

Rainsford sprang up and moved quickly to the rail, mystified. He strained his eyes in the direction from which the reports had come, but it was like trying to see through a blanket. He leaped upon the rail and balanced himself there, to get greater elevation; his pipe, striking a rope, was knocked from his mouth. He lunged for it; a short, hoarse cry came from his lips as he realized he had reached too far and had lost his balance. The cry was pinched off short as the blood-warm waters of the Caribbean Sea closed over his head.

He struggled to the surface and cried out, but the wash from the speeding yacht slapped him in the face and the salt water in his open mouth made him gag and strangle. Desperately he struck out after the receding lights of the yacht, but he stopped before he had swum fifty feet. A certain coolheadedness had come to him, for this was not the first time he had been in a tight place. There was a chance that his cries could be heard by someone aboard the yacht, but that chance was slender and grew more slender as the yacht raced on. He wrestled himself out of his clothes and shouted with all his power. The lights of the boat became faint and vanishing fireflies; then they were blotted out by the night.

Rainsford remembered the shots. They had come from the right, and doggedly he swam in that direction, swimming slowly, conserving his strength. For a seemingly endless time he fought the sea. He began to count his strokes; he could do possibly a hundred more and then—

He heard a sound. It came out of the darkness, a high, screaming sound, the cry of an animal in an extremity of anguish and terror. He did not know what animal made the sound. With fresh vitality he swam toward it. He heard it again; then it was cut short by another noise, crisp, staccato.

"Pistol shot," muttered Rainsford, swimming on.

Ten minutes of determined effort brought to his ears the most welcome sound he had ever heard, the breaking of the sea on a rocky shore. He was almost on the rocks before he saw them; on a night less calm he would have been shattered against them. With his remaining strength he dragged himself from the swirling waters. Jagged crags appeared to jut into the opaqueness; he forced himself up hand over hand. Gasping, his hands raw, he reached a flat place at the top. Dense jungle came down to the edge of the cliffs, and, careless of everything but his weariness, Rainsford flung himself down and tumbled into the deepest sleep of his life.

When he opened his eyes he knew from the position of the sun that it was late in the afternoon. Sleep had given him vigor; a sharp hunger was picking at him.

"Where there are pistol shots there are men. Where there are men there is food," he thought; but he saw no sign of a trail through the closely knit web of weeds and trees; it was easier to go along the shore. Not far from where he had landed, he stopped.

Some wounded thing, by the evidence a large animal, had crashed about in the underwood. A small glittering object caught Rainsford's eye and he picked it up. It was an empty cartridge.

"A twenty-two," he remarked. "That's odd. It must have been a fairly large animal, too. The hunter had his nerve with him to tackle it with a light gun. It is clear the brute put up a fight. I suppose the first three shots I heard were when the hunter flushed his quarry and wounded it. The last shot was when he trailed it here and finished it."

He examined the ground closely and found what he had hoped to find—the print of hunting boots. They pointed along the cliff in the direction he had been going. Eagerly he hurried along, for night was beginning to settle down on the island.

Darkness was blacking out sea and jungle before Rainsford sighted the lights. He came upon them as he turned a crook in the coastline, and his first thought was that he had come upon a village, as there were so many lights. But as he forged along he saw that all the lights were in one building—a château on a high bluff.

"Mirage," thought Rainsford. But the stone steps were real enough. He lifted the knocker and it creaked up stiffly, as if it had never before been used.

The door, opening, let out a river of glaring light. A tall man, solidly built and black-bearded to the waist, stood facing Rainsford with a revolver in his hand.

"Don't be alarmed," said Rainsford, with a smile that he hoped was disarming. "I'm no robber. I fell off a yacht. My name is Sanger Rainsford of New York City."

The man gave no sign that he understood the words or had even heard them. The menacing revolver pointed as rigidly as if the giant were a statue.

Another man was coming down the broad marble steps, an erect slender man in evening clothes. He advanced and held out his hand.

In a cultivated voice marked by a slight accent which gave it added precision and deliberateness, he said, "It is a great pleasure and honor to welcome Mr. Sanger Rainsford, the celebrated hunter, to my home."

Automatically Rainsford shook the man's hand.

"I've read your book about hunting snow leopards in Tibet," explained the man. "I am General Zaroff."

Rainsford's first impression was that the man was singularly handsome; his second, that there was a bizarre quality about the face. The general was a tall man past middle age, for his hair was white; but his eyebrows and mustache were black. His eyes, too, were black and very bright. He had the face of a man used to giving orders. Turning to the man in uniform he made a sign. The fellow put away his pistol, saluted, withdrew.

"Ivan is incredibly strong," remarked the general, "but he has the misfortune to be deaf and dumb. A simple fellow, but a bit of a savage."

"Is he Russian?"

"A Cossack," said the general, and his smile showed red lips and pointed teeth. "So am I.

"Come," he said, "we shouldn't be chatting here. You want clothes, food, rest. You shall have them. This is a most restful spot."

Ivan had reappeared and the general spoke to him with lips that moved but gave forth no sound.

"Follow Ivan if you please, Mr. Rainsford. I was about to have my dinner, but will wait. I think my clothes will fit you."

It was to a huge beam-ceilinged bedroom with a canopied bed large enough for six men that Rainsford followed the man. Ivan laid out an evening suit and Rainsford as he put it on noticed that it came from a London tailor.

"Perhaps you were surprised," said the general as they sat down to dinner in a room which suggested a baronial hall of feudal times, "that I recognized your name; but I read all books on hunting published in

English, French and Russian. I have but one passion in life, and that is the hunt."

"You have some wonderful heads here," said Rainsford, glancing at the walls. "That cape buffalo is the largest I ever saw."

"Oh, that fellow? He charged me, hurled me against a tree and fractured my skull. But I got the brute."

"I've always thought," said Rainsford, "that the cape buffalo is the most dangerous of all big game."

For a moment the general did not reply, then he said slowly, "No, the cape buffalo is not the most dangerous." He sipped his wine. "Here in my preserve on this island I hunt more dangerous game."

"Is there big game on this island?"

The general nodded. "The biggest."

"Really?"

"Oh, it isn't here naturally. I have to stock the island."

"What have you imported, General? Tigers?"

The general grinned. "No, hunting tigers ceased to interest me when I exhausted their possibilities. No thrill left in tigers, no real danger. I live for danger, Mr. Rainsford."

The general took from his pocket a gold cigarette case and offered his guest a long black cigarette with a silver tip; it was perfumed and gave off a smell like incense.

"We will have some capital hunting, you and I," said the general.

"But what game—" began Rainsford.

"I'll tell you. You will be amused, I know. I think I may say, in all modesty, that I have done a rare thing. I have invented a new sensation. May I pour you another glass of port?"

"Thank you, General."

The general filled both glasses and said, "God makes some men poets. Some he makes kings, some beggars. Me he made a hunter. But after years of enjoyment I found that the hunt no longer fascinated me. You can perhaps guess why?"

"No—why?"

"Simply this, hunting had ceased to be what you call a sporting proposition. I always got my quarry . . . always . . . and there is no greater bore than perfection."

The general lit a fresh cigarette.

"The animal has nothing but his legs and his instinct. Instinct is no match for reason. When I realized this, it was a tragic moment for me."

Rainsford leaned across the table, absorbed in what his host was saying.

"It came to me as an inspiration what I must do."

"And that was?"

"I had to invent a new animal to hunt."

"A new animal? You are joking."

"I never joke about hunting. I needed a new animal. I found one. So I bought this island, built this house, and here I do my hunting. The island is perfect for my purpose—there are jungles with a maze of trails in them, hills, swamps—"

"But the animal, General Zaroff?"

"Oh," said the general, "it supplies me with the most exciting hunting in the world. Every day I hunt, and I never grow bored now, for I have a quarry with which I can match my wits."

Rainsford's bewilderment showed in his face.

"I wanted the ideal animal to hunt, so I said, 'What are the attributes of an ideal quarry?' and the answer was, of course, 'It must have courage, cunning, and, above all, it must be able to reason.'"

"But no animal can reason," objected Rainsford.

"My dear fellow," said the general, "there is one that can."

"But you can't mean—"

"And why not?"

"I can't believe you are serious, General. This is a grisly joke."

"Why should I not be serious? I am speaking of hunting."

"Hunting? Good God, General Zaroff, what you speak of is murder."

The general regarded Rainsford quizzically. "Surely your experiences in the war—"

"Did not make me condone cold-blooded murder," finished Rainsford stiffly.

Laughter shook the general. "I'll wager you'll forget your notions when you go hunting with me. You've a genuine new thrill in store for you, Mr. Rainsford."

"Thank you, I am a hunter, not a murderer."

"Dear me," said the general, quite unruffled, "again that unpleasant word; but I hunt the scum of the earth—sailors from tramp ships—lascars, blacks, Chinese, whites, mongrels."

"Where do you get them?"

The general's left eyelid fluttered down in a wink. "This island is called Ship-Trap. Come to the window with me."

Rainsford went to the window and looked out toward the sea.

"Watch! Out there!" exclaimed the general, as he pressed a button. Far out Rainsford saw a flash of lights. "They indicate a channel where there's none. Rocks with razor edges crouch there like a sea monster. They can crush a ship like a nut. Oh, yes, that is electricity. We try to be civilized."

"Civilized? And you shoot down men?"

"But I treat my visitors with every consideration," said the general in his most pleasant manner. "They get plenty of good food and exercise. They get into splendid physical condition. You shall see for yourself tomorrow."

"What do you mean?"

"We'll visit my training school." The general smiled. "It is in the cellar. I have about a dozen there now. They're from the Spanish bark *Sanlucar*, which had the bad luck to go on the rocks out there. An inferior lot, I regret to say, and more accustomed to the deck than the jungle."

He raised his hand and Ivan brought thick Turkish coffee. "It is a game, you see," pursued the general blandly. "I suggest to one of them that we go hunting. I give him three hours' start. I am to follow, armed only with a pistol of smallest caliber and range. If my quarry eludes me for three whole days, he wins the game. If I find him"—the general smiled—"he loses."

"Suppose he refuses to be hunted?"

"I give him the option. If he does not wish to hunt I turn him over to Ivan. Ivan once served as official knouter to the Great White Tsar and he has his own ideas of sport. Invariably they choose the hunt."

"And if they win?"

The smile on the general's face widened. "To date I have not lost."

Then he added hastily, "I don't wish you to think me a braggart, Mr. Rainsford, and one did almost win. I eventually had to use the dogs."

"The dogs?"

"This way, please. I'll show you."

The general led the way to another window. The lights sent a flickering illumination that made grotesque patterns on the courtyard below, and Rainsford could see a dozen or so huge black shapes moving about. As they turned toward him he caught the green glitter of eyes.

"They are let out at seven every night. If anyone should try to get into my house—or out of it—something regrettable would happen to him. And now I want to show you my new collection of heads. Will you come to the library?"

"I hope," said Rainsford, "that you will excuse me tonight. I'm really not feeling at all well."

"Ah, indeed? You need a good restful night's sleep. Tomorrow you'll feel like a new man. Then we'll hunt, eh? I've one rather promising prospect—"

Rainsford was hurrying from the room.

"Sorry you can't go with me tonight," called the general. "I expect rather fair sport. A big, strong black. He looks resourceful—"

The bed was good and Rainsford was tired, but nevertheless he could not sleep, and had only achieved a doze when, as morning broke, he heard, far off in the jungle, the faint report of a pistol.

General Zaroff did not appear till luncheon. He was solicitous about Rainsford's health. "As for me," he said, "I do not feel so well. The hunting was not good last night. He made a straight trail that offered no problems at all."

"General," said Rainsford, "I want to leave the island at once."

He saw the dead black eyes of the general studying him. The eyes suddenly brightened. "Tonight," said he, "we will hunt—you and I."

Rainsford shook his head. "No, General," he said, "I will not hunt."

The general shrugged his shoulders. "As you wish. The choice rests with you, but I would suggest that my idea of sport is more diverting than Ivan's."

"You don't mean—" cried Rainsford.

"My dear fellow," said the general, "have I not told you I always mean what I say about hunting? This is really an inspiration. I drink to a foeman worthy of my steel at last."

The general raised his glass, but Rainsford sat staring at him. "You'll find this game worth playing," the general said enthusiastically. "Your brain against mine. Your woodcraft against mine. Your strength and stamina against mine. Outdoor chess! And the stake is not without value, eh?"

"And if I win—" began Rainsford huskily.

"If I do not find you by midnight of the third day, I'll cheerfully acknowledge myself defeated," said General Zaroff. "My sloop will place you on the mainland near a town."

The general read what Rainsford was thinking.

"Oh, you can trust me," said the Cossack. "I will give you my word as a gentleman and a sportsman. Of course, you, in turn, must agree to say nothing of your visit here."

"I'll agree to nothing of the kind."

"Oh, in that case—but why discuss that now? Three days hence we can discuss it over a bottle of Veuve Cliquot, unless—"

The general sipped his wine.

Then a businesslike air animated him. "Ivan," he said, "will supply you with hunting clothes, food, a knife. I suggest you wear moccasins; they leave a poorer trail. I suggest, too, that you avoid the big swamp in the southeast corner of the island. We call it Death Swamp. There's quicksand there. One foolish fellow tried it. The deplorable part of it was that Lazarus followed him. You can't imagine my feelings, Mr. Rainsford, I loved Lazarus; he was the finest hound in my pack. Well, I must beg you to excuse me now. I always take a siesta after lunch. You'll hardly have time for a nap, I fear. You'll want to start, no doubt. I shall not follow until dusk. Hunting at night is so much more exciting than by day, don't you think? *Au revoir*, Mr. Rainsford, *au revoir*."

As General Zaroff with a courtly bow strolled from the room, Ivan entered by another door. Under one arm he carried hunting clothes, a haversack of food, a leathern sheath containing a long-bladed hunting knife; his right hand rested on a cocked revolver thrust in the crimson sash about his waist. . . .

RAINSFORD HAD FOUGHT HIS WAY through the bush for two hours, but at length he paused, saying to himself through tight teeth, "I must keep my nerve."

He had not been entirely clearheaded when the château gates closed behind him. His first idea was to put distance between himself and General Zaroff, and to this end he had plunged along, spurred by the sharp rowels of something approaching panic. Now, having got a grip on himself, he had stopped to take stock of himself and the situation.

Straight flight was futile, for it must inevitably bring him to the sea. Being in a picture with a frame of water, his operations, clearly, must take place within that frame.

"I'll give him a trail to follow," thought Rainsford, striking off from the path into trackless wilderness. Recalling the lore of the fox hunt and the dodges of the fox, he executed a series of intricate loops, doubling again and again on his trail. Night found him leg-weary, with hands and face lashed by the branches. He was on a thickly wooded ridge. As his need for rest was imperative, he thought, "I have played the fox, now I must play the cat of the fable."

A big tree with a thick trunk and outspread branches was nearby, and, taking care to leave no marks, he climbed into the crotch and stretched out on one of the broad limbs. Rest brought him new confidence and almost a feeling of security.

An apprehensive night crawled slowly by like a wounded snake. Toward morning, when a dingy gray was varnishing the sky, the cry of a startled bird focused Rainsford's attention in its direction. Something was coming through the bush, coming slowly, carefully, coming by the same winding way that Rainsford had come. He flattened himself against the bough and, through a screen of leaves almost as thick as tapestry, watched.

It was General Zaroff. He made his way along, with his eyes fixed in concentration on the ground. He paused, almost beneath the tree, dropped to his knees and studied the ground. Rainsford's impulse was to leap on him like a panther, but he saw that the general's right hand held a small automatic.

The hunter shook his head several times as if he were puzzled. Then, straightening himself, he took from his case one of his long black cigarettes; its pungent incenselike smoke rose to Rainsford's nostrils.

Rainsford held his breath. The general's eyes had left the ground and were traveling inch by inch up the tree. Rainsford froze, every muscle tensed for a spring. But the sharp eyes of the hunter stopped before they reached the limb where Rainsford lay. A smile spread over his brown face. Very deliberately he blew a smoke ring into the air; then he turned his back on the tree and walked carelessly away along the trail he had come. The swish of the underbrush against his hunting boots grew fainter and fainter.

The pent-up air burst hotly from Rainsford's lungs. His first thought made him feel sick and numb. The general could follow a trail through the woods at night; he could follow an extremely difficult trail; he must have uncanny powers; only by the merest chance had he failed to see his quarry.

Rainsford's second thought was more terrible. It sent a shudder through him. Why had the general smiled? Why had he turned back?

Rainsford did not want to believe what his reason told him was true—the general was playing with him, saving him for another day's sport. The Cossack was the cat; he was the mouse. Then it was that Rainsford knew the meaning of terror.

"I will not lose my nerve," he told himself, "I will not."

Sliding down from the tree, he set off into the woods. Three hundred yards from his hiding place he stopped where a huge dead tree leaned precariously on a smaller, living one. Throwing off his sack of food, he took his knife from its sheath and set to work.

When the job was finished, he threw himself down behind a fallen log a hundred feet away. He did not have to wait long. The cat was coming back to play with the mouse.

Following the trail with the sureness of a bloodhound came General Zaroff. Nothing escaped those searching black eyes, no crushed blade of grass, no bent twig, no mark, no matter how faint, in the moss. So intent was the Cossack on his stalking that he was upon the thing Rainsford had made before he saw it. His foot touched the protruding bough that was the trigger. Even as he touched it, the general sensed his danger, and leaped back with the agility of an ape. But he was not quite quick enough; the dead tree, delicately adjusted to rest on the cut living one, crashed down and struck the general a glancing blow on the shoulder as it fell; but for his alertness he must have been crushed beneath it. He staggered, but he did not fall; nor did he drop his revolver. He stood there, rubbing his injured shoulder, and Rainsford, with fear again gripping his heart, heard the general's mocking laugh ring through the jungle.

"Rainsford," called the general, "if you are within sound of my voice let me congratulate you. Not many men know how to make a Malay man catcher. Luckily for me, I too have hunted in Malacca. You are proving interesting, Mr. Rainsford. I am now going to have my wound dressed; it is only a slight one. But I shall be back. I shall be back."

When the general, nursing his wounded shoulder, had gone, Rainsford again took up his flight. It was flight now, and it carried him on for some hours. Dusk came, then darkness, and still he pressed on. The ground grew softer under his moccasins; the vegetation grew ranker, denser; insects bit him savagely. He stepped forward and his foot sank into ooze. He tried to wrench it back, but the mud sucked viciously at his foot as if it had been a giant leech. With a violent effort he tore his foot loose. He knew where he was now. Death Swamp and its quicksand.

The softness of the earth had given him an idea. Stepping back from the quicksand a dozen feet, he began, like some huge prehistoric beaver, to dig.

Rainsford had dug himself in, in France, when a second's delay would have meant death. Compared to his digging now, that had been a placid pastime. The pit grew deeper; when it was above his shoulders he climbed out and from some hard saplings cut stakes, sharpening them to a fine point. These stakes he planted at the bottom of the pit with the points up. With flying fingers he wove a rough carpet of weeds and branches and with it covered the mouth of the pit. Then, wet with sweat and aching with tiredness, he crouched behind the stump of a lightning-blasted tree.

By the padding sound of feet on the soft earth he knew his pursuer was coming. The night breeze brought him the perfume of the general's cigarette. It seemed to the hunted man that the general was coming with unusual swiftness; that he was not feeling his way along, foot by foot. Rainsford, from where he was crouching, could not see the general, neither could he see the pit. He lived a year in a minute. Then he heard the sharp crackle of breaking branches as the cover of the pit gave way; heard the sharp scream of pain as the pointed stakes found their mark. Then he cowered back. Three feet from the pit a man was standing with an electric torch in his hand.

"You've done well, Rainsford," cried the general. "Your Burmese tiger pit has claimed one of my best dogs. Again you score. I must now see what you can do against my whole pack. I'm going home for a rest now. Thank you for a most amusing evening."

At daybreak Rainsford, lying near the swamp, was awakened by a distant sound, faint and wavering, but he knew it for the baying of a pack of hounds.

Rainsford knew he could do one of two things. He could stay where he was. That was suicide. He could flee. That was postponing the inevitable. For a moment he stood there thinking. An idea that held a wild chance came to him, and, tightening his belt, he headed away from the swamp.

The baying of the hounds drew nearer, nearer. Rainsford climbed a tree. Down a watercourse, not a quarter of a mile away, he could see the bush moving. Straining his eyes, he saw the lean figure of General Zaroff. Just ahead of him Rainsford made out another figure, with wide shoulders, which surged through the jungle reeds. It was the gigantic Ivan and he seemed to be pulled along. Rainsford realized that he must be holding the pack in leash.

They would be on him at any moment now. His mind worked frantically, and he thought of a native trick he had learned in Uganda. Sliding down the tree, he caught hold of a springy young sapling and to it fastened his hunting knife, with the blade pointing down the trail. With a bit of wild grapevine he tied back the sapling . . . and ran for his life. As the hounds hit the fresh scent, they raised their voices and Rainsford knew how an animal at bay feels.

He had to stop to get his breath. The baying of the hounds stopped abruptly, and Rainsford's heart stopped, too. They must have reached the knife.

Shinning excitedly up a tree, he looked back. His pursuers had stopped. But the hope in Rainsford's brain died, for he saw that General Zaroff was still on his feet. Ivan, however, was not. The knife, driven by the recoil of the springing tree, had not wholly failed.

Hardly had Rainsford got back to the ground when, once more, the pack took up the cry.

"Nerve, nerve, nerve!" he panted to himself as he dashed along. A blue gap showed through the trees dead ahead. The hounds drew nearer. Rainsford forced himself on toward that gap. He reached the sea, and across a cove could see the gray stone of the château. Twenty feet below him the sea rumbled and hissed. Rainsford hesitated. He heard the hounds. Then he leaped far out into the water.

When the general and his pack reached the opening, the Cossack stopped. For some moments he stood regarding the blue-green expanse of water. Then he sat down, took a drink of brandy from a silver flask, lit a perfumed cigarette, and hummed a bit from *Madama Butterfly*.

GENERAL ZAROFF ATE an exceedingly good dinner in his great paneled hall that evening. With it he had a bottle of Pol Roger and half a bottle of Chambertin. Two slight annoyances kept him from perfect enjoyment. One was that it would be difficult to replace Ivan; the other, that his quarry had escaped him. Of course—so thought the general, as he tasted his after-dinner liqueur—the American had not played the game.

To soothe himself, he read in his library from the works of Marcus Aurelius. At ten he went to his bedroom. He was comfortably tired, he said to himself, as he turned the key of his door.

There was a little moonlight, so before turning on the light he went to the window and looked down on the courtyard. He could see the great hounds, and he called, "Better luck another time." Then he switched on the light.

A man who had been hiding in the curtains of the bed was standing before him.

"Rainsford!" screamed the general. "How in God's name did you get here?"

"Swam. I found it quicker than walking through the jungle."

The other sucked in his breath and smiled. "I congratulate you. You have won the game."

Rainsford did not smile. "I am still a beast at bay," he said in a low, hoarse voice. "Get ready, General Zaroff."

The general made one of his deepest bows. "I see," he said. "Splendid. One of us is to furnish a repast for the hounds. The other will sleep in this very excellent bed. On guard, Rainsford. . . ."

He had never slept in a better bed, Rainsford decided.

A DAY IN THE COUNTRY

DAN JACOBSON

WE HAD SPENT the day on the farm, as we usually did every Sunday. Rather a dull day it had been, I remember, in April, too cold to go swimming in the river, and there had been nothing much else to do except sit in the car and watch my father as he helped the boys round up the cattle driven down from the veld, and then walk through them, stick in hand, prodding their sides, stopping to discuss at length what to do about the heifer who was going blind in one eye, or what a pity it was that this miserable beast should be in calf again when what it needed was a long rest. My father could spend hours like that, perfectly happy among the slow red cows and oxen, with the African herd boy who knew each head of cattle as an individual and respected it as such. And my father prodded, leaned against his stick, screwed his face up against the sun, listened to the herd boy's comments, and twisted his ankle on one of the rocks that littered the piece of veld where the cattle were gathered.

When he ricked his ankle, my father had had enough. He got back into the car and we set off home, with the herd-boy's children riding with us on the back bumper, as far as the gate. At the gate they climbed off and opened it for us; we passed through, they waved, and we waved back. Now there was just the thirty-mile run home, through Rietpan, by-passing Dors River, meeting the tarred road to take us to the Boer War Memorial—and so home. My brother was driving, my father and mother sat in front with him, and my sister and I were in the back seat. The first stretch of road was really bad, not a road at all, but a cart-track across Rietpan Commonage, a piece of veld that had been grazed to complete nudity by the donkeys of the villagers. A few donkeys, a cow or two, one or two goats: those were generally the sole possessions of the Rietpan villagers, that and a mud-walled house and five irrigated acres. But though Rietpan was poor, it had its location, even poorer, where the black-skinned inhabitants of the village lived. They were conducting some sort of religious rite as we passed the location, and a man held up a cross of plaited twigs towards us. He was wearing a blue cowl on his head. The wind blew all their clothes in bright fluttering rags as they walked behind the leader. The sun shone bare upon them through the wind.

Inside the car it was dull and dusty, with the Sunday newspapers in a mess on the floor. My sister was knitting. We passed through Rietpan quickly, in a cloud of dust, with a greeting for Major le Roy on his front stoep and a pause to give way for someone's sheep. The road between Rietpan and Dors River was better, and my brother increased his speed.

My father looked up from the comic he was reading. He read it with an air of absolute puzzlement: "Who reads these things?" he asked. Then: "Oh, oh, oh, boy, slow down." He placed a hand on my brother's arm. There was a car standing in the middle of the road, and a group of people at the side of the road, looking down at something.

We thought it was an accident. It looked like an accident. We prepared ourselves for something horrible and warily our car crept up to the other, then drove past it and stopped.

"What is it?" my sister said shrilly.

"I don't know." We couldn't see. The other car was blocking our view of what the little group was seeing. Our car went forward a few feet. Dear God, it was an accident. The group stood over a little African child, a group of white men and women. A few Africans stood a little way off, looking at what was going on, and saying nothing. The white people were talking to one another. They seemed quite unmoved, almost light-hearted, but the black child lay still on the ground. I could see its spindly legs like winter branches of a tree, lying still on the ground.

"What is it?" my father called out through the window of the car, and as he did so, one of the white men stooped and picked the child up. The black legs kicked wildly, and a shriek went up from the child. I saw one of the Africans take a pace forward, then fall back. The group turned to their car, one man still carrying the child. And then I saw a strange thing. They were laughing, all of them were laughing. The child still screamed and kicked, and then writhed over in the man's arms, away from the motor-car, butting its head into the broad grey-shirted chest, as a child turns into its mother's arms for protection. We saw white face after face, all bared in smiles, and their laughter surrounded the thin screams of the child, until one could no longer believe that what one heard was truly a scream of fear.

"What is it?" my father called again. But no one took any notice. One of the men ran forward and opened the bonnet of the car. We heard him say in Afrikaans, "Come on, put him in," and the child screamed again, awfully.

But we knew now. It wasn't an accident, it was a game. I don't know whether we felt more relief or disgust. One of the grinning men saw us watching them, and still with his grin, he waved to us that we could go on. They didn't need our help; it wasn't an accident. None of us grinned back at him. I think he saw that we weren't amused at his game for he looked away.

"For God's sake let's go."

"I've had enough of this."

My brother started the car. As we drove off I said, "What dirty swine." I looked through the back window of the car. They had put the child back on the road, one of the men was standing halfway in his car, the bonnet was down. Apparently the game was breaking up. We hoped that it was our condemnation that had broken it up. Yet there was the taste of guilt in each of our mouths that we had just looked our condemnation and not said anything to them, not made a protest in the name of humanity. But we were used to that sort of scene and that sort of guilt. Together they almost make up a way of life.

WE HAD DRIVEN on only a short distance when with a roar of wind and a cloud of dust the car passed us. As it whipped past, one of the men in it leaned his head, half his body, out of the window, and shouted something at us. None of us heard what he was shouting, it was lost in the wind and the dust. All we saw was a white shirt and a white face and a pair of bright red lips opening and closing grotesquely.

Now you don't shout insults at my father. My brother and I swore ineffectually at the billows of dust which followed their car, but my father, in a moment, was trembling with rage.

"Chase them," he shouted.

"Don't be mad," my brother said.

"Then stop the car."

"Why? What for."

"I'll show you why. Stop the car." My brother didn't, so my father leaned over and switched off the ignition key.

My brother lost his temper as the car slowed down and stopped. "All right, take your bloody car," he said and got out and came in the back, slamming the door behind him.

"Michael, what are you going to do?" my mother asked.

My brother and I were both yelling at my father to leave it, cut it out, forget the whole business and he was saying, "No one shouts at me like that. No one shouts at me like that," as we tore along the road. We could see the other car ahead of us, still raising dust. But we were catching up with it. Soon we were in the car's cloud of dust. Small stones struck against the windshield, and we could see very little through the grey murk.

"Michael, you're going to have an accident."

"I'm not going to have an accident."

"For God's sake, Dad, let's not have a scene."

"What do you mean let's not have a scene, when they shout at me like that?"

"You don't even know what he shouted."

"I know well enough what he shouted."

"What did he shout?"

"No one shouts at me like that."

We came to the crossroads of the main road to Lyndhurst and the Rietpan-Dors River road. The front car went towards Dors River, so we went that way too, still at a dangerously high speed.

"Michael, you're going to have an accident."

Dors River was about us. J. Wassenaar *Algemene Handelaar*/General Dealer. There was the station. The road passed J. Wassenaar and then turned round a corner, the hotel, the Savoy, with two petrol-pumps in front of it. Then there was a house, another, a piece of veld, two more houses, and a last shop. In front of the last shop stood the black Dodge we had been chasing. The people were climbing out of it. One of them, the man in the white shirt, the one who had shouted, saw us coming and stood looking at us with his mouth open.

Again we drew level with the car. Inside our car, everyone with the exception of my father, was dreading the scene that we knew was about to follow.

We stopped. My father said: "How dare you shout at me like that."

Now they were all out of their car. There were six of them, three men and three women. They stood at various points round their car, looking at us.

The young man in the grey shirt said, "What's the matter with you?" He was big and dirty, the one who had been carrying the child. He wore a broad-brimmed hat on the back of his head, and it made his face look round and flabby, under the circling rim of his hat. But he was big and strong, with enormous bare arms folded on his chest. I knew that if it did come to a fight he would be the one to give us the most trouble, and the one who would probably beat us at that. He walked over to our car, arms still folded, contemptuously, and said again: "What's the matter with you?"

But he was speaking English. Was that already a victory for us? He was speaking our language, we weren't speaking his. But he was big, much bigger than any of us as he stood at the driver's window of the car and said: "What's the matter with you?"

My father suddenly blazed out at him. "What sort of a person are you? First you torture a child that's done nothing to you, and then you scream at someone you're passing on the road. Well, let me tell you that I'm not a little Kaffir piccanin. You can't do what you like with me. I'll teach you manners before I'm finished with you."

The man said, "How?" He added: "You're too old." And it was true, pitifully true, my father was too old to fight him. He could have killed the old man.

This was the cue for my brother and myself. We climbed out of the car and walked round. The big man wheeled to face us. I saw his muscles tighten under the hair of his arms and I knew that if we were to win this argument it wouldn't be by force. But we stared at each other as though we weren't frightened. He probably wasn't.

My father said: "You people make me sick. You've got no idea how to behave. But if you think you can go round bullying everybody like you bully that Kaffir child you're mistaken." He opened the door of the car as though to come out, and quickly the man darted at it, to slam it on him. With me a little way behind him my brother moved towards the man. My brother said: "No you don't." He was panting as he spoke, as though he had been running in a race.

Now, if there was to be a fight, it would be now. But there was no fight, and I did not understand why, as the old man, apparently the father of the two younger ones, came up and said, "You've got no right to talk like that about my people. We weren't doing anything to the piccanin." He gestured, almost appealingly.

We stared at him. He said again, "You've got no right to talk like that about my people"—and then I realised that our fear—the fear that we would be called "Bloody Jews", the fear which perhaps had kept our mouths closed when we had seen the piccanin being tortured— was his fear too. He, the Afrikaner who spoke English to us, felt that my father was sitting in his car and despising him for the race he belonged to, and judging him and his race by what we had seen on the road; and I realised, how happily, that the father did not want to be judged by that act, and did not want his son to fight us, for even if we should fight and his son should beat us, our original and damning judgement would remain, would even be confirmed. He didn't want to beat us, he wanted us to think well of his race, and how could he do that while the piccanin screamed with terror and kicked helplessly against his son's arms? He stayed his son's arm, and said, "It was only a bit of fun and you had no right to swear at us."

"Swear at you?" my father asked.

"Yes, swear at us," the other son said, coming up. I saw then why his lips were so red. It was lipstick on his mouth. It must have come from the lips of one of the girls who were leaning against the mud-guards of the other car, watching. Like his father, this son did not want to fight. He said, "We heard you swearing as you drove off."

"You were the one," my father said, interrupting him. "You were the one who leaned out of the car and shouted." My father looked at him.

He wiped his mouth with his hand. There was another smear of lipstick on his cheek-bone. He said, "I shouted at you to mind your own business."

"But we said nothing to you. We didn't like what you were doing, but we didn't say anything to you."

"You said 'bloody swine'."

"That's simply not true," my father said.

I said nothing.

"I heard you," the man repeated.

"You couldn't have heard it because no one said it."

And despite this foolish wrangling, the tension remained where it had been all along, where it had been when it had looked as though there was to be a physical fight. The unspoken words lay heavily on our tongues: *Dutchmen, Jews.* But they were never used. Racial tensions usually hasten fights, but this time they didn't, for they were too widely shared. Our fear was theirs: it was almost as though we co-operated with one another to keep the significance of the argument hidden, yet never for a moment forgot it. Had we not been Jews, we might have reproved them more strongly for what they did to the piccanin—for kinship in oppression, or fear of oppression, has two sides, one less noble than the other; and had they not been Afrikaners who feared that their reputation was one of brutality, uncouthness and oppression —all of which they had confirmed, they feared—they might simply have fought us off. But we were all prevented from fighting, and prevented from peace.

I remember the father saying, "Do you think we would have done anything to that piccanin? We aren't mad people. It was just a bit of fun among ourselves."

And the younger son, who did not want to fight, spoke earnestly to me. "You see, this little native child ran right across our car, in front of our car, and I had to brake like hell not to knock him over. So we thought we'll give him a lesson he'll remember. It's for his own good too, you know. He'll be a damn sight more careful now. He'll look what's going on before he runs across the road. Perhaps he'll live longer that way."

Tentatively he smiled at me.

The father was saying, "You see that boy there, he goes to university. In Pretoria. Already he's in his second-year studies. A university student. Do you think that people like that, university students, gentlemen, educated people, are going to do anything that they'll be ashamed of afterwards? . . ."

I said, "You made a mistake. No one shouted 'bloody swine'." What I said was true, but it was a lie too. In all that squalor it hardly mattered, but I had to add: "But we didn't like what you were doing."

"All right, then I shouldn't have shouted at you from my car. But it was our business what we were doing with that piccanin, especially as we weren't going to hurt him. It was only a bit of sport."

"Not a very nice sport," my mother called out. We seemed to be winning all the way down the line. The big son had moved away and was being ignored by everybody. The other two continued their laboured explanations, struggling for English words to express themselves in. Once the father veered towards an aggressive tone, and then, as though remembering the faces in the car, closed and hostile, with the struggling black body in his son's arms, as guilty as blood, he became defensive again.

So a sort of peace did come, and we got back into the car. No one shook hands with anyone, there had been no reconciliation to warrant that. But no blows had been struck, and no one had called anyone a bloody Dutchman or a bloody Jew, so everything was as well as could be expected. Better really, for us, because we still despised them. We despised that family: it is not our fault they misinterpreted it. And they should have known that we were as frightened of them as they were of us. We left them there, outside their whitewashed shop with the house behind it, that looked across the sand road to the railway line and the railway paddock where one chestnut horse was growing thin in transit between two lost farms.

It was a quiet journey home. Everyone was feeling depressed and beaten, though, as I have explained, the victory was ours. But we had all lost, so much, somewhere, farther back, along that dusty road.

THE LUMBER-ROOM

"SAKI" (H. H. MUNRO)

H. H. Munro

THE CHILDREN were to be driven, as a special treat, to the sands at Jagborough. Nicholas was not to be of the party; he was in disgrace. Only that morning he had refused to eat his wholesome bread-and-milk on the seemingly frivolous ground that there was a frog in it. Older and wiser and better people had told him that there could not possibly be a frog in his bread-and-milk and that he was not to talk nonsense; he continued, nevertheless, to talk what seemed the veriest nonsense, and described with much detail the coloration and markings of the alleged frog. The dramatic part of the incident was that there really was a frog in Nicholas's basin of bread-and-milk; he had put it there himself, so he felt entitled to know something about it. The sin of taking a frog from the garden and putting it into a bowl of wholesome bread-and-milk was enlarged on at great length, but the fact that stood out clearest in the whole affair, as it presented itself to the mind of Nicholas, was that the older, wiser, and better people had been proved to be profoundly in error in matters about which they had expressed the utmost assurance.

"You said there couldn't possibly be a frog in my bread-and-milk; there *was* a frog in my bread-and-milk," he repeated, with the insistence of a skilled tactician who does not intend to shift from favourable ground.

So his boy-cousin and girl-cousin and his quite uninteresting younger brother were to be taken to Jagborough sands that afternoon and he was to stay at home. His cousins' aunt, who insisted, by an unwarranted stretch of imagination, in styling herself his aunt also, had hastily invented the Jagborough expedition in order to impress on Nicholas the delights that he had justly forfeited by his disgraceful conduct at the breakfast-table. It was her habit, whenever one of the children fell from grace, to improvise something of a festival nature from which the offender would be rigorously debarred; if all the children sinned collectively they were suddenly informed of a circus in a neighbouring town, a circus of unrivalled merit and uncounted elephants, to which, but for their depravity, they would have been taken that very day.

A few decent tears were looked for on the part of Nicholas when the moment for the departure of the expedition arrived. As a matter of fact, however, all the crying was done by his girl-cousin, who scraped her knee rather painfully against the step of the carriage as she was scrambling in. "How she did howl," said Nicholas cheerfully, as the party drove off without any of the elation of high spirits that should have characterized it.

"She'll soon get over that," said the *soi-disant* aunt; "it will be a glorious afternoon for racing about over those beautiful sands. How they will enjoy themselves!"

"Bobby won't enjoy himself much, and he won't race much either," said Nicholas with a grim chuckle; "his boots are hurting him. They're too tight."

"Why didn't he tell me they were hurting?" asked the aunt with some asperity.

"He told you twice, but you weren't listening. You often don't listen when we tell you important things."

"You are not to go into the gooseberry garden," said the aunt, changing the subject.

"Why not?" demanded Nicholas.

"Because you are in disgrace," said the aunt loftily.

Nicholas did not admit the flawlessness of the reasoning; he felt perfectly capable of being in disgrace and in a gooseberry garden at the same moment. His face took on an expression of considerable obstinacy. It was clear to his aunt that he was determined to get into the gooseberry garden, "only," as she remarked to herself, "because I have told him he is not to."

Now the gooseberry garden had two doors by which it might be entered, and once a small person like Nicholas could slip in there he could effectually disappear from view amid the masking growth of artichokes, raspberry canes, and fruit bushes. The aunt had many other things to do that afternoon, but she spent an hour or two in trivial gardening operations among flower beds and shrubberies, whence she could watch the two doors that led to the forbidden paradise. She was a woman of few ideas, with immense powers of concentration.

Nicholas made one or two sorties into the front garden, wriggling his way with obvious stealth of purpose towards one or other of the doors, but never able for a moment to evade the aunt's watchful eye. As a matter of fact, he had no intention of trying to get into the gooseberry garden, but it was extremely convenient for him that his aunt should believe that he had; it was a belief that would keep her on self-imposed sentry-duty for the greater part of the afternoon. Having thoroughly confirmed and fortified her suspicions, Nicholas slipped back into the house and rapidly put into execution a plan of action that had long germinated in his brain. By standing on a chair in the library one could reach a shelf on which reposed a fat, important-looking key. The key was as important as it looked; it was the instrument which kept the mysteries of the lumber-room secure from unauthorized intrusion, which opened a way only for aunts and such-like privileged persons. Nicholas had not had much experience of the art of fitting keys into keyholes and turning locks, but for some days past he had practised with the key of the schoolroom door; he did not believe in trusting too much to luck and accident. The key turned stiffly in the lock, but it turned. The door opened, and Nicholas was in an unknown land, compared with which the gooseberry garden was a stale delight, a mere material pleasure.

Often and often Nicholas had pictured to himself what the lumber-room might be like, that region that was so carefully sealed from youthful eyes and concerning which no questions were ever answered. It came up to his expectations. In the first place it was large and dimly lit, one high window opening onto the forbidden garden being its only source of illumination. In the second place it was a storehouse of un-imagined treasures. The aunt-by-assertion was one of those people who think that things spoil by use and consign them to dust and damp by way of preserving them. Such parts of the house as Nicholas knew best were rather bare and cheerless, but here there were wonderful things for the eye to feast on. First and foremost there was a piece of framed tapestry that was evidently meant to be a fire-screen. To Nicholas it was a living, breathing story; he sat down on a roll of Indian hangings, glowing in wonderful colours beneath a layer of dust, and took in all the details of the tapestry picture. A man, dressed in the hunting costume of some remote period, had just transfixed a stag with an arrow; it could not have been a difficult shot because the stag was only one or two paces away from him; in the thickly growing vegetation that the picture suggested it would not have been difficult to creep up to a feeding stag, and the two spotted dogs that were springing forward to join in the chase had evidently been trained to keep to heel till the arrow was discharged. That part of the picture was simple, if interesting, but did the huntsman see, what Nicholas saw, that four galloping wolves were coming in his direction through the wood? There might be more than four of them hidden behind the trees, and in any case would the man and his dogs be able to cope with the four wolves if they made an attack? The man had only two arrows left in his quiver, and he might miss with one or both of them; all one knew about his skill in shooting was that he could hit a large stag at a ridiculously short range. Nicholas sat for many golden minutes re-volving the possibilities of the scene; he was inclined to think that there were more than four wolves and that the man and his dogs were in a tight corner.

But there were other objects of delight and interest claiming his instant attention; there were quaint twisted candlesticks in the shape of snakes, and a teapot fashioned like a china duck, out of whose open beak the tea was supposed to come. How dull and shapeless the nursery teapot seemed in comparison! And there was a carved sandal-wood box packed tight with aromatic cotton-wool, and between the layers of cotton-wool were little brass figures, hump-necked bulls, and peacocks and goblins, delightful to see and to handle. Less promising in appearance was a large square book with plain black covers; Nicholas peeped into it, and, behold, it was full of coloured pictures of birds. And such birds! In the garden, and in the lanes when he went for a walk, Nicholas came across a few birds, of which the largest were an occasional magpie or wood-pigeon; here were herons and bustards, kites, toucans, tiger-bitterns, brush turkeys, ibises, golden pheasants, a whole portrait gallery of undreamed-of creatures. And as he was admiring the colouring of the mandarin duck and assigning a life-history to it, the voice of his aunt in shrill vociferation of his name came from the gooseberry garden without. She had grown suspicious at his long disappearance, and had leapt to the conclusion that he had climbed over the wall behind the sheltering screen of the lilac bushes; she was now engaged in energetic and rather hopeless search for him among the artichokes and raspberry canes.

"Nicholas, Nicholas!" she screamed, "you are to come out of this at once. It's no use trying to hide there; I can see you all the time."

It was probably the first time for twenty years that any one had smiled in that lumber-room.

Presently the angry repetitions of Nicholas's name gave way to a shriek, and a cry for somebody to come quickly. Nicholas shut the book, restored it carefully to its place in a corner, and shook some dust from a neighbouring pile of newspapers over it. Then he crept from the room, locked the door, and replaced the key exactly where he had found it. His aunt was still calling his name when he sauntered into the front garden.

"Who's calling?" he asked.

"Me," came the answer from the other side of the wall; "didn't you hear me? I've been looking for you in the gooseberry garden, and I've slipped into the rain-water tank. Luckily there's no water in it, but the sides are slippery and I can't get out. Fetch the little ladder from under the cherry tree—"

"I was told I wasn't to go into the gooseberry garden," said Nicholas promptly.

"I told you not to, and now I tell you that you may," came the voice from the rain-water tank, rather impatiently.

"Your voice doesn't sound like aunt's," objected Nicholas; "you may be the Evil One tempting me to be disobedient. Aunt often tells me that the Evil One tempts me and that I always yield. This time I'm not going to yield."

"Don't talk nonsense," said the prisoner in the tank; "go and fetch the ladder."

"Will there be strawberry jam for tea?" asked Nicholas innocently.

"Certainly there will be," said the aunt, privately resolving that Nicholas should have none of it.

"Now I know that you are the Evil One and not aunt," shouted Nicholas gleefully; "when we asked aunt for strawberry jam yesterday she said there wasn't any. I know there are four jars of it in the store cupboard, because I looked, and of course you know it's there, but *she* doesn't, because she said there wasn't any. Oh, Devil, you *have* sold yourself!"

There was an unusual sense of luxury in being able to talk to an aunt as though one was talking to the Evil One, but Nicholas knew, with childish discernment that such luxuries were not to be over-indulged in. He walked noisily away, and it was a kitchenmaid, in search of parsley, who eventually rescued the aunt from the rain-water tank.

Tea that evening was partaken of in a fearsome silence. The tide had been at its highest when the children had arrived at Jagborough Cove, so there had been no sands to play on—a circumstance that the aunt had overlooked in the haste of organizing her punitive expedition. The tightness of Bobby's boots had had a disastrous effect on his temper the whole of the afternoon, and altogether the children could not have been said to have enjoyed themselves. The aunt maintained the frozen muteness of one who has suffered undignified and unmerited detention in a rain-water tank for thirty-five minutes. As for Nicholas, he, too, was silent, in the absorption of one who has much to think about; it was just possible, he considered, that the huntsman would escape with his hounds while the wolves feasted on the stricken stag.

WINTER DREAMS

F. SCOTT FITZGERALD

Some of the caddies were poor as sin and lived in one-room houses with a neurasthenic cow in the front yard, but Dexter Green's father owned the second-best grocery store in Black Bear—the best one was The Hub, patronized by the wealthy people from Sherry Island—and Dexter caddied only for pocket money.

In the fall when the days became crisp and gray, and the long Minnesota winter shut down like the white lid of a box, Dexter's skis moved over the snow that hid the fairways of the golf course. At these times the country gave him a feeling of profound melancholy—it offended him that the links should lie in enforced fallowness, haunted by ragged sparrows for the long season. It was dreary, too, that on the tees where the gay colors fluttered in summer there were now only the desolate sandboxes knee-deep in crusted ice. When he crossed the hills the wind blew cold as misery, and if the sun was out he tramped with his eyes squinted up against the hard dimensionless glare.

In April the winter ceased abruptly. The snow ran down into Black Bear Lake, scarcely tarrying for the early golfers to brave the season with red and black balls. Without elation, without an interval of moist glory, the cold was gone.

Dexter knew that there was something dismal about this northern spring, just as he knew there was something gorgeous about the fall. Fall made him clinch his hands and tremble and repeat idiotic sentences to himself, and make brisk abrupt gestures of command to imaginary audiences and armies. October filled him with hope, which November raised to a sort of ecstatic triumph, and in this mood the fleeting brilliant impressions of the summer at Sherry Island were ready grist to his mill. He became a golf champion and defeated Mr. T. A. Hedrick in a marvelous match played a hundred times over the fairways of his imagination, a match each detail of which he changed about untiringly—sometimes he won with almost laughable ease, sometimes he came up magnificently from behind. Again, stepping from a Pierce Arrow automobile, like Mr. Mortimer Jones, he strolled frigidly into the lounge of the Sherry Island Golf Club—or perhaps, surrounded by an admiring crowd, he gave an exhibition of fancy diving from the springboard of the club raft. . . . Among those who watched him in openmouthed wonder was Mr. Mortimer Jones.

And one day it came to pass that Mr. Jones—himself and not his ghost—came up to Dexter with tears in his eyes and said that Dexter was the __ __ best caddie in the club, and wouldn't he decide not to quit if Mr. Jones made it worth his while, because every other __ __ caddie in the club lost one ball a hole for him—regularly.

"No, sir," said Dexter decisively, "I don't want to caddie anymore." Then, after a pause: "I'm too old."

"You're not more than fourteen. Why the devil did you decide just this morning that you wanted to quit? You promised that next week you'd go over to the state tournament with me."

"I decided I was too old."

Dexter handed in his A Class badge, collected what money was due him from the caddie master, and walked home to Black Bear Village.

"The best __ __ caddie I ever saw," shouted Mr. Mortimer Jones over a drink that afternoon. "Never lost a ball! Willing! Intelligent! Quiet! Honest! Grateful!"

The little girl who had done this was eleven—beautifully ugly, as little girls are apt to be who are destined after a few years to be inexpressibly lovely and bring no end of misery to a great number of men. The spark, however, was perceptible. There was a general ungodliness in the way her lips twisted down at the corners when she smiled, and in the—Heaven help us!—in the almost passionate quality of her eyes. Vitality is born early in such women. It was utterly in evidence now, shining through her thin frame in a sort of glow.

She had come eagerly out onto the course at nine o'clock with a white linen nurse and five small new golf clubs in a white canvas bag which the nurse was carrying. When Dexter first saw her she was standing by the caddie house, rather ill at ease and trying to conceal the fact by engaging her nurse in an obviously unnatural conversation graced by startling and irrelevant grimaces from herself.

"Well, it's certainly a nice day, Hilda," Dexter heard her say. She drew down the corners of her mouth, smiled, and glanced furtively around, her eyes in transit falling for an instant on Dexter.

Then to the nurse: "Well, I guess there aren't very many people out here this morning, are there?"

The smile again—radiant, blatantly artificial—convincing.

"I don't know what we're supposed to do now," said the nurse, looking nowhere in particular.

"Oh, that's all right. I'll fix it up."

Dexter stood perfectly still, his mouth slightly ajar. He knew that if he moved forward a step his stare would be in her line of vision—if he moved backward he would lose his full view of her face. For a moment he had not realized how young she was. Now he remembered having seen her several times the year before—in bloomers.

Suddenly, involuntarily, he laughed, a short abrupt laugh—then, startled by himself, he turned and began to walk quickly away.

"Boy!"

Dexter stopped.

"Boy . . ."

Beyond question he was addressed. Not only that, but he was treated to that absurd smile, that preposterous smile—the memory of which at least a dozen men were to carry into middle age.

"Boy, do you know where the golf teacher is?"

"He's giving a lesson."

"Well, do you know where the caddie master is?"

"He isn't here yet this morning."

"Oh." For a moment this baffled her. She stood alternately on her right and left foot.

"We'd like to get a caddie," said the nurse. "Mrs. Mortimer Jones sent us out to play golf, and we don't know how without we get a caddie."

Here she was stopped by an ominous glance from Miss Jones, followed immediately by the smile.

"There aren't any caddies here except me," said Dexter to the nurse, "and I got to stay here in charge until the caddie master gets here."

"Oh."

Miss Jones and her retinue now withdrew, and at a proper distance from Dexter became involved in a heated conversation, which was concluded by Miss Jones taking one of the clubs and hitting it on the ground with violence.

For further emphasis she raised it again and was about to bring it down smartly upon the nurse's bosom, when the nurse seized the club and twisted it from her hands.

"You damn little mean old *thing!*" cried Miss Jones wildly.

Another argument ensued. Realizing that the elements of the comedy were implied in the scene, Dexter several times began to laugh, but each time restrained the laugh before it reached audibility. He could not resist the monstrous conviction that the little girl was justified in beating the nurse.

The situation was resolved by the fortuitous appearance of the caddie master, who was appealed to immediately by the nurse.

"Miss Jones is to have a little caddie, and this one says he can't go."

"Mr. McKenna said I was to wait here till you came," said Dexter quickly.

"Well, he's here now." Miss Jones smiled cheerfully at the caddie master. Then she dropped her bag and set off at a haughty mince toward the first tee.

"Well?" The caddie master turned to Dexter. "What you standing there like a dummy for? Go pick up the young lady's clubs."

"I don't think I'll go out today," said Dexter.

"You don't—"

"I think I'll quit."

The enormity of his decision frightened him. He was a favorite caddie, and the thirty dollars a month he earned through the summer were not to be made elsewhere around the lake. But he had received a strong emotional shock, and his perturbation required a violent and immediate outlet.

It is not so simple as that, either. As so frequently would be the case in the future, Dexter was unconsciously dictated to by his winter dreams.

Now, OF COURSE, the quality and the seasonability of these winter dreams varied, but the stuff of them remained. They persuaded Dexter several years later to pass up a business course at the state university— his father, prospering now, would have paid his way—for the precarious advantage of attending an older and more famous university in the East, where he was bothered by his scanty funds. But do not get the impression, because his winter dreams happened to be concerned at first with musings on the rich, that there was anything merely snobbish in the boy. He wanted not association with glittering things and glittering people—he wanted the glittering things themselves. Often he reached out for the best without knowing why he wanted it—and sometimes he ran up against the mysterious denials and prohibitions in which life indulges. It is with one of those denials and not with his career as a whole that this story deals.

He made money. It was rather amazing. After college he went to the city from which Black Bear Lake draws its wealthy patrons. When he was only twenty-three and had been there not quite two years, there were already people who liked to say, "Now *there's* a boy—" All about him rich men's sons were peddling bonds precariously, or investing patrimonies precariously, or plodding through the two dozen volumes of the George Washington Commercial Course, but Dexter borrowed a thousand dollars on his college degree and his confident mouth, and bought a partnership in a laundry.

It was a small laundry when he went into it, but Dexter made a specialty of learning how the English washed fine woolen golf stockings without shrinking them, and within a year he was catering to the trade that wore knickerbockers. Men were insisting that their Shetland hose and sweaters go to his laundry, just as they had insisted on a caddie who could find golf balls. A little later he was doing their wives' lingerie as well—and running five branches in different parts of the city.

Before he was twenty-seven he owned the largest string of laundries in his section of the country. It was then that he sold out and went to New York.

But the part of his story that concerns us goes back to the days when he was making his first big success. When he was twenty-three Mr. Hart—one of the gray-haired men who like to say, "Now *there's* a boy"—gave him a guest card to the Sherry Island Golf Club for a weekend. So he signed his name one day on the register, and that afternoon played golf in a foursome with Mr. Hart and Mr. Sandwood and Mr. T. A. Hedrick. He did not consider it necessary to remark that he had once carried Mr. Hart's bag over this same links, and that he knew every trap and gully with his eyes shut—but he found himself glancing at the four caddies who trailed them, trying to catch a gleam or gesture that would remind him of himself, that would lessen the gap which lay between his present and his past.

It was a curious day, slashed abruptly with fleeting, familiar impressions. One minute he had the sense of being a trespasser—in the next he was impressed by the tremendous superiority he felt toward Mr. T. A. Hedrick, who was a bore and not even a good golfer anymore.

Then, because of a ball Mr. Hart lost near the fifteenth green, an enormous thing happened. While they were searching the stiff grasses of the rough there was a clear call of "Fore!" from behind a hill in their rear. And as they all turned abruptly from their search a bright new ball sliced abruptly over the hill and caught Mr. T. A. Hedrick in the abdomen.

"By Gad!" cried Mr. T. A. Hedrick. "They ought to put some of these crazy women off the course. It's getting to be outrageous."

A head and a voice came up together over the hill: "Do you mind if we go through?"

"You hit me in the stomach!" declared Mr. Hedrick wildly.

"Did I?" The girl approached the group of men. "I'm sorry. I yelled 'Fore!' " Her glance fell casually on each of the men—then scanned the fairway for her ball. "Did I bounce into the rough?"

It was impossible to determine whether this question was ingenuous or malicious. In a moment, however, she left no doubt, for as her partner came up over the hill she called cheerfully, "Here I am! I'd have gone on the green except that I hit something."

As she took her stance for a short mashie shot, Dexter looked at her closely. She wore a blue gingham dress, rimmed at throat and shoulders with a white edging that accentuated her tan. The quality of exaggeration, of thinness, which had made her passionate eyes and down-turning mouth absurd at eleven, was gone now. She was arrestingly beautiful. The color in her cheeks was centered like the color in a picture—it was not a high color, but a sort of fluctuating and feverish warmth, so shaded that it seemed at any moment it would recede and disappear. This color and the mobility of her mouth gave a continual impression of flux, of intense life, of passionate vitality—balanced only partially by the sad luxury of her eyes.

She swung her mashie impatiently and without interest, pitching the ball into a sandpit on the other side of the green. With a quick, insincere smile and a careless "Thank you!" she went on after it.

"That Judy Jones!" remarked Mr. Hedrick on the next tee, as they waited—some moments—for her to play on ahead. "All she needs is to be turned up and spanked for six months and then to be married off to an old-fashioned cavalry captain."

"My God, she's good-looking!" said Mr. Sandwood, who was just over thirty.

"Good-looking!" cried Mr. Hedrick contemptuously. "She always looks as if she wanted to be kissed! Turning those big cow eyes on every calf in town!"

It was doubtful if Mr. Hedrick intended a reference to the maternal instinct.

"She'd play pretty good golf if she'd try," said Mr. Sandwood.

"She has no form," said Mr. Hedrick solemnly.

"She has a nice figure," said Mr. Sandwood.

"Better thank the Lord she doesn't drive a swifter ball," said Mr. Hart, winking at Dexter.

Later in the afternoon the sun went down with a riotous swirl of gold and varying blues and scarlets, and left the dry, rustling night of western summer. Dexter watched from the veranda of the golf club, watched the even overlap of the waters in the little wind, silver molasses under the harvest moon. Then the moon held a finger to her lips and the lake became a clear pool, pale and quiet. Dexter put on his bathing suit and swam out to the farthest raft, where he stretched dripping on the wet canvas of the springboard.

There was a fish jumping and a star shining and the lights around the lake were gleaming. Over on a dark peninsula a piano was playing the songs of last summer and of summers before that—songs from *Chin-Chin* and *The Count of Luxemburg* and *The Chocolate Soldier*—and because the sound of a piano over a stretch of water had always seemed beautiful to Dexter he lay perfectly quiet and listened.

The tune the piano was playing at that moment had been gay and new five years before when Dexter was a sophomore at college. They had played it at a prom once when he could not afford the luxury of proms, and he had stood outside the gymnasium and listened. The sound of the tune precipitated in him a sort of ecstasy and it was with that ecstasy he viewed what happened to him now. It was a mood of intense appreciation, a sense that, for once, he was magnificently attune to life and that everything about him was radiating a brightness and a glamour he might never know again.

A low, pale oblong detached itself suddenly from the darkness of the island, spitting forth the reverberate sound of a racing motorboat. Two white streamers of cleft water rolled themselves out behind it and almost immediately the boat was beside him, drowning out the hot tinkle of the piano in the drone of its spray. Dexter, raising himself on his arms, was aware of a figure standing at the wheel, of two dark eyes regarding him over the lengthening space of water—then the boat had gone by and was sweeping in an immense and purposeless circle of spray round and round in the middle of the lake. With equal eccentricity one of the circles flattened out and headed back toward the raft.

"Who's that?" she called, shutting off her motor. She was so near now that Dexter could see her bathing suit, which consisted apparently of pink rompers.

The nose of the boat bumped the raft, and as the latter tilted rakishly he was precipitated toward her. With different degrees of interest they recognized each other.

"Aren't you one of those men we played through this afternoon?" she demanded.

He was.

"Well, do you know how to drive a motorboat? Because if you do I wish you'd drive this one so I can ride on the surfboard behind. My name is Judy Jones"—she favored him with an absurd smirk—rather, what tried to be a smirk, for, twist her mouth as she might, it was not grotesque, it was merely beautiful—"and I live in a house over there on the island, and in that house there is a man waiting for me. When he drove up at the door I drove out of the dock because he says I'm his ideal."

There was a fish jumping and a star shining and the lights around the lake were gleaming. Dexter sat beside Judy Jones and she explained how her boat was driven. Then she was in the water, swimming to the floating surfboard with a sinuous crawl. Watching her was without effort to the eye, watching a branch waving or a sea gull flying. Her arms, burned to butternut, moved sinuously among the dull platinum ripples, elbow appearing first, casting the forearm back with a cadence of falling water, then reaching out and down, stabbing a path ahead.

They moved out into the lake; turning, Dexter saw that she was kneeling on the low rear of the now uptilted surfboard.

"Go faster," she called, "fast as it'll go."

Obediently he jammed the lever forward and the white spray mounted at the bow. When he looked around again the girl was standing up on the rushing board, her arms spread wide, her eyes lifted toward the moon.

"It's awful cold," she shouted. "What's your name?"

He told her.

"Well, why don't you come to dinner tomorrow night?"

His heart turned over like the flywheel of the boat, and, for the second time, her casual whim gave a new direction to his life.

NEXT EVENING while he waited for her to come downstairs, Dexter peopled the soft deep summer room and the sun porch that opened from it with the men who had already loved Judy Jones. He knew the sort of men they were—the men who when he first went to college had entered from the great prep schools with graceful clothes and the deep tan of healthy summers. He had seen that, in one sense, he was better than these men. He was newer and stronger. Yet in acknowledging to himself that he wished his children to be like them he was admitting that he was but the rough, strong stuff from which they eternally sprang.

When the time had come for him to wear good clothes, he had known who were the best tailors in America, and the best tailors in America had made him the suit he wore this evening. He had acquired that particular reserve peculiar to his university, that set it off from other universities. He recognized the value to him of such a mannerism and he had adopted it; he knew that to be careless in dress and manner required more confidence than to be careful.

But carelessness was for his children. His mother's name had been Krimslich. She was a Bohemian of the peasant class and she had talked broken English to the end of her days. Her son must keep to the set patterns.

At a little after seven Judy Jones came downstairs. She wore a blue silk afternoon dress, and he was disappointed at first that she had not put on something more elaborate. This feeling was accentuated when, after a brief greeting, she went to the door of a butler's pantry and pushing it open called, "You can serve dinner, Martha." He had rather expected that a butler would announce dinner, that there would be a cocktail. Then he put these thoughts behind him as they sat down side by side on a lounge and looked at each other.

"Father and Mother won't be here," she said thoughtfully.

He remembered the last time he had seen her father, and he was glad the parents were not to be here tonight—they might wonder who he was. He had been born in Keeble, a Minnesota village fifty miles farther north, and he always gave Keeble as his home instead of Black Bear Village. Country towns were well enough to come from if they weren't inconveniently in sight and used as footstools by fashionable lakes.

They talked of his university, which she had visited frequently during the past two years, and of the nearby city which supplied Sherry Island with its patrons, and whither Dexter would return next day to his prospering laundries.

During dinner she slipped into a moody depression which gave

Dexter a feeling of uneasiness. Whatever petulance she uttered in her throaty voice worried him. Whatever she smiled at—at him, at a chicken liver, at nothing—it disturbed him that her smile could have no root in mirth, or even in amusement. When the scarlet corners of her lips curved down, it was less a smile than an invitation to a kiss.

Then, after dinner, she led him out on the dark sun porch and deliberately changed the atmosphere.

"Do you mind if I weep a little?" she said.

"I'm afraid I'm boring you," he responded quickly.

"You're not. I like you. But I've just had a terrible afternoon. There was a man I cared about, and this afternoon he told me out of a clear sky that he was poor as a church mouse. He'd never even hinted it before. Does this sound horribly mundane?"

"Perhaps he was afraid to tell you."

"Suppose he was," she answered. "He didn't start right. You see, if I'd thought of him as poor—well, I've been mad about loads of poor men, and fully intended to marry them all. But in this case, I hadn't thought of him that way, and my interest in him wasn't strong enough to survive the shock. As if a girl calmly informed her fiancé that she was a widow. He might not object to widows, but—

"Let's start right," she interrupted herself suddenly. "Who are you, anyhow?"

For a moment Dexter hesitated. Then: "I'm nobody," he announced. "My career is largely a matter of futures."

"Are you poor?"

"No," he said frankly, "I'm probably making more money than any man my age in the Northwest. I know that's an obnoxious remark, but you advised me to start right."

There was a pause. Then she smiled and the corners of her mouth drooped and an almost imperceptible sway brought her closer to him, looking up into his eyes. A lump rose in Dexter's throat, and he waited breathless for the experiment, facing the unpredictable compound that would form mysteriously from the elements of their lips. Then he saw—she communicated her excitement to him, lavishly, deeply, with kisses that were not a promise but a fulfillment. They aroused in him not hunger demanding renewal but surfeit that would demand more surfeit . . . kisses that were like charity, creating want by holding back nothing at all.

It did not take him many hours to decide that he had wanted Judy Jones ever since he was a proud, desirous little boy.

IT BEGAN like that—and continued, with varying shades of intensity, on such a note right up to the denouement. Dexter surrendered a part of himself to the most direct and unprincipled personality with which he had ever come in contact. Whatever Judy wanted, she went after with the full pressure of her charm. There was no divergence of method, no jockeying for position or premeditation of effects—there was very little mental side to any of her affairs. She simply made men conscious to the highest degree of her physical loveliness. Dexter had no desire to change her. Her deficiencies were knit up with a passionate energy that transcended and justified them.

When, as Judy's head lay against his shoulder that first night, she whispered, "I don't know what's the matter with me. Last night I thought I was in love with a man and tonight I think I'm in love with you—" it seemed to him a beautiful and romantic thing to say. It was the exquisite excitability that for the moment he controlled and owned. But a week later he was compelled to view this same quality in a different light. She took him in her roadster to a picnic supper, and after supper she disappeared, likewise in her roadster, with another man. Dexter became enormously upset and was scarcely able to be decently civil to the other people present. When she assured him that she had not kissed the other man, he knew she was lying—yet he was glad that she had taken the trouble to lie to him.

He was, as he found before the summer ended, one of a varying dozen who circulated about her. Each of them had at one time been favored above all others—about half of them still basked in the solace of occasional sentimental revivals. Whenever one showed signs of dropping out through long neglect, she granted him a brief honeyed hour, which encouraged him to tag along for a year or so longer. Judy made these forays upon the helpless and defeated without malice, indeed half unconscious that there was anything mischievous in what she did.

When a new man came to town every one dropped out—dates were automatically canceled.

The helpless part of trying to do anything about it was that she did it all herself. She was not a girl who could be "won" in the kinetic sense—she was proof against cleverness, she was proof against charm; if any of these assailed her too strongly she would immediately resolve the affair to a physical basis, and under the magic of her physical splendor the strong as well as the brilliant played her game and not their own. She was entertained only by the gratification of her desires and by the direct exercise of her own charm. Perhaps from so much youthful love, so many youthful lovers, she had come, in self-defense, to nourish herself wholly from within.

Succeeding Dexter's first exhilaration came restlessness and dissatisfaction. The helpless ecstasy of losing himself in her was opiate rather than tonic. It was fortunate for his work during the winter that those moments of ecstasy came infrequently. Early in their acquaintance it had seemed for a while that there was a deep and spontaneous mutual attraction—that first August, for example—three days of long evenings on her dusky veranda, of strange wan kisses through the late afternoon, in shadowy alcoves or behind the protecting trellises of the garden arbors, of mornings when she was fresh as a dream and almost shy at meeting him in the clarity of the rising day. There was all the ecstasy of an engagement about it, sharpened by his realization that there was no engagement. It was during those three days that, for the first time, he had asked her to marry him. She said "Maybe some day," she said "Kiss me," she said "I'd like to marry you," she said "I love you"—she said—nothing.

The three days were interrupted by the arrival of a New York man who visited at her house for half of September. To Dexter's agony, rumor engaged them. The man was the son of the president of a great trust company. But at the end of a month it was reported that Judy was yawning. At a dance one night she sat all evening in a motorboat with a local beau, while the New Yorker searched the club for her frantically. She told the local beau that she was bored with her visitor, and two days later he left. She was seen with him at the station, and it was reported that he looked very mournful indeed.

On this note the summer ended. Dexter was twenty-four, and he found himself increasingly in a position to do as he wished. He joined two clubs in the city and lived at one of them. Though he was by no means an integral part of the stag lines at these clubs, he managed to be on hand at dances where Judy Jones was likely to appear. He could have gone out socially as much as he liked—he was an eligible young man, now, and popular with downtown fathers. His confessed devotion to Judy Jones had rather solidified his position. But he had no social aspirations and rather despised the dancing men who were always on tap for the Thursday or Saturday parties and who filled in at dinners with the younger married set. Already he was playing with the idea of going east to New York. He wanted to take Judy Jones with him. No disillusion as to the world in which she had grown up could cure his illusion as to her desirability.

Remember that—for only in the light of it can what he did for her be understood.

Eighteen months after he first met Judy Jones he became engaged to another girl. Her name was Irene Scheerer, and her father was one of the men who had always believed in Dexter. Irene was light-haired and sweet and honorable, and a little stout, and she had two suitors whom she pleasantly relinquished when Dexter asked her to marry him.

Summer, fall, winter, spring, another summer, another fall—so much he had given of his active life to the incorrigible lips of Judy Jones. She had treated him with interest, with encouragement, with malice, with indifference, with contempt. She had inflicted on him the innumerable little slights and indignities possible in such a case—as if in revenge for having ever cared for him at all. She had beckoned him and yawned at him and beckoned him again and he had responded often with bitterness and narrowed eyes. She had brought him ecstatic happiness and intolerable agony of spirit. She had caused him untold inconvenience and not a little trouble. She had insulted him, and she had ridden over him, and she had played his interest in her against his interest in his work—for fun. She had done everything to him except to criticize him—this she had not done—it seemed to him only because it might have sullied the utter indifference she manifested and sincerely felt toward him.

When autumn had come and gone again it occurred to him that he could not have Judy Jones. He had to beat this into his mind but he convinced himself at last. He lay awake at night for a while and argued it over. He told himself the trouble and the pain she had caused him, he enumerated her glaring deficiencies as a wife. Then he said to himself that he loved her, and after a while he fell asleep. For a week, lest he imagined her husky voice over the telephone or her eyes opposite him at lunch, he worked hard and late, and at night he went to his office and plotted out his years.

At the end of a week he went to a dance and cut in on her once. For almost the first time since they had met he did not ask her to sit out with him or tell her that she was lovely. It hurt him that she did not miss these things—that was all. He was not jealous when he saw that there was a new man tonight. He had been hardened against jealousy long before.

He stayed late at the dance. He sat for an hour with Irene Scheerer and talked about books and about music. He knew very little about either. But he was beginning to be master of his own time now, and he had a rather priggish notion that he—the young and already fabulously successful Dexter Green—should know more about such things.

That was in October, when he was twenty-five. In January, Dexter and Irene became engaged. It was to be announced in June, and they were to be married three months later.

The Minnesota winter prolonged itself interminably, and it was almost May when the winds came soft and the snow ran down into Black Bear Lake at last. For the first time in over a year Dexter was enjoying a certain tranquillity of spirit. Judy Jones had been in Florida, and afterward in Hot Springs, and somewhere she had been engaged, and somewhere she had broken it off. At first, when Dexter had definitely given her up, it had made him sad that people still linked them together and asked for news of her, but when he began to be placed at dinner next to Irene Scheerer people didn't ask him about her anymore—they told him about her. He ceased to be an authority on her.

May at last. Dexter walked the streets at night when the darkness was damp as rain, wondering that so soon, with so little done, so much of ecstasy had gone from him. May one year back had been marked by Judy's poignant, unforgiveable, yet forgiven turbulence—it had been one of those rare times when he fancied she had grown to care for him. That old penny's worth of happiness he had spent for this bushel of content. He knew that Irene would be no more than a curtain spread behind him, a hand moving among gleaming teacups, a voice calling to children . . . fire and loveliness were gone, the magic of nights and the wonder of the varying hours and seasons . . . slender lips, down-turning, dropping to his lips and bearing him up into a heaven of eyes. . . . The thing was deep in him. He was too strong and alive for it to die lightly.

In the middle of May when the weather balanced for a few days on the thin bridge that led to deep summer he turned in one night at Irene's house. Their engagement was to be announced in a week now—no one would be surprised at it. And tonight they would sit together on the lounge at the University Club and look on for an hour at the dancers. It gave him a sense of solidity to go with her—she was so sturdily popular, so intensely "great."

He mounted the steps of the brownstone house and stepped inside.

"Irene," he called.

Mrs. Scheerer came out of the living room to meet him.

"Dexter," she said, "Irene's gone upstairs with a splitting headache. She wanted to go with you but I made her go to bed."

"Nothing serious, I—"

"Oh, no. She's going to play golf with you in the morning. You can spare her for just one night, can't you, Dexter?"

Her smile was kind. She and Dexter liked each other. In the living room he talked for a moment before he said good night.

Returning to the University Club, where he had rooms, he stood in the doorway for a moment and watched the dancers. He leaned against the doorpost, nodded at a man or two—yawned.

"Hello, darling."

The familiar voice at his elbow startled him. Judy Jones had left a man and crossed the room to him—Judy Jones, a slender enameled doll in cloth of gold: gold in a band at her head, gold in two slipper points at her dress's hem. The fragile glow of her face seemed to blossom as she smiled at him. A breeze of warmth and light blew through the room.

His hands in the pockets of his dinner jacket tightened spasmodically. He was filled with a sudden excitement.

"When did you get back?" he asked casually.

"Come here and I'll tell you about it."

She turned and he followed her. She had been away—he could have wept at the wonder of her return. She had passed through enchanted streets, doing things that were like provocative music. All mysterious happenings, all fresh and quickening hopes, had gone away with her, came back with her now.

She turned in the doorway.

"Have you a car here? If you haven't, I have."

"I have a coupe."

In then, with a rustle of golden cloth. He slammed the door. Into so many cars she had stepped—like this—like that—her back against the leather, so—her elbow resting on the door—waiting. She would have been soiled long since had there been anything to soil her—except herself—but this was her own self outpouring.

With an effort he forced himself to start the car and back into the street. This was nothing, he must remember. She had done this before, and he had put her behind him, as he would have crossed a bad account from his books.

He drove slowly downtown and, affecting abstraction, traversed the deserted streets of the business section, peopled here and there where a movie was giving out its crowd or where consumptive or pugilistic youth lounged in front of pool halls. The clink of glasses and the slap of hands on the bars issued from saloons, cloisters of glazed glass and dirty yellow light.

She was watching him closely and the silence was embarrassing, yet in this crisis he could find no casual word with which to profane the hour. At a convenient turning he began to zigzag back toward the University Club.

"Have you missed me?" she asked suddenly.

"Everybody missed you."

He wondered if she knew of Irene Scheerer. She had been back only a day—her absence had been almost contemporaneous with his engagement.

"What a remark!" Judy laughed sadly—without sadness. She looked at him searchingly. He became absorbed in the dashboard.

"You're handsomer than you used to be," she said thoughtfully. "Dexter, you have the most rememberable eyes."

He could have laughed at this, but he did not laugh. It was the sort of thing that was said to sophomores. Yet it stabbed at him.

"I'm awfully tired of everything, darling." She called everyone darling, endowing the endearment with careless, individual comradery. "I wish you'd marry me."

The directness of this confused him. He should have told her now that he was going to marry another girl, but he could not tell her. He could as easily have sworn that he had never loved her.

"I think we'd get along," she continued, on the same note, "unless probably you've forgotten me and fallen in love with another girl."

Her confidence was obviously enormous. She had said, in effect, that she found such a thing impossible to believe, that if it were true he had merely committed a childish indiscretion—and probably to show off. She would forgive him, because it was not a matter of any moment but rather something to be brushed aside lightly.

"Of course you could never love anybody but me," she continued. "I like the way you love me. Oh, Dexter, have you forgotten last year?"

"No, I haven't forgotten."

"Neither have I!"

Was she sincerely moved—or was she carried along by the wave of her own acting?

"I wish we could be like that again," she said, and he forced himself to answer:

"I don't think we can."

"I suppose not. . . . I hear you're giving Irene Scheerer a violent rush." There was not the faintest emphasis on the name, yet Dexter was suddenly ashamed.

"Oh, take me home," cried Judy suddenly; "I don't want to go back to that idiotic dance—with those children."

Then, as he turned up the street that led to the residence district, Judy began to cry quietly to herself. He had never seen her cry before.

The dark street lightened, the dwellings of the rich loomed up around them, he stopped his coupe in front of the great white bulk of the Mortimer Joneses' house, somnolent, gorgeous, drenched with the splendor of the damp moonlight. Its solidity startled him. The strong walls, the steel of the girders, the breadth and beam and pomp of it were there only to bring out the contrast with the young beauty beside him. It was sturdy to accentuate her slightness—as if to show what a breeze could be generated by a butterfly's wing.

He sat perfectly quiet, his nerves in wild clamor, afraid that if he moved he would find her irresistibly in his arms. Two tears had rolled down her wet face and trembled on her upper lip.

"I'm more beautiful than anybody else," she said brokenly, "why can't I be happy?" Her moist eyes tore at his stability—her mouth turned slowly downward with an exquisite sadness. "I'd like to marry you if you'll have me, Dexter. I suppose you think I'm not worth having, but I'll be so beautiful for you, Dexter."

A million phrases of anger, pride, passion, hatred, tenderness fought on his lips. Then a perfect wave of emotion washed over him, carrying off with it a sediment of wisdom, of convention, of doubt, of honor. This was his girl who was speaking, his own, his beautiful, his pride.

"Won't you come in?" He heard her draw in her breath sharply. Waiting.

"All right"—his voice was trembling—"I'll come in."

IT WAS strange that neither when it was over nor a long time afterward did he regret that night. Looking at it from the perspective of ten years, the fact that Judy's flare for him endured just one month seemed of little importance. Nor did it matter that by his yielding he subjected himself to a deeper agony in the end and gave serious hurt to Irene Scheerer and to Irene's parents, who had befriended him. There was nothing sufficiently pictorial about Irene's grief to stamp itself on his mind.

Dexter was at bottom hard-minded. The attitude of the city on his action was of no importance to him, not because he was going to leave the city, but because any outside attitude on the situation seemed superficial. He was completely indifferent to popular opinion. Nor, when he had seen that it was no use, that he did not possess in himself the power to move fundamentally or to hold Judy Jones, did he bear any malice toward her. He loved her, and he would love her until the day he was too old for loving—but he could not have her. So he tasted the deep pain that is reserved only for the strong, just as he had tasted for a little while the deep happiness.

Even the ultimate falsity of the grounds upon which Judy terminated the engagement, that she did not want to "take him away" from Irene—Judy who had wanted nothing else—did not revolt him. He was beyond any revulsion or any amusement.

He went east in February with the intention of selling out his laundries and settling in New York—but the war came to America in March and changed his plans. He returned to the West, handed over the management of the business to his partner, and went into the first officers' training camp in late April. He was one of those young thousands who greeted the war with a certain amount of relief, welcoming the liberation from webs of tangled emotion.

THIS STORY is not his biography, remember, although things creep into it which have nothing to do with those dreams he had when he was young. We are almost done with them and with him now. There is only one more incident to be related here, and it happens seven years farther on.

It took place in New York, where he had done well—so well that there were no barriers too high for him. He was thirty-two years old, and, except for one flying trip immediately after the war, he had not been west in seven years. A man named Devlin from Detroit came into his office to see him in a business way, and then and there this incident occurred, and closed out, so to speak, this particular side of his life.

"So you're from the Middle West," said the man Devlin. "That's funny—I thought men like you were probably born and raised on Wall Street. You know—wife of one of my best friends in Detroit came from your city. I was an usher at the wedding."

Dexter waited with no apprehension of what was coming.

"Judy Simms," said Devlin with no particular interest; "Judy Jones she was once."

"Yes, I knew her." A dull impatience spread over him. He had heard that she was married—perhaps deliberately he had heard no more.

"Awfully nice girl," brooded Devlin meaninglessly; "I'm sort of sorry for her."

"Why?" Something in Dexter was alert, receptive, at once.

"Oh, Lud Simms has gone to pieces in a way. I don't mean he ill-uses her, but he drinks and runs around—"

"Doesn't she run around?"

"No. Stays at home with her kids."

"Oh."

"She's a little too old for him," said Devlin.

"Too old!" cried Dexter. "Why, man, she's only twenty-seven."

He was possessed with a wild notion of rushing out into the streets and taking a train to Detroit. He rose to his feet spasmodically.

"I guess you're busy," Devlin apologized quickly. "I didn't realize—"

"No, I'm not busy," said Dexter, steadying his voice. "I'm not busy at all. Not busy at all. Did you say she was—twenty-seven? No, I said she was twenty-seven."

"Yes, you did," agreed Devlin dryly.

"Go on, then. Go on."

"What do you mean?"

"About Judy Jones."

Devlin looked at him helplessly.

"Well, that's—I told you all there is to it. He treats her like the devil. Oh, they're not going to get divorced or anything. When he's particularly outrageous she forgives him. In fact, I'm inclined to think she loves him. She was a pretty girl when she first came to Detroit."

A pretty girl! The phrase struck Dexter as ludicrous.

"Isn't she—a pretty girl, anymore?"

"Oh, she's all right."

"Look here," said Dexter, sitting down suddenly. "I don't understand. You say she was a 'pretty girl' and now you say she's 'all right.' I don't understand what you mean—Judy Jones wasn't a pretty girl, at all. She was a great beauty. Why, I knew her, I knew her. She was—"

Devlin laughed pleasantly.

"I'm not trying to start a row," he said. "I think Judy's a nice girl and I like her. I can't understand how a man like Lud Simms could fall madly in love with her, but he did." Then he added, "Most of the women like her."

Dexter looked closely at Devlin, thinking wildly that there must be a reason for this, some insensitivity in the man or some private malice.

"Lots of women fade just like *that*," Devlin snapped his fingers. "You must have seen it happen. Perhaps I've forgotten how pretty she was at her wedding. I've seen her so much since then, you see. She has nice eyes."

A sort of dullness settled down upon Dexter. For the first time in his life he felt like getting very drunk. He knew that he was laughing loudly at something Devlin had said, but he did not know what it was or why it was funny. When, in a few minutes, Devlin went he lay down on his lounge and looked out the window at the New York skyline into which the sun was sinking in dull lovely shades of pink and gold.

He had thought that having nothing else to lose he was invulnerable at last—but he knew that he had just lost something more, as surely as if he had married Judy Jones and seen her fade away before his eyes.

The dream was gone. Something had been taken from him. In a sort of panic he pushed the palms of his hands into his eyes and tried to bring up a picture of the waters lapping on Sherry Island and the moonlit veranda, and gingham on the golf links and the dry sun and the gold color of her neck's soft down. And her mouth damp to his kisses and her eyes plaintive with melancholy and her freshness like new fine linen in the morning. Why, these things were no longer in the world! They had existed and they existed no longer.

For the first time in years the tears were streaming down his face. But they were for himself now. He did not care about mouth and eyes and moving hands. He wanted to care, and he could not care. For he had gone away and he could never go back anymore. The gates were closed, the sun was gone down, and there was no beauty but the gray beauty of steel that withstands all time. Even the grief he could have borne was left behind in the country of illusion, of youth, of the richness of life, where his winter dreams had flourished.

"Long ago," he said, "long ago, there was something in me, but now that thing is gone. Now that thing is gone, that thing is gone. I cannot cry. I cannot care. That thing will come back no more."

HOOK

WALTER VAN TILBURG CLARK

Walter T. Clark

Hook, the hawks' child, was hatched in a dry spring among the oaks beside the seasonal river, and was struck from the nest early. In the drought his single-willed parents had to extend their hunting ground by more than twice. The range became too great for them to wish to return and feed Hook, and when they had lost interest in each other they drove Hook down into the sand and brush and went back to solitary courses over the bleaching hills.

Unable to fly yet, Hook crept over the ground, challenging all large movements with recoiled head, erected rudimentary wings, and the small rasp of his clattering beak. It was during this time of abysmal ignorance and continual fear that his eyes took on the first quality of hawk, that of being wide, alert and challenging. He dwelt, because of his helplessness, among the rattling brush which grew between the oaks and the river.

Two spacious sounds environed Hook at this time. One was the great rustle of the slopes of yellowed wild wheat, with over it the chattering rustle of the leaves of the California oaks. The other was the distant whisper of the foaming edge of the Pacific, punctuated by the hollow shoring of the waves. But these Hook did not yet hear, for he was attuned by fear and hunger to the small, spasmodic rustlings of live things. Dry, shrunken and nearly starved, and with his plumage delayed, he snatched at beetles, dragging in the sand to catch them. When swifter and stronger birds and animals did not reach them first, which was seldom, he ate the small, silver fish left in the mud by the failing river.

244

Only one sight and sound not of his world of microscopic necessity was forced upon Hook. That was the flight of the big gulls from the beaches, which sometimes, in quealing play, came spinning back over the foothills and the riverbed. For some inherited reason the big, ship-bodied birds did not frighten Hook, but angered him. Small and chewed-looking, with his wide, already yellowing eyes glaring up at them, he would stand in an open place on the sand in the sun and spread his shaping wings and clatter his bill like shaken dice. Hook was furious about the swift, easy passage of gulls.

His first opportunity to leave off living like a ground owl came accidentally. He was standing in the late afternoon under the thicket when suddenly something beside him moved, and he struck, and killed a field mouse driven out of the wheat by thirst. It was a poor mouse, shriveled and lice-ridden, but in striking, Hook had tasted blood. With started neck plumage and shining eyes, he tore and fed. When the mouse was devoured, Hook had entered hoarse adolescence. He began to seek with a conscious appetite, and to move more readily out of shelter. Impelled by the blood appetite, so glorious after his long preservation upon the flaky and bitter stuff of bugs, he ventured even into the wheat in the open sun beyond the oaks, and discovered the small trails and holes among the roots. With his belly often partially filled with flesh, he grew rapidly in strength and will. His eyes were taking on their final change, their yellow growing deeper and more opaque, their stare more constant, their challenge less desperate.

Once, during this transformation, he surprised a ground squirrel, and although he was ripped and wing-bitten and could not hold his prey, he was not dismayed by the conflict, but exalted. Even while the wing was still drooping and the pinions not grown back, he was excited by other ground squirrels and pursued them futilely, and was angered by their dusty escapes. He realized that his world was a great arena for killing, and felt the magnificence of it.

The two major events of Hook's young life occurred in the same day. A little after dawn he made the customary essay and succeeded in flight. A little before sunset he made his first sustained flight of over two hundred yards, and at its termination struck and slew a great buck squirrel, whose thrashing and terrified gnawing and squealing gave him a wild delight. When he had gorged on the strong meat, Hook stood upright, and in his eyes was the stare of the hawk, never flagging in intensity. He had mastered the first of the three hungers which are fused into the single, flaming will of a hawk, and had experienced the second.

The third and consummating hunger did not awaken in Hook until the following spring, when the exultation of space had grown slow and steady in him, so that he swept freely with the wind over the miles of coastal foothills, using without struggle the warm currents lifting from the slopes.

That spring the rains were long, and Hook sat for hours, hunched and angry under their pelting, glaring into the fogs of the river valley, and killed only small, drenched things flooded up from their tunnels. But when the rains had dissipated and there were sun and sea wind again, the game ran plentiful. Hook then was scorched by the third hunger. Ranging farther, often forgetting to kill and eat, he sailed for days with growing rage, and woke at night clattering on his dead tree limb, and struck and struck and struck at the porous wood of the trunk, tearing it away. After days, in the draft of a coastal canyon miles below his own hills, he came upon the acrid taint he did not know but had expected, and, sailing down it, felt his neck plumes rise and his wings quiver so that he swerved unsteadily. He saw the unmated female perched upon the tall and jagged stump of a tree that had been shorn by storm, and he stooped, as if upon game. But she was older than he, and wary of the gripe of his importunity, and banked off screaming, and he screamed also at the intolerable delay.

At the head of the canyon, the screaming pursuit was crossed by another male with a great wingspread. But his more skillful opening played him false against the ferocity of the twice-balked Hook. His rising maneuver for position was cut short by Hook's wild, upward swoop, and at the blow he raked desperately and tumbled off to the side. Dropping, Hook struck him again, struggled to clutch, but only raked and could not hold, and, diving, struck once more in passage, and then beat up, yelling triumph, and saw the crippled antagonist sideslip away and glide obliquely into the cover of brush. Beating hard and stationary in the wind above the bush that covered his competitor,

Hook waited an instant, but when the bush was still, screamed again, and resought the female.

On a hilltop projection of stone two miles inland, he struck her down, gripping her rustling body with his talons, beating her wings down with his wings, and, when her coy struggles had given way to stillness, succeeded.

In the early summer, Hook drove the three young ones from their nest and went back to lone circling above his own range. He was complete.

THROUGHOUT THAT summer and the cool, growthless weather of the winter, Hook was master of the sky and the hills of his range. His flight became a lovely and certain thing, so that he played with the treacherous currents of the air with a delicate ease surpassing that of the gulls. He could sail for hours, searching the blanched grasses below him with telescopic eyes, gaining height against the wind, and never beating either wing. At the swift passage of his shadow within their vision, gophers, ground squirrels and rabbits froze, or plunged gibbering into their tunnels beneath matted turf. Now, when he struck, he killed easily in one hard-knuckled blow. Occasionally, in sport, he soared up over the river and drove the heavy and weaponless gulls downstream again, until they would no longer venture inland.

There was nothing which Hook feared now, and his spirit was wholly belligerent, swift and sharp, like his gaze. Only the mixed smells and incomprehensible activities of the people at the Japanese farmer's home, inland of the coastwise highway, troubled him. The smells were strong, unsatisfactory and never clear, and the people, though they behaved foolishly, constantly running in and out of their built-up holes, were large and appeared capable, with fearless eyes looking up at him, so that he instinctively swerved aside from them. He cruised over their gardens and their crate-cluttered chicken yard, but he would not alight close to their buildings.

Four times that year he was challenged by other hawks blowing up from behind the coastal hills to scud down his slopes, but two of these he slew in midair and saw hurtle down to thump on the ground and lie still while he circled, and a third, whose wing he tore, he followed closely to earth and beat to death in the grass. The fourth was a strong flier and experienced fighter, and theirs was a long, running battle, with brief, rising flurries of striking and screaming, from which down and plumage soared off.

Here, for the first time, Hook felt doubts and at moments wanted to drop away from the scoring, burning talons and the twisted hammer-strokes of the strong beak, drop away shrieking and take cover and be still. In the end, when Hook, having outmaneuvered his enemy and come above him, wholly in control, and going with the wind, tilted and plunged for the death rap, the other, in desperation, threw over on his back and struck up. Talons locked, beaks raking, they dived earthward. The earth grew and spread under them amazingly, and they were not fifty feet above it when Hook, feeling himself turning toward the underside, tore free and beat up again on heavy, wrenched wings. The other, stroking swiftly, and so close to down that he lost wing plumes to a bush, righted himself and flew away lumberingly between the hills. Hook screamed the triumph and made a brief pretense of pursuit, but was glad to return, slow and victorious, to his dead tree.

In all these encounters Hook was injured, but experienced only the fighter's pride and exultation from the sting of wounds received in successful combat. And in each of them he learned new skill.

In the next spring the third hunger returned upon Hook with a new violence. In this quest he came into the taint of a young hen. Others too were drawn by the unnerving perfume, but only one of them, the same with which Hook had fought his great battle, was a worthy competitor. This hunter drove off two, while two others, game but neophytes, were glad enough that Hook's impatience would not permit him to follow and kill. Then the battle between the two champions fled inland, and was a tactical marvel, but Hook lodged the neck-breaking blow as they dropped past the treetops. The blood had already begun to pool on the gray, fallen foliage as Hook flapped up between branches, too spent to cry his victory. Yet his hunger would not let him rest until, on the second day, he drove the female to ground in a strange river canyon.

When the two fledglings of this second brood had been driven from the nest and Hook had returned to his own range, he was not only complete, but supreme. He slept without concealment on his bare limb, and did not open his eyes when in the night the heavy-billed cranes coughed in the shallows below him.

THE TURNING point of Hook's career came in the autumn, when the brush in the canyons rustled dryly and the hills, mowed close by the cattle, smoked under the wind as if burning. One midafternoon Hook rode the wind diagonally across the river mouth. His great eyes, focused for small things stirring in the dust and leaves, overlooked the large, slow movement of the farmer rising from the brush and lifting the two black eyes of his shotgun. Too late Hook saw and swerved. The surf muffled the reports, and, nearly without sound, Hook felt the minute whips of the first shot, and the astounding, breath-breaking blow of the second.

Beating his good wing, tasting the blood that quickly swelled into his beak, he tumbled off with the wind and struck into the thickets on the far side of the river mouth. The branches tore him. Wild with rage, he thrust up and clattered his beak, challenging, but when he had fallen over twice, he knew that the trailing wing would not carry, and then heard the boots of the hunter among the stones in the riverbed, and, seeing him loom at the edge of the bushes, crept back among the thickest brush and was still. When he saw the boots pause before him, he reared back, his beak open but soundless, his great eyes hard and very shining. The boots passed on.

When Hook could hear nothing but the surf and the wind in the thicket, he let the sickness and shock overcome him. The fine film of the inner lid dropped over his big eyes. His heart beat frantically, so that it made the plumage of his shot-aching breast throb. But this was nothing compared to the lightning of pain in his left shoulder, where the shot had shattered the airy bones so the pinions could not be lifted. Yet, when a sparrow lit in the bush over him, Hook's eyes flew open again, hard and challenging, his good wing was lifted, and his beak strained open. The startled sparrow darted piping out over the river.

Throughout two days and three nights Hook remained stationary, enduring his sickness. At midday of the third day he was so weak that his good wing also trailed to prop him upright, and his eyes were lusterless. But his wounds were hardened and he felt the return of hunger. Beyond his shelter he heard the gulls flying in great numbers and crying their joy. From the fringe of the river came the ecstatic bubblings and chirpings of the small birds.

With the aid of his hunger, and on the crutches of his wings, Hook came down to stand in the sun beside the beach. Through the white foam writing of surf on sand the long-billed pipers twinkled in bevies, escaping each wave, then racing down after it to plunge their fine drills into the minute double holes where the sand crabs bubbled. Among the stones at the foot of the cliff, small red and green crabs made a little, continuous rattling and knocking. The cliff swallows glittered and twanged on aerial forays.

The afternoon began auspiciously. One of two gulls which came squabbling above him dropped a freshly caught fish to the sand. Quickly Hook was upon it. Gripping it, he raised his good wing and cocked his head with open beak at the many gulls which had circled down at once toward the fall of the fish. The gulls sheered off, cursing raucously. Left alone on the sand, Hook devoured the fish and, after resting in the sun, withdrew again to his shelter.

IN THE succeeding days, between rains, he foraged on the beach. He learned to kill and crack the small green crabs. Along the edge of the river mouth, he found the drowned bodies of mice and squirrels and even sparrows. He grew stronger slowly, but the shot sail continued to drag. Often, at the choking thought of soaring and striking and the good, hot-blood kill, he strove to take off, but only the one wing came up, winnowing with a hiss, and drove him over onto his side in the sand. After these futile trials he would rage and clatter. But gradually he learned that he could not fly, that his life must be that of the discharged nestling again. Denied the joy of space, the joy of battle and killing—the bloodlust—became his whole concentration. It was his hope, as he charged feeding gulls, that they would turn and offer battle, but they never did. The sandpipers, at his approach, fled peeping or, like a quiver of arrows shot together, streamed out over the surf in a long curve.

Hook's shame, and hunger too, began to keep him awake at night.

When he became aware that the gulls slept at night in flocks on the sand, each with one leg tucked under him, evil delight filled him at the thought of protracted striking among them.

There was only half of a sick moon in the sky on the night when he managed to stalk into the center of the sleeping gulls. This was light enough, but so great was his vengeful pleasure that there broke from him a shrill scream of challenge as he first struck. Without the power of flight behind it, the blow was not murderous, and this newly discovered impotence made Hook crazy, so that he screamed again and again as he struck and tore at the felled gull. He slew the one, but was twice knocked over by its heavy flounderings, and all the others rose above him, weaving and screaming in the thin moonlight, to settle elsewhere, beyond his pitiful range. He was left alone beside the single kill. It was a disappointing victory. He fed with lowering spirit.

Thereafter he stalked silently. At sunset he would watch where the gulls settled along the miles of beach, and after dark he would come like a sharp shadow among them and drive with his hook on all sides of him. In his best night he killed five, but his ire was so great that he could eat little. It was not the joyous, controlled hunting anger of a sane hawk, but something which made him dizzy and left him unsatisfied with any kill.

One day, when he had very nearly struck a gull while driving it from a gasping yellowfin, the gull's wing rapped against him and he was knocked over. He flurried awkwardly in the sand to regain his feet, but his mastery of the beach was ended. Seeing him, in clear sunlight, struggling after the chance blow, the gulls returned about him in a flashing cloud, circling and pecking on the wing. Hook's plumage showed quick little jets of irregularity here and there. He was forced to turn and dance awkwardly on the sand, trying to clash bills with each tormentor. Again he fell sideways. Before he could right himself he was bowled over, and was struck three times by three successive gulls, shrieking their flock triumph.

Finally he managed to roll to his breast, and to crouch, only his snake head, with its now silent scimitar, erect. One great eye blazed under its level brow, but where the other had been was a shallow hole from which thin blood trickled. In this crouch, by short stages, stopping to turn and drive the gulls up repeatedly, he dragged into the river canyon and under the stiff cover of the bitter-leafed laurel. There the gulls left him, soaring up with great clatter of their valor. Till nearly sunset, Hook, broken-spirited and enduring his hardening eye socket, heard them celebrating over the waves.

When his will was somewhat replenished and his empty eye socket had stopped twitching, Hook ventured from the protective lacings of his thicket. He knew fear again, and the challenge of his remaining eye was once more strident, as in adolescence. He dared not return to the beaches, and with a new weak hunger, the home hunger, made his way by short hunting journeys back to the wild wheat slopes and the crisp oaks. There was in Hook an unwonted sensation now, that of the ever neighboring possibility of death.

At first the familiar surroundings of the bend in the river and the tree with the dead limb to which he could not ascend aggravated his humiliation, but in time, forced to live cunningly and half starved, he lost much of his savage pride. At the first flight of a strange hawk over his realm he was wild at his helplessness, and kept spinning in the grass like a small, feathered dervish to keep the hateful beauty of the wind rider in sight. But in the succeeding weeks, as one after another coasted his beat, his resentment declined and the second of his great hungers was gone. He had no longer the true lust to kill, no joy of battle, but only the poor desire to fill his belly.

Then truly he lived in the wheat and the brush like a ground owl, ridden with ground lice, dusty or muddy, ever half starved, forced to sit for hours by small holes for petty and unsatisfying kills. Only once during the final months before his end did he make a kill where the breath of danger recalled his valor, and then the danger was such as a hawk with wings and eyes would scorn. Waiting beside a gopher hole, surrounded by the high yellow grass, he saw the head emerge, and struck, and was amazed that there writhed in his clutch the neck and dusty coffin skull of a rattlesnake. Holding his grip, Hook saw the great, thick body slither up after, the tip an erect, strident blur, and writhe on the dirt of the gopher's mound. The weight of the snake pushed Hook about, and once threw him down, and the rising and falling whine of the rattles made the moment terrible, but the gaping, vaulted mouth could not reach him. When Hook replaced the grip of his beak with the grip of his talons, and was free to strike again and again at the base of the head, the struggle was over.

THE RAINS returned, and then the season of love and the nesting season, leaving Hook's love hunger shriveled in him. It was during another long period of drought, with Hook starved on dry and fleshless kills, that one night his weary hunting brought him again close to the chicken farm. In the dark he stood outside the wire of the run. The scent of fat and blooded birds reached him from the shelter, and also within the enclosure was water. At the breath of the water, Hook's gorge contracted, and his tongue quivered and clove in its groove of horn. But there was the wire. He stalked its perimeter and found no opening. He beat it with his good wing, wrenched at it with his beak in many places, but could not tear it. Finally, in a fury, he leaped at it, clawed up the wire, and tumbled within.

First he drank at the chill metal trough hung for the chickens. Then he walked stiffly, to stalk down the scent. He trailed it up the runway. Then there was the stuffy, body-warm air, full of soft rustlings as his talons clicked on the board floor. The thick white shapes showed faintly in the darkness. Hook struck quickly, driving a hen to the floor with one blow, its neck broken. He leaped the still pulsing body, and tore it. The rich, streaming blood was overpowering to his dried senses, his starved, leathery body. After a few swallows the flesh choked him. In his rage he struck down another hen. The urge to kill took him again, as on that night on the beach. Clattering, he struck again and again. The henhouse was suddenly filled with the squawking and helpless rushing and buffeting of the terrified, brainless fowls.

Hook reveled in mastery. Here was game big enough to offer weight against a strike, and yet unable to soar away from his blows. When the hens finally discovered the outlet and streamed into the yard to run around the fence, beating and squawking, Hook followed them, scraping down the incline, clumsy and joyous. In the yard, the cock, a bird as large as he and much heavier, found him out and gave valiant battle. In the dark, and both earthbound, there was little skill, but blow upon blow, and only chance parry. While the duel went on, a dog began to bark, running back and forth along the fence on one side. A light flashed on in the farmhouse.

Enthralled by his old battle joy, Hook knew only the burly cock before him. The farmer, with his gun and lantern, was already at the gate when the finish came. The great cock leaped to jab with his spurs, and, toppling forward as he fell, was struck and extinguished. Blood had loosened Hook's throat. Shrilly he cried his triumph. It was a thin and exhausted cry, but within him as good as when he shrilled in midair over the plummeting descent of a fine foe in his best spring.

The light from the lantern partially blinded Hook. He essayed the fence, and, on the second try, in his desperation, was out. But in the open dust the dog was on him, circling, dashing in, snapping. The farmer, who at first had not fired because of the chickens, now did not fire because of the dog, and, when he saw that the hawk was unable to fly, relinquished the sport to the dog, holding the lantern up in order to see better. His wife, in a stained wrapper, joined him hesitantly, but watched, fascinated and a little horrified. Courageous and cruel death, however it may afterward sicken the one who has watched it, is impossible to look away from.

In the circle of the light, Hook turned to keep the dog in front of him. His one eye gleamed with malevolence. Each time the dog pounced, Hook stood ground, raising his good wing, and, at the closest approach, hissed furiously and at once struck. Hit and ripped twice by the whetted horn, the dog recoiled more quickly from several subsequent jumps, and, infuriated by his own cowardice, began to bark wildly.

"Oh, kill the poor thing," the woman begged.

But the man encouraged the dog again, saying, "Sic him; sic him."

The dog rushed bodily. Unable to avoid him, Hook was bowled down, snapping and raking. When the dog leaped away, Hook could not rise to use his talons.

Once again the dog charged, this time throwing the weight of his forepaws against Hook's shoulder and furiously worrying the feathered bulk. Hook's neck went limp, and between his gaping clappers came only a faint chittering, as from some small kill of his own in the grasses.

In this last conflict, however, there had been some minutes of the supreme fire of the hawk whose three hungers are perfectly fused in the one will; enough to burn off a year of shame.

Between the great sails the light body lay caved and perfectly still. The dog, smarting from his cuts, came to the master and was praised. The woman, joining them slowly, looked at the great wingspread, her husband raising the lantern that she might see it better.

"Oh, the brave bird," she said.

THE DESERT FLOWER

OLAF RUHEN

Olaf Ruhen

I NEVER SEE the parakeelya spread its dainty lace of cool rose-lilac flower-cups over the scorching rust-coloured stones of the Australian inland, or the orange-pink of its desert sand, but I think of Lacey Soak and the family that lived there, gambling their living and their lives against the chance of the waters failing.

I was there just twice, and I have never forgotten them. The tall, gaunt and silent cattleman MacDonnel, his silent, grey and pudding-faced wife, even the crippled ailing child were figures common enough. It was the girl who blossomed like the parakeelya. She was strangely like the parakeelya blossom, with her flower-face and her thin limbs, and the way she was rooted, as the parakeelya seems always rooted, in an alien soil.

And perhaps there was another less physical resemblance too; for the parakeelya spells life, and at the same time it spells death. So succulent are the finger-length leaves that cattle can feed and fatten on them when there is no water anywhere. They can travel miles from the waterholes and never feel thirst; and then there comes a time when the parakeelya is finished, and, panic-stricken, they look for water; but there is no water anywhere and they die in the dry lands: big well-nourished beasts, they stumble and fall and perish in an agony mercifully fast.

It happens often. It happens every year; but the sweet drifts of blossoms that paint the whole land in beauty are joy to the cattleman nevertheless; they spell money in his pocket, and he is only dimly aware of the menace in their impermanence, the menace of unalloyed goodness that has no lasting power. I've eaten parakeelya myself. It carries a poison so they say, and its taste is bitter on a man's tongue; but when that tongue is dry in your mouth, rasping against dry teeth, and your saddle canteen is empty, a few parakeelya leaves can evoke the blessed relief of flowing saliva, and carry you on to the waters.

The first time I came through Lacey Soak it was a season of rain, with pools of water here and there in the normally dry riverbeds, and the desert everywhere safe for travelling. That was why I was there. I had delivered the cattle in the south, sold most of my plant of horses, and sent the four native stockmen back to their own country by air. Now I was travelling fast with half a dozen horses I didn't want to part with and, because the water was so plentiful, cutting across country away from the meandering stock route. Besides, I like new country. I always want to see the other side of the next hill.

I was riding through a carpet of parakeelya blossoms, and stiff, butter-yellow everlastings; and the whitewood trees were flowering and I could smell the scented white snapdragons of the duboisia blooms, when I saw this smoke go up a mile or so on my right. It faded quickly enough; it was only a spinifex clump; but as soon as it had died another went up in exactly the same place. I thought there might have been aborigines there signalling to one another; and rode on; but when the third fire rose I headed the horses over and went to find out about it; and not long before I reached there I cut the tracks of a single horse.

Alongside the burnt grass there was a man on the ground. He was on his back, propped up on his elbows, watching me.

"A man can be lucky," he said when I got near. "I saw your dust. I've got a broken leg, kid. You'll have to help me in."

"Your horse lit out?" I asked, though it was obvious enough. He must have thought so, for he just grunted.

He was a tall man, but he looked weak, some ways, not frail, but ineffective. I wouldn't have bet on his horse-sense. He was dark-complected, and hadn't shaved for a few days, and his grey hair showed through a tear in the crown of his felt hat. His shirt had patches over the patches, very neatly made; but his boots were worn beyond saving. So he was not a man who could look after his gear, but somewhere, I guessed, there was a woman doing all she could for him. He didn't seem to want to say more, and after I'd waited awhile I asked him straight.

"What happened?"

"Took a shot at a snake. Young horse. Not trained to the rifle. Threw me and bolted." The rifle was there, near him.

He was true to his looks. He'd been acting silly, and I let him know that I thought so.

"This is a hell of a place to train a young horse when you're by yourself."

"A man can make mistakes, kid."

"Bob," I said. "Bob Corcoran." I outgrew that "kid" stuff years ago, but at nineteen I've still got a young kind of a face, I suppose. Some people do.

"You don't like being called 'kid'?"

"Would you? I've been old enough to do a man's work for years. I'm old enough to pack you in to where you're going. Can you sit a saddle?"

"I reckon. If you can strap me up."

When I'd rigged a splint to make his leg easy I put my palomino through one of her circus tricks and sat her down so it was easy to get him in the saddle. I rode a sorrel gelding I had, bareback, for I'd shipped my spare gear with the men. We took four hours to reach Lacey Soak, and he didn't say more than fourteen words the whole way. He was in some pain, but the reason he didn't talk, I thought, was that he didn't have anything to say.

His homestead was like a hundred others I've seen, an unlined shed of corrugated iron with earthen floors standing perhaps a hundred yards from the tank, the windmill and the watering-troughs of an artesian bore. Iron partitions divided the house into four rooms. There were no connecting doors; instead they all opened onto a kind of veranda, a structure of poles supporting a framework that kept the worst of the afternoon sun from the front wall of the house. Iron cots had been pulled out into the open. Such houses were too hot for sleeping in in summer.

This homestead had something else: a pitiful attempt at a garden; but of the flowers that had been planted the survivors had only a pathetic, small hold on life. I supposed that the water with which they had been drenched was carrying too high a concentration of salts; later, when I dismounted and gulped down a pint or so from the canvas waterbag hanging in the shade, I was sure of it. A little distance from the house some athel pines from Arabia and parkinsonias from Africa had been planted for shade, and were beginning to thrive. For half a mile beyond, no other tree had survived the attentions of the cattle brought to the water; the plain was barren, and it, with the pathetic garden plots, made a sorry contrast to the country I had been riding through, with its blaze of native herbage, the cassias and the desert willows and the casuarinas and the high grained heads of the grasses, the spinifex and the neverfail.

There was a dove-grey carpet flecked with rose spread over some acres of the ground near the troughs, and as we rode up and my loose horses made for the water it lifted, changing like a miracle into a sky-filling flock of screaming galahs.

"Bloody parrots," said MacDonnel.

A grey woman was at the doorway, crying out "Mac, Mac" in surprised delight. He did not answer.

"He's hurt, Mrs. MacDonnel," I replied. "He's broken a leg."

She released her hands from the folds of her apron and came running.

"It's all right," I said. "Steady a minute. I'll get him down. The horse won't scare, but take it easy."

There was no doubt about it, she was almost in a panic. I led the palomino as close as I could to the doorway, and took the bridle-rein up close and sat her down there. After that it was easy to stand by MacDonnel's bad leg and get his arm round my shoulder.

"This way," his wife said, and opened the second door.

There was a double-bed in there, a blanketed mattress on an iron bedstead. There was one cheap rug on the earth floor beside the bed, a small chest of drawers standing unevenly by the iron wall, two trunks and two kitchen chairs. It was a room that matched the patched and over-patched shirt and denim trousers MacDonnel had been wearing. The partitions stopped short of the roof and there was no ceiling, but the room was like an oven. For that matter there was no coolness anywhere.

"Deborah's in the kitchen. She'll get you something to eat. I'll come in a little while," the woman told me.

The leg was splinted all right. There was little that needed doing, but a woman fussing makes a sick man comfortable, so I went to the room at the chimney end of the house. There was a table set with clean but ragged linen and standing on the floor between two rough benches; there was a bright-coloured grocer's calendar hung against the black iron walls; there was a child lying on his back on a sofa playing with a braid of kangaroo-hide; and there was a girl standing near the stove, with wide and frightened eyes, with spindly arms and legs and a skin as pallid as though she lived in a city cellar.

"MacDonnel's hurt?" she asked. Though it was just a simple question she somehow managed to make it sound aggressive.

"He'll be all right," I told her. "Give him a month he'll be as good as new."

"A month?"

"Broken leg."

"We can call the doctor in the morning." There was a battery-powered transmitter on a bench near the door. Even the poorest homesteads had them.

"Just as well," I nodded.

I don't get to see many girls, the way I travel; I guess I looked at her too much. She was like a fragile scented flower, and she was the only thing beautiful in that bare and ugly house. As soon as my meal was on the table she picked up the child and left the room. He was too big for her to carry, but she did it effortlessly.

The woman offered me a bed that night, but instead I threw down my swag near the water-tank. A tarp and a blanket is all a man needs, and I sleep better on the ground. But she brought out a pillow for my head, and took my roll of clothes inside. In the morning my shirts

THE DESERT FLOWER / Olaf Ruhen

were hanging on the line, and one or two rips that had been there for a long time were patched, and all the missing buttons were replaced.

I would have pulled out, but I happened to notice that the water-tank was half empty and the windmill pump not working because of a couple of sheared bolts at the top of the shaft. I poked around and found what was needed, and fixed that; but by that time I'd seen a lot of things that needed a man's hand, things that the women couldn't manage, and in the end I stayed three weeks. In mid-morning, that first day, the doctor flew in, piloting an old-fashioned de Havilland. He taxied right up to the house, and he took the patient away with him when he left. So I felt obliged to stay for a day or two.

And I don't mind admitting I had the thought of getting to know Deborah better. So even though I'd imagined myself in a hurry I stayed and fixed the engine that drove the circular saw, and cut enough mulga wood and blackheart to keep the stove burning half the year, and cleaned the tank and troughs—it was a good time with so much surface water and parakeelya about—and fixed a lot of gear that needed it, and tightened down the roof where it had been lifted by the wind. And tried to get friendly with the girl.

But she was like a frightened wildcat that's found itself in a house and can't get away. She'd accept a good turn as a wild thing will accept food, warily, with a guarded gratitude that kept her still untouchable. I could call her "Deborah", but she never called me "Bob". It was the woman who spoke with me in the evenings and summoned me to meals.

"Why don't you want to be friendly, Deborah?" I asked her once; and she turned to me, surprised.

"I'm friendly," she said.

"Not so much."

She just looked at me with those big eyes dark in her pallid face and said nothing.

"You've never got much to say," I tried again. "We could be real friendly, you and I."

"Men are all the same," she said. "I came here to get away from them. I could live my life without seeing a man—I'd like to."

"You have to be fond of somebody, though."

260

"There's Freddie," she said. Freddie was the child.

"He'll be a man someday," I reminded her.

"Maybe. He doesn't stand too much of a chance, poor kid."

He was a fretful, ailing child with some weakness in his legs. I never did ask what was the matter with him, but he wasn't well. He played quietly in the house, in the heat; mostly lying on his back holding something in his hands, usually the half-plaited braid of shiny kangaroo leather.

"You've grown though," I said. "And you can't keep running away all your life."

"I'm not running," she snapped. "And it's my life." Her eyes were steady on me with that queer defensive look, bold and hesitant at the same time. "I've stopped running," she corrected herself after a pause, and she kicked aside a log of firewood that had fallen off the top of the filled box.

"Here?" I asked. "This is no place to stop. There's nothing here. You've run from nothing to nothing."

"Maybe I like this nothing better," she said, and then she didn't talk any more.

"She's had hard knocks, poor thing," Mrs. MacDonnel told me once.

"What happened?"

"I don't know. She's never told me. I don't know anything about her. She came to me a year ago. My sister, before she died, sent her on out to me; and she's worked for me ever since without a word of complaint. And she's good to Freddie. But if there's a man comes round the place she stands and shivers like a filly in a yard ablaze. As yourself, for example; not that you'd do her harm, a good lad like you, but you put her on edge. Or any other man. God knows what happened to her, but the one who did it deserves shooting."

"She doesn't mind your husband?"

"MacDonnel? Lord love you, no. He doesn't know she's there half the time, and she likes it that way. He's a good man, that man of mine. He's been unlucky; the luck's against him when it comes to making money, and he's a bit of a dreamer; he doesn't see when things are going wrong. But he's a good man. He takes no notice of her, nor she of him; though she'll do things for him. He never notices. He takes a power of looking after sometimes, but he doesn't know it himself. She doesn't mind that. And she likes to look to Freddie."

When the word came through on the radio that MacDonnel would soon be starting for home I rounded up my plant and left. I reined in as I passed the doorway, and the girl came and looked out, the child in her arms where she'd picked him up to take him somewhere. She didn't let him walk enough.

"Goodbye, Deborah," I called.

"You've been a help. Goodbye," she said, and she sounded friendly, but she didn't use my name.

She didn't use it the second time I saw her, and that was more than a year later. I'd been travelling all that time; I'd been travelling some lonely country; and there was many a night I lay back in my blankets and looked at the lake of darkness at the foot of the Milky Way that the natives called the Emu's Nest, and thought I could see the big dark frightened eyes of the girl from Lacey Soak stare back at me. And sometimes I wondered whether she was frightened of me, and sometimes whether it was just her fear that the mirror of her loneliness might be shattered.

You think all sorts of things if you lie down in the sharp-textured air of the desert night to watch its big bright stars, and sometimes the night will draw you up until you'd believe that you'd left the world behind, except that the drifting tang of wood-smoke and the smell of the night-horse nearby and the cattle a little beyond will tie you to reality. And I used to imagine myself at Lacey Soak, and think about the girl, and wonder if she would ever turn to meet the world waiting for her, and how; and just what her world would be when she'd accepted it, and whether she would find a true friend waiting for her, and how she would recognize him. I saw her as a kind of Sleeping Beauty and I wondered what would wake her. In all my wildest dreams I never would have guessed.

For in the end I rode a hundred miles out of my way, one season, to camp at Lacey Soak; and once again I found that I was needed. This time it was the woman. She was ill. She was worse than ill; she was dying; though she was the only one who knew.

I didn't see her when I came, but they must have told her I was there. The girl Deborah was still the same, silent and frightened. The child was bigger, but he was still sickly; he haunted the girl, and went after her wherever she moved. McDonnel was the same silent man I'd found disabled on the plain, and half his gear was out of order again. He didn't say much, even now he was well.

He spent most of his time in the bedroom with his wife, and I tried to talk to the girl, but she was as remote as the face I'd seen in the stars.

"I've been thinking of you, Deborah," I told her, and she looked at me sharply.

"You've had little to do, then."

"No, it's true. I've been thinking of you a lot."

"I dare say I can't stop you."

I wanted to say some more, but how could I? It didn't seem real to sit and watch that fragile beauty move around that harsh and ugly room; to know that though physically she was near, she was otherwise remote, that she walked in an invisible unbreakable shell as impenetrable as star-distance.

MacDonnel came into the room.

"She wants some paper and a pen," he said. He made no attempt to find them for himself, but just stood there, waiting for the girl to hand him what he needed.

"Paper?" she asked, not moving.

"Paper," he said. "Where's that paper I write orders on? And the pen?"

"Oh, yes."

She rummaged in a wooden box, one of a series stacked one above the other against the wall, with the openings outwards so they could be used for shelves, and she brought him a block of paper and a pen and an inkbottle.

"What's it for?" she asked, but he just shook his head as he went out.

He came back in a moment or two and sat with us. We were all silent; I was wishing I was outside, where the stars at least and the horses were company. We sat so long in silence I was ready to go when a knocking came on the partition wall. MacDonnel got up and answered it. He reappeared in a moment and beckoned the girl.

"She wants you," he said.

I was stretching out my legs when he came to the door again.

"You too," he said. "She asked for you."

She was greyer than ever propped up with pillows against the iron paint-chipped railings of the bedhead. She looked grey and tired, no longer pudding-faced, and older than I had remembered her.

"I want you to listen," she said to me and turned her face to the others.

"I want you all to listen. I'm going to die."

"Now, mother," MacDonnel said tenderly. It was the first time I had heard emotion in his voice. "The doctor will be here in the morning. We'll send for him at first light."

"You'd better tell him to bring the parson then," she said. "I'll not last so long."

I believed her. I'd seen men die, more than once; die of accidents, and one of a long illness; but it was an awesome thing to ride to this place from the wide surrounding desert, and to find a woman ready for death, and accepting it.

"But. . . ." MacDonnel was beginning.

"Listen to me," she said again.

"I want a Christian burial. I want the parson to come out here and bury me. But that's not the end. For when he goes there'll be you, MacDonnel, and young Freddie; and you, Deborah, and the lad will ride on. And I've been thinking of it these hours. You need a woman, MacDonnel, to look after you, and so does Freddie; and Deborah has a need for something of her own, a man and a home and the child. So I brought you in here, MacDonnel, to ask you if I die tonight, will you marry her?"

MacDonnel was staring at her, his mouth open, his face twisted between astonishment and despair. I looked past him to Deborah; her eyes were so big they seemed to pulse in the lamplight; she had put her hand to cover her mouth. She was sitting bolt upright on the edge of the wooden chair; I'd have expected her to leap up and run away. No one else was looking at her.

"If you want me to go happy, promise me you'll marry her," the grey woman said.

MacDonnel stood up and came to the bed.

"Maisie, dear," he said; and it was the first time I'd heard a name for her.

"You can do this one thing right, MacDonnel. Will you marry her?"

"All right, mother. If she'll have me."

I thought that the girl cried out then; a tiny cry out of a torment, but no one else seemed to notice. The woman on the bed turned to her.

"Deborah?"

She didn't move or speak.

"Will you marry him, Deborah?"

She put her hand down, and there were long seconds of silence while she seemed to struggle for a sound. Her mouth worked. She caught her breath. When she did speak the sound came abruptly, explosively. But it was "yes".

It satisfied the grey woman.

"All right. Then that's the beginning. You've a head on your shoulders, Deborah, and a heart too big for your body. But now I was thinking beyond, and it wouldn't be fit for you two to live here awhile and then go in to get married; so you'll make me this promise: that the parson that buries me shall marry you before he leaves."

We all stared at her.

"That's the way it's got to be," she said, and her voice was weak, but it was determined. "Promise me."

"All right, mother," MacDonnel said soothingly.

"Deborah?"

"Yes."

"Now as for neighbours they're far enough away. But as like as not the parson will never believe you if you tell him that this was a wish of mine," she said. "So I've written it all out here in my own hand and signed it; and you sign to show you agree, and young Bob will sign it for a witness, or else it will be thought to be something arranged between the two of you."

Her voice was clear, but the hand that reached for the paper on the box beside the bed shook and trembled, and MacDonnel jumped forward to help, but she had the paper in her hand before he could.

"Sign it all three of you, where I've written it out, and I'll go happy," she said.

MacDonnel signed like a man in a trance. The girl took the paper from him and put her name to it firmly and quickly, and passed it to me.

It read, "It is my last dying wish that my husband shall marry Deborah Knight, and that the parson that buries me shall marry them without delay, so that they will be married in the same hour and in proof of this their names shall appear below mine and it shall be witnessed by R. Corkran. And this is my dearest wish and they shall do this in honour of my memory."

She had signed it, and the other two names were below. She had spelt my name wrong; but I signed it with my usual "Bob Corcoran" and then put the wrong spelling in brackets beneath.

"You'll wait for the parson," she said to me. "He might take convincing." Her voice was suddenly very weak and halting.

Then she said, "Bring Freddie in," and I slipped out of the room ahead of the girl.

In the early morning I saw MacDonnel carrying a pick and a shovel. I got up and pulled my boots on and went over to him as he started to dig.

"Not here," I said. "It's not a good place. Leave it to me. I'll fix it all."

I didn't ask him was she dead; I knew it would happen the way she had said, and it did. They were married by the parson that buried her; and the doctor who'd flown the plane out stood with me as witness; and the earth was still crumbling down from the pile over the grave I'd dug beneath the parkinsonias, where the cattle wouldn't trample it.

But the last time I went to town I saw Deborah again, and the child was with her, and her eyes were serene and confident. She had grown in some way; she was a woman complete. She didn't see me; she was too full of her business in the town and I thought it better to leave it that way; for there's nothing now would take me back to Lacey Soak.

And I've thought it over with the stars and tossed it this way and that; for I marvel that the weak and awkward man and the even weaker child should furnish the food for her final growth. It seemed an unlikely place to find such food, or love, or safety. It was a place to find nothing, except their need of her.

Perhaps that was it. I had no need of her, anyway. Sometimes, thinking back, I see her face yet in the dark place amongst the stars; and it is a glory and a wonder to see the frightened eyes turn free and confident; and I think, too, of the moment of revelation that was the grey woman's, before she died. As when I ride amongst the blossoming parakeelya I marvel at the way its frail daintiness thrives in the blazing heat, on the harsh and arid sand.

THE REUNION
MARGARET DRABBLE

Margaret Drabble

THERE MUST HAVE been a moment at which she decided to go down the street and round the corner and into the café, a moment dividing innocence from guilt, a moment of weakness, of falling: for at first she was walking along quite idly, quite innocently, with no recollection or association in her head but the dimmest faintest palest shadow of long past knowledge, and yet somehow, within ten yards, twenty yards perhaps, of that innocence, the distance of two frontages of those ancient crumbling small tall buildings, now so uniformly shoddy warehouses, she had made up her mind that she would go and have her lunch there in that place where they had always had their lunch together, that place which she had not seen since their parting. Or no, she said to herself (excusing herself, embarking on the casuistry of deceit, already diminishing any possible responsibility for her act)—they had not had their lunch there *always*, they had had it there merely occasionally, once a fortnight or so over that long and lovely year; and the first time that they had gone there had had no significance at all, for it was simply that being in such an area, an area that they did not know well, they had had lunch in the only place that they could find. And they had gone back there, not because they liked it, but because it was the kind of place where nobody that they knew would ever go, although it was at the same time not impossibly inconvenient, not so very far from Holborn, where both of them could find good reasons to be. They had felt safe in there, as safe as they could ever feel, and yet they did not have to feel that they had been driven into grotesque and undignified precautions. They had found the place themselves by chance, and they did not think that anyone they knew could chance, so aimlessly, to walk that way.

And now, after so long, after three years, she had found herself there again, almost on the threshold, and at lunch time too. She was hungry. There is nothing more to it than that, she said to herself, as she found herself walking, with so little conscious intention, towards it: I happened to be near, and wanting some lunch, and the fact that I wanted some lunch merely reminded me of this place, the only place within walking distance. She had done enough walking: she had never liked walking: it had been quite enough of a walk from the tube station to the place where they had made her new tooth. She ran her tongue over her new front tooth, reassuringly, slightly ashamed of the immense relief that she felt at being once more presentable, no longer disfigured by that humiliating gap: being beautiful, she had made much of caring little for her beauty, and was always profoundly disturbed by the accidents which from time to time brought her face to face with her own mirrored vanity—the inconvenient pimple, the unperceived smudge on the cheek, the heavy cold. And that lost tooth had been something of a test case, ever since she had had it knocked out while still at school. Her dentist had made for her the most elaborate and delicate bridge, so that not even she herself would ever have to endure the sight of herself toothless, but the night before last she had fallen downstairs after a party and broken it. She had rung up her dentist in the morning, and made a dreadful fuss, and he had promised her a temporary plate to last her until he had made her a new elaborate and delicate bridge: and when he had told her the name of the place that she should go to collect the plate, she had noticed in herself a small, hardly noticeable flicker of recollection. He went on explaining to her, obliging yet irritable, "You've got that then, Mrs. Harvey, 82, St. Luke's Street? You go to Old Street station, then turn right . . ." and she heard herself saying, "Oh yes, St. Luke's Street, that's just off Tunstall Square." As though anybody might be expected to know about Tunstall Square. And he had agreed, without surprise, about its proximity to Tunstall Square, and then had continued to explain to her about the fact that he was doing her a special favour, and that she should suitably express her gratitude to the man at the works, in view of the shortness of the notice: and she had duly expressed it to the man at the works when he had handed her, ten minutes ago, her new tooth, all wrapped up somewhat brutally she thought in a brown paper bag. She had been effusive, in the gratitude, and the man had looked at her blankly and said oh that was quite all right, no trouble at all.

And then she had come out, and walked along this street. And as she paused at the café door, she knew that she had been thinking of him and of that other year all the time, that she could not very well have avoided the thought of him, amongst so much familiar scenery. There they had sat in the car, and kissed and endlessly discussed the impossibility of kissing: there they had stood by that lamp-post, transfixed, unable to move. The pavement seemed still to bear the marks of their feet. And yet it was all so long ago, so thoroughly slaughtered and decayed. She did not care at all: it was two years since she had cared, more than two years since she had suffered, since she had suffered more for the loss of him than for the old tedium of her life, and the old anxieties, which had existed before him, and which would exist forever, because they were what she was made of. Inadequacy, loneliness, panic, vanity, decay. These words she said to herself, because such words, in their vague grand size, consoled her.

Though she was not unhappy. She was content, she was occupied, she had got her tooth back, everything was under control; the evening would be fine now that the horror and strain of pretending not to mind that one had a tooth missing had been so successfully averted. She had quite enjoyed going to that odd place where they made teeth: it was the kind of place that she enjoyed seeing, and she would even be able to tell people about her panic about her tooth, now that the real panic was truly over. And perhaps in a way it made her almost happy, to be back in this place, to find how thoroughly dead it all was, how most efficiently she had died. She saw no ghosts of him here: for a year after their parting she had seen him on every street corner, in every passing car, in shapes of head and hand and forms of movement, but now he was nowhere any more, not even here. For as long as she had imagined that she saw him, she had imagined that he had remembered: that those false ghosts had been in some way the projected shadows of his love: but now she knew that surely they had both forgotten. Remembering him, she thought that this was what she knew.

She pushed open the door and went in. It looked the same. Nothing had changed. She realised that she had been imagining that it must look different, had been preparing herself for heaven knows what ugly transformations and redecorations, but it looked the same. The sameness of it made her pause, took her breath away, though even as she stood there she said to herself: how foolish to imagine it takes my breath away, for I am breathing quite regularly, quite normally. It is simply that I have become, for an instant, aware of the fact that I am breathing.

She went to the side of the room that they had always favoured, the wall side, away from the door and the window, and sat on the corner table, which they had always taken when they could. She sat there, and looked down at the red-veined Formica table top, with its cluster of salt pot, pepper pot, mustard pot, sauce bottle, and ash tray: the salt pot was of thick-ribbed Perspex, and she remembered the exact common mounting scallops of its edges. She took it in her hand, and felt it. She did not often lunch now in places where such objects might be found. Then she looked up at the dark yellow ceiling, with its curiously useless trelliswork hung with plastic lemons and bananas: and then at the wall, the wall papered as before in a strange delicate dirty flowered print, with paper badly cut, and joining badly at the seams, and broken up by protruding obsolescent functionless bits of woodwork, dating from former decorative schemes. On the wall hung the only thing that was different. It was a calendar, a gift from a garage, and the picture showed an Alpine hut in snowy mountains, for all that the month was May. In their day, the calendar had been one donated by a fruit juice firm, and they had seen it through three seasons: she recalled the anguish with which she had seen its leaves turn, more relentless even than those leaves falling so dreadfully and ominously from more natural trees, and she recalled the appalling photograph of their parting, which had portrayed an autumn evening in a country garden, with an old couple sitting by their creeper-covered door. They had both been insatiable, merciless deliverers of ultimatums, the one upon the other, and she had selected in her own soul that month, and one day of that month—the twenty-third, she knew it even now, the twenty-third—for her final, last, unalterable decision; she had watched it come up upon them, she had sat at this table, or perhaps after all not at this one but at the one next to it, and she had said, "Look, that's it, on the twenty-third, that's it, and I mean it this time." She wondered if he had known that she had meant it: whether an indefinable resolution in her, so small that she did not trust it, had somehow communicated itself to him, so that he had known that for this one last time it was for real. Because he had taken her at her word. It was the first time that she had not relented, nor he persisted; each other time that he had left her forever, a phone call had been enough to regain him, and each time she had left him, she had sat by the telephone biting her nails and waiting for it to ring. But this time he did not ring, and after a couple of days she ceased to leave the receiver off when nobody was looking. She said to herself from time to time, perhaps in those two days he rang, and rang repeatedly, rang every hour and found me perpetually engaged, and knew what I had done, and knew that at last I meant what I had said: but she knew that she would never never know, and that for her it was all the same if he had rung once, or twenty times, or never. It had happened, after so many false attempts, it had finally happened: preparations for death had been in a way like death itself, and she supposed that was why they must so incessantly have made them, more merciful to each other than they knew, for the experience of losing him, so often endured in imagination, had solidified from imagination into reality so slowly, with such obdurate slow accretions, that there was no point at which she said, Look, it is done and done for good. There had always seemed a point at which it might be undone. But not now, not now. She looked at the snowy hut upon the wall, at the icy mountains and the frozen glaciers, and she thought, Ah well, there was a point at which I feared we did not have it in us to part. And a kind of admiration for her past self possessed her, a respect for a woman who had been so thoroughly capable of so sizeable a renunciation.

The menu, when it was brought to her, had not altered much. She was glad of this, for without her glasses she doubted whether she would have made much of its faded violet overduplicated manuscript. Though she never knew why she bothered to read menus, for she always with unfailing regularity wherever she was ate the same lunch: she always had cheese omelette and chips. So she ordered her meal, and then sat back to wait. Usually, whenever left alone in a public place, she would read, and through habit she propped her book up against the sauce bottle and rested her eyes upon it, but she did not look at the words. Nor was she dwelling entirely upon the past, for a certain pleasurable anxiety about her evening's engagement was stealing most of her attention, and she found herself wondering whether she had adequately prepared her piece, and whether David Rathbone would offer to drive her home, and whether her hair would look all right, for the last time she had been on the television there had been a girl in the make-up place who had messed it about dreadfully, and cut bits off her fringe, and generally made her look like some quite other kind of person. And most of all, she wondered if she ought to wear her grey skirt. She was really worried about the grey skirt question: all the anxiety that had previously attached itself to the importance of getting her tooth in time had now transferred itself to the skirt, for although she liked it very much she was not at all sure that it was not just a very very little bit tight. If it wasn't, then it was perfect, for it was the kind of thing that she always looked good in: but just supposing that it was? There was nobody in the whole world who could tell her, who could decide for her this delicate point: she had even asked her husband about it, the night before, and he had looked at it and nodded his head and said it looked lovely, and she knew exactly how much and how little that meant.

There was nobody but herself with the finesse, with the information to decide such a point, and she could not decide; and she was just saying to herself, the very fact that I'm *worrying* about it must mean that it must be too tight after all, or the thought of it's being too tight wouldn't have crossed my mind, would it? when she saw him.

What was really most shocking about it was the way that they noticed each other at exactly the same moment, simultaneously, without a chance of turning away or in any way managing the shock. They were both such managers, but this time they had not a chance. Their eyes met, and they both jerked, beyond hope of dissimulation.

"Oh Christ," he said, after a second or two, and stood there and went on looking at her.

And she felt at such a loss, sitting there with her book propped up against the tomato ketchup, and her head full of skirts and false teeth, that she said, hurriedly, throwing away in panic what might to such as her have been really quite a moment,

"Oh Lord, oh well, since you're there, do sit down, I mean you might as well sit down," and she moved up the small two-seater bench, pushing her bag along, losing a shoe, for she had kicked them off under the table, inelegantly dragging her jacket out of his way, closing up her book with a rapid snap, averting her eyes, confused, deprecating, unable to look.

And he sat down by her, and then said quite suddenly and intimately, as though perfectly at home with her after so many years of silence, as though perfectly confident that she would share whatever he might have to think or say,

"Oh Lord, my darling, what a dreadful dreadful surprise, I don't think I shall ever recover."

"Oh, I don't know," she said, as though she too had discovered exactly where she was, "Oh, I don't know. One gets over these things quite quickly. I feel better already, don't you?"

"Why, yes, I suppose I do," he said. "I feel better now I'm sitting down. I thought I was going to faint, standing there and looking at you."

"Well," she said, "it wasn't quite a fair test of me, was it, because after all I was sitting down already. I mean, nobody ever fainted sitting down, surely?"

"Oh, I'm sure it has been done," he said. "If you'd fainted, I'd have had to put your head between your knees. And God knows how we'd have managed that at one of these tables. I'd forgotten how cramped it all was. But we used to like that, I suppose, didn't we?"

"Yes, I suppose we did," she said.

"Even though you didn't faint," he said, "didn't you feel some sort of slight tremor? Surely you must have done?"

"It's hard to tell," she said, "when one's sitting down. It isn't a fair test. Even of tremors."

"No," he said, "no."

Then they were silent for a moment or two, and then she said, very precisely and carefully, offering her first generous signal of intended retreat,

"I suppose that what *is* odd, really, is that we haven't come across one another before?"

"Oh, I don't know," he said, with equal, disappointing neutrality. "Where would we have met? It's not as though we ever belonged to what you might call the same world."

"No," she said, "no, I suppose not."

"Have you ever been back here before?" he asked.

"No, never," she said. "Have you?"

"Yes," he said. "Yes, I have. And if you had been back, you might have seen me. I looked for you."

"You're lying," she said quickly, elated, looking at him for the first time since he had sat down by her, and then looking away again quickly, horrified by the dangerous and appalling proximity of his head, but nevertheless keeping her nerve, being more or less sure that he was in fact lying.

"No, I'm not," he said. "I came here, and I looked for you. I was sure that you would come."

"It's a safe lie," she said, "like all your lies. A lie I could never catch you out in. Unless I had been here, looking for you, and simply hadn't wanted to admit it."

"And even then," he said, "we might merely have missed each other."

"Yes," she conceded.

"But," he said with conviction, "you weren't here at all. I know you weren't here. *I* was here, *I* came, but you didn't. You were faithless, weren't you, my darling?"

"Faithless?"

"You forgot me quicker than I forgot you, didn't you? When you had so promised to remember."

"Oh," she said, wondering if she should admit so much, but unable to resist the ominous luxury of admission, "oh, I didn't forget you."

"Didn't you? How long did you remember me for?"

"Oh, how can one say?" she said. "After all, there are degrees of remembrance."

"Tell me," he said, "tell me. What harm can it do, to tell me now?"

She moved a little on the seat, away from him, but settling at the same time into a more comfortable pose of confidence: because she wanted to tell him, she had been waiting for years to tell him.

"I suffered quite horribly," she said. "Really quite horribly. That's what you want to hear, isn't it?"

"Of course it is," he said.

"Oh, I really did," she said. "I can't tell you. I cried, all the time, for weeks. For a month. For at least a month. And whenever the phone went, I started, I jumped as though I'd been shot. It was pathetic, it was ludicrous. In the end I had to invent some bloody silly story about waiting for a call about a job, though what job could ever have got anyone in such a state I can hardly imagine, and each time I answered and it wasn't you I could hardly speak, I could somehow hardly make the effort to speak. It's odd how people don't notice when one doesn't reply. I would stand there listening, and they would go on talking, and sometimes I would say yes or no, as I waited for them to ring off, and when they did ring off I don't think they'd even noticed I hadn't spoken. And then I would sit down and cry. Is that what you want me to say?"

"I want to hear it," he said, "but it can't, it can't be true."

"It's as true as that you came to this place to look for me," she said.

"I did come," he said.

"And I did weep," she said.

"Did you ever try to ring me?" he asked, then, unable to resist.

"No!" she said with some pride. "No, not once. I never tried, not once. I said I wouldn't, and I didn't."

"I rang you, once," he said.

"You didn't," she said, "you didn't," and became aware at that instant that her knees under the table were trembling; they were, quite unmistakably.

"I did," he said. "It was just over a year ago, and we'd just got back from a party, about three in the morning it was, and I rang you. But you didn't answer. He answered."

"Oh God," she said, "oh God. It's true, it's true, it's not a lie, because I remember it. Oliver said it was burglars. A Friday night. Wasn't it a Friday night?"

"Yes," he said, "my darling darling, it was. Did you think it might have been me?"

"I didn't think it could have been you," she said. "Not you, after so long a time. But I thought of you. When the phone rang and woke us, I thought of you, and when Oliver said there was no answer, I thought of you. Oh God, I can't tell you how I've had to stop myself ringing you, how I've sat there by the phone and lifted the receiver and dialled the first numbers of your number, and then stopped, and not let myself do it, and the receiver would be dripping with sweat when I put it down, but I stopped myself, I did stop myself."

"Oh," he said, "if you knew how I'd wanted you to ring."

"I did write to you once," she said. "But I couldn't bring myself to post it. But I'll tell you what I did, I typed out an envelope to you, and I put one of those circulars from that Poetry Club of mine into it, and I sent it off to you, because I thought at least it might create in you a passing thought of me. And I liked the thought of something from my house reaching your house. Though perhaps she threw it away before it even got to you."

"I remember it," he said. "I did think of you. But I didn't think you sent it, because the postmark was Croydon."

"Oh," she said, weakly. "You got it. You did get it. Oh Lord, how alarmingly faithful we have both been."

"Did you expect us not to be? We swore that we would be. Oh look, here's your lunch, are you still eating cheese omelettes every day; now that really *is* what I call alarming consistency. And I haven't even ordered. What shall I have, what about some Moussaka, it was always rather nice, in its own disgusting way. One Moussaka, please."

"I *like* cheese omelettes," she said. "And after all, I don't see why one shouldn't have the same lunch every day. I mean, most people always have the same breakfast, don't they? Nobody complains when people go on eating toast and marmalade, do they?"

"I wasn't complaining," he said. "I was just remarking. I like your habits, I always did. You don't think I've changed, do you?"

"How should I know?" she said, and ate her first mouthful. Then she put down her knife and fork, and said, reflectively,

"You know, from my point of view at least, the whole business was quite unnecessary. What I mean is, Oliver hadn't the faintest suspicion. The thought of you had never even crossed his mind. Which, considering how ludicrously careless we were, is quite astonishing. We could have carried on forever, and he'd never have known. He was far too preoccupied himself with his own affairs to notice. I got it all out of him in the end, and I forgave him very nicely, and do you know what he said at the end of it all, at the end of all my forgiveness? He said that he'd had his suspicions that I'd been carrying on at the time with Robert Bennington. Have you ever heard of such a thing? I was so horrified by the very idea that I flew into a terrible rage and defended myself so vehemently that I quite frightened him. I mean to say, Robert, what a choice that would have been, what a ghastly mistake that would have been. I was never so offended in my life. What a pleasure it was, all that virtuous indignation, it was like getting rid of a whole year's guilt. I can't tell you what a relief it was."

"Robert Bennington," he said, "Robert Bennington. Who was he? Was he that tall fellow in advertising, with that fat wife?"

"Oh," she said, "he's nobody, just nobody, I mean he's quite nice, but as for anyone thinking him more than quite nice . . ."

And she noticed as she spoke that her voice had taken on, somehow, as with age-old habit, those provocative, defensive tones in which they would always discuss others, other people, the stray characters with which they would decorate from time to time their charmed and passionate dialogue and she knew that he, in reply, would use that note of confident and yet in some way truly, dreadfully suspicious jealousy.

"I seem to remember," he said, sure enough, "that Robert

Bennington took you out to the cinema one evening, when Oliver was in Ireland. That was him, wasn't it?"

"You remember everything," she said.

"And you said that you thought of me when you were in the cinema, but you didn't, I know you didn't," he said.

"Oh, I did, I did," she protested. "I thought of you everywhere, and what better place to think of you than in the cinema, especially when with a dull fellow like Robert?"

"I thought you said he was quite nice," he said, and she started to say "Yes, he is quite nice", and then instead she started to laugh, and said,

"You are absurd, darling, it was Oliver that introduced that Robert motif, there's no need for *you* to start on it, especially so long after the event, I mean any concern you might now feel would be well and truly irrelevant."

"After what event?" he said, incurable.

"No event, there wasn't any event," she said, "the whole point of the story was that Oliver had got it so wrong, so pointlessly wrong; I mean suspecting Robert instead of you. . . ."

"It's no good," he said, "whatever you say, I simply can't prevent myself feeling annoyed that anyone might have had any reasons for thinking that you were in love with anyone but me . . ." and then, the word "love" being mentioned, that fatal syllable, they were both reduced to silence, and they sat there, still, in their ridiculous proximity, until she managed to take another mouthful of her omelette.

"You know," he said, when the movement of her jaws had sufficiently disrupted the connection, "all those continual threats of separation, that was really corrupt, you know, that was as bad as nagging. I feel bad about it now, looking back. Don't you?"

"How do you mean, bad about it?" she said.

"I feel we ought to have been able to do better than that. Though, come to think of it, it was you that did nearly all the threatening. Every time I saw you, you said it was for the last time. Every time. And I must have seen you nearly six days in every week for over a year. You can't have meant it, each time."

"I *did* mean it," she said. "I *did* mean it. Though each time I stopped meaning it and fixed up the next time to see you, I felt that of course I hadn't meant it. But then again, I did mean it, because I finally did it. Didn't I?"

"You mean *we* did it," he said. "You couldn't have done it without my help. If I'd rung you, if I'd written to you, it would have started all over again."

"Do you really think so?" she said, sadly, without even a pretence of indignation. "Yes, I suppose you might be right. I could never decide whether I could do it on my own or not. Evidently I couldn't. It takes two to part, just as it takes two to love."

"It was corrupt, though," he said, "to make ourselves live under that perpetual threat."

"Yes," she said, "but remember how lovely it was, how horribly lovely, each time that one relented. Each time one said, 'I'll never see you again, all right I'll meet you tomorrow in the usual place at half past one.' It was lovely."

"Lovely but wicked," he said.

"Oh, that sensation of defeat," she said, "it was so lovely, every time, every time I saw you . . . and I felt so sure, so entirely sure that what you felt was what I felt, that you were as weak as me, and as capable of enduring such ghastly self-inflicted wounds . . . Lord, we were so alike, and to think that when I first knew you I couldn't think of anything to say to you at all, I thought you came from another world, that we had nothing in common. That was the true disaster, our being so alike."

"It was that that made it so hard," he said. "The reverse of the irresistible force and unbreakable object principle, whatever that might be."

"Two objects most infinitely breakable, perhaps," she said.

"I liked it though," he said. "I liked it, breaking up together. Better than having it done to one, better than doing it."

"Better?"

"Perhaps even after all less corrupt," he said.

"Yes, but more seriously incurable," she said. And silence threatening to fall once more, she said quickly, "Anyway, tell me what you're doing round here. I mean to say, one has to have some reason, for coming to a place like this."

"I told you," he said, "I was looking for you."

"You *are* a liar," she said, smiling, amazed that she still even here could allow herself to be amused.

"What are you doing here then?" he said.

"Oh, I had a perfectly good reason," she said, "perfectly good, though rather embarrassing, I don't know if I'll tell you, but I suppose I will. You know that false front tooth? Well, yesterday evening I lost it, and I've got to be on a television thing tonight, and the thought of being without a tooth was so alarming so I went to my dentist's and he made them make me a new one, and I had to come round here to the warehouse to pick it up."

"Have you got it in?"

"Yes," she said, and turned to face him, smiling, lifting her upper lip. "Look, there it is."

"Do you mean," he said, "that if you'd had lunch *before* collecting your tooth, I would at last have seen you without it in?"

"Theoretically," she said, "but it wouldn't in fact have been possible, because how could I ever have had my lunch in a public place without my front tooth?"

"I'd hardly call this a public place," he said. "What a vain woman you are. You always were."

"I don't see anything wrong with vanity," she said. "And look, if you really want to see me without my tooth, there you are," and she took it out, and turned to him, and showed him.

"You look lovely," he said. "You look like a school child. You look like my daughter, she's got three missing at the moment."

"You still haven't told me what you're doing here," she said, putting her plate back in again. "I bet you haven't got as good a reason as me. Mine is entirely convincing, don't you think? I mean, where else could I have had lunch? I think my reason clears me entirely of any suspicion of any kind, don't you?"

"Any suspicion of sentiment?"

"That's what I meant."

He thought for a moment, and then he said,

"I had to call on a man about my Income Tax. Look, here's his address." And he got an envelope out of his pocket and showed her.

"Ah," she said.

"You see," he said.

"See what?" she said.

"*I* came here on purpose," he said. "To think of you. I could have had lunch at lots of places between London Wall and here."

"Yes, I suppose so," she said, "but you always were rather conservative about eating places. Suspicious, almost. You didn't come here because of me, you came here because it's the only place you know about."

"It comes to the same thing," he said.

"No, it doesn't," she said, firmly. She felt creeping upon her the familiar illusion of control, created as always before by a concentration upon trivialities, which could no longer even momentarily disguise the gravity of the outcome: and she reflected that their conversations had always so closely followed the patterns of their dialogues in bed, and that these idle points of contention were like those frivolous, delaying gestures in which she would turn aside, in which he would lie still and stare at the ceiling, hardly touching her, not daring, as he said, to touch her, and thus merely deferring, in their own studiously developed amorous dialectic, the inevitable: and thinking this, and able to live only in the deferment, for now there was no inevitability, no outcome that she could see, she said, eating her last chip,

"And how are your children?"

"They're fine," he said, "fine. What about yours?"

"Oh, they're all right too. I've had some dreadful nights with Laura recently, I must say I thought I was through with all that, I mean the child's five now, but she says she can't sleep and has these dreadful nightmares, so she's been every night in my bed for the last fortnight. It's wearing me out. Then in the morning she just laughs. And then at night it starts all over again. She doesn't kick, she's not as bony and awful as Fred used to be, it's just that I can't sleep with anyone else in the bed."

"What does Oliver say?" he asked, and she said, without thinking, having said it so often to others,

"Oh, I don't sleep with Oliver any more," and realising as she said it precisely what she had said, wondering how she could have made such a mistake, and wondering how to get out of it. But fortunately at that instant his Moussaka arrived, and the depositing of the plate and the redeployment of cutlery made it unnecessary to pursue the subject. Though once it had become unnecessary, she regretted the subject's disappearance: and she thought of saying what was very nearly the truth, she thought of saying that she had slept with nobody since she had slept with him, that for three years she had slept alone, and was quite prepared to sleep alone forever. But she was not sure, not entirely sure that he would want to hear it, and she knew that such a remark once made could never be retracted, so she said nothing.

He stared at his Moussaka, at the browned yellow crust.

"It looks all right," he said, and took a mouthful, and chewed it, and then he put his fork down and said, "Oh Lord, oh Lord, what a Proustian experience. I can't believe it. I can't believe that I'm sitting here with you. It tastes of you, that stuff, Oh God it reminds me of you. You look so beautiful, you look so lovely, my darling, Oh God I loved you so much. I really loved you, can you still believe that I really loved you?"

"I haven't slept with anyone," she said, "since I last slept with you."

"Oh darling," he said: and she could feel herself fainting and sighing away, drifting downwards on that fatefully descending eddying spiral, like Paolo and Francesca in hell, helpless, the mutually entwined drifting fall of all true lovers, unresisting, finally unresisting, as though three years of solitude had been nothing but a pause, nothing but a long breath before this final acknowledgement of nature, damnation and destiny; she turned towards him, and said, "Oh my darling, I love you, what can I do, I love you," and he with the same breath said, "I love you, I all the time love you, I want you," and they kissed there, their faces already so close that little inclination was needed, they kissed there above the Moussaka and chips, because they believed in such things, because that was what they believed in, because, like disastrous romantics, they habitually connived with fate by remembering the names of restaurants and the streets they had once walked along as lovers.

Those who forget, forget, he said to her later: and those who do not forget will meet again.

THE YELLOW
WALL PAPER

CHARLOTTE PERKINS GILMAN

IT IS VERY seldom that mere ordinary people like John and myself
secure ancestral halls for the summer.

A colonial mansion, a hereditary estate, I would say a haunted house,
and reach the height of romantic felicity—but that would be asking too
much of fate!

Still, there is something queer about it. Else, why should it be let so
cheaply? And why have stood so long untenanted?

John laughs at me, of course, but one expects that in marriage.

John is a physician, and practical in the extreme. He scoffs openly at
any talk of things not to be felt and seen and put down in figures, and
perhaps (I would not say it to a living soul, of course, but this is dead
paper and a great relief to my mind)—*perhaps* that is one reason I do not
get well faster.

You see, he does not believe I am sick!

If a physician of high standing, and one's own husband, assures
friends and relatives that there is really nothing the matter with one but
temporary nervous depression—a slight hysterical tendency—what is
one to do? My brother is also a physician, and also of high standing, and
he says the same thing.

So I take phosphates, and tonics, and journeys, and air, and exercise
and am absolutely forbidden to "work" until I am well again.

I did write for a while in spite of them; but it does exhaust me a
good deal—having to be so sly about it, or else meet with heavy
opposition.

Personally I sometimes fancy that in my condition if I had less opposition and more society and stimulus—but John says the very worst thing I can do is to think about my condition, and I confess it always makes me feel bad.

So I will let it alone and talk about the house.

The most beautiful place! It is quite alone, standing well back from the road, three miles from the village. There are hedges, and walls and gates that lock, and lots of separate little houses for the gardeners and people.

There is a *delicious* garden! I never saw such a garden—large and shady, full of box-bordered paths, and lined with long grape-covered arbors with seats under them. There were greenhouses, but they are all broken now. There was some legal trouble, I believe, something about the heirs and coheirs; anyhow, the place has been empty for years.

There is something strange and ghostly about the house—I can feel it. I even said so to John one moonlight evening, but he said what I felt was a *draft*, and shut the window. I get unreasonably angry with John sometimes. I think it is due to this nervous condition.

I don't like our room a bit. I wanted one downstairs that opened on the piazza and had roses all over the window, and such pretty, old-fashioned chintz hangings! But John would not hear of it.

He said there was only one window and no room for two beds. He said we came here solely on my account, that I was to have perfect rest and all the air I could get. He is very careful and loving, and hardly lets me stir without special direction. So we took the nursery, at the top of the house.

It is a big, airy room, the whole floor nearly, with windows that look all ways, and air and sunshine galore. It was nursery first and then playroom and gymnasium, I should judge; for the windows are barred for little children, and there are rings and things in the walls.

The paint and paper look as if a boys' school had used it. It is stripped off—the paper—in great patches all around the head of my bed, about as far as I can reach, and in a great place on the other side of the roof, low down.

I never saw a worse paper in my life. One of those sprawling flamboyant patterns committing every artistic sin. It is dull enough to confuse the eye, pronounced enough to constantly irritate, and provoke study. When you follow the lame, uncertain curves for a little distance they suddenly commit suicide—destroy themselves in unheard-of contradictions. The color is repellent, almost revolting; a smoldering, unclean yellow, strangely faded by the slow-turning sunlight. It is a dull yet lurid orange in some places, a sickly sulfur tint in others.

No wonder the children hated it! I should hate it myself if I had to live in this room long.

There comes John, and I must put this away—he hates to have me write a word.

WE HAVE BEEN here two weeks, and I haven't felt like writing since that first day. I am sitting by the window now, up in this atrocious nursery, and there is nothing to hinder my writing as much as I please. John is away all day, and even some nights when his cases are serious.

I am glad my case is not serious!

But these nervous troubles are dreadfully depressing. I meant to be such a help to John, and here I am a comparative burden already! Nobody would believe what an effort it is to do what little I am able.

It is fortunate Mary is so good with the baby. Such a dear baby! And yet I *cannot* be with him, it makes me so nervous.

I suppose John never was nervous in his life. He laughs at me so about this wall paper! At first he meant to repaper the room, but afterward he said that I was letting it get the better of me, and that nothing was worse for a nervous patient than to give way to such fancies. He said that after the wall paper was changed it would be the heavy bedstead, and then the barred windows, and then that gate at the head of the stairs. "You know the place is doing you good," he said, "and really, dear, I don't care to renovate the house just for a three months' rental." Then he took me in his arms and called me a blessed little goose.

But he is right enough about the beds and windows. It is as airy and comfortable a room as anyone need wish, and I'm really getting quite fond of it, all but that horrid wall paper.

It looks to me as if it *knew* what a vicious influence it had!

There is a recurrent spot where the pattern lolls like a broken neck and two bulbous eyes stare at you upside down. I got positively angry at the impertinence of it. In one place the two breadths didn't match, and the eyes go all up and down the line, one a little higher than the other.

I never saw so much expression in an inanimate thing before, and we all know how much expression they have! I used to lie awake as a child and get more entertainment and terror out of blank walls and plain furniture than most children could find in a toy store. I remember what a kindly wink the knobs of our big old bureau used to have, and there was one chair that always seemed like a strong friend.

The furniture in this room is no worse than inharmonious, however, for we had to bring it all from downstairs. I suppose when it was used as a playroom they had to take the nursery things out, and no wonder! I never saw such ravages as the children have made here.

The wall paper, as I said before, is torn off in spots. Then the floor is scratched and gouged and splintered, the plaster itself is dug out here and there, and this great heavy bed, which is all we found in the room, looks as if it had been through the wars.

But I don't mind it a bit—only the paper.

It has a kind of subpattern in a different shade, a particularly irritating one, for you can only see it in certain lights, and not clearly then. But in the places where it isn't faded, and where the sun is just so, I can see a strange, provoking, formless sort of figure that seems to sulk about that silly front design.

There's Jennie, John's sister, on the stairs! Such a dear girl as she is, and so careful of me! I must not let her find me writing. I believe she thinks it is the writing which made me sick!

WELL, THE Fourth of July is over! The people are all gone and I am tired out. John thought it might do me good to see a little company, so we just had Mother and Nellie and the children down for a week.

Of course I didn't do a thing. Jennie sees to everything now. She is a perfect, an enthusiastic housekeeper, and hopes for no better profession. But the visit tired me all the same.

John says if I don't pick up faster he shall send me to Weir Mitchell in the fall. But I don't want to go there at all. I had a friend who was in his hands once, and she says he is just like John and my brother, only more so!

I'm getting dreadfully fretful and querulous. I cry at nothing, and cry most of the time. Of course I don't when John is here, or anybody else, but when I am alone.

And I am alone a good deal just now. John is kept in town very often by serious cases, and Jennie is good and lets me alone when I want her to.

So I walk a little in the garden or sit on the porch under the roses, and lie down up here a good deal.

I'm getting really fond of the room in spite of the wall paper. Perhaps *because* of the wall paper. It dwells in my mind so!

I lie here on this great immovable bed—it is nailed down, I believe—and follow that pattern about by the hour. It is as good as gymnastics, I assure you. I start, we'll say at the bottom, down in the corner over there where it has not been touched, and I determine for the thousandth time that I *will* follow that pointless pattern to some sort of a conclusion.

It is repeated, of course, by the breadths, but not otherwise. Looked at in one way, each breadth stands alone, the bloated curves and flourishes go waddling up and down in isolated columns. But, on the other hand, they connect diagonally, and the sprawling outlines run off in great slanting waves of optic horror, like a lot of wallowing seaweeds in full chase.

It makes me tired to follow it. I will take a nap, I guess.

JOHN SAYS I mustn't lose my strength, and has me take cod-liver oil and tonics, to say nothing of ale and wine and rare meat.

Dear John! He loves me very dearly, and hates to have me sick. I tried to have a reasonable talk with him the other day, and tell him how I wished he would let me go and make a visit to Cousin Henry and Julia. But he said I wasn't able to go, nor able to stand it after I got there; and I did not make out a very good case for myself, for I was crying before I had finished.

And dear John gathered me up in his arms, and just carried me upstairs and laid me on the bed, and sat by me and read to me till he tired my head.

He said I was his darling and his comfort, and that I must take care of myself for his and the baby's sake, and keep well. He says no one but myself can help me out of it, that I must use my will and self-control and not let my silly fancies run away with me.

Of course I never mention the wall paper to him anymore—I am too wise—but I keep watch of it all the same.

There are things in that paper that nobody knows but me, or ever will. Behind that outside pattern the dim shapes get clearer every day. It is always the same shape, only very numerous. And it is like a woman stooping down and creeping about behind that pattern. I don't like it a bit. I wonder—I begin to think—I wish John would take me away from here!

It is so hard to talk with John about my case, because he is so wise, and because he loves me so. But I tried it last night.

John was asleep and I hated to waken him, so I kept still and watched the moonlight on that undulating wall paper till I felt creepy. The faint figure behind seemed to shake the pattern, just as if she wanted to get out.

I got up softly and went to feel and see if the paper *did* move, and when I came back John was awake.

"What is it, little girl?" he said. "Don't go walking about like that— you'll get cold."

I thought it was a good time to talk, so I told him that I really was not gaining here, and that I wished he would take me away.

"Why, darling!" said he. "Our lease will be up in three weeks, and I can't see how to leave before. The repairs are not done at home, and you really are better, dear, whether you can see it or not. You are gaining flesh and color, your appetite is better. I feel really much easier about you."

"I don't weigh a bit more," said I, "nor as much; and my appetite may be better in the evening, when you are here, but it is worse in the morning, when you are away."

"Bless her little heart!" said he with a big hug. "She shall be as sick as she pleases. It is only three weeks more and then we will take a nice little trip while Jennie is getting the house ready. Really, dear, you are better!"

"Better in body, perhaps—" I began, and stopped short, for he sat up straight and looked at me sternly.

"My darling," said he, "I beg that you will never for one instant let that idea enter your mind! There is nothing so dangerous, so fascinating, to a temperament like yours. Can you not trust me as a physician when I tell you so? But now let's sleep, and talk about it in the morning."

So of course I said no more. He thought I was asleep, but I wasn't—I lay there for hours trying to decide whether that front pattern and the back pattern really did move together or separately.

On a pattern like this, by daylight, there is a lack of sequence, a defiance of law, that is a constant irritant to a normal mind. The color is hideous enough, and unreliable enough, and infuriating enough, but the pattern is torturing. It slaps you in the face, knocks you down, and tramples upon you. It is like a bad dream.

The outside pattern is a florid arabesque, reminding one of a fungus. If you can imagine a toadstool in joints, an interminable string of toadstools, budding and sprouting in endless convolutions—why, that is something like it.

That is, sometimes!

There is one marked peculiarity about this paper, a thing nobody seems to notice but myself, and that is that it changes as the light changes. When the first sun shoots in through the east window, it changes so quickly that I never can quite believe it. That is why I watch it always. At night in any kind of light, in twilight, candlelight, lamplight, and worst of all by moonlight, it becomes bars! The outside pattern, I mean, and the woman behind it is as plain as can be.

I didn't realize for a long time what the thing was that showed behind—that dim subpattern—but now I am quite sure it is a woman.

By daylight she is subdued, quiet. I fancy it is the pattern that keeps her so still. It is so puzzling. It keeps me quiet by the hour.

I lie down ever so much now. John started the habit by making me lie down for an hour after each meal. It is a very bad habit, I am convinced, for, you see, I don't sleep. And that cultivates deceit, for I don't tell them I'm awake—oh, no!

The fact is, I am getting a little afraid of John. He seems very queer sometimes, and even Jennie has an inexplicable look. It strikes me occasionally, just as a scientific hypothesis, that perhaps it is the paper! I have watched John when he did not know I was looking, and I've caught him several times *looking at the paper!* And Jennie, too. I caught Jennie with her hand on it once.

She didn't know I was in the room, and when I asked her in a very quiet voice what she was doing with the paper she turned around as if she had been caught stealing, and looked quite angry—asked me why I should frighten her so! Then she said that the paper stained everything it touched, and that she had found yellow smooches on all my clothes and John's, and she wished we would be more careful!

Did not that sound innocent? But I know she was studying that pattern, and I am determined that nobody shall find it out but myself! I don't want to leave now until I have found it out. There is a week more, and I think that will be enough.

I'M FEELING EVER so much better! I don't sleep much at night, for it is so interesting to watch developments; but I sleep a good deal in the daytime.

It is the strangest yellow, that wall paper! It makes me think of all the yellow things I ever saw—not beautiful ones like buttercups, but old foul, bad yellow things.

But there is something else about that paper—the smell! I noticed it the moment we came into the room, but with so much air and sun it was not bad! Now we have had a week of fog and rain, and whether the windows are open or not the smell is here.

It creeps all over the house. I find it hovering in the dining room, skulking in the parlor, hiding in the hall, lying in wait for me on the stairs. It gets into my hair.

Even when I go to ride, if I turn my head suddenly and surprise it— there is that smell! Such a peculiar odor, too! In this damp weather it is awful. I wake up in the night and find it hanging over me.

It used to disturb me at first. I thought seriously of burning the house—to reach the smell.

But now I am used to it. The only thing I can think of that it is like is the *color* of the paper—a yellow smell!

There is a very funny mark on the walls, low down, near the mopboard. A streak that runs around the room. It goes behind every piece of furniture, except the bed, a long, straight, even *smooch,* as if it had been rubbed over and over.

I wonder how it was done and who did it, and what they did it for. Round and round and round—round and round and round—it makes me dizzy!

I REALLY HAVE discovered something at last. Through watching so much at night, I have finally found out. The front pattern *does* move— and no wonder! The woman behind shakes it!

Sometimes I think there are a great many women behind, and sometimes only one, and she crawls around fast, and her crawling shakes it all over. Then in the very bright spots she keeps still, and in the very shady spots she takes hold of the bars and shakes them hard.

And she is all the time trying to climb through. But nobody could climb through that pattern—it strangles so; I think that is why it has so many heads. They get through, and then the pattern strangles them off and turns them upside down, and makes their eyes white!

If those heads were covered or taken off it would not be half so bad.

I THINK THAT woman gets out in the daytime!

And I'll tell you why—privately—I've seen her! I can see her out of every one of my windows! It is the same woman, I know, for she is always creeping, and most women do not creep by daylight. I see her in the long shaded lane, creeping up and down, as fast as a cloud shadow in a high wind. I see her in those dark grape arbors, creeping all around the garden. I see her on that long road under the trees, creeping along, and when a carriage comes she hides under the blackberry vines. I don't blame her a bit. It must be very humiliating to be caught creeping by daylight!

I always lock the door when I creep by daylight. I can't do it at night, for I know John would suspect something at once. And John is so queer, now, that I don't want to irritate him. I wish he would take another room! Besides, I don't want anybody to get that woman out at night but myself.

IF ONLY THAT TOP PATTERN could be gotten off from the under one! I mean to try it, little by little.

There are only two more days to get this wall paper off, and I believe John is beginning to notice. I don't like the look in his eyes. He knows I don't sleep very well at night, for all I'm so quiet! He asked me all sorts of questions, and pretended to be very loving and kind.

As if I couldn't see through him!

Still, I don't wonder he acts so, sleeping under this paper for three months. It only interests me, but I feel sure John and Jennie are secretly affected by it.

HURRAH! THIS is the last day, but it is enough. John is to stay in town overnight, and won't be out until this evening. Jennie wanted to sleep with me—the sly thing! But I told her I should undoubtedly rest better for a night all alone.

That was clever, for really I wasn't alone a bit! As soon as it was moonlight, and that poor thing began to crawl and shake the pattern, I got up and ran to help her.

I pulled and she shook, I shook and she pulled, and before morning we had peeled off yards of that paper. A strip about as high as my head and half around the room. And then when the sun came and that awful pattern began to laugh at me I declared I would finish it today!

We go away tomorrow, and they are moving all my furniture down again to leave things as they were before. Jennie looked at the wall in amazement, but I told her merrily that I did it out of pure spite at the vicious thing. She laughed and said she wouldn't mind doing it herself, but I must not get tired.

How she betrayed herself that time!

But I am here, and no person touches this paper but me—not *alive!*

Jennie tried to get me out of the room. But I said it was so quiet and empty and clean now that I believed I would lie down and sleep all I could; and not to wake me even for dinner—I would call when I woke.

So now she is gone, and the servants are gone, and the things are gone, and there is nothing left but that great bedstead nailed down, with the canvas mattress we found on it. How those children did tear about here! The bedstead is fairly gnawed!

But I must get to work.

I have locked the door and thrown the key down into the front path.

I've got a rope up here that even Jennie did not find. If that woman does get out, and tries to get away, I can tie her!

But I forgot I could not reach far without anything to stand on! This bed will *not* move!

I tried to lift and push it until I was lame, and then I got so angry I bit off a little piece at one corner—but it hurt my teeth.

Then I peeled off all the paper I could reach standing on the floor. It sticks horribly and the pattern just enjoys it! All those strangled heads and bulbous eyes and the waddling fungus growths just shriek with derision!

I am getting angry enough to do something desperate. To jump out of the window would be admirable exercise, but the bars are too strong even to try.

Besides, I wouldn't do it. Of course not. I know well enough that a step like that is improper and might be misconstrued.

I don't like to *look* out of the windows even—there are so many of those creeping women, and they creep so fast.

I wonder if they all come out of that wall paper, as I did?

But I am securely fastened now by my well-hidden rope—you don't get *me* out in the road there!

I suppose I shall have to get back behind the pattern when it comes night, and that is hard! It is so pleasant to be out in this great room and creep around as I please!

I don't want to go outside. I won't, even if Jennie asks me to.

For outside you have to creep on the ground, and everything is green instead of yellow.

But here I can creep smoothly on the floor, and my shoulder just fits in that long smooch around the wall, so I cannot lose my way.

Why, there's John at the door!

It is no use, young man, you can't open it!

How he does call and pound!

Now he's crying for an ax.

"John, dear," said I in the gentlest voice, "the key is down by the front steps, under a plantain leaf!"

That silenced him for a few moments.

Then he said—very quietly indeed, "Open the door, my darling!"

"I can't," said I. "The key is down by the front door, under a plantain leaf!"

And then I said it again, several times, very gently and slowly, and said it so often that he had to go and see, and he got it, of course, and came in. He stopped short by the door.

"What is the matter?" he cried. "For God's sake, what are you doing?"

I kept on creeping just the same, but I looked at him over my shoulder.

"I've got out at last," said I, "in spite of you and Jennie! And I've pulled off most of the paper, so you can't put me back!"

Now why should that man have fainted? But he did, and right across my path by the wall, so that I had to creep over him every time!

SECOND BEST

D. H. LAWRENCE

D. H. Lawrence [signature]

"Oh, I'm tired!" Frances exclaimed petulantly, and in the same instant she dropped down on the turf, near the hedge-bottom. Anne stood a moment surprised, then, accustomed to the vagaries of her beloved Frances, said:

"Well, and aren't you always likely to be tired, after travelling that blessed long way from Liverpool yesterday?" and she plumped down beside her sister. Anne was a wise young body of fourteen, very buxom, brimming with common sense. Frances was much older, about twenty-three, and whimsical, spasmodic. She was the beauty and the clever child of the family. She plucked the goose-grass buttons from her dress in a nervous, desperate fashion. Her beautiful profile, looped above with black hair, warm with the dusky-and-scarlet complexion of a pear, was calm as a mask, her thin brown hand plucked nervously.

"It's not the journey," she said, objecting to Anne's obtuseness. Anne looked inquiringly at her darling. The young girl, in her self-confident, practical way, proceeded to reckon up this whimsical creature. But suddenly she found herself full in the eyes of Frances; felt two dark, hectic eyes flaring challenge at her, and she shrank away. Frances was peculiar for these great, exposed looks, which disconcerted people by their violence and their suddenness.

"What's a matter, poor old duck?" asked Anne, as she folded the slight, wilful form of her sister in her arms. Frances laughed shakily, and nestled down for comfort on the budding breasts of the strong girl.

"Oh, I'm only a bit tired," she murmured, on the point of tears.

"Well, of course you are, what do you expect?" soothed Anne. It was a joke to Frances that Anne should play elder, almost mother to her. But then, Anne was in her unvexed teens; men were like big dogs to her: while Frances, at twenty-three, suffered a good deal.

The country was intensely morning-still. On the common everything shone beside its shadow, and the hillside gave off heat in silence. The brown turf seemed in a low state of combustion, the leaves of the oaks were scorched brown. Among the blackish foliage in the distance shone the small red and orange of the village.

The willows in the brook-course at the foot of the common suddenly shook with a dazzling effect like diamonds. It was a puff of wind. Anne resumed her normal position. She spread her knees, and put in her lap a handful of hazel nuts, whity-green leafy things, whose one cheek was tanned between brown and pink. These she began to crack and eat. Frances, with bowed head, mused bitterly.

"Eh, you know Tom Smedley?" began the young girl, as she pulled a tight kernel out of its shell.

"I suppose so," replied Frances sarcastically.

"Well, he gave me a wild rabbit what he'd caught, to keep with my tame one—and it's living."

"That's a good thing," said Frances, very detached and ironic.

"Well, it *is*! He reckoned he'd take me to Ollerton Feast, but he never did. Look here, he took a servant from the rectory; I saw him."

"So he ought," said Frances.

"No, he oughtn't! And I told him so. And I told him I should tell you—an' I have done."

Click and snap went a nut between her teeth. She sorted out the kernel, and chewed complacently.

"It doesn't make much difference," said Frances.

"Well, 'appen it doesn't; but I was mad with him all the same."

"Why?"

"Because I was; he's no right to go with a servant."

"He's a perfect right," persisted Frances, very just and cold.

"No, he hasn't, when he'd said he'd take me."

Frances burst into a laugh of amusement and relief.

"Oh, no; I'd forgot that," she said, adding, "and what did he say when you promised to tell me?"

"He laughed and said, 'She won't fret her fat over that'."

"And she won't," sniffed Frances.

There was silence. The common, with its sere, blonde-headed thistles, its heaps of silent bramble, its brown-husked gorse in the glare of sunshine, seemed visionary. Across the brook began the immense pattern of agriculture, white chequering of barley stubble, brown squares of wheat, khaki patches of pasture, red stripes of fallow, with the woodland and the tiny village dark like ornaments, leading away to the distance, right to the hills, where the check-pattern grew smaller and smaller, till, in the blackish haze of heat, far off, only the tiny white squares of barley stubble showed distinct.

"Eh, I say, here's a rabbit hole!" cried Anne suddenly. "Should we watch if one comes out? You won't have to fidget, you know."

The two girls sat perfectly still. Frances watched certain objects in her surroundings: they had a peculiar, unfriendly look about them: the weight of greenish elderberries on their purpling stalks; the twinkling of the yellowing crab-apples that clustered high up in the hedge, against the sky: the exhausted, limp leaves of the primroses lying flat in the hedgebottom: all looked strange to her. Then her eyes caught a movement. A mole was moving silently over the warm, red soil, nosing, shuffling hither and thither, flat, and dark as a shadow, shifting about, and as suddenly brisk, and as silent, like a very ghost of *joie de vivre*. Frances started, from habit was about to call on Anne to kill the little pest. But, today her lethargy of unhappiness was too much for her. She watched the little brute paddling, snuffing, touching things to discover them, running in blindness, delighted to ecstasy by the sunlight and the hot, strange things that caressed its belly and its nose. She felt a keen pity for the little creature.

"Eh, our Fran, look there! It's a mole."

Anne was on her feet, standing watching the dark, unconscious beast. Frances frowned with anxiety.

"It doesn't run off, does it?" said the young girl softly. Then she stealthily approached the creature. The mole paddled fumblingly away. In an instant Anne put her foot upon it, not too heavily. Frances could see the struggling, swimming movement of the little pink hands of the brute, the twisting and twitching of its pointed nose, as it wrestled under the sole of the boot.

"It *does* wriggle!" said the bonny girl, knitting her brows in a frown at the eerie sensation. Then she bent down to look at her trap. Frances could now see, beyond the edge of the boot-sole, the heaving of the velvet shoulders, the pitiful turning of the sightless face, the frantic rowing of the flat, pink hands.

"Kill the thing," she said, turning away her face.

"Oh—I'm not," laughed Anne, shrinking. "You can, if you like."

"I *don't* like," said Frances, with quiet intensity.

After several dabbing attempts, Anne succeeded in picking up the little animal by the scruff of its neck. It threw back its head, flung its long blind snout from side to side, the mouth open in a peculiar oblong, with tiny pinkish teeth at the edge. The blind, frantic mouth gaped and writhed. The body, heavy and clumsy, hung scarcely moving. "Isn't it a snappy little thing?" observed Anne, twisting to avoid the teeth.

"What are you going to do with it?" asked Frances sharply.

"It's got to be killed—look at the damage they do. I s'll take it home and let dadda or somebody kill it. I'm not going to let it go."

She swaddled the creature clumsily in her pocket-handkerchief and sat down beside her sister. There was an interval of silence, during which Anne combated the efforts of the mole.

"You've not had much to say about Jimmy this time. Did you see him often in Liverpool?" Anne asked suddenly.

"Once or twice," replied Frances, giving no sign of how the question troubled her.

"And aren't you sweet on him any more, then?"

"I should think I'm not, seeing that he's engaged."

"Engaged? Jimmy Barrass! Well, of all things! I never thought *he*'d get engaged."

"Why not? he's as much right as anybody else," snapped Frances.

Anne was fumbling with the mole.

"'Appen so," she said at length; "but I never thought Jimmy would, though."

"Why not?" snapped Frances.

"*I* don't know—this blessed mole, it'll not keep still!—who's he got engaged to?"

"How should I know?"

"I thought you'd ask him; you've known him long enough. I s'd think he thought he'd get engaged now he's a Doctor of Chemistry."

Frances laughed in spite of herself.

"What's that got to do with it?" she asked.

"I'm sure it's got a lot. He'll want to feel *somebody* now, so he's got engaged. Hey, stop it; go in!"

But at this juncture the mole almost succeeded in wriggling clear. It wrestled and twisted frantically, waved its pointed blind head, its mouth standing like a little shaft, its big, wrinkled hands spread out.

"Go in with you!" urged Anne, poking the little creature with her forefinger, trying to get it back into the handkerchief. Suddenly the mouth turned like a spark on her finger.

"Oh!" she cried, "he's bit me."

She dropped him to the floor. Dazed, the blind creature fumbled around. Frances felt like shrieking. She expected him to dart away in a flash, like a mouse, and there he remained groping; she wanted to cry to him to be gone. Anne, in a sudden decision of wrath, caught up her sister's walking-cane. With one blow the mole was dead. Frances was startled and shocked. One moment the little wretch was fussing in the heat, and the next it lay like a little bag, inert and black—not a struggle, scarce a quiver.

"Is it dead?" Frances said breathlessly. Anne took her finger from her mouth, looked at the tiny pinpricks, and said:

"Yes, he is, and I'm glad. They're vicious little nuisances, moles are."

With which her wrath vanished. She picked up the dead animal.

"Hasn't it got a beautiful skin?" she mused, stroking the fur with her forefinger, then with her cheek.

"Mind," said Frances sharply. "You'll have the blood on your skirt!"

One ruby drop of blood hung on the small snout, ready to fall. Anne shook it off on to some hare-bells. Frances suddenly became calm; in that moment, grown-up.

"I suppose they have to be killed," she said, and a certain rather dreary indifference succeeded to her grief. The twinkling crab-apples, the glitter of brilliant willows now seemed to her trifling, scarcely worth the notice. Something had died in her, so that things lost their poignancy. She was calm, indifference overlying her quiet sadness. Rising, she walked down to the brook course.

"Here, wait for me," cried Anne, coming tumbling after.

Frances stood on the bridge, looking at the red mud trodden into pockets by the feet of cattle. There was not a drain of water left, but everything smelled green, succulent. Why did she care so little for Anne, who was so fond of her? she asked herself. Why did she care so little for anyone? She did not know, but she felt a rather stubborn pride in her isolation and indifference.

They entered a field where stooks of barley stood in rows, the straight, blonde tresses of the corn streaming on to the ground. The stubble was bleached by the intense summer, so that the expanse glared white. The next field was sweet and soft with a second crop of seeds; thin, straggling clover whose little pink knobs rested prettily in the dark green. The scent was faint and sickly. The girls came up in single file, Frances leading.

Near the gate a young man was mowing with the scythe some fodder for the afternoon feed of the cattle. As he saw the girls he left off working and waited in an aimless kind of way. Frances was dressed in white muslin, and she walked with dignity, detached and forgetful. Her lack of agitation, her simple, unheeding advance made him nervous. She had loved the far-off Jimmy for five years, having had in return his half-measures. This man only affected her slightly.

Tom was of medium stature, energetic in build. His smooth, fair-skinned face was burned red, not brown, by the sun, and this ruddiness enhanced his appearance of good humour and easiness. Being a year older than Frances, he would have courted her long ago had she been so inclined. As it was, he had gone his uneventful way amiably, chatting with many a girl, but remaining unattached, free of trouble for the most part. Only he knew he wanted a woman. He hitched his trousers just a trifle self-consciously as the girls approached. Frances was a rare, delicate kind of being, whom he realized with a queer and delicious stimulation in his veins. She gave him a slight sense of suffocation. Somehow this morning she affected him more than usual. She was dressed in white. He, however, being matter-of-fact in his mind, did not realize. His feeling had never become conscious, purposive.

Frances knew what she was about. Tom was ready to love her as soon as she would show him. Now that she could not have Jimmy, she did not poignantly care. Still, she would have something. If she could not have the best— Jimmy, whom she knew to be something of a snob —she would have the second best, Tom. She advanced rather indifferently.

"You are back, then!" said Tom. She marked the touch of un-certainty in his voice.

"No," she laughed, "I'm still in Liverpool," and the undertone of intimacy made him burn.

"This isn't you, then?" he asked.

Her heart leapt up in approval. She looked in his eyes, and for a second was with him.

"Why, what do you think?" she laughed.

He lifted his hat from his head with a distracted little gesture. She liked him, his quaint ways, his humour, his ignorance, and his slow masculinity.

"Here, look here, Tom Smedley," broke in Anne.

"A moudiwarp! Did you find it dead?" he asked.

"No, it bit me," said Anne.

"Oh, aye! An' that got your rag out, did it?"

"No, it didn't!" Anne scolded sharply. "Such language!"

"Oh, what's up wi' it?"

"I can't bear you to talk broad."

"Can't you?"

He glanced at Frances.

"It isn't nice," Frances said. She did not care, really. The vulgar speech jarred on her as a rule; Jimmy was a gentleman. But Tom's manner of speech did not matter to her.

"I like you to talk *nicely*," she added.

"Do you," he replied, tilting his hat, stirred.

"And generally you *do*, you know," she smiled.

"I s'll have to have a try," he said, rather tensely gallant.

"What?" she asked brightly.

"To talk nice to you," he said. Frances coloured furiously, bent her head for a moment, then laughed gaily, as if she liked this clumsy hint.

"Eh now, you mind what you're saying," cried Anne, giving the young man an admonitory pat.

"You wouldn't have to give yon mole many knocks like that," he teased, relieved to get on safe ground, rubbing his arm.

"No indeed, it died in one blow," said Frances, with a flippancy that was hateful to her.

"You're not so good at knockin' 'em?" he said, turning to her.

"I don't know, if I'm cross," she said decisively.

"No?" he replied, with alert attentiveness.

"I could," she added, harder, "it if was necessary."

He was slow to feel her difference.

"And don't you consider it *is* necessary?" he asked, with misgiving.

"W-ell—is it?" she said. looking at him steadily, coldly.

"I reckon it is," he replied, looking away, but standing stubborn.

She laughed quickly.

"But it isn't necessary for *me*," she said, with slight contempt.

"Yes, that's quite true," he answered.

She laughed in a shaky fashion.

"*I know it is*," she said; and there was an awkward pause.

"Why, would you *like* me to kill moles then?" she asked tentatively, after a while.

"They do us a lot of damage," he said, standing firm on his own ground, angered.

"Well, I'll see the next time I come across one," she promised, defiantly. Their eyes met, and she sank before him, her pride troubled. He felt uneasy and triumphant and baffled, as if fate had gripped him. She smiled as she departed.

"Well," said Anne, as the sisters went through the wheat stubble; "I don't know what you two's been jawing about, I'm sure."

"Don't you?" laughed Frances significantly.

"No, I don't. But, at any rate, Tom Smedley's a good deal better to my thinking than Jimmy, so there—and nicer."

"Perhaps he is," said Frances coldly.

And the next day, after a secret, persistent hunt, she found another mole playing in the heat. She killed it, and in the evening, when Tom came to the gate to smoke his pipe after supper, she took him the dead creature. "Here you are then!" she said.

"Did you catch it?" he replied, taking the velvet corpse into his fingers and examining it minutely. This was to hide his trepidation.

"Did you think I couldn't?" she asked, her face very near his.

"Nay, I didn't know."

She laughed in his face, a strange little laugh that caught her breath, all agitation, and tears, and recklessness of desire. He looked frightened and upset. She put her hand to his arm.

"Shall you go out wi' me?" he asked, in a difficult, troubled tone.

She turned her face away, with a shaky laugh. The blood came up in him, strong, overmastering. He resisted it. But it drove him down, and he was carried away. Seeing the winsome, frail nape of her neck, fierce love came upon him for her, and tenderness.

"We s'll 'ave to tell your mother," he said. And he stood, suffering, resisting his passion for her.

"Yes," she replied, in a dead voice. But there was a thrill of pleasure in this death.

IF GRANT HAD BEEN DRINKING AT APPOMATTOX

JAMES THURBER

James Thurber

THE MORNING of the ninth of April, 1865, dawned beautifully. General Meade was up with the first streaks of crimson in the eastern sky. General Hooker and General Burnside were up, and had breakfasted, by a quarter after eight. The day continued beautiful. It drew on toward eleven o'clock. General Ulysses S. Grant was still not up. He was asleep in his famous old navy hammock, swung high above the floor of his headquarters' bedroom. Headquarters was distressingly disarranged: papers were strewn on the floor; confidential notes from spies scurried here and there in the breeze from an open window; the dregs of an overturned bottle of wine flowed pinkly across an important military map.

Corporal Shultz, of the Sixty-fifth Ohio Volunteer Infantry, aide to General Grant, came into the outer room, looked around him, and sighed. He entered the bedroom and shook the General's hammock roughly. General Ulysses S. Grant opened one eye.

"Pardon, sir," said Corporal Shultz, "but this is the day of surrender. You ought to be up, sir."

"Don't swing me," said Grant, sharply, for his aide was making the hammock sway gently. "I feel terrible," he added, and he turned over and closed his eye again.

"General Lee will be here any minute now," said the Corporal firmly, swinging the hammock again.

"Will you cut that out?" roared Grant. "D'ya want to make me sick, or what?" Shultz clicked his heels and saluted. "What's he coming here for?" asked the General.

303

"This is the day of surrender, sir," said Shultz. Grant grunted bitterly.

"Three hundred and fifty generals in the Northern armies," said Grant, "and he has to come to *me* about this. What time is it?"

"You're the Commander-in-Chief, that's why," said Corporal Shultz. "It's eleven twenty-five, sir."

"Don't be crazy," said Grant. "Lincoln is the Commander-in-Chief. Nobody in the history of the world ever surrendered before lunch. Doesn't he know that an army surrenders on its stomach?" He pulled a blanket up over his head and settled himself again.

"The generals of the Confederacy will be here any minute now," said the Corporal. "You really ought to be up, sir."

Grant stretched his arms above his head and yawned.

"All right, all right," he said. He rose to a sitting position and stared about the room. "This place looks awful," he growled.

"You must have had quite a time of it last night, sir," ventured Shultz.

"Yeh," said General Grant, looking around for his clothes. "I was wrassling some general. Some general with a beard."

Shultz helped the commander of the Northern armies in the field to find his clothes.

"Where's my other sock?" demanded Grant. Shultz began to look around for it. The General walked uncertainly to a table and poured a drink from a bottle.

"I don't think it wise to drink, sir," said Shultz.

"Nev' mind about me," said Grant, helping himself to a second, "I can take it or let it alone. Didn' ya ever hear the story about the fella went to Lincoln to complain about me drinking too much? 'So-and-So says Grant drinks too much,' this fella said. 'So-and-So is a fool,' said Lincoln. So this fella went to What's-His-Name and told him what Lincoln said and he came roarin' to Lincoln about it. 'Did you tell So-and-So I was a fool?' he said. 'No,' said Lincoln, 'I thought he knew it.' " The General smiled, reminiscently, and had another drink. "*That's* how I stand with Lincoln," he said, proudly.

The soft thudding sound of horses' hooves came through the open window. Shultz hurriedly walked over and looked out.

"Hoof steps," said Grant, with a curious chortle.

"It is General Lee and his staff," said Shultz.

"Show him in," said the General, taking another drink. "And see what the boys in the back room will have."

Shultz walked smartly over to the door, opened it, saluted, and stood aside. General Lee, dignified against the blue of the April sky, magnificent in his dress uniform, stood for a moment framed in the doorway. He walked in, followed by his staff. They bowed, and stood silent. General Grant stared at them. He only had one boot on and his jacket was unbuttoned.

"I know who you are," said Grant. "You're Robert Browning, the poet."

"This is General Robert E. Lee," said one of his staff, coldly.

"Oh," said Grant. "I thought he was Robert Browning. He certainly looks like Robert Browning. There was a poet for you, Lee: Browning. Did ja ever read 'How They Brought the Good News from Ghent to Aix'? 'Up Derek, to saddle, up Derek, away; up Dunder, up Blitzen, up Prancer, up Dancer, up Bouncer, up Vixen, up—' "

"Shall we proceed at once to the matter in hand?" asked General Lee, his eyes disdainfully taking in the disordered room.

"Some of the boys was wrassling here last night," explained Grant. "I threw Sherman, or some general a whole lot like Sherman. It was pretty dark." He handed a bottle of Scotch to the commanding officer of the Southern armies, who stood holding it, in amazement and discomfiture. "Get a glass, somebody," said Grant, looking straight at General Longstreet. "Didn't I meet you at Cold Harbor?" he asked. General Longstreet did not answer.

"I should like to have this over with as soon as possible," said Lee. Grant looked vaguely at Shultz, who walked up close to him, frowning.

"The surrender, sir, the surrender," said Corporal Shultz in a whisper.

"Oh sure, sure," said Grant. He took another drink. "All right," he said. "Here we go." Slowly, sadly, he unbuckled his sword. Then he handed it to the astonished Lee. "There you are, General," said Grant. "We dam' near licked you. If I'd been feeling better we *would* of licked you."

NIGHT CLUB

KATHARINE BRUSH

Katharine Brush

PROMPTLY AT quarter of ten p.m. Mrs. Brady descended the steps of the elevated. She purchased from the news dealer in the cubbyhole beneath them a next month's magazine and a tomorrow morning's paper and, with these tucked under one plump arm, she walked. She walked two blocks north on Sixth Avenue; turned and went west. But not far west. Westward half a block only, to the place where the gay green awning marked "Club Français" paints a stripe of shade across the glimmering sidewalk. Under this awning Mrs. Brady halted briefly, to remark to the six-foot doorman that it looked like rain and to await his performance of his professional duty. When the small green door yawned open, she sighed deeply and plodded in.

The foyer was a blackness, an airless velvet blackness like the inside of a jeweler's box. Four drum-shaped lamps of golden silk suspended from the ceiling gave it light (a very little) and formed the jewels: gold signets, those, or cuff links for a giant. At the far end of the foyer there were black stairs, faintly dusty, rippling upward toward an amber radiance. Mrs. Brady approached and ponderously mounted the stairs, clinging with one fist to the mangy velvet rope that railed their edge.

From the top, Miss Lena Levin observed the ascent. Miss Levin was the checkroom girl. She had dark-at-the-roots blond hair, and slender hips upon which, in moments of leisure, she wore her hands, like buckles of ivory loosely attached.

This was a moment of leisure. Miss Levin waited behind her counter. Row upon row of hooks, empty as yet, and seeming to beckon—wee curved fingers of iron—waited behind her.

"Late," said Miss Levin, "again."

"Go wan!" said Mrs. Brady. "It's only ten to ten. *Whew!* Them *stairs!*" She leaned heavily, sideways, against Miss Levin's counter, and, applying one palm to the region of her heart, appeared at once to listen and to count. "Feel!" she cried then in a pleased voice.

Miss Levin obediently felt.

"Them stairs," continued Mrs. Brady darkly, "with my bad heart, will be the death of me. Whew! Well, dearie? What's the news?"

"You got a paper," Miss Levin languidly reminded her.

"Yeah!" agreed Mrs. Brady with sudden vehemence. "I got a paper!" She slapped it upon the counter. "An' a lot of time I'll get to *read* my paper, won't I now? On a Saturday night!" She moaned. "Other nights is bad enough, dear knows—but *Saturday* nights! How I dread 'em! Every Saturday night I say to my daughter, I say, 'Geraldine, I can't,' I say, 'I can't go through it again, an' that's all there is to it,' I say. 'I'll *quit!*' I say. An' I *will*, too!" added Mrs. Brady firmly, if indefinitely.

Miss Levin, in defense of Saturday nights, mumbled some vague something about tips.

"Tips!" Mrs. Brady hissed it. She almost spat it. Plainly money was nothing, nothing at all, to this lady. "I just wish," said Mrs. Brady, and glared at Miss Levin, "I just wish *you* had to spend one Saturday night, just one, in that dressing room! Bein' pushed an' stepped on and near knocked down by that gang of hussies, an' them orderin' an' bossin' you round like you was *black*, an' usin' your things an' then sayin' they're sorry, they got no change, they'll be back. Yeah! They *never* come back!"

"There's Mr. Costello," whispered Miss Levin through lips that, like a ventriloquist's, scarcely stirred.

"An' as I was sayin'," Mrs. Brady said at once brightly, "I got to leave you. Ten to ten, time I was on the job."

She smirked at Miss Levin, nodded, and right-about-faced. There, indeed, Mr. Costello was. Mr. Billy Costello, manager, proprietor, monarch of all he surveyed. From the doorway of the big room where the little tables herded in a ring around the waxen floor, he surveyed Mrs. Brady, and in such a way that Mrs. Brady, momentarily forgetting her bad heart, walked fast, scurried faster, almost ran.

The door of her domain was set politely in an alcove, beyond silken curtains looped up at the sides. Mrs. Brady reached it breathless, shouldered it open, and groped for the electric switch. Lights sprang up, a bright white blaze, intolerable for an instant to the eyes, like sun on snow. Blinking, Mrs. Brady shut the door.

The room was a spotless, white-tiled place, half beauty shop, half dressing room. Along one wall stood washstands, sturdy triplets in a row, with pale green liquid soap in glass balloons afloat above them. Against the opposite wall there was a couch. A third wall backed an elongated glass-topped dressing table; and over the dressing table and over the washstands long rectangular sheets of mirror reflected lights, doors, glossy tiles, lights multiplied. . . .

Mrs. Brady moved across this glitter like a thick dark cloud in a hurry. At the dressing table she came to a halt, and upon it she laid her newspaper, her magazine, and her purse—a black purse worn gray with much clutching. She divested herself of a rusty black coat and a hat of the mushroom persuasion, and hung both up in a corner cupboard which she opened by means of one of a quite preposterous bunch of keys. From a nook in the cupboard she took down a lace-edged handkerchief with long streamers. She untied the streamers and tied them again around her chunky black alpaca waist. The handkerchief became an apron's baby cousin.

Mrs. Brady relocked the cupboard door, fumbled her key ring over, and unlocked a capacious drawer of the dressing table. She spread a fresh towel on the plate glass top, in the geometrical center, and upon the towel she arranged with care a procession of things fished from the drawer. Things for the hair. Things for the complexion. Things for the eyes, the lashes, the brows, the lips, and the finger-nails. Things in boxes and things in jars and things in tubes and tins. Also an ashtray, matches, pins, a tiny sewing kit, a pair of scissors. Last of all, a hand-printed sign, a nudging sort of sign: NOTICE! THESE ARTICLES, PLACED HERE FOR YOUR CONVENIENCE, ARE THE PROPERTY OF THE MAID. And directly beneath the sign, propping it up against the looking glass, a china saucer, in which Mrs. Brady now slyly laid decoy money: two quarters and two dimes, in four-leaf clover formation.

Another drawer yielded a bottle of Bromo Seltzer, a bottle of aromatic spirits of ammonia, a tin of sodium bicarbonate, and a teaspoon. These were lined up on a shelf above the couch.

Mrs. Brady was now ready for anything. And (from the grim, thin pucker of her mouth) expecting it.

Music came to her ears. Rather, the beat of music, muffled, rhythmic, remote. *Umpa-um, umpa-um, umpa-um-umm*—Mr. "Fiddle" Baer and his band, hard at work on the first fox-trot of the night. It was teasing, foot-tapping music; but the large solemn feet of Mrs. Brady were still. She sat on the couch and opened her newspaper; and for some moments she read uninterruptedly, with special attention to the murders, the divorces, the breaches of promise, the funnies.

Then the door swung inward, admitting a blast of Mr. Fiddle Baer's best, a whiff of perfume, and a girl.

Mrs. Brady put her paper away.

The girl was petite and darkly beautiful; wrapped in fur and mounted on tall jeweled heels. She entered humming the ragtime song the orchestra was playing, and while she stood near the dressing table, stripping off her gloves, she continued to hum it softly to herself: *"Oh! I know my baby loves me, I can tell my baby loves me."* Here the dark little girl got the left glove off, and Mrs. Brady glimpsed a platinum wedding ring. *"Cause there ain't no maybe in my baby's eyes."*

The right glove came off. The dark little girl sat down in one of the chairs that faced the dressing table. She doffed her wrap, casting it carelessly over the chair back. It had a cloth-of-gold lining, and the name of a Paris house was embroidered in curlicues on the label. Mrs. Brady hovered solicitously near.

The dark little girl, still humming, looked over the articles, "placed here for your convenience," and picked up the scissors. Having cut off a very small hangnail with the air of one performing a perilous major operation, she seized and used the manicure buffer, and after that the eyebrow pencil. Mrs. Brady's mind, hopefully calculating the tip, jumped and jumped again like a taximeter.

"Oh! I know my baby loves me—" The dark little girl applied powder and lipstick belonging to herself. She examined the result searchingly in the mirror and sat back, satisfied. She cast some silver, *Klink! Klink!*

into Mrs. Brady's saucer, and half rose. Then, remembering something, she settled down again.

The ensuing thirty seconds were spent by her in pulling off her platinum wedding ring, tying it in a corner of a lace handkerchief, and tucking the handkerchief down the bodice of her tight white velvet gown.

"There!" she said.

She swooped up her wrap and trotted toward the door, jeweled heels merrily twinkling. *"Cause there ain't no maybe—"* The door fell shut.

Almost instantly it opened again, and another girl came in. A blonde, this. She was pretty in a round-eyed, doll-like way; but Mrs. Brady, regarding her, mentally grabbed the spirits of ammonia bottle. For she looked terribly ill. The round eyes were dull, the pretty, silly little face was drawn. The thin hands, picking at the fastenings of a specious beaded bag, trembled and twitched.

Mrs. Brady cleared her throat. "Can I do something for you, miss?"

Evidently the blond girl had believed herself alone in the dressing room. She started violently and glanced up, panic in her eyes. Panic, and something else. Something very like murderous hate—but for an instant only, so that Mrs. Brady, whose perceptions were never quick, missed it altogether.

"A glass of water?" suggested Mrs. Brady.

"No," said the girl, "no." She had one hand in the beaded bag now. Mrs. Brady could see it moving, causing the bag to squirm like a live thing, and the fringe to shiver. "Yes!" she cried abruptly. "A glass of water—please—you get it for me." She dropped onto the couch.

Mrs. Brady scurried to the water cooler in the corner, pressed the spigot with a determined thumb. Water trickled out thinly. Mrs. Brady pressed harder, and scowled, and thought, "Something's wrong with this thing. I mustn't forget, next time I see Mr. Costello—"

When again she faced her patient, the patient was sitting erect. She was thrusting her clenched hand back into the beaded bag again.

She took only a sip of the water, but it seemed to help her quite miraculously. Almost at once color came to her cheeks, life to her eyes. She grew young again—as young as she was. She smiled up at Mrs. Brady.

"Well!" she exclaimed. "What do you know about that!" She shook her honey-colored head. "I can't imagine what came over me."

"Are you better now?" inquired Mrs. Brady.

"Yes. Oh, yes. I'm better now. You see," said the blond girl confidentially, "we were at the theater, my boy friend and I, and it was hot and stuffy—I guess that must have been the trouble."

She paused, and the ghost of her recent distress crossed her face. "God! I thought that last act *never* would end!" she said.

While she attended to her hair and complexion, she chattered gaily to Mrs. Brady, chattered on with scarcely a stop for breath, and laughed much. She said, among other things, that she and her "boy friend" had not known one another very long, but that she was "gaga" about him. "He is about me, too," she confessed. "He thinks I'm grand."

She fell silent then, and in the looking glass her eyes were shadowed, haunted. But Mrs. Brady, from where she stood, could not see the looking glass; and half a minute later the blond girl laughed and began again. When she went out she seemed to dance out on little winged feet; and Mrs. Brady, sighing, thought it must be nice to be young . . . and happy like that.

The next arrivals were two. A tall, extremely smart young woman in black chiffon entered first, and held the door open for her companion; and the instant the door was shut, she said, as though it had been on the tip of her tongue for hours, "Amy, what under the sun *happened?*"

Amy, who was brown-eyed, brown-bobbed-haired, and patently annoyed about something, crossed to the dressing table and flopped into a chair before she made reply.

"Nothing," she said wearily then.

"That's nonsense!" snorted the other. "Tell me. Was it something she said? She's a tactless ass, of course. Always was."

"No, not anything she said. It was—" Amy bit her lip. "All right! I'll tell you. Before we left your apartment I just happened to notice that Tom had disappeared. So I went to look for him—I wanted to ask him if he'd remembered to tell the maid where we were going— Skippy's subject to croup, you know, and we always leave word. Well, so I went into the kitchen, thinking Tom might be there mixing cocktails—and there he was—and there *she* was!"

The full red mouth of the other young woman pursed itself slightly. Her arched brows lifted. "Well?"

Her matter-of-factness appeared to infuriate Amy. "He was *kissing* her!" she flung out.

"Well?" said the other again. She chuckled softly and patted Amy's shoulder, as if it were the shoulder of a child. "You're surely not going to let *that* spoil your whole evening? Amy *dear!* Kissing may once have been serious and significant—but it isn't nowadays. Nowadays it's like shaking hands. It means nothing."

But Amy was not consoled. "I hate her!" she cried desperately. "Redheaded *thing!* Calling me darling and honey, and s-sending me handkerchiefs for C-Christmas—and then sneaking off behind closed doors and k-kissing my h-h-husband—"

At this point Amy broke down, but she recovered herself sufficiently to add with venom, "I'd like to slap her!"

"Oh, oh, oh," smiled the tall young woman, "I wouldn't do that!"

Amy wiped her eyes with what might well have been one of the Christmas handkerchiefs, and confronted her friend. "Well, what *would* you do, Vera? If you were I?"

"I'd forget it," said Vera, "and have a good time. I'd kiss somebody myself. You've no idea how much better you'd feel!"

"I don't do—" Amy began indignantly; but as the door behind her opened and a third young woman—redheaded, earringed, exquisite— lilted in, she changed her tone. "Oh, hello!" she called sweetly, beaming at the newcomer via the mirror. "We were wondering what had become of you!"

The redheaded girl, smiling easily back, dropped her cigarette on the floor and crushed it out with a silver-shod toe. "Tom and I were talking to Fiddle Baer," she explained. "He's going to play 'Clap Yo' Hands' next, because it's my favorite. Lend me a comb, will you?"

"There's a comb," said Vera, indicating Mrs. Brady's business comb.

"But imagine using it!" murmured the redheaded girl. "Amy, darling, haven't you one?"

Amy produced a tiny comb from her rhinestone purse. "Don't forget to bring it when you come," she said, and stood up. "I'm going on out, I want to tell Tom something." She went.

The redheaded young woman and the tall black-chiffon one were alone, except for Mrs. Brady. The redheaded one beaded her incredible lashes. The tall one, the one called Vera, sat watching her. Presently she said, "Sylvia, look here." And Sylvia looked. Anybody, addressed in that tone, would have.

"There is one thing," Vera went on quietly, holding the other's eyes, "that I want understood. And that is, *'Hands off!'* Do you hear me?"

"I don't know what you mean."

"You do know what I mean!"

The redheaded girl shrugged her shoulders. "Amy told you she saw us, I suppose."

"Precisely. And," went on Vera, gathering up her possessions and rising, "as I said before, you're to keep away." Her eyes blazed sudden white-hot rage. "Because, as you very well know, he belongs to *me*," she said, and departed, slamming the door.

BETWEEN ELEVEN o'clock and one Mrs. Brady was very busy indeed. Never for more than a moment during those two hours was the dressing room empty. Often it was jammed, full to overflowing with curled cropped heads, with ivory arms and shoulders, with silk and lace and chiffon, with legs. The door flapped in and back, in and back. The mirrors caught and held—and lost—a hundred different faces. Powder veiled the dressing table with a thin white dust; cigarette stubs, scarlet at the tips, choked the ashtray. Dimes and quarters clattered into Mrs. Brady's saucer—and were transferred to Mrs. Brady's purse. The original seventy cents remained. That much, and no more, would Mrs. Brady gamble on the integrity of womankind.

She earned her money. She threaded needles and took stitches. She powdered the backs of necks. She supplied towels for soapy, dripping hands. She removed a speck from a teary blue eye and pounded the heel on a slipper. She curled the straggling ends of a black bob and a gray bob, pinned a velvet flower on a lithe round waist, mixed three doses of bicarbonate of soda, took charge of a shed pink satin girdle, collected, on hands and knees, several dozen fake pearls that had wept from a broken string.

She served chorus girls and schoolgirls, gay young matrons and gayer young mistresses, a lady who had divorced four husbands, and a lady who had poisoned one, the secret (more or less) sweetheart of a Most Distinguished Name, and the Brains of a bootleg gang. . . . She saw things. She saw a yellow check, with the ink hardly dry. She saw four tiny bruises, such as fingers might make, on an arm. She saw a girl strike another girl, not playfully. She saw a bundle of letters some man wished he had not written, safe and deep in a brocaded handbag.

ABOUT MIDNIGHT the door flew open and at once was pushed shut, and a gray-eyed, lovely child stood backed against it, her palms flattened on the panels at her sides, the draperies of her white chiffon gown settling lightly to rest around her.

There were already five damsels of varying ages in the dressing room. The latest arrival marked their presence with a flick of her eyes and, standing just where she was, she called peremptorily, "Maid!"

Mrs. Brady, standing just where *she* was, said, "Yes, miss?"

"Please come here," said the girl.

Mrs. Brady, as slowly as she dared, did so.

The girl lowered her voice to a tense half whisper. "Listen! Is there any way I can get out of here except through this door I came in?"

Mrs. Brady stared at her stupidly.

"Any window?" persisted the girl. "Or anything?"

Here they were interrupted by the exodus of two of the damsels of varying ages. Mrs. Brady opened the door for them—and in so doing caught a glimpse of a man who waited in the hall outside, a debonair, old-young man with a girl's furry wrap hung over his arm, and his hat in his hand.

The door clicked. The gray-eyed girl moved out from the wall, against which she had flattened herself—for all the world like one eluding pursuit in a cinema.

"What about that window?" she demanded, pointing.

"That's all the farther it opens," said Mrs. Brady.

"Oh! And it's the only one—isn't it?"

"It is."

"Damn," said the girl. "Then there's *no* way out?"

"No way but the door," said Mrs. Brady testily.

The girl looked at the door. She seemed to look *through* the door, and to despise and to fear what she saw. Then she looked at Mrs. Brady. "Well," she said, "then I s'pose the only thing for me to do is to stay in here."

She stayed. Minutes ticked by. Jazz crooned distantly, stopped, struck up again. Other girls came and went. Still the gray-eyed girl sat on the couch, with her back to the wall and her shapely legs crossed, smoking cigarettes, one from the stub of another.

After a long while she said, "Maid!"

"Yes, miss?"

"Peek out that door, will you, and see if there's anyone standing there."

Mrs. Brady peeked, and reported that there was a gentleman with a little bit of a black mustache standing there. The same gentleman, in fact, who was standing there "just after you came in."

"Oh, Lord," sighed the gray-eyed girl. "Well . . . I can't stay here all *night*, that's one sure thing." She slid off the couch and went listlessly to the dressing table. There she occupied herself for a minute or two. Suddenly, without a word, she darted out.

Thirty seconds later Mrs. Brady was elated to find two crumpled one-dollar bills lying in her saucer. Her joy, however, died a premature death. For she made an almost simultaneous second discovery. A saddening one. Above all, a puzzling one.

"Now what for," marveled Mrs. Brady, "did she want to walk off with them *scissors?*"

This at twelve twenty-five.

At twelve thirty a quartet of excited young things burst in, babbling madly. All of them had their evening wraps with them; all talked at once. One of them, a Dresden-china girl with a heart-shaped face, was the center of attraction. Around her the rest fluttered like monstrous butterflies; to her they addressed their shrill exclamatory cries. "Babe," they called her.

Mrs. Brady heard snatches: "Not in this state unless . . ." "Well, you can in Maryland, Jimmy says." "Oh, there must be someplace nearer than . . ." "Isn't this marvelous?" "When did it happen, Babe? When did you decide?"

315

"Just now," the girl with the heart-shaped face sang softly, "when we were dancing."

The babble resumed, "But listen, Babe, what'll your mother and father . . . ?" "Oh, never mind, let's hurry." "Shall we be warm enough with just these thin wraps, do you think? Babe, will you be warm enough? Sure?"

Powder flew and little pocket combs marched through bright marcels. Flushed cheeks were painted pinker still.

"My pearls," said Babe, "are *old*. And my dress and my slippers are *new*. Now, let's see—what can I *borrow?*"

A lace handkerchief, a diamond bar pin, a pair of earrings were proffered. She chose the bar pin, and its owner unpinned it proudly.

"I've got blue garters!" exclaimed a shrill little girl in a silver dress.

"Give me one, then," directed Babe. "I'll trade with you. . . . There! That fixes that."

More babbling, "Hurry! Hurry up!" . . . "Listen, are you *sure* we'll be warm enough? Because we can stop at my house, there's nobody home." "Give me that puff, Babe, I'll powder your back." "And just to think a week ago you'd never even met each other!" "Oh, hurry *up*, let's get *started!*" "I'm ready." "So'm I." "Ready, Babe? You look adorable." "Come on, everybody."

They were gone again, and the dressing room seemed twice as still and vacant as before.

A minute of grace, during which Mrs. Brady wiped the spilled powder away with a damp gray rag. Then the door jumped open again. Two evening gowns appeared and made for the dressing table in a beeline. Slim tubular gowns they were, one green, one palest yellow. Yellow hair went with the green gown, brown hair with the yellow. The green-gowned, yellow-haired girl wore gardenias on her left shoulder, four of them, and a flashing bracelet on each fragile wrist. The other girl looked less prosperous; still, you would rather have looked at her.

Both ignored Mrs. Brady's cosmetic display as utterly as they ignored Mrs. Brady, producing full field equipment of their own.

"Well," said the girl with gardenias, rouging energetically, "how do you like him?"

"Oh-h—all right."

"Meaning, 'Not any,' hmm? I suspected as much!" The girl with gardenias turned in her chair and scanned her companion's profile with disapproval. "See here, Marilee," she drawled, "are you going to be a damn fool *all* your life?"

"He's fat," said Marilee dreamily. "Fat, and—greasy, sort of. I mean, greasy in his mind. Don't you know what I mean?"

"I know *one* thing," declared the other. "I know Who He Is! And if I were you, that's all I'd need to know. *Under the circumstances.*"

The last three words, stressed meaningly, affected the girl called Marilee curiously. She grew grave. Her lips and lashes drooped. For some seconds she sat frowning a little, breaking a black-sheathed lipstick in two and fitting it together again.

"She's worse," she said finally, low.

"Worse?"

Marilee nodded.

"Well," said the girl with gardenias, "there you are. It's the climate. She'll never be anything *but* worse, if she doesn't get away. Out west. Arizona or somewhere."

"I know," murmured Marilee.

The other girl opened a tin of eye shadow. "Of course," she said dryly, "suit yourself. She's not *my* sister."

Marilee said nothing. Quiet she sat, breaking the lipstick, mending it, breaking it.

"Oh, well," she breathed finally, wearily, and straightened up. She propped her elbows on the plate glass dressing-table top and leaned toward the mirror, and with the lipstick she began to make her coral-pink mouth very red and gay and reckless and alluring.

NIGHTLY AT ONE o'clock Vane and Moreno dance for the Club Français. They dance a tango, they dance a waltz; then, by way of encore, they do a Black Bottom, and a trick of their own called the Wheel. They dance for twenty, thirty minutes. And while they dance you do not leave your table—for this is what you came to see. Vane and Moreno. The new New York thrill. The sole justification for the five-dollar *couvert* extorted by Billy Costello.

From one until half past, then, was Mrs. Brady's recess. She had been looking forward to it all the evening long. When it began—when the opening chords of the tango music sounded stirringly from the room outside—Mrs. Brady brightened. With a right good will she sped the parting guests.

Alone, she unlocked her cupboard and took out her magazine—the magazine she had bought three hours before. Heaving a great breath of relief and satisfaction, she plumped herself on the couch and fingered the pages.

Immediately she was absorbed, her eyes drinking up printed lines, her lips moving soundlessly.

The magazine was Mrs. Brady's favorite. Its stories were true stories, taken from life (so the editor said); and to Mrs. Brady they were live, vivid threads in the dull, drab pattern of her night.

THE SILK

JOY COWLEY

Joy Cowley

WHEN MR. BLACKIE took bad again that autumn both he and Mrs. Blackie knew that it was for the last time. For many weeks neither spoke of it; but the understanding was in their eyes as they watched each other through the days and nights. It was a look, not of sadness or despair, but of quiet resignation tempered with something else, an unnamed expression that is seen only in the old and the very young.

Their acceptance was apparent in other ways, too. Mrs. Blackie no longer complained to the neighbours that the old lazy-bones was running her off her feet. Instead she waited on him tirelessly, stretching their pension over chicken and out-of-season fruits to tempt his appetite; and she guarded him so possessively that she even resented the twice-weekly visits from the District Nurse. Mr. Blackie, on the other hand, settled into bed as gently as dust. He had never been a man to dwell in the past, but now he spoke a great deal of their earlier days and surprised Mrs. Blackie by recalling things which she, who claimed the better memory, had forgotten. Seldom did he talk of the present, and never in these weeks did he mention the future.

Then, on the morning of the first frost of winter, while Mrs. Blackie was filling his hot water bottle, he sat up in bed, unaided, to see out the window. The inside of the glass was streaked with tears of condensation. Outside, the frost had made an oval frame of crystals through which he could see a row of houses and lawns laid out in front of them, like white carpets.

"The ground will be hard," he said at last. "Hard as nails."

Mrs. Blackie looked up quickly. "Not yet," she said.

"Pretty soon, I think." His smile was apologetic.

She slapped the hot water bottle into its cover and tested it against her cheek. "Lie down or you'll get a chill." she said.

Obediently, he dropped back against the pillow, but as she moved about him, putting the hot water bottle at his feet, straightening the quilt, he stared at the frozen patch of window.

"Amy, you'll get a double plot, won't you?" he said. "I wouldn't rest easy thinking you were going to sleep by someone else."

"What a thing to say!" The corner of her mouth twitched. "As if I would."

"It was your idea to buy single beds," he said accusingly.

"Oh Herb—" She looked at the window, away again. "We'll have a double plot," she said. For a second or two she hesitated by his bed, then she sat beside his feet, her hands placed one on top of the other in her lap, in a pose that she always adopted when she had something important to say. She cleared her throat.

"You know, I've been thinking on and off about the silk."

"The silk?" He turned his head towards her.

"I want to use it for your laying out pyjamas."

"No Amy," he said. "Not the silk. That was your wedding present, the only thing I brought back with me."

"What would I do with it now?" she said. When he didn't answer, she got up, opened the wardrobe door and took the camphorwood box from the shelf where she kept her hats. "All these years and us not daring to take a scissors to it. We should use it sometime."

"Not on me," he said.

"I've been thinking about your pyjamas." She fitted a key into the brass box. "It'd be just right."

"A right waste, you mean," he said. But there was no protest in his voice. In fact, it had lifted with a childish eagerness. He watched her hands as she opened the box and folded back layers of white tissue paper. Beneath them lay the blue of the silk. There was a reverent silence as she took it out and spread it under the light.

"Makes the whole room look different, doesn't it?" he said. "I nearly forgot it looked like this." His hands struggled free of the sheet and moved across the quilt. Gently, she picked up the blue material and poured it over his fingers.

"Aah," he breathed, bringing it closer to his eyes. "All the way from China." He smiled. "Not once did I let it out of me sight. You know that, Amy? There were those on board as would have pinched it quick as that. I kept it pinned round me middle."

"You told me," she said.

He rubbed the silk against the stubble of his chin. "It's the birds that take your eye," he said.

"At first," said Mrs. Blackie. She ran her fingers over one of the peacocks that strutted in the foreground of a continuous landscape. They were proud birds, irridescent blue, with silver threads in their tails. "I used to like them best, but after a while you see much more, just as fine only smaller." She pushed her glasses onto the bridge of her nose and leaned over the silk, her finger guiding her eyes over islands where waterfalls hung, eternally suspended, between pagodas and dark blue conifers, over flat lakes and tiny fishing boats, over mountains where the mists never lifted, and back again to a haughty peacock caught with one foot suspended over a rock. "It's a work of art like you never see in this country," she said.

Mr. Blackie inhaled the scent of camphorwood. "Don't cut it, Amy. It's too good for an old blighter like me." He was begging her to contradict him.

"I'll get the pattern tomorrow," she said.

The next day, while the District Nurse was giving him his injection, she went down to the store and looked through a pile of pattern books. Appropriately, she chose a mandarin style with a high collar and piped cuffs and pockets. But Mr. Blackie, who had all his life worn striped flannel in the conventional design, looked with suspicion at the pyjama pattern and the young man who posed so easily and shamelessly on the front of the packet.

"It's the sort them teddy bear boys have," he said.

"Nonsense," said Mrs. Blackie.

"That's exactly what they are," he growled. "You're not laying me out in a lot of new-fangled nonsense."

Mrs. Blackie put her hands on her hips. "You'll not have any say in the matter," she said.

"Won't I just? I'll get up and fight—see if I don't."

The muscles at the corner of her mouth twitched uncontrollably. "All right, Herb, if you're so set against it—"

But now, having won the argument, he was happy. "Get away with you, Amy. I'll get used to the idea." He threw his lips back against his gums. "Matter of fact, I like them fine. It's that nurse that done it. Blunt needle again." He looked at the pattern. "When d'you start?"

"Well—"

"This afternoon?"

"I suppose I could pin the pattern out after lunch."

"Do it in here," he said. "Bring in your machine and pins and things and set them up so I can watch."

She stood taller and tucked in her chin. "I'm not using the machine," she said with pride. "Every stitch is going to be done by hand. My eyes mightn't be as good as they were once, mark you, but there's not a person on this earth can say I've lost my touch with a needle."

His eyes closed in thought. "How long?"

"Eh?"

"Till it's finished."

She turned the pattern over in her hands. "Oh—about three or four weeks. That is—if I keep it."

"No," he said. "Too long."

"Oh Herb, you'd want a good job done, wouldn't you?" she pleaded.

"Amy—" Almost imperceptibly, he shook his head on the pillow.

"I can do the main seams on the machine," she said, lowering her voice.

"How long?"

"A week," she whispered.

When she took down the silk that afternoon, he insisted on an extra pillow in spite of the warning he'd had from the doctor about lying flat with his legs propped higher than his head and shoulders.

She plumped up the pillow from her own bed and put it behind his neck; then she unrolled her tape measure along his body, legs, arms, around his chest.

"I'll have to take them in a bit," she said, making inch-high black figures on a piece of cardboard. She took the tissue-paper pattern into the kitchen to iron it flat. When she came back, he was waiting, wide-eyed with anticipation and brighter, she thought, than he'd been for many weeks.

As she laid the silk out on her bed and started pinning down the first of the pattern pieces, he described, with painstaking attempts at accuracy, the boat trip home, the stop at Hong Kong, and the merchant who had sold him the silk. "Most of his stuff was rubbish," he said. "You wouldn't look twice at it. This was the only decent thing he had and even then he done me. You got to argue with these devils. Beat him down, they told me. But there was others as wanted that silk and if I hadn't made up me mind there and then I'd have lost it." He squinted at her hands. "What are you doing now? You just put that bit down."

"It wasn't right," she said, through lips closed on pins. "I have to match it—like wallpaper."

She lifted the pattern pieces many times before she was satisfied. Then it was evening and he was so tired that his breathing had become laboured. He no longer talked. His eyes were watering from hours of concentration; the drops spilled over his red lids and soaked into the pillow.

"Go to sleep," she said. "Enough's enough for one day."

"I'll see you cut it out first," he said.

"Let's leave it till the morning," she said, and they both sensed her reluctance to put the scissors to the silk.

"Tonight," he said.

"I'll make the tea first."

"After," he said.

She took the scissors from her sewing drawer and wiped them on her apron. Together they felt the pain as the blades met cleanly, almost without resistance, in that first cut. The silk would never again be the same. They were changing it, rearranging the pattern of fifty-odd years to form something new and unfamiliar. When she had cut out the first piece, she held it up, still pinned to the paper, and said, "The back of the top." Then she laid it on the dressing table and went on as quickly as she dared, for she knew that he would not rest until she had finished.

One by one the garment pieces left the body of silk. With each touch of the blades, threads sprang apart; mountains were divided, peacocks split from head to tail; waterfalls fell on either side of fraying edges. Eventually, there was nothing on the bed but a few shining snippets. Mrs. Blackie picked them up and put them back in the camphorwood box, and covered the pyjama pieces on the dressing table with a cloth. Then she removed the extra pillow from Mr. Blackie's bed and laid his head back in a comfortable position before she went into the kitchen to make the tea.

He was very tired the next morning but refused to sleep while she was working with the silk. She invented a number of excuses for putting it aside and leaving the room. He would sleep then, but never for long. No more than half an hour would pass and he would be calling her. She would find him lying awake and impatient for her to resume sewing.

In that day and the next, she did all the machine work. It was a tedious task, for first she tacked each seam by hand, matching the patterns in the weave so that the join was barely noticeable. Mr. Blackie silently supervised every stitch. At times she would see him studying the silk with an expression that she still held in her memory. It was the look he'd given her in their courting days. She felt a prick of jealousy, not because she thought that he cared more for the silk than he did for her, but because he saw something in it that she didn't share. She never asked him what it was. At her age a body did not question these things or demand explanations. She would bend her head lower and concentrate her energy and attention into the narrow seam beneath the needle.

On the Friday afternoon, four days after she'd started the pyjamas, she finished the buttonholes and sewed on the buttons. She'd deliberately hurried the last of the hand sewing. In the four days, Mr. Blackie had become weaker, and she knew that the sooner the pyjamas were completed and put back in the camphorwood box out of sight, the sooner he would take an interest in food and have the rest he needed.

She snipped the last thread and put the needle in its case.

"That's it, Herb," she said, showing him her work.

He tried to raise his head. "Bring them over here." he said.

"Well—what do you think?" As she brought the pyjamas closer, his eyes relaxed and he smiled.

"Try them on?" he said.

She shook her head. "I got the measurements," she said. "They'll be the right fit."

"Better make sure," he said.

She hesitated but could find no reason for her reluctance.

"All right," she said, switching on both bars of the electric heater and drawing it closer to his bed. "Just to make sure I've got the buttons right."

She peeled back the bedclothes, took off his thick pyjamas and put on the silk. She stepped back to look at him.

"Well, even if I do say so myself, there's no one could have done a better job. I could move the top button over a fraction, but apart from that they're a perfect fit."

He grinned. "Light, aren't they?" He looked down the length of his body and wriggled his toes. "All the way from China. Never let it out of me sight. Know that, Amy?"

"Do you like them?" she said.

He sucked his lips in over his gums to hide his pleasure. "All right. A bit on the tight side."

"They are not, and you know it," Mrs. Blackie snapped. "Never give a body a bit of credit, would you? Here, put your hands down and I'll change you before you get a chill."

He tightened his arms across his chest. "You made a right good job, Amy. Think I'll keep them on a bit."

"No." She picked up his thick pyjamas.

"Why not?"

"Because you can't," she said. "It—it's disrespectful. And the nurse will be here soon."

"Oh, get away with you, Amy." He was too weak to resist further but as she changed him, he still possessed the silk with his eyes. "Wonder who made it?"

Although she shrugged his question away, it brought to her a definite picture of a Chinese woman seated in front of a loom surrounded by blue and silver silkworms. The woman was dressed from a page in a geographic magazine, and except for the Oriental line of her eyelids, she looked like Mrs. Blackie.

"D'you suppose there's places like that?" Mr. Blackie asked.

She snatched up the pyjamas and put them in the box. "You're the one that's been there," she said briskly. "Now settle down and rest or you'll be bad when the nurse arrives."

The District Nurse did not come that afternoon. Nor in the evening. It was at half-past three the following morning that her footsteps, echoed by the doctor's sounded along the gravel path.

Mrs. Blackie was in the kitchen, waiting. She sat straight-backed and dry-eyed, her hands placed one on top of the other in the lap of her dressing gown.

"Mrs. Blackie. I'm sorry—"

She ignored the nurse and turned to the doctor. "He didn't say goodbye," she said with an accusing look. "Just before I phoned. His hand was over the side of the bed. I touched it. It was cold."

The doctor nodded.

"No sound of any kind," she said. "He was good as gold last night."

Again, the doctor nodded. He put his hand, briefly, on her shoulder, then went into the bedroom. Within a minute he returned, fastening his leather bag and murmuring sympathy.

Mrs. Blackie sat still, catching isolated words. Expected. Peacefully.

Brave. They dropped upon her—neat, geometrical shapes that had no meaning.

"He didn't say goodbye." She shook her head. "Not a word."

"But look, Mrs. Blackie," soothed the nurse. "It was inevitable. You knew that. He couldn't have gone on—"

"I know, I know." She turned away, irritated by their lack of understanding. "He just might have said goodbye. That's all."

The doctor took a white tablet from a phial and tried to persuade her to swallow it. She pushed it away; refused, too, the cup of tea that the District Nurse poured and set in front of her. When they picked up their bags and went towards the bedroom, she followed them.

"In a few minutes," the doctor said. "If you'll leave us—"

"I'm getting his pyjamas," she said. 'There's a button needs changing. I can do it now."

As soon as she entered the room, she glanced at Mr. Blackie's bed and noted that the doctor had pulled up the sheet. Quickly, she lifted the camphorwood box, took a needle, cotton, scissors, her spectacle case, and went back to the kitchen. Through the half-closed door she heard the nurse's voice, "Poor old thing," and she knew, instinctively, that they were not talking about her.

She sat down at the table to thread the needle. Her eyes were clear but her hands were so numb that for a long time they refused to work together. At last, the thread knotted, she opened the camphorwood box. The beauty of the silk was always unexpected. As she spread the pyjamas out on the table, it warmed her, caught her up and comforted her with the first positive feeling she'd had that morning. The silk was real. It was brought to life by the electric light above the table, so that every fold of the woven landscape moved. Trees swayed towards rippling water and peacocks danced with white fire in their tails. Even the tiny bridges—

Mrs. Blackie took off her glasses, wiped them, put them on again. She leaned forward and traced her thumbnail over one bridge, then another. And another. She turned over the pyjama coat and closely examined the back. It was there, on every bridge; something she hadn't noticed before. She got up, and from the drawer where she kept her tablecloths, she took out a magnifying glass.

As the bridge in the pattern of the silk grew, the figure which had been no larger than an ant, became a man.

Mrs. Blackie forgot about the button and the murmur of voices in the bedroom. She brought the magnifying glass nearer her eyes.

It was a man and he was standing with one arm outstretched, on the highest span between two islands. Mrs. Blackie studied him for a long time, then she straightened up and smiled. Yes, he was waving. Or perhaps, she thought, he was beckoning to her.

ACTION
LEN DEIGHTON

Len Deighton

JOHN DOVER knew how his story must begin. Not in the imposing old mansion that was used as an Officers' Mess. That was full of leather armchairs, Irish linen and passable food. It was like a London club, except that the voices from the anteroom were too shrill and guest nights too much of a rumpus. The Mess was a warm comfortable place. That came later, much later.

John Dover's story began in a place that was cold, wet and miserable: a place where men would go only to sleep. Or try to sleep. B Flight pits was such a place. "Pit" was slang for bed, and there were forty beds in tiny hardboard cubicles in the four tar-black corrugated-iron huts on the exposed side of the RAF airfield at Warley. They were far beyond B Flight. Even beyond the Repair Party hangar, where crippled bombers were parked waiting to be dissected and disembowelled by factory-trained civvies who made more money each week than the commanding officer.

Originally the pits were a shelter for ground crews who spent their duty hours out there on the edge of the world where the wind honed its edge on the wet fenland of East Anglia. It was only after a Canadian squadron had arrived the previous autumn—bringing an unusually high proportion of officer air crews—that the pits became the "Officers" Mess annexe. Out of bounds to other ranks except on duty. The notice had long since been mud spattered, knocked askew and broken. Finally it disappeared into one of the temperamental iron stoves that kept a haze of dirty smoke hanging over the place.

In winter there was nowhere colder than the pits. Anything that might help to warm the huts was tried. Parachute elastic was fixed to the doors to spring them closed; stolen coal was piled under the beds and every window was sealed with yards of insulating tape. Devoid of ventilation, the huts smelled of unwashed bodies and ancient blankets. There was no running water, and the duty crews had grown tired of refilling the fire buckets that hung in the corridors. They were now cobwebbed and dusty.

Pilot Officer John Dover was the man in Room 33. It was the third room on the right if you entered Hut 4 from the village side. Not that you could get in from the other end—the draughty end—because that was permanently locked to prevent the hut being used as a short-cut in rainy weather. Dover couldn't remember any other sort of weather. The rain dripping from his overcoat had made a large white mark on the lino inside the door. However, compared with some of the rooms, Dover's was luxurious. There was a crudely fashioned reading-light rigged over the iron bedstead, a shelf full of battered paperbacks and a torn armchair—rescued from the dump—with its stuffing supplemented with a buckshee overcoat.

On the wall there was a snapshot photo of Dover's Lancaster bomber—"Santa Claus"—with Dover standing under the nose. He wouldn't allow the whole crew to be photographed together because so many of the old-timers vowed that Fortune took a fast revenge upon crews that did so.

Under the photo there was a sectional drawing of an Avro Lancaster clipped from *The Aeroplane* magazine. It was almost indecent in its revelation of each nut and bolt, each spar and former of the great machine that Dover had flown to within ten thousand feet of so many German cities. There was a calendar above the drawing. Red pencil marks dated each trip: twenty-three red marks, seven to go.

Dover wished that there were no more to go. Not even the most genial of his instructors had seen Dover as a natural pilot. In fact he suspected that he passed the flying course only because he'd never once complained about the airsickness that dogged him right through it. Even now, after two hundred and fifty hours in Lancs, he still suffered nausea when the weather was bad. On his twentieth trip—to Essen— the weather had closed in to ten-tenths cloud. He'd circled the whole of Yorkshire trying to find an aerodrome clear enough to land upon. The strain of this, following the stress he'd suffered over the heavily defended target, had caused him to vomit for almost an hour. Luckily his engineer had been close enough to take the controls. Dover himself had taken over for the actual landing, but after that he'd been almost carried from the aircraft. The blokes were wonderful: not one of them mentioned the fact at any time. But now Dover knew that airsickness could be totally incapacitating. Sometimes he worried what would happen to his crew if he suffered it again.

John Dover inhaled deeply of the cold air. In winter dusk came early, just as it had nearly thirty years ago when he lived on this field, in this dilapidated hut that became a pigsty. He could hear a Lanc on the circuit. The trees of Dirty Lane hid the great machines as they passed over Warley Fen village. When they came into sight to the right of the church steeple you could watch out for the bank of the wings as they came on to finals. You could tell then: you could tell if they were badly shot up or the driver was not at his best. "Not at his best" was the Wingo's way of saying half dead. That Wingo: a cold fish. The red Very lights had already been fired to keep the other planes circling and clear of the cripple. The sky behind the church was dark, and he couldn't see the aeroplane. He felt for his spectacles and put them on before he realized that the sound he could hear was traffic on the Great North Road. The planes had all landed a quarter of a century ago; there were no more to come. The blackboards had long since been wiped clean, the telegrams sent, the widows paid, the war won.

"Have you seen enough, John?"

"I thought it was . . ."

"Yes."

"The sky was like this. But it wasn't quite as cold."

"You were younger then, John. You feel the cold more now."

"Remember?"

"Yes, I remember."

The young pilot watched the electric kettle boil as he measured two spoonfuls of tea into a battered metal pot.

"It's dangerous to plug a kettle into the light," said Childs. He was younger than Dover. A fresh-faced youngster with medical officer's badges on his lapels.

Dover poured the hot water carefully. He had no wish to scald himself. "More dangerous," he inquired affably, "than flying to Essen?"

"Why find out?" said Childs. He put milk into both cups.

"It's only bad weather that frightens me," admitted Dover. "And that's when I get sick."

"It's evasive action that makes most chaps queasy," said Childs. "Everyone has a weak spot: I knew one fellow who'd done two tours. He said he always felt sick over the target. O.K. all the way there, O.K. all the way back, just over the target."

"Is that neurotic?"

"Of course it is, we're all neurotic. The way I see it, Ben, if you weren't neurotic you wouldn't be alert enough to do the job you do." They called him Ben as a joke.

"Is that what your old man says, Childsy?" Childs's father was a doctor too. His opinion was often quoted.

Childs nodded. He watched Dover going through all the pockets of his best blue uniform. "What is it, John?"

"The doll."

"When did you see it last?"

"This morning. I had it this morning." Dover tipped three dirty blue shirts, some collars and a torn vest out of a box that came from under his bed. He raked through the soiled clothing with his fingers. He squeezed each pocket to be sure that no celluloid doll was hiding in them. "No one could have taken it," murmured John Dover, "surely?"

"For Christ's sake, Ben!"

"The trouble is, if it dropped into the mud it would be trodden in and no one would see it now that it's dark."

"It will turn up in the morning."

"Perhaps we'll . . ." Dover didn't finish what he was about to say. He rubbed his face and loosened the sheepskin flying-jacket. His face was flushed and shiny. Perhaps he'd not return in the morning; Childs knew he'd been about to say.

The old man shivered as he remembered his fears. Some of the words he heard, others were merely inside his head. He moved nearer to the windows of the hut in order to peer inside. He could see the two airmen and wanted to shout advice to them. One learned a lot in twenty-five years, or was it nearer thirty years? A man learns a different set of values.

"If you think your lucky doll is that important, you shouldn't fly," said Childs.

"That would look great on my medical file, wouldn't it?"

"Just unfit to fly. I don't have to give a reason. That's why they have reserve crews, isn't it?"

"Keep looking, Doc. It's here somewhere."

"It's five to," said Childs.

"Will you keep looking? It's a little pink doll with a green-paper skirt. Parson—my Rear Gunner—won it at a shooting gallery in Blackpool."

"You told me."

"Seemed like a good omen; him being the Rear Gunner and all."

"The crew bus will be leaving."

"You'll keep looking, Stan?" It was the first time that Dover had used his friend's name. Until now it had been Childsy or Doc, but never his real name.

"I'll start at the door and go through everything again."

"We won't take off for another hour." Dover put his peaked cap on and glanced in the mirror. Then he shuffled through the postcards and official forms that were tucked behind the mirror frame, but no doll was there.

"Ben," said Childs, pushing the door closed again, "on my last unit some of the pilots tested their magnetos too many times before take-off."

"Did they?" said Dover impassively.

"The motors overheated. They had to scrub in case of a mechanical fault."

Dover didn't answer.

Childs continued, "They couldn't be blamed for making sure about the mags."

"How did you hear about it?"

"The Engineering Officer noticed it. He mentioned it to me so . . ." His voice trailed away.

"And you want me to try it?" Dover flushed at the thought of having his name mentioned to the M.O. as a possible "lack of confidence." The fact that the M.O. was his friend made the prospect not better but far worse.

"Once. It can happen to anyone once: just nerves, a natural thing."

"O.K., Childsy," said Dover. Childs didn't understand whether Dover meant he had understood him or not. Dover gave a jerky palms-down salute like they had seen in some old Hollywood film. His smile didn't hide the tight lines of anxiety that had appeared on his grey, shrivelled face.

"If I don't—" said Childs.

"Then forget it. It's not that important." The outside door slammed as Dover stamped out over the metal grating that was clogged with ancient mud. There was a rattle as his bicycle was moved from the rack alongside the corrugated hut. "Good luck, Ben," said Childs softly. It was more prayer than farewell, for Dover was far out of earshot.

One after another Childs heard the Lancasters run-up their engines. Dabs of rain hit the dirty windows, and the reading light, by which Childs continued his search, made a tiny dot of gold inside each raindrop. The storm clouds had sunk lower and lower until the ceiling became dangerously little, but tonight was ordered as "a maximum effort" and it would not be scrubbed.

Childs wondered how much of his friend's anxiety was due to the lost mascot, how much to the tough target—Essen again—and how much to the bad weather. Predisposition poor, thought Childs.

"Did I call you Childsy, Stanley?"

"Sometimes you did."

"How frightful," said Dover.

"We were young."

"As young as those two?"

"Younger," said Childs, "and far more stupid."

"A man shouldn't be allowed this agony," said Dover.

"It was your own decision, John."

Even as the two old men watched, the night passed and dawn came. Easy now to say that it was magical, but his life had passed just as quickly. He looked across to the control tower. It was newly painted, and as pristine as it had been that day in 1943 when he'd first arrived here as a sprog officer with the wings still bright on his tunic.

Childs went back to the pits at midday. It had been a bad one: Santa Claus hadn't returned, nor had O Orange. The Admin. Officer was acting as "effects bod" that week. There was a young airman with him who bundled up Dover's uniforms and dirty linen as the Admin. Officer ticked a list. They worked quietly because the pits were full of sleeping officers who had returned from the raid. Now and again there was an anxious cry or some snores, and in the last room someone who could not sleep was stifling his coughs.

"That would be Davidson," said the old man. "He got bronchitis. Never finished his tour, as I remember."

"No," said Childs, "shot down over Hamburg in July '43. During the week of fire raids. One of the first to go, Davidson. On the Monday, I think."

"Really," said Dover. It was funny that it had taken him thirty years to find that out. He'd always faintly resented Davidson getting released from his tour so easily.

"And a celluloid doll," said the airman. He was making three piles: photos and maps for return to the Intelligence Officer, personal effects to be auctioned for the next of kin and a third pile of letters and sometimes photos that were best destroyed. Sometimes the airmen stole the pornographic photos and sold them in the NAAFI.

"Doll," acknowledged the Admin. Officer, adding it to his list. "Put it with the letters." He looked up suddenly as Childs came in, "Hello, Doc, what are you doing here?" He blushed. "Oh, of course, young Dover. I'm awfully sorry."

"Where did you find the doll?" said Childs. He picked it up off the dressing-table.

"The doll? Oh, I don't know, just among all this stuff."

"I didn't go!" shouted the old man. "The inner port engine was overheating. Ask my engineer, ask any of the fitters, they'll tell you why we didn't go." His voice had been so loud that everyone stopped to stare at him. They were angry with him, and rightly so. They were doing a job that was difficult enough, without criticism across thirty years from another generation.

"I'm sorry," said Dover. "I didn't mean to interrupt." After all, it was his idea to come, just as Childs had reminded him. They'd all been awfully kind, too, letting him pry and peer into places he had no right to go.

The young man was very understanding. It was not the first time such a thing had happened. Watching one's past unfold before one's eyes must be a terrible strain. Especially when—as now—a man remembered it all so differently.

Dover tried to explain. "It's just that it wasn't like that."

"Like what?" said the man.

"That business about the magneto switches. I must explain to you."

"Magneto switches?" said the young man. He smiled awkwardly and tried to imagine what the old dotard was talking about. "'Leave it to me sir, we'll wipe out the U-boat pens if it's the last thing we do,'" he read from a large book. "They were the only words spoken, sir."

"I don't remember anything about U-boat pens," said Dover.

"Don't you worry about it, sir. Even the rushes you saw are nothing like the real thing. Once we get the sound effects and the music on it and get a proper graded print, it will look different again."

"It was nothing like this," said Dover sadly. "Nothing like this at all."

"You heard that great music?"

"Yes, I heard it," said Dover.

Childs took the old hero by the arm and spoke quietly to him. "These film people are leaving out the business about you being afraid, John. And also the mix-up when you tested your magnetos and the Wingo threatened to court-martial you for cowardice. In the film you get shot down over Berlin in the end."

"But that was in 1945," said Dover, "that was my third tour. That was two years later, and it was Graz."

"Yes, yes, yes," said Childs gently. He was a Harley Street specialist and well used to the petulance of old age. "But they don't want our war, John. They have writers."

"It wasn't like that," protested Air-Marshal Dover, v.c., d.s.o., d.f.c. "Our war wasn't like that."

"It might have been," said Childs, "if we'd had their incidental music."

INNOCENT PLEASURES

OLIVIA MANNING

Olivia Manning

It was the tram-car in the Transport Museum that reconstituted Mr. Limestone. Before that he had been no more than a little dust buried beneath Emily's rejected and done-for memories of Camber. She had not given him a thought for years. He was probably dead. There might be no one left in Camber who had even heard of him; yet, suddenly, there he was in her mind, as alive as he had ever been, which was not saying much.

When she went closer to read the tram-car's particulars, she was startled, for it was one of Camber's own old tram-cars. There had never been many of them and she must have ridden in this one dozens of times. It had probably taken her again and again to Mr. Limestone's door and now, by some afflatus of its own, it had conjured up the man himself. It had said across the floor: "Limestone", yet she would not have recognised it as a Camber tram-car.

Giving herself distance as though in front of a painting, she viewed the car from the front. She was struck by its elegance. With that tall, narrow prow it might have been built, like a clipper, for speed; instead, it had been a mere public conveyance, scarcely able to get under way before once more grinding to a halt.

The line had run from the north of Camber to the Pier. The tram simply went straight down and back again. She and Edward had called it "the brown tram" to distinguish it from the green, open-topped tram that went into the country; but now she saw it was not brown at all; it was maroon. The maroon outer casing was beautifully bright. Inside, the slatted honey-coloured seats were polished like satin, the brasswork shone. In its present shape, it was as much a museum piece as some handmade engine of Victorian times. It certainly had not looked like this when she and Edward, a critical, impatient pair, had watched it come swinging and pinging through the dusty sunlight, or ploughing, like some lighted bathysphere, the sea-blue murk of a winter's afternoon.

Mr. Limestone lived halfway between the termini. The Worples were in north Camber, which Emily condemned as "a nothing place", and when the tram left her at Mr. Limestone's door and went on to the sea and pier and the promenade where the band played on Sundays, she wished she were going with it.

The Limestones' house, a carmine semi-detached with yellow brick-work, was finer than the Worples' house, at least on the outside. It had a front garden where a wooden palette stood on an easel and told passersby that Mr. Limestone was a dentist. Because of the palette there was a general belief that Mr. Limestone was "artistic". Nothing was said about his being a children's dentist but the patients—and these were few enough—all seemed to be children.

There was a dentist in north Camber, but someone had told Mrs. Worple that Mr. Limestone was good with children. In those early days, when she had to accompany her children, she took the long tram journey in the belief that he, and he alone, could "manage" them. She boasted that she could not manage them herself, a fact for which she apportioned blame equally between them and their father. Of course there had been uproar before she could persuade them to a first visit. She described the awful remorse suffered by grown-ups who neglected their teeth in childhood: "You wouldn't like false teeth, would you?" she demanded. "Why not?" said Edward: "False teeth don't ache." When nothing else would move them, she promised them two bars of chocolate apiece. As most occasions began with threats and ended with chocolate bars, the years ahead were filled with visits to Mr. Limestone.

Mr. Limestone had another virtue: he was cheap. It took him months, years even, to concoct his account, and then several items would be forgotten. But small though his accounts were, and overdue, they led to painful discussions about money and Mrs. Worple would say that Emily and Edward did not appreciate the sacrifices that were being made for them.

"In my young day," she said, "children looked up to their parents. They were grateful for being alive."

"I bet," said Edward, bringing from Mrs. Worple the bitter comment:

"Unruly children!"

This riposte, a favourite of hers, dated back to the time when a Mr. Greening, a business acquaintance of Mr. Worple, had called on the Worples at tea-time and been invited to join them at the table. He was a stout, pompous man who did most of the talking, and while he talked his moustache waggled in a manner that gripped the attention of the children. At first they watched, scarcely believing, then dire amusement set in. They began to laugh until, losing control, their laughter became wild. When Mrs. Worple frowned at them, they exploded helplessly and rolled round and round in their chairs. It slowly came to Mr. Greening that he, of all people, was the cause of this shocking exhibition. He looked at Mr. Worple, but Mr. Worple had a weakness. It was a serious weakness of a sort that had been unknown in fathers when Mrs. Worple was young. Whenever Emily and Edward started to laugh, Mr. Worple had to laugh, too.

He did his best to admonish them: "Now, Emily," he said, "Now, Edward," but he was already beginning to shake and his face was red and his eyes damp with the effort to suppress his laughter.

Emily's voice rose in a shriek: "Listen to daddy trying to talk like mummy," and both children collapsed on the table, weeping in an anguish of mirth.

It was then that Mr. Greening, observing them with disgust, said "Unruly children!" and Mrs. Worple was deeply impressed. Although he never came back to the Worples' house, she remembered him as a champion against her unsatisfactory husband and intolerable children.

If he had not made his historic indictment, she might never have realised the extent of her own grievance. When things were at their worst—which usually meant, when some *jeu d'esprit* thrown off by one of them had thrown both into hysterics—she would say, as though the phrase might quell them: "Unruly children!"

In view of this, it was all the more remarkable that Mr. Limestone, with nothing but his professional mystery, could manage them. He did not look like a manager. Mrs. Worple gave him one look and began to say, "I'm afraid you'll find them very difficult. I don't know why they behave so badly. I'm sure they couldn't have a better home."

Mr. Limestone murmured "Oh, yes?" without interest, and the children felt he was on their side.

He was so small that they outgrew him in no time. He was pale, with sandy hair and a nose that looked over-large because it was almost the whole of his face. His cheeks, brow and chin seemed to have receded, leaving the nose in possession. His shoulders, too, had shrunk so his white jackets were all too big for him and his collar always stood out at the back as though a hand had seized him by the scruff. He was gentle, but never smiled. Emily and Edward, used to their father's quick response, sometimes tried to entertain Mr. Limestone, but it meant nothing to him. Whether he heard them or not, he remained melancholy, perhaps intent on more serious things.

When he had to drill a tooth, he kept up a reassuring murmur of "There, there, shan't be long now," and at the slightest wince or whimper, he withdrew the cutting point, saying "Easy does it. No hurry. We'll just take a little rest," then he would go and browse among his instruments. The danger was that he might wander out of the room and not come back for half an hour or more. Once, returning and finding Emily, miserable prisoner of the chair, he said, as though he had been seeking her all over the house, "Oh, that's where you are!"

Unlike most other people in those spacious times, the Limestones did not keep a maid. The front door was opened by Mrs. Limestone with her pink, empty, melted face above a long neck, a lace blouse and a lace-edged apron. She acted as assistant when her husband was forced to extract a tooth, an extreme measure that he would avoid whenever possible, and would show her strength by letting the patient grip her hand and by wordlessly guiding the movements of Mr. Limestone whose fear was such he scarcely knew what he was doing.

When she was home, she kept an eye on the waiting-room and saw that no one was forgotten. When she was out, anything might happen. Once Emily had arrived for a three o'clock appointment and getting no answer, had been about to go when the door was opened by Mr. Limestone, hair towsled, eyes pink like those of a white rabbit, who hoarsely whispered, "Yes, what is it?" Then, recognising Emily, he put her into the waiting-room where another patient, a small boy, was curled up asleep in a chair. "Won't be a minute," Mr. Limestone said and left them, and there they remained, Emily and the sleeping boy, until Mrs. Limestone came back at five o'clock. "Better go home," Mrs. Limestone said, waking the boy and packing them off as though she scarcely knew what she might find below.

Emily had spent so long in the waiting-room, she could have listed every item in it. The wallpaper was aflash with shaded squares, orange, fawn and brown. A large yellowish table crowded the centre of the room. It was littered with old copies of *Little Folks* and surrounded by eight straight-backed chairs whose leatherette seats were as good as new. No one sat in them. The children always threw themselves into the broken-down, tapestry armchairs that stood, one on either side of the fireplace. Though the grate held nothing but crumpled red paper, the whole area of the fireplace was hung with brass toasting-forks, chestnut pans and ornamental bellows, and there were so many fire-irons, dogs and hobs, it was scarcely possible to fit in the little electric fire which held a bar of heat on very cold days.

On either side of the chimney-breast there were built-in cupboards which, Emily early discovered, were filled with grown-up books. It was years before she took them out and looked at them. On the shelves above the cupboards there were, beside the electro-plated toast-racks, jam-dishes and other useful unused objects, statuettes of tall girls leading Alsatian dogs and small girls cuddling bunnies.

The years passed and there were changes outside in Camber, but none in the waiting-room. Even in Camber nothing changed completely. The tram-cars gave way to buses but the buses followed the arbitrary route of the tram-lines that were still there under the tarmac and could be seen in places where the tarmac rubbed away. The Band of Hope Hall opposite Mr. Limestone's house was turned into a cinema, but when the Council permitted it to open on Sunday, the massed Baptist choirs sang outside, making so much noise that people asked for their money back.

As for Emily, waiting in the waiting-room, she had started to rummage in the fireside cupboards, hoping the hidden books would help her to solve some of life's mysteries. They did solve mysteries, but not those of this world. They all treated of one subject: Spiritualism.

At first Emily was excited by them. She had been discouraged by the picture of Heaven given at St. Luke's, Camber (N), and had rejected it as soon as she discovered Bernard Shaw. Now she found that people called mediums were in direct touch with the Other Side and showed it to be nothing like the boring hymn-singing Heaven of St. Luke's. In fact, the spirits revealed, the Other Side was much like this Side, only nicer. Innocent pleasures enjoyed here by the few, could there be enjoyed by everyone. Supposing, one writer said, you occasionally indulge in the luxury of a cigar! On the Other Side you had only to wish for a cigar and a box of the Very Best would appear in your hand.

"Chocolates, too," Emily hoped.

The *mise en scène* where these wonders occurred was all green lawns, trees, roses, lilies, crystal fountains, sweet breezes and balmy airs. Book after book assured the reader that the Other Side was a garden set in perpetual summer. "It's beautiful," the mediums said: "Everything's beautiful."

"And then what happens?" Emily wondered, but nothing, it seemed, happened. The Other Side was as static as the garden painted on the safety curtain at the Pier concert hall, and soon it looked to Emily just as dusty and faded.

Between visits, caught up in the rough and tumble of reality, she forgot the spirit world, but when she returned to the Limestones' waiting-room, she would remember the nectar of the Hereafter and feel drawn back to it and read avidly a while, then find it as insipid as before.

In one book a seance was described for those who, like Emily, knew nothing of procedure. When she learnt that the researchers sat round a dining-room table, she looked anew at the Limestones' table and imagined them sitting round it, fingers touching, and Mr. Limestone with head raised and eyes shut, saying in his sad little voice, "It's beautiful. Everything's beautiful."

Emily now towered over Mr. Limestone and, feeling there was something ridiculous about their relationship, she resented the hours wasted in the waiting-room and said she should go to a grown-up dentist. Soon it became what Mrs. Worple called "a battle" to get her to go at all, and the battle became grim when Emily was invited to Lilac Mittens' birthday party on the same half-term afternoon that had been appointed for a session with Mr. Limestone. Emily demanded that the appointment be changed. Mrs. Worple refused to change it.

Though she boasted of her inability to control her children, Mrs. Worple could on occasions be adamant. These occasions always related to any suggested alteration in the scheme of things. She could not bear a picture, ornament or piece of furniture to be moved from its place in the household. Arrangements made for the future must not be unmade. Appointments that had been made by letter had a rigidity all their own. Nothing would induce Mrs. Worple to write to Mr. Limestone and change Emily's appointment, and it was a measure of Emily's immaturity that she dare not write herself or fail to keep it. As a last resort, she burst into tears and Mrs. Worple hit back by raising her eyes to heaven and asking. "Haven't I borne enough?"

When she addressed the Almighty, Mrs. Worple would do so in an anguished wail that always defeated Emily. So Emily argued no more, but when the afternoon came she set out early, wearing her party frock under her coat, determined to get Mr. Limestone over and done with. Mrs. Limestone appeared at the door with her hat on. A bad omen. Emily appealed to her in a confiding manner: "I'm going to a party, Mrs. Limestone. Do you think Mr. Limestone could do my tooth straight away?"

"We'll see," Mrs. Limestone said, not committing herself, but she went straight down to the basement where Mr. Limestone had his being, and a few minutes later, he appeared, abject, in a newly starched jacket, his wife at his heels, self-satisfied and a little breathless as though she had taken him by the collar and pushed him up the stairs. She now had on her rat-grey coat and imitation silver-fox fur: "I'm off," she said, and off she went.

Mr. Limestone said resignedly, "Come along, Emily," and led the way to the back room where the blue plush dental chair stood in the chilly, silvery light of the half frosted window. The upper pane that sometimes held the distraction of clouds, held nothing now but the flat, grey February sky.

Emily, sitting down, tried to hurry Mr. Limestone by mentioning the party. Not listening, he said, "Put your head back. Open your mouth. *There's* a good girl," and went with maddening slowness from tooth to tooth. He tapped with his mirror: "That one ought to come out." The tooth, crowded sideways into Emily's lower jaw, had been condemned months before and Mr. Limestone would never have the nerve to pull it unsupported by his wife. When Emily said nothing, he sighed and moved on to the tooth that had to be filled. Changing the mirror for a sort of button-hook, he picked for several minutes at the decay before saying sombrely: "I'll have to cut it."

Snatching at his natural unwillingness to act, she said, "I could come another time." He reflected deeply, then said with decision: "No. Let's get it over."

He packed her mouth with cotton-wool, an exacting process, then brought over the drill. Knowing that any squeak or shudder would delay the operation, Emily gripped the chair-arms and watched Mr. Limestone's nose that moved, too close for comfort, like a half moon around her vision. She could smell the peppermint which he sucked to sustain himself while he worked. Her fortitude was such that he said several times: "There's a brave girl," then: "I think that will do. It's only a small cavity."

The worst over, Emily relaxed, thinking that even Mr. Limestone must soon be done, but it was amazing how long it took him to mix the little dab of filling. As he bent to apply it, hand trembling with creative effort, his anxiety was such that he swallowed his peppermint. He pushed and scraped at the filling, breathing loudly, taking so long that when he stepped back to survey his handiwork, Emily was ready to leap from the chair. "We're not finished yet," he warned her and she reluctantly put her head back on the rest and reopened her mouth.

Mr. Limestone went to his table and searched among his equipment. He came back with a sliver of whalebone which he wedged between the newly filled tooth and its neighbour, saying: "Don't touch that. I want the filling to dry out. It's very important it shouldn't be disturbed."

Gagged with cotton-wool and whalebone, Emily watched Mr. Limestone to see he did not leave the room. Should he try to go, she was ready, or almost ready, to jump down and seize him. Yet he got away. One moment he was replacing his instruments in their box, the next he had gone. He went so quickly, quietly and suddenly, he seemed to dissolve among the shadows at the door. She gave a cry, but too late. She listened.

Sometimes, when Mrs. Limestone was home, there could be heard slight creaks and murmurs from the rooms below. Now there was no sound at all.

She felt tricked and could do nothing but wait. The waiting went on and on. There were no clocks in the waiting-room or surgery, no means of measuring time except by the change in the light. As she watched the sky turn from grey to pewter, she began to panic.

The party began at four-thirty and tea was at five. In Emily's circle it was not correct to arrive late, and one could lose by doing so. Emily had been late for the first meeting of the Drama Club and found that the elocution mistress had cast the play and left no part for her. She had never got over that and the rebuff may, for all she knew, have destroyed her chance of becoming a great actress. It was possible that Lilac's party had already begun and she sat in agony, imaging the bright room, the talk, the expectation, the brilliance of it all.

At last, unable to bear more, she sat up and considered her position. The silence was such, Mr. Limestone might have sunk down into the grave; yet he must be somewhere in the house. As the shadows deepened about her, she began to imagine him down in the basement with his hands on the table, his eyes shut, his little pale face raised as he whispered to himself, "It's beautiful. Everything's beautiful." Fearful, she longed for Mrs. Limestone to come back. "Oh, Mrs. Limestone," she pleaded in her solitude, "*please* ask Mr. Limestone to finish my tooth!" But Mrs. Limestone did not come.

Growing desperate, Emily did what she had never done before:

she disobeyed Mr. Limestone. First she took the soaking cotton-wool out of her mouth, then she touched the whalebone filament. It was firmly fixed between the teeth and protruded so slightly, she could not get a grip on it. She might have gone, whalebone and all, but without the protecting cotton-wool, the filament cut into her lip.

She sat for some minutes on the chair edge, listening to silence, giving Mr. Limestone a last chance, then she slid down and tip-toed into the hall. She leant over the basement stairs and called in a small voice, "Mr. Limestone." There was not a breath below.

Had he abandoned her completely? Had he left the house? She descended a few steps and spoke his name more boldly. Her voice died and not a sound returned to her. She went down further, breathing the lower air redolent with cooking-fat and old floor-cloths, and saw through the shadows a daylight glimmer from a half-open door. When she paused again, she knew he was there. She could hear him breathing.

She stood, daunted by the fact he did not answer, then it occurred to her that he might be ill. He may have fainted or had a heart attack or a stroke. With this excuse for trespass, she ran on down, ready to save Mr. Limestone's life. The half-open door led to the kitchen. She saw a scrubbed deal table, an old dresser, a gas-stove, a sink—but no Mr. Limestone. Yet he was near. His breathing came more loudly. An inner door led to a scullery or pantry and knowing he must be there, she advanced cautiously until she could see inside. And there he was. An old dental chair, its plush bursting and spilling the interior wadding, stood inside the door and Mr. Limestone was sitting in it. She edged round to view him and saw his head propped on the rest, his eyes, shut, his breath puffing out between his parted lips. His expression, tranquil, almost felicitous, told her he was not ill. He must be asleep; and before going to sleep, he had pulled up the sleeve of his white jacket and thrust a hypodermic needle into his arm. His poor, thin, little arm lay on his lap with the tip of the needle still clinging to the flesh.

What an extraordinary thing to do! Having a dislike of injections herself, Emily edged nearer, repelled and bewildered, yet curious, and at her movement, Mr. Limestone's eyelids fluttered. He gave her an unseeing glance then seemed to sleep again.

She said, "I must go, Mr. Limestone. I'm invited to a party," and for the first time in their long acquaintance, Mr. Limestone smiled. His smile was joyous, as though he had already reached the Other Side where pleasures were innocent and everything was beautiful.

In front of him, on a work-table, there were some small tools and a row of false teeth set in ruby gums and mounted on a base of chalk. Among the tools Emily saw a pair of pliers and, stretching round Mr. Limestone's chair, she picked these up and used them to pluck the whalebone cleanly from between her teeth. Her relief was such, she became flippant and said with a giggle:

"I'm sorry, Mr. Limestone. I couldn't wait."

As she spoke, the front door banged on the floor above and the sound sobered Mr. Limestone. He did not wake, but his smile was gone in an instant. Emily, guilty, an intruder who must not be discovered, fled from the kitchen and made her escape through the back garden door. Running round the side of the house, she jumped on a bus and reached Lilac's party just as the guests were going in to tea.

Imagining she would be at fault, Emily decided to tell her mother nothing of this episode, but somehow it all came out.

Mrs. Worple was surprisingly indignant: "I sometimes thought . . . I suspected," she said: "Well, what a disgraceful thing!"

"What do you mean?" Emily asked. Mrs. Worple would say no more but when Emily next complained of Mr. Limestone's slowness, her mother at once agreed it was time for both the children to attend a "grown-up" dentist. They never saw Mr. Limestone again.

Almost at once he disappeared from Emily's mind and it was only now, twenty years later, that she remembered and understood. Mr. Limestone's blissful smile. Her mother had disapproved, yet Emily could not disapprove. His may not have been an innocent pleasure, yet it seemed to her the pleasure of the innocent.

She came to the end of the Transport Museum feeling she had had enough of the past. She had had enough of Mr. Limestone, too. Faced with the Clapham traffic and the struggle to get home, she turned her back on his memory and said again, "I must go, Mr. Limestone."

After a moment she thought to add "Goodbye." And that was all she could say to Mr. Limestone in an age that had given up innocence and received nothing in return.

BARN BURNING

WILLIAM FAULKNER

[signature: Will Faulkner]

T**HE STORE** in which the justice of the peace's court was sitting smelled of cheese. The boy, crouched on his nail keg at the back of the crowded room, knew he smelled cheese, and more: from where he sat he could see the ranked shelves close-packed with the solid, squat, dynamic shapes of tin cans whose labels his stomach read, not from the lettering which meant nothing to his mind but from the scarlet devils and the silver curve of fish—this, the cheese which he knew he smelled and the hermetic meat which his intestines believed he smelled coming in intermittent gusts momentary and brief between the other constant one, the smell and sense just a little of fear because mostly of despair and grief, the old fierce pull of blood. He could not see the table where the justice sat and before which his father and his father's enemy *(our enemy* he thought in that despair; *ourn! mine and hisn both! He's my father!)* stood, but he could hear them, the two of them that is, because his father had said no word yet:

"But what proof have you, Mr. Harris?"

"I told you. The hog got into my corn. I caught it up and sent it back to him. He had no fence that would hold it. I told him so, warned him. The next time I put the hog in my pen. When he came to get it I gave him enough wire to patch up his pen. The next time I put the hog up and kept it. I rode down to his house and saw the wire I gave him still rolled onto the spool in his yard. I told him he could have the hog when he paid me a dollar pound fee. That evening a nigger came with the dollar and got the hog. He was a strange nigger. He said, 'He say to tell you wood and hay kin burn.' I said, 'What?' 'That whut he say to

346

tell you,' the nigger said. 'Wood and hay kin burn.' That night my barn burned. I got the stock out but I lost the barn."

"Where is the nigger? Have you got him?"

"He was a strange nigger, I tell you. I don't know what became of him."

"But that's not proof. Don't you see that's not proof?"

"Get that boy up here. He knows." For a moment the boy thought too that the man meant his older brother until Harris said, "Not him. The little one. The boy," and, crouching, small for his age, small and wiry like his father, in patched and faded jeans even too small for him, with straight, uncombed, brown hair and eyes gray and wild as storm scud, he saw the men between himself and the table part and become a lane of grim faces, at the end of which he saw the justice, a shabby, collarless, graying man in spectacles, beckoning him. He felt no floor under his bare feet; he seemed to walk beneath the palpable weight of the grim turning faces. His father, stiff in his black Sunday coat donned not for the trial but for the moving, did not even look at him. *He aims for me to lie,* he thought, again with that frantic grief and despair. *And I will have to do hit.*

"What's your name, boy?" the justice said.

"Colonel Sartoris Snopes," the boy whispered.

"Hey?" the justice said. "Talk louder. Colonel Sartoris? I reckon anybody named for Colonel Sartoris in this country can't help but tell the truth, can they?" The boy said nothing. *Enemy! Enemy!* he thought; for a moment he could not even see, could not see that the justice's face was kindly nor discern that his voice was troubled when he spoke to the man named Harris: "Do you want me to question this boy?" But he could hear, and during those subsequent long seconds while there was absolutely no sound in the crowded little room save that of quiet and intent breathing it was as if he had swung outward at the end of a grapevine, over a ravine, and at the top of the swing had been caught in a prolonged instant of mesmerized gravity, weightless in time.

"No!" Harris said violently, explosively. "Damnation! Send him out of here!" Now time, the fluid world, rushed beneath him again, the voices coming to him again through the smell of cheese and sealed meat, the fear and despair and the old grief of blood:

"This case is closed. I can't find against you, Snopes, but I can give you advice. Leave this country and don't come back to it."

His father spoke for the first time, his voice cold and harsh, level, without emphasis: "I aim to. I don't figure to stay in a country among people who . . ." he said something unprintable and vile, addressed to no one.

"That'll do," the justice said. "Take your wagon and get out of this country before dark. Case dismissed."

His father turned, and he followed the stiff black coat, the wiry figure walking a little stiffly from where a Confederate provost's man's musket ball had taken him in the heel on a stolen horse thirty years ago, followed the two backs now, since his older brother had appeared from somewhere in the crowd, no taller than the father but thicker, chewing tobacco steadily, between the two lines of grim-faced men and out of the store and across the worn gallery and down the sagging steps and among the dogs and half-grown boys in the mild May dust, where as he passed a voice hissed:

"Barn burner!"

Again he could not see, whirling; there was a face in a red haze, moonlike, bigger than the full moon, the owner of it half again his size, he leaping in the red haze toward the face, feeling no blow, feeling no shock when his head struck the earth, scrabbling up and leaping again, feeling no blow this time either and tasting no blood, scrabbling up to see the other boy in full flight and himself already leaping into pursuit as his father's hand jerked him back, the harsh, cold voice speaking above him: "Go get in the wagon."

It stood in a grove of locusts and mulberries across the road. His two hulking sisters in their Sunday dresses and his mother and her sister in calico and sunbonnets were already in it, sitting on and among the sorry residue of the dozen and more movings which even the boy could remember—the battered stove, the broken beds and chairs, the clock inlaid with mother-of-pearl, which would not run, stopped at some fourteen minutes past two o'clock of a dead and forgotten day and time, which had been his mother's dowry. She was crying, though when she saw him she drew her sleeve across her face and began to descend from the wagon. "Get back," the father said.

348

"He's hurt. I got to get some water and wash his—"

"Get back in the wagon," his father said. He got in too, over the tailgate. His father mounted to the seat where the older brother already sat, and struck the gaunt mules two savage blows with the peeled willow, but without heat. It was not even sadistic; it was exactly that same quality which in later years would cause his descendants to overrun the engine before putting a motorcar into motion, striking and reining back in the same movement. The wagon went on, the store with its quiet crowd of grimly watching men dropped behind; a curve in the road hid it. *Forever* he thought. *Maybe he's done satisfied now, now that he has* . . . stopping himself, not to say it aloud even to himself. His mother's hand touched his shoulder.

"Does hit hurt?" she said.

"Naw," he said. "Hit don't hurt. Lemme be."

"Can't you wipe some of the blood off before hit dries?"

"I'll wash tonight," he said. "Lemme be, I tell you."

The wagon went on. He did not know where they were going. None of them ever did or ever asked, because it was always somewhere, always a house of sorts waiting for them a day or two days or even three days away. Likely his father had already arranged to make a crop on another farm before he— Again he had to stop himself. He (the father) always did. There was something about his wolflike independence and even courage when the advantage was at least neutral which impressed strangers, as if they got from his latent ravening ferocity not so much a sense of dependability as a feeling that his ferocious conviction in the rightness of his own actions would be of advantage to all whose interest lay with his.

That night they camped, in a grove of oaks and beeches where a spring ran. The nights were still cool and they had a fire against it, of a rail lifted from a nearby fence and cut into lengths—a small fire, neat, niggard almost, a shrewd fire; such fires were his father's habit and custom always, even in freezing weather. Older, the boy might have remarked this and wondered why not a big one; why should not a man who had not only seen the waste and extravagance of war, but who had in his blood an inherent voracious prodigality with material not his own, have burned everything in sight? Then he might have gone a step farther and thought that that was the reason: that niggard blaze was the living fruit of nights passed during those four years in the woods hiding from all men, blue or gray, with his strings of horses (captured horses, he called them). And older still, he might have divined the true reason: that the element of fire spoke to some deep mainspring of his father's being, as the element of steel or of powder spoke to other men, as the one weapon for the preservation of integrity, else breath were not worth the breathing, and hence to be regarded with respect and used with discretion.

But he did not think this now and he had seen those same niggard blazes all his life. He merely ate his supper beside it and was already half asleep over his iron plate when his father called him, and once more he followed the stiff back, the stiff and ruthless limp, up the slope and onto the starlit road where, turning, he could see his father against the stars but without face or depth—a shape black, flat, and bloodless, as though cut from tin in the iron folds of the frock coat which had not been made for him, the voice harsh like tin and without heat like tin: "You were fixing to tell them. You would have told him."

He didn't answer. His father struck him with the flat of his hand on the side of the head, hard but without heat, exactly as he had struck the two mules at the store, exactly as he would strike either of them with any stick in order to kill a horsefly, his voice still without heat or anger: "You're getting to be a man. You got to learn. You got to learn to stick to your own blood or you ain't going to have any blood to stick to you. Do you think either of them, any man there this morning, would? Don't you know all they wanted was a chance to get at me because they knew I had them beat? Eh?" Later, twenty years later, he was to tell himself, "If I had said they wanted only truth, justice, he would have hit me again." But now he said nothing. He was not crying. He just stood there. "Answer me," his father said.

"Yes," he whispered. His father turned.

"Get on to bed. We'll be there tomorrow."

Tomorrow they were there. In the early afternoon the wagon stopped before a paintless two-room house identical almost with the dozen others it had stopped before even in the boy's ten years, and again, as on the other dozen occasions, his mother and aunt got down and began to unload the wagon, although his two sisters and his father and brother had not moved.

"Likely hit ain't fitten for hawgs," one of the sisters said.

"Nevertheless, fit it will and you'll hog it and like it," his father said. "Get out of them chairs and help your ma unload."

The two sisters got down, big, bovine, in a flutter of cheap ribbons; one of them drew from the jumbled wagon bed a battered lantern, the other a worn broom. His father handed the reins to the older son and began to climb stiffly over the wheel. "When they get unloaded, take the team to the barn and feed them." Then he said, and at first the boy thought he was still speaking to his brother, "Come with me."

"Me?" he said.

"Yes," his father said. "You."

"Abner," his mother said. His father paused and looked back—the harsh level stare beneath the shaggy, graying, irascible brows.

"I reckon I'll have a word with the man that aims to begin tomorrow owning me body and soul for the next eight months."

They went back up the road. A week ago—or before last night, that is—he would have asked where they were going, but not now. His father had struck him before last night but never before had he paused afterward to explain why; it was as if the blow and the following calm, outrageous voice still rang, repercussed, divulging nothing to him save the terrible handicap of being young, the light weight of his few years, just heavy enough to prevent his soaring free of the world as it seemed to be ordered but not heavy enough to keep him footed solid in it, to resist it and try to change the course of its events.

Presently he could see the grove of oaks and cedars and the other flowering trees and shrubs where the house would be, though not the house yet. They walked beside a fence massed with honeysuckle and Cherokee roses and came to a gate swinging open between two brick pillars, and now, beyond a sweep of drive, he saw the house for the first time and at that instant he forgot his father and the terror and despair both, and even when he remembered his father again (who had not stopped) the terror and despair did not return. Because, for all the twelve movings, they had sojourned until now in a poor country, a land of small farms and fields and houses, and he had never seen a house like this before. *Hit's big as a courthouse* he thought quietly, with a surge of peace and joy whose reason he could not have thought into words, being too young for that: *They are safe from him. People whose lives are a part of this peace and dignity are beyond his touch, he no more to them than a buzzing wasp: capable of stinging for a little moment but that's all; the spell of this peace and dignity rendering even the barns and stable and cribs which belong to it impervious to the puny flames he might contrive . . .* this, the peace and joy, ebbing for an instant as he looked again at the stiff black back, the stiff and implacable limp of the figure which was not dwarfed by the house, for the reason that it had never looked big anywhere and which now, against the serene columned backdrop, had more than ever that impervious quality of something cut ruthlessly from tin, depthless, as though, sidewise to the sun, it would cast no shadow. Watching him, the boy remarked the absolutely undeviating course which his father held and saw the stiff foot come squarely down in a pile of fresh droppings where a horse had stood in the drive and which his father could have avoided by a simple change of stride. But it ebbed only for a moment, though he could not have thought this into words either, walking on in the spell of the house, which he could even want but without envy, without sorrow, certainly never with that ravening and jealous rage which unknown to him walked in the ironlike black coat before him: *Maybe he will feel it too. Maybe it will even change him now from what maybe he couldn't help but be.*

They crossed the portico. Now he could hear his father's stiff foot as it came down on the boards with clocklike finality, a sound out of all proportion to the displacement of the body it bore and which was not dwarfed either by the white door before it, as though it had attained to a sort of vicious and ravening minimum not to be dwarfed by anything—the flat, wide, black hat, the formal coat of broadcloth which had once been black but which had now that friction-glazed greenish cast of the bodies of old houseflies, the lifted sleeve which was too large, the lifted hand like a curled claw. The door opened so promptly that the boy knew the Negro must have been watching them all the time, an old man with neat grizzled hair, in a linen jacket, who stood barring the door with his body, saying, "Wipe yo foots, white man, fo you come in here. Major ain't home nohow."

"Get out of my way, nigger," his father said, without heat too, flinging the door back and the Negro also and entering, his hat still on his head. And now the boy saw the prints of the stiff foot on the doorjamb and saw them appear on the pale rug behind the machinelike deliberation of the foot which seemed to bear (or transmit) twice the weight which the body compassed. The Negro was shouting, "Miss Lula! Miss Lula!" somewhere behind them; then the boy, deluged as though by a warm wave by a suave turn of carpeted stair and a pendant glitter of chandeliers and a mute gleam of gold frames, heard the swift feet and saw her too, a lady—perhaps he had never seen her like before either—in a gray, smooth gown with lace at the throat and an apron tied at the waist and the sleeves turned back, wiping cake or biscuit dough from her hands with a towel as she came up the hall, looking not at his father at all but at the tracks on the blond rug with an expression of incredulous amazement.

"I tried," the Negro cried. "I tole him to . . ."

"Will you please go away?" she said in a shaking voice. "Major de Spain is not at home. Will you please go away?"

His father had not spoken again. He did not speak again. He did not even look at her. He just stood stiff in the center of the rug, in his hat, the shaggy iron-gray brows twitching slightly above the pebble-colored eyes as he appeared to examine the house with brief deliberation. Then with the same deliberation he turned; the boy watched him pivot on the good leg and saw the stiff foot drag round the arc of the turning, leaving a final long and fading smear. His father never looked at it, he never once looked down at the rug. The Negro held the door. It closed behind them, upon the hysteric and indistinguishable woman-wail. His father stopped at the top of the steps and scraped his boot clean on the edge of it. At the gate he stopped again. He stood for a moment, planted stiffly on the stiff foot, looking back at the house. "Pretty and white, ain't it?" he said. "That's sweat. Nigger sweat. Maybe it ain't white enough yet to suit him. Maybe he wants to mix some white sweat with it."

Two hours later the boy was chopping wood behind the house within which his mother and aunt and the two sisters (the mother and aunt, not the two girls, he knew that; even at this distance and muffled by walls the flat loud voices of the two girls emanated an incorrigible idle inertia) were setting up the stove to prepare a meal, when he heard the hooves and saw the linen-clad man on a fine sorrel mare, whom he recognized even before he saw the rolled rug in front of the Negro youth following on a fat bay carriage horse—a suffused, angry face vanishing, still at full gallop, beyond the corner of the house where his father and brother were sitting in the two tilted chairs; and a moment later, almost before he could have put the ax down, he heard the hooves again and watched the sorrel mare go back out of the yard, already galloping again. Then his father began to shout one of the sisters' names, who presently emerged backward from the kitchen door dragging the rolled rug along the ground by one end while the other sister walked behind it.

"If you ain't going to tote, go on and set up the washpot," the first said.

"You, Sarty!" the second shouted. "Set up the washpot!" His father appeared at the door, framed against that shabbiness, as he had been against that other bland perfection, impervious to either, the mother's anxious face at his shoulder.

"Go on," the father said. "Pick it up." The two sisters stooped, broad, lethargic; stooping, they presented an incredible expanse of pale cloth and a flutter of tawdry ribbons.

"If I thought enough of a rug to have to git hit all the way from France, I wouldn't keep hit where folks coming in would have to tromp on hit," the first said. They raised the rug.

"Abner," the mother said. "Let me do it."

"You go back and git dinner," his father said. "I'll tend to this."

From the woodpile through the rest of the afternoon the boy watched them, the rug spread flat in the dust beside the bubbling washpot, the two sisters stooping over it with that profound and lethargic reluctance, while the father stood over them in turn, implacable and grim, driving them though never raising his voice again. He could smell the harsh homemade lye they were using; he saw his mother come to the door once and look toward them with an expression not anxious now but very like despair; he saw his father turn, and he fell to with the ax and saw from the corner of his eye his father raise from the ground a flattish fragment of fieldstone and examine it and return to the pot, and this time his mother actually spoke: "Abner. Abner. Please don't. Please, Abner."

Then he was done too. It was dusk; the whippoorwills had already begun. He could smell coffee from the room where they would presently eat the cold food remaining from the midafternoon meal, though when he entered the house he realized they were having coffee again probably because there was a fire on the hearth, before which the rug now lay spread over the backs of the two chairs. The tracks of his father's foot were gone. Where they had been were now long, water-cloudy scoriations resembling the sporadic course of a lilliputian mowing machine.

It still hung there while they ate the cold food and then went to bed, scattered without order or claim up and down the two rooms, his mother in one bed, where his father would later lie, the older brother in the other, himself, the aunt and the two sisters on pallets on the floor. But his father was not in bed yet. The last thing the boy remembered was the depthless, harsh silhouette of the hat and coat bending over the rug, and it seemed to him that he had not even closed his eyes when the silhouette was standing over him, the fire almost dead behind it, the stiff foot prodding him awake. "Catch up the mule," his father said.

When he returned with the mule his father was standing in the black door, the rolled rug over his shoulder. "Ain't you going to ride?" he said.

"No. Give me your foot."

He bent his knee into his father's hand, the wiry, surprising power flowed smoothly, rising, he rising with it, onto the mule's bare back (they had owned a saddle once; the boy could remember it though not when or where) and with the same effortlessness his father swung the rug up in front of him. Now in the starlight they retraced the afternoon's path, up the dusty road rife with honeysuckle, through the gate and up the black tunnel of the drive to the lightless house, where he sat on the mule and felt the rough warp of the rug drag across his thighs and vanish.

"Don't you want me to help?" he whispered. His father did not answer and now he heard again that stiff foot striking the hollow portico with that wooden and clocklike deliberation, that outrageous overstatement of the weight it carried. The rug, hunched, not flung (the boy could tell that even in the darkness) from his father's shoulder struck the angle of wall and floor with a sound unbelievably loud, thunderous, then the foot again, unhurried and enormous; a light came on in the house and the boy sat, tense, breathing steadily and quietly and just a little fast, though the foot itself did not increase its beat at all, descending the steps now; now the boy could see him.

"Don't you want to ride now?" he whispered. "We kin both ride now," the light within the house altering now, flaring up and sinking. *He's coming down the stairs now,* he thought. He had already ridden the mule up beside the horse block; presently his father was up behind him and he doubled the reins over and slashed the mule across the neck, but before the animal could begin to trot the hard, thin arm came round him, the hard, knotted hand jerking the mule back to a walk.

In the first red rays of the sun they were in the lot, putting plow gear on the mules. This time the sorrel mare was in the lot before he heard it at all, the rider collarless and even bareheaded, trembling, speaking in a shaking voice as the woman in the house had done, his father merely looking up once before stooping again to the hame he was buckling, so that the man on the mare spoke to his stooping back:

"You must realize you have ruined that rug. Wasn't there anybody here, any of your women . . ." he ceased, shaking, the boy watching him, the older brother leaning now in the stable door, chewing, blinking slowly and steadily at nothing apparently. "It cost a hundred dollars. But you never had a hundred dollars. You never will. So I'm going to charge you twenty bushels of corn against your crop. I'll add it in your contract and when you come to the commissary you can sign it. That won't keep Mrs. de Spain quiet but maybe it will teach you to wipe your feet off before you enter her house again."

Then he was gone. The boy looked at his father, who still had not spoken or even looked up again, who was now adjusting the logger-head in the hame.

"Pap," he said. His father looked at him—the inscrutable face, the shaggy brows beneath which the gray eyes glinted coldly. Suddenly the boy went toward him, fast, stopping as suddenly. "You done the best you could!" he cried. "If he wanted hit done different, why didn't he wait and tell you how? He won't git no twenty bushels! He won't git none! We'll gether hit and hide hit! I kin watch . . ."

"Did you put the cutter back in that straight stock like I told you?"

"No, sir," he said.

"Then go do it."

That was Wednesday. During the rest of that week he worked steadily, at what was within his scope and some which was beyond it, with an industry that did not need to be driven nor even commanded twice; he had this from his mother, with the difference that some at least of what he did he liked to do, such as splitting wood with the half-size ax which his mother and aunt had earned, or saved money somehow, to present him with at Christmas. In company with the two older women (and on one afternoon, even one of the sisters), he built pens for the shoat and the cow which were a part of his father's contract with the landlord, and one afternoon, his father being absent, gone somewhere on one of the mules, he went to the field.

They were running a middlebuster now, his brother holding the plow straight while he handled the reins, and walking beside the straining mule, the rich black soil shearing cool and damp against his bare ankles, he thought, *Maybe this is the end of it. Maybe even that twenty bushels that seems hard to have to pay for just a rug will be a cheap price for him to stop forever and always from being what he used to be;* thinking, dreaming now, so that his brother had to speak sharply to him to mind the mule: *Maybe he even won't collect the twenty bushels. Maybe it will all add up and balance and vanish—corn, rug, fire; the terror and grief, the being pulled two ways like between two teams of horses—gone, done with for ever and ever.*

Then it was Saturday; he looked up from beneath the mule he was harnessing and saw his father in the black coat and hat. "Not that," his father said. "The wagon gear." And then, two hours later, sitting in the wagon bed behind his father and brother on the seat, the wagon accomplished a final curve, and he saw the weathered paintless store with its tattered tobacco and patent-medicine posters and the tethered wagons and saddle animals below the gallery. He mounted the gnawed steps behind his father and brother, and there again was the lane of quiet, watching faces for the three of them to walk through. He saw the man in spectacles sitting at the plank table and he did not need to be told this was a justice of the peace; he sent one glare of fierce, exultant, partisan defiance at the man in collar and cravat now, whom he had seen but twice before in his life, and that on a galloping horse, who now wore on his face an expression not of rage but of amazed unbelief which the boy could not have known was at the incredible circumstance of being sued by one of his own tenants, and came and stood against his father and cried at the justice: "He ain't done it! He ain't burnt . . ."

"Go back to the wagon," his father said.

"Burnt?" the justice said. "Do I understand this rug was burned too?"

"Does anybody here claim it was?" his father said. "Go back to the wagon." But he did not, he merely retreated to the rear of the room, crowded as that other had been, but not to sit down this time, instead, to stand pressing among the motionless bodies, listening to the voices:

"And you claim twenty bushels of corn is too high for the damage you did to the rug?"

"He brought the rug to me and said he wanted the tracks washed out of it. I washed the tracks out and took the rug back to him."

"But you didn't carry the rug back to him in the same condition it was in before you made the tracks on it."

His father did not answer, and now for perhaps half a minute there was no sound at all save that of breathing, the faint, steady suspiration of complete and intent listening.

"You decline to answer that, Mr. Snopes?" Again his father did not answer. "I'm going to find against you, Mr. Snopes. I'm going to find that you were responsible for the injury to Major de Spain's rug and hold you liable for it. But twenty bushels of corn seems a little high for a man in your circumstances to have to pay. Major de Spain claims it cost a hundred dollars. October corn will be worth about fifty cents. I figure that if Major de Spain can stand a ninety-five-dollar loss on something he paid cash for, you can stand a five-dollar loss you haven't earned yet. I hold you in damages to Major de Spain to the amount of ten bushels of corn over and above your contract with him, to be paid to him out of your crop at gathering time. Court adjourned."

It had taken no time hardly, the morning was but half begun. He thought they would return home and perhaps back to the field, since they were late, far behind all other farmers. But instead his father passed on behind the wagon, merely indicating with his hand for the older brother to follow with it, and crossed the road toward the blacksmith shop opposite; pressing on after his father, overtaking him, speaking, whispering up at the harsh, calm face beneath the weathered hat: "He won't git no ten bushels neither. He won't git one. We'll . . ." until his father glanced for an instant down at him, the face absolutely calm, the grizzled eyebrows tangled above the cold eyes, the voice almost pleasant, almost gentle: "You think so? Well, we'll wait till October anyway."

The matter of the wagon—the setting of a spoke or two and the tightening of the tires—did not take long either, the business of the tires accomplished by driving the wagon into the spring branch behind the shop and letting it stand there, the mules nuzzling into the water from time to time, and the boy on the seat with the idle reins, looking up the slope and through the sooty tunnel of the shed where the slow hammer rang and where his father sat on an upended cypress bolt, easily, either talking or listening, still sitting there when the boy brought the dripping wagon up out of the branch and halted it before the door.

"Take them on to the shade and hitch," his father said. He did so and returned. His father and the smith and a third man squatting on his heels inside the door were talking, about crops and animals; the boy, squatting too in the ammoniac dust and hoof parings and scales of rust, heard his father tell a long and unhurried story out of the time before the birth of the older brother even, when he had been a professional horse trader. And then his father came up beside him where he stood before a tattered last year's circus poster on the other side of the store, gazing rapt and quiet at the scarlet horses, the incredible poisings and convolutions of tulle and tights and the painted leers of comedians, and said, "It's time to eat."

But not at home. Squatting beside his brother against the front wall, he watched his father emerge from the store and produce from a paper sack a segment of cheese and divide it carefully and deliberately into three with his pocketknife and produce crackers from the same sack. They all three squatted on the gallery and ate, slowly, without talking; then in the store again, they drank from a tin dipper tepid water smelling of the cedar bucket and of living beech trees. And still they did not go home. It was a horse lot this time, a tall rail fence upon and along which men stood and sat and out of which one by one horses were led, to be walked and trotted and then cantered back and forth along the road while the slow swapping and buying went on and the sun began to slant westward, they—the three of them—watching and listening, the older brother with his muddy eyes and his steady, inevitable tobacco, the father commenting now and then on certain of the animals, to no one in particular.

It was after sundown when they reached home. They ate supper by lamplight, then, sitting on the doorstep, the boy watched the night fully accomplish, listening to the whippoorwills and the frogs, when he heard his mother's voice: "Abner! No! No! Oh, God. Oh, God. Abner!" and he rose, whirled, and saw the altered light through the door where a candle stub now burned in a bottle neck on the table and his father, still in the hat and coat, at once formal and burlesque as though dressed carefully for some shabby and ceremonial violence, emptying the reservoir of the lamp back into the five-gallon kerosene can from which it had been filled, while the mother tugged at his arm until he shifted the lamp to the other hand and flung her back, not savagely or viciously, just hard, into the wall, her hands flung out against the wall for balance, her mouth open and in her face the same quality of hopeless despair as had been in her voice. Then his father saw him standing in the door.

"Go to the barn and get that can of oil we were oiling the wagon with," he said.

The boy did not move. Then he could speak.

"What . . ." he cried. "What are you . . ."

"Go get that oil," his father said. "Go."

Then he was moving, running, outside the house, toward the stable: this the old habit, the old blood which he had not been permitted to choose for himself, which had been bequeathed him willy-nilly and which had run for so long (and who knew where, battening on what of outrage and savagery and lust) before it came to him. *I could keep on,* he thought. *I could run on and on and never look back, never need to see his face again. Only I can't. I can't,* the rusted can in his hand now, the liquid sploshing in it as he ran back to the house and into it, into the sound of his mother's weeping in the next room, and handed the can to his father.

"Ain't you going to even send a nigger?" he cried. "At least you sent a nigger before!"

This time his father didn't strike him. The hand came even faster than the blow had, the same hand which had set the can on the table with almost excruciating care flashing from the can toward him too quick for him to follow it, gripping him by the back of his shirt and onto tiptoe before he had seen it quit the can, the face stooping at him in breathless and frozen ferocity, the cold, dead voice speaking over him to the older brother who leaned against the table, chewing with that steady, curious, sidewise motion of cows:

"Empty the can into the big one and go on. I'll catch up with you."

"Better tie him up to the bedpost," the brother said.

"Do like I told you," the father said. Then the boy was moving, his bunched shirt and the hard, bony hand between his shoulder blades, his toes just touching the floor, across the room and into the other one, past the sisters sitting with spread heavy thighs in the two chairs over the cold hearth, and to where his mother and aunt sat side by side on the bed, the aunt's arms about his mother's shoulders.

"Hold him," the father said. The aunt made a startled movement. "Not you," the father said. "Lennie. Take hold of him. I want to see you do it." His mother took him by the wrist. "You'll hold him better than that. If he gets loose, don't you know what he is going to do? He will go up yonder." He jerked his head toward the road. "Maybe I'd better tie him."

"I'll hold him," his mother whispered.

"See you do then." Then his father was gone, the stiff foot heavy and measured upon the boards, ceasing at last.

Then he began to struggle. His mother caught him in both arms, he jerking and wrenching at them. He would be stronger in the end, he knew that. But he had no time to wait for it. "Lemme go!" he cried. "I don't want to have to hit you!"

"Let him go!" the aunt said. "If he don't go, before God, I am going up there myself!"

"Don't you see I can't?" his mother cried. "Sarty! Sarty! No! No! Help me, Lizzie!"

Then he was free. His aunt grasped at him but it was too late. He whirled, running, his mother stumbled forward onto her knees behind him, crying to the nearer sister: "Catch him, Net! Catch him!" But that was too late too, the sister (the sisters were twins, born at the same time, yet either of them now gave the impression of being, encompassing as much living meat and volume and weight as any other two of the family) not yet having begun to rise from the chair, her head, face, alone merely turned, presenting to him in the flying instant an astonishing expanse of young female features untroubled by any surprise even, wearing only an expression of bovine interest. Then he was out of the room, out of the house, in the mild dust of the starlit road and the heavy rifeness of honeysuckle, the pale ribbon unspooling with terrific slowness under his running feet, reaching the gate at last and turning in, running, his heart and lungs drumming, on up the drive toward the lighted house, the lighted door. He did not knock, he burst in, sobbing for breath, incapable for the moment of speech; he saw the astonished face of the Negro in the linen jacket without knowing when the Negro had appeared.

"De Spain!" he cried, panted. "Where's . . ." then he saw the white man too emerging from a white door down the hall. "Barn!" he cried. "Barn!"

"What?" the white man said. "Barn?"

"Yes!" the boy cried. "Barn!"

"Catch him!" the white man shouted.

But it was too late this time too. The Negro grasped his shirt, but the entire sleeve, rotten with washing, carried away, and he was out that door too and in the drive again, and had actually never ceased to run even while he was screaming into the white man's face.

Behind him the white man was shouting, "My horse! Fetch my horse!" and he thought for an instant of cutting across the park and climbing the fence into the road, but he did not know the park nor how high the vine-massed fence might be and he dared not risk it. So he ran on down the drive, blood and breath roaring; presently he was in the road again though he could not see it. He could not hear either: the galloping mare was almost upon him before he heard her, and even then he held his course, as if the very urgency of his wild grief and need must in a moment more find him wings, waiting until the ultimate instant to hurl himself aside and into the weed-choked roadside ditch as the horse thundered past and on, for an instant in furious silhouette against the stars, the tranquil early summer night sky which, even before the shape of the horse and rider vanished, stained abruptly and violently upward: a long, swirling roar incredible and soundless, blotting the stars, and he springing up and into the road again, running again, knowing it was too late yet still running even after he heard the shot and, an instant later, two shots, pausing now without knowing he had ceased to run, crying "Pap! Pap!", running again before he knew he had begun to run, stumbling, tripping over something and scrabbling up again without ceasing to run, looking backward over his shoulder at the glare as he got up, running on among the invisible trees, panting, sobbing, "Father! Father!"

At midnight he was sitting on the crest of a hill. He did not know it was midnight and he did not know how far he had come. But there was no glare behind him now and he sat now, his back toward what he had called home for four days anyhow, his face toward the dark woods which he would enter when breath was strong again, small, shaking steadily in the chill darkness, hugging himself into the remainder of his thin, rotten shirt, the grief and despair now no longer terror and fear but just grief and despair. *Father. My father,* he thought. "He was brave!" he cried suddenly, aloud but not loud, no more than a whisper: "He was! He was in the war! He was in Colonel Sartoris' cav'ry!" not knowing that his father had gone to that war a private in the fine old European sense, wearing no uniform, admitting the authority of and giving fidelity to no man or army or flag, going to war as Malbrouck himself did: for booty—it meant nothing and less than nothing to him if it were enemy booty or his own.

The slow constellations wheeled on. It would be dawn and then sun-up after a while and he would be hungry. But that would be tomorrow and now he was only cold, and walking would cure that. His breathing was easier now and he decided to get up and go on, and then he found that he had been asleep because he knew it was almost dawn, the night almost over. He could tell that from the whippoorwills. They were everywhere now among the dark trees below him, constant and inflectioned and ceaseless, so that, as the instant for giving over to the day birds drew nearer and nearer, there was no interval at all between them. He got up. He was a little stiff, but walking would cure that too as it would the cold, and soon there would be the sun. He went on down the hill, toward the dark woods within which the liquid silver voices of the birds called unceasing—the rapid and urgent beating of the urgent and quiring heart of the late spring night. He did not look back.

THE GENTLE ART

NADINE GORDIMER

IN THE HEAT of the day the huge, pale silky width of river put out your eyes, so that when you turned away from it everything else looked black and jumped. There was a one-roomed square reed house on the bank, with a reed-mat door that rolled up and let down. Inside was a camp bed with an animal skin on it, and a table with an enamelled teapot, an assortment of flowered china cups, a tin of tea and a tin of powdered milk. There was a stool with a battery radio set that played all the time. The enormous trees of Africa, ant-eaten and ancient, hung still, over the hut; down on the margin of the river, in the sun, the black-and-lemon checkered skin of a crocodile made a bladder of air in the water and, right on the verge, the body of the creature lay in its naked flesh, stripped, except for the head and jaws and four gloves of skin left on its claws. The flesh looked pink, fresh and edible. The water stirred it like a breeze in feathers.

At night there was nothing—no river, no hut, no crocodile, no trees; only a vast soft moonless darkness that made the couple giggle with excitement as they bumped along the river track in the path of their headlights. "Shall we ever find it?" said Vivien, and her husband knew that he must. "This is it, all right," he said. "Do you think you're on the right path, Ricks?" she asked, ignoring him. Just then they heard the intimate, dramatic, triumphant, wheedling voice of the radio, finishing off a commercial in a squall of music; they were there, upon it, at the very hut. There was the dull red of a camp fire, an oil lamp came towards them, Rick's torch leapt from branch to branch, figures emerged like actors coming onto a stage.

"We have been waiting for you people since half-past seven," said a large blond man, half-challengingly.

Vivien broke into the exaggerated apologies of a woman anxious to make good in a world other than her own; at home in Johannesburg she was never punctual, and disdained any reproach about it, but here in the bush, she was abject at the thought that she might have kept the crocodile hunters waiting. She was sorry; she was terribly, terribly sorry, the hotel was so small, they couldn't upset regular meal hours by giving dinner a little earlier. . . . She really was *terribly* sorry. "I should jolly well think so," said the blond man, no longer challenging, no longer even listening. Although the night was warm as milk he had a muffler round his neck, and his blue-eyed, red face wore the perpetual bright smile of short temper. The other man, in shorts and ribbed stockings, stood about with his hands on his hips. "Ruddy motor's been kicking up hell," he said. "Jimmy and I've been friggin around with the damned thing best part of the afternoon." In the light of the oil lamp he had piggy good looks; handsome turned-up nose, bristling moustache, narrow, blinking eyes.

A man's voice called, "Davie? Davie, old man? You all ready." Another oil lamp came out of the hut, circling with light a stripling and a woman. As they came nearer, the stripling became a forty-year-old man whose thin, hard body stored up nothing; simply acted as a conductor of energy. . . . He was skinny and brown as an urchin, and he had dusty straight brown hair and large, deeply-recessed black eyes in a small, lined face. He looked like one of those small boys who look like old men, and the others watched him come towards them.

He was the host of the couple and the boss of the two men. Vivien followed his approach with parted lips; each time she saw him, since they had met by a miracle of accident on the river bank three days before, he materialized to her unbelievably out of all the stories she had heard about him. "Mr. Baird!" she called. "Hullo there! I'm so terribly sorry . . ." and she went off into her elaborate obeisance of apology all over again. "That's all right, that's all right." His voice was quick, light and friendly. "Only I want you people to enjoy your-selves and see some action, that's the idea, isn't it? Haven't you got a coat along with you Mr. McEwen? It gets pretty chilly on the river at night, you want to wrap up . . . Mike, can you spare a jersey or some-thing for Mr. McEwen?—Nothing of mine'd go near you, I'm afraid."

Vivien spoke up for her husband, "Oh Rick's fine, Mr. Baird, he's tough, really, he never wears a thing, even in winter. He spent his childhood running wild in Rhodesia, he's not really a soft city boy at all." He was one of those huge, thick-set young men who have gone almost bald by the time they are twenty. He passed a hand over his head and said, "Oh Vivien . . ."

"He c'n have my coat," said the smiling blond man, over his muffler.

Jimmy Baird turned to him with quick concern, "No, no Mike old man, you better hang on to that, you're not yourself yet. Give him one of your jerseys, there's a good chap."

"I'm not comin'," said Mike, "I don't need it."

Vivien drew back, her head on one side. "Not coming? Oh but you must, why, we wouldn't think of you staying behind alone."

"He can keep me company," said Mrs. Baird. She stood beside her husband, her arms folded across her body, that was young but made soft and comfortable with frequent childbearing. She had the air of the wife who, as usual, is walking down the garden path with her husband to see him off to work. Vivien turned to her. "Mrs. Baird! *You're* coming?"

"No, I think I'll just stay here. There's the children and everything."

She moved her head in the direction of a tent that was pitched in the shadowy darkness beside a truck.

"Aren't they asleep?"

"Yes, but the little one might wake up, and it's so close to the river . . . I don't like the idea of one of them wandering around. It's strange to the little one, we usually leave her at home, you see, it's her first time camping out up here with her Daddy."

Jimmy Baird, talking, giving orders, making suggestions all the time, disappeared into Mike's reed hut—this was Mike's headquarters, of the three that belonged to Jimmy Baird's river concession—and came out shaking himself into a pair of overalls.

"Doesn't he look wonderful?" said Vivien. "Doesn't your husband look wonderful, Mrs. Baird! That's how I like a man to look, as if he's really got a job to do. It drives me mad to see poor Ricks shut up in a blue suit in town. Isn't that a wonderful outfit, Ricks? Is that the sort of thing you had on the night the hippo overturned the boat, Mr. Baird? I can imagine it's not too easy to swim in that, unless you're a terrifically strong swimmer."

But Jimmy Baird was not so easily to be led to repeat, first-hand, as she longed to hear it, the story of one of his exploits famous in the territory; one of the stories out of which she had built up her idea of what such men are like. That idea had had to go through some modification already; she had always loathed "tiny men"—that was any man under the standard of 185 cm which she had set when she married Ricks. But although her picture of a man had shrunk to fit Jimmy Baird, three days ago, other aspects of it had not changed. Everything he said and did she saw as a manifestation of the qualities she read into his exploits and that she admired most—ruthlessness, recklessness, animal courage.

She said to Mrs. Baird, "I still can't believe this really is the famous Jimmy Baird. Oh yes, you know it. Your husband is the most talked-about man in the territory, wherever we've been on this trip up here, it's been Jimmy Baird, Jimmy Baird. And now we're actually going crocodile-hunting with him!" "*Ag*, yes." Mrs. Baird came from South Africa and had the usual off-hand, careless way of speaking, putting in a word of Afrikaans here and there; tongue-tied and yet easy, shy and yet forthright. "The Bairds have lived in the territory for donkey's years. Everybody knows them."

"We're off now girl," said Jimmy Baird, coming up to her and putting his arm round her.

Out on the river the boat kicked and roared and puttered into silence again under the experimental hands of Davie; he brought it back into the submerged reeds with a skidding rush. "Right-o," he yelled.

"Enjoy yourself," said Mrs. Baird.

"It's awful you not being able to come. Are you sure you won't?— But I suppose you've been dozens of times before—" said Vivien.

Mrs. Baird held her arms and looked round the limit of the camp fire's light as if it were a room. "I don't like water," she said. "They say if you don't like it, that's a warning to keep away from it."

At the last moment, the man Mike got into the boat with them after all. He wore an old army overcoat in addition to his muffler—Ricks put the borrowed sweater round his shoulders as a concession to Jimmy Baird's insistence. Davie handed Vivien into the boat, while she called out, "Now where do you want me to sit? Don't let us be in the way, please." The light of an oil lamp ran over their faces like liquid; the boat grated heavily in the mud. Two Africans, enclosed in a sullen cocoon of silence, pushed and shoved beneath the shouts of the men in the boat.

"Ricks, you're too heavy," said Vivien, laughing excitedly. They began to argue about the distribution of weight, changing places with each other.

"No—wait—" Jimmy Baird rolled up the legs of his overalls, kicked off his shoes and jumped out of the boat. "That's it—that's it—" his strong thin hands spread in a straining grip on the prow, his head lifted with effort. With one last concerted shove, along with the Africans, he freed the boat and jumped in.

They saw the two black men, for a moment, gasping, leaning forward with hands hanging where the boat had been wrenched from their grasp; they heard the reeds hissing away on either side; they felt the sky open, enormous, above them. The black water took them; between one moment and the next, they left the downward pull of the land, and were afloat on an element that made nothing of their weight. "Oh!"

said Vivien, like a child on a swing. "Oh, it's lovely." And at once remembered that she was on a crocodile hunt, and fell silent.

They were drifting without sound or sensation in the dark. Far away already, there was the small glowing centre that was the camp fire, throwing up a fading orbit of light that caught the trees architecturally, here a branch, there the column of a trunk, like the planes of a lost temple half-hidden in the jungle. They were out in deep water; the middle of the river offered them to the sky.

The oil lamps had been left on shore and Mike, who was to steer, switched on the long, stiff, powerful beam of a portable searchlight. It shot through the dark and plucked out of nothing the reeds of the opposite bank, rose like a firework steeply into the sky, plunged, shortening, down into the water. "O.K.," said Mike, and Davie started up the engine at the first kick. They began to cleave smoothly up river at a steady pace.

"Now we let the light travel all over the show, like this," Jimmy Baird was explaining. "Along the reeds and so on, specially when we get further up, in the shallows, and we watch out to pick up the eyes of a croc. You can see them quite distinctly, you'll see, Mrs. McEwen, you can pick them up quite a way off, and then when you do you just make straight for them, keep the light on them all the time. They're like rabbits, you know, in the headlights of a car. They seem to be fascinated by the glare or something; so long's you keep the light full on them they don't move. Then we go right close up, right up, and shoot them at about two metres—Bit lower down, Mike, that's it.— There you are Mrs. McEwen, you can see the mudbank over there, that's the sort of place the old croc likes, nice and soft for his belly."

"Two metres!" said Ricks.

Jimmy Baird turned sympathetically. He was standing up in the boat with his gun in his hand. "Yes. Two metres or even less. It's not sport, you see, Mr. McEwen. You must get them, and you must kill first shot. Then we usually give them another one, anyway just to make sure. It's pretty nasty if you get one coming alive in the boat. We've had some scares, eh, Mike?"

"I'll say," said the blond man, bright-eyed, grinning into the night.

"Yes," said Jimmy Baird. "You must be quite sure they're knocked right out. Can you see Mrs. McEwen? I'm sorry to be standing right here half in front of you like this. But I promise I'll skip out of the way the moment there's anything to see. Are you comfy? Wait a minute— there ought to be a cushion down here—" "Oh no, please, I'm wonderful," protested Vivien, rapt. "Davie," Jimmy Baird called to him, "isn't there that old leather cushion down there?" "Oh please, Mr. Baird, don't worry—I am perfect—here!"

"Over there," said Mike's voice drily.

Jimmy Baird excusing himself, slipped past Vivien and came up behind her so that he could direct her. "There you are! Yes, there he is, fair-sized chappie, I should say. See those red eyes?"

The long beam of light led across the dark to a small reedy island. Vivien half-rose from the box she had been huddled on; "Where," she whispered urgently, "where?"

"There, there," said Jimmy Baird soothingly. "There he is . . ."

Ricks said, "I've got it. Like two little bits of coal! I'll be damned!"

"Oh where?" Vivien was desperate.

Jimmy Baird took her hand and pointed: "Straight ahead, my dear. Got him?"

Then she saw, low down in the dark tangle, two glowing red points. The boat bore down upon them. Nobody spoke except Jimmy. He kept up a quiet running commentary, a soothing incantation to keep the crocodile unmoving. But as they reached the reeds, there was a movement quicker than a blink. "He's gone!" said Jimmy. "There he goes."

The boat kicked, turned, made for open water again.

"I saw him!" said Vivien. "I saw his tail!"

"Never mind, lots more to come," said Jimmy Baird, promising.

"I think you'll find 'em a bit shy down this way," said Davie. "We been giving 'em hell the last week, Jimmy. I think we ought to go right up a bit."

"O.K. Davie, if you think so," said Jimmy politely.

In a few minutes they caught another pair of eyes in the beam of the searchlight; but again the unseen creature got away without even a splash. To the two visitors, the unlikelihood of the whole business— that men could earn a living on a tropical river, at night, shooting crocodiles in order to sell their skins—seemed the answer. They could not believe that they themselves really were *there*; so it did not seem strange that there was no crocodile lying dead in the boat. Then Jimmy Baird said in his encouraging, friendly voice, "On the right, Davie, please." As the boat swerved neatly and closed in, Vivien said, "Oh yes, I see it," although she could see nothing.

"It's a babe, I'm afraid—yes, just a babe," said Jimmy, who had explained earlier that they did not shoot crocodiles below a certain minimum size, though they took them as big as they came. "You can see how close together the eyes are; that's a little head, that one." The boat nosed into the reeds and the engine cut out. Suddenly Jimmy Baird said, "Bring her right in, Davie! Right up!" and as the boat shot by the mud bank where the light had settled, he leant swiftly out of the boat and with a movement of incredible balance and strength, like a circus performer, he brought up in his hands a struggling sixty centimetre-long crocodile.

Vivien was so astonished that she looked quickly round the boat, from one to another, as if she were afraid she had been fooled. "There you are," said Jimmy Baird, with both small hard hands rigid as steel round the long snout of the frantic creature. "Now you can have a good look at him, Mrs. McEwen—Ah-ah, you wicked one," he added to the crocodile in the special voice of admonishment you would use for a young child. "Look at him, look at him trying to lever himself loose with his tail." The crocodile had slapped his strong tail round the man's slender right forearm and was using a wrestler's muscular pressure to free himself.

The young woman put out a hand. "Go on," said Jimmy Baird. "He's all right, the little blighter," and she touched the creature's cool, hard back, a horny hide of leather medallions, fresh, strange, alive; from a life unknown to the touch of humans, beneath the dark river. In the light of the searchlight, turned upon the creature and the faces of those around it, she saw the scissor jaws—parted a little as the man moved his grip a shade back toward the throat—with the ugly, uneven rows of razor-jagged teeth. In the light, she met the eyes; slits of pale brilliant green, brilliant as fire; in their beast's innocence of such things, they held for humans the projection of hate, cunning and evil.

There was a moment when the eyes saw her, of all the others. She felt that the thing knew her, as God knew her; there was an incomparable thrill of fear.

The creature suddenly bellowed hoarsely with the yell of an infuriated and desperate baby; and they all laughed.

"Ma-ma! Ma-ma!"

"Jesus, how he'd like one of your fingers!"

"Could he really?" asked Vivien.

"You bet," said Mike. "Just like that. Clean as a whistle."

Jimmy Baird bent over the water, with care. Then his hands sprang back like a released trap. "That's the last we'll see of him," he said, wiping his wet hands down his overalls.

Vivien was excited and boastful. "Oh, I'm sure you'll get him. You'll get him next year, when he's bigger."

Davie was using a pole to shove the boat off from the mud bank.

"They live a long time . . . Their lives are slower than ours. Probably he'll be lying here in the sun long after I've finished banging away up and down this river or anywhere else," said Jimmy Baird. His face was serene, in the light, then the light left him and went out over the darkness again.

"We should have put a mark on him," Vivien went on joyfully. "Couldn't we have branded him or something, so that you'd know him if you caught him?"

Mike turned with his perpetual ill-tempered grin. "We got six hundred last season and we didn't know any of 'em by name."

"Sure you're O.K. Mike?" Jimmy Baird asked, and touched him on the shoulder.

"Fine, fine," he said, looking out into the dark with his eyes wide open like a blind man.

"Isn't he well tonight?" said Vivien.

"He's had a nasty temperature all day," said Jimmy Baird, concertedly. "Bit of malaria—he says it's flu, old Mike."

IN AN HOUR the haze had cleared from the sky and, although there was only a thin new moon, the stars were bright; their faint silvering, that is put out by the glow of cities in countries where there are cities, came out in a night silence hundreds of kilometres away from even the most distant sound of a train. The mere touch of light lay on the water, a membrane upon the darkness; touched the reeds; penetrated nothing of the great massed mansions of wild fig trees on the banks. There were low calls and whoops, a snatch of far-off human laughter from the jackals—the behind-the-hand noises of the river's secret life. Awe invaded the heart and took the tongue of Vivien McEwen; at the same time, she wanted to giggle, like a child watching a Hollywood adventure film. At one point, where the right bank of the river opened out on what must have been treeless scrub, small glowing points jumped about; it looked as if, out there in the waste where no one lived, someone was throwing cigarette butts away in the dark. Jimmy Baird explained that they were the eyes of spring-hares, who had a big warren just there.

"Slow down, Davie old man, perhaps we can spot them."

The searchlights swivelled obediently and made low sweeps on the bank, but it was too far away; they could see nothing but the light itself, the colour of strong tea, reaching out.

They went on and twice they entered a water-maze, where the river closed in to alleys and lanes and passages enclosed by high walls of reeds, but to the crocodile hunters these were the streets of their own neighbourhood. They glided by narrow mud-bars where heavy wet bodies had made a resting-place like the place in long grass where a dog has made a bed. The propellor was lifted clear of the water, bearded with debris, and their progress was silent, as Davie poled them along. Jimmy Baird held back the reeds that came to splatter and hit at Vivien's face. This was a closely inhabited place; like a ghetto or a souk, it had the atmosphere of an interior, of the particular quality and kind of life lived there. It was a closed saurian world of mud, dankness, sun, unmeasured time.

The boat emerged again, into the broad main flow and the power of the engine coming to life like a great fish carrying them along on its back. The big blond Mike sat hunched in his place, his face turned smiling into the dark, not following the purposeful wandering of the light his hands directed. There were stretches where he whistled, piercingly and professionally, tunes that had gone round in people's

heads exhaustively, then died, like spinning tops, of their own repeti-
tion, over the past twenty years. When the young woman heard a tune
that was recent enough to have pleasant associations for her, she asked
him what it was called.

"I wooden know," he said, not looking at her. "I pick 'em up from
the radio." The searchlight pushed aside the darkness from the reeds,
first on this side, then on that; occasionally, as you might lift your eyes
from a trying task in order to rest them with a change of focus, it ran
lightly over the bank, discovering trees, caves of undergrowth, sudden
clearings, and the crook of the terrible finger, grey and five metres
high, of an ant-heap.

"What d'you think?" Davie called.

"Well, yes, I suppose we should think about getting back, you know
Davie," said Jimmy Baird, and paused to consider a moment. "What
d'you say, Mike?" It seemed that it was not out of an inability to make
up his own mind about things that he consulted his companions with
great care, on every point, but rather out of a fear that, always knowing
exactly what he wanted to do, he might impose his will thoughtlessly.

"Nothing up here tonight," said Mike, as if someone were arguing
with him. "This's where I got these two big fellers yesterday."

"Oh we'll raise something yet," said Jimmy Baird. "We'll go back
down slowly and see what we can find. I must say, this's been disappointing for you so far, Mrs. McEwen—are you sure you're warm
enough? Hands not too cold?" He added to Mike, "You missing your
teatime tonight, Mike, eh?—Mike always pumps up the old primus and
gives us a cuppa tea round about this time, it makes all the difference,
you know, specially when it's cold—you just long for that cuppa tea."

Mike looked at his watch. "Half-past ten. Yes, just about time."

"We'll have something hot when we get back, to make up," promised
Jimmy Baird. Vivien and her husband protested that they were not
thirsty, needed nothing.

Davie, who could not always follow what was being said, because
of his closeness to the noise of the motor, suddenly called out, "Mike!
D'jou forget the tea tonight? S'half-past ten."

"He didn't bring the primus."

"Well, of all the lousy chumps . . ."

"We're not working," said Mike. "That's why I didn't think of it, man, just fooling around."

While the discussion about the tea was going on, Jimmy Baird, still talking, spotted a crocodile with that third eye of alertness that was constantly awake in him. He had been telling Vivien and her husband how Davie and Mike always argued over the cups—Davie had a flowered china cup, the last of three he had brought with him from town life two years ago, and he didn't want Mike to risk it on the river. "I must say, it is a very pretty cup, Royal Doulton or something posh like that—" he was saying, when he suddenly changed his manner beneath his voice, which went on in exactly the same tone: "On the left there, Davie. Come on, now—" and he bent down and picked up his gun. "Excuse me, Mrs. McEwen," he said with concern, because he had brushed her shoulder as he moved—and he was looking at the two red eyes fifty metres ahead, and he was loading the gun that he insisted must always be kept unloaded the moment it was not in use. Mike thrust the light into the hands of Ricks McEwen, saying, "Keep that dead steady, eh?" and picked up the gaff.

With the numb swiftness of a piece of surgery it was accomplished; Vivien seemed to hear Jimmy Baird's voice through ether, kind and confident, the voice of the doctor doing what has to be done, without the futility of pity and with the mercy of skill.

"Right up, now, quickly, Davie."

The boat bore down fast on the reeds and the two pencil-torch eyes glowed nearer, and there it was, in the space of a second, the horny-looking, greenish-black forehead with the frontal ridges over the eyes above the water, and the nostrils breaking the water again at the end of the lumpy snout—there it was, gazing, in the eternity of a split second, not a metre away, and Jimmy Baird's calm, compassionate voice saying, "Right", and the gun swiftly on his shoulder and the crack beside her where she stood. Then the pale gaze coming from the dark forehead exploded; it blew up as if from within, and where the gaze had been there was a soft pink mess of brain with the scarlet wetness of blood and the mother-of-pearl sheen of muscle. There was violent threshing of the water, and although the crocodile was dead—had been completely alive one second and quite dead the next—Jimmy Baird shot it again and the great gaff swooped down and hooked it out of the pull of the river. The men heaved it aboard. "All over. O.K. O.K. Let's get him down here, that's it." Jimmy Baird saw the creature laid out carefully on the bottom of the boat, out of the way, but so that Vivien and Ricks could see it well. It was nearly two metres long, less than half-grown. The broad, soft-looking belly part, which was the part for which it had been hunted, was beautifully marked in lozenge-shaped plates, cream-coloured with tinges of black, that were perfectly articulated as the segments of a tortoise-shell. The lizard legs and the belly twitched occasionally, as if the blown communications had left some unfinished message of impulse.

Vivien McEwen was on her feet. "Oh my God," she cried, grinning, laughing "What a man! Wasn't that wonderful, Ricks? Did you ever see anything like it! What a man! Oh Mr. Baird, that was terrific. Terrific!" She was in such a state of excitement that she was unsteady, like a drunk; the boat rocked and her husband had to hold her elbow. "That's the most wonderful thing I've ever seen," she appealed from one to the other. "Wasn't that splendid? Oh my God, what do you think of him?—The way he simply goes up and blazes the hell out of that thing—Those eyes! Staring at you! Crash—Whoom—Finished!"

Mike took a look at the crocodile. "Just a teenager, eh, Jimmy?"

"Well, not too bad, Mike, he'll pay for the petrol."

Ricks McEwen said, as one man to another, "You certainly don't give yourself time to fumble. Hardly a chance to aim, even."

Jimmy Baird gave him his attention. "You're so close, you don't have to aim, really. It's instantaneous, you know. The old croc doesn't suffer at all. I don't like to kill. I haven't shot a buck, for instance, since just after the war. But I often think these old crocs have a better end than most of us will ever have. We come up so close, you see, it's only a second . . ."

"Ricks, look at this!"

Davie had taken a spanner and knocked off one of the crocodile's teeth for the young woman. She was a dark woman, rather plain, with a very small head; the scarf she had worn over it had fallen back and now, bared, with its smooth brown hair in a bun, her head emerged, rather reptilian itself—the little black moles, one beside her left eye, one beside the corner of her mouth, and two on her cheek, added to the suggestion. She might have come out of the night river, a creature cunningly marked for concealment in the ambiguous, shifting, blotchy light-and-dark of reeds and water. "Just look," her teeth and small eyes shone in the light. "Imagine that crunching into your leg! And if he breaks this one, he's got another inside!" She showed her husband how the big mossy yellowed tooth held a spare one wedged within it.

At last they all settled themselves in the boat again, and Davie poled off from the mudbank where a cloud of blood, suspended in the shallows, was slowly threading away into the mass of water.

Vivien McEwen sat back, plumping herself with sighs of triumph. She could not control her excited laughter; it rippled over with everything she said. "Ricks? Ricks? How do you feel about Johannesburg now?" She wrapped the crocodile tooth carefully in a handkerchief and put it in among the cigarettes and cosmetics that made a perfumed jumble in her handbag.

"Oh fine, Vivien, fine."

Her brow wrinkled, she drew her head back on her shoulder with intensity, as she confided to Mike. "This'll make my poor husband just impossible. He loathes cities, anyway. This is a life for a man."

Jimmy Baird had unloaded the gun and put it away and was squatting next to Ricks McEwen. He took out his pipe and began to fill it, but McEwen said, "Oh come on, try some of this."

"May I really? That's jolly nice," Jimmy Baird took the proffered pouch, a pigskin-and-suède affair that Vivien had made for her husband last Christmas.

The two men sat feeding the tobacco into their pipes and tamping it down. The light of matches opened and closed on their faces, and a spasm of muscle made the dead beast at their feet nudge suddenly at the shoes. "Sometimes when I've got five or six big crocs in one night, I look at them spread out on the river bank and I think, that's a thousand years of life lying there. It seems kind of awful, a thousand years of life," Jimmy Baird said.

THE NIGHT river closed away behind them. It went back where it came from; from the world of sleep, of eternity and darkness, the place

before birth, after death—all those ideas with which the flowing con-
tinuity of dark water is bound up. And the boat came back; brought
them within sight of the light of the camp fire and the shapes it touched,
and then back to the camp itself, existence itself, a fire, the reed house,
the smell of food, and a human figure. A moment, between boat and
bank, when each one of them saw the dark water beneath him, wriggling with light from the oil lamp an African held—and then they were
on land, lively and stretching. "Are you all ready for us, my girlie?"
said Jimmy Baird, putting his arm around his wife and looking at her
tenderly. "Yes, yes, there's coffee there, and sandwiches," she said,
making as if to put him away, but staying within his arm. Mike stamped
around, hunching his shoulders and hitting the fist of one hand in the
palm of the other, and Davie kicked the big logs closer into the fire
so that sparks flew. "I didn't see you coming, you know," she said
smiling. "You gave me quite a scare. You can't see beyond the light of
the fire, when you're sitting there in it."

Vivien McEwen was glowing, even panting a little, "Ah Mrs. Baird,"
she said, "your husband! It was sensational! I thought I'd die! Oh you
should've been there! You should've been there, really!" She stood
dramatically, as if the other woman, who was smiling at her kindly
with a polite smile, might catch alight from her. "I'll bring you a cup of
coffee, eh," said Jimmy Baird's wife, and as Vivien, who had followed
her to the table, stood beside her while she poured the coffee out of a
big enamel jug. Vivien looked at her and suddenly said, curiously,
"What did you do, all the time we were gone? Did you read or something?"

"I waited," said Mrs. Baird.

"Yes, but I mean how did you pass the time," Vivien said. She had
taken the cup and, although the coffee was boiling hot, was taking
quick, darting sips at it.

The other woman looked up from the coffee jug a moment, apologetic
because her visitor hadn't caught what she had said.

"I waited," she said.

For a moment, Vivien looked as if, this time, she really hadn't heard.
Then she gave the woman a big brilliant, dazed smile and wandered
off back to the company of the men.

CORONER'S INQUEST

MARC CONNELLY

"WHAT IS your name?"

"Frank Wineguard."

"Where do you live?"

"A hundred and eighty-five West Fifty-fifth Street."

"What is your business?"

"I'm stage manager for *Hello, America*."

"You were the employer of James Dawle?"

"In a way. We both worked for Mr. Bender, the producer, but I have charge backstage."

"Did you know Theodore Robel?"

"Yes, sir."

"Was he in your company, too?"

"No, sir. I met him when we started rehearsals. That was about three months ago, in June. We sent out a call for midgets and he and Jimmy showed up together, with a lot of others. Robel was too big for us. I didn't see him again until we broke into their room Tuesday."

"You discovered their bodies?"

"Yes, sir. Mrs. Pike, there, was with me."

"You found them both dead?"

"Yes, sir."

"How did you happen to be over in Jersey City?"

"Well, I'd called up his house at curtain time Monday night when I found Jimmy hadn't shown up for the performance. Mrs. Pike told me they were both out, and I asked her to have either Jimmy or Robel call me when they came in. Then Mrs. Pike called me Tuesday morning and said she tried to get into the room but she'd found the door was bolted. She said all her other roomers were out and she was alone and scared.

"I'd kind of suspected something might be wrong. So I said to wait and I'd come over. Then I took the tube over and got there about noon. Then we went up and I broke down the door."

"Did you see this knife there?"

"Yes, sir. It was on the floor, about a foot from Jimmy."

"You say you suspected something was wrong. What do you mean by that?"

"I mean I felt something might have happened to Jimmy. Nothing like this, of course. But I knew he'd been feeling very depressed lately, and I knew Robel wasn't helping to cheer him up any."

"You mean that they had had quarrels?"

"No, sir. They just both had the blues. Robel had had them for a long time. Robel was Jimmy's brother-in-law. He'd married Jimmy's sister—she was a midget, too—about five years ago, but she died a year or so later. Jimmy had been living with them and after the sister died he and Robel took a room in Mrs. Pike's house together."

"How did you learn this?"

"Jimmy and I were pretty friendly at the theater. He was a nice little fellow and seemed grateful that I'd given him his job. We'd only needed one midget for an Oriental scene in the second act and the agencies had sent about fifteen. Mr. Gehring, the director, told me to pick one of them as he was busy and I picked Jimmy because he was the littlest.

"After I got to know him he told me how glad he was I'd given him the job. He hadn't worked for nearly a year. He wasn't little enough to be a featured midget with circuses or in museums so he had to take whatever came along. Anyway, we got to be friendly and he used to tell me about his brother-in-law and all."

"He never suggested that there might be ill feeling between him and his brother-in-law?"

"No, sir. I don't imagine he'd ever had any words at all with Robel. As a matter of fact from what I could gather I guess Jimmy had quite a lot of affection for him and he certainly did everything he could to help him. Robel was a lot worse off than Jimmy. Robel hadn't worked for a couple of years and Jimmy practically supported him. He used to tell me how Robel had been sunk ever since he got his late growth."

"His what?"

"His late growth. I heard it happens among midgets often, but Jimmy told me about it first. Usually a midget will stay as long as he lives at whatever height he reaches when he's fourteen or fifteen, but every now and then one of them starts growing again just before he's thirty, and he can grow a foot or even more in a couple of years. Then he stops growing for good. But of course he don't look so much like a midget anymore.

"That's what had happened to Robel about three years ago. Of course he had trouble getting jobs and it hit him pretty hard.

"From what Jimmy told me and from what Mrs. Pike says, I guess he used to talk about it all the time. Robel used to come over and see his agent in New York twice a week, but there was never anything for him. Then he'd go back to Jersey City. Most of the week he lived alone because after the show started Jimmy often stayed in New York with a cousin or somebody that lived uptown.

"Lately Robel hadn't been coming over to New York at all. But every Saturday night Jimmy would go over to Jersey City and stay till Monday with him, trying to cheer him up. Every Sunday they'd take a walk and go to a movie. I guess as they walked along the street Robel realized most the difference in their heights. And I guess that's really why they're both dead now."

"How do you mean?"

"Well, as I told you, Jimmy would try to sympathize with Robel and cheer him up. He and Robel both realized that Jimmy was working and supporting them and that Jimmy would probably keep right on working, according to the ordinary breaks of the game, while Robel would always be too big. It simply preyed on Robel's mind.

"And then three weeks ago Monday, Jimmy thought he saw the ax fall.

"I was standing outside the stage door—it was about seven thirty—and Jimmy came down the alley. He looked down in the mouth, which I thought was strange seeing that he usually used to come in swinging his little cane and looking pretty cheerful. I said, 'How are you feeling,

Jimmy?' and he said, 'I don't feel so good, Mr. Wineguard.' So I said, 'Why, what's the matter, Jimmy?' I could see there really was something the matter with him by this time.

" 'I'm getting scared,' he said, and I says, 'Why?'

" 'I'm starting to grow again,' he says. He said it the way you'd say you just found out you had some disease that was going to kill you in a week. He looked like he was shivering.

" 'Why, you're crazy, Jimmy,' I says. 'You ain't growing.'

" 'Yes, I am,' he says. 'I'm thirty-one and it's that late growth like my brother-in-law has. My father had it, but his people had money, so it didn't make much difference to him. It's different with me. I've got to keep working.'

"He went on like that for a while and then I tried to kid him out of it.

" 'You look all right to me,' I said. 'How tall have you been all along?'

" 'Thirty-seven inches,' he says. So I says, 'Come on into the prop room and I'll measure you.'

"He backed away from me. 'No,' he says, 'I don't want to know how much it is.' Then he went up to the dressing room before I could argue with him.

"All week he looked awful sunk. When he showed up the next Monday evening he looked almost white.

"I grabbed him as he was starting upstairs to make up.

" 'Come on out of it,' I says. I thought he'd make a break and try to get away from me, but he didn't. He just sort of smiled as if I didn't understand. Finally he says, 'It ain't any use, Mr. Wineguard.'

" 'Listen,' I says, 'you've been over with that brother-in-law of yours, haven't you?' He said yes, he had. 'Well,' I says, 'that's what's bothering you. From what you tell me about him he's talked about his own tough luck so much that he's given you the willies, too. Stay away from him the end of this week.'

"He stood there for a second without saying anything. Then he says, 'That wouldn't do any good. He's all alone over there and he needs company. Anyway, it's all up with me, I guess. I've grown nearly two inches already.'

"I looked at him. He was pretty pathetic, but outside of that there wasn't any change in him as far as I could see.

"I says, 'Have you been measured?' He said he hadn't. Then I said, 'Then how do you know? Your clothes fit you all right, except your pants, and as a matter of fact they seem a little longer.'

"'I fixed my suspenders and let them down a lot farther,' he says. 'Besides they were always a little big for me.'

"'Let's make sure,' I says. 'I'll get a yardstick and we'll make absolutely sure.'

"But I guess he was too scared to face things. He wouldn't do it.

"He managed to dodge me all week. Then, last Saturday night, I ran into him as I was leaving the theater. I asked him if he felt any better.

"'I feel all right,' he says. He really looked scared to death.

"That's the last time I saw him before I went over to Jersey City after Mrs. Pike phoned me Tuesday morning."

"Patrolman Gorlitz has testified that the bodies were in opposite ends of the room when he arrived. They were in that position when you - forced open the door?"

"Yes, sir."

"The medical examiner has testified that they were both dead of knife wounds, apparently from the same knife. Would you assume the knife had fallen from Dawle's hand as he fell?"

"Yes, sir."

"Has it been your purpose to suggest that both men were driven to despondency by a fear of lack of employment for Dawle, and that they might have committed suicide?"

"No, sir. I don't think anything of the kind."

"What do you mean?"

"Well, when Mrs. Pike and I went in the room and I got a look at the knife, I said to Mrs. Pike that that was a funny kind of a knife for them to have in the room. You can see it's a kind of a butcher knife. Then Mrs. Pike told me it was one that she'd missed from her kitchen a few weeks before. She'd never thought either Robel or Jimmy had taken it. It struck me as funny Robel or Jimmy had stolen it, too. Then I put two and two together and found out what really happened. Have you got the little broken cane that was lying on the bed?"

"Is this it?"

"Yes, sir. Well, I'd never been convinced by Jimmy that he was really growing. So when Mrs. Pike told me about the knife I started figuring. I figured that about five minutes before that knife came into play Jimmy must have found it, probably by accident."

"Why by accident?"

"Because Robel had gone a little crazy, I guess. He'd stolen it and kept it hidden from Jimmy. And when Jimmy found it he wondered what Robel had been doing with it. Then Robel wouldn't tell him and Jimmy found out for himself. Or maybe Robel did tell him. Anyway, Jimmy looked at the cane. It was the one he always carried. He saw where, when Jimmy wasn't looking, Robel had been cutting little pieces off the end of it."

HOTEL DU COMMERCE
ELIZABETH TAYLOR

Elizabeth Taylor

THE HALLWAY, with its reception desk and hat-stand, was gloomy. Madame Bertail reached up to the board where the keys hung, took the one for Room Eight, and led the way upstairs. Her daughter picked up the heavier suitcase, and begun to lurch, lopsidedly, across the hall with it until Leonard, blushing as he always (and understandably) did when he was obliged to speak French, insisted on taking it from her.

Looking offended, she grabbed instead Melanie's spanking-new wedding-present suitcase, and followed them grimly, as *they* followed Madame Bertail's stiffly corseted back. Level with her shoulder-blades, the corsets stopped and the massive flesh moved gently with each step she took, as if it had a life of its own.

In Room Eight was a small double bed and wallpaper with a paisley pattern, on which what looked like curled-up blood-red embryos were repeated every two inches upon a sage-green background. There were other patterns for curtains and chair covers and the thin eiderdown. It was a depressing room, and a smell of some previous occupier's *Ambre Solaire* still hung about it.

"I'm so sorry, darling," Leonard apologised, as soon as they were alone.

Melanie smiled. For a time, they managed to keep up their spirits. "I'm so tired, I'll sleep anywhere," she said, not knowing about the mosquito hidden in the curtains, or the lumpiness of the bed, and other horrors to follow.

They were both tired. A day of driving in an open car had made them feel, now they had stopped, quite dull and drowsy. Conversation was an effort.

Melanie opened her case. There was still confetti about. A crescent-shaped white piece fluttered onto the carpet, and she bent quickly and picked it up. So much about honeymoons was absurd—even little reminders like this one. And there had been awkwardnesses they could never have forseen—especially that of having to make their way in a foreign language. (*Lune de miel* seemed utterly improbable to her.) She did not know how to ask a maid to wash a blouse, although she had pages of irregular verbs somewhere in her head, and odd words, from lists she had learned as a child—the Parts of the Body, the Trees of the Forest, the Days of the Week—would often spring gratifyingly to her rescue.

When she had unpacked, she went to the window and leaned out, over a narrow street with lumpy cobbles all ready for an early-morning din of rattling carts and slipping hooves.

Leonard kept glancing nervously at her as he unpacked. He did everything methodically, and at one slow pace. She was quick and untidy, and spent much time hanging about waiting for him, growing depressed, then exasperated, leaning out of windows, as now, strolling impatiently in gardens.

He smoked in the bedroom: she did not, and often thought it would have been better the other way about, so that she could have had something to do while she waited.

He hung up his dressing-gown, paused, then trod heavily across to his suitcase and took out washing things, which he arranged neatly on a shelf. He looked at her again. Seen from the back, hunched over the window-sill, she seemed to be visibly drooping, diminishing, like melting wax; and he knew that her mood was because of him. But a lifetime's habit—more than that, something inborn—made him feel helpless. He also had a moment of irritation himself, seeing her slippers thrown anyhow under a chair.

"Ready, then," he said, in a tone of anticipation and decision.

She turned eagerly from the window, and saw him take up his comb. He stood before the glass, combing, combing his thin hair, lapsing once more into dreaminess, intent on what he was doing. She sighed quietly and turned back to look out of the window.

"I can see a spire of the Cathedral," she said presently; but her head was so far out of the window—and a lorry was going by—that he did not hear her.

Well, we've *had* the Cathedral, she thought crossly. It was too late for the stained glass. She would never be able to make him see that every minute counted, or that there should not be some preordained method but, instead, a shifting order of priorities. Unpacking can wait; but the light will not.

By the time they got out for their walk, and saw the Cathedral, it was floodlit, bone-white against the dark sky, bleached, flat, stagey, though beautiful in this unintended and rather unsuitable way. Walking in the twisting streets, Leonard and Melanie had glimpsed the one tall spire above roof-tops, then lost it. Arm-in-arm, they had stopped to look in shop windows, at huge *terrines* and glazed *pates en croûte,* tarts full of neatly arranged strawberries, sugared almonds on stems, in bunches, tied with ribbons. Leonard lingered, comparing prices of watches and cameras with those at home in England; Melanie, feeling chilly, tried gently to draw him on. At last, without warning, they came to the square where the Cathedral stood, and here there were more shops, all full of little plaster statues and rosaries, and antiques for the tourists.

"Exorbitant," Leonard kept saying. "My God, how they're out to fleece you!"

Melanie stood staring up at the Cathedral until her neck ached. The great rose window was dark, the light glaring on the stone façade too static. The first sense of amazement and wonder faded. It was part of her impatient nature to care most for her first impressions. On their way south, the sudden, and faraway sight of Chartres Cathedral across the plain, crouched on the horizon, with its lopsided spires, like a giant, had meant much more to her than the close-up details of it. Again, for *that*, they had been too late. Before they reached the town, storm-clouds had gathered. It might as well have been dusk inside the Cathedral. She, for her part, would not have stopped to fill up with petrol on the road. She would have risked it, parked the car anywhere, and run.

Staring up at *the* Cathedral, she felt dizzy from leaning backwards, and swayed suddenly, and laughed. He caught her close to him and so, walking rather unevenly, with arms about the other's waist, moved on, out of the square, and back to the hotel.

Such moments, of more-than-usual love, gave them both great confidence. This time, their mood of elation lasted much longer than a moment.

Although the hotel dining-room was dark, and they were quite alone in it, speaking in subdued voices, their humour held; and held, as they took their key from impassive Madame Bertail, who still sat at the desk, doing her accounts; it even held as they undressed in their depressing room, and had no need to hold longer than that. Once in bed, they had always been safe.

"DON'T TELL ME! Don't tell me!"

They woke at the same instant and stared at the darkness, shocked, wondering where they were.

"Don't tell me! I'll spend my money how I bloody well please."

The man's voice, high and hysterical, came through the wall, just behind their heads.

A woman was heard laughing softly, with obviously affected amusement.

Something was thrown, and broke.

"I've had enough of your nagging."

"I've had enough of *you*," the woman answered coolly.

Melanie buried her head against Leonard's shoulder and he put an arm round her.

"I had enough of *you*, a very long time ago," the woman's voice went on. "I can't honestly remember a time when I *hadn't* had enough of you."

"What I've gone through!"

"What *you've* gone through?"

"Yes, that's what I said. What I've gone through."

"Don't shout. It's so common." She had consciously lowered her own voice, then said, forgetting, in almost a shout, "It's a pity for both our sakes you were so greedy. For Daddy's money, I mean. That's all you ever cared about—my father's money."

"All *you* cared about was getting into bed with me."

"You great braggart. I've always loathed going to bed with you. Who wouldn't?"

Leonard heaved himself up, and knocked on the damp wall.

"I always felt sick," the woman's voice went on, taking no notice. She was as strident now as the man, had begun to lose her grip on the situation, as he had done. "And God knows," she said, "how many other women you've made feel sick."

Leonard knocked louder, with his fist this time. The wall seemed as soft as if it were made from cardboard.

"I'm scared," said Melanie. She sat up and switched on the light. "Surely he'll kill her, if she goes on like that."

"You little strumpet!" The man slurred this word, tried to repeat it and dried up, helplessly, goaded into incoherence.

"Be careful! Just be careful!" A dangerous, deliberate voice hers was now.

"Archie Durrant? Do you think I don't know about Archie Durrant? Don't take me for a fool."

"I'll warn you; don't put ideas into my head, my precious husband. At least Archie Durrant wouldn't bring me to a lousy place like this."

She then began to cry. They reversed their roles and he in his turn became the cool one.

"He won't take you anywhere, my pet. Like me, he's had enough. *Un*like me, *he* can skedaddle."

"Why doesn't someone *do* something!" asked Melanie, meaning, of course, that Leonard should. "Everyone must be able to hear. And they're English, too. It's so shaming, and horrible."

"Go on, then, skedaddle, skedaddle!" The absurd word went on and on, blurred, broken by sobs. Something more was thrown—something with a sharp, hard sound; perhaps a shoe or book.

Leonard sprang out of bed and put on his dressing-gown and slippers.

Slippers! thought Melanie, sitting up in bed, shivering.

As Leonard stepped out into the passage, he saw Madame Bertail coming along it, from the other direction. She, too, wore a dressing-gown, corded round her stout stomach; her grey hair was thinly braided. She looked steadily at Leonard, as if dismissing him, classing him with his loose compatriots, then knocked quickly on the door and at once tried the door-handle. The key had been turned in the lock. She knocked again, and there was silence inside the room. She knocked once more, very loudly, as if to make sure of this silence, and then, without a word to Leonard, seeming to feel satisfied that she had dealt successfully with the situation, she went off down the corridor.

Leonard went back to the bedroom and slowly took off his dressing-gown and slippers.

"I think that will be that," he said, and got back into bed and tried to warm poor Melanie.

"You talk about your father's money," the man's voice went on, almost at once. "But I wouldn't want any truck with that kind of money."

"You just want it."

Their tone was more controlled, as if they were temporarily calmed. However, although the wind had dropped they still quietly angled for it, keeping things going for the time-being.

"I'll never forget the first time I realised how you got on my nerves," he said, in the equable voice of an old friend reminiscing about happier days. "That way you walk upstairs with your bottom waggling from side to side. My God, I've got to walk upstairs and downstairs behind that bottom for the rest of my life, I used to think."

Such triviality! Melanie thought fearfully, pressing her hands against her face. To begin with such a thing—for the hate to grow from it—not nearly as bad as being slow and keeping people waiting.

"I wasn't seriously loathing you then," the man said in a conversational tone. "Even after that fuss about Archie Durrant. I didn't seriously *hate* you."

"Thank you very much, you . . . . cuckold."

If Leonard did not snore at that moment, he certainly breathed sonorously.

During that comparative lull in the next room, he had dropped off to sleep leaving Melanie wakeful and afraid.

"She called him a cuckold," she hissed into Leonard's ear.

"No, the time, I think," said the man behind the wall, in the same deadly flat voice, "the time I first really hated you, was when you threw the potatoes at me."

"Oh, yes, that was a *great* evening," she said, in tones chiming with affected pleasure.

"In front of my own mother."

"She seemed to enjoy it as much as I did. Probably longed for years to do it herself."

"That was when I first realised."

"Why did you stay?" There was silence. Then, "Why stay now? Go on! Go now! I'll help you to pack. There's your bloody hairbrush for a start. My God, you look ridiculous when you duck down like that. You sickening little coward."

"I'll kill you."

"Oh God, he'll kill her," said Melanie, shaking Leonard roughly.

"You won't, you know," shouted the other woman.

The telephone rang in the next room.

"Hallo?" The man's voice was cautious, ruffled. The receiver was quietly replaced. "You see what you've done?" he said. "Someone ringing up to complain about the noise we're making."

"You don't think I give a damn for anyone in a crummy little hotel like this, do you?"

"Oh, my nerves, my nerves, my nerves," the man suddenly groaned. Bedsprings creaked, and Melanie imagined him sinking down on the edge of the bed, his face buried in his hands.

Silence lasted only a minute or two. Leonard was fast asleep now. Melanie lay very still, listening to a mosquito coming and going above her head.

Then the crying began, at first a little sniffing, then a quiet sobbing.

"Leonard, you must wake up. I can't lie here alone listening to it. Or *do* something, for heaven's sake."

He put out a hand, as if to stave her off, or calm her, without really disturbing his sleep, and this gesture infuriated her. She slapped his hand away roughly.

"There's nothing I can do," he said, still clinging to the idea of sleep; then, as she flounced over in the bed, turning her back to him, he resignedly sat up and turned on the light. Blinking and tousled, he stared before him, and then leaned over and knocked on the wall once more.

"*That* won't do any good," said Melanie.

"Well, their door's locked, so what else can I do?"

"Ring up the police."

"I can't do that. Anyhow, I don't know how to in French."

"Well, try. If the hotel was on fire, you'd do something, wouldn't you?"

Her tone was new to him, and alarming.

"It's not really our business."

"If he kills? While you were asleep, she called him a cuckold. I thought he was going to kill her then. And even if he doesn't, we can't hope to get any sleep. It's perfectly horrible. It sounds like a child crying."

"Yes, with temper. Your feet are frozen."

"Of course, they're frozen." Her voice blamed him for this.

"My dear, don't let *us* quarrel."

"I'm so tired. Oh, that—damned mosquito." She sat up, and tried to smack it against the wall, but it had gone. "It's been such an awful day."

"I thought it was a perfectly beautiful day."

She pressed her lips together and closed her eyes, drawing herself away from him, as if determined now, somehow or other, to go to sleep.

"Didn't you like your day?" he asked.

"Well, you must have known I was disappointed about the Cathedral. Getting there when it was too dark."

"I didn't know. You didn't give me an inkling. We can go first thing in the morning."

"It wouldn't be the same. Oh, you're so hopeless. You hang about, and hang about, and drive me mad with impatience."

She lay on her side, well away from him on the very edge of the bed, facing the horribly patterned curtains, her mouth so stiff, her eyes full of tears. He made an attempt to draw her close, but she became rigid, her limbs were iron.

"You see, she's quietening down," he said. The weeping had gone through every stage—from piteous sobbing, gasping, angry moans, to —now—a lulled whimpering, dying off, hardly heard. And the man was silent. Had he dropped senseless across the bed, Melanie wondered, or was he still sitting there, staring at the picture of his own despair.

"I'm so sorry about the Cathedral. I had no idea . . . ." said Leonard, switching off the light, and sliding down in bed. Melanie kept her cold feet to herself.

"We'll say no more about it," she said, in a grim little voice.

THEY SLEPT LATE. When he awoke, Leonard saw that Melanie was almost falling out of bed in her attempt to keep away from him. Disquieting memories made him frown. He tried to lay his thoughts out in order. The voices in the next room, the nightmare of weeping and abuse; but worse, Melanie's cold voice, her revelation of that harboured disappointment; then, worse again, even worse, her impatience with him. He drove her nearly mad, she had said. Always? Since they were married? When?

At last Melanie awoke, and seemed uncertain of how to behave. Unable to make up her mind, she assumed a sort of non-behaviour to be going on with, which he found most mystifying.

"Shall we go to the Cathedral?" he asked.

"Oh, I don't think so," she said carelessly. She even turned her back to him while she dressed.

There was silence from the next room, but neither of them referred to it. It was as if some shame of their own were shut up in there. The rest of the hotel was full of noises—kitchen clatterings and sharp voices. A vacuum cleaner bumped and whined along the passage outside, and countrified traffic went by in the cobbled street.

Melanie's cheeks and forehead were swollen with mosquito bites, which gave her an angry look. She scratched one on her wrist and made it water. They seemed the stigmata of her irritation.

They packed their cases.

"Ready?" he asked.

"When you are," she said sullenly.

"Might as well hit the trail as soon as we've had breakfast," he said, trying to sound optimistic, as if nothing were wrong. He had no idea of how they would get through the day. They had no plans, and she seemed disinclined to discuss any.

They breakfasted in silence in the empty dining-room. Some of the tables had chairs stacked on them.

"You've no idea where you want to go, then?" he asked.

She was spreading apricot jam on a piece of bread and he leaned over and gently touched her hand. She laid down the knife, and put her hand in her lap. Then picked up the bread with her left hand and began to eat.

They went upstairs, to fetch their cases and, going along the passage, could see that the door of the room next to theirs now stood wide open. Before they reached it, a woman came out and hesitated in the doorway, looking back into the room. There was an appearance of shine and freshness about her—her glowing face, shining hair, starched dress. Full of gay anticipation as it was, her voice, as she called back into the room, was familiar to Melanie and Leonard.

"Ready, darling?"

The other familiar voice replied. The man came to the doorway, carrying the case. He put his arm round the woman's waist and they went off down the passage. Such a well turned-out couple, Melanie thought, staring after them, as she paused at her own doorway, scratching her mosquito bites.

"Let's go to that marvellous place for lunch," she heard the man suggesting. They turned a corner to the landing, but as they went on downstairs, their laughter floated up after them.

THE MAGIC BARREL

BERNARD MALAMUD

Bernard Malamud

Not long ago there lived in uptown New York, in a small, almost meager room, though crowded with books, Leo Finkle, a rabbinical student in the Yeshivah University. Finkle, after six years of study, was to be ordained in June and had been advised by an acquaintance that he might find it easier to win himself a congregation if he were married. Since he had no present prospects of marriage, after two tormented days of turning it over in his mind, he called in Pinye Salzman, a marriage broker whose two-line advertisement he had read in the *Forward*.

The matchmaker appeared one night out of the dark fourth-floor hallway of the gray stone rooming house where Finkle lived, grasping a black, strapped portfolio that had been worn thin with use. Salzman, who had been long in the business, was of slight but dignified build, wearing an old hat, and an overcoat too short and tight for him. He smelled frankly of fish, which he loved to eat, and although he was missing a few teeth, his presence was not displeasing, because of an amiable manner curiously contrasted with mournful eyes. His voice, his lips, his wisp of beard, his bony fingers were animated, but give him a moment of repose and his mild blue eyes revealed a depth of sadness, a characteristic that put Leo a little at ease although the situation, for him, was inherently tense.

He at once informed Salzman why he had asked him to come, explaining that his home was in Cleveland, and that but for his parents, who had married comparatively late in life, he was alone in the world. He had for six years devoted himself almost entirely to his studies, as a result of which, understandably, he had found himself without time for a social life and the company of young women. Therefore he thought it the better part of trial and error—of embarrassing fumbling—to call in an experienced person to advise him on these matters. He remarked in passing that the function of the marriage broker was ancient and honorable, highly approved in the Jewish community, because it made practical the necessary without hindering joy. Moreover, his own parents had been brought together by a matchmaker. They had made, if not a financially profitable marriage—since neither had possessed any worldly goods to speak of—at least a successful one in the sense of their everlasting devotion to each other. Salzman listened in embarrassed surprise, sensing a sort of apology. Later, however, he experienced a glow of pride in his work, an emotion that had left him years ago, and he heartily approved of Finkle.

The two went to their business. Leo had led Salzman to the only clear place in the room, a table near a window that overlooked the lamplit city. He seated himself at the matchmaker's side but facing him, attempting by an act of will to suppress the unpleasant tickle in his throat. Salzman eagerly unstrapped his portfolio and removed a loose rubber band from a thin packet of much-handled cards. As he flipped through them, a gesture and sound that physically hurt Leo, the student pretended not to see and gazed steadfastly out the window. Although it was still February, winter was on its last legs, signs of which he had for the first time in years begun to notice. He now observed the round white moon, moving high in the sky through a cloud menagerie, and watched with half-open mouth as it penetrated a huge hen, and dropped out of her like an egg laying itself. Salzman, though pretending, through eyeglasses he had just slipped on, to be engaged in scanning the writing on the cards, stole occasional glances at the young man's distinguished face, noting with pleasure the long, severe scholar's nose, brown eyes heavy with learning, sensitive yet ascetic lips, and a certain almost hollow quality of the dark cheeks. He gazed around at shelves upon shelves of books and let out a soft, contented sigh.

When Leo's eyes fell upon the cards, he counted six spread out in Salzman's hand.

"So few?" he asked in disappointment.

"You wouldn't believe me how much cards I got in my office," Salzman replied. "The drawers are already filled to the top, so I keep them now in a barrel, but is every girl good for a new rabbi?"

Leo blushed at this, regretting all he had revealed of himself in a curriculum vitae he had sent to Salzman. He had thought it best to acquaint him with his strict standards and specifications, but in having done so, felt he had told the marriage broker more than was absolutely necessary.

He hesitantly inquired, "Do you keep photographs of your clients on file?"

"First comes family, amount of dowry, also what kind promises," Salzman replied, unbuttoning his tight coat and settling himself in the chair. "After comes pictures, rabbi."

"Call me Mr. Finkle. I'm not yet a rabbi."

Salzman said he would, but instead called him doctor, which he changed to rabbi when Leo was not listening too attentively.

Salzman adjusted his horn-rimmed spectacles, gently cleared his throat and read in an eager voice the contents of the top card:

"Sophie P. Twenty-four years. Widow one year. No children. Educated high school and two years college. Father promises eight thousand dollars. Has wonderful wholesale business. Also real estate. On the mother's side comes teachers, also one actor. Well known on Second Avenue."

Leo gazed up in surprise. "Did you say a widow?"

"A widow don't mean spoiled, rabbi. She lived with her husband maybe four months. He was a sick boy, she made a mistake to marry him."

"Marrying a widow has never entered my mind."

"This is because you have no experience. A widow, especially if she is young and healthy like this girl, is a wonderful person to marry. She will be thankful to you the rest of her life. Believe me, if I was looking now for a bride, I would marry a widow."

Leo reflected, then shook his head.

Salzman hunched his shoulders in an almost imperceptible gesture of disappointment. He placed the card down on the wooden table and began to read another:

"Lily H. High school teacher. Regular. Not a substitute. Has savings and new Dodge car. Lived in Paris one year. Father is successful dentist thirty-five years. Interested in professional man. Well-Americanized family. Wonderful opportunity."

"I knew her personally," said Salzman. "I wish you could see this girl. She is a doll. Also very intelligent. All day you could talk to her about books and theyater and whatnot. She also knows current events."

"I don't believe you mentioned her age?"

"Her age?" Salzman said, raising his brows. "Her age is thirty-two years."

Leo said after a while, "I'm afraid that seems a little too old."

Salzman let out a laugh. "So how old are you, rabbi?"

"Twenty-seven."

"So what is the difference, tell me, between twenty-seven and thirty-two? My own wife is seven years older than me. So what did I suffer? Nothing. If Rothschild's daughter wants to marry you, would you say on account her age, no?"

"Yes," Leo said dryly.

Salzman shook off the no in the yes. "Five years don't mean a thing. I give you my word that when you will live with her for one week you will forget her age. What does it mean five years—that she lived more and knows more than somebody who is younger? On this girl, God bless her, years are not wasted. Each one that it comes makes better the bargain."

"What subject does she teach in high school?"

"Languages. If you heard the way she speaks French, you will think it is music. I am in the business twenty-five years, and I recommend her with my whole heart. Believe me, I know what I'm talking, rabbi."

"What's on the next card?" Leo said abruptly.

Salzman reluctantly turned up the third card:

"Ruth K. Nineteen years. Honor student. Father offers thirteen thousand cash to the right bridegroom. He is a medical doctor. Stomach specialist with marvelous practice. Brother-in-law owns own garment business. Particular people."

Salzman looked as if he had read his trump card.

"Did you say nineteen?" Leo asked with interest.

"On the dot."

"Is she attractive?" He blushed. "Pretty?"

Salzman kissed his fingertips. "A little doll. On this I give you my word. Let me call the father tonight and you will see what means pretty."

But Leo was troubled. "You're sure she's that young?"

"This I am positive. The father will show you the birth certificate."

"Are you positive there isn't something wrong with her?" Leo insisted.

"Who says there is wrong?"

"I don't understand why an American girl her age should go to a marriage broker."

A smile spread over Salzman's face.

"So for the same reason you went, she comes."

Leo flushed. "I am pressed for time."

Salzman, realizing he had been tactless, quickly explained. "The father came, not her. He wants she should have the best, so he looks around himself. When we will locate the right boy he will introduce him and encourage. This makes a better marriage than if a young girl without experience takes for herself. I don't have to tell you this."

"But don't you think this young girl believes in love?" Leo spoke uneasily.

Salzman was about to guffaw but caught himself and said soberly, "Love comes with the right person, not before."

Leo parted dry lips but did not speak. Noticing that Salzman had snatched a glance at the next card, he cleverly asked, "How is her health?"

"Perfect," Salzman said, breathing with difficulty. "Of course, she is a little lame on her right foot from an auto accident that it happened to her when she was twelve years, but nobody notices on account she is so brilliant and also beautiful."

Leo got up heavily and went to the window. He felt curiously bitter and upbraided himself for having called in the marriage broker. Finally, he shook his head.

"Why not?" Salzman persisted, the pitch of his voice rising.

"Because I detest stomach specialists."

"So what do you care what is his business? After you marry her do you need him? Who says he must come every Friday night in your house?"

Ashamed of the way the talk was going, Leo dismissed Salzman, who went home with heavy, melancholy eyes.

Though he had felt only relief at the marriage broker's departure, Leo was in low spirits the next day. He explained it as arising from Salzman's failure to produce a suitable bride for him. He did not care for his type of clientele. But when Leo found himself hesitating whether to seek out another matchmaker, one more polished than Pinye, he wondered if it could be—his protestations to the contrary, and although he honored his father and mother—that he did not, in essence, care for the matchmaking institution? This thought he quickly put out of mind yet found himself still upset. All day he ran around in the woods—missed an important appointment, forgot to give out his laundry, walked out of a Broadway cafeteria without paying and had to run back with the ticket in his hand; had even not recognized his landlady in the street when she passed with a friend and courteously called out, "A good evening to you, Doctor Finkle." By nightfall, however, he had regained sufficient calm to sink his nose into a book and there found peace from his thoughts.

Almost at once there came a knock on the door. Before Leo could say enter, Salzman, commercial cupid, was standing in the room. His face was gray and meager, his expression hungry, and he looked as if he would expire on his feet. Yet the marriage broker managed, by some trick of the muscles, to display a broad smile.

"So good evening. I am invited?"

Leo nodded, disturbed to see him again, yet unwilling to ask the man to leave.

Beaming still, Salzman laid his portfolio on the table. "Rabbi, I got for you tonight good news."

"I've asked you not to call me rabbi. I'm still a student."

"Your worries are finished. I have for you a first-class bride."

"Leave me in peace concerning this subject." Leo pretended lack of interest.

"The world will dance at your wedding."

"Please, Mr. Salzman, no more."

"But first must come back my strength," Salzman said weakly. He fumbled with the portfolio straps and took out of the leather case an oily paper bag, from which he extracted a hard seeded roll and a small smoked whitefish. With a quick motion of his hand he stripped the fish out of its skin and began ravenously to chew. "All day in a rush," he muttered.

Leo watched him eat.

"A sliced tomato you have maybe?" Salzman hesitantly inquired.

"No."

The marriage broker shut his eyes and ate. When he had finished he carefully cleaned up the crumbs and rolled up the remains of the fish in the paper bag. His spectacled eyes roamed the room until he discovered, amid some piles of books, a one-burner gas stove. Lifting his hat he humbly asked, "A glass tea you got, rabbi?"

Conscience-stricken, Leo rose and brewed the tea. He served it with a chunk of lemon and two cubes of lump sugar, delighting Salzman.

After he had drunk his tea, Salzman's strength and good spirits were restored.

"So tell me, rabbi," he said amiably, "you considered some more the three clients I mentioned yesterday?"

"There was no need to consider."

"Why not?"

"None of them suits me."

"What then suits you?"

Leo let it pass because he could give only a confused answer.

Without waiting for a reply, Salzman asked, "You remember this girl I talked to you—the high school teacher?"

"Age thirty-two?"

But, surprisingly, Salzman's face lit in a smile. "Age twenty-nine."

Leo shot him a look. "Reduced from thirty-two?"

"A mistake," Salzman avowed. "I talked today with the dentist. He took me to his safety-deposit box and showed me the birth certificate. She was twenty-nine years last August. They made her a party in the mountains where she went for her vacation. When her father spoke to me the first time I forgot to write the age and I told you thirty-two, but now I remember this was a different client, a widow."

"The same one you told me about? I thought she was twenty-four?"

"A different. Am I responsible that the world is filled with widows?"

"No, but I'm not interested in them, nor for that matter, in schoolteachers."

Salzman pulled his clasped hands to his breast. Looking at the ceiling he devoutly exclaimed, "*Yiddishe kinder*, what can I say to somebody that he is not interested in high school teachers? So what then you are interested?"

Leo flushed but controlled himself.

"In what else will you be interested," Salzman went on, "if you not interested in this fine girl that she speaks four languages and has personally in the bank ten thousand dollars? Also her father guarantees further twelve thousand. Also she has a new car, wonderful clothes, talks on all subjects, and she will give you a first-class home and children. How near do we come in our life to paradise?"

"If she's so wonderful, why wasn't she married ten years ago?"

"Why?" said Salzman with a heavy laugh. "Why? Because she is *partikiler*. This is why. She wants the *best*."

Leo was silent, amused at how he had entangled himself. But Salzman had aroused his interest in Lily H., and he began seriously to consider calling on her. When the marriage broker observed how intently Leo's mind was at work on the facts he had supplied, he felt certain they would soon come to an agreement.

LATE SATURDAY afternoon, conscious of Salzman, Leo Finkle walked with Lily Hirschorn along Riverside Drive. He walked briskly and erectly, wearing with distinction the black fedora he had that morning taken with trepidation out of the dusty hatbox on his closet shelf, and the heavy black Saturday coat he had thoroughly whisked clean. Leo also owned a walking stick, a present from a distant relative, but quickly put temptation aside and did not use it. Lily, petite and not unpretty, had on something signifying the approach of spring. She was *au courant*, animatedly, with all sorts of subjects, and he weighed her words and found her surprisingly sound—score another for Salzman, whom he uneasily sensed to be somewhere around, hiding perhaps high in a tree along the street, flashing the lady signals with a pocket mirror; or perhaps a cloven-hoofed Pan, piping nuptial ditties as he danced his invisible way before them, strewing wild buds on the walk and purple grapes in their path, symbolizing fruit of a union, though there was of course still none.

Lily startled Leo by remarking, "I was thinking of Mr. Salzman, a curious figure, wouldn't you say?"

Not certain what to answer, he nodded.

She bravely went on, blushing, "I for one am grateful for his introducing us. Aren't you?"

He courteously replied, "I am."

"I mean," she said with a little laugh—and it was all in good taste, or at least gave the effect of being not in bad—"do you mind that we came together so?"

He was not displeased with her honesty, recognizing that she meant to set the relationship aright, and understanding that it took a certain amount of experience in life, and courage, to want to do it quite that way. One had to have some sort of past to make that kind of beginning.

He said that he did not mind. Salzman's function was traditional and honorable—valuable for what it might achieve, which, he pointed out, was frequently nothing.

Lily agreed with a sigh. They walked on for a while and she said after a long silence, again with a nervous laugh, "Would you mind if I asked you something a little bit personal? Frankly, I find the subject fascinating." Although Leo shrugged, she went on half embarrassedly, "How was it that you came to your calling? I mean, was it a sudden passionate inspiration?"

Leo, after a time, slowly replied, "I was always interested in the Law."

"You saw revealed in it the presence of the Highest?"

He nodded and changed the subject. "I understand that you spent a little time in Paris, Miss Hirschorn?"

"Oh, did Mr. Salzman tell you, Rabbi Finkle?" Leo winced, but she went on, "It was ages ago and almost forgotten. I remember I had to return for my sister's wedding."

And Lily would not be put off. "When," she asked in a trembly voice, "did you become enamored of God?"

He stared at her. Then it came to him that she was talking not about Leo Finkle, but of a total stranger, some mystical figure, perhaps even passionate prophet that Salzman had dreamed up for her—no relation to the living or dead. Leo trembled with rage and weakness. The trickster had obviously sold her a bill of goods, just as he had him, who'd expected to become acquainted with a young lady of twenty-nine, only to behold, the moment he laid eyes upon her strained and anxious face, a woman past thirty-five and aging rapidly. Only his self-control had kept him this long in her presence.

"I am not," he said gravely, "a talented religious person," and in seeking words to go on, found himself possessed by shame and fear. "I think," he said in a strained manner, "that I came to God not because I loved Him, but because I did not."

This confession he spoke harshly because its unexpectedness shook him.

Lily wilted. Leo saw a profusion of loaves of bread go flying like ducks high over his head, not unlike the winged loaves by which he had counted himself to sleep last night. Mercifully, then, it snowed, which he would not put past Salzman's machinations.

HE WAS INFURIATED with the marriage broker and swore he would throw him out of the room the minute he reappeared. But Salzman did not come that night, and when Leo's anger had subsided, an unaccountable despair grew in its place. At first he thought this was caused by his disappointment in Lily, but before long it became evident that he had involved himself with Salzman without a true knowledge of his own intent. He gradually realized—with an emptiness that seized him with six hands—that he had called in the broker to find him a bride because he was incapable of doing it himself. This terrifying insight he had derived as a result of his meeting and conversation with Lily Hirschorn. Her probing questions had somehow irritated him into revealing—to himself more than her—the true nature of his relationship to God, and from that it had come upon him, with shocking force, that apart from his parents, he had never loved anyone. Or perhaps it went the other way, that he did not love God so well as he might, because he had not loved man. It seemed to Leo that his whole life stood starkly revealed and he saw himself for the first time as he truly was—unloved and loveless. This bitter but somehow not fully unexpected revelation brought him to a point of panic, controlled only by extraordinary effort. He covered his face with his hands and cried.

The week that followed was the worst of his life. He did not eat and lost weight. His beard darkened and grew ragged. He stopped attending seminars and almost never opened a book. He seriously considered leaving the Yeshivah, although he was deeply troubled at the thought of the loss of all his years of study—saw them like pages torn from a book, strewn over the city—and at the devastating effect of this decision upon his parents. But he had lived without knowledge of himself, and never in the Five Books and all the Commentaries—*mea culpa*—had the truth been revealed to him. He did not know where to turn, and in all this desolating loneliness there was no *to whom*, although he often thought of Lily but not once could bring himself to go downstairs and make the call. He became touchy and irritable, especially with his landlady, who asked him all manner of personal questions; on the other hand, sensing his own disagreeableness, he waylaid her on the stairs and apologized abjectly, until mortified, she ran from him. Out of this, however, he drew the consolation that he was a Jew and that a Jew suffered. But gradually, as the long and terrible week drew to a close, he regained his composure and some idea of purpose in life: to go on as planned. Although he was imperfect, the ideal was not. As for his quest of a bride, the thought of continuing afflicted him with anxiety and heartburn, yet perhaps with this new knowledge of himself he would be more successful than in the past. Perhaps love would now come to him, and a bride to that love. And for this sanctified seeking who needed a Salzman?

The marriage broker, a skeleton with haunted eyes, returned that very night. He looked, withal, the picture of frustrated expectancy—as if he had steadfastly waited the week at Miss Lily Hirschorn's side for a telephone call that never came.

Casually coughing, Salzman came immediately to the point: "So how did you like her?"

Leo's anger rose and he could not refrain from chiding the matchmaker: "Why did you lie to me, Salzman?"

Salzman's pale face went dead white, the world had snowed on him.

"Did you not state that she was twenty-nine?" Leo insisted.

"I give you my word—"

"She was thirty-five, if a day. *At least* thirty-five."

"Of this don't be too sure. Her father told me—"

"Never mind. The worst of it was that you lied to her."

"How did I lie to her, tell me?"

"You told her things about me that weren't true. You made me out to be more, consequently less than I am. She had in mind a totally different person, a sort of semimystical Wonder Rabbi."

"All I said, you was a religious man."

"I can imagine."

Salzman sighed. "This is my weakness that I have," he confessed. "My wife says to me I shouldn't be a salesman, but when I have two fine people that they would be wonderful to be married, I am so happy that I talk too much." He smiled wanly. "This is why Salzman is a poor man."

Leo's anger left him. "Well, Salzman, I'm afraid that's all."

The marriage broker fastened hungry eyes on him.

"You don't want anymore a bride?"

"I do," said Leo, "but I have decided to seek her in a different way. I am no longer interested in an arranged marriage. To be frank, I now admit the necessity of premarital love. That is, I want to be in love with the one I marry."

"Love?" said Salzman, astounded. After a moment he remarked, "For us, our love is our life, not for the ladies. In the ghetto they—"

"I know, I know," said Leo. "I've thought of it often. Love, I have said to myself, should be a by-product of living and worship rather than its own end. Yet for myself I find it necessary to establish the level of my need and fulfill it."

Salzman shrugged but answered, "Listen, rabbi, if you want love, this I can find for you also. I have such beautiful clients that you will love them the minute your eyes will see them."

Leo smiled unhappily. "I'm afraid you don't understand."

But Salzman hastily unstrapped his portfolio and withdrew a manila packet from it.

"Pictures," he said, quickly laying the envelope on the table.

Leo called after him to take the pictures away, but as if on the wings of the wind, Salzman had disappeared.

March came. Leo had returned to his regular routine. Although he felt not quite himself yet—lacked energy—he was making plans for a more active social life. Of course it would cost something, but he was an expert in cutting corners; and when there were no corners left he would make circles rounder. All the while Salzman's pictures had lain on the table, gathering dust. Occasionally as Leo sat studying, or enjoying a cup of tea, his eyes fell on the manila envelope, but he never opened it.

The days went by and no social life to speak of developed with a member of the opposite sex—it was difficult, given the circumstances of his situation. One morning Leo toiled up the stairs to his room and stared out the window at the city. Although the day was bright his view of it was dark. For some time he watched the people in the street below hurrying along and then turned with a heavy heart to his little room. On the table was the packet. With a sudden relentless gesture he tore it open. For a half hour he stood by the table in a state of excitement, examining the photographs of the ladies Salzman had included. Finally, with a deep sigh he put them down. There were six, of varying degrees of attractiveness, but look at them long enough and they all became Lily Hirschorn: all past their prime, all starved behind bright smiles, not a true personality in the lot. Life, despite their frantic yoo-hooings, had passed them by; they were pictures in a briefcase that stank of fish. After a while, however, as Leo attempted to return the photographs into the envelope, he found in it another, a snapshot of the type taken by a machine for a quarter. He gazed at it a moment and let out a cry.

Her face deeply moved him. Why, he could at first not say. It gave him the impression of youth—spring flowers, yet age—a sense of having been used to the bone, wasted; this came from the eyes, which were hauntingly familiar, yet absolutely strange. He had a vivid impression that he had met her before, but try as he might he could not place her although he could almost recall her name, as if he had read it in her own handwriting. No, this couldn't be; he would have remembered her. It was not, he affirmed, that she had an extraordinary beauty—no, though her face was attractive enough; it was that *something* about her moved him. Feature for feature, even some of the ladies of the photographs could do better; but she leaped forth to his heart—had *lived*, or wanted to—more than just wanted, perhaps regretted how she had lived—had somehow deeply suffered: it could be seen in the depths of those reluctant eyes, and from the way the light enclosed and shone from her, and within her, opening realms of possibility: this was her own. Her he desired. His head ached and eyes narrowed with the intensity of his gazing, then as if an obscure fog had blown up in the mind, he experienced fear of her and was aware that he had received an impression, somehow, of evil. He shuddered, saying softly, it is thus with us all. Leo brewed some tea in a small pot and sat sipping it without sugar, to calm himself. But before he had finished drinking, again with excitement he examined the face and found it good: good for Leo Finkle. Only such a one could understand him and help him seek whatever he was seeking. She might, perhaps, love him. How she had happened to be among the discards in Salzman's barrel he could never guess, but he knew he must urgently go find her.

Leo rushed downstairs, grabbed up the Bronx telephone book, and searched for Salzman's home address. He was not listed, nor was his office. Neither was he in the Manhattan book. But Leo remembered having written down the address on a slip of paper after he had read Salzman's advertisement in the "personals" column of the *Forward*. He ran up to his room and tore through his papers, without luck. It was exasperating. Just when he needed the matchmaker he was nowhere to be found. Fortunately Leo remembered to look in his wallet. There on a card he found his name written and a Bronx address. No phone number was listed, the reason—Leo now recalled—he had originally communicated with Salzman by letter. He got on his coat, put a hat on over his skullcap and hurried to the subway station. All the way to the far end of the Bronx he sat on the edge of his seat. He was more than once tempted to take out the picture and see if the girl's face was as he remembered it, but he refrained, allowing the snapshot to remain in his inside coat pocket, content to have her so close. When the train pulled into the station he was waiting at the door and bolted out. He quickly located the street Salzman had advertised.

The building he sought was less than a block from the subway, but it was not an office building, nor even a loft, nor a store in which one could rent office space. It was a very old tenement house. Leo found Salzman's name in pencil on a soiled tag under the bell and climbed three dark flights to his apartment. When he knocked, the door was opened by a thin, asthmatic, gray-haired woman in felt slippers.

"Yes?" she said, expecting nothing. She listened without listening. He could have sworn he had seen her, too, before but knew it was an illusion.

"Salzman—does he live here? Pinye Salzman," he said, "the matchmaker?"

She stared at him a long minute. "Of course."

He felt embarrassed. "Is he in?"

"No." Her mouth, though left open, offered nothing more.

"The matter is urgent. Can you tell me where his office is?"

"In the air." She pointed upward.

"You mean he has no office?" Leo asked.

"In his socks."

He peered into the apartment. It was sunless and dingy, one large room divided by a half-open curtain, beyond which he could see a sagging metal bed. The near side of the room was crowded with rickety chairs, old bureaus, a three-legged table, racks of cooking utensils, and all the apparatus of a kitchen. But there was no sign of Salzman or his magic barrel, probably also a figment of the imagination. An odor of frying fish made Leo weak to the knees.

"Where is he?" he insisted. "I've got to see your husband."

At length she answered, "So who knows where he is? Every time he thinks a new thought he runs to a different place. Go home, he will find you."

"Tell him Leo Finkle."

She gave no sign she had heard.

He walked downstairs, depressed.

But Salzman, breathless, stood waiting at his door.

Leo was astounded and overjoyed. "How did you get here before me?"

"I rushed."

"Come inside."

They entered. Leo fixed tea, and a sardine sandwich for Salzman. As they were drinking he reached behind him for the packet of pictures and handed them to the marriage broker.

Salzman put down his glass and said expectantly, "You found somebody you like?"

"Not among these."

The marriage broker turned away.

"Here is the one I want." Leo held forth the snapshot.

Salzman slipped on his glasses and took the picture into his trembling hand. He turned ghastly and let out a groan.

"What's the matter?" cried Leo.

"Excuse me. Was an accident this picture. She isn't for you."

Salzman frantically shoved the manila packet into his portfolio. He thrust the snapshot into his pocket and fled down the stairs.

Leo, after momentary paralysis, gave chase and cornered the marriage broker in the vestibule. The landlady made hysterical outcries but neither of them listened.

"Give me back the picture, Salzman."

"No." The pain in his eyes was terrible.

"Tell me who she is then."

"This I can't tell you. Excuse me."

He made to depart, but Leo, forgetting himself, seized the matchmaker by his tight coat and shook him frenziedly.

"Please," sighed Salzman. *"Please."*

Leo ashamedly let him go. "Tell me who she is," he begged. "It's very important for me to know."

"She is not for you. She is a wild one—wild, without shame. This is not a bride for a rabbi."

"What do you mean wild?"

"Like an animal. Like a dog. For her to be poor was a sin. This is why to me she is dead now."

"In God's name, what do you mean?"

"Her I can't introduce to you," Salzman cried.

"Why are you so excited?"

"Why, he asks," Salzman said, bursting into tears. "This is my baby, my Stella, she should burn in hell."

LEO HURRIED UP to bed and hid under the covers. Under the covers he thought his life through. Although he soon fell asleep he could not sleep her out of his mind. He woke, beating his breast. Though he prayed to be rid of her, his prayers went unanswered. Through days of torment he endlessly struggled not to love her; fearing success, he escaped it. He then concluded to convert her to goodness, himself to God. The idea alternately nauseated and exalted him.

He perhaps did not know that he had come to a final decision until he encountered Salzman in a Broadway cafeteria. He was sitting alone at a rear table, sucking the bony remains of a fish. The marriage broker appeared haggard, and transparent to the point of vanishing.

Salzman looked up at first without recognizing him. Leo had grown a pointed beard and his eyes were weighted with wisdom.

"Salzman," he said, "love has at last come to my heart."

"Who can love from a picture?" mocked the marriage broker.

"It is not impossible."

"If you can love her, then you can love anybody. Let me show you some new clients that they just sent me their photographs. One is a little doll."

"Just her I want," Leo murmured.

"Don't be a fool, doctor. Don't bother with her."

"Put me in touch with her, Salzman," Leo said humbly. "Perhaps I can be of service."

Salzman had stopped eating and Leo understood with emotion that it was now arranged.

Leaving the cafeteria, he was, however, afflicted by a tormenting suspicion that Salzman had planned it all to happen this way.

LEO WAS INFORMED by letter that she would meet him on a certain corner, and she was there one spring night, waiting under a streetlamp. He appeared, carrying a small bouquet of violets and rosebuds. Stella stood by the lamppost, smoking. She wore white with red shoes, which fitted his expectations, although in a troubled moment he had imagined the dress red, and only the shoes white. She waited uneasily and shyly. From afar he saw that her eyes—clearly her father's—were filled with desperate innocence. He pictured, in her, his own redemption. Violins and lit candles revolved in the sky. Leo ran forward with flowers outthrust.

Around the corner, Salzman, leaning against a wall, chanted prayers for the dead.

LAMB TO THE SLAUGHTER

ROALD DAHL

THE ROOM WAS warm and clean, the curtains drawn, the two table lamps alight—hers and the one by the empty chair opposite. On the sideboard behind her, two tall glasses, soda water, whisky. Fresh ice cubes in the Thermos bucket.

Mary Maloney was waiting for her husband to come home from work.

Now and again she would glance up at the clock, but without anxiety, merely to please herself with the thought that each minute gone by made it nearer the time when he would come. There was a slow smiling air about her, and about everything she did. The drop of the head as she bent over her sewing was curiously tranquil. Her skin—for this was her sixth month with child—had acquired a wonderful translucent quality, the mouth was soft, and the eyes, with their new placid look, seemed larger, darker than before.

When the clock said ten minutes to five, she began to listen, and a few moments later, punctually as always, she heard the tyres on the gravel outside, and the car door slamming, the footsteps passing the window, the key turning in the lock. She laid aside her sewing, stood up, and went forward to kiss him as he came in.

"Hullo, darling," she said.

"Hullo," he answered.

She took his coat and hung it in the closet. Then she walked over and made the drinks, a strongish one for him, a weak one for herself; and soon she was back again in her chair with the sewing, and he in the other, opposite, holding the tall glass with both his hands, rocking it so the ice cubes tinkled against the side.

For her, this was always a blissful time of day. She knew he didn't want to speak much until the first drink was finished, and she, on her side, was content to sit quietly, enjoying his company after the long hours alone in the house. She loved to luxuriate in the presence of this man, and to feel—almost as a sunbather feels the sun—that warm male glow that came out of him to her when they were alone together. She loved him for the way he sat loosely in a chair, for the way he came in a door, or moved slowly across the room with long strides. She loved the intent, far look in his eyes when they rested on her, the funny shape of the mouth, and especially the way he remained silent about his tiredness, sitting still with himself until the whisky had taken some of it away.

"Tired, darling?"

"Yes," he said. "I'm tired." And as he spoke, he did an unusual thing. He lifted his glass and drained it in one swallow although there was still half of it, at least half of it left. She wasn't really watching him, but she knew what he had done because she heard the ice cubes falling back against the bottom of the empty glass when he lowered his arm. He paused a moment, leaning forward in the chair, then he got up and went slowly over to fetch himself another.

"I'll get it!" she cried, jumping up.

"Sit down," he said.

When he came back, she noticed that the new drink was dark amber with the quantity of whisky in it.

"Darling, shall I get your slippers?"

"No."

She watched him as he began to sip the dark yellow drink, and she could see little oily swirls in the liquid because it was so strong.

"I think it's a shame," she said, "that when a policeman gets to be as senior as you, they keep him walking about on his feet all day long."

He didn't answer, so she bent her head again and went on with her sewing; but each time he lifted the drink to his lips, she heard the ice cubes clinking against the side of the glass.

"Darling," she said. "Would you like me to get you some cheese? I haven't made any supper because it's Thursday."

"No," he said.

"If you're too tired to eat out," she went on, "it's still not too late. There's plenty of meat and stuff in the freezer, and you can have it right here and not even move out of the chair."

Her eyes waited on him for an answer, a smile, a little nod, but he made no sign.

"Anyway," she went on, "I'll get you some cheese and crackers first."

"I don't want it," he said.

She moved uneasily in her chair, the large eyes still watching his face. "But you *must* have supper. I can easily do it here. I'd like to do it. We can have lamb chops. Or pork. Anything you want. Everything's in the freezer."

"Forget it," he said.

"But, darling, you *must* eat! I'll fix it anyway, and then you can have it or not, as you like."

She stood up and placed her sewing on the table by the lamp.

"Sit down," he said. "Just for a minute, sit down."

It wasn't till then that she began to get frightened.

"Go on," he said. "Sit down."

She lowered herself back slowly into the chair, watching him all the time with those large, bewildered eyes. He had finished the second drink and was staring down into the glass, frowning.

"Listen," he said. "I've got something to tell you."

"What is it, darling? What's the matter?"

He had now become absolutely motionless, and he kept his head down so that the light from the lamp beside him fell across the upper part of his face, leaving the chin and mouth in shadow. She noticed there was a little muscle moving near the corner of his left eye.

"This is going to be a bit of a shock to you, I'm afraid," he said. "But I've thought about it a good deal and I've decided the only thing do is to tell you right away. I hope you won't blame me too much."

And he told her. It didn't take long, four or five minutes at most, and she sat very still through it all, watching him with a kind of dazed horror as he went further and further away from her with each word.

"So there it is," he added. "And I know it's kind of a bad time to be telling you, but there simply wasn't any other way. Of course I'll give you money and see you're looked after. But there needn't really be any fuss. I hope not anyway. It wouldn't be very good for my job."

Her first instinct was not to believe any of it, to reject it all. It occurred to her that perhaps he hadn't even spoken, that she herself had imagined the whole thing. Maybe, if she went about her business and acted as though she hadn't been listening, then later, when she sort of woke up again, she might find none of it had ever happened.

"I'll get the supper," she managed to whisper, and this time he didn't stop her.

When she walked across the room she couldn't feel her feet touching the floor. She couldn't feel anything at all—except a slight nausea and a desire to vomit. Everything was automatic now—down the steps to the cellar, the light switch, the deep freeze, the hand inside the cabinet taking hold of the first object it met. She lifted it out, and looked at it. It was wrapped in paper, so she took off the paper and looked at it again.

A leg of lamb.

All right then, they would have lamb for supper. She carried it upstairs, holding the thin bone-end of it with both her hands, and as she went through the living-room, she saw him standing over by the window with his back to her, and she stopped.

"For God's sake," he said, hearing her, but not turning round. "Don't make supper for me. I'm going out."

At that point, Mary Maloney simply walked up behind him and without any pause she swung the big frozen leg of lamb high in the air and brought it down as hard as she could on the back of his head.

She might just as well have hit him with a steel club.

She stepped back a pace, waiting, and the funny thing was that he remained standing there for at least four or five seconds, gently swaying.

Then he crashed to the carpet.

The violence of the crash, the noise, the small table overturning, helped bring her out of the shock. She came out slowly, feeling cold and surprised, and she stood for a while blinking at the body, still holding the ridiculous piece of meat tight with both hands.

All right, she told herself. So I've killed him.

It was extraordinary, now, how clear her mind became all of a sudden. She began thinking very fast. As the wife of a detective, she knew quite well what the penalty would be. That was fine. It made no difference to her. In fact, it would be a relief. On the other hand, what about the child? What were the laws about murderers with unborn children? Did they kill them both—mother and child? Or did they wait until the tenth month? What did they do?

Mary Maloney didn't know. And she certainly wasn't prepared to take a chance.

She carried the meat into the kitchen, placed it in a pan, turned the oven on high, and shoved it inside. Then she washed her hands and ran upstairs to the bedroom. She sat down before the mirror, tidied her face, touched up her lips and face. She tried a smile. It came out rather peculiar. She tried again.

"Hullo Sam," she said brightly, aloud.

The voice sounded peculiar too.

"I want some potatoes please, Sam. Yes, and I think a can of peas."

That was better. Both the smile and the voice were coming out better now. She rehearsed it several times more. Then she ran downstairs, took her coat, went out the back door, down the garden, into the street.

It wasn't six o'clock yet and the lights were still on in the grocery shop.

"Hullo Sam," she said brightly, smiling at the man behind the counter.

"Why, good evening, Mrs. Maloney. How're *you*?"

"I want some potatoes please, Sam. Yes, and I think a can of peas."

The man turned and reached up behind him on the shelf for the peas.

"Patrick's decided he's tired and doesn't want to eat out tonight," she told him. "We usually go out Thursdays, you know, and now he's caught me without any vegetables in the house."

"Then how about meat, Mrs. Maloney?"

"No, I've got meat, thanks. I got a nice leg of lamb, from the freezer."

"Oh."

"I don't much like cooking it frozen, Sam, but I'm taking a chance on it this time. You think it'll be all right?"

"Personally," the grocer said, "I don't believe it makes any difference. You want those Idaho potatoes?"

"Oh yes, that'll be fine. Two of those."

"Anything else?" The grocer cocked his head on one side, looked at her pleasantly. "How about afterwards? What you going to give him for afterwards?"

"Well—what would you suggest, Sam?"

The man glanced around his shop. "How about a nice big slice of cheesecake? I know he likes that."

"Perfect," she said. "He loves it."

And when it was all wrapped and she had paid, she put on her brightest smile and said, "Thank you, Sam. Good night."

"Good night, Mrs. Maloney. And thank *you*."

And now, she told herself as she hurried back, all she was doing now, she was returning home to her husband and he was waiting for his supper; and she must cook it good, and make it as tasty as possible because the poor man was tired; and if, when she entered the house, she happened to find anything unusual, or tragic, or terrible, then naturally it would be a shock and she'd become frantic with grief and horror. Mind you, she wasn't *expecting* to find anything. She was just going home with the vegetables. Mrs. Patrick Maloney going home with the vegetables on Thursday evening to cook supper for her husband.

That's the way, she told herself. Do everything right and natural. Keep things absolutely natural and there'll be no need for any acting at all.

Therefore, when she entered the kitchen by the back door, she was humming a little tune to herself and smiling.

"Patrick!" she called. "How are you, darling?"

She put the parcel down on the table and went through into the living-room; and when she saw him lying there on the floor with his legs doubled up and one arm twisted back underneath his body, it really was rather a shock. All the old love and longing for him welled up inside her, and she ran over to him, knelt down beside him, and began to cry her heart out. It was easy. No acting was necessary.

A few minutes later she got up and went to the phone. She knew the number of the police station, and when the man at the other end answered, she cried to him, "Quick! Come quick! Patrick's dead!"

"Who's speaking?"

"Mrs. Maloney. Mrs. Patrick Maloney."

"You mean Patrick Maloney's dead?"

"I think so," she sobbed. "He's lying on the floor and I think he's dead."

"Be right over," the man said.

The car came very quickly, and when she opened the front door, two policemen walked in. She knew them both—she knew nearly all the men at that precinct—and she fell right into Jack Noonan's arms, weeping hysterically.

He put her gently into a chair, then went over to join the other one, who was called O'Malley, kneeling by the body.

"Is he dead?" she cried.

"I'm afraid he is. What happened?"

Briefly, she told her story about going out to the grocer and coming back to find him on the floor. While she was talking, crying and talking, Noonan discovered a small patch of congealed blood on the dead man's head. He showed it to O'Malley who got up at once and hurried to the phone.

Soon, other men began to come into the house. First a doctor, then two detectives, one of whom she knew by name. Later, a police photographer arrived and took pictures, and a man who knew about fingerprints. There was a great deal of whispering and muttering beside the corpse, and the detectives kept asking her a lot of questions. But they always treated her kindly. She told her story again, this time right from the beginning, when Patrick had come in, and she was sewing, and he was tired, so tired he hadn't wanted to go out for supper. She told how she'd put the meat in the oven—"it's there now, cooking"—and how she'd slipped out to the grocer for vegetables, and come back to find him lying on the floor.

"Which grocer?" one of the detectives asked.

She told him, and he turned and whispered something to the other detective who immediately went outside into the street.

In fifteen minutes he was back with a page of notes, and there was more whispering, and through her sobbing she heard a few of the whispered phrases—". . . acted quite normal . . . very cheerful . . . wanted to give him a good supper . . . peas . . . cheesecake . . . impossible that she . . ."

After a while, the photographer and the doctor departed and two other men came in and took the corpse away on a stretcher. Then the fingerprint man went away. The two detectives remained, and so did the two policemen. They were exceptionally nice to her, and Jack Noonan asked if she wouldn't rather go somewhere else, to her sister's house perhaps, or to his own wife who would take care of her and put her up for the night.

No, she said. She didn't feel she could move even a yard at the moment. Would they mind awfully if she stayed just where she was until she felt better? She didn't feel too good at the moment, she really didn't.

Then hadn't she better lie down on the bed? Jack Noonan asked.

No, she said. She'd like to stay right where she was, in this chair. A little later perhaps, when she felt better, she would move.

So they left her there while they went about their business, searching the house. Occasionally one of the detectives asked her another question. Sometimes Jack Noonan spoke to her gently as he passed by. Her husband, he told her, had been killed by a blow on the back of the head administered with a heavy blunt instrument, almost certainly a large piece of metal. They were looking for the weapon. The murderer may have taken it with him, but on the other hand he may've thrown it away or hidden it somewhere on the premises.

"It's the old story," he said. "Get the weapon, and you've got the man."

Later, one of the detectives came up and sat beside her. Did she know, he asked, of anything in the house that could've been used as the weapon? Would she mind having a look around to see if anything was missing—a very big spanner, for example, or a heavy metal vase.

They didn't have any heavy metal vases, she said.

"Or a big spanner?"

She didn't think they had a big spanner. But there might be some things like that in the garage.

The search went on. She knew that there were other policemen in the garden all around the house. She could hear their footsteps on the gravel outside, and sometimes she saw the flash of a torch through a chink in the curtains. It began to get late, nearly nine she noticed by the clock on the mantel. The four men searching the rooms seemed to be growing weary, a trifle exasperated.

"Jack," she said, the next time Sergeant Noonan went by. "Would you mind giving me a drink?"

"Sure I'll give you a drink. You mean this whisky?"

"Yes, please. But just a small one. It might make me feel better."

He handed her the glass.

"Why don't you have one yourself," she said. "You must be awfully tired. Please do. You've been very good to me."

"Well," he answered. "It's not strictly allowed, but I might take just a drop to keep me going."

One by one the others came in and were persuaded to take a little nip of whisky. They stood around rather awkwardly with the drinks in their hands, uncomfortable in her presence, trying to say consoling things to her. Sergeant Noonan wandered into the kitchen, came out quickly and said, "Look, Mrs. Maloney. You know that oven of yours is still on, and the meat still inside."

"Oh *dear* me!" she cried. "So it is!"

"I better turn it off for you, hadn't I?"

"Will you do that, Jack. Thank you so much."

When the sergeant returned the second time, she looked at him with her large, dark, tearful eyes. "Jack Noonan," she said.

"Yes?"

"Would you do me a small favour—you and these others?"

"We can try, Mrs. Maloney."

"Well," she said. "Here you all are, and good friends of dear Patrick's too, and helping to catch the man who killed him. You must be terrible hungry by now because it's long past your supper time, and I know Patrick would never forgive me, God bless his soul, if I allowed you to remain in his house without offering you decent hospitality. Why don't you eat up that lamb that's in the oven? It'll be cooked just right by now.

"Wouldn't dream of it," Sergeant Noonan said.

"Please," she begged. "Please eat it. Personally I couldn't touch a thing, certainly not what's been in the house when he was here. But it's all right for you. It'd be a favour to me if you'd eat it up. Then you can go on with your work again afterwards."

There was a good deal of hesitating among the four policemen, but they were clearly hungry, and in the end they were persuaded to go into the kitchen and help themselves. The woman stayed where she was, listening to them through the open door, and she could hear them speaking among themselves, their voices thick and sloppy because their mouths were full of meat.

"Have some more, Charlie?"

"No. Better not finish it."

"She *wants* us to finish it. She said so. Be doing her a favour."

"O.K. then. Give me some more."

"That's the hell of a big club the guy must've used to hit poor Patrick," one of them was saying. "The doc says his skull was smashed all to pieces just like from a sledge-hammer."

"That's why it ought to be easy to find."

"Exactly what I say."

"Whoever done it, they're not going to be carrying a thing like that around with them longer than they need."

One of them belched.

"Personally, I think it's right here on the premises."

"Probably right under our very noses. What you think, Jack?"

And in the other room, Mary Maloney began to giggle.

THE LAST GAS STATION

SHIRLEY ANN GRAU

Shirley Ann Grau (signature)

WE HAVE lived here with our father for years and years. Joe, who's the oldest—then Mark, then me—says he can remember our other place real well: the house we used to live in, and the kitchen with yellow roses on the wallpaper. He says there were tall trees, real tall trees where you could lie on your back and watch the sun spin in the leaves. (There's no trees that big around here.) He says that there was a high bluff where you could look down on a river that was twenty feet across. He caught crawfish in the pools there sometimes.

Joe tells that our father had a whole pack of spotted hounds, and when they went hunting you could hear them for hours, our father shouting and the dogs fighting and howling. Joe says on nights when the moon was full the country was plain crowded with animals running.

Joe says all of that—only thing he won't talk about is our mother. Now, I know we got to have had one, but Joe won't answer, and Mark, being younger, don't remember more than some old black lady who took care of us for a while.

Of course I don't even remember that, being the youngest. For all I know, I never been anywhere but here. Our gas station. Our house next door, sitting high on its foundations against the damp and the snakes. The highway, four lanes straight down from the north and straight off to the south, not a curve nor a bend in it. And all around everywhere, far as you can see, palmettos. Low and yellow green, and good for nothing except making fans. There's a fair number of snakes out there and some mice and rabbits but not much else. You can see

421

it—the scrub's no higher than a man's shoulder—and that's all there is.

Once Mark told me that if I climbed to the very top of the roof and looked to the west, I'd see a big lake shining. But he was just fooling. All I saw was heat haze, and I don't have to climb a roof for that.

In one way it's a good thing we don't have our father's hunting pack anymore. The scrub's full of sinkholes, and dogs are pretty like to fall in. I suppose that's what happened to Lucky—he was a dog we had for a while. He came off a Buick sedan—the people, they slowed down and threw him out a window. He bounced two or three times and landed on his back, but he wasn't any more than scared. That's why we called him Lucky. He was small and long-haired and he suffered from ticks during the spring and ear infections the rest of the year. Never was a time when both his ears stood up straight—always something draining out one or the other. But he sure did like running in the palmettos. And one day he never came back.

We went looking, Joe and Mark and me, but there was too many holes and too much ground. We never even found a sign of him.

We had a cat too, you know that? She got killed on the highway by a big semi, name of Beatons Long Distance Moving.

When Joe scraped her up with a shovel and tossed her way back in the scrub, I started crying. I really did love that cat. I kept on crying until Joe and our father beat the tears out of me. They said it wasn't decent.

After that I felt different about the highway. Before, I used to like it, especially the sounds: the tires whistling and singing on the wet, and hissing on the dry. The soft growling sound—kind of like a sigh—when some trucker tested his air brakes. The way horns echo way off in the distance. The thin little screech of car brakes, too, almost like a laugh. And something else—a steady even whisper. Day and night, no different. It ran along the whole length of highway, like electric wires singing. Or maybe kind of like breathing.

And I got to admit that sometimes the highway was a pretty thing too. When the moon was on it. When quick summer rains fell and clouds of steam rose up and cleared away leaving just a heat mirage in the distance. The wind was nice too. On a hot August day, those passing cars and trucks really stirred up a nice little breeze for you.

But I didn't like the highway anymore. Not at all. There just wasn't no getting away from it. If I didn't hear it or see it, if I closed my eyes and stuck my fingers in my ears, I still could smell it. The different exhausts, gas and diesel. The smell of oil that's burning clean and oil that's not. The paint smell of engines overheating with the load of their air conditioners.

Like Joe would say, the highway brought everything to us, and took it away too. Joe's always been the religious one around here, the one who put a Bible on the top shelf in the kitchen. He used to read a little from it now and then. It was a comfort to him, I guess, specially after Bruce left.

You see, when we first came here, there were four boys, not three. The oldest was Bruce. And this was how he come to leave.

Every December there was a big increase in southbound traffic. Out of that crowd there'd always be some who'd made the trip before, and who always made a point of coming back to the same places.

Take this one car now; it had stopped every winter for four or five years. It was a man and his wife and their girl. She got prettier each year, her blond hair hanging long and loose down her back. The last time the man wasn't with them. They stayed quite a while, parked off to one side of the station, talking to Bruce. Afterward, Bruce was very excited: he smashed his thumb with a tire iron, something he don't ever do.

Anyhow, right after they left, he marked a date on the wall calendar with a big red star, and on that day he packed his clothes in a paper bag and told us he was going north with them. Then he walked across the highway to wait.

I remember that: Bruce walking across the road, putting his feet down heavily, as if they hurt him, crossing the wide median, kicking at the pine trees the state planted there. (Funny thing, those trees, been there five or six years and don't hardly reach to your knee.) He waited a long time, swatting at the flies and slapping at the mosquitoes—they're both pretty bad sometimes.

Joe and Mark and me, we sat on the curb by the gas pumps and watched and waited with him. We only moved when a car came in. Then the three of us rushed to fill the tank, clean the windshield, and check the tires. (I always checked the tires because I was the smallest.) We worked so fast we even got a couple of tips.

The sun got hotter and hotter. Bruce kept taking off his hat to fan himself with it, and now and then he'd spit to clear the dust out his mouth.

Along toward the middle of the afternoon, Joe said, "Maybe he won't get to go after all." And he went in the house to tell our father. Minute or two later he was back. "He said it don't matter none about Bruce."

Then a Mercedes pulled in, a 220 with special order extra green glass—made the people with their big sunglasses look just like frogs.

They wanted diesel fuel, which we never had.

"We may not make it," the man said accusingly to us. Like we had let his tank run low. "We just may not."

"She won't burn gas, mister," Joe said firmly. He figures he knows a lot about cars because he's filled so many tanks.

"How far to the next station?"

"I don't know," Joe said. "I never been down that way."

They pulled out very slowly to avoid wasting any fuel. With a shrug Joe moved the sign that said LAST GAS a little closer to the road. It was one of those folding tripod things that we had to take in at night so the big trucks wouldn't backwind it over. It could make an awful racket in the middle of the night.

All of a sudden the three of us remembered and looked across the highway. Bruce was gone. We never even saw the car that stopped for him.

YOU'D THINK we'd be lonely living in a place like this. But we weren't. There was the cars stopping for gas. And once a week the company truck came to fill the underground tanks. That man always stayed to pass the time of day with us. Sometimes he'd bring the newspapers, and he'd always bring our groceries and take our order for the next week. We didn't ever go to town. Our father's car was parked behind the house, next to the cistern, a '59 Pontiac. It was up on blocks, nice and neat, and the hens liked to nest under it. Used to be, too, that the school bus picked us up, and made a big U-turn through the highway median. But we stopped going to school, and the big tracks filled in and grass grew over them.

We had plenty to do what with running the station, and keeping house, and doing the cooking, and feeding the chickens, and hunting after their eggs, and repairing the roof, and keeping the screens patched. Our father, he didn't do anything. He was so tired that he could only sit all day long on the front porch. He used to chew tobacco, but finally he even stopped fooling with the plug.

One day Joe and Mark told me he was dead. "You come see for yourself."

I'd seen dead things before but never a man. Even so, just the way he sat there, head a little on one side—and the big blue-and-green flies banging away at the porch screen to get at him—I'd have known by myself.

That night Joe and Mark (they wouldn't let me go with them) carried our father way far out into the scrub and dropped him into one of the sinkholes there. They took a couple of tire irons and a piece or two of rusted junk from the backyard—to make sure he stayed down.

Nothing changed after his death. Joe went on signing his name on the receipts from the company. He'd been doing it so long that nobody, not the driver of the gas truck nor the company office, seemed to notice the difference.

So, like I said, things went on, quiet except for that one busy season in the winter when all the campers and the trailers and the baggage-packed cars poured south over the road.

"Look at that," Joe said one day when four Pace Arrows and six Winnebagos passed, bumper to bumper. All the Winnebagos had little Christmas trees in the back windows. "Don't it look like something's chasing them?"

And that was exactly the way it looked: drivers scowling, staring hard ahead, concentrating on the road, just like something awful was right behind them.

FEW MONTHS after that, Joe and Mark got in a fight. I didn't see the start; when I walked in the kitchen Mark had ahold of a broken bottle and Joe had his knife out, the big switchblade he kept from our father. I

425

could tell that Mark was beginning to have second thoughts; he'd have turned and run only he was scared of getting that knife in his back. He just kept moving in the general direction of the door. Me, I was too scared to say anything.

Mark managed to back around the table, past the stove, and down the steps leading to the yard, pushing open the screen as he went. He had his left hand on the rail and he was trying to get down the three steps without taking his eyes off Joe. Well, we all knew that the railing was loose, been loose for years I guess, but neither Joe nor I knew that all you had to do was pick it up.

And that was very lucky for Mark. Because once he got to the steps, Joe closed on him, holding the knife low and flat, just the right position.

Well, Mark faked a stumble and Joe moved in. Joe was so busy watching the broken bottle he wasn't paying no attention to Mark's left hand. The long piece of two-by-two rail caught him square alongside the head. And he slid face down the steps into the yard.

Mark watched Joe for a long time. But whatever he was waiting for, it didn't come. Slowly, in an easy underhand, Mark tossed the broken bottle at Joe's back, the way you'd throw something on a pile of garbage. The railing he dropped right where he stood.

He came back inside, walked straight by me into the bedroom. He pushed the mattress off his bed so that the whole set of springs showed. He kept his special secret things hidden in a black plastic zipper case stuffed down in one of the center coils. He took that case, and his good jacket from where it hung on a nail by his bed, and his special clean cap from the shelf.

"Cain killed Abel," he said to me as he left. And, "The end of the world is coming."

You see that he was really the religious one in the family.

He got a hitch almost immediately, a big truck with a load of cattle, going south. I never saw him again.

LIKE I SAID, Mark used his left hand. I guess that's why the side of Joe's head wasn't caved in. But he looked pretty terrible lying there, not moving, bleeding into the gravel, half his ear knocked off. I pulled him up the steps and inside; took me a long time and I couldn't hardly do it: he was a big man. I stopped the bleeding and kept ice on his head, but it was days before he came around. And then he couldn't do nothing but talk foolishness and vomit all over the kitchen floor.

He got well after a while and was just like always. Except for the headaches and the limp in his left leg. That never did feel right, he said.

Now I was really busy. I had to do the cars all by myself and of course I had to take care of him. That's why lots of things that should have been done, didn't get done. Like the light bulb over the round orange sign GAS. I wasn't tall enough to reach it, not even with our ladder; Joe didn't feel like fooling with it; and the sign stayed dark. I took to leaving the porch light on, so people could see where we were in all that empty stretch of road. I even found some reflectors and put them along the highway too.

We got along, one season after the other. Just Joe and me.

THEN SOMETHING changed, really changed. All of a sudden there was too much traffic on the highway. Now, it gets pretty busy during the holiday season, but this was fifty times more. Thousands and thousands of cars, and this was the middle of the summer. The ground was shaking with their weight, all the windows were rattling in the back draft, like a storm blowing up.

We'd have four, five cars in the gas station at once. They weren't the usual crowd, wanting to get out and stretch, complaining because we didn't have a Coke machine or any rest rooms. They wanted gas and they wanted oil, forget the windshield, they wanted to be gone.

"Something's going on up north there," Joe said.

Nobody would stop long enough to talk. They were in that much a hurry.

Pretty soon our tanks were empty, regular and super both. And the truck from the company, the one that always came on Wednesdays, it didn't come. So I took in the sign that said LAST GAS and leaned it against the house wall, and at night I turned off the porch light.

Now the traffic raced by us without stopping. And on the sides of the road abandoned cars began to appear. Nothing wrong with them, they were just out of gas.

427

The people from those cars, they'd thumb a ride if they could. If they couldn't, they'd start walking—not talking, nor anything like that—just following the highway.

Soon the roadsides were lined solid with empty cars, and then the left lane was closed completely by an eight-car smashup. And then, well, then it began slowing down. Just as suddenly as it started, it was stopping.

This upset Joe, really upset him. "I know it ain't right," he said. He got more and more nervous, and that brought on his headaches, like it always did. In a couple of hours he was limping up and down by the empty gas pumps, holding his head with both hands.

All of a sudden he spun around, rubber heel squealing on the asphalt. "Now look"—he jabbed me right in the middle of the chest with his finger. "If they're going, we're going too. Let's get together right now. Before we miss the last car."

While his back was turned, I took off, running. There was this one particular sinkhole I'd known about for years—I'd found it myself. You could climb down into it (limestone is nothing but layers) to a nice wide shelf, under the overhanging ground. You were out of sight unless somebody happened to climb down after you. And I didn't think Joe was going to look for me in every single sink, not with the pain he had in his leg.

He sure did look for quite a while. He yelled and he cursed after me for hours and hours, before he finally gave up.

Even when I knew he was gone, I stayed hidden, just to be sure. I'd rather met a coral snake where I was than run into Joe on the surface, mad as he was. So I waited a long, long time. When I came out, it was late evening and the highway was empty and I thought, Maybe Joe really did get the last car. Maybe he really did.

THAT WAS yesterday. And there's things I didn't think about before that's bothering me now. Like, when I went to turn on the light, there wasn't any electricity. And food. Joe left everything for me, but it isn't all that much. And the quiet. I'm not used to the quiet. Nor the way winds sound in the dark, hollow and big. And most of all, being alone.

I should have gone with him. Sometimes I think I'll walk along after

him, but it's got to be too far. I climbed on the roof to look off that
way; I could see for miles and miles, and there wasn't a single thing
moving.

And I wonder if there's anything there either, in that direction
where all the people were rushing.

I sure wish I'd gone with Joe.

When the next car passes I think I'm going to run out in the
highway so they have to hit me or stop for me. I know that's what I'm
going to do.

If there ever is another car.

THE SONG OF THE NARRANGUY

BRIAN JAMES

Brian James,

In THE SINGING of many little rivers, the song of the Narranguy persists
the clearest, and I hear it now as I write this. The Narranguy came out
of the dawn and the great dark mysterious ranges and circled and
looped its way by the little hills to the setting of all the suns. Our place
was set on the rising ground just above the rich black river-flats.
"Riverview", father had called it: from our front verandah we saw so
much of the river and the river country, and it all became, without
our knowing it, a very big part of ourselves. Also, if we looked to the
left, we could see something of the ranges, with Coolangubra rising
above them, a giant among giants. He watched continually over us in
his frowning dominance and majesty, in all ways like the God who
lived once a week in our catechism. Bleak and black against the rising
day, he was; but he caught the last of its going. And then he smiled,
distantly, a trifle grimly; but for the moment his great face lit up in a
smile, and that somehow reconciled us a little to the awful Deity who

so pitilessly watched our lives. Occasionally, too, the great bow or double bow, after the violence of a summer storm, would be fully bent in all its beauty and glory right over Coolangubra. And that gave us a glimpse of the Heaven reserved for us, if we were very good, in some impossibly distant future.

Mother was romantic; even six children hadn't cured her of that, as it does most women long since. As we grew a bit older and she should have been gloomily instructing us, the girls anyway, in the facts of life, and getting us to adjust ourselves in the correct modern gloomy fashion, and teaching us that life was a pretty gloomy affair anyhow, she wasted many an hour, when the mood was on her, in painting life in bright colours. Ah well, she didn't prate of Security, for she seemed to find life more interesting without it. Not that she was feckless or lazy or improvident either: but she knew how to clip from time the golden moments. And she was always singing scraps of the old songs, lovely songs we thought they were: "Sweet Belle Mahone", "Prairie Flower", "The Land of the Leal", "White Wings", and "What are the Wild Waves Saying?".

Father was very different from mother. A very quiet man and full of reserves where she was so voluble. Very patient, easy-going was the expression. Sometimes he would tell us stories round the fire at night, when he was in the mood: old stories they were, well worn, graduating, as we grew older, from fairies, giants, ogres, to smugglers and so forth. Or he read to us: Fenimore Cooper, Jane Porter, Bunyan, and even Mark Twain. And often he told us stories from the Old Testament. He certainly had an eye for a good story and he told it well. We never tired of Joseph and Abraham and Ruth and Daniel. Perhaps we liked more than any of them Pharaoh's pursuit of the Children of Israel—what time the mighty host was swallowed up by the Red Sea. It had a local setting and application: "You see," father would say, "it was just as if Pharaoh was right in the middle of the old Narranguy, at the crossing before there was a bridge at all, and down comes the river with a rush." It certainly did make it all very real.

Father was much less enjoyable on Sunday afternoon. For after dinner he lined us up and "went through our catechisms". He'd ask the questions and we had to give the answers. Not a paraphrase either:

he insisted on our being word perfect. In any case, a paraphrase was mostly impossible for, as like as not, we hadn't the faintest notion what it was all about. Father's theory apparently was that the meaning would come to us all right some day, and then we'd be very glad. All the years have not yet brought the gladness.

But life at "Riverview", with a few definite drawbacks, was a happy one and a fair proportion of the good sunlight fell upon us. Time flowed on, inexorably though we knew it not, like the water of the Narranguy, under the bridge, singing its song as it went, on to the west. Never to come back any more.

There had been a drought all that summer. Eaglehawks floated as specks in the hard blue of the sky, or described their wide and endless circles; never before so many crows, dreary crowds of them, black as Satan, sinister choruses, hark-harking at the drought and its spoils: dusty, bony, skinny cattle moving in listless mobs from somewhere to the shelter of the river country. The tanks at our place went dry, the two round tanks and the two square tanks, and we carted water from the river for household use; or rather we dragged it up on the sled. The Narranguy was a mere thread now, a trickle only, and all its old-time murmuring, its song and croon had gone. No one had ever seen the river so low, not even the old hands. And then it stopped flowing altogether; that more than anything made the drought a fearsome thing.

Then fires broke out in the ranges and filled the air with smoke by day; and by night there were a thousand twinkling lights to mock the pale stars. Even Coolangubra, so aloof and stately, was burning. Coolangubra whose final peak had been so often sifted over with snow. And now on fire! It was the end of the world, and the world was burning up. "No man knows" said the catechism of this event. But here it was now, consummation, and the dreaded general judgment was at hand.

One night when summer had shaded into unnatural autumn, for there was no harvest, no fulfilment, a voice from the past, from the dead, called to us. From under the stand of the back tank came the croak of old grandfather frog, as we used to call him. A confident and prophetic croak. God knows how grandfather had survived all those months. But there he was in the darkness croaking away. "Drought done," he said as plain as could be. "I believe him," said father, "there is rain coming."

Grandfather was right. Next day clouds piled up in the north-west, and filled all the sky and sat on the top of Coolangubra; and all the air was still and hushed, listening for the forgotten patter of raindrops, waiting for the smell of wetted dust. And that night it began to rain, lightly and shyly. The wetted dust smelled sweet. Grandfather frog reproved our former doubts. "Said so," he croaked.

The rain grew heavier, ever so gradually. But it made music on the iron roof now. There was the laughter and gurgle of falling water in the empty tanks. Mother had made us come in. "No use getting soaked," she said. And we danced and sang in the sheer relief of purgatory done with.

We went to bed with the rain drumming heavily in our ears. There was no deception about it, no false alarm. When we woke in the morning there was still the heavy drumming on the galvanized iron. It was a "real set-in". The grey light came grudgingly from the hidden sun. All the tanks were full, and the two round ones were spurting great arcs from their overflows. Heavy splash of unwanted water. Water everywhere: the whole world turning to water.

Father and Jack, in long-unused oilskins, slopped through the falling rain and the puddles and mud to feed the horses and cows. The hungry fowls came right to the back verandah to beg. We laughed at the sight of them, so dejected looking they were with tails depressed.

We didn't go to school that day, for once father said we'd have to stay home. We grew tired of the tedious hours. Even the fowls, sad and solemn as they looked, were having a better time. And we wondered, too, what the old Narranguy was doing about all the rain. And in the midst of the wondering we heard him. Yes, we heard him. A heavy booming that rose above the monotonous beating upon the roof. It was quite exciting to hear the river, and not a little terrifying.

Ted, second youngest and nearly two years older than myself, and I managed to sneak off down the lane. We had corn-bags over us made into hoods and capes. It was great to be out of the house. We squelched through mud and went knee-deep at times through the sheets of water.

And then the river. From bank to bank, nearly over-brimming them, was this great monster, yellow and grey, tearing along. We stood on the bridge now, and from its safety looked upon this fearsome thing that thrilled us so. And so close beneath us. Grey tumult. Splotches of yellow foam, like islands, only they shot along and made us dizzy to watch them. We ventured further along, to the very middle of the bridge, and then we felt it jar and quiver and tremble. Some big object, no doubt a huge log, had bumped against one of the supports. And the whole bridge trembled. It wasn't safe any more.

"Come on," said Ted daringly, "to the other end."

"Back," I said.

"Afraid?" said Ted.

"Afraid—what of?" No younger brother can own fear when an older brother taunts him. And Ted and I raced to the far end. There was now the whole length of bridge between us and home. I strove hard to beat back the trembles within myself, and that queer vacant feeling that assails one at the top of the stomach. I daresay Ted was much in the same way. After all, he was only twelve. But then I was only just ten.

We had enough sense to realize that, if the bridge was unsafe (and we knew now in our very bones that it was unsafe) the sooner we re-crossed the better it was for us. We got our breaths again, and took one look at the tumbling waves, bigger than ever. The whole flooring of the bridge would soon be awash.

"Off we go!" said Ted. Fear put springs in our feet. There was no doubt about it, the bridge was rocking. Not trembling, but rocking. We flew, unconscious of the pains and stitches that must have been in our sides. Nor did we look any more at the flood. I stumbled and fell, sprawled out yards ahead of the stumble. This was It—the very end of everything. I could hear mother singing "Wait for me at Heaven's gate, sweet Belle Mahone"; and father, with the steel-rim spectacles on his nose, asking so severely, "What is sanctifying grace?" . . . Ted slowed down while I bounced to my feet again. "All right?" he gasped. And as my feet bounded away I managed, "I'm all right."

We did reach our side, heaving and puffing, sucking in the air that would not fill the emptiness within. "A narrow squeak, that was," said

Ted at last. I felt then, and know now, that Ted was bitterly disappointed that the whole bridge didn't crash before our eyes, dissolve and be no more, now we were safe!

And then out of the dull curtain of rain, came father. "Hey, you fellows, what do you think you're doing?" Anxiety, tempered with relief, was in his voice. He had been out looking for us, and should have been angry at finding us. But he was not. He must have been mortally afraid for us. We had to admit having been on the bridge.

"Come along," said father, "your mother is dreadfully upset, thinking all kinds of terrible things have happened to you." Then he noticed my knee. "What on earth have you done to your leg?" For the first time I felt the pain of it. There was a big gash—the mark of it is still there.

"I fell, I think."

"On the bridge, of course." And father made me ride pick-a-back, despite demurring on my part. Even that made the wounded leg worth while.

Mother cleansed the gash on my knee with "karroseen", a universal remedy then, and bound it neatly with clean rag strips. And cooed and clucked and scolded and fussed. Which showed how afraid she had been for us, too. After all, our greatest fears are for others. In the ultimate we can face fate for ourselves, steel and nerve ourselves to it; but we cannot quite do that for others, for those we really love. Then the coward in us reveals himself. We did not know that then, but we do now. We do now.

And it still rained. And rained. Ted was saying "Forty days and forty nights," grinning to show how funny he thought it. Mother said it was not nice to joke about the Scriptures. No doubt we were all scared, Ted as much as any of us. Towards evening there was a great crash and a ripping and rending. "That," said father, "is the bridge. There won't be a stick of it left."

Morning, and still raining. We looked out, and there was the flood right at our door, for all our living on a slope that overlooked the flats. Quiet water this. Quiet and deadly in purpose. No tumbling waves in it. It ran slowly the other way. And that puzzled us greatly in our fears. Father told us it was a back-water, but how and why we did not understand. Father also assured us that the house was safe, we need not worry about that. I could see he did not quite believe it himself. Ted did not say anything more about Noah and the Ark.

Father warned us to stay inside. He and Jack went out to look after the stock. They came back and said all was well and that the rain was starting to ease up. And even a small patch of pale and washed-out blue showed in the north-west. But it was sky. There *was* sky behind the low clouds, however hard it was to believe it. The blue patch winked and disappeared and the rain went on. But it was not so heavy.

Young Eric Martin, the first outsider we had seen for days, appeared on the back verandah. We hailed him gladly therefore, though at school we did not like him much. A big fellow, well over thirteen, on whom with a deal of malicious satisfaction we had bestowed the name "Turkey Eggs" on account of his freckles.

Ted said, "By cripes, Eric, the bridge is gone."

"I know, Ted, we heard it go."

"You didn't see it, did you?" His voice was curiously low and strained.

"No, but Jim here and I crossed it just before she went. All wobbly she was then, I can tell you."

Mother came out of the kitchen. She was very fond of boys, all sorts of boys. Mothers who are always singing, as she was, mostly are. The sour sort cling to the daughters, so we used to think, perhaps a kind of feminine conspiracy against Man. Be that as it may, mother had a very sympathetic understanding of boys. She summed up Eric now at a glance. "What's wrong, Eric? she asked.

And Eric broke down and blubbered, great bubbles of weeping coming through a narrow-necked bottle, as it were. Not much of tears either, except through his nose, which he restrained by great intaking sniffs.

"There, there!" said mother, patting the huge fellow on the shoulders. "There, there! You're out of wind—get your breath and tell us."

"It's father!" This came up and out with a very big bubble.

"Yes, yes," said mother anxiously and paling a little. "What is it, Eric?"

"He's gone."

"Gone!"

"We can't find him, and he hasn't come back."

"Run over," said mother to Ted, "and get father."

It took a long time for Eric to tell the tale. It seemed that Mr. Martin had gone to shift some cows from a paddock.

"On foot was he, Eric?"

"No, he was riding Nellie. And she's gone, too."

And that was hours ago. They had waited and waited. And he did not come back. They went down to the edge of the water. Some of the cows were on the higher slopes of the next paddock. And some were missing. No sign of them, nor of Mr. Martin, nor of Nellie either.

Father had heard enough. "I'll be coming across, lad," he said. "And Jack, too."

Early evening was falling. Rain certainly lighter now, but a kind of fog with it. And the booming of the river and a gentle, mocking lap-lap of water at the front of the house.

"Do be careful," said mother as father and Jack and Eric set out. And to Eric—"Never fear, he's all right."

Then she had a quiet cry herself, and made herself busy and bossy to hide it. She had us pile up a great fire in the wide kitchen fireplace. "They'll be soaked and frozen," she said, "when they get back." Then she made us kneel down and say prayers, specifying for God's convenience and better understanding what the prayers were for: for father and Jack; that Mr. Martin turned up all right; that the rain would stop; that the water would come no higher; and that we did not lose too many head of stock. Lastly, that the fences did not get washed away. I think she had the turkeys in mind, too, but did not like to worry God too much.

Mother got the long black fork and told Ted to make toast; there were lovely coals now, simply inviting toast. "Watch it," she said, "and don't let it burn." I assisted, largely in the capacity of critic. Ted was a realist which meant, like most realists, he was morbid. Cheerfully morbid he was. Our adventure on the bridge had greatly stimulated his realism.

"He's a goner, I reckon," said Ted.

"Who, Mr. Martin?"

"Sure. And as like as not they won't find him for days and days. Sometimes they never do at all, you know."

I shivered. Ted went on. "And when they do they're horrible. All puffed up and hard to know, except by buttons and pipe and pocket-knife. . . . And such like things. . . ."

Mother returned just then and heard the tail-end of Ted's prophecy for Mr. Martin. "Not another word like that," she said—fiercely for mother.

The hours went by. Mother was just on the point of sending up a new lot of petitions, and a reminder of the old ones, to the Lord, when Ted announced: "Here they come, I do believe! Someone's coming! And the water's under the front of the house."

We all went out to the side of the back verandah and joined Ted. A weird sort of light came from the gloom, an uncertain light that bobbed and jerked, grew big and grew small, came close and receded. And around it a vague, luminous sphere. Voices. It was father and Jack, with hurricane lamp, skirting the grey limitless sea of the Narranguy.

"Did you find him?" called Ted. Father didn't answer; he only gave a look and a shrug to mother. We understood that it was all up with Mr. Martin.

"Oh dear!" said mother. "And did you. . . ."

"We didn't," said father, "and there's not a hope. He's gone. We'll be lucky ever to find him now."

"Miles and miles lower down, and days after—like that Chinaman at Wellington. . . ." Ted's prophecies evidently derived from an old newspaper account of a big fresh in the Macquarie and the drowning of a Chinaman.

Father and Jack were very wet and cold, and father was much dejected. Mr. Martin was a close friend. Mother hustled and bustled and gave them steaming cups of tea. She was a great believer in tea. Tea ran a very close second to prayers as a comforter. Better sometimes, for tea was never a complete failure. Then she got them something to eat.

"And how is she—poor thing?" asked mother.

"Pretty badly, naturally. And calm enough, too, if you understand."

Mother understood. "I must go over and see her," she said.

"A long way round now, and not very nice going either. Wait till morning I'd say."

"No, tonight," And she got herself ready.

Father had the trip over again with mother, and Jack was to stay with us. He sent us to bed and sat up late himself.

The sun was actually shining next morning when he woke up. Very much watered down sunlight it was. But the rain had stopped, and there was a very pale blue sky. Like someone's eyes we knew once—awful weak eyes, with the blue of them nearly white, and the white nearly as blue. And the water had dropped a little overnight below the gate. But the river was still a raging sea, miles wide, and the hills seemed to have got farther away. There was more water than land. There was the view in front. Behind, Coolangubra and the high ranges stood out, not so sharply defined now, but triumphant.

Word had gone round somehow that Mr. Martin was missing. Neighbours, men and young fellows, dropped into our place. Father was looked to for leadership in the community.

The search for the missing man was simple and restricted. Ted and I were not allowed to go, and after Ted's talk of finding the body I was secretly glad. There was just one chance, Martin might be brought in by a backwater somewhere. Well over a mile down-stream, the river tore at the hills that came on to the left bank; but on the right was a great stretch of slightly calmer water, covering what had been paddocks of corn and lucerne. It was here that they found Martin—at least what seemed to be he. A quick eye detected a something caught in the lower branches of a river-gum, just above the water. The gum itself was one of a scattered group of dumpy green islands, for the tree trunks were all under water. The something was a man, wedged in a fork, slumped, with feet and legs in water. Dead or unconscious, for there was no response to hail and shout. It must be Martin, washed into the tree most likely, caught by the branches and jammed there.

How to rescue him? There were no boats, not on the Narranguy, and it was nearly two hundred yards out to that tree. All kinds of suggestions were made, ropes, rafts, logs, but none of them was practicable. Father studied the current carefully.

"We can reach him all right," he said. "That is not the big difficulty. It's getting him to shore." He looked hard again. "But one could use the current and slant across to somewhere about Tully's. What do you think?"

That was all very well, but who could undertake such a swim? Not a few hundred yards, it might be a mile. More, perhaps. And all the risks of the swift current and the flood's fearful harvest of driftwood and debris. Still, there were volunteers, too, not such good swimmers either. Father turned them down. He himself was by far the best swimmer along the Narranguy. In fact, of all present he was the only one likely to succeed. "I'll give it a flutter," he said, "and I feel sure I can do it."

"Look, Tom," said old man George to father, "if you wait a few hours the river will drop. Wait, I say."

"He may be alive now and dead then," said father.

He gave instructions to the party to wait lower down, at least four hundred yards and farther, and to keep a good look-out. He himself would enter the water a few hundred yards up-stream. He made it seem not so hard after all.

"Your own wife and kids, you know," said old man George. "Is it fair to them?" Apparently this nettled father somewhat. "Charlie," he remarked, "I am the only man here who can do this. Could I face the wife and kids again if I didn't try to do it?" I can't doubt now that there was more than a touch of the melodramatic in all this. But father was a brave man, too, and it is good to think that he was. Old Charlie George gave it up with a shrug. "All right, Tom. All right, and good luck."

Father waded out as far as he could; heavens, but the water must have been cold! Then he struck out at a slant across the powerful current. There were many obstacles in his way, and bigger than they seemed from the shore; floating stuff that had to be avoided, travelling down-stream faster than father.

One large mass of debris hove down upon him when he was close to the big gum where Martin was. No doubt it was right upon him before he noticed it. It seemed to go over him entirely, they said. And partly turn over, too. For a moment, they said, father was seen to struggle against it, and then he disappeared. And the floating snag, whatever it was, passed on.

But there was no longer any sight of father.

"God!" said old man George. "He's under it! Caught and tangled in it! Barbed wire in it, perhaps, or wire netting. God, but what did I tell him! Tangled up and caught!"

They watched the spot where he had disappeared, but father didn't show up. They watched the mass of rubbish swiftly floating on, but no sign of father in that either. Not a sign, and no one could know exactly what had happened. But not a soul could do a thing about it. That treacherous moving island, dancing and bobbing a deal in the stream, moved on, now caught by some cross current, to stop and circle a moment, and then on again, farther out than before.

As simply—and as uselessly—as that, it happened.

They followed down on the right bank till they came to the junction of the Narranguy and Bluett's Creek. The creek was a river now itself, fifty yards wide at least, and swifter than the river. There was no crossing it, even if there had been any use in doing so.

So that was that. If there was any hope for Martin, jammed and caught in the river-gum, there was none at all for father.

At last they gathered together again, full of unspoken guilt. They had witnessed tragedy, stood by and seen it, and had been powerless to avert it. Only old man George voiced his thought: "He shouldn't you know, but he went like a man."

There were still small straws to clutch—to save themselves. "Charlie," someone said, "we'll have to tell her." And that meant there was no one so fitting as old George to do it. There are men of course who do not mind breaking the news, the bad news. Some have even a horrible relish in doing it. Many more women enjoy it still more. But this little crowd shrank from it. There was no gleam of credit for them in it.

"All right," said old man George. "I'll do it." He selected some of the older men to go with him. "But," he said stubbornly, "I'm not taking his clothes. I can't face her with them. Do something with them till later on. It wouldn't be decent now." I think old man George must have wept over those empty clothes on the bank.

And so he came to our place and broke the news; and from his account, and from those of others later on, I tell this tale of the last of father in the Big Flood. The river to this day has never given him up. Buried somewhere, farther down, beneath the silt and mud, or caught for ever in the reedy swamps. We never learned where, but there he sleeps.

The river went down rapidly after the rain ceased. It almost seemed as if the flood had been waiting for father. And now that it had him it subsided. Coolangubra, progenitor of the river and flood, was no great distance from us, so the water got away quickly. Very soon they were able to get out to the big gum with Mr. Martin in it. High up, caught tightly in the branches, in a nest of rubbish and mud. And he was not dead either, though nearly as good as dead. Terribly knocked about, to say nothing of what the doctor called shock and exposure. But still alive. And he lived, broken and crippled. Worse off really than father.

Mother took it well—how much it was to her we could not know. But she said it was God's will, and that God knew best. Great faith, it seems, can only go with great optimism. For a long time we did not hear her sing, not very much. And then in more plaintive note, "The Land of the Leal" over and over. And then in scraps of hymns, over and over too. Otherwise busy and cheerful as ever. A wonderful woman, she was. It is largely, I suppose, a matter of what one is born to be.

Ted, poor Ted, was completely cured of his romantic fallacies, or morbidness, or whatever it was. We never heard him mention again that Chinaman who was drowned in the Macquarie.

Floods and droughts have followed each other down the years. Cycles, they call them, with ordinary seasons in between. But never a drought like the Big Drought, or a flood like the Great Flood. And now a new crop of old hands speak of them, possessively, exclusively. I am one of the old hands myself. Time has mellowed it all: that raging sea of water and father going to his death in it.

Two songs go on for ever, sadly sweetest of all, when Coolangubra catches the last of the suns in late spring evenings: the Narranguy singing to itself in its gravelly bed, and the giant oaks singing the refrains of all the yesterdays.

THE MUSIC
OF ERICH ZANN

H. P. LOVECRAFT

H P Lovecraft

I HAVE EXAMINED maps of the city with the greatest care, yet have
never again found the Rue d'Auseil. These maps have not been modern
maps alone, for I know that names change. I have, on the contrary,
delved deeply into all the antiquities of the place, and have personally
explored every region, of whatever name, which could possibly answer
to the street I knew as the Rue d'Auseil. But despite all I have done, it
remains a humiliating fact that I cannot find the house, the street, or
even the locality, where, during the last months of my impoverished
life as a student of metaphysics at the university, I heard the music of
Erich Zann.

That my memory is broken I do not wonder; for my health, physical
and mental, was gravely disturbed throughout the period of my
residence in the Rue d'Auseil, and I recall that I took none of my few
acquaintances there. But that I cannot find the place again is both
singular and perplexing; for it was within a half hour's walk of the
university and was distinguished by peculiarities which could hardly be
forgotten by anyone who had been there. I have never met a person
who has seen the Rue d'Auseil.

The Rue d'Auseil lay across a dark river bordered by precipitous
brick blear-windowed warehouses and spanned by a ponderous bridge
of dark stone. It was always shadowy along that river, as if the smoke of
neighboring factories shut out the sun perpetually. The river was also
odorous with evil stenches which I have never smelled elsewhere, and
which may someday help me to find it, since I should recognize them at
once. Beyond the bridge were narrow cobbled streets with rails; and

then came the ascent, at first gradual, but incredibly steep as the Rue d'Auseil was reached.

I have never seen another street as narrow and steep as the Rue d'Auseil. It was almost a cliff, closed to all vehicles, consisting in several places of flights of steps, and ending at the top in a lofty ivied wall. Its paving was irregular, sometimes stone slabs, sometimes cobblestones, and sometimes bare earth with struggling greenish gray vegetation.

The houses were tall, peaked-roofed, incredibly old, and crazily leaning backward, forward, and sidewise. Occasionally an opposite pair, both leaning forward, almost met across the street like an arch; and certainly they kept most of the light from the ground below. There were a few overhead bridges from house to house across the street.

The inhabitants of that street impressed me peculiarly. At first I thought it was because they were all silent and reticent; but later decided it was because they were all very old. I do not know how I came to live on such a street, but I was not myself when I moved there. I had been living in many poor places, always evicted for want of money; until at last I came upon that tottering house in the Rue d'Auseil kept by the paralytic Blandot. It was the third house from the top of the street, and by far the tallest of them all.

My room was on the fifth story; the only inhabited room there, since the house was almost empty. On the night I arrived I heard strange music from the peaked garret overhead, and the next day asked old Blandot about it. He told me it was an old German viol player, a strange dumb man who signed his name as Erich Zann, and who played evenings in a cheap theater orchestra; adding that Zann's desire to play in the night after his return from the theater was the reason he had chosen this lofty and isolated garret room, whose single gable window was the only point on the street from which one could look over the terminating wall at the declivity and panorama beyond.

Thereafter I heard Zann every night, and although he kept me awake, I was haunted by the weirdness of his music. Knowing little of the art myself, I was yet certain that none of his harmonies had any relation to music I had heard before; and concluded that he was a composer of highly original genius. The longer I listened, the more I was fascinated, until after a week I resolved to make the old man's acquaintance.

One night as he was returning from his work, I intercepted Zann in the hallway and told him that I would like to know him and be with him when he played. He was a small, lean, bent person, with shabby clothes, blue eyes, grotesque, satyr-like face, and nearly bald head; and at my first words seemed both angered and frightened. My obvious friendliness, however, finally melted him; and he grudgingly motioned to me to follow him up the dark, creaking, and rickety attic stairs.

His room, one of only two in the steeply pitched garret, was on the west side, toward the high wall that formed the upper end of the street. Its size was very great, and seemed the greater because of its extraordinary barrenness and neglect. Of furniture there was only a narrow iron bedstead, a dingy washstand, a small table, a large bookcase, an iron music rack, and three old-fashioned chairs. Sheets of music were piled in disorder about the floor. The walls were of bare boards, and had probably never known plaster; while the abundance of dust and cobwebs made the place seem more deserted than inhabited. Evidently Erich Zann's world of beauty lay in some far cosmos of the imagination.

Motioning me to sit down, the dumb man closed the door, turned the large wooden bolt, and lighted a candle to augment the one he had brought with him. He now removed his viol from its moth-eaten covering, and taking it, seated himself in the least uncomfortable of the chairs. He did not employ the music rack, but, offering no choice and playing from memory, enchanted me for over an hour with strains I had never heard before; strains which must have been of his own devising. To describe their exact nature is impossible for one unversed in music. They were a kind of fugue, with recurrent passages of the most captivating quality, but to me were notable for the absence of any of the weird notes I had overheard from my room below on other occasions.

Those haunting notes I had remembered, and had often hummed and whistled inaccurately to myself, so when the player at length laid down his bow I asked him if he would render some of them. As I began my request the wrinkled satyr-like face lost the bored placidity it had possessed during the playing, and seemed to show the same curious mixture of anger and fright which I noticed when first I accosted the old man. For a moment I was inclined to use persuasion, regarding rather lightly the whims of senility; and even tried to awaken my host's weirder mood by whistling a few of the strains to which I had listened the night before. But I did not pursue this course for more than a moment; for when the dumb musician recognized the whistled air his face grew suddenly distorted with an expression wholly beyond analysis, and his long, cold, bony right hand reached out to stop my mouth and silence the crude imitation. As he did this he further demonstrated his eccentricity by casting a startled glance toward the lone curtained window, as if fearful of some intruder—a glance doubly absurd, since the garret stood high and inaccessible above all the adjacent roofs, this window being the only point on the steep street, as the concierge had told me, from which one could see over the wall at the summit.

The old man's glance brought Blandot's remark to my mind, and with a certain capriciousness I felt a wish to look out over the wide and dizzying panorama of moonlit roofs and city lights beyond the hilltop, which of all the dwellers in the Rue d'Auseil only this crabbed musician could see. I moved toward the window and would have drawn aside the nondescript curtains, when with a frightened rage even greater than before, the dumb lodger was upon me again; this time motioning with his head toward the door as he nervously strove to drag me thither with both hands. Now thoroughly disgusted with my host, I ordered him to release me, and told him I would go at once. His clutch relaxed, and as he saw my disgust and offense, his own anger seemed to subside. He tightened his relaxing grip, but this time in a friendly manner, forcing me into a chair; then with an appearance of wistfulness crossing to the littered table, where he wrote many words with a pencil, in the labored French of a foreigner.

The note which he finally handed me was an appeal for tolerance and forgiveness. Zann said that he was old, lonely, and afflicted with strange fears and nervous disorders connected with his music and with other things. He had enjoyed my listening to his music, and wished I would come again and not mind his eccentricities. But he could not play to another his weird harmonies, and could not bear hearing them from another; nor could he bear having anything in his room touched by another. He had not known until our hallway conversation that I could overhear his playing in my room, and now asked me if I would arrange with Blandot to take a lower room where I could not hear him in the night. He would, he wrote, defray the difference in rent.

As I sat deciphering the execrable French, I felt more lenient toward the old man. He was a victim of physical and nervous suffering, as was I; and my metaphysical studies had taught me kindness. In the silence there came a slight sound from the window—the shutter must have rattled in the night wind, and for some reason I started almost as violently as did Erich Zann. So when I had finished reading, I shook my host by the hand, and departed as a friend.

The next day Blandot gave me a more expensive room on the third floor, between the apartments of an aged moneylender and the room of a respectable upholsterer. . . . There was no one on the fourth floor.

It was not long before I found that Zann's eagerness for my company was not as great as it had seemed while he was persuading me to move down from the fifth story. He did not ask me to call on him, and when I did call he appeared uneasy and played listlessly. This was always at night—in the day he slept and would admit no one. My liking for him did not grow, though the attic room and the weird music seemed to hold an odd fascination for me. I had a curious desire to look out of that window, over the wall and down the unseen slope at the glittering roofs and spires which must lie outspread there. Once I went up to the garret during theater hours, when Zann was away, but the door was locked.

What I did succeed in doing was to overhear the nocturnal playing of the dumb old man. At first I would tiptoe up to my old fifth floor, then I grew bold enough to climb the last creaking staircase to the peaked garret. There in the narrow hall, outside the bolted door with the covered keyhole, I often heard sounds which filled me with an indefinable dread—the dread of vague wonder and brooding mystery. It was not that the sounds were hideous, for they were not; but that they held vibrations suggesting nothing on this globe of earth, and that at certain intervals they assumed a symphonic quality which I could hardly conceive as produced by one player. Certainly, Erich Zann was a genius of wild power. As the weeks passed, the playing grew wilder, while the old musician acquired an increasing haggardness and furtiveness pitiful to behold. He now refused to admit me at any time, and shunned me whenever we met on the stairs.

Then one night as I listened at the door, I heard the shrieking viol swell into a chaotic babel of sound; a pandemonium which would have led me to doubt my own shaking sanity had there not come from behind that barred portal a piteous proof that the horror was real—the awful, inarticulate cry which only a mute can utter, and which rises only in moments of the most terrible fear or anguish. I knocked repeatedly at the door, but received no response. Afterward I waited in the black hallway, shivering with cold and fear, till I heard the poor musician's feeble effort to rise from the floor by the aid of a chair. Believing him just conscious after a fainting fit, I renewed my rapping, at the same time calling out my name reassuringly. I heard Zann stumble to the window and close both shutter and sash, then stumble to the door, which he falteringly unfastened to admit me. This time his delight at having me present was real; for his distorted face gleamed with relief while he clutched at my coat as a child clutches at its mother's skirts.

Shaking pathetically, the old man forced me into a chair while he sank into another, beside which his viol and bow lay carelessly on the floor. He sat for some time inactive, nodding oddly, but having a paradoxical suggestion of intense and frightened listening. Subsequently he seemed to be satisfied, and crossing to a chair by the table wrote a brief note, handed it to me, and returned to the table, where he began to write rapidly and incessantly.

The note implored me in the name of mercy, and for the sake of my own curiosity, to wait where I was while he prepared a full account in German of all the marvels and terrors which beset him. I waited, and the dumb man's pencil flew.

It was perhaps an hour later, while I still waited and while the old musician's feverishly written sheets still continued to pile up, that I saw Zann start as from the hint of a horrible shock. Unmistakably he was looking at the curtained window and listening shudderingly. Then I half fancied I heard a sound myself; though it was not a horrible sound, but rather an exquisitely low and infinitely distant musical note, suggesting a player in one of the neighboring houses, or in some abode beyond the lofty wall over which I had never been able to look. Upon Zann the effect was terrible, for, dropping his pencil, suddenly he rose, seized his viol, and commenced to rend the night with the wildest playing I had ever heard from his bow save when listening at the barred door.

It would be useless to describe the playing of Erich Zann on that dreadful night. It was more horrible than anything I had ever overheard, because I could now see the expression of his face, and could realize that this time the motive was stark fear. He was trying to make a noise; to ward something off or drown something out—what, I could not imagine, awesome though I felt it must be. The playing grew fantastic, delirious, and hysterical, yet kept to the last the qualities of supreme genius which I knew this strange old man possessed. I recognized the air—it was a wild Hungarian dance popular in the theaters, and I reflected for a moment that this was the first time I had ever heard Zann play the work of another composer.

Louder and louder, wilder and wilder, mounted the shrieking and whining of that desperate viol. The player was dripping with an uncanny perspiration and twisted like a monkey, always looking frantically at the curtained window. In his frenzied strains I could almost see shadowy satyrs and bacchanals dancing and whirling insanely through seething abysses of clouds and smoke and lightning. And then I thought I heard a shriller, steadier note that was not from the viol; a calm, deliberate, purposeful, mocking note from far away in the west.

At this juncture the shutter began to rattle in a howling night wind which had sprung up outside as if in answer to the mad playing within. Zann's screaming viol now outdid itself, emitting sounds I had never thought a viol could emit. The shutter rattled more loudly, unfastened, and commenced slamming against the window. Then the glass broke shiveringly under the persistent impacts, and the chill wind rushed in, making the candles sputter and rustling the sheets of paper on the table where Zann had begun to write out his horrible secret. I looked at

Zann, and saw that he was past conscious observation. His blue eyes were bulging, glassy and sightless, and the frantic playing had become a blind, mechanical unrecognizable orgy that no pen could even suggest.

A sudden gust, stronger than the others, caught up the manuscript and bore it toward the window. I followed the flying sheets in desperation, but they were gone before I reached the demolished panes. Then I remembered my old wish to gaze from this window, the only window in the Rue d'Auseil from which one might see the slope beyond the wall, and the city outspread beneath. It was very dark, but the city's lights always burned, and I expected to see them there amid the rain and wind. Yet when I looked from that highest of all gable windows, looked while the candles sputtered and the insane viol howled with the night wind, I saw no city spread below, and no friendly lights gleamed from remembered streets, but only the blackness of space illimitable; unimagined space alive with motion and music, and having no semblance of anything on earth. And as I stood there looking in terror, the wind blew out both the candles in that ancient peaked garret, leaving me in savage and impenetrable darkness with chaos and pandemonium before me, and the demon madness of that night-baying viol behind me.

I staggered back in the dark, without the means of striking a light, crashing against the table, overturning a chair, and finally groping my way to the place where the blackness screamed with shocking music. To save myself and Erich Zann I could at least try, whatever the powers opposed to me. Once I thought some chill thing brushed me, and I screamed, but my scream could not be heard above that hideous viol. Suddenly out of the blackness the madly sawing bow struck me, and I knew I was close to the player. I felt ahead, touched the back of Zann's chair, and then found and shook his shoulder in an effort to bring him to his senses.

He did not respond, and still the viol shrieked on without slackening. I moved my hand to his head, whose mechanical nodding I was able to stop, and shouted in his ear that we must both flee from the unknown things of the night. But he neither answered me nor abated the frenzy of his unutterable music, while all through the garret strange currents of wind seemed to dance in the darkness and babel. When my hand touched his ear I shuddered, though I knew not why—knew not why till I felt of the still face; the ice-cold, stiffened, unbreathing face whose glassy eyes bulged uselessly into the void. And then, by some miracle, finding the door and the large wooden bolt, I plunged wildly away from that glassy-eyed thing in the dark, and from the ghoulish howling of that accursed viol whose fury increased even as I plunged.

Leaping, floating, flying down those endless stairs through the dark house; racing mindlessly out into the narrow, steep, and ancient street of steps, and tottering houses; clattering down steps and over cobbles to the lower streets and the putrid canyon-walled river; panting across the dark bridge to the broader, healthier streets and boulevards we know; all these are terrible impressions that linger with me. And I recall that there was no wind, and that the moon was out, and that all the lights of the city twinkled.

Despite my most careful searches and investigations, I have never since been able to find the Rue d'Auseil. But I am not wholly sorry; either for this or for the loss in undreamable abysses of the closely written sheets which alone could have explained the music of Erich Zann.

HIS FIRST FLIGHT
LIAM O'FLAHERTY

Liam O'Flaherty

THE YOUNG SEAGULL was alone in his ledge. His two brothers and his sister had already flown away the day before. He had been afraid to fly with them. Somehow when he had taken a little run forward to the brink of the ledge and attempted to flap his wings he became afraid. The great expanse of sea stretched down beneath, and it was such a long way down—miles down. He felt certain that his wings would never support him, so he bent his head and ran away back to the little hole under the ledge where he slept at night.

Even when each of his brothers and his little sister, whose wings were far shorter than his own, ran to the brink, flapped their wings, and flew away he failed to muster up courage to take that plunge which appeared to him so desperate. His father and mother had come around calling to him shrilly, upbraiding him, threatening to let him starve on his ledge unless he flew away. But for the life of him he could not move.

That was twenty-four hours ago. Since then nobody had come near him. The day before, all day long he had watched his parents flying about with his brothers and sister, perfecting them in the art of flight, teaching them how to skim the waves and how to dive for fish. He had, in fact, seen his older brother catch his first herring and devour it, standing on a rock, while his parents circled around raising a proud cackle. And all the morning the whole family had walked about on the big plateau midway down the opposite cliff, taunting him with his cowardice.

The sun was now ascending the sky, blazing warmly on his ledge that faced south. He felt the heat because he had not eaten since the previous nightfall. Then he had found a dried piece of mackerel's tail at the far end of his ledge. Now there was not a single scrap of food left. He had searched every inch, rooting among the rough, dirt-caked straw nest where he and his brothers and sister had been hatched. He even gnawed at the dried pieces of eggshell. It was like eating part of himself.

He had then trotted back and forth from one end of the ledge to the other, his grey body the colour of the cliff, his long grey legs stepping daintily, trying to find some means of reaching his parents without having to fly. But on each side of him the ledge ended in a sheer fall of precipice, with the sea beneath. And between him and his parents there was a deep, wide chasm.

Surely he could reach them without flying if he could only move northwards along the cliff face? But then on what could he walk? There was no ledge, and he was not a fly. And above him he could see nothing. The precipice was sheer, and the top of it was perhaps farther away than the sea beneath him.

He stepped slowly out to the brink of the ledge, and, standing on one leg with the other leg hidden under his wing, he closed one eye, then the other, and pretended to be falling asleep. Still they took no notice of him. He saw his two brothers and his sister lying on the plateau dozing, with their heads sunk into their necks. His father was preening the feathers on his white back. Only his mother was looking at him.

She was standing on a little high hump on the plateau, her white breast thrust forward. Now and again she tore at a piece of fish that lay at her feet, and then scraped each side of her beak on the rock. The sight of the food maddened him. How he loved to tear food that way, scraping his beak now and again to whet it! He uttered a low cackle. His mother cackled too, and looked over at him.

Ga, ga, ga, he cried, begging her to bring him over some food. *Gawl-ool-ah,* she screamed back derisively. But he kept calling plaintively, and after a minute or so he uttered a joyful scream. His mother had picked up a piece of the fish and was flying across to him with it. He leaned out eagerly, tapping the rock with his feet, trying to get nearer to her as she flew across. But when she was just opposite to him, abreast of the ledge, she halted, her legs hanging limp, her wings motionless, the piece of fish in her beak almost within reach of his beak.

He waited a moment in surprise, wondering why she did not come nearer, and then maddened by hunger, he dived at the fish. With a loud scream he fell outwards and downwards into space. His mother had swooped upwards. As he passed beneath her he heard the swish of her wings.

Then a monstrous terror seized him and his heart stood still. He could hear nothing. But it only lasted a moment. The next moment he felt his wings spread outwards. The wind rushed against his breast feathers, then under his stomach and against his wings. He could feel the tips of his wings cutting through the air. He was not falling headlong now. He was soaring gradually downwards and outwards. He was no longer afraid. He just felt a bit dizzy. Then he flapped his wings once and he soared upwards.

He uttered a joyous scream and flapped them again. He soared higher. He raised his breast and banked against the wind. *Ga, ga, ga. Ga, ga, ga.*

Gawl-ool-ah. His mother swooped past him, her wings making a loud noise. He answered her with another scream. Then his father flew over him screaming. Then he saw his two brothers and sister flying around him, curvetting and banking and soaring and diving.

Then he completely forgot that he had not always been able to fly, and commenced himself to dive and soar and curvet, shrieking shrilly.

He was near the sea now, flying straight over it, facing out over the ocean. He saw a vast green sea beneath him, with little ridges moving over it, and he turned his beak sideways and crowed amusedly. His parents and his brothers and sister had landed on this green floor in front of him. They were beckoning to him, calling shrilly. He dropped his legs to stand on the green sea. His legs sank into it. He screamed with fright and attempted to rise again, flapping his wings. But he was tired and weak with hunger and he could not rise, exhausted by the strange exercise. His feet sank into the green sea, and then his belly touched it and he sank no farther.

He was floating on it. And around him his family was screaming, praising him, and their beaks were offering him scraps of dog-fish.

He had made his first flight.

THROUGH THE TUNNEL
DORIS LESSING

GOING TO THE SHORE on the first morning of the holiday, the young English boy stopped at a turning of the path and looked down at a wild and rocky bay, and then over to the crowded beach he knew so well from other years. His mother walked on in front of him, carrying a bright-striped bag in one hand. Her other arm, swinging loose, was very white in the sun. The boy watched that white, naked arm, and turned his eyes, which had a frown behind them, towards the bay and back again to his mother. When she felt he was not with her, she swung around. "Oh, there you are, Jerry!" she said. She looked impatient, then smiled. "Why, darling, would you rather not come with me? Would you rather—" She frowned, conscientiously worrying over what amusements he might secretly be longing for which she had been too busy or too careless to imagine. He was very familiar with that anxious, apologetic smile. Contrition sent him running after her. And yet, as he ran, he looked back over his shoulder at the wild bay; and all morning, as he played on the safe beach, he was thinking of it.

Next morning, when it was time for the routine of swimming and sunbathing, his mother said, "Are you tired of the usual beach, Jerry? Would you like to go somewhere else?"

"Oh, no!" he said quickly, smiling at her out of that unfailing impulse of contrition—a sort of chivalry. Yet, walking down the path with her, he blurted out, "I'd like to go and have a look at those rocks down there."

She gave the idea her attention. It was a wild-looking place, and there was no one there, but she said, "Of course, Jerry. When you've had enough, come to the big beach. Or just go straight back to the villa, if you like." She walked away, that bare arm, now slightly reddened from yesterday's sun, swinging. And he almost ran after her again, feeling it unbearable that she should go by herself, but he did not.

She was thinking, Of course he's old enough to be safe without me. Have I been keeping him too close? He mustn't feel he ought to be with me. I must be careful.

He was an only child, eleven years old. She was a widow. She was determined to be neither possessive nor lacking in devotion. She went worrying off to her beach.

As for Jerry, once he saw that his mother had gained her beach, he began the steep descent to the bay. From where he was, high up among the red-brown rocks, it was a scoop of moving bluish green fringed with white. As he went lower, he saw that it spread among small promontories and inlets of rough, sharp rock, and the crisping, lapping surface showed stains of purple and darker blue. Finally, as he ran sliding and scraping down the last few yards, he saw an edge of white surf, and the shallow, luminous movement of water over white sand, and, beyond that, a solid, heavy blue.

He ran straight to the water and began swimming. He was a good swimmer. He went out fast over the gleaming sand, over a middle region where rocks lay like discoloured monsters under the surface, and then he was in the real sea—a warm sea where irregular cold currents from the deep water shocked his limbs.

When he was so far out that he could look back not only on the little bay but past the promontory that was between it and the big beach, he floated on the buoyant surface and looked for his mother. There she was, a speck of yellow under an umbrella that looked like a slice of orange peel. He swam back to shore, relieved at being sure she was there, but all at once very lonely.

On the edge of the small cape that marked the side of the bay away from the promontory was a loose scatter of rocks. Above them, some boys were stripping off their clothes. They came running, naked, down to the rocks. The English boy swam towards them, and kept his distance at a stone's throw. They were of that coast, all of them burned smooth dark brown and speaking a language he did not understand. To be with them, of them, was a craving that filled his whole body. He swam a little closer; they turned and watched him with narrowed, alert eyes. Then one smiled and waved. It was enough. In a minute, he had swum in and was on the rocks beside them, smiling with a desperate, nervous supplication. They shouted cheerful greetings at him, and then, as he preserved his nervous uncomprehending smile, they understood that he was a foreigner strayed from his own beach, and they proceeded to forget him. But he was happy. He was with them.

They began diving again and again from a high point into a well of blue sea between rough, pointed rocks. After they had dived and come up, they swam around, hauled themselves up, and waited their turn to dive again. They were big boys—men to Jerry. He dived, and they watched him, and when he swam around to take his place, they made way for him. He felt he was accepted, and he dived again, carefully, proud of himself.

Soon the biggest of the boys poised himself, shot down into the water, and did not come up. The others stood about, watching. Jerry, after waiting for the sleek brown head to appear, let out a yell of warning; they looked at him idly and turned their eyes back towards the water. After a long time, the boy came up on the other side of a big dark rock, letting the air out of his lungs in a sputtering gasp and a shout of triumph. Immediately, the rest of them dived in. One moment, the morning seemed full of chattering boys; the next, the air and the surface of the water were empty. But through the heavy blue, dark shapes could be seen moving and groping.

Jerry dived, shot past the school of underwater swimmers, saw a black wall of rock looming at him, touched it, and bobbed up at once to the surface, where the wall was a low barrier he could see across. There was no one visible; under him, in the water, the dim shapes of the swimmers had disappeared. Then one, and then another of the boys came up on the far side of the barrier of rock, and he understood that they had swum through some gap or hole in it. He plunged down again. He could see nothing through the stinging salt water but the blank rock. When he came up, the boys were all on the diving rock, preparing to attempt the feat again. And now, in a panic of failure, he yelled up, in English, "Look at me! Look!" and he began splashing and kicking in the water like a foolish dog.

They looked down gravely, frowning. He knew the frown. At moments of failure, when he clowned to claim his mother's attention, it was just this grave, embarrassed inspection that she rewarded him. Through his hot shame, feeling the pleading grin on his face like a scar that he could never remove, he looked up at the group of big brown boys on the rock and shouted, *"Bonjour! Merci! Au revoir! Monsieur, monsieur!"* while he hooked his fingers round his ears and waggled them.

Water surged into his mouth; he choked, sank, came up. The rock, lately weighted with boys, seemed to rear up out of the water as their weight was removed. They were flying down past him, now, into the water; the air was full of falling bodies. Then the rock was empty in the hot sunlight. He counted one, two, three . . .

At fifty, he was terrified. They must all be drowning beneath him, in the water caves of the rock! At a hundred, he stared around him at the empty hillside, wondering if he should yell for help. He counted faster, faster, to hurry them up, to bring them to the surface quickly, to drown them quickly—anything rather than the terror of counting on and on into the blue emptiness of the morning. And then, at a hundred and sixty, the water beyond the rock was full of boys blowing like brown whales. They swam back to the shore without a look at him.

He climbed back to the diving rock and sat down, feeling the hot roughness of it under his thighs. The boys were gathering up their bits of clothing and running off along the shore to another promontory. They were leaving to get away from him. He cried openly, fists in his eyes. There was no one to see him, and he cried himself out.

It seemed to him that a long time had passed, and he swam out to where he could see his mother. Yes, she was still there, a yellow spot under an orange umbrella.

He swam back to the big rock, climbed up, and dived into the blue pool among the fanged and angry boulders. Down he went, until he touched the wall of rock again. But the salt was so painful in his eyes that he could not see.

He came to the surface, swam to shore, and went back to the villa to wait for his mother. Soon she walked slowly up the path, swinging her striped bag, the flushed, naked arm dangling beside her. "I want some swimming goggles," he panted, defiant and beseeching.

She gave him a patient, inquisitive look as she said casually, "Well, of course, darling."

But now, now, now! He must have them this minute, and no other time. He nagged and pestered until she went with him to a shop. As soon as she had bought the goggles, he grabbed them from her hand as if she were going to claim them for herself, and was off, running down the steep path to the bay.

Jerry swam out to the big barrier rock, adjusted the goggles, and dived. The impact of the water broke the rubber-enclosed vacuum, and the goggles came loose. He understood that he must swim down to the base of the rock from the surface of the water. He fixed the goggles tight and firm, filled his lungs, and floated, face down, on the water. Now he could see. It was as if he had eyes of a different kind—

fish-eyes that showed everything clear and delicate and wavering in the bright water.

Under him, six or seven feet down, was a floor of perfectly clean, shining white sand, rippled firm and hard by the tides. Two greyish shapes steered there, like long, rounded pieces of wood or slate. They were fish. He saw them nose towards each other, poise motionless, make a dart forward, swerve off, and come around again. It was like a water dance. A few inches above them, the water sparkled as if sequins were dropping through it. Fish again—myriads of minute fish, the length of his fingernail, were drifting through the water, and in a moment he could feel the innumerable tiny touches of them against his limbs. It was like swimming in flaked silver. The great rock the big boys had swum through rose sheer out of the white sand, black, tufted lightly with greenish weed. He could see no gap in it. He swam down to its base.

Again and again he rose, took a big chestful of air, and went down. Again and again he groped over the surface of the rock, feeling it, almost hugging it in the desperate need to find the entrance. And then once, while he was clinging to the black wall, his knees came up and he shot his feet out forward and they met no obstacle. He had found the hole.

He gained the surface, clambered about the stones that littered the barrier rock until he found a big one, and, with this in his arms, let himself down over the side of the rock. He dropped, with the weight, straight to the sandy floor. Clinging tight to the anchor of stone, he lay on his side and looked in under the dark shelf at the place where his feet had gone. He could see the hole. It was an irregular, dark gap, but he could see not deep into it. He let go of his anchor, clung with his hands to the edges of the hole, and tried to push himself in.

He got his head in, found his shoulders jammed, moved them in sidewise, and was inside as far as his waist. He could see nothing ahead. Something soft and clammy touched his mouth, he saw a dark frond moving against the greyish rock, and panic filled him. He thought of octopuses, of clinging weed. He pushed himself out backward and caught a glimpse, as he retreated, of a harmless tentacle of seaweed drifting in the mouth of the tunnel. But it was enough. He reached the sunlight, swam to shore, and lay on the diving rock. He looked down into the blue well of water. He knew he must find his way through that cave, or hole, or tunnel, and out the other side.

First, he thought, he must learn to control his breathing. He let himself down into the water with another big stone in his arms, so that he could lie effortlessly on the bottom of the sea. He counted. One, two, three. He counted steadily. He could hear the movement of blood in his chest. Fifty-one, fifty-two. . . . His chest was hurting. He let go of the rock and went up into the air. He saw that the sun was low. He rushed to the villa and found his mother at her supper. She said only "Did you enjoy yourself?" and he said "Yes."

All night, the boy dreamed of the water-filled cave in the rock, and as soon as breakfast was over he went to the bay.

That night, his nose bled badly. For hours he had been underwater, learning to hold his breath, and now he felt weak and dizzy. His mother said, "I shouldn't overdo things, darling, if I were you."

That day and the next, Jerry exercised his lungs as if everything, the whole of his life, all that he would become, depended upon it. And again his nose bled at night, and his mother insisted on his coming with her the next day. It was a torment to him to waste a day of his careful self-training, but he stayed with her on that other beach, which now seemed a place for small children, a place where his mother might lie safe in the sun. It was not his beach.

He did not ask for permission, on the following day, to go to his beach. He went, before his mother could consider the complicated rights and wrongs of the matter. A day's rest, he discovered, had improved his count by ten. The big boys had made the passage while he counted a hundred and sixty. He had been counting fast, in his fright. Probably now, if he tried, he could get through that long tunnel, but he was not going to try yet. A curious, most unchildlike persistence, a controlled impatience, made him wait. In the meantime, he lay underwater on the white sand, littered now by stones he had brought down from the upper air, and studied the entrance to the tunnel. He knew every jut and corner of it, as far as it was possible to see. It was as if he already felt its sharpness about his shoulders.

He sat by the clock in the villa, when his mother was not near, and checked his time. He was incredulous and then proud to find he could hold his breath without strain for two minutes. The words "two minutes", authorized by the clock, brought the adventure that was so necessary to him close.

In another four days, his mother said casually one morning, they must go home. On the day before they left, he would do it. He would do it if it killed him, he said defiantly to himself. But two days before they were to leave—a day of triumph when he increased his count by fifteen—his nose bled so badly that he turned dizzy and had to lie limply over the big rock like a bit of seaweed, watching the thick red blood flow on to the rock and trickle slowly down to the sea. He was frightened. Supposing he turned dizzy in the tunnel? Supposing he died there, trapped? Supposing—his head went around, in the hot sun, and he almost gave up. He thought he would return to the house and lie down, and next summer, perhaps, when he had another year's growth in him—*then* he would go through the hole.

But even after he had made the decision, or thought he had, he found himself sitting up on the rock and looking down into the water, and he knew that now, this moment, when his nose had only just stopped bleeding, when his head was still sore and throbbing—this was the moment when he would try. If he did not do it now, he never would. He was trembling with fear that he would not go, and he was trembling with horror at that long, long tunnel under the rock, under the sea. Even in the open sunlight, the barrier rock seemed very wide and very heavy; tons of rock pressed down on where he would go. If he died there, he would lie until one day—perhaps not before next year—those big boys would swim into it and find it blocked.

He put on his goggles, fitted them tight, tested the vacuum. His hands were shaking. Then he chose the biggest stone he could carry and slipped over the edge of the rock until half of him was in the cool, enclosing water and half in the hot sun. He looked up once at the empty sky, filled his lungs once, twice, and then sank fast to the bottom with the stone. He let it go and began to count. He took the edges of the hole in his hands and drew himself into it, wriggling his shoulders in sideways as he remembered he must, kicking himself along with his feet.

Soon he was clear inside. He was in a small rock-bound hole filled with yellowish-grey water. The water was pushing him up against the roof. The roof was sharp and pained his back. He pulled himself along with his hands—fast, fast—and used his legs as levers. His head knocked against something; a sharp pain dizzied him. Fifty, fifty-one, fifty-two. . . . He was without light, and the water seemed to press upon him with the weight of rock. Seventy-one, seventy-two. . . . There was no strain on his lungs. He felt like an inflated balloon, his lungs were so light and easy, but his head was pulsing.

He was being continually pressed against the sharp roof, which felt slimy as well as sharp. Again he thought of octopuses, and wondered if the tunnel might be filled with weed that could tangle him. He gave himself a panicky, convulsive kick forward, ducked his head, and swam. His feet and hands moved freely, as if in open water. The hole must have widened out. He thought he must be swimming fast, and he was frightened of banging his head if the tunnel narrowed.

A hundred, a hundred and one. . . . The water paled. Victory filled him. His lungs were beginning to hurt. A few more strokes and he would be out. He was counting wildly; he said a hundred and fifteen, and then, a long time later, a hundred and fifteen again. The water was a clear jewel-green all round him. Then he saw, above his head, a crack running up through the rock. Sunlight was falling through it, showing the clean dark rock of the tunnel, a single mussel shell, and darkness ahead.

He was at the end of what he could do. He looked up at the crack as if it were filled with air and not water, as if he could put his mouth to it to draw in air. A hundred and fifteen, he heard himself say inside his head—but he had said that long ago. He must go on into the blackness ahead, or he would drown. His head was swelling, his lungs cracking. A hundred and fifteen, a hundred and fifteen pounded through his head, and he feebly clutched at rocks in the dark, pulling himself forward, leaving the brief space of sunlit water behind. He felt he was dying. He was no longer quite conscious. He struggled on in the darkness between lapses into unconsciousness. An immense, swelling pain filled his head, and then the darkness cracked with an explosion of green light. His hands, groping forward, met nothing, and his feet, kicking back, propelled him out into the open sea.

He drifted to the surface, his face turned up to the air. He was gasping like a fish. He felt he would sink now and drown; he could not swim the few feet back to the rock. Then he was clutching it and pulling himself up on to it. He lay face down, gasping. He could see nothing but a red-veined, clotted dark. His eyes must have burst, he thought; they were full of blood. He tore off his goggles and a gout of blood went into the sea. His nose was bleeding, and the blood had filled the goggles.

He scooped up handfuls of water from the cool, salty sea, to splash on his face, and did not know whether it was blood or salt water he tasted. After a time, his heart quieted, his eyes cleared, and he sat up. He could see the local boys diving and playing half a mile away. He did not want them. He wanted nothing but to get back home and lie down.

In a short while, Jerry swam to shore and climbed slowly up the path to the villa. He flung himself on his bed and slept, waking at the sound of feet on the path outside. His mother was coming back. He rushed to the bathroom, thinking she must not see his face with bloodstains, or tearstains, on it. He came out of the bathroom and met her as she walked into the villa, smiling, her eyes lighting up.

"Have a nice morning?" she asked, laying her hand on his warm brown shoulder a moment.

"Oh, yes, thank you," he said.

"You look a bit pale." And then, sharp and anxious, "How did you bang your head?"

"Oh, just banged it," he told her.

She looked at him closely. He was strained. His eyes were glazed-looking. She was worried. And then she said to herself, "Oh, don't fuss! Nothing can happen. He can swim like a fish."

They sat down to lunch together.

"Mummy," he said, "I can stay under water for two minutes—three minutes, at least." It came bursting out of him.

"Can you, darling?" she said. "Well, I shouldn't overdo it. I don't think you ought to swim any more today."

She was ready for a battle of wills, but he gave in at once. It was no longer of the least importance to go to the bay.

462

CHRISTMAS IS A SAD SEASON FOR THE POOR

JOHN CHEEVER

John Cheever

CHRISTMAS IS A SAD season. The phrase came to Charlie an instant after the alarm clock had waked him, and named for him an amorphous depression that had troubled him all the previous evening. The sky outside his window was black. He sat up in bed and pulled the light chain that hung in front of his nose. Christmas is a very sad day of the year, he thought. Of all the millions of people in New York, I am practically the only one who has to get up in the cold black of six a.m. on Christmas Day in the morning; I am practically the only one.

He dressed, and when he went downstairs from the top floor of the rooming house in which he lived, the only sounds he heard were the coarse sounds of sleep; the only lights burning were lights that had been forgotten. Charlie ate some breakfast in an all-night lunch wagon and took an elevated train uptown. From Third Avenue, he walked over to Sutton Place. The neighborhood was dark. House after house put into the shine of the streetlights a wall of black windows. Millions and millions were sleeping, and this general loss of consciousness generated an impression of abandonment, as if this were the fall of the city, the end of time.

He opened the iron-and-glass doors of the apartment building where he had been working for six months as an elevator operator, and went through the elegant lobby to a locker room at the back. He put on a striped vest with brass buttons, a false ascot, a pair of pants with a light blue stripe on the seam, and a coat. The night elevator man was dozing on the little bench in the car. Charlie woke him. The night elevator man told him thickly that the day doorman had been taken sick and wouldn't be in that day. With the doorman sick, Charlie wouldn't have any relief for lunch, and a lot of people would expect him to whistle for cabs.

CHARLIE HAD BEEN on duty a few minutes when 14 rang—a Mrs. Hewing, who, he happened to know, was kind of immoral. Mrs. Hewing hadn't been to bed yet, and she got into the elevator wearing a long dress under her fur coat. She was followed by her two funny-looking dogs. He took her down and watched her go out into the dark and take her dogs to the curb. She was outside for only a few minutes. Then she came in and he took her up to 14 again. When she got off the elevator, she said, "Merry Christmas, Charlie."

"Well, it isn't much of a holiday for me, Mrs. Hewing," he said. "I think Christmas is a very sad season of the year. It isn't that people around here ain't generous—I mean I got plenty of tips—but, you see, I live alone in a furnished room and I don't have any family or anything, and Christmas isn't much of a holiday for me."

"I'm sorry, Charlie," Mrs. Hewing said. "I don't have any family myself. It is kind of sad when you're alone, isn't it?" She called her dogs and followed them into her apartment. He went down.

It was quiet then, and Charlie lighted a cigarette. The heating plant in the basement encompassed the building at that hour in a regular and profound vibration, and the sullen noises of arriving steam heat began to resound, first in the lobby and then to reverberate up through all the sixteen stories, but this was a mechanical awakening, and it didn't lighten his loneliness or his petulance. The black air outside the glass doors had begun to turn blue, but the blue light seemed to have no source; it appeared in the middle of the air. It was a tearful light, and as it picked out the empty street he wanted to cry. Then a cab drove up, and the Walsers got out, drunk and dressed in evening clothes, and he took them up to their penthouse. The Walsers got him to brooding about the difference between his life in a furnished room and the lives of the people overhead. It was terrible.

Then the early churchgoers began to ring, but there were only three of these that morning. A few more went off to church at eight o'clock, but the majority of the building remained unconscious, although the smell of bacon and coffee had begun to drift into the elevator shaft.

At a little after nine, a nursemaid came down with a child. Both the nursemaid and the child had a deep tan and had just returned, he knew, from Bermuda. He had never been to Bermuda. He, Charlie, was a prisoner, confined eight hours a day to a six-by-eight elevator cage, which was confined, in turn, to a sixteen-story shaft. In one building or another, he had made his living as an elevator operator for ten years. He estimated the average trip at about an eighth of a mile, and when he thought of the thousands of miles he had traveled, when he thought that he might have driven the car through the mists above the Caribbean and set it down on some coral beach in Bermuda, he held the narrowness of his travels against his passengers, as if it were not the nature of the elevator but the pressure of their lives that confined him, as if they had clipped his wings.

He was thinking about this when the DePauls, on 9, rang. They wished him a merry Christmas.

"Well, it's nice of you to think of me," he said as they descended, "but it isn't much of a holiday for me. Christmas is a sad season when you're poor. I live alone in a furnished room. I don't have any family."

"Who do you have dinner with, Charlie?" Mrs. DePaul asked.

"I don't have any Christmas dinner," Charlie said. "I just get a sandwich."

"Oh, Charlie!" Mrs. DePaul was a stout woman with an impulsive heart, and Charlie's plaint struck at her holiday mood as if she had been caught in a cloudburst. "I do wish we could share our Christmas dinner with you, you know," she said. "I come from Vermont, you know, and when I was a child, you know, we always used to have a great many people at our table. The mailman, you know, and the schoolteacher, and just anybody who didn't have any family of their own, you know, and I wish we could share our dinner with you the way we used to, you know, and I don't see any reason why we can't. We can't have you at the table, you know, because you couldn't leave the elevator—could you?—but just as soon as Mr. DePaul has carved the goose, I'll give you a ring, and I'll arrange a tray for you, you know, and I want you to come up and at least share our Christmas dinner."

Charlie thanked them, and their generosity surprised him, but he wondered if, with the arrival of friends and relatives, they wouldn't forget their offer.

Then old Mrs. Gadshill rang, and when she wished him a merry Christmas, he hung his head.

"It isn't much of a holiday for me, Mrs. Gadshill," he said. "Christmas is a sad season if you're poor. You see, I don't have any family. I live alone in a furnished room."

"I don't have any family either, Charlie," Mrs. Gadshill said. She spoke with a pointed lack of petulance, but her grace was forced. "That is, I don't have any children with me today. I have three children and seven grandchildren, but none of them can see their way to coming east for Christmas with me. Of course, I understand their problems. I know that it's difficult to travel with children during the holidays, although I always seemed to manage it when I was their age, but people feel differently, and we mustn't condemn them for the things we can't understand. But I know how you feel, Charlie. I haven't any family either. I'm just as lonely as you."

Mrs. Gadshill's speech didn't move him. Maybe she was lonely, but she had a ten-room apartment and three servants and bucks and bucks and diamonds and diamonds, and there were plenty of poor kids in the slums who would be happy at a chance at the food her cook threw away. Then he thought about poor kids. He sat down on a chair in the lobby and thought about them.

They got the worst of it. Beginning in the fall, there was all this excitement about Christmas and how it was a day for them. After Thanksgiving, they couldn't miss it. It was fixed so they couldn't miss it. The wreaths and decorations everywhere, and bells ringing, and trees in the park, and Santa Clauses on every corner, and pictures in the magazines and newspapers and on every wall and window in the city told them that if they were good, they would get what they wanted. Even if they couldn't read, they couldn't miss it. They couldn't miss it even if they were blind. It got into the air the poor kids inhaled. Every time they took a walk, they'd see all the expensive toys in the store windows, and they'd write letters to Santa Claus, and their mothers and fathers would promise to mail them, and after the kids had gone to sleep, they'd burn the letters in the stove. And when it came Christmas morning, how could you explain it, how could you tell them that Santa Claus only visited the rich, that he didn't know about the good? How could you face them when all you had to give them was a balloon or a lollipop?

On the way home from work a few nights earlier, Charlie had seen a woman and a little girl going down Fifty-ninth Street. The little girl was crying. He guessed she was crying, he knew she was crying, because she'd seen all the things in the toy-store windows and couldn't understand why none of them were for her. Her mother did housework, he guessed; or maybe was a waitress, and he saw them going back to a room like his, with green walls and no heat, on Christmas Eve, to eat a can of soup. And he saw the little girl hang up her ragged stocking and fall asleep, and he saw the mother looking through her purse for something to put into the stocking— This reverie was interrupted by a bell on 11. He went up, and Mr. and Mrs. Fuller were waiting.

When they wished him a merry Christmas, he said, "Well, it isn't much of a holiday for me, Mrs. Fuller. Christmas is a sad season when you're poor."

"Do you have any children, Charlie?" Mrs. Fuller asked.

"Four living," he said. "Two in the grave." The majesty of his lie overwhelmed him. "Mrs. Leary's a cripple," he added.

"How sad, Charlie," Mrs. Fuller said. She started out of the elevator when it reached the lobby, and then she turned. "I want to give your children some presents, Charlie," she said. "Mr. Fuller and I are going to pay a call now, but when we come back, I want to give you some things for your children."

He thanked her. Then the bell rang on 4, and he went up to get the Westons.

"It isn't much of a holiday for me," he told them when they wished him a merry Christmas. "Christmas is a sad season when you're poor. You see, I live alone in a furnished room."

"Poor Charlie," Mrs. Weston said. "I know just how you feel. During the war, when Mr. Weston was away, I was all alone at Christmas. I didn't have any Christmas dinner or a tree or anything. I just scrambled myself some eggs and sat there and cried." Mr. Weston, who had gone into the lobby, called impatiently to his wife. "I know just how you feel, Charlie," Mrs. Weston said.

BY NOON, THE climate in the elevator shaft had changed from bacon and coffee to poultry and game, and the house, like an enormous and complex homestead, was absorbed in the preparations for a domestic feast. The children and their nursemaids had all returned from the park. Grandmothers and aunts were arriving in limousines. Most of the people who came through the lobby were carrying packages wrapped in colored paper, and were wearing their best furs and new clothes. Charlie continued to complain to most of the tenants when they wished him a merry Christmas, changing his story from the lonely bachelor to the poor father, and back again, as his mood changed, but this outpouring of melancholy, and the sympathy it aroused, didn't make him feel any better.

At half past one, 9 rang, and when he went up, Mr. DePaul was standing in the door of their apartment holding a cocktail shaker and a glass. "Here's a little Christmas cheer, Charlie," he said, and he poured Charlie a drink. Then a maid appeared with a tray of covered dishes, and Mrs. DePaul came out of the living room. "Merry Christmas, Charlie," she said. "I had Mr. DePaul carve the goose early, so that you could have some, you know. I didn't want to put the dessert on the tray, because I was afraid it would melt, you know, so when we have our dessert, we'll call you."

"And what is Christmas without presents?" Mr. DePaul said, and he brought a large, flat box from the hall and laid it on top of the covered dishes.

"You people make it seem like a real Christmas to me," Charlie said. Tears started into his eyes. "Thank you, thank you."

"Merry Christmas! Merry Christmas!" they called, and they watched him carry his dinner and his present into the elevator. He took the tray and the box into the locker room when he got down. On the tray, there was a soup, some kind of creamed fish, and a serving of goose. The bell rang again, but before he answered it, he tore open the DePaul's box and saw that it held a dressing gown. Their generosity and their cocktail had begun to work on his brain, and he went jubilantly up to 12. Mrs. Gadshill's maid was standing in the door with a tray, and Mrs. Gadshill stood behind her. "Merry Christmas, Charlie!" she said. He thanked her, and tears came into his eyes again. On the way down, he drank off the glass of sherry on Mrs. Gadshill's tray. Mrs. Gadshill's contribution was a mixed grill. He ate the lamb chop with his fingers. The bell was ringing again, and he wiped his face with a paper towel and went up to 11. "Merry Christmas, Charlie," Mrs. Fuller said, and she was standing in the door with her arms full of packages wrapped in silver paper, just like a picture in an advertisement, and Mr. Fuller was beside her with an arm around her, and they both looked as if they were going to cry. "Here are some things I want you to take home to your children," Mrs. Fuller said. "And here's something for Mrs. Leary and here's something for you. And if you want to take these things out to the elevator, we'll have your dinner ready for you in a minute." He carried the things into the elevator and came back for the tray. "Merry Christmas, Charlie!" both of the Fullers called after him as he closed the door. He took their dinner and their presents into the locker room and tore open the box that was marked for him. There was an alligator wallet in it, with Mr. Fuller's initials in the corner. Their dinner was also goose, and he ate a piece of the meat with his fingers and was washing it down with a cocktail when the bell rang. He went up again. This time it was the Westons. "Merry Christmas, Charlie!" they said, and they gave him a cup of eggnog, a turkey dinner, and a present. Their gift was also a dressing gown. Then 7 rang, and when he went up, there was another dinner and some more toys. Then 14 rang, and when he went up, Mrs. Hewing was standing in the hall, in a kind of negligee, holding a pair of riding boots in one hand and some neckties in the other. She had been crying and drinking. "Merry Christmas, Charlie," she said tenderly. "I wanted to give you something, and I've been thinking about you all morning, and I've been all over the apartment, and these are the only things I could find that a man might want. These are the only things that Mr. Brewer left. I don't suppose you'd have any use for the riding boots, but wouldn't you like the neckties?" Charlie took the neckties and thanked her and hurried back to the car, for the elevator bell had rung three times.

BY THREE O'CLOCK CHARLIE HAD fourteen dinners spread on the table and the floor of the locker room, and the bell kept ringing. Just as he started to eat one, he would have to go up and get another, and he was in the middle of the Parsons' roast beef when he had to go up and get the DePaul's dessert.

He kept the door of the locker room closed, for he sensed that the quality of charity is exclusive and that his friends would have been disappointed to find that they were not the only ones to try to lessen his loneliness. There were goose, turkey, chicken, pheasant, grouse, and pigeon. There were trout and salmon, creamed scallops and oysters, lobster, crabmeat, whitebait, and clams. There were plum puddings, mince pies, mousses, puddles of melted ice cream, layer cakes, torten, éclairs, and two slices of Bavarian cream. He had dressing gowns, neckties, cuff links, socks, and handkerchiefs, and one of the tenants had asked for his neck size and then given him three green shirts. There were a glass teapot filled, the label said, with jasmine honey, four bottles of after-shave lotion, some alabaster bookends, and a dozen steak knives.

The avalanche of charity he had precipitated filled the locker room and made him hesitant, now and then, as if he had touched some well-spring in the female heart that would bury him alive in food and dressing gowns.

He had made almost no headway on the food, for all the servings were preternaturally large, as if loneliness had been counted on to generate in him a brutish appetite. Nor had he opened any of the presents that had been given to him for his imaginary children, but he had drunk everything they sent down, and around him were the dregs of Martinis, Manhattans, Old-Fashioneds, champagne-and-raspberry-shrub cocktails, eggnogs, Bronxes, and Side Cars.

His face was blazing. He loved the world, and the world loved him. When he thought back over his life, it appeared to him in a rich and wonderful light, full of astonishing experiences and unusual friends. He thought that his job as an elevator operator—cruising up and down through hundreds of feet of perilous space—demanded the nerve and the intellect of a birdman. All the constraints of his life—the green walls of his room and the months of unemployment—dissolved. No one was ringing, but he got into the elevator and shot it at full speed up to the penthouse and down again, up and down, to test his wonderful mastery of space.

A bell rang on 12 while he was cruising, and he stopped in his flight long enough to pick up Mrs. Gadshill. As the car started to fall, he took his hands off the controls in a paroxysm of joy and shouted, "Strap on your safety belt, Mrs. Gadshill! We're going to make a loop-the-loop!"

Mrs. Gadshill shrieked. Then, for some reason, she sat down on the floor of the elevator. Why was her face so pale, he wondered; why was she sitting on the floor? She shrieked again. He grounded the car gently, and cleverly, he thought, and opened the door.

"I'm sorry if I scared you, Mrs. Gadshill," he said meekly. "I was only fooling."

She shrieked again. Then she ran out into the lobby, screaming for the superintendent.

The superintendent fired Charlie and took over the elevator himself. The news that he was out of work stung Charlie for a minute. It was his first contact with human meanness that day. He sat down in the locker room and gnawed on a drumstick. His drinks were beginning to let him down, and while it had not reached him yet, he felt a miserable soberness in the offing. The excess of food and presents around him began to make him feel guilty and unworthy. He regretted bitterly the lie he had told about his children. He was a single man with simple needs. He had abused the goodness of the people upstairs. He was unworthy.

Then up through this drunken train of thought surged the sharp figure of his landlady and her three skinny children. He thought of them sitting in their basement room. The cheer of Christmas had passed them by. This image got him to his feet. The realization that he was in a position to give, that he could bring happiness easily to someone else, sobered him.

He took a big burlap sack, which was used for collecting waste, and began to stuff it, first with his presents and then with the presents for his imaginary children. He worked with the haste of a man whose train is approaching the station, for he could hardly wait to see those long faces light up when he came in the door. He changed his clothes, and, fired by a wonderful and unfamiliar sense of power, he slung his

CHRISTMAS IS A SAD SEASON FOR THE POOR / John Cheever

bag over his shoulder like a regular Santa Claus, went out the back way, and took a taxi to the Lower East Side.

The landlady and her children had just finished off a turkey, which had been sent to them by the local Democratic club, and they were stuffed and uncomfortable when Charlie began pounding on the door, shouting "Merry Christmas!"

He dragged the bag in after him and dumped the presents for the children onto the floor. There were dolls and musical toys, blocks, sewing kits, an Indian suit, and a loom, and it appeared to him that, as he had hoped, his arrival in the basement dispelled its gloom.

When half the presents had been opened, he gave the landlady a bathrobe and went upstairs to look over the things he had been given for himself.

Now, THE LANDLADY's children had already received so many presents by the time Charlie arrived that they were confused with receiving, and it was only the landlady's intuitive grasp of the nature of charity that made her allow the children to open some of the presents while Charlie was still in the room, but as soon as he had gone, she stood between the children and the presents that were still unopened.

"Now, you kids have had enough already," she said. "You kids have got your share. Just look at the things you got there. Why, you ain't even played with the half of them. Mary Anne, you ain't even looked at that doll the Fire Department give you. Now, a nice thing to do would be to take all this stuff that's left over to those poor people on Hudson Street—them Dekkers. They ain't got nothing." A beatific light came into her face when she realized that she could give, that she could bring cheer, that she could put a healing finger on a case needier than hers, and—like Mrs. DePaul and Mrs. Weston, like Charlie himself and like Mrs. Dekker, when Mrs. Dekker was to think, subsequently, of the poor Shannons—first love, then charity, and then a sense of power drove her. "Now, you kids help me get all this stuff together. Hurry, hurry, hurry," she said, for it was dark then, and she knew that we are bound, one to another, in licentious benevolence for only a single day, and that day was nearly over. She was tired, but she couldn't rest, she couldn't rest.

472

THE FURNISHED ROOM

O. HENRY

O Henry

Restless, shifting, fugacious as time itself is a certain vast bulk of the population of the red brick district of the lower West Side. Homeless, they have a hundred homes. They flit from furnished room to furnished room, transients forever—transients in abode, transients in heart and mind. They sing "Home, Sweet Home" in ragtime; they carry their *lares et penates* in a bandbox; their vine is entwined about a picture hat; a rubber plant is their fig tree.

Hence the houses of this district, having had a thousand dwellers, should have a thousand tales to tell, mostly dull ones, no doubt; but it would be strange if there could not be found a ghost or two in the wake of all these vagrant guests.

One evening after dark a young man prowled among these crumbling red mansions, ringing their bells. At the twelfth he rested his lean hand baggage upon the step and wiped the dust from his hatband and forehead. The bell sounded faint and far away in some remote, hollow depths.

To the door of this, the twelfth house whose bell he had rung, came a housekeeper who made him think of an unwholesome, surfeited worm that had eaten its nut to a hollow shell and now sought to fill the vacancy with edible lodgers.

He asked if there was a room to let.

"Come in," said the housekeeper. Her voice came from her throat; her throat seemed lined with fur. "I have the third-floor-back, vacant since a week back. Should you wish to look at it?"

The young man followed her up the stairs. A faint light from no particular source mitigated the shadows of the halls. They trod noiselessly upon a stair carpet that its own loom would have forsworn. It seemed to have become vegetable; to have degenerated in that rank, sunless air to lush lichen or spreading moss that grew in patches to the staircase and was viscid under the foot like organic matter. At each turn of the stairs were vacant niches in the wall. Perhaps plants had once been set within them. If so, they had died in that foul and tainted air. It may be that statues of the saints had stood there, but it was not difficult to conceive that imps and devils had dragged them forth in the darkness and down to the unholy depths of some furnished pit below.

"This is the room," said the housekeeper, from her furry throat. "It's a nice room. It ain't often vacant. I had some most elegant people in it last summer—no trouble at all, and paid in advance to the minute. The water's at the end of the hall. Sprowls and Mooney kept it three months. They done a vaudeville sketch. Miss B'retta Sprowls—you may have heard of her—oh, that was just the stage names—right there over the dresser is where the marriage certificate hung, framed. The gas is here, and you see there is plenty of closet room. It's a room everybody likes. It never stays idle long."

"Do you have many theatrical people rooming here?" asked the young man.

"They comes and goes. A good proportion of my lodgers is connected with the theaters. Yes, sir, this is the theatrical district. Actor people never stays long anywhere. I get my share. Yes, they comes and they goes."

He engaged the room, paying for a week in advance. He was tired, he said, and would take possession at once. He counted out the money. The room had been made ready, she said, even to towels and water. As the housekeeper moved away he put, for the thousandth time, the question that he carried at the end of his tongue.

"A young girl—Miss Vashner—Miss Eloise Vashner—do you remember such a one among your lodgers? She would be singing on the stage, most likely. A fair girl, of medium height and slender, with reddish gold hair and a dark mole near her left eyebrow."

"No, I don't remember the name. Them stage people has names they change as often as their rooms. No, I don't call that one to mind."

No. Always no. Five months of ceaseless interrogation and the inevitable negative. So much time spent by day in questioning managers, agents, schools and choruses; by night among the audiences of theaters from all-star casts down to music halls so low that he dreaded to find what he most hoped for. He who had loved her best had tried to find her. He was sure that since her disappearance from home this great, water-girt city held her somewhere, but it was like a monstrous quicksand, shifting its particles constantly, with no foundation, its upper granules of today buried tomorrow in ooze and slime.

The furnished room received its latest guest with a first glow of pseudo hospitality, a hectic, haggard, perfunctory welcome like the specious smile of a demirep. The sophistical comfort came in reflected gleams from the decayed furniture, the ragged brocade upholstery of a couch and two chairs, a foot-wide cheap pier glass between the two windows, from one or two gilt picture frames and a brass bedstead in a corner.

The guest reclined, inert, upon a chair, while the room, confused in speech as though it were an apartment in Babel, tried to discourse to him of its divers tenantry.

A polychromatic rug like some brilliant-flowered, rectangular, tropical islet lay surrounded by a billowy sea of soiled matting. Upon the gay-papered wall were those pictures that pursue the homeless one from house to house—*The Huguenot Lovers, The First Quarrel, The Wedding Breakfast, Psyche at the Fountain.* The mantel's chastely severe outline was ingloriously veiled behind some pert drapery drawn rakishly askew like the sashes of the Amazonian ballet. Upon it was some desolate flotsam cast aside by the room's marooned when a lucky sail had borne them to a fresh port—a trifling vase or two, pictures of actresses, a medicine bottle, some stray cards out of a deck.

One by one, as the characters of a cryptograph became explicit, the little signs left by the furnished room's procession of guests developed a significance. The threadbare space in the rug in front of the dresser told that lovely women had marched in the throng. The tiny fingerprints on the wall spoke of little prisoners trying to feel their way to sun and air. A splattered stain, raying like the shadow of a bursting bomb, witnessed where a hurled glass or bottle had splintered with its contents against the wall. Across the pier glass had been scrawled with a diamond in staggering letters the name Marie. It seemed that the succession of dwellers in the furnished room had turned in fury—perhaps tempted beyond forbearance by its garish coldness—and wreaked upon it their passions. The furniture was chipped and bruised; the couch, distorted by bursting springs, seemed a horrible monster that had been slain during the stress of some grotesque convulsion. Some more potent upheaval had cloven a great slice from the marble mantel. Each plank in the floor owned its particular cant and shriek as from a separate and individual agony. It seemed incredible that all this malice and injury had been wrought upon the room by those who had called it for a time their home; and yet it may have been the cheated home instinct surviving blindly, the resentful rage at false household gods that had kindled their wrath. A hut that is our own we can sweep and adorn and cherish.

The young tenant in the chair allowed these thoughts to file, soft-shod, through his mind, while there drifted into the room furnished sounds and furnished scents. He heard in one room a tittering and incontinent, slack laughter; in others the monologue of a scold, the rattling of dice, a lullaby, and one crying dully; above him a banjo tinkled with spirit. Doors banged somewhere; the elevated trains roared intermittently; a cat yowled miserably upon a back fence. And he breathed the breath of the house—a dank savor rather than a smell—a cold, musty effluvium as from underground vaults mingled with the reeking exhalations of linoleum and mildewed and rotten woodwork.

Then suddenly, as he rested there, the room was filled with the strong, sweet odor of mignonette. It came as upon a single buffet of wind with such sureness and fragrance and emphasis that it almost seemed a living visitant. And the man cried aloud, "What, dear?" as if he had been called, and sprang up and faced about. The rich odor clung to him and wrapped him around. He reached out his arms for it, all his senses for the time confused and commingled. How could one be peremptorily called by an odor? Surely it must have been a sound. But was it not the sound that had touched, that had caressed him?

"She has been in this room," he cried, and he sprang to wrest from it a token, for he knew he would recognize the smallest thing that had belonged to her or that she had touched. This enveloping scent of mignonette, the odor that she had loved and made her own—whence came it?

The room had been but carelessly set in order. Scattered upon the flimsy dresser scarf were half a dozen hairpins—those discreet, indistinguishable friends of womankind, feminine of gender, infinite of mood and uncommunicative of tense. These he ignored, conscious of their triumphant lack of identity. Ransacking the drawers of the dresser he came upon a discarded, tiny, ragged handkerchief. He pressed it to his face. It was racy and insolent with heliotrope; he hurled it to the floor. In another drawer he found odd buttons, a theater program, a pawnbroker's card, two lost marshmallows, a book on the divination of dreams. In the last was a woman's black satin hair bow, which halted him, poised between ice and fire. But the black satin hair bow also is femininity's demure, impersonal common ornament and tells no tales.

And then he traversed the room like a hound on the scent, skimming the walls, considering the corners of the bulging matting on his hands and knees, rummaging mantel and tables, the curtains and hangings, the drunken cabinet in the corner, for a visible sign, unable to perceive that she was there beside, around, against, within, above him, clinging to him, wooing him, calling him so poignantly through the finer senses that even his grosser ones became cognizant of the call. Once again he answered loudly, "Yes, dear!" and turned, wild-eyed, to gaze on vacancy, for he could not yet discern form and color and love and outstretched arms in the odor of mignonette. Oh, God! Whence that odor, and since when have odors had a voice to call? Thus he groped.

He burrowed in crevices and corners, and found corks and cigarettes. These he passed in passive contempt. But once he found in a fold of the matting a half-smoked cigar, and this he ground beneath his heel with a green and trenchant oath. He sifted the room from end to end. He found dreary and ignoble small records of many a peripatetic tenant; but of her whom he sought, and who may have lodged there, and whose spirit seemed to hover there, he found no trace.

And then he thought of the housekeeper.

He ran from the haunted room downstairs and to a door that showed a crack of light. She came out to his knock. He smothered his excitement as best he could.

"Will you tell me, madam," he besought her, "who occupied the room I have before I came?"

"Yes, sir. I can tell you again. 'Twas Sprowls and Mooney, as I said. Miss B'retta Sprowls it was in the theaters, but Missis Mooney she was. My house is well known for respectability. The marriage certificate hung, framed, on a nail over—"

"What kind of a lady was Miss Sprowls—in looks, I mean?"

"Why, black-haired, sir, short, and stout, with a comical face. They left a week ago Tuesday."

"And before they occupied it?"

"Why, there was a single gentleman connected with the draying business. He left owing me a week. Before him was Missis Crowder and her two children, that stayed four months; and back of them was old Mr. Doyle, whose sons paid for him. He kept the room six months. That goes back a year, sir, and further I do not remember."

He thanked her and crept back to his room. The room was dead. The essence that had vivified it was gone. The perfume of mignonette had departed. In its place was the old, stale odor of moldy house furniture, of atmosphere in storage.

The ebbing of his hope drained his faith. He sat staring at the yellow, singing gaslight. Soon he walked to the bed and began to tear the sheets into strips. With the blade of his knife he drove them tightly into every crevice around windows and door. When all was snug and taut he turned out the light, turned the gas full on again and laid himself gratefully upon the bed.

IT WAS Mrs. McCool's night to go with the can for beer. So she fetched it and sat with Mrs. Purdy in one of those subterranean retreats where housekeepers forgather and the worm dieth seldom.

"I rented out my third-floor-back this evening," said Mrs. Purdy, across a fine circle of foam. "A young man took it. He went up to bed two hours ago."

"Now, did ye, Mrs. Purdy, ma'am?" said Mrs. McCool, with intense admiration. "You do be a wonder for rentin' rooms of that kind. And did ye tell him, then?" she concluded in a husky whisper laden with mystery.

"Rooms," said Mrs. Purdy, in her furriest tones, "are furnished for to rent. I did not tell him, Mrs. McCool."

" 'Tis right ye are, ma'am; 'tis by renting rooms we kape alive. Ye have the rale sense for business, ma'am. There be many people will rayjict the rentin' of a room if they be tould a suicide has been after dyin' in the bed of it."

"As you say, we has our living to be making," remarked Mrs. Purdy.

"Yis, ma'am; 'tis true. 'Tis just one wake ago this day I helped ye lay out the third-floor-back. A pretty slip of a colleen she was to be killin' herself wid the gas—a swate little face she had, Mrs. Purdy, ma'am."

"She'd a-been called handsome, as you say," said Mrs. Purdy, assenting but critical, "but for that mole she had a-growin' by her left eyebrow. Do fill up your glass again, Mrs. McCool."

THE ELEPHANT'S CHILD
RUDYARD KIPLING

Rudyard Kipling [signature]

IN THE HIGH and Far-Off Times the Elephant, O Best Beloved, had no trunk. He had only a blackish, bulgy nose, as big as a boot, that he could wriggle about from side to side; but he couldn't pick up things with it. But there was one Elephant—a new Elephant—an Elephant's Child— who was full of 'satiable curtiosity, and that means he asked ever so many questions. *And* he lived in Africa, and he filled all Africa with his 'satiable curtiosities. He asked his tall aunt, the Ostrich, why her tail-feathers grew just so, and his tall aunt the Ostrich spanked him with her hard, hard claw. He asked his tall uncle, the Giraffe, what made his skin spotty, and his tall uncle, the Giraffe, spanked him with his hard, hard hoof. And still he was full of 'satiable curtiosity! He asked his broad aunt, the Hippopotamus, why her eyes were red, and his broad aunt, the Hippopotamus, spanked him with her broad, broad hoof; and he asked his hairy uncle, the Baboon, why melons tasted just so, and his hairy uncle, the Baboon, spanked him with his hairy, hairy paw. And *still* he was full of 'satiable curtiosity! He asked questions about everything that he saw, or heard, or felt, or smelt, or touched, and all his uncles and his aunts spanked him. And still he was full of 'satiable curtiosity!

One fine morning in the middle of the Precession of the Equinoxes this 'satiable Elephant's Child asked a new fine question that he had never asked before. He asked, "What does the Crocodile have for dinner?" Then everybody said, "Hush!" in a loud and dretful tone, and they spanked him immediately and directly, without stopping, for a long time. By and by, when that was finished, he came upon Kolokolo Bird sitting in the middle of a wait-a-bit thorn-bush, and he said, "My father has spanked me, and my mother has spanked me; all my aunts and uncles have spanked me for my 'satiable curtiosity; and *still* I want to know what the Crocodile has for dinner!"

Then Kolokolo Bird said, with a mournful cry, "Go to the banks of the great grey-green, greasy Limpopo River, all set about with fever-trees, and find out."

That very next morning, when there was nothing left of the Equinoxes, because the Precession had preceded according to precedent, this 'satiable Elephant's Child took a hundred pounds of bananas (the little short red kind), and a hundred pounds of sugar-cane (the long purple kind), and seventeen melons (the greeny-crackly kind), and said to all his dear families, "Goodbye. I am going to the great grey-green, greasy Limpopo River, all set about with fever-trees, to find out what the Crocodile has for dinner." And they all spanked him once more for luck, though he asked them most politely to stop.

Then he went away, a little warm, but not at all astonished, eating melons, and throwing the rind about, because he could not pick it up.

He went from Graham's Town to Kimberley, and from Kimberley to Khama's Country, and from Khama's Country he went east by north, eating melons all the time, till at last he came to the banks of the great grey-green, greasy Limpopo River, all set about with fever-trees, precisely as Kolokolo Bird had said.

Now you must know and understand, O Best Beloved, that till that very week, and day, and hour, and minute, this 'satiable Elephant's Child had never seen a Crocodile, and did not know what one was like. It was all his 'satiable curtiosity.

The first thing that he found was a Bi-Coloured-Python-Rock-Snake curled round a rock.

"'Scuse me," said the Elephant's Child most politely, "but have you seen such a thing as a Crocodile in these promiscuous parts?"

"*Have* I seen a Crocodile?" said the Bi-Coloured-Python-Rock-Snake, in a voice of dretful scorn. "What will you ask me next?"

"'Scuse me," said the Elephant's Child, "but could you kindly tell me what he has for dinner?"

Then the Bi-Coloured-Python-Rock-Snake uncoiled himself very quickly from the rock, and spanked the Elephant's Child with his scalesome, flailsome tail.

"That is odd," said the Elephant's Child, "because my father and my mother, and my uncle and my aunt, not to mention my other aunt, the Hippopotamus, and my other uncle, the Baboon, have all spanked me for my 'satiable curtiosity—and I suppose this is the same thing."

So he said goodbye very politely to the Bi-Coloured-Python-Rock-Snake, and helped to coil him up on the rock again, and went on, a little warm, but not at all astonished, eating melons, and throwing the rind about, because he could not pick it up, till he trod on what he thought was a log of wood at the very edge of the great grey-green, greasy Limpopo River, all set about with fever-trees.

But it was really the Crocodile, O Best Beloved, and the Crocodile winked one eye—like this!

"'Scuse me," said the Elephant's Child most politely, "but do you happen to have seen a Crocodile in these promiscuous parts?"

Then the Crocodile winked the other eye, and lifted half his tail out of the mud; and the Elephant's Child stepped back most politely, because he did not wish to be spanked again.

"Come hither, Little One," said the Crocodile. "Why do you ask?"

"'Scuse me," said the Elephant's Child most politely, "but my father has spanked me, my mother has spanked me, not to mention my tall aunt, the Ostrich, and my tall uncle, the Giraffe, who can kick ever so hard, as well as my broad aunt, the Hippopotamus, and my hairy uncle, the Baboon, *and* including the Bi-Coloured-Python-Rock-Snake, with the scalesome, flailsome tail, just up the bank, who spanks harder than any of them; and *so*, if it's quite all the same to you, I don't want to be spanked any more."

"Come hither, Little One," said the Crocodile, "for I am the Crocodile," and he wept crocodile-tears to show it was quite true.

Then the Elephant's Child grew all breathless, and panted, and kneeled down on the bank and said, "You are the very person I have been looking for all these long days. Will you please tell me what you have for dinner?"

"Come hither, Little One," said the Crocodile, "and I'll whisper."

Then the Elephant's Child put his head down close to the Crocodile's musky, tusky mouth, and the Crocodile caught him by his little nose, which up to that very week, day, hour, and minute, had been no bigger than a boot, though much more useful.

"I think," said the Crocodile—and he said it between his teeth, like this—"I think today I will begin with Elephant's Child!"

At this, O Best Beloved, the Elephant's Child was much annoyed, and he said, speaking through his nose, like this, "Led go! You are hurtig be!"

Then the Bi-Coloured-Python-Rock-Snake scuffled down from the bank and said, "My young friend, if you do not now, immediately and instantly, pull as hard as ever you can, it is my opinion that your acquaintance in the large-pattern leather ulster" (and by this he meant the Crocodile) "will jerk you into yonder limpid stream before you can say Jack Robinson."

This is the way Bi-Coloured-Python-Rock-Snakes always talk.

Then the Elephant's Child sat back on his little haunches, and pulled, and pulled, and pulled, and his nose began to stretch. And the Crocodile floundered into the water, making it all creamy with great sweeps of his tail, and *he* pulled, and pulled, and pulled.

And the Elephant's Child's nose kept on stretching; and the Elephant's Child spread all his little four legs and pulled, and pulled, and pulled, and his nose kept on stretching; and the Crocodile threshed his tail like an oar, and *he* pulled, and pulled, and pulled, and at each pull the Elephant's Child's nose grew longer and longer—and it hurt him hijjus!

Then the Elephant's Child felt his legs slipping, and he said through his nose, which was now nearly five feet long, "This is too butch for be!"

Then the Bi-Coloured-Python-Rock-Snake came down from the bank, and knotted himself in a double-clove-hitch round the Elephant's Child's hind-legs, and said, "Rash and inexperienced traveller, we will now seriously devote ourselves to a little high tension, because if we do not, it is my impression that yonder self-propelling man-of-war with the armour-plated upper deck" (and by this, O Best Beloved, he meant the Crocodile) "will permanently vitiate your future career."

That is the way all Bi-Coloured-Python-Rock-Snakes always talk.

So he pulled, and the Elephant's Child pulled, and the Crocodile pulled; but the Elephant's Child and the Bi-Coloured-Python-Rock-Snake pulled hardest; and at last the Crocodile let go of the Elephant's Child's nose with a plop that you could hear all up and down the Limpopo.

Then the Elephant's Child sat down most hard and sudden; but first he was careful to say "Thank you" to the Bi-Coloured-Python-Rock-Snake; and next he was kind to his poor pulled nose, and wrapped it all up in cool banana leaves, and hung it in the great grey-green, greasy Limpopo to cool.

"What are you doing?" said the Bi-Coloured-Python-Rock-Snake.

"'Scuse me," said the Elephant's Child, "but my nose is badly out of shape, and I am waiting for it to shrink."

"Then you will have to wait a long time," said the Bi-Coloured-Python-Rock-Snake. "Some people do not know what is good for them."

The Elephant's Child sat there for three days waiting for his nose to shrink. But it never grew any shorter, and, besides, it made him squint. For, O Best Beloved, you will see and understand that the Crocodile had pulled it out into a really truly trunk same as all Elephants have today.

At the end of the third day a fly came and stung him on the shoulder, and before he knew what he was doing he lifted up his trunk and hit that fly dead with the end of it.

"'Vantage number one!" said the Bi-Coloured-Python-Rock-Snake. "You couldn't have done that with a mere-smear nose. Try and eat a little now."

Before he thought what he was doing the Elephant's Child put out his trunk and plucked a large bundle of grass, dusted it clean against his fore-legs, and stuffed it into his own mouth.

"'Vantage number two!" said the Bi-Coloured-Python-Rock-Snake. "You couldn't have done that with a mere-smear nose. Don't you think the sun is very hot here?"

"It is," said the Elephant's Child, and before he thought what he was doing he schlooped up a schloop of mud from the banks of the great grey-green, greasy Limpopo, and slapped it on his head, where it made a cool schloopy-sloshy mud-cap all trickly behind his ears.

"'Vantage number three!" said the Bi-Coloured-Python-Rock-Snake. "You couldn't have done that with a mere-smear nose. Now how do you feel about being spanked again?"

"'Scuse me," said the Elephant's Child, "but I should not like it at all."

"How would you like to spank somebody?" said the Bi-Coloured-Python-Rock-Snake.

"I should like it very much indeed," said the Elephant's Child.

"Well," said the Bi-Coloured-Python-Rock-Snake, "you will find that new nose of yours very useful to spank people with."

"Thank you," said the Elephant's Child, "I'll remember that; and now I think I'll go home to all my dear families and try."

So the Elephant's Child went home across Africa frisking and whisking his trunk. When he wanted fruit to eat he pulled fruit down from a tree, instead of waiting for it to fall as he used to do. When he wanted grass he plucked grass up from the ground, instead of going on his knees as he used to do. When the flies bit him he broke off the branch of a tree and used it as a fly-whisk; and he made himself a new cool, slushy-squashy mud-cap whenever the sun was hot. When he felt lonely walking through Africa he sang to himself down his trunk, and the noise was louder than several brass bands. He went especially out of his way to find a broad Hippopotamus (she was no relation of his), and he spanked her very hard, to make sure that the Bi-Coloured-Python-Rock-Snake had spoken the truth about his new trunk. The rest of the time he picked up the melon rinds that he had dropped on his way to the Limpopo—for he was a Tidy Pachyderm.

One dark evening he came back to all his dear families, and he coiled up his trunk and said, "How do you do?" They were very glad to see him, and immediately said, "Come here and be spanked for your 'satiable curtiosity."

"Pooh," said the Elephant's Child. "I don't think you peoples know anything about spanking, but *I* do, and I'll show you." Then he un-curled his trunk and knocked two of his dear brothers head over heels.

"O Bananas!" said they, "where did you learn that trick, and what have you done to your nose?"

"I got a new one from the Crocodile on the banks of the great grey-green, greasy Limpopo River," said the Elephant's Child. "I asked him what he had for dinner, and he gave me this to keep."

"It looks very ugly," said his hairy uncle, the Baboon.

"It does," said the Elephant's Child. "But it's very useful," and he picked up his hairy uncle, the Baboon, by one hairy leg, and hove him into a hornet's nest.

Then that bad Elephant's Child spanked all his dear families for a long time, till they were very warm and greatly astonished. He pulled out his tall Ostrich aunt's tail-feathers; and he caught his tall uncle, the Giraffe, by the hind-leg, and dragged him through a thorn-bush; and he shouted at his broad aunt, the Hippopotamus, and blew bubbles into her ear when she was sleeping in the water after meals; but he never let any one touch Kolokolo Bird.

At last things grew so exciting that his dear families went off one by one in a hurry to the banks of the great grey-green, greasy Limpopo River, all set about with fever-trees, to borrow new noses from the Crocodile. When they came back nobody spanked anybody any more; and ever since that day, O Best Beloved, all the Elephants you will ever see, besides all those that you won't, have trunks precisely like the trunk of the 'satiable Elephant's Child.

THE DAEMON LOVER

SHIRLEY JACKSON

Shirley Jackson

She HAD NOT slept well; from one thirty, when Jamie left and she went lingeringly to bed, until seven, when she at last allowed herself to get up and make coffee, she had slept fitfully, stirring awake to open her eyes and look into the half-darkness, remembering over and over, slipping again into a feverish dream. She spent almost an hour over her coffee—they were to have a real breakfast on the way—and then, unless she wanted to dress early, had nothing to do. She washed her coffee cup and made the bed, looking carefully over the clothes she planned to wear, worried unnecessarily, at the window, over whether it would be a fine day. She sat down to read, thought that she might write a letter to her sister instead, and began, in her finest handwriting, "Dearest Anne, by the time you get this I will be married. Doesn't it sound funny? I can hardly believe it myself, but when I tell you how it happened, you'll see it's even stranger than that. . . ."

Sitting, pen in hand, she hesitated over what to say next, read the lines already written, and tore up the letter. She went to the window and saw that it was undeniably a fine day. It occurred to her that perhaps she ought not to wear the blue silk dress; it was too plain, almost severe, and she wanted to be soft, feminine. Anxiously she pulled through the dresses in the closet, and hesitated over a print she had worn the summer before; it was too young for her, and it had a ruffled neck, and it was very early in the year for a print dress, but still . . .

She hung the two dresses side by side on the outside of the closet door and opened the glass doors carefully closed upon the small closet that was her kitchenette. She turned on the burner under the coffeepot, and went to the window; it was sunny. When the coffeepot began to crackle she came back and poured herself coffee, into a clean cup. I'll have a headache if I don't get some solid food soon, she thought, all this coffee, smoking too much, no real breakfast. A headache on her wedding day; she went and got the tin box of aspirin from the bathroom closet and slipped it into her blue pocketbook. She'd have to change to a brown pocketbook if she wore the print dress, and the only brown pocketbook she had was shabby. Helplessly, she stood looking from the blue pocketbook to the print dress, and then put the pocketbook down and went and got her coffee and sat down near the window, drinking her coffee, and looking carefully around the one-room apartment. They planned to come back here tonight and everything must be correct. With sudden horror she realized that she had forgotten to put clean sheets on the bed; the laundry was freshly back and she took clean sheets and pillowcases from the top shelf of the closet and stripped the bed, working quickly to avoid thinking consciously of why she was changing the sheets. The bed was a studio bed, with a cover to make it look like a couch, and when it was finished no one would have known she had just put clean sheets on it. She took the old sheets and pillowcases into the bathroom and stuffed them down into the hamper, and put the bathroom towels in the hamper too, and clean towels on the bathroom racks. Her coffee was cold when she came back to it, but she drank it anyway.

When she looked at the clock, finally, and saw that it was after nine, she began at last to hurry. She took a bath, and used one of the clean towels, which she put into the hamper and replaced with a clean one. She dressed carefully, all her underwear fresh and most of it new; she put everything she had worn the day before, including her nightgown, into the hamper. When she was ready for her dress, she hesitated before the closet door. The blue dress was certainly decent, and clean, and fairly becoming, but she had worn it several times with Jamie, and there was nothing about it which made it special for a wedding day. The print dress was overly pretty, and new to Jamie, and yet wearing such a print this early in the year was certainly rushing the season. Finally she thought, This is my wedding day, I can dress as I please, and she took the print dress down from the hanger. When she slipped it on over her head it felt fresh and light, but when she looked at herself in the mirror she remembered that the ruffles around the neck did not show her throat to any great advantage, and the wide swinging skirt looked irresistibly made for a girl, for someone who would run freely, dance, swing it with her hips when she walked. Looking at herself in the mirror she thought with revulsion, It's as though I was trying to make myself look prettier than I am, just for him; he'll think I want to look younger because he's marrying me; and she tore the print dress off so quickly that a seam under the arm ripped. In the old blue dress she felt comfortable and familiar, but unexciting. It isn't what you're wearing that matters, she told herself firmly, and turned in dismay to the closet to see if there might be anything else. There was nothing even remotely suitable for her marrying Jamie, and for a minute she thought of going out quickly to some little shop nearby, to get a dress. Then she saw that it was close on ten, and she had no time for more than her hair and her makeup. Her hair was easy, pulled back into a knot at the nape of her neck, but her makeup was another delicate balance between looking as well as possible, and deceiving as little. She could not try to disguise the sallowness of her skin, or the lines around her eyes, today, when it might look as though she were only doing it for her wedding, and yet she could not bear the thought of Jamie's bringing to marriage anyone who looked haggard and lined. You're thirty-four years old after *all*, she told herself cruelly in the bathroom mirror. Thirty, it said on the license.

It was two minutes after ten; she was not satisfied with her clothes, her face, her apartment. She heated the coffee again and sat down in the chair by the window. Can't do anything more now, she thought, no sense trying to improve anything the last minute.

Reconciled, settled, she tried to think of Jamie and could not see his face clearly, or hear his voice. It's always that way with someone you love, she thought, and let her mind slip past today and tomorrow, into the farther future, when Jamie was established with his writing and she had given up her job, the golden house-in-the-country future they had been preparing for the past week. "I used to be a wonderful cook," she had promised Jamie; "with a little time and practice I could remember how to make angel food cake. And fried chicken," she said, knowing how the words would stay in Jamie's mind, half tenderly. "And hollandaise sauce."

Ten thirty. She stood up and went purposefully to the phone. She dialed, and waited, and the girl's metallic voice said, ".., the time will be exactly ten twenty-nine." Half consciously she set her clock back a minute; she was remembering her own voice saying last night, in the doorway, "Ten o'clock then. I'll be ready. Is it really *true?*"

And Jamie laughing down the hallway.

By eleven o'clock she had sewn up the ripped seam in the print dress and put her sewing box away carefully in the closet. With the print dress on, she was sitting by the window drinking another cup of coffee. I could have taken more time over my dressing after all, she thought; but by now it was so late he might come any minute, and she did not dare try to repair anything without starting all over. There was nothing to eat in the apartment except the food she had carefully stocked up for their life beginning together: the unopened package of bacon, the dozen eggs in their box, the unopened bread and the unopened butter; they were for breakfast tomorrow. She thought of running downstairs to the drugstore for something to eat, leaving a note on the door. Then she decided to wait a little longer.

By eleven thirty she was so dizzy and weak that she had to go downstairs. If Jamie had had a phone she would have called him then. Instead, she opened her desk and wrote a note: "Jamie, have gone downstairs to the drugstore. Back in five minutes." Her pen leaked onto her fingers and she went into the bathroom and washed, using a clean towel which she replaced. She tacked the note on the door, surveyed the apartment once more to make sure that everything was perfect, and closed the door without locking it, in case he should come.

In the drugstore she found that there was nothing she wanted to eat except more coffee, and she left it half finished because she suddenly realized that Jamie was probably upstairs waiting and impatient, anxious to get started.

But upstairs everything was prepared and quiet, as she had left it, her note unread on the door, the air in the apartment a little stale from too many cigarettes. She opened the window and sat down next to it until she realized that she had been asleep and it was twenty minutes to one.

Now, suddenly, she was frightened. Waking without preparation into the room of waiting and readiness, everything clean and untouched since ten o'clock, she was frightened, and felt an urgent need to hurry. She got up from the chair and almost ran across the room to the bathroom, dashed cold water on her face, and used a clean towel; this time she put the towel carelessly back on the rack without changing it; time enough for that later. Hatless, still in the print dress with a coat thrown on over it, the wrong blue pocketbook with the aspirin inside in her hand, she locked the apartment door behind her, no note this time, and ran down the stairs. She caught a taxi on the corner and gave the driver Jamie's address.

It was no distance at all; she could have walked it if she had not been so weak, but in the taxi she suddenly realized how imprudent it would be to drive brazenly up to Jamie's door, demanding him. She asked the driver, therefore, to let her off at a corner near Jamie's address and, after paying him, waited till he drove away before she started to walk down the block. She had never been here before; the building was pleasant and old, and Jamie's name was not on any of the mailboxes in the vestibule, nor on the doorbells. She checked the address; it was right, and finally she rang the bell marked SUPERINTENDENT. After a minute or two the door buzzer rang and she opened the door and went into the dark hall where she hesitated until a door at the end opened and someone said, "Yes?"

She knew at the same moment that she had no idea what to ask, so she moved forward toward the figure waiting against the light of the open doorway. When she was very near, the figure said, "Yes?" again and she saw that it was a man in his shirt sleeves, unable to see her any more clearly than she could see him.

With sudden courage she said, "I'm trying to get in touch with someone who lives in this building and I can't find the name outside."

"What's the name you wanted?" the man asked, and she realized that she would have to answer.

"James Harris," she said. "Harris."

The man was silent for a minute and then he said, "Harris." He turned around to the room inside the lighted doorway and said, "Margie, come here a minute."

"What now?" a voice said from inside, and after a wait long enough for someone to get out of a comfortable chair a woman joined him in the doorway, regarding the dark hall. "Lady here," the man said. "Lady looking for a guy name of Harris, lives here. Anyone in the building?"

"No," the woman said. Her voice sounded amused. "No men named Harris here."

"Sorry," the man said. He started to close the door. "You got the wrong house, lady," he said, and added in a lower voice, "or the wrong guy," and he and the woman laughed.

When the door was almost shut and she was alone in the dark hall she said to the thin lighted crack still showing, "But he *does* live here; I know it."

"Look," the woman said, opening the door again a little, "it happens all the time."

"Please don't make any mistake," she said, and her voice was very dignified, with thirty-four years of accumulated pride. "I'm afraid you don't understand."

"What did he look like?" the woman said wearily, the door still only part open.

"He's rather tall, and fair. He wears a blue suit very often. He's a writer."

"No," the woman said, and then, "Could he have lived on the third floor?"

"I'm not sure."

"There was a fellow," the woman said reflectively. "He wore a blue suit a lot, lived on the third floor for a while. The Roysters lent him their apartment while they were visiting her folks upstate."

"That might be it; I thought, though . . ."

"This one wore a blue suit mostly, but I don't know how tall he was," the woman said. "He stayed there about a month."

"A month ago is when—"

"You ask the Roysters," the woman said. "They come back this morning. Apartment 3B."

The door closed, definitely. The hall was very dark and the stairs looked darker.

On the second floor there was a little light from a skylight far above.

The apartment doors lined up, four on the floor, uncommunicative and silent. There was a bottle of milk outside 2C.

On the third floor, she waited for a minute. There was the sound of music beyond the door of 3B, and she could hear voices. Finally she knocked, and knocked again. The door was opened and the music swept out at her, an early afternoon symphony broadcast. "How do you do," she said politely to this woman in the doorway. "Mrs. Royster?"

"That's right." The woman was wearing a housecoat and last night's makeup.

"I wonder if I might talk to you for a minute?"

"Sure," Mrs. Royster said, not moving.

"About Mr. Harris."

"*What* Mr. Harris?" Mrs. Royster said flatly.

"Mr. James Harris. The gentleman who borrowed your apartment."

"Oh, Lord," Mrs. Royster said. She seemed to open her eyes for the first time. "What'd he do?"

"Nothing. I'm just trying to get in touch with him."

"Oh, Lord," Mrs. Royster said again. Then she opened the door wider and said, "Come in," and then, "Ralph!"

Inside, the apartment was still full of music, and there were suitcases half unpacked on the couch, on the chairs, on the floor. A table in the corner was spread with the remains of a meal, and the young man sitting there, for a minute resembling Jamie, got up and came across the room.

"What about it?" he said.

"Mr. Royster," she said. It was difficult to talk against the music. "The superintendent downstairs told me that this was where Mr. James Harris has been living."

"Sure," he said. "If that was his name."

"I thought you lent him the apartment," she said, surprised.

"I don't know anything about him," Mr. Royster said. "He's one of Dottie's friends."

"Not *my* friends," Mrs. Royster said. "No friend of mine." She had gone over to the table and was spreading peanut butter on a piece of bread. She took a bite and said thickly, waving the bread and peanut butter at her husband. "Not *my* friend."

"You picked him up at one of those damn meetings," Mr. Royster said. He shoved a suitcase off the chair next to the radio and sat down, picking up a magazine from the floor next to him. "I never said more'n ten words to him."

"You said it was okay to lend him the place," Mrs. Royster said before she took another bite. "You never said a word against him, after *all*."

"*I* don't say anything about *your* friends," Mr. Royster said.

"If he'd of been a friend of mine you would have said *plenty*, believe me," Mrs. Royster said darkly. She took another bite and said, "Believe me, he would have said *plenty*."

"That's all I want to hear," Mr. Royster said, over the top of the magazine. "No more, now."

"You see." Mrs. Royster pointed the bread and peanut butter at her husband. "That's the way it is, day and night."

There was silence except for the music bellowing out of the radio next to Mr. Royster, and then she said, in a voice she hardly trusted to be heard over the radio noise, "Has he gone, then?"

"Who?" Mrs. Royster demanded, looking up from the peanut butter jar.

"Mr. James Harris."

"Him? He must've left this morning, before we got back. No sign of him anywhere."

"Gone?"

"Everything was fine, though, perfectly fine. I told you," she said to Mr. Royster, "I told you he'd take care of everything fine. I can always tell."

"You were lucky," Mr. Royster said.

"Not a thing out of place," Mrs. Royster said. She waved her bread and peanut butter inclusively. "Everything just the way we left it," she said.

"Do you know where he is now?"

"Not the slightest idea," Mrs. Royster said cheerfully. "But, like I said, he left everything fine. Why?" she asked suddenly. "You looking for *him*?"

"It's very important."

"I'm sorry he's not here," Mrs. Royster said. She stepped forward politely when she saw her visitor turn toward the door.

"Maybe the super saw him," Mr. Royster said into the magazine.

When the door was closed behind her the hall was dark again, but the sound of the radio was deadened. She was halfway down the first flight of stairs when the door was opened and Mrs. Royster shouted down the stairwell, "If I see him I'll tell him you were looking for him."

What can I do? she thought, out on the street again. It was impossible to go home, not with Jamie somewhere between here and there. She stood on the sidewalk so long that a woman, leaning out of a window across the way, turned and called to someone inside to come and see. Finally, on an impulse, she went into the small delicatessen next door to the apartment house, on the side that led to her own apartment. There was a small man reading a newspaper, leaning against the counter; when she came in he looked up and came down inside the counter to meet her.

Over the glass case of cold meats and cheese she said, timidly, "I'm trying to get in touch with a man who lived in the apartment house next door, and I just wondered if you know him."

"Whyn't you ask the people there?" the man said, his eyes narrow, inspecting her.

It's because I'm not buying anything, she thought, and she said, "I'm sorry. I asked them, but they don't know anything about him. They think he left this morning."

"I don't know what you want *me* to do," he said, moving a little back toward his newspaper. "I'm not here to keep track of guys going in and out next door."

She said quickly, "I thought you might have noticed, that's all. He would have been coming past here, a little before ten o'clock. He was rather tall, and he usually wore a blue suit."

"Now how many men in blue suits go past here every day, lady?" the man demanded. "You think I got nothing to do but—"

"I'm sorry," she said. She heard him say, "For God's sake," as she went out the door.

As she walked toward the corner, she thought, He must have come this way, it's the way he'd go to get to my house, it's the only way for him to walk. She tried to think of Jamie: Where would he have crossed the street? What sort of person was he actually—would he cross in front of his own apartment house, at random in the middle of the block, at the corner?

On the corner was a newsstand; they might have seen him there. She hurried on and waited while a man bought a paper and a woman asked directions. When the newsstand man looked at her she said, "Can you possibly tell me if a rather tall young man in a blue suit went past here this morning around ten o'clock?" When the man only looked at her, his eyes wide and his mouth a little open, she thought, He thinks it's a joke, or a trick, and she said urgently, "It's very important, please believe me. I'm not teasing you."

"*Look*, lady," the man began, and she said eagerly, "He's a writer. He might have bought magazines here."

"What you want him for?" the man asked. He looked at her, smiling, and she realized that there was another man waiting in back of her and the news dealer's smile included him. "Never mind," she said, but the news dealer said, "Listen, maybe he did come by here." His smile was knowing and his eyes shifted over her shoulder to the man in back of her. She was suddenly horribly aware of her overyoung print dress, and pulled her coat around her quickly. The news dealer said, with vast thoughtfulness, "Now I don't know for sure, mind you, but there might have been someone like your gentleman friend coming by this morning."

"About ten?"

"About ten," the news dealer agreed. "Tall fellow, blue suit. I wouldn't be at all surprised."

"Which way did he go?" she said eagerly. "Uptown?"

"Uptown," the news dealer said, nodding. "He went uptown. That's just exactly it. What can I do for you, sir?"

She stepped back, holding her coat around her. The man who had been standing behind her looked at her over his shoulder and then he and the news dealer looked at one another. She wondered for a minute whether or not to tip the news dealer, but when both men began to laugh she moved hurriedly on across the street.

Uptown, she thought, that's right, and she started up the avenue, thinking, He wouldn't have to cross the avenue, just go up six blocks and turn down my street, so long as he started uptown. About a block farther on she passed a florist's shop; there was a wedding display in the window and she thought, This is my wedding day after all, he might have gotten flowers to bring me, and she went inside. The florist came out of the back of the shop, smiling and sleek, and she said, before he could speak, so that he wouldn't have a chance to think she was buying anything, "It's *terribly* important that I get in touch with a gentleman who may have stopped in here to buy flowers this morning. *Terribly* important."

She stopped for breath, and the florist said, "Yes, what sort of flowers were they?"

"I don't know," she said, surprised. "He never—" She stopped and said, "He was a rather tall young man, in a blue suit. It was about ten o'clock."

"I see," the florist said. "Well, *really*, I'm afraid . . ."

"But it's *so* important," she said. "He may have been in a hurry," she added helpfully.

"Well," the florist said. He smiled genially, showing all his small teeth. "For a *lady*," he said. He went to a stand and opened a large book. "Where were they to be sent?" he asked.

"Why," she said, "I don't think he'd have sent them. You see, he was coming—that is, he'd *bring* them."

"Madam," the florist said; he was offended. His smile became deprecatory, and he went on, "Really, you must realize that unless I have *something* to go on . . ."

"*Please* try to remember," she begged. "He was tall, and had a blue suit, and it was about ten this morning."

The florist closed his eyes, one finger to his mouth, and thought deeply. Then he shook his head. "I simply *can't*," he said.

"Thank you," she said despondently, and started for the door, when the florist said, in a shrill, excited voice, "Wait! Wait just a moment, madam." She turned and the florist, thinking again, said finally, "Chrysanthemums?" He looked at her inquiringly.

"Oh, *no*," she said; her voice shook a little and she waited for a minute before she went on. "Not for an occasion like this, I'm sure."

The florist tightened his lips and looked away coldly. "Well, of *course* I don't know the *occasion*," he said, "but I'm almost certain that the gentleman you were inquiring for came in this morning and purchased one dozen chrysanthemums. No delivery."

"You're *sure?*" she asked.

"Positive," the florist said emphatically. "That was absolutely the man." He smiled brilliantly, and she smiled back and said, "Well, thank you very much."

He escorted her to the door. "Nice corsage?" he said, as they went through the shop. "Red roses? Gardenias?"

"It was very kind of you to help me," she said at the door.

"Ladies always look their best in flowers," he said, bending his head toward her. "Orchids, perhaps?"

"No, thank you," she said, and he said, "I hope you find your young man," and gave it a nasty sound.

Going on up the street she thought, Everyone thinks it's so *funny;* and she pulled her coat tighter around her, so that only the ruffle around the bottom of the print dress was showing.

There was a policeman on the corner, and she thought, Why don't I go to the police—you go to the police for a missing person. And then thought, What a fool I'd look like.

She had a quick picture of herself standing in a police station, saying, "Yes, we were going to be married today, but he didn't come," and the policemen, three or four of them standing around listening, looking at her, at the print dress, at her too-bright makeup, smiling at one another. She couldn't tell them any more than that, could not say, "Yes, it looks silly, doesn't it, me all dressed up and trying to find the young man who promised to marry me, but what about all of it you don't know? I have more than this, more than you can see: talent, perhaps, and humor of a sort, and I'm a lady and I have pride and affection and delicacy and a certain clear view of life that might make a man satisfied and productive and happy; there's more than you think when you look at me."

The police were obviously impossible, leaving out Jamie and what he might think when he heard she'd set the police after him. "No, no," she said aloud, hurrying her steps, and someone passing stopped and looked after her.

On the coming corner—she was three blocks from her own street—was a shoeshine stand, an old man sitting almost asleep in one of the chairs. She stopped in front of him and waited, and after a minute he opened his eyes and smiled at her.

"Look," she said, the words coming before she thought of them, "I'm sorry to bother you, but I'm looking for a young man who came up this way about ten this morning, did you see him?" And she began her description, "Tall, blue suit, carrying a bunch of flowers?"

The old man began to nod before she was finished. "I saw him," he said. "Friend of yours?"

"Yes," she said, and smiled back involuntarily.

The old man blinked his eyes and said, "I remember I thought, You're going to see your girl, young fellow. They all go to see their girls," he said, and shook his head tolerantly.

"Which way did he go? Straight on up the avenue?"

"That's right," the old man said. "Got a shine, had his flowers, all dressed up, in an awful hurry. You got a girl, I thought."

"Thank you," she said, fumbling in her pocket for her loose change.

"She sure must of been glad to see him, the way he looked," the old man said.

"Thank you," she said again, and brought her hand empty from her pocket.

For the first time she was really sure he would be waiting for her, and she hurried up the three blocks, the skirt of the print dress swinging under her coat, and turned into her own block. From the corner she could not see her own windows, could not see Jamie looking out, waiting for her, and going down the block she was almost running to get to him. Her key trembled in her fingers at the downstairs door, and as she glanced into the drugstore she thought of her panic, drinking coffee there this morning, and almost laughed. At her own door she could wait no longer, but began to say, "Jamie, I'm here, I was so worried," even before the door was open.

Her own apartment was waiting for her, silent, barren, afternoon shadows lengthening from the window. For a minute she saw only the empty coffee cup, thought, He has been here waiting, before she recognized it as her own, left from the morning. She looked all over the room, into the closet, into the bathroom.

"I never saw him," the clerk in the drugstore said. "I know because I would of noticed the flowers. No one like that's been in."

The old man at the shoeshine stand woke up again to see her standing in front of him. "Hello again," he said, and smiled.

"Are you *sure?*" she demanded. "Did he go on up the avenue?"

"I watched him," the old man said, dignified against her tone. "I thought, There's a young man's got a girl, and I watched him right into the house."

"What house?" she said remotely.

"Right there," the old man said. He leaned forward to point. "The next block. With his flowers and his shine and going to see his girl. Right into her house."

"Which one?" she said.

"About the middle of the block," the old man said. He looked at her with suspicion, and said, "What you trying to do, anyway?"

She almost ran, without stopping to say "Thank you." Up on the next block she walked quickly, searching the houses from the outside to see if Jamie looked from a window, listening to hear his laughter somewhere inside.

A woman was sitting in front of one of the houses, pushing a baby carriage monotonously back and forth the length of her arm. The baby inside slept, moving back and forth.

The question was fluent, by now. "I'm sorry, but did you see a young man go into one of these houses about ten this morning? He was tall, wearing a blue suit, carrying a bunch of flowers."

A boy about twelve stopped to listen, turning intently from one to the other, occasionally glancing at the baby.

"Listen," the woman said tiredly, "the kid has his bath at ten. Would I see strange men walking around? I ask you."

"Big bunch of flowers?" the boy asked, pulling at her coat. "Big bunch of flowers? I seen him, missus."

She looked down and the boy grinned insolently at her. "Which house did he go in?" she asked wearily.

"You gonna divorce him?" the boy asked insistently.

"That's not nice to ask the lady," the woman rocking the carriage said.

"Listen," the boy said, "I seen him. He went in there." He pointed to the house next door. "I followed him," the boy said. "He give me a quarter." The boy dropped his voice to a growl, and said, " 'This is a big day for me, kid,' he says. Give me a quarter."

She gave him a dollar bill. "Where?" she said.

"Top floor," the boy said. "I followed him till he give me the quarter. Way to the top." He backed up the sidewalk, out of reach, with the dollar bill. "You gonna divorce him?" he asked again.

"Was he carrying flowers?"

"Yeah," the boy said. He began to screech. "You gonna divorce him, missus? You got something on him?" He went careening down the street, howling, "She's got something on the poor guy," and the woman rocking the baby laughed.

The street door of the apartment house was unlocked; there were no bells in the outer vestibule, and no lists of names. The stairs were narrow and dirty; there were two doors on the top floor. The front one was the right one; there was a crumpled florist's paper on the floor outside the door, and a knotted paper ribbon, like a clue, like the final clue in the paper chase.

She knocked, and thought she heard voices inside, and she thought, suddenly, with terror, What shall I say if Jamie is there, if he comes to the door? The voices seemed suddenly still. She knocked again and there was silence, except for something that might have been laughter far away. He could have seen me from the window, she thought, it's the front apartment and that little boy made a dreadful noise. She waited, and knocked again, but there was silence.

Finally she went to the other door on the floor, and knocked. The door swung open beneath her hand and she saw the empty attic room, bare lath on the walls, floorboards unpainted. She stepped just inside, looking around; the room was filled with bags of plaster, piles of old newspapers, a broken trunk. There was a noise which she suddenly realized was a rat, and then she saw it, sitting very close to her, near the wall, its evil face alert, bright eyes watching her. She stumbled in her haste to be out with the door closed, and the skirt of the print dress caught and tore.

She knew there was someone inside the other apartment, because she was sure she could hear low voices and sometimes laughter. She came back many times, every day for the first week. She came on her way to work, in the mornings; in the evenings, on her way to dinner alone, but no matter how often or how firmly she knocked, no one ever came to the door.

THE LOVE POTION
HERMAN CHARLES BOSMAN

H C Bosman

You MENTION the juba-plant (Oom Schalk Lourens said). Oh, yes, everybody in the Marico knows about the juba-plant. It grows high up on the krantzes, and they say you must pick off one of its little red berries at midnight, under the full moon. Then, if you are a young man, and you are anxious for a girl to fall in love with you, all you have to do is to squeeze the juice of the juba-berry into her coffee.

They say that after the girl has drunk the juba-juice she begins to forget all sorts of things. She forgets that your forehead is rather low, and that your ears stick out, and that your mouth is too big. She even forgets having told you, the week before last, that she wouldn't marry you if you were the only man in the Transvaal.

All she knows is that the man she gazes at, over her empty coffee-cup, has grown remarkably handsome. You can see from this that the plant must be very potent in its effects. I mean, if you consider what some of the men in the Marico look like.

One young man I knew, however, was not very enthusiastic about juba-juice. In fact, he always said that before he climbed up the krantz one night, to pick one of those red berries, he was more popular with the girls than he was afterwards. This young man said that his decline in favour with the girls of the neighbourhood might perhaps be due to the fact that, shortly after he had picked the juba-berry, he lost most of his front teeth.

This happened when the girl's father, who was an irascible sort of fellow, caught the young man in the act of squeezing juba-juice into his daughter's cup.

And afterwards, while others talked of the magic properties of this love potion, the young man would listen in silence, and his lip would curl in a sneer over the place where his front teeth used to be.

"Yes, kerels," he would lisp at the end, "I suppose I must have picked that juba-berry at the wrong time. Perhaps the moon wasn't full enough, or something. Or perhaps it wasn't just exactly midnight. I am only glad now that I didn't pick off two of those red berries while I was about it."

We all felt it was a sad thing what the juba-plant had done to that young man.

But with Gideon van der Merwe it was different.

One night I was out shooting in the veld with a lamp fastened on my hat. You know that kind of shooting: in the glare of the lamplight you can see only the eyes of the thing you are aiming at, and you get three months if you are caught. They made it illegal to hunt by lamplight since the time a policeman got shot in the foot, this way, when he was out tracking cattle-smugglers on the Lesotho border.

The magistrate at Zeerust, who did not know the ways of the cattle-smugglers, found that the shooting was an accident. The verdict satisfied everybody except the policeman, whose foot was still bandaged when he came into court. But the men in the Volksraad, some of whom had been cattle-smugglers themselves, knew better than the magistrate did as to how the policeman came to have a couple of buck-shot in the soft part of his foot, and accordingly they brought in this new law.

Therefore I walked very quietly that night on the krantz.

Frequently I put on my lamp and stood very still amongst the trees, and waited long moments to make sure I was not being followed. Ordinarily, there would have been little to fear, but a couple of days before two policemen had been seen disappearing into the bush. By their looks they seemed young policemen, who were anxious for promotion, and who didn't know that it is more becoming for a policeman to drink an honest farmer's peach-brandy than to arrest him for hunting by lamplight.

I was walking along, turning the light from side to side, when suddenly, about a hundred paces from me, in the full brightness of the lamp, I saw a pair of eyes. When I also saw, about the eyes, a policeman's khaki helmet, I remembered that a moonlight night, such as that was, was not good for finding buck.

So I went home.

I took the shortest way, too, which was over the side of the krantz— the steep side—and on my way down I clutched at a variety of branches tree-roots, stone ledges and tufts of grass. Later on, at the foot of the krantz, when I came to and was able to sit up there was that policeman bending over me.

"Oom Schalk," he said, "I was wondering if you would lend me your lamp."

I looked up. It was Gideon van der Merwe, a young policeman who had been stationed for some time at Derdepoort. I had met him on several occasions and had found him very likeable.

"You can have my lamp," I answered, "but you must be careful. It's worse for a policeman to get caught breaking the law than for an ordinary man."

Gideon van der Merwe shook his head.

"No, I don't want to go shooting with the lamp," he said, "I want to . . ." And then he paused.

He laughed nervously.

"It seems silly to say it, Oom Schalk," he said, "but perhaps you'll understand. I have come to look for a juba-plant. I need it for my studies. For my third-class sergeant's examination. And it will soon be midnight, and I can't find one of those plants anywhere."

I felt sorry for Gideon. It struck me that he would never make a good policeman. If he couldn't find a juba-plant, of which there were thousands on the krantz, it would be much harder for him to find the spoor of a cattle-smuggler.

So I handed him my lamp and explained where he had to go and look. Gideon thanked me and walked off.

About half-an-hour later he was back.

He took a red berry out of his tunic-pocket and showed it to me. For fear he should tell any more lies about needing that juba-berry for his studies, I spoke first.

"Lettie Cordier?" I asked.

Gideon nodded. He was very shy, though, and wouldn't talk much at the start. But I had guessed long ago that Gideon van der Merwe was not calling at Krisjan Cordier's house so often just to hear Krisjan relate the story of his life.

Nevertheless, I mentioned Krisjan Cordier's life-story.

"Yes," Gideon replied, "Lettie's father has got up to what he was like at the age of seven. It has taken him a month, so far."

"He must be glad to get you to listen," I said, "the only other who listened for any length of time was an insurance agent. But he left after a fortnight. By that time Krisjan had reached to only a little beyond his fifth birthday."

"But Lettie is wonderful, Oom Schalk," Gideon went on. "I have never spoken more than a dozen words to her. And, of course, it is ridiculous to expect her even to look at a policeman. But to sit there, in the voorkamer, with her father talking about all the things he could do before he was six—and Lettie coming in now and again with more coffee—that is love, Oom Schalk."

I agreed with him that it must be.

"I have worked it out," Gideon explained, "that at the rate he is going now, Lettie's father will have come to the end of his life-story in two years' time, and after that I won't have any excuse for going there. That worries me."

I said that no doubt it was disconcerting.

"I have tried often to tell Lettie how much I think of her," Gideon said, "but every time, as soon as I start, I get a foolish feeling. My uniform begins to look shabby. My boots seem to curl up at the toes. And my voice gets shaky, and all I can say to her is that I will come round again, soon, as I have simply got to hear the rest of her father's life-story."

"Then what is your idea with the juba-juice?" I asked.

"The juba-juice," Gideon van der Merwe said wistfully, "might make her say something first."

We parted shortly afterwards. I took up my lamp and gun, and as I saw Gideon's figure disappear among the trees I thought of what a good fellow he was. And very simple. Still, he was best off as a policeman, I reflected. For if he was a cattle-smuggler it seemed to me that he would get arrested every time he tried to cross the border.

Next morning I rode over to Krisjan Cordier's farm to remind him about a tin of sheep-dip that he still owed me from the last dipping season.

As I stayed for only an hour, I wasn't able to get in a word about the sheep-dip, but Krisjan managed to tell me quite a lot about the things he did at the age of nine. When Lettie came in with the coffee I made a casual remark to her father about Gideon van der Merwe.

"Oh, yes, he's an interesting young man," Krisjan Cordier said, "and very intelligent. It is a pleasure for me to relate to him the story of my life. He says the incidents I describe to him are not only thrilling, but very helpful. I can quite understand that. I wouldn't be surprised if he is made a sergeant one of these days. For these reasons I always dwell on the more helpful parts of my story."

I didn't take much notice of Krisjan's remarks, however. Instead, I looked carefully at Lettie when I mentioned Gideon's name. She didn't give much away, but I am quick at these things, and I saw enough. The colour that crept into her cheeks. The light that came in her eyes.

On my way back I encountered Lettie. She was standing under a thorn-tree. With her brown arms and her sweet, quiet face and her full bosom, she was a very pretty picture. There was no doubt that Lettie Cordier would make a fine wife for any man. It wasn't hard to understand Gideon's feeling about her.

"Lettie," I asked, "do you love him?"

"I love him, Oom Schalk," she answered.

It was as simple as all that.

Lettie guessed I meant Gideon van der Merwe, without my having spoken his name. Accordingly, it was easy for me to acquaint Lettie with what had happened the night before, on the krantz, in the moonlight. At least, I only told her the parts that mattered to her, such as the way I explained to Gideon where the juba-plant grew. Another man might have wearied her with a long and unnecessary description of the way he fell down the krantz, clutching at branches and tree-roots. But I am different. I told her that it was Gideon who fell down the krantz.

After all, it was Lettie's and Gideon's love affair, and I didn't want to bring myself into it too much.

"Now you'll know what to do, Lettie," I said. "Put your coffee on the table within easy reach of Gideon. Then give him what you think is long enough to squeeze the juba-juice into your cup."

"Perhaps it will be even better," Lettie said, "if I watch through a crack in the door."

I patted her head approvingly.

"After that you come into the voorkamer and drink your coffee," I said.

"Yes, Oom Schalk," she answered simply.

"And when you have drunk the coffee," I concluded, "you'll know what to do next. Only don't go too far."

It was pleasant to see the warm blood mount to her face. As I rode off I said to myself Gideon van der Merwe was a lucky fellow.

There isn't much more to tell about Lettie and Gideon.

When I saw Gideon some time afterwards, he was very elated, as I had expected he would be.

"So the juba-plant worked?" I enquired.

"It was wonderful, Oom Schalk," Gideon answered, "and the funny part of it was that Lettie's father was not there, either, when I put the juba-juice into her coffee. Lettie had brought him a message, just before then, that he was wanted in the mealie-lands."

"And was the juba-juice all they claim for it?" I asked.

"You'd be surprised how quickly it acted," he said, "Lettie just took one sip at the coffee and then jumped straight onto my lap."

But then Gideon van der Merwe winked in a way that made me believe that he was not so very simple, after all.

"I was pretty certain that the juba-juice would work, Oom Schalk," he said, "after Lettie's father told me that you had been there that morning."

BARTLEBY
THE SCRIVENER

HERMAN MELVILLE

Herman Melville.

I AM A rather elderly man. The nature of my avocations for the last
thirty years has brought me into more than ordinary contact with an
interesting and somewhat singular set of men, of whom, as yet,
nothing that I know of has ever been written—I mean the law copyists,
or scriveners. I have known very many of them, professionally and
privately, and, if I pleased, could relate divers histories at which good-
natured gentlemen might smile and sentimental souls might weep. But
I waive the biographies of all other scriveners for a few passages in the
life of Bartleby, who was a scrivener, the strangest I ever saw or heard
of. While of other law copyists I might write the complete life, of
Bartleby nothing of that sort can be done. What my own astonished
eyes saw of Bartleby, *that* is all I know of him, except, indeed, one
vague report which will appear in the sequel.

I am a man who, from his youth upwards, has been filled with a
profound conviction that the easiest way of life is the best. Though I
belong to a profession proverbially energetic and nervous, yet I am one
of those unambitious lawyers who never address a jury or in any way
draw public applause, but in the cool tranquillity of a snug retreat do a
snug business among rich men's bonds and mortgages and title deeds.
All who know me consider me an eminently *safe* man. The late John
Jacob Astor, a personage little given to poetic enthusiasm, had no
hesitation in pronouncing my first grand point to be prudence; my
next, method. I do not speak it in vanity, but simply record the fact
that I was employed in my profession by the late John Jacob Astor, a
name which, I admit, I love to repeat, for it hath a rounded and

orbicular sound to it, and rings like unto bullion. I will add that I was not insensible to the late John Jacob Astor's opinion.

Some time prior to the period at which this little history begins, the office of a Master in Chancery had been conferred upon me. It was not a very arduous office, but very pleasantly remunerative. My chambers were upstairs at No. —— Wall Street. At one end they looked upon the white wall of the interior of a spacious skylight shaft penetrating the building from top to bottom. The view from the other end of my chambers offered, at least, a contrast, if nothing more. In that direction my windows commanded an unobstructed view of a lofty brick wall, black by age and everlasting shade, pushed up to within ten feet of my windowpanes.

At the period just preceding the advent of Bartleby, I had two persons as copyists in my employment, and a promising lad as an office boy. First, Turkey; second, Nippers; third, Ginger Nut. These were nicknames conferred upon each other by my three clerks, expressive of their respective persons or characters.

Turkey was a short, pursy Englishman of about my own age—that is, somewhere not far from sixty. In the morning his face was of a fine florid hue, but after twelve o'clock—his dinner hour—it blazed like a grate full of Christmas coals. When Turkey displayed his fullest beams from his red and radiant countenance, just then, too, began the daily period when I considered his business capacities as seriously disturbed for the remainder of the day. Not that he was absolutely idle, or averse to business then; far from it. He was apt to be altogether too energetic. There was a strange, inflamed, flurried, flighty recklessness of activity about him. He made an unpleasant racket with his chair; spilled his sandbox; in mending his pens, impatiently split them all to pieces, and threw them on the floor in a sudden passion; stood up and leaned over his table, boxing his papers about in a most indecorous manner, very sad to behold in an elderly man like him. Nevertheless, as he was in many ways a most valuable person to me, and all the time before twelve o'clock was the quickest, steadiest creature, I was willing to overlook his eccentricities, though, indeed, occasionally I remonstrated with him. I did this very gently, however, because, though the civilest, nay, the blandest and most reverential of men in the morning, yet, in the afternoon, he was disposed, upon provocation, to be slightly rash with his tongue—in fact, insolent.

Nippers was a whiskered, sallow, rather piratical-looking young man of about five-and-twenty. I always deemed him the victim of two evil powers—ambition and indigestion. The ambition was evinced by a certain impatience of the duties of a mere copyist, an unwarrantable usurpation of strictly professional affairs. The indigestion seemed betokened in an occasional nervous testiness and grinning irritability, causing the teeth to audibly grind together over mistakes committed in copying; unnecessary maledictions, hissed rather than spoken, in the heat of business, and especially by a continual discontent with the height of the table where he worked. Though of a very ingenious mechanical turn, Nippers could never get this table to suit him. He put chips under it, blocks of various sorts, and at last went so far as to attempt an exquisite adjustment by final pieces of folded blotting paper. But no invention would answer. The truth of the matter was, Nippers knew not what he wanted. Or, if he wanted anything, it was to be rid of a scrivener's table altogether. Among the manifestations of his diseased ambition was a fondness he had for receiving visits from certain ambiguous-looking fellows in seedy coats, whom he called his clients. Indeed, I was aware that not only was he, at times, considerable of a ward politician, but he occasionally did a little business at the justices' courts, and was not unknown on the steps of the Tombs.

But with all his failings, and the annoyances he caused me, Nippers, like his compatriot Turkey, was a very useful man to me, wrote a neat, swift hand, and, when he chose, was not deficient in a gentlemanly sort of deportment. Though concerning the self-indulgent habits of Turkey I had my own private surmises, yet, touching Nippers, I was well persuaded that he was, at least, a temperate young man. But, indeed, nature herself seemed to have charged him at his birth so thoroughly with an irritable, brandylike disposition, that all subsequent potations were needless.

It was fortunate for me that, owing to its cause—indigestion—the irritability and consequent nervousness of Nippers were mainly observable in the morning, while in the afternoon he was comparatively mild. So that, Turkey's paroxysms only coming on about twelve o'clock, I never had to do with their eccentricities at one time. Their fits relieved each other, like guards.

Ginger Nut, the third on my list, was a lad some twelve years old. His father, a carman, sent him to my office as student at law, errand boy, cleaner and sweeper, at the rate of one dollar a week. He had a little desk to himself, but he did not use it much. Upon inspection, the drawer exhibited a great array of the shells of various sorts of nuts. Indeed, to this quick-witted youth the whole noble science of the law was contained in a nutshell. Not the least among his employments was his duty as cake and apple purveyor for Turkey and Nippers. Copying law papers being a dry, husky sort of business, my two scriveners were fain to moisten their mouths very often with Spitzenbergs, to be had at the numerous stalls nigh the customhouse and post office. Also, they sent Ginger Nut very frequently for that peculiar cake—small, flat, round, and very spicy—after which he had been named by them. Of all the fiery afternoon blunders of Turkey was his once moistening a ginger cake between his lips and clapping it onto a mortgage, for a seal. I came within an ace of dismissing him then.

Now my original business—that of a conveyancer and title hunter, and drawer-up of documents of all sorts—was considerably increased by receiving the Master's office. There was now great work for scriveners. Not only must I push the clerks already with me, but I must have additional help.

In answer to my advertisement, a motionless young man one morning stood upon my office threshold, the door being open, for it was summer. I can see that figure now—pallidly neat, pitiably respectable, incurably forlorn! It was Bartleby.

After a few words touching his qualifications, I engaged him, glad to have among my corps of copyists a man of so singularly sedate an aspect, which I thought might operate beneficially upon the flighty temper of Turkey and the fiery one of Nippers.

I should have stated before that ground-glass folding doors divided my premises into two parts, one of which was occupied by my scriveners, the other by myself. According to my humor, I threw open these doors, or closed them. I resolved to assign Bartleby a corner by the folding doors, but on my side of them, so as to have this quiet man within easy call, in case any trifling thing was to be done. I placed his desk close up to a small side window, which commanded no view at all, though it gave some light. Within three feet of the panes was a wall, and the light came down from far above, between two lofty buildings. I procured a high green folding screen, which might entirely isolate Bartleby from my sight, though not remove him from my voice. And thus, in a manner, privacy and society were conjoined.

At first Bartleby did an extraordinary quantity of writing. As if long famishing for something to copy, he seemed to gorge himself on my documents. I should have been quite delighted with his application had he been cheerfully industrious. But he wrote on silently, palely, mechanically.

It is, of course, an indispensable part of a scrivener's business to verify the accuracy of his copy, word by word. Where there are two or more scriveners in an office, they assist each other in this examination, one reading from the copy, the other holding the original. It is a very dull, wearisome, and lethargic affair.

Now and then, in the haste of business, it had been my habit to assist in comparing some brief document myself, calling Turkey or Nippers for this purpose. One object I had in placing Bartleby so handy to me behind the screen was to avail myself of his services on such trivial occasions. It was on the third day, I think, of his being with me that, being hurried to complete an affair, I abruptly called Bartleby to examine a paper with me. Imagine my surprise when, without moving from his privacy, Bartleby, in a singularly mild, firm voice, replied, "I would prefer not to."

I sat awhile in perfect silence, rallying my stunned faculties. Immediately it occurred to me that Bartleby had entirely misunderstood my meaning. I repeated my request in the clearest tone I could assume; but in quite as clear a one came the previous reply, "I would prefer not to."

"Prefer not to," echoed I, rising in high excitement and crossing the room with a stride. "What do you mean? Are you moonstruck? I want you to help me compare this sheet here—take it," and I thrust it towards him.

"I would prefer not to," said he.

I looked at him steadfastly. His face was leanly composed; his gray eyes dimly calm. Had there been the least uneasiness, anger, impatience, or impertinence in his manner; in other words, had there been anything ordinarily human about him, doubtless I should have violently dismissed him from the premises. But as it was, I should have as soon thought of turning my pale plaster of paris bust of Cicero out of doors.

I reseated myself at my desk. This is very strange, thought I. What had one best do? But my business hurried me. I concluded to forget the matter for the present, reserving it for my future leisure. So, calling Nippers from the other room, the paper was speedily examined.

A few days after this, Bartleby concluded four lengthy documents, being quadruplicates of a week's testimony taken before me in my High Court of Chancery. It was an important suit, and great accuracy was imperative. Having all things arranged, I called Turkey, Nippers, and Ginger Nut from the next room, meaning to place the four copies in the hands of my four clerks, while I should read from the original. Accordingly, Turkey, Nippers, and Ginger Nut had taken their seats in a row, each with his document in his hand, when I called to Bartleby to join this interesting group.

"Bartleby! Quick, I am waiting."

I heard a slow scrape of his chair legs on the uncarpeted floor, and soon he appeared, standing at the entrance of his hermitage.

"What is wanted?" said he mildly.

"The copies, the copies," said I hurriedly. "We are going to examine them. There"—and I held towards him the fourth quadruplicate.

"I would prefer not to," he said, and gently disappeared behind the screen.

For a few moments I was turned into a pillar of salt, standing at the head of my seated column of clerks. Recovering myself, I advanced towards the screen.

"*Why* do you refuse?"

"I would prefer not to."

There was something about Bartleby that not only strangely disarmed me, but, in a wonderful manner, touched and disconcerted me. I began to reason with him.

"These are your own copies we are about to examine. It is labor saving to you, because one examination will answer for your four papers. It is common usage. Every copyist is bound to help examine his copy. Is it not so? Will you not speak? Answer!"

"I prefer not to," he replied in a flutelike tone. It seemed to me that he had carefully revolved every statement that I made and could not gainsay the irresistible conclusion; but, at the same time, some paramount consideration prevailed with him to reply as he did.

"You are decided, then, not to comply with my request—a request made according to common usage and common sense?"

He briefly gave me to understand that on that point my judgment was sound. Yes: his decision was irreversible.

It is not seldom the case that when a man is browbeaten in some violently unreasonable way, he begins to stagger in his own plainest faith. Accordingly, if any disinterested persons are present, he turns to them for some reinforcement for his own faltering mind.

"Turkey," said I, "what do you think of this? Am I not right?"

"With submission, sir," said Turkey in his blandest tone, "I think that you are."

"Nippers," said I, "what do *you* think of it?"

"I think I should kick him out of the office."

(The reader of nice perceptions will here perceive that, it being morning, Nipper's ugly mood was on duty, and Turkey's off.)

"Ginger Nut," said I, willing to enlist the smallest suffrage in my behalf, "what do *you* think of it?"

"I think, sir, he's a little *loony*," replied Ginger Nut, with a grin.

"You hear what they say," said I, turning towards the screen, "come forth and do your duty."

But he vouchsafed no reply. Once more business hurried me. I determined again to postpone the consideration of this dilemma to my future leisure. With a little trouble we made out to examine the papers without Bartleby, who sat in his hermitage, oblivious to everything but his own peculiar business there.

Some days passed, the scrivener being employed upon another lengthy work. His late remarkable conduct led me to regard his ways narrowly. I observed that he never went to dinner; indeed, that he never went anywhere. As yet I had never, of my personal knowledge, known him to be outside of my office. At about eleven o'clock, though, in the morning, I noticed that Ginger Nut would advance towards the opening in Bartleby's screen, as if silently beckoned thither by a gesture invisible to me. The boy would then leave the office, jingling a few pence, and reappear with a handful of ginger nuts, which he delivered in the hermitage, receiving two of the cakes for his trouble. Bartleby lives, then, on ginger nuts, thought I; never eats a dinner, properly speaking.

Poor fellow! thought I. He means no mischief; his eccentricities are involuntary. He is useful to me. I can get along with him. If I turn him away, the chances are he will fall in with some less indulgent employer, and then he will be rudely treated, and perhaps driven forth miserably to starve. Yes. Here I can cheaply purchase a delicious self-approval. To befriend Bartleby, to humor him in his strange willfulness, will cost me little or nothing, while I lay up in my soul what will eventually prove a sweet morsel for my conscience.

But this mood was not invariable with me. The passiveness of Bartleby sometimes irritated me. One afternoon I felt strangely goaded to encounter him in new opposition—to elicit some angry spark from him answerable to my own.

"Bartleby," said I, "Ginger Nut is away; just step around to the post office, won't you" (it was but a three minutes' walk) "and see if there is anything for me?"

"I would prefer not to."

"You *will* not?"

"I *prefer* not."

I staggered to my desk, and sat there in a deep study. Was there any other thing in which I could procure myself to be ignominiously repulsed by this lean, penniless wight—my hired clerk? What added thing is there, perfectly reasonable, that he will be sure to refuse to do?

"Bartleby!"

No answer.

"Bartleby," in a louder tone.

No answer.

"Bartleby," I roared.

Like a ghost he appeared at the entrance of his hermitage.

"Go to the next room and tell Nippers to come to me."

"I prefer not to," he respectfully and slowly said, and mildly disappeared.

"Very good, Bartleby," said I in a quiet, self-possessed tone, intimating some terrible retribution very close at hand. At the moment I half intended something of the kind. But upon the whole, as it was drawing towards my dinner hour, I thought it best to put on my hat and walk home for the day, suffering much from perplexity and distress of mind.

Shall I acknowledge it? The conclusion of this whole business was that it soon became a fixed fact of my chambers that a pale young scrivener by the name of Bartleby had a desk there; that he copied for me at the usual rate of four cents for one hundred words, but was permanently exempt from examining the work done by him, and was never, on any account, to be dispatched on the most trivial errand of any sort.

As days passed on, I became considerably reconciled to Bartleby. His steadiness, his freedom from all dissipation, his incessant industry (except when he chose to throw himself into a standing reverie behind his screen), his great stillness, his unalterableness of demeanor under all circumstances, made him a valuable acquisition. One prime thing was this—*he was always there*—first in the morning, continually through the day, and the last at night.

ONE SUNDAY morning I happened to go to Trinity Church to hear a celebrated preacher, and finding myself rather early, I thought I would walk round to my chambers for a while. Upon applying my key to the lock, I found it resisted by something inserted from the inside. Quite surprised, I called out, when to my consternation a key was turned from within; and thrusting his lean visage at me, and holding the door ajar, Bartleby appeared, in his shirt sleeves and otherwise in a strangely tattered dishabille, saying quietly that he was sorry, but he was deeply engaged just then and preferred not admitting me at present. In a brief word or two he moreover added that perhaps I had better walk round the block two or three times, and by that time he would probably have concluded his affairs.

Now, the utterly unsurmised appearance of Bartleby, tenanting my law chambers of a Sunday morning, with his cadaverously gentlemanly nonchalance, had such a strange effect upon me that I slunk away from my own door and did as desired. But not without sundry twinges of impotent rebellion against Bartleby's mild effrontery. Indeed, it was his wonderful mildness chiefly, which not only disarmed me, but un-manned me, as it were. For I consider that one, for the time, is unmanned when he tranquilly permits his hired clerk to dictate to him and order him away from his own premises. Furthermore, I was uneasy as to what Bartleby could possibly be doing in my office in his shirt sleeves and in an otherwise dismantled condition of a Sunday morning. Was anything amiss going on? Nay, that was out of the question. It was not to be thought of for a moment that Bartleby was an immoral person. But what could he be doing there—copying? Nay again, whatever might be his eccentricities, Bartleby was an eminently decorous person. He would be the last man to sit down to his desk in any state approaching to nudity.

Nevertheless, my mind was not pacified, and full of a restless curiosity, at last I returned to the door. Without hindrance I inserted my key, opened it, and entered. I looked round anxiously, peeped behind Bartleby's screen; but it was very plain that he was gone. Upon more closely examining the place, I surmised that for an indefinite period Bartleby must have eaten, dressed, and slept in my office, and that too without plate, mirror, or bed. The cushioned seat of a rickety old sofa in one corner bore the faint impress of a lean, reclining form. Rolled away under his desk was a blanket; on a chair, a tin basin, with soap and a ragged towel; in a newspaper, a few crumbs of ginger nuts and a morsel of cheese. Yes, thought I, it is evident enough that Bartleby has been making his home here, keeping bachelor's hall all by himself. Immediately then the thought came sweeping across me, What miserable friendlessness and loneliness are here revealed! Think of it. Of a Sunday, Wall Street is deserted, and every night of every day it is an emptiness.

For the first time in my life a feeling of overpowering stinging melancholy seized me. The bond of a common humanity drew me irresistibly to gloom. I remembered the bright silks and sparkling faces

I had seen that day, and I contrasted them with the pallid copyist, and thought to myself, Ah, happiness courts the light, so we deem the world is gay; but misery hides aloof, so we deem that misery there is none. Presentiments of strange discoveries hovered round me. The scrivener's pale form appeared to me laid out, among uncaring strangers, in its shivering winding-sheet.

Suddenly I was attracted by Bartleby's closed desk, the key in open sight left in the lock.

I mean no mischief, seek the gratification of no heartless curiosity, thought I; besides, the desk is mine, and its contents, too, so I will make bold to look within. Everything was methodically arranged, the papers smoothly placed. The pigeonholes were deep, and removing the files of documents, I groped into their recesses. Presently I felt something there, and dragged it out. It was an old bandanna handkerchief, heavy and knotted. I opened it, and saw it was a savings bank.

I now recalled all the quiet mysteries which I had noted in the man. I remembered that he never spoke but to answer; that, though at intervals he had considerable time to himself, yet I had never seen him reading—no, not even a newspaper; that for long periods he would stand looking out, at his pale window behind the screen, upon the dead brick wall; I was quite sure he never visited any refectory or eating house; that he never went out for a walk; that though so thin and pale, he never complained of ill health. And more than all, I remembered a certain unconscious air of pallid—how shall I call it?—of pallid haughtiness, say, or rather an austere reserve about him, which had positively awed me into my tame compliance with his eccentricities.

As the forlornness of Bartleby grew and grew to my imagination, so did melancholy merge into fear, pity into repulsion. Up to a certain point misery enlists our best affections, but in certain special cases beyond that point it does not. To a sensitive being, pity is not seldom pain. And when at last it is perceived that such pity cannot lead to effectual succor, common sense bids the soul be rid of it. What I saw that morning persuaded me that the scrivener was the victim of innate and incurable disorder. I might give alms to his body, but it was his soul that suffered, and his soul I could not reach.

I did not accomplish the purpose of going to Trinity Church.

Somehow, the things I had seen disqualified me. I walked homeward, thinking what I would do with Bartleby. Finally, I resolved upon this—I would put certain calm questions to him the next morning, touching his history, etc., and if he declined to answer them openly and unreservedly (and I supposed he would prefer not), then to give him a twenty-dollar bill over and above whatever I might owe him, and tell him his services were no longer required; but that if in any other way I could assist him, I would be happy to do so, especially if he desired to return to his native place, wherever that might be. Moreover, if after reaching home he found himself at any time in want of aid, a letter from him would be sure of a reply.

The next morning came.

"Bartleby," said I, gently calling to him behind his screen.

No reply.

"Bartleby," said I in a still gentler tone, "come here; I am not going to ask you to do anything you would prefer not to do—I simply wish to speak to you."

Upon this he noiselessly slid into view.

"Will you tell me, Bartleby, where you were born?"

"I would prefer not to."

"Will you tell me *anything* about yourself?"

"I would prefer not to."

"But what reasonable objection can you have to speak to me? I feel friendly towards you."

He did not look at me while I spoke, but kept his glance fixed upon my bust of Cicero, which, as I then sat, was directly behind me, some six inches above my head.

"What is your answer, Bartleby?" said I, after waiting a considerable time for a reply.

"At present I prefer to give no answer," he said, and retired into his hermitage.

Mortified as I was at his behavior, and resolved as I had been to dismiss him when I entered my office, nevertheless I strangely felt something superstitious knocking at my heart, denouncing me for a villain if I dared to breathe one bitter word against this forlornest of mankind. At last, familiarly drawing my chair behind his screen, I sat down and said, "Bartleby, never mind, then, about revealing your history; but let me entreat you, as a friend, to comply as far as may be with the usages of this office. Say now, you will help to examine papers tomorrow or next day: in short, say now that in a day or two you will begin to be a little reasonable. Say so, Bartleby."

"At present I would prefer not to be a little reasonable," was his mildly cadaverous reply.

Just then the folding doors opened and Nippers approached. He seemed suffering from an unusually bad night's rest, induced by severer indigestion than common. He overheard Bartleby's answer.

"*Prefer not*, eh?" gritted Nippers. "I'd *prefer* him, if I were you, sir"—addressing me—"I'd give him preferences, the stubborn mule! What is it, sir, pray, that he *prefers* not to do now?"

Bartleby moved not a limb.

"Mr. Nippers," said I, "I'd prefer that you would withdraw for the present."

Somehow, of late, I had got into the way of involuntarily using this word prefer upon all sorts of not exactly suitable occasions. And I trembled to think that my contact with the scrivener had already and seriously affected me in a mental way. What further and deeper aberration might it not yet produce? Surely I must get rid of this demented man. But I thought it prudent not to break the dismissal at once.

The next day I noticed that Bartleby did nothing but stand at his window in his dead-wall reverie. Upon asking him why he did not write, he said that he had decided upon doing no more writing.

"Why, how now? What next!" exclaimed I. "Do no more writing?"

"No more."

"And what is the reason?"

"Do you not see the reason for yourself?" he indifferently replied.

I looked steadfastly at him, and perceived that his eyes looked dull and glazed. Instantly it occurred to me that his diligence in copying by his dim window might have temporarily impaired his vision.

I was touched. I said something in condolence with him. I hinted that of course he did wisely in abstaining from writing for a while, and urged him to embrace that opportunity of taking wholesome exercise in the open air. This, however, he did not do.

A few days went by. Whether Bartleby's eyes improved or not, I could not say. To all appearance, I thought they did. But when I asked him if they did, he vouchsafed no answer. At all events, he would do no copying. At last, in reply to my urgings, he informed me that he had permanently given up copying.

"What!" exclaimed I. "Suppose your eyes should get entirely well—better than ever before—would you not copy then?"

"I have given up copying," he answered, and slid aside.

He remained as ever, a fixture in my chamber. What was to be done? He would do nothing in the office; why should he stay there? In plain fact, he had now become a millstone to me. Yet I was sorry for him. If he would but have named a single relative or friend, I would instantly have written, and urged their taking the poor fellow away to some convenient retreat. But he seemed alone, absolutely alone in the universe. At length, necessities connected with my business tyrannized over all other considerations. Decently as I could, I told Bartleby that in six days' time he must unconditionally leave the office. I warned him to take measures, in the interval, for procuring some other abode. I offered to assist him in this endeavor, if he himself would but take the first step towards a removal. "And when you finally quit me, Bartleby," added I, "I shall see that you go not away entirely unprovided. Six days from this hour, remember."

At the expiration of that period, I peeped behind the screen, and lo! Bartleby was there.

I buttoned up my coat, balanced myself, advanced slowly towards him, touched his shoulder, and said, "The time has come; you must quit this place; I am sorry for you; here is money; but you must go."

"I would prefer not," he replied, with his back still towards me.

"You *must*."

He remained silent.

"Bartleby," said I, "I owe you twelve dollars on account; here are thirty-two; the odd twenty are yours. Will you take it?" and I handed the bills towards him.

But he made no motion.

"I will leave them here, then," putting them under a weight on the table. Then taking my hat and cane and going to the door, I tranquilly turned and added, "After you have removed your things from these offices, Bartleby, you will of course lock the door and, if you please, slip your key underneath the mat, so that I may have it in the morning. I shall not see you again; so good-by to you. If, hereafter, in your new place of abode, I can be of any service to you, do not fail to advise me by letter. Good-by, Bartleby, and fare you well."

But he answered not a word; like the last column of some ruined temple, he remained standing mute and solitary in the middle of the otherwise deserted room.

As I walked home in a pensive mood, my vanity got the better of my pity. I could not but highly plume myself on my masterly management in getting rid of Bartleby. The beauty of my procedure seemed to consist in its perfect quietness. There was no vulgar bullying, no bravado of any sort. Without loudly bidding Bartleby depart—as an inferior genius might have done—I *assumed* the ground that depart he must, and upon that assumption built all I had to say. The more I thought over my procedure, the more I was charmed with it. Nevertheless, next morning, upon awakening, I had my doubts—I had somehow slept off the fumes of vanity. One of the coolest and wisest hours a man has is just after he awakes in the morning. My procedure seemed as sagacious as ever—but only in theory. How it would prove in practice—there was the rub.

After breakfast I walked downtown, arguing the probabilities pro and con. As I had intended, I was earlier than usual at my office door. I stood listening for a moment. All was still. He must be gone. I tried the knob. The door was locked. Yes, my procedure had worked to a charm; he indeed must be vanished. Yet a certain melancholy mixed with this: I was almost sorry for my brilliant success. I was fumbling under the doormat for the key, which Bartleby was to have left there for me, when accidentally my knee knocked against a panel, producing a summoning sound, and in response a voice came to me from within— "Not yet; I am occupied."

It was Bartleby.

I was thunderstruck. For an instant I stood like the man who, pipe in mouth, was killed one cloudless afternoon long ago in Virginia by summer lightning; at his own warm open window he was killed, and remained leaning out there upon the dreamy afternoon till someone touched him, when he fell.

"Not gone!" I murmured at last. But again obeying that wondrous ascendancy which the inscrutable scrivener had over me, I slowly went downstairs and out into the street and, while walking round the block, considered what I should next do in this unheard-of perplexity. Turn the man out by an actual thrusting I could not; to drive him away by calling him hard names would not do; calling in the police was an unpleasant idea; and yet, permit him to enjoy his cadaverous triumph over me—this, too, I could not think of. What was to be done? Finally, I resolved to argue the matter over with him again.

"Bartleby," said I, entering the office with a quietly severe expression, "I am seriously displeased. I am pained, Bartleby. I had thought better of you. I had imagined you of such a gentlemanly organization that in any delicate dilemma a slight hint would suffice. But it appears I am deceived. Why," I added, unaffectedly starting, "you have not even touched that money yet," pointing to it, just where I had left it the evening previous.

He answered nothing.

"Will you, or will you not, quit me?" I now demanded in a sudden passion, advancing close to him.

"I would prefer *not* to quit you," he replied, gently emphasizing the not.

"What earthly right have you to stay here? Do you pay any rent? Do you pay my taxes? Or is this property yours?"

He answered nothing.

"Are you ready to go on and write now? Are your eyes recovered? Could you copy a small paper for me this morning? Or help examine a few lines? Or step round to the post office? In a word, will you do anything at all to give a coloring to your refusal to depart the premises?"

He silently retired into his hermitage.

I was now in such a state of nervous resentment that I thought it but prudent to check myself at present from further demonstrations. I endeavored immediately to occupy myself, and at the same time to comfort my despondency. I tried to fancy that in the course of the morning, at such time as might prove agreeable to him, Bartleby, of his own free accord, would emerge from his hermitage and take up some decided line of march in the direction of the door. But no. Half past twelve o'clock came; Turkey began to glow in the face, overturn his inkstand, and become generally obstreperous; Nippers abated into quietude and courtesy; Ginger Nut munched his noon apple; and Bartleby remained standing at his window in one of his profoundest dead-wall reveries. Will it be credited? Ought I to acknowledge it? That afternoon I left the office without saying one further word to him.

Some days now passed, during which at leisure intervals I looked a little into Edwards' *Freedom of the Will* and Priestley on *Necessity*. Under the circumstances, those books induced a salutary feeling. Gradually I slid into the persuasion that Bartleby was billeted upon me for some mysterious purpose of an all-wise Providence, which it was not for a mere mortal like me to fathom. Yes, Bartleby, stay there behind your screen, thought I; I shall persecute you no more; you are harmless and noiseless as any of these old chairs. At last I see it, I feel it; I penetrate to the predestinated purpose of my life. Others may have loftier parts to enact, but my mission in this world, Bartleby, is to furnish you with office room for such period as you may see fit to remain.

I believe that this wise and blessed frame of mind would have continued with me had it not been for the unsolicited and uncharitable remarks obtruded upon me by my professional friends who visited the rooms. Sometimes an attorney, calling at my office and finding no one but the scrivener there, would undertake to obtain some sort of precise information from him touching my whereabouts; but without heeding his idle talk, Bartleby would remain standing immovable in the middle of the room. So after contemplating him in that position for a time, the attorney would depart, no wiser than he came.

Also, when a reference was going on, and the room full of lawyers and witnesses, and business driving fast, some deeply occupied legal gentleman present, seeing Bartleby wholly unemployed, would request him to run round to his office and fetch some papers for him. Thereupon, Bartleby would tranquilly decline, and yet remain idle as before. Then the lawyer would give a great stare, and turn to me. And what could I say? At last I was made aware that all through the circle of my professional acquaintance a whisper of wonder was running round, having reference to the strange creature I kept at my office. And as my friends continually intruded their relentless remarks upon this apparition, a great change was wrought in me. I resolved to gather all my faculties together, and forever rid me of this intolerable incubus.

Ere revolving any complicated project, however, I first simply suggested to Bartleby the propriety of his permanent departure. In a calm and serious tone I commended the idea to his careful and mature consideration. But, having taken three days to meditate upon it, he apprised me that his original determination remained the same; in short, that he still preferred to abide with me.

What shall I do? I now said to myself, buttoning up my coat to the last button. What shall I do? What ought I to do? What does conscience say I *should* do with this man, or, rather, ghost. Rid myself of him, I must; go, he shall. But how? You will not thrust him, the poor, pale, passive mortal—you will not thrust such a helpless creature out of your door? You will not dishonor yourself by such cruelty? No, I will not, I cannot do that. What, then, will you do? For all your coaxing, he will not budge. Bribes he leaves under your own paperweight on your table; in short, it is quite plain that he prefers to cling to you.

Then something severe, something unusual must be done. What! Surely you will not have him collared by a constable, and commit his innocent pallor to the common jail? No more, then. Since he will not quit me, I must quit him. I will change my offices; I will move elsewhere, and give him fair notice that if I find him on my new premises, I will then proceed against him as a common trespasser.

Acting accordingly, next day I thus addressed him: "I find these chambers too far from the city hall; the air is unwholesome. In a word, I propose to remove my offices next week, and shall no longer require your services. I tell you this now, in order that you may seek another place."

He made no reply, and nothing more was said.

On the appointed day I engaged carts and men, proceeded to my chambers, and, having but little furniture, everything was removed in a few hours. Throughout, the scrivener remained standing behind the screen, which I directed to be removed the last thing. It was withdrawn; and, being folded up like a huge folio, left him the motionless occupant of a naked room. I stood in the entry watching him a moment, while something from within me upbraided me.

I reentered, with my hand in my pocket—and—and my heart in my mouth.

"Good-by, Bartleby; I am going—good-by, and God someway bless you; and take that," slipping something in his hand. But it dropped upon the floor, and then—strange to say—I tore myself from him whom I had so longed to be rid of.

Established in my new quarters, for a day or two I kept the door locked, and started at every footfall in the passages. When I returned to my rooms after any little absence, I would pause at the threshold for an instant, and attentively listen, ere applying my key. But these fears were needless. Bartleby never came nigh me.

I thought all was going well, when a perturbed-looking stranger visited me, inquiring whether I was the person who had recently occupied rooms at No. —— Wall Street.

Full of forebodings, I replied that I was.

"Then, sir," said the stranger, who proved a lawyer, "you are responsible for the man you left there. He refuses to do any copying; he refuses to do anything; he says he prefers not to; and he refuses to quit the premises."

"I am very sorry, sir," said I, with assumed tranquillity, but an inward tremor, "but, really, the man you allude to is nothing to me— he is no relation or apprentice of mine, that you should hold me responsible for him."

"In mercy's name, who is he?"

"I certainly cannot inform you. I know nothing about him. Formerly I employed him as a copyist; but he has done nothing for me now for some time past."

"I shall settle him, then. Good morning, sir."

Several days passed, and I heard nothing more; and, though I often felt a charitable prompting to call at the place and see poor Bartleby, yet a certain squeamishness, of I know not what, withheld me.

All is over with him by this time, thought I at last, when, through another week, no further intelligence reached me. But, coming to my room the day after, I found several persons waiting at my door in a high state of nervous excitement.

"That's the man—here he comes," cried the foremost one, whom I recognized as the lawyer who had previously called upon me alone.

"You must take him away, sir, at once," cried a portly person among them, advancing upon me, and whom I knew to be the landlord of No. —— Wall Street. "These gentlemen, my tenants, cannot stand it any longer; Mr. B——"—pointing to the lawyer—"has turned him out of his room, and he now persists in haunting the building generally, sitting upon the banisters of the stairs by day, and sleeping in the entry by night. Everybody is concerned; clients are leaving the offices; some fears are entertained of a mob; something you must do, and that without delay."

Aghast at this torrent, I fell back before it, and would fain have locked myself in my new quarters. In vain I persisted that Bartleby was nothing to me—no more than to anyone else. In vain—I was the last person known to have anything to do with him, and they held me to the terrible account. I considered the matter, and at length said that if the lawyer would give me a confidential interview with the scrivener in his (the lawyer's) own room, I would, that afternoon, strive my best to rid them of the nuisance they complained of.

Going upstairs to my old haunt, there was Bartleby silently sitting upon the banister at the landing.

"What are you doing here, Bartleby?" said I.

"Sitting upon the banister," he mildly replied.

I motioned him into the lawyer's room; the lawyer left us.

"Bartleby," said I, "are you aware that you are the cause of great tribulation to me, by persisting in occupying the entry after being dismissed from the office?"

No answer.

"Now one of two things must take place. Either you must do something, or something must be done to you. Now what sort of business would you like to engage in? Would you like to reengage in copying for someone?"

"No; I would prefer not to make any change."

"Would you like a clerkship in a dry-goods store?"

"There is too much confinement about that. No, I would not like a clerkship; but I am not particular."

"Too much confinement!" I cried. "Why, you keep yourself confined all the time!"

"I would prefer not to take a clerkship," he rejoined, as if to settle that little item at once.

"How would a bartender's business suit you? There is no trying of the eyesight in that."

"I would not like it at all; though, as I said before, I am not particular."

His unwonted wordiness inspirited me. I returned to the charge.

"Well, then, would you like to travel through the country collecting bills for the merchants? That would improve your health."

"No; I would prefer to be doing something else."

"How, then, would going as a companion to Europe, to entertain some young gentleman with your conversation—how would that suit you?"

"Not at all. It does not strike me that there is anything definite about that. I like to be stationary. But I am not particular."

Despairing of all further efforts, I was precipitately leaving him when a final thought occurred to me—one which had not been wholly unindulged before.

"Bartleby," said I, in the kindest tone I could assume under such existing circumstances, "will you go home with me now—not to my office, but my dwelling—and remain there till we can conclude upon some convenient arrangement for you at our leisure? Come, let us start now, right away."

"No; at present I would prefer not to make any change at all."

I answered nothing; but, effectually dodging everyone by the suddenness and rapidity of my flight, rushed from the building and, jumping into the first omnibus, was soon removed from pursuit. As soon as tranquillity returned, I distinctly perceived that I had now done all that I possibly could, both in respect to the demands of the landlord and his tenants, and with regard to my own desire and sense of duty, to shield Bartleby from rude persecution. I now strove to be entirely carefree and quiescent. But so fearful was I of being again hunted out by the incensed landlord and his exasperated tenants, that, surrendering my business to Nippers for a few days, I drove in my carriage about the upper part of the town and through the suburbs, crossed over to Jersey City and Hoboken, and paid fugitive visits to Manhattanville and Astoria. In fact, I almost lived in my carriage for the time.

When again I entered my office, lo, a note from the landlord lay upon the desk. I opened it with trembling hands. It informed me that the writer had sent to the police and had Bartleby removed to the Tombs as a vagrant. Moreover, since I knew more about him than anyone else, he wished me to appear at that place and make a suitable statement of the facts. These tidings had a conflicting effect upon me. At first I was indignant; but, at last, almost approved. The landlord's energetic, summary disposition had led him to adopt a procedure which I do not think I would have decided upon myself; and yet, as a last resort, under such peculiar circumstances, it seemed the only plan.

As I afterwards learned, the poor scrivener, when told that he must be conducted to the Tombs, offered not the slightest obstacle, but, in his pale unmoving way, silently acquiesced.

Some of the compassionate and curious bystanders joined the party; and, headed by one of the constables arm in arm with Bartleby, the silent procession filed its way through all the noise and heat and joy of the roaring thoroughfares at noon.

The same day I received the note I went to the Tombs. Seeking the right officer, I stated the purpose of my call, and was informed that the individual I described was, indeed, within. I then assured the officer that Bartleby was a perfectly honest man and greatly to be pitied, however unaccountably eccentric. I narrated all I knew, and closed by suggesting the idea of letting him remain in as indulgent confinement as possible, till something less harsh might be done—though, indeed, I hardly knew what. At all events, if nothing else could be decided upon, the almshouse must receive him. I then begged to have an interview.

Being under no disgraceful charge, and quite serene and harmless in all his ways, they had permitted him freely to wander about the prison and, especially, in the enclosed grass-platted yards thereof. And so I found him there, standing all alone in the quietest of the yards, his face towards a high wall, while all around, from the narrow slits of the jail windows, I thought I saw peering out upon him the eyes of murderers and thieves.

"Bartleby!"

"I know you," he said, without looking round, "and I want nothing to say to you."

"It was not I that brought you here, Bartleby," said I, keenly pained at his implied suspicion. "And to you, this should not be so vile a place. Nothing reproachful attaches to you by being here. And see, it is not so sad a place as one might think. Look, there is the sky, and here is the grass."

"I know where I am," he replied, but would say nothing more, and so I left him.

As I entered the corridor again, a broad meatlike man in an apron accosted me and, jerking his thumb over his shoulder, said, "Is that your friend?"

"Yes."

"Does he want to starve? If he does, let him live on the prison fare, that's all."

"Who are you?" asked I, not knowing what to make of such an unofficially speaking person in such a place.

"I am the grub man. Such gentlemen as have friends here hire me to provide them with something good to eat."

"Is this so?" said I, turning to the turnkey.

He said it was.

"Well, then," said I, slipping some silver into the grub man's hands, "I want you to give particular attention to my friend there; let him have the best dinner you can get. And you must be as polite to him as possible."

"Introduce me, will you?" said the grub man, looking at me with an expression which seemed to say he was all impatience for an opportunity to give a specimen of his breeding.

Thinking it would prove of benefit to the scrivener, I acquiesced; and, asking the grub man his name, went up with him to Bartleby.

"Bartleby, this is a friend; you will find him very useful to you."

"Your sarvant, sir, your sarvant," said the grub man, making a low salutation behind his apron. "Hope you find it pleasant here, sir; nice grounds—cool apartments—hope you'll stay with us some time—try to make it agreeable. What will you have for dinner today?"

"I prefer not to dine today," said Bartleby, turning away. "It would disagree with me; I am unused to dinners." So saying, he slowly moved to the other side of the enclosure and took up a position fronting the dead wall.

"How's this?" said the grub man, addressing me with a stare of astonishment. "He's odd, ain't he?"

"I think he is a little deranged," said I sadly.

"Deranged? Deranged is it? Well, now, upon my word, I thought that friend of yourn was a gentleman forger; they are always pale and genteellike, them forgers. I can't help pity 'em—can't help it, sir," he added touchingly.

"I cannot stop longer, but look to my friend yonder. You will not lose by it. I will see you again."

Some few days after this I again obtained admission to the Tombs, and went through the corridors in quest of Bartleby, but without finding him.

"I saw him coming from his cell not long ago," said a turnkey. "Maybe he's gone to loiter in the yards."

So I went in that direction.

"Are you looking for the silent man?" said another turnkey, passing me. "Yonder he lies—sleeping in the yard there. 'Tis not twenty minutes since I saw him lie down."

The yard was entirely quiet. It was not accessible to the common prisoners. The surrounding walls, of amazing thickness, kept off all sounds behind them. The Egyptian character of the masonry weighed upon me with its gloom. But a soft imprisoned turf grew underfoot. The heart of the eternal pyramids, it seemed, wherein, by some strange magic, through the clefts, grass seed, dropped by birds, had sprung.

Strangely huddled at the base of the wall, his knees drawn up, and lying on his side, his head touching the cold stones, I saw the wasted Bartleby. But nothing stirred. I paused, then went close up to him; stooped over, and saw that his dim eyes were open; otherwise he seemed profoundly sleeping. Something prompted me to touch him. I felt his hand, when a tingling shiver ran up my arm and down my spine to my feet.

The round face of the grub man peered upon me now. "His dinner is ready. Won't he dine today, either? Or does he live without dining?"

"Lives without dining," said I, and closed the eyes.

"Eh! He's asleep, ain't he?"

"With kings and counselors," murmured I.

ERE PARTING with the reader, let me divulge one little item of rumor which came to my ear a few months after the scrivener's decease. How true it is I cannot now tell, but the report was this: that before he came to me Bartleby had been a subordinate clerk in the dead letter office at Washington, from which he had been suddenly removed by a change in the administration. Dead letters! Does it not sound like dead men? Conceive a man by nature and misfortune prone to a pallid hopelessness, can any business seem more fitted to heighten it than that of continually handling these dead letters, and assorting them for the flames? For by the cartload they are annually burned. On errands of life, these letters speed to death. Ah, Bartleby! Ah, humanity!

•

LOUISE
W. SOMERSET MAUGHAM

W. S. Maugham

I COULD NEVER understand why Louise bothered with me. She disliked me and I knew that behind my back, in that gentle way of hers, she seldom lost the opportunity of saying a disagreeable thing about me. She had too much delicacy ever to make a direct statement, but with a hint and a sigh and a little flutter of her beautiful hands she was able to make her meaning plain. She was a mistress of cold praise. It was true that we had known one another almost intimately, for five-and-twenty years, but it was impossible for me to believe that she could be affected by the claims of old association. She thought me a coarse, brutal, cynical, and vulgar fellow. I was puzzled at her not taking the obvious course and dropping me. She did nothing of the kind; indeed, she would not leave me alone; she was constantly asking me to lunch and dine with her and once or twice a year invited me to spend a weekend at her house in the country. At last I thought that I had discovered her motive. She had an uneasy suspicion that I did not believe in her; and if that was why she did not like me, it was also why she sought my acquaintance: it galled her that I alone should look upon her as a comic figure and she could not rest till I acknowledged myself mistaken and defeated. Perhaps she had an inkling that I saw the face behind the mask and because I alone held out was determined that sooner or later I too should take the mask for the face. I was never quite certain that she was a complete humbug. I wondered whether she fooled herself as thoroughly as she fooled the world or whether there was some spark of humour at the bottom of her heart. If there was it might be that she was attracted to me, as a pair of crooks might be attracted to one another, by the knowledge that we shared a secret that was hidden from everybody else.

I knew Louise before she married. She was then a frail, delicate girl with large and melancholy eyes. Her father and mother worshipped her with an anxious adoration, for some illness, scarlet fever I think, left her with a weak heart and she had to take the greatest care of herself. When Tom Maitland proposed to her they were dismayed, for they were convinced that she was much too delicate for the strenuous state of marriage. But they were not too well off and Tom Maitland was rich. He promised to do everything in the world for Louise and finally they entrusted her to him as a sacred charge. Tom Maitland was a big, husky fellow, very good-looking, and a fine athlete. He doted on Louise.

With her weak heart he could not hope to keep her with him long and he made up his mind to do everything he could to make her few years on earth happy. He gave up the games he excelled in, not because she wished him to, she was glad that he should play golf and hunt, but because by a coincidence she had a heart attack whenever he proposed to leave her for a day. If they had a difference of opinion she gave in to him at once, for she was the most submissive wife a man could have, but her heart failed her and she would be laid up, sweet and uncomplaining, for a week. He could not be such a brute as to cross her. Then they would have a quiet little tussle about which should yield and it was only with difficulty that at last he persuaded her to have her own way. On one occasion seeing her walk eight miles on an expedition that she particularly wanted to make, I suggested to Tom Maitland that she was stronger than one would have thought. He shook his head and sighed.

"No, no, she's dreadfully delicate. She's been to all the best heart specialists in the world, and they all say that her life hangs on a thread. But she has an unconquerable spirit."

He told her that I had remarked on her endurance.

"I shall pay for it tomorrow," she said to me in her plaintive way. "I shall be at death's door."

"I sometimes think that you're quite strong enough to do the things you want to," I murmured.

I had noticed that if a party was amusing she could dance till five in the morning, but if it was dull she felt very poorly and Tom had to take her home early. I am afraid she did not like my reply, for though she gave me a pathetic little smile I saw no amusement in her large blue eyes.

"You can't very well expect me to fall down dead just to please you," she answered.

Louise outlived her husband. He caught his death of cold one day when they were sailing and Louise needed all the rugs there were to keep her warm. He left her a comfortable fortune and a daughter. Louise was inconsolable. It was wonderful that she managed to survive the shock. Her friends expected her speedily to follow poor Tom Maitland to the grave. Indeed they already felt dreadfully sorry for Iris, her daughter, who would be left an orphan. They redoubled their attentions towards Louise. They would not let her stir a finger; they insisted on doing everything in the world to save her trouble. They had to, because if she was called upon to do anything tiresome or inconvenient her heart went back on her and there she was at death's door. She was entirely lost without a man to take care of her, she said, and she did not know how, with her delicate health, she was going to bring up her dear Iris. Her friends asked why she did not marry again. Oh, with her heart it was out of the question, though of course she knew that dear Tom would have wished her to, and perhaps it would be the best thing for Iris if she did; but who would want to be bothered with a wretched invalid like herself? Oddly enough more than one young man showed himself quite ready to undertake the charge and a year after Tom's death she allowed George Hobhouse to lead her to the altar. He was a fine, upstanding fellow, and he was not at all badly off. I never saw anyone so grateful as he for the privilege of being allowed to take care of this frail little thing.

"I shan't live to trouble you long," she said.

He was a soldier and an ambitious one, but he resigned his commission.

Louise's health forced her to spend the winter at Monte Carlo and the summer at Deauville. He hesitated a little at throwing up his career, and Louise at first would not hear of it; but at last she yielded as she always yielded, and he prepared to make his wife's last few years as happy as might be.

"It can't be very long now," she said. "I'll try not to be troublesome."

For the next two or three years Louise managed, notwithstanding her weak heart, to go beautifully dressed to all the most lively parties, to gamble very heavily, to dance and even to flirt with tall, slim young men. But George Hobhouse had not the stamina of Louise's first husband and he had to brace himself now and then with a stiff drink for his day's work as Louise's second husband. It is possible that the habit would have grown on him, which Louise would not have liked at all, but very fortunately (for her) the war broke out. He rejoined his regiment and three months later was killed. It was a great shock to Louise.

She felt, however, that in such a crisis she must not give way to a private grief; and if she had a heart attack nobody heard of it. In order to distract her mind, she turned her villa at Monte Carlo into a hospital for convalescent officers. Her friends told her that she would never survive the strain.

"Of course it will kill me," she said, "I know that. But what does it matter? I must do my bit."

It didn't kill her. She had the time of her life. There was no convalescent home in France that was more popular. I met her by chance in Paris. She was lunching at the Ritz with a tall and very handsome Frenchman. She explained that she was there on business connected with the hospital. She told me that the officers were too charming to her. They knew how delicate she was and they wouldn't let her do a single thing. They took care of her, well—as though they were all her husbands. She sighed.

"Poor George, who would ever have thought that I, with my heart, should survive him?"

"And poor Tom!" I said.

I don't know why she didn't like my saying that. She gave me her plaintive smile and her beautiful eyes filled with tears.

"You always speak as though you grudged me the few years that I can expect to live."

"By the way, you heart's much better, isn't it?"

"It'll never be better. I saw a specialist this morning and he said I must be prepared for the worst."

"Oh, well, you've been prepared for that for nearly twenty years now, haven't you?"

When the war came to an end Louise settled in London. She was now a woman of over forty, thin and frail still, with large eyes and pale cheeks, but she did not look a day more than twenty-five. Iris, who had been at school and was now grown up, came to live with her.

"She'll take care of me," said Louise. "Of course it'll be hard on her to live with such a great invalid as I am, but it can only be for such a little while, I'm sure she won't mind."

Iris was a nice girl. She had been brought up with the knowledge that her mother's health was precarious. As a child she had never been allowed to make a noise. She had always realized that her mother must on no account be upset. And though Louise told her now that she would not hear of her sacrificing herself for a tiresome old woman the girl simply would not listen. It wasn't a question of sacrificing herself, it was a happiness to do what she could for her poor dear mother. With a sigh her mother let her do a great deal.

"It pleases the child to think she's making herself useful," she said.

"Don't you think she ought to go out and about more?" I asked.

"That's what I'm always telling her. I can't get her to enjoy herself. Heaven knows, I never want anyone to put themselves out on my account."

And Iris, when I remonstrated with her, said: "Poor dear mother, she wants me to go and stay with friends and go to parties, but the moment I start off anywhere she has one of her heart attacks, so I much prefer to stay at home."

But presently she fell in love. A young friend of mine, a very good lad, asked her to marry him and she consented. I liked the child and was glad that she was to be given the chance to lead a life of her own. She had never seemed to suspect that such a thing was possible. But one day the young man came to me in great distress and told me that his marriage was indefinitely posponed. Iris felt that she could not desert her mother.

Of course it was really no business of mine, but I made the opportunity to go and see Louise. She was always glad to receive her friends at tea-time and now that she was older she cultivated the society of painters and writers.

"Well, I hear that Iris isn't going to be married," I said after a while.

"I don't know about that. She's not going to be married quite as soon as I could have wished. I've begged her on my bended knees not to consider me, but she absolutely refuses to leave me."

"Don't you think it's rather hard on her?"

"Dreadfully. Of course it can only be for a few months, but I hate the thought of anyone sacrificing themselves for me."

"My dear Louise, you've buried two husbands, I can't see the least reason why you shouldn't bury at least two more."

"Do you think that's funny?" she asked me in a tone that she made as offensive as she could.

"I suppose it's never struck you as strange that you're always strong enough to do anything you want to and that your weak heart only prevents you from doing things that bore you?"

"Oh, I know, I know what you've always thought of me. You've never believed that I had anything the matter with me, have you?"

I looked at her full and square.

"Never. I think you've carried out for twenty-five years a stupendous bluff. I think you're the most selfish and monstrous woman I have ever known. You ruined the lives of those two wretched men you married and now you're going to ruin the life of your daughter."

I should not have been surprised if Louise had had a heart attack then. I fully expected her to fly into a passion. She merely gave me a gentle smile.

"My poor friend, one of these days you'll be so dreadfully sorry you said this to me."

"Have you quite determined that Iris shall not marry this boy?"

"I've begged her to marry him. I know it'll kill me, but I don't mind. Nobody cares for me. I'm just a burden to everybody."

"Did you tell her it would kill you?"

"She made me."

"As if anyone ever made you do anything that you were not yourself quite determined to do."

"She can marry her young man tomorrow if she likes. If it kills me, it kills me."

"Well, let's risk it, shall we?"

"Haven't you got any compassion for me?"

"One can't pity anyone who amuses one as much as you amuse me," I answered.

A faint spot of colour appeared on Louise's pale cheeks and though she smiled still her eyes were hard and angry.

"Iris shall marry in a month's time," she said, "and if anything happens to me I hope you and she will be able to forgive yourselves."

Louise was as good as her word. A date was fixed, a trousseau of great magnificence was ordered, and invitations were issued. Iris and the very good lad were radiant. On the wedding-day, at ten o'clock in the morning, Louise, that devilish woman, had one of her heart attacks —and died. She died gently forgiving Iris for having killed her.

TO BUILD A FIRE

JACK LONDON

Jack London

Day had broken cold and gray, exceedingly cold and gray, when the man turned aside from the main Yukon trail and climbed the high earth bank, where a dim and little-traveled trail led eastward through the fat spruce timberland. It was a steep bank, and he paused for breath at the top, excusing the act to himself by looking at his watch. It was nine o'clock. There was no sun nor hint of sun, though there was not a cloud in the sky. It was a clear day, and yet there seemed an intangible pall over the face of things, a subtle gloom that made the day dark, and that was due to the absence of sun. This fact did not worry the man. He was used to the lack of sun. It had been days since he had seen the sun, and he knew that a few more days must pass before that cheerful orb, due south, would just peep above the skyline and dip immediately from view.

The man flung a look back along the way he had come. The Yukon lay a mile wide and hidden under three feet of ice. On top of this ice were as many feet of snow. It was all pure white, rolling in gentle undulations where the ice jams of the freeze-up had formed. North and south, as far as his eye could see, it was unbroken white, save for a dark hairline that curved and twisted from around the spruce-covered island to the south, and that curved and twisted away into the north, where it disappeared behind another spruce-covered island. This hairline was the main trail that led south five hundred miles to the Chilcoot Pass, Dyea, and salt water; and that led north seventy miles to Dawson, and still on to the north a thousand miles to Nulato, and finally to St. Michael on Bering Sea, a thousand miles and half a thousand more.

But all this—the mysterious, far-reaching hairline trail, the absence of sun from the sky, the tremendous cold, and the strangeness and weirdness of it all—made no impression on the man. It was not because he was long used to it. He was a newcomer in the land, a cheechako, and this was his first winter. The trouble with him was that he was without imagination. He was quick and alert in the things of life, but only in the things, and not in the significances. Fifty degrees below zero meant eighty-odd degrees of frost. Such fact impressed him as being cold and uncomfortable, and that was all. It did not lead him to meditate upon his frailty as a creature of temperature, and upon man's frailty in general, able only to live within certain narrow limits of heat and cold; and from there on it did not lead him to the conjectural field of immortality and man's place in the universe. Fifty degrees below zero stood for a bite of frost that hurt and that must be guarded against by the use of mittens, earflaps, warm moccasins, and thick socks. Fifty degrees below zero was to him just precisely fifty degrees below zero. That there should be anything more to it than that was a thought that never entered his head.

As he turned to go on, he spat speculatively. There was a sharp, explosive crackle that startled him. He spat again. And again, in the air, before it could fall to the snow, the spittle crackled. He knew that at fifty below spittle crackled on the snow, but this spittle had crackled in the air. Undoubtedly it was colder than fifty below—how much colder he did not know. But the temperature did not matter. He was bound for the old claim on the left fork of Henderson Creek, where the boys were already. They had come over across the divide from the Indian Creek country, while he had come the roundabout way to take a look at the possibilities of getting out logs in the spring from the islands in the Yukon. He would be into camp by six o'clock; a bit after dark, it was true, but the boys would be there, a fire would be going, and a hot supper would be ready. As for lunch, he pressed his hand against the protruding bundle under his jacket. It was also under his shirt, wrapped up in a handkerchief and lying against the naked skin. It was the only way to keep the biscuits from freezing. He smiled agreeably to himself as he thought of those biscuits, each cut open and sopped in bacon grease, and each enclosing a generous slice of fried bacon.

He plunged in among the big spruce trees. The trail was faint. A foot of snow had fallen since the last sled had passed over, and he was glad he was without a sled, traveling light. In fact, he carried nothing but the lunch wrapped in the handkerchief. He was surprised, however, at the cold. It certainly was cold, he concluded, as he rubbed his numb nose and cheekbones with his mittened hand. He was a warm-whiskered man, but the hair on his face did not protect the high cheekbones and the eager nose that thrust itself aggressively into the frosty air.

At the man's heels trotted a dog, a big native husky, the proper wolf dog, gray-coated and without any visible or temperamental difference from its brother, the wild wolf. The animal was depressed by the tremendous cold. It knew that it was no time for traveling. Its instinct told it a truer tale than was told to the man by the man's judgment. In reality, it was not merely colder than fifty below zero; it was colder than sixty below, than seventy below. It was seventy-five below zero. Since the freezing point is thirty-two above zero, it meant that one hundred and seven degrees of frost obtained. The dog did not know anything about thermometers. Possibly in its brain there was no sharp consciousness of a condition of very cold such as was in the man's brain. But the brute had its instinct. It experienced a vague but menacing apprehension that subdued it and made it slink along at the man's heels, and that made it question eagerly every unwonted movement of the man as if expecting him to go into camp or to seek shelter somewhere and build a fire. The dog had learned fire, and it wanted fire, or else to burrow under the snow and cuddle its warmth away from the air.

The frozen moisture of its breathing had settled on its fur in a fine powder of frost, and especially were its jowls, muzzle, and eyelashes whitened by its crystaled breath. The man's red beard and mustache were likewise frosted, but more solidly, the deposit taking the form of ice and increasing with every warm, moist breath he exhaled. Also, the man was chewing tobacco, and the muzzle of ice held his lips so rigidly that he was unable to clear his chin when he expelled the juice. The result was that a crystal beard of the color and solidity of amber was increasing its length on his chin. If he fell down it would shatter itself, like glass, into brittle fragments. But he did not mind the appendage. It was the penalty all tobacco chewers paid in that country, and he had been out before in two cold snaps. They had not been so cold as this, he knew, but by the spirit thermometer at Sixty Mile he knew they had been registered at fifty below and at fifty-five.

He held on through the level stretch of woods for several miles and dropped down a bank to the frozen bed of a small stream. This was Henderson Creek, and he knew he was ten miles from the forks. He looked at his watch. It was ten o'clock. He was making four miles an hour, and he calculated that he would arrive at the forks at half past twelve. He decided to celebrate that event by eating his lunch there.

The dog dropped in again at his heels, with a tail drooping discouragement, as the man swung along the creek bed. The furrow of the old sled trail was visible, but a dozen inches of snow covered the marks of the last runners. In a month no man had come up or down that silent creek. The man held steadily on. He was not much given to thinking, and just then particularly he had nothing to think about save that he would eat lunch at the forks and that at six o'clock he would be in camp with the boys. There was nobody to talk to; and, had there been, speech would have been impossible because of the ice muzzle on his mouth. So he continued monotonously to chew tobacco and to increase the length of his amber beard.

Once in a while the thought reiterated itself that it was very cold and that he had never experienced such cold. As he walked along he rubbed his cheekbones and nose with the back of his mittened hand. He did this automatically, now and again changing hands. But rub as he would, the instant he stopped his cheekbones went numb, and the following instant the end of his nose went numb. He was sure to frost his cheeks; he knew that, and experienced a pang of regret that he had not devised a nose strap of the sort Bud wore in cold snaps. Such a strap passed across the cheeks, as well, and saved them. But it didn't matter much, after all. What were frosted cheeks? A bit painful, that was all; they were never serious.

Empty as the man's mind was of thoughts, he was keenly observant, and he noticed the changes in the creek, the curves and bends and timber jams, and always he sharply noted where he placed his feet. Once, coming around a bend, he shied abruptly, like a startled horse, curved away from the place where he had been walking, and retreated

541

several paces back along the trail. The creek he knew was frozen clear to the bottom—no creek could contain water in that arctic winter—but he knew also that there were springs that bubbled out from the hillsides and ran along under the snow and on top the ice of the creek. He knew that the coldest snaps never froze these springs, and he knew likewise their danger. They were traps. They hid pools of water under the snow that might be three inches deep, or three feet. Sometimes a skin of ice half an inch thick covered them, and in turn was covered by the snow. Sometimes there were alternate layers of water and ice skin, so that when one broke through he kept on breaking through for a while, sometimes wetting himself to the waist.

That was why he had shied in such panic. He had felt the give under his feet and heard the crackle of a snow-hidden ice skin. And to get his feet wet in such a temperature meant trouble and danger. At the very least it meant delay, for he would be forced to stop and build a fire, and under its protection to bare his feet while he dried his socks and moccasins. He stood and studied the creek bed and its banks, and decided that the flow of water came from the right. He reflected a while, rubbing his nose and cheeks, then skirted to the left, stepping gingerly and testing the footing for each step. Once clear of the danger, he took a fresh chew of tobacco and swung along at his four-mile gait.

In the course of the next two hours he came upon several similar traps. Usually the snow above the hidden pools had a sunken, candied appearance that advertised the danger. Once again, however, he had a close call; and once, suspecting danger, he compelled the dog to go on in front. The dog did not want to go. It hung back until the man shoved it forward, and then it went quickly across the white, unbroken surface. Suddenly it broke through, floundered to one side, and got away to firmer footing. It had wet its forefeet and legs, and almost immediately the water that clung to it turned to ice. It made quick efforts to lick the ice off its legs, then dropped down in the snow and began to bite out the ice that had formed between the toes. This was a matter of instinct. To permit the ice to remain would mean sore feet. It did not know this. It merely obeyed the mysterious prompting that arose from the deep crypts of its being. But the man knew, having achieved a judgment on the subject, and he removed the mitten from his right hand and helped tear out the ice particles. He did not expose his fingers more than a minute, and was astonished at the swift numbness that smote them. It certainly was cold. He pulled on the mitten hastily, and beat the hand savagely across his chest.

At twelve o'clock the day was at its brightest. Yet the sun was too far south on its winter journey to clear the horizon. The bulge of the earth intervened between it and Henderson Creek, where the man walked under a clear sky at noon and cast no shadow. At half past twelve, to the minute, he arrived at the forks of the creek. He was pleased at the speed he had made. If he kept it up, he would certainly be with the boys by six. He unbuttoned his jacket and shirt and drew forth his lunch. The action consumed no more than a quarter of a minute, yet in that brief moment the numbness laid hold of the exposed fingers. He did not put the mitten on, but, instead, struck the fingers a dozen sharp smashes against his leg. Then he sat down on a snow-covered log to eat. The sting that followed upon the striking of his fingers against his leg ceased so quickly that he was startled. He had had no chance to take a bite of biscuit. He struck the fingers repeatedly and returned them to the mitten, baring the other hand for the purpose of eating. He tried to take a mouthful, but the ice muzzle prevented. He had forgotten to build a fire and thaw out. He chuckled at his foolishness, and as he chuckled he noted the numbness creeping into the exposed fingers. Also, he noted that the stinging which had first come to his toes when he sat down was already passing away. He wondered whether the toes were warm or numb. He moved them inside the moccasins and decided that they were numb.

He pulled the mitten on hurriedly and stood up. He was a bit frightened. He stamped up and down until the stinging returned into the feet. It certainly was cold, was his thought. That man from Sulphur Creek had spoken the truth when telling how cold it sometimes got in the country. And he had laughed at him at the time! That showed one must not be too sure of things. There was no mistake about it, it *was* cold. He strode up and down, stamping his feet and threshing his arms, until reassured by the returning warmth. Then he got out matches and proceeded to make a fire. From the undergrowth, where high water of the previous spring had lodged a supply of seasoned twigs, he got his firewood. Working carefully from a small beginning, he soon had a roaring fire, over which he thawed the ice from his face and in the protection of which he ate his biscuits. For the moment the cold of space was outwitted. The dog took satisfaction in the fire, stretching out close enough for warmth and far enough away to escape being singed.

When the man had finished, he filled his pipe and took his comfortable time over a smoke. Then he pulled on his mittens, settled the earflaps of his cap firmly about his ears, and took the creek trail up the left fork. The dog was disappointed and yearned back toward the fire. This man did not know cold. Possibly all the generations of his ancestry had been ignorant of cold, of real cold, of cold one hundred and seven degrees below freezing point. But the dog knew; all its ancestry knew, and it had inherited the knowledge. And it knew that it was not good to walk abroad in such fearful cold. It was the time to lie snug in a hole in the snow and wait for a curtain of cloud to be drawn across the face of outer space whence this cold came. On the other hand, there was no keen intimacy between the dog and the man. The one was the toil slave of the other, and the only caresses it had ever received were the caresses of the whiplash and of harsh and menacing throat sounds that threatened the whiplash. So the dog made no effort to communicate its apprehension to the man. It was not concerned in the welfare of the man; it was for its own sake that it yearned back toward the fire. But the man whistled, and spoke to it with the sound of whiplashes, and the dog swung in at the man's heel and followed after.

The man took a chew of tobacco and proceeded to start a new amber beard. Also, his moist breath quickly powdered with white his mustache, eyebrows, and lashes. There did not seem to be so many springs on the left fork of the Henderson, and for half an hour the man saw no signs of any. And then it happened. At a place where there were no signs, where the soft, unbroken snow seemed to advertise solidity beneath, the man broke through. It was not deep. He wet himself halfway to the knees before he floundered out to the firm crust.

He was angry, and cursed his luck aloud. He had hoped to get into camp with the boys at six o'clock, and this would delay him an hour, for he would have to build a fire and dry out his footgear. This was imperative at that low temperature—he knew that much; and he turned aside to the bank, which he climbed. On top, tangled in the underbrush about the trunks of several small spruce trees, was a high-water deposit of dry firewood—sticks and twigs, principally, but also larger portions of seasoned branches and fine, dry, last-year's grasses. He threw down several large pieces on top of the snow. This served for a foundation and prevented the young flame from drowning itself in the snow it otherwise would melt. The flame he got by touching a match to a small shred of birch bark that he took from his pocket. This burned even more readily than paper. Placing it on the foundation, he fed the young flame with wisps of dry grass and with the tiniest dry twigs.

He worked slowly and carefully, keenly aware of his danger. Gradually, as the flame grew stronger, he increased the size of the twigs with which he fed it. He squatted in the snow, pulling the twigs out from their entanglement in the brush and feeding directly to the flame. He knew there must be no failure. When it is seventy-five below zero, a man must not fail in his first attempt to build a fire—that is, if his feet are wet. If his feet are dry, and he fails, he can run along the trail for half a mile and restore his circulation. But the circulation of wet and freezing feet cannot be restored by running when it is seventy-five below. No matter how fast he runs, the wet feet will freeze the harder.

All this the man knew. The old-timer on Sulphur Creek had told him about it the previous fall, and now he was appreciating the advice. Already all sensation had gone out of his feet. To build the fire he had been forced to remove his mittens, and the fingers had quickly gone numb. His pace of four miles an hour had kept his heart pumping blood to the surface of his body and to all the extremities. But the instant he stopped, the action of the pump eased down. The cold of space smote the unprotected tip of the planet, and he, being on that unprotected tip, received the full force of the blow. The blood of his body recoiled before it. The blood was alive, like the dog, and like the dog it wanted to hide away and cover itself up from the fearful cold. So long as he walked four miles an hour, he pumped that blood, willy-nilly, to the surface; but now it ebbed away and sank down into the recesses of his body. The extremities were the first to feel its absence.

His wet feet froze the faster, and his exposed fingers numbed the faster, though they had not yet begun to freeze. Nose and cheeks were already freezing, while the skin of all his body chilled as it lost its blood.

But he was safe. Toes and nose and cheeks would be only touched by the frost, for the fire was beginning to burn with strength. He was feeding it with twigs the size of his finger. In another minute he would be able to feed it with branches the size of his wrist, and then he could remove his wet footgear, and, while it dried, he could keep his naked feet warm by the fire, rubbing them at first, of course, with snow. The fire was a success. He was safe. He remembered the advice of the old-timer on Sulphur Creek, and smiled. The old-timer had been very serious in laying down the law that no man must travel alone in the Klondike after fifty below. Well, here he was; he had had the accident; he was alone; and he had saved himself. Those old-timers were rather womanish, some of them, he thought. All a man had to do was to keep his head, and he was all right. Any man who was a man could travel alone. But it was surprising, the rapidity with which his cheeks and nose were freezing. And he had not thought his fingers could go lifeless in so short a time. Lifeless they were, for he could scarcely make them move together to grip a twig, and they seemed remote from his body and from him. When he touched a twig, he had to look and see whether or not he had hold of it. The wires were pretty well down between him and his finger ends.

All of which counted for little. There was the fire, snapping and crackling and promising life with every dancing flame. He started to untie his moccasins. They were coated with ice; the thick German socks were like sheaths of iron halfway to the knees; and the moccasin strings were like rods of steel all twisted and knotted as by some conflagration. For a moment he tugged with his numb fingers, then, realizing the folly of it, he drew his sheath knife.

But before he could cut the strings, it happened. It was his own fault or, rather, his mistake. He should not have built the fire under the spruce tree. He should have built it in the open. But it had been easier to pull the twigs from the brush and drop them directly on the fire. Now the tree under which he had done this carried a weight of snow on its boughs. No wind had blown for weeks, and each bough was fully freighted. Each time he had pulled a twig he had communicated a slight agitation to the tree—an imperceptible agitation, so far as he was concerned, but an agitation sufficient to bring about the disaster. High up in the tree one bough capsized its load of snow. This fell on the boughs beneath, capsizing them. This process continued, spreading out and involving the whole tree. It grew like an avalanche, and it descended without warning upon the man and the fire, and the fire was blotted out! Where it had burned was a mantle of fresh and disordered snow.

The man was shocked. It was as though he had just heard his own sentence of death. For a moment he sat and stared at the spot where the fire had been. Then he grew very calm. Perhaps the old-timer on Sulphur Creek was right. If he had only had a trail mate, he would have been in no danger now. The trail mate could have built the fire. Well, it was up to him to build the fire over again, and this second time there must be no failure. Even if he succeeded, he would most likely lose some toes. His feet must be badly frozen by now, and there would be some time before the second fire was ready.

Such were his thoughts, but he did not sit and think them. He was busy all the time they were passing through his mind. He made a new foundation for a fire, this time in the open, where no treacherous tree could blot it out. Next, he gathered dry grasses and tiny twigs from the high-water flotsam. He could not bring his fingers together to pull them out, but he was able to gather them by the handful. In this way he got many rotten twigs and bits of green moss that were undesirable, but it was the best he could do. He worked methodically, even collecting an armful of the larger branches to be used later when the fire gathered strength. And all the while the dog sat and watched him, a certain yearning wistfulness in its eyes, for it looked upon him as the fire provider, and the fire was slow in coming.

When all was ready, the man reached in his pocket for a second piece of birch bark. He knew the bark was there, and, though he could not feel it with his fingers, he could hear its crisp rustling as he fumbled for it. Try as he would, he could not clutch hold of it. And all the time, in his consciousness, was the knowledge that each instant his feet were freezing. This thought tended to put him in a panic, but he fought against it and kept calm. He pulled on his mittens with his teeth, and threshed his arms back and forth, beating his hands with all his might against his sides. He did this sitting down, and he stood up to do it; and all the while the dog sat in the snow, its wolf brush of a tail curled around warmly over its forefeet, its sharp wolf ears pricked forward intently as it watched the man. And the man, as he beat and threshed with his arms and hands, felt a great surge of envy as he regarded the creature that was warm and secure in its natural covering.

After a time he was aware of the first faraway signals of sensation in his beaten fingers. The faint tingling grew stronger till it evolved into a stinging ache that was excruciating, but which the man hailed with satisfaction. He stripped the mitten from his right hand and fetched forth the birch bark. The exposed fingers were quickly going numb again. Next he brought out his bunch of sulphur matches. But the tremendous cold had already driven the life out of his fingers. In his effort to separate one match from the others, the whole bunch fell in the snow. He tried to pick it out of the snow, but failed. The dead fingers could neither touch nor clutch. He was very careful. He drove the thought of his freezing feet, and nose, and cheeks, out of his mind, devoting his whole soul to the matches. He watched, using the sense of vision in place of that of touch, and when he saw his fingers on each side the bunch, he closed them—that is, he willed to close them, for the wires were down, and the fingers did not obey. He pulled the mitten on the right hand, and beat it fiercely against his knee. Then, with both mittened hands, he scooped the bunch of matches, along with much snow, into his lap. Yet he was no better off.

After some manipulation he managed to get the bunch between the heels of his mittened hands. In this fashion he carried it to his mouth. The ice crackled and snapped when by a violent effort he opened his mouth. He drew the lower jaw in, curled the upper lip out of the way, and scraped the bunch with his upper teeth in order to separate a match. He succeeded in getting one, which he dropped on his lap. He was no better off. He could not pick it up. Then he devised a way. He picked it up in his teeth and scratched it on his leg. Twenty times he scratched before he succeeded in lighting it. As it flamed he held it with his teeth to the birch bark. But the burning brimstone went up his nostrils and into his lungs, causing him to cough spasmodically. The match fell into the snow and went out.

The old-timer on Sulphur Creek was right, he thought in the moment of controlled despair that ensued: after fifty below, a man should travel with a partner. He beat his hands, but failed in exciting any sensation. Suddenly he bared both hands, removing the mittens with his teeth. He caught the whole bunch between the heels of his hands. His arm muscles not being frozen enabled him to press the hand heels tightly against the matches. Then he scratched the bunch along his leg. It flared into flame, seventy sulphur matches at once! There was no wind to blow them out. He kept his head to one side to escape the strangling fumes, and held the blazing bunch to the birch bark. As he so held it, he became aware of sensation in his hand. His flesh was burning. He could smell it. Deep down below the surface he could feel it. The sensation developed into pain that grew acute. And still he endured it, holding the flame of the matches clumsily to the bark that would not light readily because his own burning hands were in the way, absorbing most of the flame.

At last, when he could endure no more, he jerked his hands apart. The blazing matches fell sizzling into the snow, but the birch bark was alight. He began laying dry grasses and the tiniest twigs on the flame. He could not pick and choose, for he had to lift the fuel between the heels of his hands. Small pieces of rotten wood and green moss clung to the twigs, and he bit them off as well as he could with his teeth. He cherished the flame carefully and awkwardly. It meant life, and it must not perish. The withdrawal of blood from the surface of his body now made him begin to shiver, and he grew more awkward. A large piece of green moss fell squarely on the little fire. He tried to poke it out with his fingers, but his shivering frame made him poke too far, and he disrupted the nucleus of the little fire, the burning grasses and tiny twigs separating and scattering. He tried to poke them together again, but in spite of the tenseness of the effort, his shivering got away with him, and the twigs were hopelessly scattered. Each twig gushed a puff of smoke and went out. The fire provider had failed. As he looked apathetically about him, his eyes chanced on the dog, sitting across the ruins of the fire from him, in the snow, making restless, hunching movements, slightly lifting one forefoot and then the other, shifting its weight back and forth on them with wistful eagerness.

The sight of the dog put a wild idea into his head. He remembered the tale of the man, caught in a blizzard, who killed a steer and crawled inside the carcass, and so was saved. He would kill the dog and bury his hands in the warm body until the numbness went out of them. Then he could build another fire. He spoke to the dog, calling it to him; but in his voice was a strange note of fear that frightened the animal, who had never known the man to speak in such way before. Something was the matter, and its suspicious nature sensed danger—it knew not what danger, but somewhere, somehow, in its brain arose an apprehension of the man. It flattened its ears down at the sound of the man's voice, and its restless, hunching movements and the liftings and shiftings of its forefeet became more pronounced; but it would not come to the man. He got on his hands and knees and crawled toward the dog. This unusual posture again excited suspicion, and the animal sidled mincingly away.

The man sat up in the snow for a moment and struggled for calmness. Then he pulled on his mittens, by means of his teeth, and got upon his feet. He glanced down at first in order to assure himself that he was really standing up, for the absence of sensation in his feet left him unrelated to the earth. His erect position in itself started to drive the webs of suspicion from the dog's mind; and when he spoke peremptorily, with the sound of whiplashes in his voice, the dog rendered its customary allegiance and came to him. As it came within reaching distance, the man lost his control. His arms flashed out to the dog, and he experienced genuine surprise when he discovered that his hands could not clutch, that there was neither bend nor feeling in the fingers. He had forgotten for the moment that they were frozen and that they were freezing more and more. All this happened quickly, and before the animal could get away, he encircled its body with his arms. He sat down in the snow, and in this fashion held the dog, while it snarled and whined and struggled.

But it was all he could do, hold its body encircled in his arms and sit there. He realized that he could not kill the dog. There was no way to do it. With his helpless hands he could neither draw nor hold his sheath knife nor throttle the animal. He released it, and it plunged wildly away, with tail between its legs, and still snarling. It halted forty feet away and surveyed him curiously, with ears sharply pricked forward.

The man looked down at his hands in order to locate them, and found them hanging on the ends of his arms. It struck him as curious that one should have to use his eyes in order to find out where his hands were. He began threshing his arms back and forth, beating the mittened hands against his sides.

He did this for five minutes, violently, and his heart pumped enough blood up to the surface to put a stop to his shivering. But no sensation was aroused in the hands. He had an impression that they hung like weights on the ends of his arms, but when he tried to run the impression down, he could not find it.

A certain fear of death, dull and oppressive, came to him. This fear quickly became poignant as he realized that it was no longer a mere matter of freezing his fingers and toes, or of losing his hands and feet, but that it was a matter of life and death with the chances against him. This threw him into a panic, and he turned and ran up the creek bed along the old, dim trail. The dog joined in behind and kept up with him.

He ran blindly, without intention, in fear such as he had never known in his life. Slowly, as he plowed and floundered through the snow, he began to see things again—the banks of the creek, the old timber jams, the leafless aspens, and the sky.

The running made him feel better. He did not shiver. Maybe, if he ran on, his feet would thaw out; and, anyway, if he ran far enough, he would reach camp and the boys. Without doubt he would lose some fingers and toes and some of his face; but the boys would take care of him, and save the rest of him when he got there. And at the same time there was another thought in his mind that said he would never get to the camp and the boys; that it was too many miles away, that the freezing had too great a start on him, and that he would soon be stiff and dead. This thought he kept in the background and refused to consider. Sometimes it pushed itself forward and demanded to be heard, but he thrust it back and strove to think of other things.

It struck him as curious that he could run at all on feet so frozen that he could not feel them when they struck the earth and took the weight of his body. He seemed to himself to skim along above the surface, and to have no connection with the earth. Somewhere he had once seen a winged Mercury, and he wondered if Mercury felt as he felt when skimming over the earth.

His theory of running until he reached camp and the boys had one flaw in it: he lacked the endurance. Several times he stumbled, and finally he tottered, crumpled up, and fell. When he tried to rise, he failed. He must sit and rest, he decided, and next time he would merely walk and keep on going.

As he sat and regained his breath, he noted that he was feeling quite warm and comfortable. He was not shivering, and it even seemed that a warm glow had come to his chest and trunk. And yet, when he touched his nose or cheeks, there was no sensation. Running would not thaw them out. Nor would it thaw out his hands and feet. Then the thought came to him that the frozen portions of his body must be extending. He tried to keep this thought down, to forget it, to think of something else; he was aware of the panicky feeling that it caused, and he was afraid of the panic. But the thought asserted itself, and persisted, until it produced a vision of his body totally frozen. This was too much, and he made another wild run along the trail. Once he slowed down to a walk, but the thought of the freezing extending itself made him run again.

And all the time the dog ran with him, at his heels. When he fell down a second time, it curled its tail over its forefeet and sat in front of him, facing him, curiously eager and intent. The warmth and security of the animal angered him, and he cursed it till it flattened down its ears appeasingly.

This time the shivering came more quickly upon the man. He was losing in his battle with the frost. It was creeping into his body from all sides. The thought of it drove him on, but he ran no more than a hundred feet, when he staggered and pitched headlong.

It was his last panic. When he had recovered his breath and control, he sat up and entertained in his mind the conception of meeting death with dignity.

However, the conception did not come to him in such terms. His idea of it was that he had been making a fool of himself, running around like a chicken with its head cut off—such was the simile that occurred to him. Well, he was bound to freeze anyway, and he might as well take it decently.

With this newfound peace of mind came the first glimmerings of drowsiness. A good idea, he thought, to sleep off to death. It was like taking an anaesthetic. Freezing was not so bad as people thought. There were lots worse ways to die.

He pictured the boys finding his body next day. Suddenly he found himself with them, coming along the trail and looking for himself. And, still with them, he came around a turn in the trail and found himself lying in the snow. He did not belong with himself anymore, for even then he was out of himself, standing with the boys and looking at himself in the snow. It certainly was cold, was his thought. When he got back to the States he could tell the folks what real cold was.

He drifted on from this to a vision of the old-timer on Sulphur Creek. He could see him quite clearly, warm and comfortable, and smoking a pipe.

"You were right, old hoss; you were right," the man mumbled to the old-timer of Sulphur Creek.

Then the man drowsed off into what seemed to him the most comfortable and satisfying sleep he had ever known.

The dog sat facing him and waiting. The brief day drew to a close in a long, slow twilight. There were no signs of a fire to be made, and, besides, never in the dog's experience had it known a man to sit like that in the snow and make no fire. As the twilight drew on, its eager yearning for the fire mastered it, and with a great lifting and shifting of forefeet, it whined softly, then flattened its ears down in anticipation of being chided by the man. But the man remained silent. Later, the dog whined loudly. And still later it crept close to the man and caught the scent of death. This made the animal bristle and back away. A little longer it delayed, howling under the stars that leaped and danced and shone brightly in the cold sky. Then it turned and trotted up the trail in the direction of the camp it knew, where were the other food providers and fire providers.

MATHIESON'S WIFE

VANCE PALMER

Vance Palmer

How well I remember that morning when the fair-haired young
woman who had come to live with old Mathieson made my heart jump
by dropping from the mulberry-tree to the grass beside me! A rustle of
the branches, a soft plop—and there she was as if she had fallen right out
of a cloud. I stumbled back a pace or two and the billy of milk I was
holding nearly slipped from my hand. It was partly the shock, partly
the look of her as she stood laughing down at me, her blue eyes dancing
and the mulberry-stains red on her lips. The blood crept up my neck,
and I tried to stutter out something, but my voice lost itself in the furry
depths of my throat.

"Did I scare you?" she said, ruffling my hair with a quick teasing
movement. "That's nothing to what you did to me. When I heard the
gate click I thought I'd been caught by one of the church people.
Wouldn't that have settled my reputation for good and all!"

She took the milk from me and led me into the kitchen, her arm
lightly around my shoulder. It was as if she had caught me up and was
carrying me off into a world of her own where everything moved at a
dance. All the while, pouring the milk into a jug and washing out the
billy, she rattled on as if she were no older than I, as if there were things
she was just bursting to ask me, but every now and then she stopped to
glance at me sideways and broke into a little bubble of laughter.
Enjoying the joke of being caught in the mulberry-tree and the way
she turned it on me! I could do nothing but gape at her, dazzled by the
dancing life in her face and the way unexpected words formed on her
lips. She was the most wonderful creature I had ever set eyes upon:

554

even with her hair tumbling over her eyes and her mouth smeared with mulberry-juice. The frock she had on was a skimpy one, torn down the front, and her bare feet were thrust into old sandshoes, but she gave me the feeling of a princess dressed in silks.

For days there'd been a bobbery among the neighbours because of the news that old Mathieson had brought a bit of a girl home with him as his wife: old Mathieson, who looked like the prophet Elijah, and made the stairs of the pulpit creak beneath his weight when he mounted them in church. He was not far off sixty and had been a navvy, it was said, in the days when they built the railway over the ranges, but that was so long ago only the old people remembered. You couldn't think of old Mathieson except with a greyish beard and heavy, stooped shoulders, coming down the track from church with a Bible under his arm or setting off on his stiff-legged chestnut for a service at one of the settlements away from the line.

The cottage he lived in was a dark old place, back from the road, covered by grape-vines in front and with a tangle of greenery at the sides. Sometimes, dawdling home from school, we caught sight of him in his shirt-sleeves splitting wood by the outhouse, and it gave us a queer feeling, as if we'd come upon grown-up people bathing naked in the creek. His black alpaca coat and buttoned-up waistcoat always seemed as much part of old Mathieson as his skin, and you felt he went to bed in them. Who could believe he'd taken it into his head to get married, and to a girl who looked as if she'd laugh at anyone but a rich farmer's son or a young and handsome squatter?

Yet there she was sitting sideways on the corner of the kitchen table, swinging her left leg and asking me about the neighbours: about my mother and grandmother, how long we had lived there, what I was going to do when I left school. Was it my father who was building the new hall at Forest Ridge? And how often did he come home? It was as if she'd just lighted there like a bird and was curious to know what sort of a place it was.

For over a week I was the only one who caught more than a glimpse of her, and something queer and secret in me made me not want to talk about her with anyone. Certainly not with my grandmother, whose sharp tongue and searching eyes could strip other women to the bone. But wherever I went I'd hear the older people gossiping:

"What could have come over the man? She's not more than twenty-three or four."

"She's thirty if she's a day. Brought up on buttermilk by the colour of her and never been asked to do a hand's turn in her life. One of a family just out from Ireland."

"Nonsense; who put that around? Would he be marrying an Irish girl, a tough old Presbyterian like him?"

"I don't believe they're married. More than likely she's a niece of his, come up here to look after him."

"Couldn't be. Hasn't he said time and again he hasn't a relative in the country?"

There was a good deal of feeling against old Mathieson, for he had kept this marriage of his a secret from everyone. Even from my grandmother, who had known him since he was a raw Scots working-boy in moleskins. It wasn't his way to talk except in the pulpit, and then words came rolling up as if from somewhere deep inside him. Words you could only understand through hearing them used over and over. When he met people on the road he had nothing to say; nothing but the same old questions about their health and their families. For a minute or two he would stand absentmindedly mopping his bald head with a handkerchief, his kind, vague eyes looking around him as if anxious to find an excuse to move on. . . . Aye, aye, it's an uncertain wurrld at the best o' times. Nothing you can count on a day ahead. . . . Although he was liked well enough, both men and women contrived to give him a wide berth, and as for us youngsters—we could spot his big, slow figure half a mile off. "Old Sandy's coming," someone would call out, and there would be a run for cover.

Why hadn't the fair-headed woman run, too? I wondered, as I lay awake thinking about her. Skipped away at the sight of his spindle-legged chestnut and hidden in some mulberry-tree. It would have been so easy for her to have escaped his notice; he always rode with his eyes fixed stolidly on the road ahead. I could imagine her looking out from between the leaves and laughing to herself as he passed by.

It soon leaked out that she came from Forest Ridge, one of the settlements he visited on his service-rounds—a terrible place, we believed, right out of the world, a place filled with big raw-boned Irish who ran about barefoot and lived on wallabies. She had come from town, they said, to live with some skinflint relatives—an old Scandinavian farmer and his wife—and had never managed to get away. That was enough to make people soften toward her. You couldn't blame anyone, trapped at Forest Ridge, for marrying even an Indian hawker to escape.

Our own little township was nothing to boast about, but it had been well in the boom when the main line to Sydney was being built over the range, and the ghost of that life remained still. There was still the big half-deserted brickyard with its dams of yellow water, the three pubs, two of them falling to pieces, and the rambling goods-yard, filled with broken-down sheds and rusted rails. Then there was the line of small shops by the station, most of them empty but with the name of some cobbler or saddler on their peeling signboards. In the days when the cuttings were being blasted and the tunnels driven, navvies had poured down from their camps on Saturday nights and made the place roar with their drinking and horse-play. A good many of them had left their bones there, if you could judge by the number of fallen gravestones in the old cemetery that was overgrown with weeds.

But the place was still a centre, for the Sydney Mail stopped there before its long pull up the range, and everyone gathered at the station of an evening to see the passengers tumble out for tea and sandwiches. It was the event of the day for us. Walking along the train we gaped in at the empty carriages, gaped at the luggage in the racks and the gaudy rugs strewn along the seats. The sleeping-cars were dark and shuttered and had a look of mystery. What a sense of strange, unexplored worlds the train left behind when it rolled off over the bridge and was lost in the night!

Mathieson's young wife had some of that strangeness. The first morning she appeared in church every eye was on her and there was a stillness even among the small boys at the back, so that you could hear the slightest rustle in the leaves of the big apple-box outside. There she sat in a front pew looking as if she had floated down from the roof, her hands folded in her lap and a small toque perched on her head, which was tilted a little to one side. Not a move out of her the whole service. Her back was as straight as a young seedling, and she looked up at the old man in the pulpit as if she was seeing him for the first time, watching the way his lips moved, trying to understand what he said.

Old Mathieson didn't catch her gaze or anyone else's. With his heavy hands grasping the edge of the pulpit he let his voice roll on over our heads and come back to him in echoes from the rafters, though his eyes wandered now and then in a lost way, as if he were wondering where he was and what had happened to him.

It was that lost look, I think, that made sympathy swing back to him. Everyone knew the story of how, as a young man, he had volunteered to go back to one of the cuttings to see what had happened when a charge failed to explode. His last job on the railway, for he was buried under a fall of rock and had to lie on his back for a year—longer, some said. That had happened half a life-time ago, but it was enough to account for his being different from other people. A bit simple, inclined to live in the next world rather than this one, too soft and kind-hearted to cope with a scheming young woman out to use him for her own ends.

It made my blood rise to hear what was said of her; now by the old women, now by the young fellows loafing at the station in the dusk. My grandmother couldn't speak of her without dropping her voice and putting a slight hiss into her words; the young fellows had all sorts of jokes about what happened to old plugs when a spring came to the grass. As for Mathieson's wife, their minds were made up. There was only one reason why a woman as young and good-looking as she was should leave town and take cover at a place like Forest Ridge. They were annoyed they had missed their chance of tin-kettling the parson on the night he had brought his bride home; it was a ceremony that was organized for couples when there was anything dubious about the marriage. Going over with the milk of a morning, I felt I carried a smear of their talk on me and was ashamed.

But with the first look the woman gave me I was free from it, lifted up and treading on air. How my heart turned over every time I came round the corner of the tank and found her sitting on the back steps eating her breakfast in the sun. Bread and honey it would be, nearly always, with a mug of tea. She sat on the steps with her bare feet curled beneath her, her corn-coloured hair twined in plaits round her head, a mischievous look in her eyes as she tossed bits of bread to the lame magpie. Sometimes she would be in her dressing-gown, sometimes in a loose cotton frock that came just below the knees. The old boy himself was never around. I always thought of him, asleep in the dark front room, as being far away as if he were dead and in his coffin. He had to go off every afternoon on his slow old chestnut and it was always late at night when he came back, so he lay in till the sun was well above the dark mulberries in the garden.

And I would hang around vaguely, trying to find jobs to do, hating the thought that soon the first bell would go for school. The woman was making a kitchen garden and asked my advice on all sorts of things. She had a teasing way of putting awkward questions, and when I was stumped she laughed and rumpled my hair. Her hands were never still; they fluttered about like butterflies, picking up a leaf and tearing it to pieces, twisting her ring off and on, fondling the ear of the blue heeler that lay at her feet.

What did she talk to the old boy about when they were together? I wondered. It was hard to guess, for no one ever saw them together, even on Sundays. The old boy was shy of having to meet people in her company, and after the service he lingered in the vestry till she had gone downhill in that swift way of hers, usually with a couple of youngsters skipping round her. On week-days they had no time to go visiting.

Yet no one could say she neglected him or failed in her duty as housewife. She seemed intent on brightening up the dark old place, and before long had cleared most of the straggling bushes from the overgrown garden, put a coat of new paint on the fence, and made a gravelled path up to the gate.

"Can you milk?" she asked me one morning.

I told her I had milked our two cows since I was ten.

"Then you must come and teach me, clever boy. I'm going to get a cow. Over at Forest Ridge I wouldn't learn, because I was scared it might become my job for life. O, what fibs I told to get out of it—tender hands, a mortal dread of the big bull down at the bails! You'd never believe."

She glanced back over her shoulder at the house where the old man

559

was sleeping, then jumped up with a laugh, putting her hands on my shoulders and tilting my chin back.

"Don't look so shocked, young poker-face. Haven't you ever learnt to fib your way out of trouble? It's much easier than milking."

If cows were strange to her, she knew all about horses, and the very smell of the old chestnut nosing round the yard excited her and put a light into her eyes. She had had her own pony as a girl, she told me, and had ridden it at some show in town, getting the blue ribbon one year and a yellow one the next. Her father had been a trainer of racehorses— a really first-class one—and had once handled the winner of the Sydney Cup. You couldn't get an idea of what her life had been from the little things she dropped, but I had a picture of her prancing about among other riders on a stretch of green turf, nursing her pony when the noise made it flighty, keeping a shrewd eye on the judges in the centre, sailing over the jumps with her fair hair floating behind her. That hair held me fascinated, it was so shining and alive.

Before long she'd broken down most of the prejudices people had against her. Partly because she never noticed them and took for granted she was liked; partly because of the way she danced all over the place, doing things for everybody—for people who never came near the church as well as for those who did. She wasn't often to be seen at the week-night meetings, but if there was a youngster down with measles, or an old woman to be nursed through the night, she'd be up at the place before anyone else heard about it, shaking out blankets and putting things straight in the kitchen. There was a ripple in the way she moved that made her seem twice as alive as other people. A few quick steps, then a little run, and back to a quick walk again. It was the same whether she was hurrying to a neighbour's house or just going out for a few sticks from the wood-heap.

The youngsters all hung round her, particularly the dirty little brats from the shanties by the railway bridge, where the lengthsmen lived. She spent a lot of time down there, yarning with the women and looking after their babies for them; sometimes you'd see her going round all afternoon with a baby on her hip, carrying it lightly as a fly even when she was playing hopscotch in a cleared space with the girls. All morning she'd be busy with her housework, washing, sweeping, bringing old Mathieson his morning tea as he sat on the veranda in the sun, and getting him his midday meal; she even caught the lean chestnut and saddled it for him, fussing over him so much at the gate that people said she tied him on; but as soon as he was over the hill by the church she'd be out of the house and away, a handkerchief tied over her head and her feet moving so quickly they hardly seemed to touch the turf.

"There's that woman gallivanting about again," my grandmother would say, watching her from her chair on the veranda.

Grandmother had a perch from which she could command the whole sweep of flat from the railway bridge to the station, and two birds could hardly settle together on a post without meeting the disapproval of her bitter old eye. My mother would gently defend Mathieson's wife.

"She has a lonely time there, all by herself most evenings. And she's so warm-hearted she must always be looking for someone to do a kind turn to."

"Rubbish," was my grandmother's retort. "That woman never lay awake because of anyone's troubles. I know the kind. She'd make love to any old horse hanging its head over the roadside fence, because that's the nature of her, but it's herself she's thinking about all the time. Herself and the figure she's cutting. She's cold as any fish underneath."

Left alone by themselves all the week, because my father was away on his building jobs, they continually discussed the Mathieson woman—who her people were, what had brought her to Forest Ridge in the first place—and I listened without saying a word; but every time her name came up my heart stopped dead a moment and then went thumping on again. I lived for the hour between breakfast and school. The cows turned out, the milk left to set in the dairy, and I would be hurrying up the road with my billy. Never a look to left or right till I reached Mathieson's gate, and a pounding in my ears as I walked past the vine-covered front where the old man slept.

The woman teased me when she saw the flush on my face.

"You funny boy; why are you always so breathless?"

"I'm not. . . . It's just that breakfast was late."

"Again? And you thought I'd keep you talking, didn't you? Thought I'd make you miss your game of rounders before school. Own up; that's it, isn't it?"

Her eyes mocking me, jollying me, filling me with confusion! It was as if she took pleasure in bringing the blood to my cheeks. Often she'd put her hands on my shoulders and lean back looking at me, then bend forward and kiss me in a challenging way as if daring me to make a protest. I'd go off with her laugh in my ears, inwardly disturbed, afraid when I reached school the other boys would notice the spot where her lips had touched.

I think she guessed I counted a good deal on my visits there of a morning. But did she know I'd have thrown myself on the ground any moment and let her wipe her boots on me? And had she any notion of the way I dreamed of her, sometimes asleep and sometimes fully awake and wandering by the creek?

In these dreams I was no longer a boy of thirteen, but ageless, older at any rate than she was, and so strong I could lift her to the saddle with a sweep of the arm when she ran to me for protection as I rode by. It was always from old Mathieson she was running. Now he was a mumbling giant who had hidden her in his cave above the railway cutting, now a hairy ape like the one in the school-books, swinging from one branch to another with his long arms, peering down through the leaves. Nearer and nearer he came through the dark trees overhead as we galloped beneath them, and I could feel the woman's heart beating as she clung to my neck and hid her eyes. But there was always a stretch of sea at the end of the forest, and a little boat waiting to take us to an island on the skyline.

That was all very well, but I couldn't live on dreams, and there were times when I was crushed with the weight of years between us. Times when my feeling for her was just a mumbling ache. No good trying to think of the fine sport I'd have next year at boarding-school. No good telling myself there'd come a day when I'd laugh at it all. I could only lie on my back in the grass and wish there weren't so many years of living ahead of me.

She had a little black-and-white heifer now, with its first calf, and usually they fed with our cows in the pockets of the creek. It was my job to bring them in of an afternoon, and often she'd come with me, gathering cress by the spring and taking off her shoes to wade in the shallows, sometimes sending me ahead and peeling off all her clothes for a swim. It was a wonderful place, that creek-bed, a wide channel cut by the flood-waters that came gushing out of the range in the wet months; three parts of it were sand and smooth stones, but a clear stream flowed through, with deep holes overhung with tea-tree and swiftly running stretches where the water foamed round your ankles. Rainbow-birds flashing from their nests in the sandy banks wheeled and dipped in the air above. What times we had when the cows travelled far afield and had to be tracked up the steep gorges!

But the excitement that summer was the travelling dairy that came with its wagon-load of machinery and set up its stand in the school playshed. For weeks placards on every post had announced the date it was due and had called on farmers to bring in their milk to be tested. It was a government project to wake up country folk to the importance of good stock and the need for improving the quality of their dairying, but that wasn't what appealed to most people. The travelling dairy was a circus. It couldn't have made a bigger sensation if it had brought a band and a string of elephants. From miles around carts and buggies rattled in to the school paddock every morning, while the people with only a cow or two came from nearby homes with their buckets of milk. Power for the machinery was created by the two heavy draught-horses moving round in the gin.

What a hum of life it brought to the place! The big separator whirred, the leather belting slid round on its smooth wheels, and people stood about listening to the manager's patter and running their fingers along the polished vats that stretched across the sheds. Vats soon brimming with cream to be turned into butter and cheese. Everything looked clean and glistening, from the spinning discs on the separator to the white overalls of the young men moving among the vats. A rich smell hovered over the playground—a smell of buttermilk, of oats scattered by the feeding horses, of cheese fresh from the presses.

The centre of it all was Bob Curdie, manager of the dairy. Black-eyed, smooth-skinned, with a moustache that looked hardly more than a dark smudge, he kept everyone entertained, whether he was guying some of the old cockies or giving a lecture on winter feeding. The women crowded round him and took every word he said for gospel. He had worked up a competition among them, offering a five-pound cheese every week to the one whose milk came out best in the tests for butter fat. It was thought a great joke when Mathieson's wife won the first one with her black-and-white heifer.

She was there every morning bright and early, getting me to carry her milk down before school and lifting the covers of the vats to have a peek before the other people came and the machinery started moving. Now she was asking Bob Curdie questions, now sniffing at the big cheeses as if she was all nose. She was like one of the wrens picking oats from the straws besides the feeding-bins. This is life, she seemed to be saying; why do we spend so much time hidden away in our own little nests? It was the horses, filling the little paddock with their snorts and whinnying, that went to her head as much as anything else. Bob Curdie had a jumper he was training for a show in town—a big brown gelding with a short barrel and legs clean as a bird's—and every afternoon when the crowd had gone he saddled it and put it at the two-railed fence of the school paddock. What a thrill to see him sail over it, turning round in the saddle to make sure the gelding didn't brush the top rail with its heels!

More often than not the only woman looking on was Mathieson's wife. She would come stealing back when the midday meal was finished and the old chestnut safely over the skyline, and leaning against a post of the shed she would watch Curdie with the cool, knowing eyes of one who had ridden over jumps herself. Though her body drooped slackly her face had the wistful eagerness of a child shut out of a game. One afternoon he noticed her and came riding over. "Game to give it a fly?"

She flushed and threw him a half-shy, half-roguish look.

"Don't poke fun at me now, or I might take up your challenge."

"Well, why not?"

"Other people would tell you quick enough. I'd have to ride astride in this skirt. Out to raise a scandal, are you?"

His eyes rested on her as if he were really looking at her for the first time, and then he said with a twinkle, "O Lord, no! Neither of us could afford that. I'll have to put a brake on myself."

But he smiled back over his shoulder as he cantered off, and from the way he took his jumps afterwards you could see that putting a brake on himself wasn't a notion that entered his head.

The other boys thought the world of Bob Curdie, and I followed him round with the rest, helping to clean the parts of the big separator when he took it to pieces, watching him groom the brown gelding, hanging about his tent in the school paddock. It wasn't like an ordinary tent, and it excited us to peer inside. Curdie was used to travelling round the country and knew how to make himself comfortable with flood-boards, kangaroo-skin rugs, and rigged-up bookshelves. Then there were his trophies—cups and medals—won at agricultural shows with his jumper, and photographs of the travelling dairy at all the townships along the line. He laughed when he told us it was his last year with the circus. He was taking a little place in the West, he said, where he could breed horses and forget the smell of butter and cheese.

His jaunty figure, his confident smile, his air of having knocked about the world, fascinated me for a while and took my mind off Mathieson's wife. I even dropped the habit of going over after breakfast to help her with the milking; perhaps I was piqued because she didn't seem to notice whether I was about or not, now that the travelling dairy had come. Bob Curdie had told me I could ride the brown horse down to the creek for a drink in the mornings, and there was always the thrill of putting it at a low log on the way back. Clinging to it bareback I could feel the lift of its withers under me as if we were flying a fence.

And so the days went on. I dreaded the thought of the empty after-noons that lay ahead when the time came for the travelling dairy to pack its machinery in the big wagons and roll off again. So, I guessed, did Mathieson's wife. She had taken a fancy to the brown gelding and didn't seem able to keep away from it, coming down to Curdie's tent to watch him rug it and turn it out for the night, arguing with him about whether it would make a better hunter or high jumper, sometimes staying to help him cook his evening meal. Trailing home with the cows in the dusk, I'd see her bending over the camp-oven or hurrying back to the house through the purple-tops of the paddock, stopping to give the feeding horse a hug on the way. She was even more shook on that horse than I was. She looked as if she'd lost her heart to it, and from the pleased twinkle in Curdie's eyes when she was fussing over it you felt he'd have made it over to her if she'd raised a hand.

I remember nursing a bit of resentment about the way it was beginning to snare all her attention. She seemed to have lost interest in the black-and-white heifer, and took for granted I would bring it home every afternoon with our cows and pen up the calf. But when I met her she would quiz me as if I were the defaulter.

"A fine follower you are, leaving me in the lurch of a morning! What's come over you these days?"

"Nothing has. But it's my only chance of a ride, taking the horse down for a drink in the morning."

"Oh, it's that horse, is it? I suppose nothing else counts with you now. What fickle creatures you men are! I feel jilted. Am I to carry my own milk over to the dairy from now on?"

She could always set something fluttering in me when she struck that note, glancing down with a pouting offended look. Did she really miss our morning talks, after all, and the sport we had dragging the young calf away when the mother had begun to let down her milk? Perhaps she did, but a little hard core of resistance was beginning to develop in me. Why was she letting me go alone on that long afternoon search for the cows?

I knew well enough, of course. She couldn't drag herself away from the playshed, and Bob Curdie's jumper, and the joking down at the tent when they were getting the camp-oven going. Nothing else really concerned her.

Then one night I awoke in my room on the veranda feeling that something was happening, not sure whether I was still in a dream. Where had the light come from that had flickered across my eyes? Had I really caught sight of an old man pressing his forehead to the pane of my mother's bedroom window? It was certain she had been aroused. There were feet padding about the house, a whisper of voices, and when I looked out of the door, a lantern moving down through the fruit-trees to the lower gate.

"Get back to bed," my mother said quietly, "it's nothing."

"But there was someone here."

"Only Mr. Mathieson. Poor old fellow, he's been getting queer lately. Imagining all sorts of things."

"His wife?" I stuttered. "She's sick—she's had an accident."

"No, no; nothing at all. He woke up and found she wasn't in the room so he came looking for her here, half in his sleep. Most likely he'll find her sound asleep in another room when he gets back."

She was quite tranquil as she shepherded me back to bed again and took away the candle. But I couldn't sleep; the night became filled with my fevered fancies. What had been happening in that gloomy little house covered with vines? I had the sense of a violence whose causes I could only dimly guess at being released and running wild, of passionate voices carrying on quarrels just beyond my range of hearing. Lurid scenes flitted before my vision—scenes of cruelty and terror—old Mathieson worked up to a pitch of madness, lightning shooting from his eyes, his great chest heaving, his hands grappling at his wife's throat. Sitting up in bed I stared out into the dark, seeing her rush into the garden and crouch by the gate, hearing her frightened sobbing as she hurried blindly down toward the creek. A curley wailed from the flat. Trembling, I sat waiting for the withered peach-tree to take shape and the roosters to begin crowing in the fowlyard.

But with the morning it all seemed just a nightmare. A rattle of crockery sounded from the kitchen, smoke curled up from the shanties by the bridge, the two cows hung about the bail in the bright sunlight waiting to be milked. Neither my mother nor grandmother said a word at breakfast about the disturbance during the night, but plied me with questions about the scholarship I was working for and whether Carney, the teacher, was taking it seriously enough. Afterwards the carts and buggies came rolling up as usual to the travelling dairy and the line of harnessed horses was strung out along the fence. Nothing had changed. The separator whirred, the rich smell of cheeses filled the shed, the farmers and their wives clustered round Bob Curdie as he stood on a box pointing out something on the coloured chart with his stick. And there, leaning against one of the vats, was Mathieson's wife, a yellow kerchief round her head and a quizzing smile in her eyes as she caught me staring at her.

What's the matter, sober-sides? that smile said. You're looking at me as if I were a ghost.

Well, what was the matter? I couldn't have explained for the life of me. Somehow, standing there with that gay look, she seemed less real than the pictures of her my mind had formed during the night: crouch-

ing terrified at the lower end of the garden, dodging about in the dark
to escape the frenzied old man with his lantern, running desperately at
last over the flat to the creek.

It was late next afternoon when, bringing the cows home from where
they had strayed to open country beyond the bridge, I saw her in the
dusk mounted on Bob Curdie's jumper. She was sitting astride with the
skirts tucked up around her knees, and the brown gelding danced
beneath her as she waited for Curdie to fix a rail in a broken fence.
There was no one else near. It was half a mile on the farther side of the
railway—a deserted holding where only the fire-blackened stumps of
the house and a few panels of fence remained. Watching from halfway
down the bed of the creek I saw Curdie stand back and lift his hand; the
woman gathered up her reins and, putting the horse at the fence,
skimmed it like a swallow. Her hair was over her eyes and she was
patting her mount's neck as she wheeled round and cantered back to
where Curdie was standing: I saw her slip out of the saddle into his
arms, saw him hold her there without moving.

There are happenings that fill a boy with a confused darkness he
doesn't wish to explore. Forget all about it, a voice urges him; soon
enough you'll be a man, and then nothing will have power to hurt. I
wasn't conscious of any resentment against Bob Curdie; none of the
fantastic black hatred I had sometimes felt for poor old Mathieson. I
could even think of him as a deliverer acting in place of me. But I was
glad when the travelling dairy moved on, and the grass grew over the
ring where the gin-horses had tramped their round.

As for the Mathieson woman, I didn't want to meet her again, and
took pains to avoid her. For the time being, I couldn't help seeing her
through my grandmother's eyes.

"If you haven't made up your mind about her now you never will," I
heard the old woman arguing with my mother. "She's light—that's the
best you can say about her and the worst. No more weight to her mind
and feelings than's in a handful of feathers."

That was what, in a confused way, I had been thinking myself. For,
struggling with a dull sense of hurt, I was going over the things about
her that had dazzled me, and trying to believe they were put on for
show. All that overflow of life that made her smile come so easily and

sent a warmth through everyone she spoke to seemed now no more than a trap for the affections. She could set things moving in other people without being moved herself. I felt this when Bob Curdie began coming back to the place for odd visits, hanging round the pub with a lost look, and drinking himself blind when it became plain he had been shaken off and forgotten.

Mathieson's wife was once more playing at being everybody's sweetheart and no one's. Joining in the games of the youngsters at the navvies' huts, stopping to joke with the men at the brickfields—giving little pieces of herself to all sorts of people and nothing very much to anybody.

"Hullo, moody boy," she greeted me one morning on her way back from the post. "When are you coming over again to help me in the garden? Didn't you know the mulberries were ripe?"

"I'm studying," I told her, "going up for a scholarship."

"Oho! So that's what's put the dark look on your face! It used to be as bright as a new billy-can once."

Yet even when she was standing there, laughing down at me, her voice only reached me across a gulf. Mumbling some excuse, I got away from her. She had floated out of my particular world and become remote.

Remote, yet with power over some part of my imagination no one else had. She was at the back of whatever I read that moved me by its beauty, heartlessness, or mystery. Away next year at school, I gathered that all was not well with old Mathieson, that he had had a bad fall from his horse, that his mind was a little affected, and that his wife (this was only hinted at vaguely) had gone off on a visit some months before and showed no signs of coming back.

"That woman!" I could hear my grandmother say.

But for a long time I dreamed of her quite often, and gradually without bitterness, as a radiant figure in the far sky. A winged horse bore her along. Careering through those boundless spaces, she leapt cloud after cloud triumphantly, an aura of light round her, completely absorbed in herself and her own airy freedom, yet looking down now and then with gay benignity to the three wistful figures below—Bob Curdie, the boy I had been, and poor old Mathieson.

THE COFFIN

UYS KRIGE

IN THE EARLY hours of the morning on which I, his first great-grandchild, was born, Great Oupa Lourens was the first to be up. And when later he heard of my safe and happy entry into life, he tiptoed through the house and stooping to get his large frame through the kitchen door, came out under the bright, still stars.

In the wagon-house he took his whip from its hook, slung it over his shoulder and strode out onto the veld. There, amongst the dark hills about a kilometre from the homestead, he let fly at the sleeping world around him. The long lash curled and writhed, tearing apart the deep, early morning stillness as if the peace of the fields were something fragile and brittle. With his feet planted wide apart and his tall figure—supple in spite of his sixty years—slightly bent, Great Oupa stood on the ridge, outlined against the starry sky. With powerful arms—on which the muscles stretched taut as wires—he plied the whipstock: a mobile pitch-black shape against the immobility of everything around him and the faint, grey light now touching the hilltops.

Now the lash would coil round the long stock like a nest of snakes. Then it would rustle like a scythe. And when Great Oupa laid about him with greater gusto, the whip would crack continuously, the echoes rippling away down the dark kloof.

A dim light was stealing over the veld. Through the gaps among the sombre clouds, massed over the horizon, the day, bronze and scarlet, was breaking. Then the light came so quickly, it was as if the whip had split the clouds, letting in the new life and investing that spacious world with another dawn.

A last lazy flick of the *voorslag* and a cluster of dewdrops on a tuft of grass splintered into sparks.

With his boots wet from the dew, Great Oupa Lourens stood in the *voorkamer,* gazing pensively up at the framed family tree that occupied a place of honour on the wall. An old Dutch tramp who had arrived on the farm one morning with a little bundle and a black case full of paint and brushes on his back, had painted the tree with great care according to the details provided him by Great Oupa. No one could have said to what species the family tree belonged, but there was no doubt about it . . . it was the Lourens tree, gnarled and old, with its roots deep in an unknown fruitful soil, and with spreading branches and many fresh shoots reaching to the heights.

And now Francina would have to take down that picture and paint in as meticulously as the old pedlar—the new green bough . . . Why, for a whole year, he, Great Oupa, had paid for special drawing lessons for Francina in the village and he hadn't sent her to that old English spinster to gather pumpkins . . . .

It was in the *voorkamer* that the old coloured woman, Ai Rosie, who had helped Great Ouma bring me into the world, came upon her master. A few years older than he, she had looked after him when he was a baby, often carrying him on her back about the house or outside on the wide, sloping *werf.*

"Why on earth is Oubaas looking at a dead painted old tree," she broke into his reverie, "when there's a fat bouncing baby shouting to be looked at in that room over there?"

"You're right, Ai Rosie!" Great Oupa said gaily. "But how strange to think you are only a branch of the tree, yet you feel as old and as strong as one of its deepest roots . . . ."

Somewhat ill at ease, he stood in front of the bed where Mother and I were lying. He bent over me, looked at me with a frown, and gave Mother's pale forehead a slight caress with his large, rough hand.

"Anna, child, it's a fine strong son," was his only remark. "We are proud of you."

In the kitchen he drank three cups of coffee and finished off a plate of rusks; then walked slowly towards the sheepkraal where he slaughtered six sheep, hanging the skins in a row to dry among the cobwebs in a far corner of the wagon-house. One for the new Petrus Lafras Lourens who this morning for the first time had opened his eyes to God's fair world; the second for Ai Rosie and her family; the third for his coloured labourers who were dipping sheep at Kleinplaas; another for the dominee who would later come and baptise the child; number five for the first visitor to set foot on the farm. And the last sheep for his neighbour, pig-headed old Kobus van Graan, with whom he was always at loggerheads—for two long years the two families hadn't spoken a Christian word to one another and all because of a cursed patch of grazing land; once the Van Graans, by planting an open garden right on the boundary between the two farms, had even enticed some of his cattle beyond the disputed piece of grazing land on to the garden and then whisked the cattle off to have them impounded in the village kilometres away; but that was an old story, he did not want to think about it any more . . . .

About noon that day Great Ouma was at last free to fetch the apples she needed for the midday meal from the loft. The door at the top of the stone staircase stood ajar, and a greyish-blue mistiness lingered about the loft. Broad tobacco leaves—a ripe gold and deep brown— hung in rows from the roof; and in the dim corners there was a reddish glow where apples lay in heaps.

Great Oupa's coffin stood in its customary place in the middle; but the small bags of dried fruit, tea and sugar, and the tinned food that were usually stored inside the coffin, now surrounded it in disorder, either dumped on one side or clumsily stacked one on top of the other. On a tin of sardines, at the head of the coffin, lay Great Oupa's pipe. Puzzled, Great Ouma walked towards the coffin, and stopped beside it. There, stretched out on his back, lay Great Oupa, fast asleep.

Nonplussed, Great Ouma stood gazing down at her sleeping husband. When she had been a young girl people had said, "Young Lafras has got a screw loose . . ." or, "Sure as eggs that pokkel of a Piet Lourens hasn't got all his little pigs in his sty . . ." But during all the years of their happy marriage it had been precisely his sudden whims or "inspirations"—something spontaneous and boyish in his character— that had given her some of the happiest hours of her life.

He looked contented lying there . . . Then her lips tightened and her small, square chin set in its usual firm lines. What nonsense was this, lying in his coffin in broad daylight! Bending over, she shook him by the arm.

Without stirring, Great Oupa gazed up at her with a happy, calm expression on his face. Then, with his voice a little drowsy from the sleep, he explained.

"I was standing here, thinking. . . . My bed I know only too well, I have long since got used to it. My parents slept in it, I was born in it, you and I have slept in it these many years. And I must die in it. But what of my bed later on—the coffin in which I shall have to lie so much longer—until this teak wood and I, my very bones, are dust and ashes? So I climbed in just to see what it feels like. I lit my pipe, lay looking at the cobwebs up there"—he had picked up his pipe and was pointing at the cobwebs—"and with the pleasant smell from the tobacco leaves and the apples, my thoughts started drifting . . ." And Great Oupa made several slow gestures with the pipe as if to indicate just how smooth and elegant had been the drift of his thoughts.

"But old Santa"—he now sat upright in his coffin—"what about those mutton chops of yours? You know it is my favourite dish. . . . And I am so hungry my insides are shouting for food!"

Laughing happily, they went arm in arm down the broad staircase.

In those days the farmers whose farms, like that of Great Oupa were a long way from Swellendam, went very seldom into the village. Death, like a hailstorm in the wheat, rinderpest among the cattle, blue tongue among the sheep, could come at any moment. So everyone had his coffin ready in the loft.

Great Oupa's coffin must have cost quite a sum. It had stood there, a glossy brown, among half a dozen black coffins in the undertaker's shop at Swellendam. Great Oupa did not hesitate for a moment. "This is it, my cot!" and he drummed with his knuckles against the coffin lid. He had it put on his wagon and then drove to the house of his friend, Jan Steyn, where he, his host and three or four of their cronies had a long "session" on the Drosdy stoep, swilling their gullets with old Cape wine until the shadows crowded around them so, they couldn't see the glasses in their hands.

I often saw the coffin up there in the loft. I remember distinctly when

I first came upon it. I had crept into the loft to steal some dried fruit; and suddenly I saw it—slim but solidly built, dark but with a gleam to it in that half-light among the red and green tins, white boxes, warmly-glowing apples and the pendant tobacco leaves with their warm tones. Without knowing it I had removed my cap; and I remained standing there, unable to take my eyes off the coffin. But it wasn't long before I got busy on the dried fruit. The next time I saw the coffin, the lid was off and Great Ouma was again using it as a larder for her tea, sugar and tinned foods.

When Great Oupa with Francina, his favourite grandchild, seated on the *wakis* beside him, drove off from Bonteboskloof on his 1500 kilometre trek to the Transvaal to visit relations he hadn't seen for years and also to do some business there, the coffin, filled to the brim with provisions, stood jammed amongst a clutter of other bulky articles at the back of the covered wagon.

Great Oupa cracked his whip, bellowed to the oxen, for the last time Francina waved her spotted bonnet—her head, tilted back, fair as ripe corn in the sun—and soon the groaning, creaking wagon had dropped behind the ridge.

Nine months later they returned from their long trip—without the coffin. When Oom Lewies of Tant Sarie had died there in the wilderness of the bushveld of the poison from the lion's claws, Great Oupa had ceded his "teak bed" to him. Why, he asked, should he worry about so small a thing as death? He was as strong as an ox and felt stronger every day.

But when communion came round again, he took the precaution of making a fresh choice from a bunch of brand-new "black sheep" in the undertaker's shop at Swellendam.

In those parts it was the custom among the farmers to give their coffins in loan to one another. For instance, if there was a sudden death with no coffin handy and the village was too far away for a wagon or cart and horse to get there in time, well, then you just had to help your neighbour to a "last haven".

I remember Great Oupa's coffin making at least three changes up there in the loft. First Koos Badenhorst was carried in Great Oupa's coffin to the Badenhorst churchyard near the old homestead at Soetwater. In its substitute, provided by the Badenhorsts, "Squint-eye" Frans de Vries, of Ouplaas, found his last resting-place. And a year later, if I remember correctly, it was old "Barrel-belly" Hans Boshoff, of Heuningrant, who went to his grave in Great Oupa's "cot".

Once again I was spending the long summer vacation on the old farm. The second afternoon after my arrival the old dispute between the two families was again nagging at Great Oupa's mind. Beside the kraal gate he discussed it with his eldest son, Oom Piet.

"What a contrary fellow Neef Kobus is!" he was saying. "Just like a sheep that won't go into the kraal gate! Everything I could do to make an end of this eternal squabbling I have done—but nothing helps! I even suggested that he take threequarters of that piece of grazing land. He can do what he likes with it, plough and sow there, even put a fence round it. I hear some of our farmers have no more use for beacons. They're beginning to use barbed wire now, strange idea—then we'll call it our Wire of Peace! Only we must retain that small strip next to the stream so that we can have some of the water. They get most of it, in any case, higher up."

The long summer days passed quickly. Great Oupa, I soon discovered, had developed a new habit. During the day one would suddenly miss him, find him neither in the wheatfield nor at the dam.

One afternoon I was walking along the riverbed, about two kilometres from the homestead. There, in a desolate kloof against the mountain, I was startled by a weird protracted sound from somewhere nearby. It stopped, then began again. It was like a long drawn-out groan; that of an animal, I thought, in great pain. I had come to a dead stop, listening. Then I walked forward mechanically and, forcing my way through some undergrowth, came upon Great Oupa sitting on a grassy bank. He was bending over with his hands clenching his knees. On his contorted face there was an expression I shall never forget; and while he clenched and unclenched his hands, fierce groans broke from his lips.

A cold had seemed to touch my heart. Then Great Oupa noticed me where I stood, bewildered and speechless, beside a shrub.

At once the agonised expression had disappeared, the face was normal again, the gaze calm and the eyes had the first little spark of a smile.

575

He beckoned to me. I sat down beside him. Within a few minutes he was as amusing as ever, telling me about the good old days when he and his three brothers were small boys; how they practically lived down here in the riverbed; how with enormous guns that today would kick grown-up people clean out of their boots, they had hunted wild animals, yes, even leopards, all on their own, here, in this same tangled kloof. But I had a strong feeling something was wrong and I could hear my heart throbbing. Beads of sweat, I noticed, stood on Great Oupa's forehead; and now and again his fingers would tremble slightly.

We walked through the veld. Great Oupa was still talking animatedly; and as he talked, he would flick off the head of a veld flower with his horse-whip, something I had never seen him do before.

At table that evening he was as humorous as ever. But I did not sleep much that night.

The feeling of fear and horror, the cruel assault on my young mind and imagination that I had experienced that afternoon in the kloof, was repeated with shattering immediacy when a few months later I learned in one of my first Latin lessons that the word cancer meant "crab".

When with the passing of time the disease struck deeper roots into that big strong body and Great Oupa was often so exhausted that he no longer felt capable of repairing to his old sanctuary, the veld, he and Great Ouma changed their bedroom—moving to the old part of the house where the walls were more than a metre thick. It would be cooler there in summer, Great Oupa said. And as far as winter was concerned, it was the only room in the house with a decent fireplace . . . .

Nobody knew what actually was happening behind those thick walls. Only as time went by Great Ouma's face became more wrinkled and her back more bent; as if in her efforts to draw on all her resources of love, patience and an obstinate resistance, her small body was gradually shrinking.

Always after one of those terrible attacks, Great Oupa would be at his gayest. Then there was no coping with his high spirits, his debonair sense of humour. A group of us would sit round the dining-room table or in the warm, late afternoon sun on the stoep, listening spellbound to everything he said. No one would interrupt him. Only one person would be speaking, Great Oupa.

At times his humour would have a light touch—subtle, playful, ironical. But his irony was directed mostly against himself; and where it touched on the failings of his fellow-men, it never hurt.

On other occasions his mood was warm and human, full of understanding—gentle as sunlight on green hills after rain. Sometimes, however, it became boisterous, extravagant. Then his laughter would come in great gusts of bawdy humour; he would be so forthright, so exuberantly coarse that many of us, especially the older ones, would have tears running down our cheeks and Great Ouma, if she were present, would lift up her hands as if to ward off a blow, and then quietly but very effectively put an end to all this "godlessness". It was then I always felt his humour was vital and earthy; and it had something physical like sea-water streaming over you on a hot summer's day and making your whole body tingle with coolness.

"Laughter is a glorious, sacred thing," Great Oupa once said, "a gift from God. . . . In this old life of ours that can be so hard and bitter, laughter is often our only defence against life. And also our only defence against death, enabling us to look it straight in the face and even, sometimes, play the fool with it. . . .

"Laughter is of us humans, the land, the earth; and the nearer you get to the earth, the nearer you get to heaven."

In her lean-to against the hill old Mieta was found dead one morning. More than a hundred years old, she had been one of the slaves of Great Oupa's grandfather down at the Cape many, many years ago, and had served the Lourens family faithfully all her long life. She had had, even in her old age, a vivid personality and a great fund of humour; and with her store of Malay folklore, her Boer simples for every ailment and her endless picturesque anecdotes from the past, she had been Great Oupa's favourite among his coloured servants. Quite often I would see him standing in front of her shack talking to her where she sat with her back propped up against the mud wall, turning her wizened old face now up at him and then at the sun; and not infrequently during our long talks on the stoep he would embellish some tale he had heard, I knew, from Mieta.

Now Great Oupa again stood in front of old Mieta's lean-to, but this time he seemed angry—rebuking her grandson, Adoons, who until a few minutes ago had been busy nailing together some planks for a coffin for his grandmother.

"Shame on you, Adoons!" he exclaimed. "Surely your old Granny deserves something better than that? To think of that awful contraption being her crib for all eternity! Go and fetch my coffin from the loft!"

So the small, shrivelled body was laid out in the large, heavy coffin with its glistening copper fittings. Carefully Adoons filled up the large gap at Mieta's feet with two of her own blankets, "just to balance poor old Oumatjie . . ."

The burial service was conducted by Great Oupa himself.

He sat in the driver's seat with beside him his brother Nicolaas, "Crazy Nick" or "Nick the Noodle," as he was called in the neighbourhood. In the middle of the open wagon stood the beautiful dark-brown coffin, the sun striking sparks from its handles. Slowly the wagon rolled over the *werf*.

A little ahead, sexton for the occasion, Adoons paced with slow, measured tread—elegant and dignified, conscious of his importance in this last solemn rite; the tails of the morning coat Great Oupa had given him some years ago almost trailing, in spite of the large tuck at the back, in the dust.

The procession swung away from the *werf* to follow the road where a thick aloe hedge shut it off on both sides from the wheatfields.

"Lafras, man, charge Adoons! Get him!" Oom Nicolaas shouted.

I do not know what it was—the fine day, the vitality Great Oupa suddenly felt surging within him in this long pause between two attacks or perhaps Oom Nic's suggestion—but the next moment the great whip thong curled through the air. Three loud cracks and the mules had jerked into action, the wagon lurching forward and gravel flying in all directions.

Adoons's first great oath was swept away on the wind. With coat tails spread out almost horizontally, he ran down the road as if the devil and all his imps were jabbing him in the heels.

The first mule was almost on top of Adoons, when he swerved off the road, dashed through a large opening in the hedge and went racing over the open veld. Great Oupa swung the wagon through the opening and started chasing Adoons over the uneven stubble land, the coffin bouncing up and down on the wagon.

Against the still, golden surface of the freshly mown fields, Adoons was a pitch-black charging form with whirling arms and long coat tails flapping in the wind. After some distance of clattering progress Great Oupa came to his senses, halting the wagon. On top of a small rise, about a hundred metres off, stood Adoons, breathless but full of righteous indignation.

Great Oupa beckoned Adoons with the whip to come and resume his office in the ceremony. Against the ridge above the drift he conducted the service, together the three of them sang "Rest, My Soul, Thy God Is King," each dropped a handful of red earth upon the coffin. Adoons filled up the grave with a spade Oom Nic had placed in the wagon for the purpose, and Great Oupa, seeing a couple of hawks circling high above his head, marched off to fetch his gun and fix those blasted pests that were always gobbling up Great Ouma's eggs.

Death was slow in coming to Great Oupa.

On an afternoon when the last sheaves of the loveliest harvest Great Oupa had ever seen were being gathered into his sheds, Great Ouma died suddenly of a heart attack.

And Great Oupa had to bear his cross in solitude until Francina resigned her teaching post at Swellendam to come and keep house at Bontebokskloof.

Shortly after Great Ouma's death, Great Oupa wrote Oom Kobus a long, friendly letter—but there was no answer.

It was then, in the first few months after her death, that I noticed how deeply the folds and wrinkles had bitten into Great Oupa's face. Above the broad arched forehead the hair had become whiter, scarcer. Great Oupa's long coat now hung loose around his body, he looked thinner and his collars were too wide for him. Under his chin the skin hung slack; and once, when I was sitting next to him on the stoep, I thought of the peculiar neck of the mountain tortoise that I had come upon near the kraal the day before, and that I had finally coaxed into pushing its head out of its shell.

It was at the beginning of the Great Drought that Great Oupa came to hear of the sudden death overnight of his old neighbour and "bosom enemy", Kobus van Graan; and that the oubaas had no provision for himself and was now lying cold and without a coffin in his large four-poster at Blouklip.

One of Oom Kobus's coloured servants had told Adoons about it down at the spruit. The old quarrel about the grazing land had recently flared up again. Lourens and Van Graans no longer greeted one another, not even in front of the church door. Great Oupa told his grandson, Mattheus, to get his new coffin from the loft, put it on the wagon and take it to Blouklip.

"When I let Kobus van Graan know the other day he should pay us a visit so that we could clear up this matter once and for all," Great Oupa said quietly, "he did not even answer my letter. But he told Neef Jan Louw he would never set foot in my house again. Now he'll be my house's guest till Judgment Day . . ."

The Great Drought had scorched the earth a grey-black when Great Oupa eventually came to die. Spent, with his face bonier than ever, he lay in his large wide bed as if for the first time he was utterly abandoned and helpless—and with at times such a calm expression on his face he seemed already dead.

At his bedside Francina wept without restraint and in a bunched group near the farther window the menfolk whispered together; for the eldest among them, Oom Piet, had only just discovered that the coffin in the loft would be too small for his father.

Berend, Kobus van Graan's youngest son, careless bungler that he was, had brought a coffin that in no way conformed to Great Oupa's stature. And to get to Swellendam today or tomorrow, or even this week, was quite out of the question. Where before there had been a wide sheet of water in the pan, the earth now was as cracked as a dead leaf; the few remaining horses had just enough strength to plod from one patch of shadow to the other in their vain search for food; and in the parched riverbed, the skulls and bones of oxen lay bleaching in the flat, white glare of the sun.

Of their neighbours, the three De Villiers were short men, and all the other men of medium height. . . . Nowhere in the neighbourhood would they find a coffin to fit Great Oupa's 191 centimetres.

Great Oupa, whose ear was so acute he could hear from the front stoep the call of a tarentaal against the ridge, slowly opened eyes and turned his head in the direction of his children.

"Francina, don't cry anymore, my child. Life is much too precious for you to mourn over someone's death. Life goes on. It's only death that comes to a dead-end like the cave I showed you one day in the mountain up there." And lifting his hand, he pointed through the window beside his bed at the distant Langeberg. "Be glad that we've had such pleasant times together. And for your heartache, the days that lie ahead will be good doctors.

"And Petrus, Mattheus, Johannes, Jacobus, Christoffel, Arnoldus"— it was the first time I heard him solemnly calling his sons by their full, sonorous names and not merely Piet, Tewis, Jan, Koos, Chris, and Nols—"you have your hands full enough just keeping your families alive until the drought breaks for you to be worrying your heads about such a trifle as a coffin that's too small. Do you think I don't know it's too small? I measured it myself the week before last. Funny, that even in death Kobus van Graan should have caught me out . . .

"Look, Piet, get Adoons. He is a good carpenter. Those deal planks at the back of the wagon-shed, let him knock them together and give them a good lick of varnish. It'll be dry by tomorrow. And don't break your necks because I won't be put away in a teak coffin. Sailors used to wrap some of our ancestors in a piece of sail and drop them into the sea . . .

"Piet, you are the eldest. This eternal quarrel with the Van Graans must stop now for good and all. With our everlasting bickering old Kobus and I were thorn enough in the side of our good Lord. Give Berend and the others the grazing land or what remans of it and *Basta*! Then if I meet Kobus van Graan on the other side, he'll probably greet me. . . ." A little laugh and Great Oupa turned his head to the window gazing at the mountains for some time. Then he closed his eyes. He never spoke again.

On a windstill afternoon full of scorching sunlight, grey bone-dry old Mother Earth took back her son in a plain deal coffin without a single fitting.

On the night after the funeral Great Oupa's twentieth grandchild was born.

I CAN'T BREATHE

RING LARDNER

Ring W. Lardner

July 12

I AM STAYING here at the Inn for two weeks with my Uncle Nat and Aunt Jule and I think I will keep a kind of diary while I am here to help pass the time and so I can have a record of things that happen though goodness knows there isn't likely to anything happen, that is anything exciting with Uncle Nat and Aunt Jule making the plans as they are both at least 35 years old and maybe older.

Dad and mother are abroad to be gone a month and me coming here is supposed to be a recompence for them not taking me with them. A fine recompence to be left with old people that come to a place like this to rest. Still it would be a heavenly place under different conditions, for instance if Walter were here, too. It would be heavenly if he were here, the very thought of it makes my heart stop.

I can't stand it. I won't think about it.

This is our first separation since we have been engaged, nearly 17 days. It will be 17 days tomorrow. And the hotel orchestra at dinner this evening played that old thing "Oh, how I miss you tonight" and it seemed as if they must be playing it for my benefit though of course the person in that song is talking about how they miss their mother though of course I miss mother too, but a person gets used to missing their mother and it isn't like Walter or the person you are engaged to.

But there won't be any more separations much longer, we are going to be married in December even if mother does laugh when I talk to her about it because she says I am crazy to even think of getting married at 18. She got married herself when she was 18, but of course that was "different," she wasn't crazy like I am, she knew whom she was marrying. As if Walter were a policeman or a foreigner or something. And she says she was only engaged once while I have been engaged at least five times a year since I was 14, of course it really isn't as bad as that and I have really only been really what I call engaged six times altogether, but is getting engaged my fault when they keep insisting and hammering at you and if you didn't say yes they would never go home.

But it is different with Walter. I honestly believe if he had not asked me I would have asked him. Of course I wouldn't have, but I would have died. And this is the first time I have ever been engaged to be really married. The other times when they talked about when we should get married I just laughed at them, but I hadn't been engaged to Walter ten minutes when he brought up the subject of marriage and I didn't laugh. I wouldn't be engaged to him unless it was to be married. I couldn't stand it.

Anyway mother may as well get used to the idea because it is "No Foolin'" this time and we have got our plans all made and I am going to be married at home and go out to California and Hollywood on our honeymoon. December, five months away. I can't stand it. I can't wait.

There were a couple of awfully nice looking boys sitting together alone in the dining-room tonight. One of them wasn't so much, but the other was cute. And he—

There's the dance orchestra playing "Always," what they played at the Biltmore the day I met Walter. "Not for just an hour, not for just a day." I can't live. I can't breathe.

July 13

THIS HAS BEEN a much more exciting day than I expected under the circumstances. In the first place I got two long night letters, one from Walter and one from Gordon Flint. I don't see how Walter ever had the nerve to send his, there was everything in it and it must have been horribly embarrassing for him while the telegraph operator was reading it over and counting the words to say nothing of embarrassing the operator.

But the one from Gordon was a kind of a shock. He just got back from a trip around the world, left last December to go on it and got back yesterday and called up our house and Helga gave him my address, and his telegram, well it was nearly as bad as Walter's. The trouble is that Gordon and I were engaged when he went away, or at least he thought so and he wrote to me right along all the time he was away and sent cables and things and for a while I answered his letters, but then I lost track of his itinerary and couldn't write to him any more and when I got really engaged to Walter I couldn't let Gordon know because I had no idea where he was besides not wanting to spoil his trip.

And now he still thinks we are engaged and he is going to call me up tomorrow from Chicago and how in the world can I explain things and get him to understand because he is really serious and I like him ever and ever so much and in lots of ways he is nicer than Walter, not really nicer but better looking and there is no comparison between their dancing. Walter simply can't learn to dance, that is really dance. He says it is because he is flat footed, he says that as a joke, but it is true and I wish to heavens it wasn't.

All forenoon I thought and thought and thought about what to say to Gordon when he calls up and finally I couldn't stand thinking about it any more and just made up my mind I wouldn't think about it any more. But I will tell the truth though it will kill me to hurt him.

I went down to lunch with Uncle Nat and Aunt Jule and they were going out to play golf this afternoon and were insisting that I go with them, but I told them I had a headache and then I had a terrible time getting them to go without me. I didn't have a headache at all and just wanted to be alone to think about Walter and besides when you play with Uncle Nat he is always correcting your stance or your swing or something and always puts his hands on my arms or shoulders to show me the right way and I can't stand it to have old men touch me, even if they are your uncle.

I finally got rid of them and I was sitting watching the tennis when that boy that I saw last night, the cute one, came and sat right next to me and of course I didn't look at him and I was going to smoke a cigarette and found I had left my lighter upstairs and I started to get up and go after it when all of a sudden he was offering me his lighter and I couldn't very well refuse it without being rude. So we got to talking and he is even cuter than he looks, the most original and wittiest person I believe I ever met and I haven't laughed so much in I don't know how long.

For one thing he asked me if I had heard Rockefeller's song and I said no and he began singing "Oil alone." Then he asked me if I knew the orange juice song and I told him no again and he said it was "Orange juice sorry you made me cry." I was in hysterics before we had been together ten minutes.

His name is Frank Caswell and he has been out of Darthmouth a year and is 24 years old. That isn't so terribly old, only two years older than Walter and three years older than Gordon. I hate the name Frank, but Caswell is all right and he is so cute.

He was out in California last winter and visited Hollywood and met everybody in the world and it is fascinating to listen to him. He met Norma Shearer and he said he thought she was the prettiest thing he had ever seen. What he said was "I did think she was the prettiest girl in the world, till today." I was going to pretend I didn't get it, but I finally told him to be sensible or I would never be able to believe anything he said.

Well, he wanted me to dance with him tonight after dinner and the next question was how to explain how we had met each other to Uncle Nat and Aunt Jule. Frank said he would fix that all right and sure enough he got himself introduced to Uncle Nat when Uncle Nat came in from golf and after dinner Uncle Nat introduced him to me and Aunt Jule too and we danced together all evening, that is not Aunt Jule. They went to bed, thank heavens.

He is a heavenly dancer, as good as Gordon. One dance we were dancing and for one of the encores the orchestra played "Just a cottage small by a waterfall" and I simply couldn't dance to it. I just stopped still and said "Listen, I can't bear it, I can't breathe" and poor Frank thought I was sick or something and I had to explain that that was the tune the orchestra played the night I sat at the next table to Jack Barrymore at Barney Gallant's.

I made him sit out that encore and wouldn't let him talk till they got through playing it. Then they played something else and I was all right again and Frank told me about meeting Jack Barrymore. Imagine meeting him. I couldn't live.

I promised Aunt Jule I would go to bed at eleven and it is way past that now, but I am all ready for bed and have just been writing this. Tomorrow Gordon is going to call up and what will I say to him? I just won't think about it.

July 14

GORDON CALLED UP this morning from Chicago and it was wonderful to hear his voice again though the connection was terrible. He asked me if I still loved him and I tried to tell him no, but I knew that would mean an explanation and the connection was so bad that I never could make him understand so I said yes, but I almost whispered it purposely, thinking he wouldn't hear me, but he heard me all right and he said that made everything all right with the world. He said he thought I had stopped loving him because I had stopped writing.

I wish the connection had been decent and I could have told him how things were, but now it is terrible because he is planning to get to New York the day I get there and heaven knows what I will do because Walter will be there, too. I just won't think about it.

Aunt Jule came in my room just after I was through talking to Gordon, thank heavens. The room was full of flowers. Walter had sent me some and so had Frank. I got another long night letter from Walter, just as silly as the first one. I wish he would say those things in letters instead of night letters so everybody in the world wouldn't see them. Aunt Jule wanted me to read it aloud to her. I would have died.

While she was still in the room, Frank called up and asked me to play golf with him and I said all right and Aunt Jule said she was glad my headache was gone. She was trying to be funny.

I played golf with Frank this afternoon. He is a beautiful golfer and it is thrilling to watch him drive, his swing is so much more graceful than Walter's. I asked him to watch me swing and tell me what was the matter with me, but he said he couldn't look at anything but my face and there wasn't anything the matter with that.

He told me the boy who was here with him had been called home and he was glad of it because I might have liked him, the other boy, better than himself.

I told him that couldn't be possible and he asked me if I really meant that and I said of course, but I smiled when I said it so he wouldn't take it too seriously.

We danced again tonight and Uncle Nat and Aunt Jule sat with us a while and danced a couple of dances themselves, but they were really there to get better acquainted with Frank and see if he was all right for me to be with. I know they certainly couldn't have enjoyed their own dancing, no old people really can enjoy it because they can't really *do* anything. They were favorably impressed with Frank I think, at least Aunt Jule didn't say I must be in bed at eleven, but just not to stay up too late. I guess it is a big surprise to a girl's parents and aunts and uncles to find out that the boys you go around with are all right, they always seem to think that if I seem to like somebody and the person pays a little attention to me, why he must be a convict or a policeman or a drunkard or something queer.

Frank had some more songs for me tonight. He asked me if I knew the asthma song and I said I didn't and he said "Oh, you must know that. It goes yes, sir, asthma baby." Then he told me about the underwear song, "I underwear my baby is tonight." He keeps you in hysterics and yet he has his serious side, in fact he was awfully serious when he said good night to me and his eyes simply shown. I wish Walter were more like him, but I mustn't think about that.

July 15

I SIMPLY CAN'T live and I know I'll never sleep tonight. I am in a terrible predicament or rather I won't know whether I really am or not till tomorrow and that is what makes it so terrible.

After we had danced two or three dances, Frank asked me to go for a ride with him and we went for a ride in his car and he had had some cocktails and during the ride he had some drinks out of a flask and finally he told me he loved me and I said not to be silly, but he said he was perfectly serious and he certainly acted that way. He asked me if I loved anybody else and I said yes and he asked if I didn't love him more than anybody else and I said yes, but only because I thought he had probably had too much to drink and wouldn't remember it anyway and the best thing to do was humor him under the circumstances.

Then all of a sudden he asked me when I could marry him and I said, just as a joke, that I couldn't possibly marry him before December. He said that was a long time to wait, but I was certainly worth waiting for and he said a lot of other things and maybe I humored him a little too much, but that is just the trouble, I don't know.

I was absolutely sure he was tight and would forget the whole thing, but that was early in the evening, and when we said good night he was a whole lot more sober than he had been and now I am not sure how it stands. If he doesn't remember anything about it, of course I am all right. But if he does remember and if he took me seriously, I will simply have to tell him about Walter and maybe about Gordon, too. And it isn't going to be easy. The suspense is what is maddening and I know I'll never live through this night.

July 16

I CAN'T STAND it, I can't breathe, life is impossible. Frank remembered everything about last night and firmly believes we are engaged and going to be married in December. His people live in New York and he says he is going back when I do and have them meet me.

Of course it can't go on and tomorrow I will tell him about Walter or Gordon or both of them. I know it is going to hurt him terribly, perhaps spoil his life and I would give anything in the world not to have had it happen. I hate so to hurt him because he is so nice besides being so cute and attractive. He sent me the loveliest flowers this morning and called up at ten and wanted to know how soon he could see me and I hope the girl wasn't listening in because the things he said were, well, like Walter's night letters.

And that is another terrible thing, today I didn't get a night letter from Walter, but there was a regular letter instead and I carried it around in my purse all this afternoon and evening and never remembered to read it till ten minutes ago when I came up in the room. Walter is worried because I have only sent him two telegrams and written him one letter since I have been here, he would be a lot more worried if he knew what has happened now, though of course it can't make any difference because he is the one I am really engaged to be married to and the one I told mother I was going to marry in December and I wouldn't dare tell her it was somebody else.

I met Frank for lunch and we went for a ride this afternoon and he was so much in love and so lovely to me that I simply did not have the heart to tell him the truth, I am surely going to tell him tomorrow and telling him today would have just meant one more day of unhappiness for both of us.

He said his people had plenty of money and his father had offered to take him into partnership and he might accept, but he thinks his true vocation is journalism with a view to eventually writing novels and if I was willing to undergo a few hardships just at first we would probably both be happier later on if he was doing something he really liked. I didn't know what to say, but finally I said I wanted him to suit himself and money wasn't everything.

He asked me where I would like to go on my honeymoon and I suppose I ought to have told him my honeymoon was all planned, that I was going to California, with Walter, but all I said was that I had always wanted to go to California and he was enthusiastic and said that is where we would surely go and he would take me to Hollywood and introduce me to all those wonderful people he met there last winter. It nearly takes my breath away to think of it, going there with someone who really knows people and has the entrée.

We danced again tonight, just two or three dances, and then went out and sat in the tennis-court, but I came upstairs early because Aunt Jule had acted kind of funny at dinner. And I wanted to be alone, too, and think, but the more I think the worse it gets.

Sometimes I wish I were dead, maybe that is the only solution and it would be best for everyone concerned. I *will* die if things keep on the way they have been. But of course tomorrow it will be all over, with Frank I mean, for I must tell him the truth no matter how much it hurts us both. Though I don't care how much it hurts me. The thought of hurting him is what is driving me mad. I can't bear it.

July 18

I HAVE SKIPPED a day. I was busy every minute of yesterday and so exhausted when I came upstairs that I was tempted to fall into bed with all my clothes on. First Gordon called me up from Chicago to remind me that he would be in New York the day I got there and that when he comes he wants me all to himself all the time and we can make plans for our wedding. The connection was bad again and I just couldn't explain to him about Walter.

I had an engagement with Frank for lunch and just as we were going in another long distance call came, from Walter this time. He wanted to know why I haven't written more letters and sent him more telegrams and asked me if I still loved him and of course I told him yes because I really do. Then he asked if I had met any men here and I told him I had met one, a friend of Uncle Nat's. After all it was Uncle Nat who introduced me to Frank. He reminded me that he would be in New York on the 25th which is the day I expect to get home, and said he would have theater tickets for that night and we would go somewhere afterwards and dance. Frank insisted on knowing who had kept me talking so long and I told him it was a boy I had known a long while, a very dear friend of mine and a friend of my family's. Frank was jealous and kept asking questions till I thought I would go mad. He was so serious and kind of cross and gruff that I gave up the plan of telling him the truth till some time when he is in better spirits.

I played golf with Frank in the afternoon and we took a ride last night and I wanted to get in early because I had promised both Walter and Gordon that I would write them long letters, but Frank wouldn't bring me back to the Inn till I had named a definite date in December. I finally told him the 10th and he said all right if I was sure that wasn't a Sunday. I said I would have to look it up, but as a matter of fact I know the 10th falls on a Friday because the date Walter and I have agreed on for our wedding is Saturday the 11th.

Today has just been the same thing over again, two more night letters, a long distance call from Chicago, golf and a ride with Frank, and the room full of flowers. But tomorrow I am going to tell Frank and I am going to write Gordon a long letter and tell him, too, because this simply can't go on any longer. I can't breathe. I can't live.

July 21

I WROTE TO Gordon yesterday, but I didn't say anything about Walter because I don't think it is a thing a person ought to do by letter. I can tell him when he gets to New York and then I will be sure that he doesn't take it too hard and I can promise him that I will be friends with him always and make him promise not to do anything silly, while if I told it to him in a letter there is no telling what he would do, there all alone.

And I haven't told Frank because he hasn't been feeling well, he is terribly sunburned and it hurts him terribly so he can hardly play golf or dance, and I want him to be feeling his best when I do tell him, but whether he is all right or not I simply must tell him tomorrow because he is actually planning to leave here on the same train with us Saturday night and I can't let him do that.

Life is so hopeless and it could be so wonderful. For instance how heavenly it would be if I could marry Frank first and stay married to him five years and he would be the one who would take me to Hollywood and maybe we could go on parties with Norman Kerry and Jack Barrymore and Buster Collier and Marion Davies and Lois Moran.

And at the end of five years Frank could go into journalism and write novels and I would only be 23 and I could marry Gordon and he would be ready for another trip around the world and he could show me things better than someone who had never seen them before.

Gordon and I would separate at the end of five years and I would be 28 and I know of lots of women that never even got married the first time till they were 28 though I don't suppose that was their fault, but I would marry Walter then, for after all he is the one I really love and want to spend most of my life with and I wouldn't care whether he could dance or not when I was that old. Before long we would be as old as Uncle Nat and Aunt Jule and I certainly wouldn't want to dance at their age when all you can do is just hobble around the floor. But Walter is so wonderful as a companion and we would enjoy the same things and be pals and maybe we would begin to have children.

But that is all impossible though it wouldn't be if older people just had sense and would look at things the right way.

It is only half past ten, the earliest I have gone to bed in weeks, but I am worn out and Frank went to bed early so he could put cold cream on his sunburn.

Listen, diary, the orchestra is playing "Limehouse Blues." The first tune I danced to with Merle Oliver, two years ago. I can't stand it. And how funny that they should play that old tune tonight of all nights, when I have been thinking of Merle off and on all day, and I hadn't thought of him before in weeks and weeks. I wonder where he is, I wonder if it is just an accident or if it means I am going to see him again. I simply mustn't think about it or I'll die.

July 22

I KNEW IT wasn't an accident. I knew it must mean something, and it did.

Merle is coming here today, here to this Inn, and just to see me. And there can only be one reason. And only one answer. I knew that when I heard his voice calling from Boston. How could I ever had thought I loved anyone else? How could he ever have thought I meant it when I told him I was engaged to George Morse?

A whole year and he still cares and I still care. That shows we were always intended for each other and for no one else. I won't make *him* wait till December. I doubt if we even wait till dad and mother get home. And as for a honeymoon I will go with him to Long Beach or the Bronx Zoo, wherever he wants to take me.

After all this is the best way out of it, the only way. I won't have to say anything to Frank, he will guess when he sees me with Merle. And when I get home Sunday and Walter and Gordon call me up, I will invite them both to dinner and Merle can tell them himself, with two of them there it will only hurt each one half as much as if they were alone.

The train is due at 2:40, almost three hours from now. I can't wait. And what if it should be late? I can't stand it.

THE AUTHORS

JAMES BALDWIN *1924–*
Son of a pastor in Harlem, New York City, James Baldwin thought briefly of studying for the ministry. In his early twenties he went to Paris, where he began to write short stories deeply rooted in the black experience. Recognition, especially of his importance as a commentator on the plight of black America, came in 1953 with his first novel, *Go Tell It on the Mountain*. Besides his short stories, collected in *Going to Meet the Man*, and five well-received novels, he has written magazine articles, a number of brilliant essays and three plays. Page 35

H. E. BATES *1905–1974*
Herbert Ernest Bates learned his craft as a provincial journalist. The first of his many popular novels was published when he was only twenty. He was most successful perhaps as a writer of short stories, many of which reflect a deep love and understanding of his native English countryside. During World War II he held the rank of Squadron Leader and wrote the famous Flying Officer X stories. Page 13

HERMAN CHARLES BOSMAN *1905–1951*
Born in Cape Town, Herman Charles Bosman worked for much of his life as a teacher in the Western Transvaal. Though his writings were principally in a humorous vein, his own life became one of stark tragedy. In a fierce family quarrel he shot and killed his step-brother. His death sentence was commuted and he spent four and a half years in prison. His most powerful novel, *Stone Cold Jug*, was based on that part of his life. Page 501

KAY BOYLE *1903–*
Born in St. Paul, Minnesota, into a household where books were a staple, Kay Boyle began writing early. Prolific, even while working as a college teacher, she has produced novels, novelettes, short stories, war correspondence, poetry, magazine articles and children's books. But she is best known for her short stories, many dealing with the infinitely subtle ways in which the human need for love reveals itself. Page 67

KATHARINE BRUSH *1902–1952*
A best-selling novelist of the 1930s, Katharine Brush was known for her deft, caustic portraits of café society in the Prohibition era. Born in Middletown, Connecticut, at sixteen she was writing for the Boston *Traveler*. Her literary career began with light verse and short fiction contributed to leading magazines. Later she became a scriptwriter in Hollywood. Her permanent home was in New York City, the setting of many of her stories. Page 306

JOHN CHEEVER *1912–*

Born in Quincy, Massachusetts, of old New England stock, John Cheever was expelled from school at the age of seventeen. He then spent four years in the army. He wrote scripts for radio and eventually for television and became a teacher of advanced composition at Barnard College, New York City. His elegant prose, shrewd observation and wry humour have won him a distinguished place in contemporary literature.   Page 463

WALTER VAN TILBURG CLARK *1909–1971*

Most of Walter Van Tilburg Clark's early life was spent in Reno, Nevada, where his father served as president of the University of Nevada. That state also gave him the setting for his best-known novel, *The Ox-Bow Incident*, the book in which the Western came suddenly of age. He attended schools in Nevada, Vermont and New York, where he was a teacher and a coach of athletics. He wrote two other novels and more than twenty short stories.   Page 244

RICHARD CONNELL *1893–1949*

Author of about three hundred short stories, Richard Connell was also a successful writer of advertising copy and Hollywood screenplays. Born in Poughkeepsie, New York, where his father edited a newspaper, he attended Harvard, and served in France during World War I. After living in New York, he moved permanently to California.   Page 193

MARC CONNELLY *1890–*

While working as a columnist for a Pittsburgh newspaper, Marc Connelly began writing musical-comedy lyrics. Visiting New York in 1915 to hear his words set to music, he fell in love with the theatre and stayed on to become one of its most notable authors and directors, writing short stories and verse as well. His greatest Broadway hit, *Green Pastures*, is as widely beloved today as when it won a Pulitzer Prize in 1930.   Page 379

JOY COWLEY *1936–*

Joy Cowley was born in New Zealand. After working three years' apprenticeship as a pharmacist she left to get married and became in due course the mother of four children. Her first novel was published in 1967. Since then she has written four more novels and a number of short stories both for adults and children.   Page 318

ROALD DAHL *1916–*

"Violence accompanied by wit and humour is loved". This master of the macabre (who was born in Wales of Norwegian parents and who now lives in England) was speaking of his highly successful children's books. Equally well, he might have been referring to his bizarre and world-famous short stories, many of which have been televised.   Page 411

LEN DEIGHTON *1929–*

In 1962, the former art student, railway platelayer, airline steward, and expert cook, was hailed throughout the book world for his brilliantly inventive spy novel, *The Ipcress File*. Since then, he has established his reputation with several novels and short stories, many on the subject of men at war.   Page 327

MARGARET DRABBLE *1939–*

To look at, Margaret Drabble is everybody's idea of a Hampstead literary lady (which is indeed what she is). Married, she has three children. Intellectually formidable, she is also deeply compassionate—except towards the phoney, which she detests. Her novels are widely admired. Her short stories are novels in miniature, tender, witty, precise.   Page 267

WILLIAM FAULKNER *1897–1962*
William Faulkner was born and raised in Mississippi, the son of an aristocratic tradition. In a series of distinguished novels set in his hometown of Oxford and the surrounding county, fictionalized as Yoknapatawpha, he mirrored the decline of the old South under the onslaught of technology. In World War I he served with the Royal Air Force. Later he worked as a newspaperman and screenwriter before earning international fame with such novels as *The Sound and the Fury* and *Sanctuary*. In 1950 he received the Nobel Prize in Literature.

Page 346

F. SCOTT FITZGERALD *1896–1940*
Only twenty-four when his first book, *This Side of Paradise*, brought him fame, the flamboyant F. Scott Fitzgerald soon became the living symbol of America's Jazz Age. Then, in mid-career, came tragedy. His wife, Zelda, suffered a mental breakdown, more or less permanent. He fell ill, took heavily to drink and was plunged into financial trouble. In Hollywood, where he wrote film scripts, the downward slide accelerated. *The Last Tycoon*, the novel left unfinished at his death, was published in 1941. His masterpiece, *The Great Gatsby*, had appeared in 1925.

Page 222

MAVIS GALLANT *1922–*
Born in Montreal, Mavis Gallant attended schools in Canada and the United States. For a time she worked for the Canadian National Film Board and then was film critic for the Montreal *Standard*. In 1951 she left North America for Paris, where she has lived ever since. Most of her stories have appeared first in *The New Yorker*.

Page 104

CHARLOTTE PERKINS GILMAN *1860–1935*
That haunting study of insanity, "The Yellow Wall Paper," published in 1892, was one of Charlotte Gilman's few works of fiction. An early campaigner for women's rights, she devoted most of her time to writing and lecturing on social reform. Her book, *Women and Economics*, published in 1898, was translated into six languages. Born in Hartford, Connecticut, she died in Pasadena, California.

Page 283

ERNEST GLANVILLE *1856–1925*
This prolific South African author of romantic adventure stories was also a professional journalist. During the Zulu War of 1879 he was a war correspondent for the London *Daily Chronicle*. Later he worked in Fleet Street before returning home to edit *The Cape Argus*.

Page 44

NADINE GORDIMER *1923–*
Nadine Gordimer began writing at the age of twelve, when confined to bed for several months. Born in the Transvaal, she was at that time attending a convent school and she went on to Witwatersrand University. As her work matured she contributed to prominent overseas magazines. Living now in Johannesburg, she has written two novels and several volumes of short stories.

Page 364

SHIRLEY ANN GRAU *1929–*
In all her novels and short stories Shirley Ann Grau writes of the South she knows so well in a style that is distinctly and hauntingly her own. Born and educated in New Orleans, Louisiana, she still resides there with her husband and three children. In 1965 she was awarded a Pulitzer Prize for her novel *The Keepers of the House*.

Page 421

ERNEST HEMINGWAY *1899–1961*

A believer in the vigorous life, he himself always seemed a little larger than life. His first thirty years of writing were capped in 1954 with the Nobel Prize in Literature. He had richly earned the honour with his many compelling short stories and his world-famous novels, *The Sun Also Rises, A Farewell to Arms* and *The Old Man and the Sea*. Born in Oak Park, Illinois, he began his career as a newsman in Kansas City. After service in World War I, he lived for a time in Paris, where his first book was published. His deceptively simple style has had a large influence on modern writers.   Page 137

O. HENRY *1862–1910*

One of the most prolific, and once the most popular, of America's short-story writers, he was born William Sydney Porter in Greensboro, North Carolina. At twenty he went to Texas, where he wrote for a Houston newspaper after having been employed as a teller in an Austin bank. Convicted later of embezzlement, he served a gaol term, then went to New York. There, in the lives of ordinary people, he found the themes for a host of memorable stories.   Page 473

SHIRLEY JACKSON *1919–1965*

As novelist, writer of short stories and radio and television scripts, Shirley Jackson reveals a preoccupation with the darker regions of human consciousness. Her novel *The Haunting of Hill House* was made into a successful film, and her story "The Lottery" became a play. But she could also write delightfully about ordinary life, as in *Life Among the Savages*, a series of essays on her children. She was born in San Francisco and lived most of her adult life in rural Vermont.   Page 486

DAN JACOBSON *1929–*

Dan Jacobson was born in Johannesburg and grew up in Kimberley. For the last twenty years he has lived in London, where recently he has taken an appointment as lecturer in English Literature at University College. As well as essays and short stories, he has written several novels.   Page 208

BRIAN JAMES *1892–1972*

Brian James is the pen-name of John Laurence Tierney. Born in New South Wales, Australia, of an Irish father and a German mother, he worked there as a schoolteacher for nearly forty years. His writing career began in 1942, on his fiftieth birthday, when he published his first short story. After that he went on to write many short stories and two distinguished novels.
                                                                            Page 429

JAMES JOYCE *1882–1941*

Perhaps the most important literary figure of his time, James Joyce developed a "stream of consciousness" style that influenced the art of the novel in the twentieth century. Born in Dublin and educated at Jesuit schools, Joyce nonetheless held political and religious views that caused him to exile himself from Ireland for most of his life. Publication of his famous novel, *Ulysses*, touched off an international furore as well as an historic court case on the freedom of the press in the United States.   Page 168

RUDYARD KIPLING *1865–1936*

Born in Bombay, Rudyard Kipling was returned to England when he was six, his health being extremely delicate. Later he rejected his parents' offer of a university education and went back to India, where he became a journalist. He soon showed himself to be a writer of genius and perhaps the master story-teller of his age. He died the recipient of many high honours, including, in 1907, the Nobel Prize in Literature.   Page 479

UYS KRIGE 1910–

This accomplished South African born author and translator served as a War Correspondent in North Africa during World War II, being captured by the Italians and held prisoner for two years till he finally escaped. Since the war he has lived and worked in South Africa, and has received several awards for his writings and translations. Page 570

RING LARDNER 1885–1933

Author of eight volumes of short stories and a novel, *The Big Town*, and co-author with George S. Kaufman of a comedy, *June Moon*, Ring Lardner first gained recognition as a sportswriter of unusual talent. A gregarious man who mixed with all sorts of people from prizefighters to stockbrokers, his subtle command of colloquial American speech became a trademark. Page 582

D. H. LAWRENCE 1885–1930

David Herbert Lawrence was the son of an English coal miner and a schoolteacher mother. One of five children, he was brought up in an atmosphere of poverty and drunken brutality which he was to immortalize in his great autobiographical novel, *Sons and Lovers*. Determined from an early age to be a writer, he persevered through a lifetime of sickness, controversy and non-acceptance, and today is secure in his position as an author of the very first magnitude.
Page 294

DORIS LESSING 1919–

Although she has lived in England since 1949, Doris Lessing was born in Persia and brought up on a farm in Rhodesia. She began writing when she was seventeen, and continued to do so through a variety of jobs: telephone operator, nursemaid, lawyers' clerk, chauffeuse. Her novels and short stories have been acclaimed the world over, and in 1954 she received the Somerset Maugham Award for work showing outstanding originality and promise. Page 453

JACK LONDON 1876–1916

By the age of twenty-two Jack London had been a cannery worker in San Francisco (his birth-place), an oyster pirate, a deckhand on a sealing vessel, a hobo, a Socialist agitator, a college student and finally a gold miner in the Klondike. It was this trip to the far North that inspired his most famous novel, *The Call of the Wild*, and many of his best stories. His vivid adventure tales became so popular that by 1913 he was said to be the world's highest-paid author. At forty, in despair over his health, finances and deteriorating talents, he died by an overdose of drugs, thought to have been deliberate. Page 538

H. P. LOVECRAFT 1890–1937

Recognition as a master of horror and fantasy tales came to H. P. Lovecraft only after he had been writing for twenty years, publishing in such specialized periodicals as *Weird Tales* and *Amazing Stories*. He was writing newspaper articles on science at the early age of sixteen, but frail health kept him from attending college, and most of his life was spent in Providence, Rhode Island, his birthplace. Much of his work anticipates the modern vogue of science fiction. Page 442

CARSON McCULLERS 1917–1967

Author of such modern classics as *The Member of the Wedding* and *The Ballad of the Sad Café*, Carson McCullers belongs to that school of writing known as Southern Gothic. All of her novels and short stories are laid in the South, evoking a world of loneliness and alienation. Born in Columbus, Georgia, she began writing at sixteen, and for a time had an ambition to become a concert pianist. She studied creative writing at New York University and when only twenty-three achieved wide fame with her first novel, *The Heart is a Lonely Hunter*. Page 180

OLIVIA MANNING *1920–1980*

The daughter of an English naval officer and an Irish mother, she was born in Portsmouth, then spent much of her childhood in Northern Ireland. She wanted to be a painter but, unable to afford the materials, started to write and completed a long first novel when she was seventeen. In 1939, she married a British Council lecturer in Bucharest. During the war, they were cut off from England and Miss Manning managed to travel extensively in unoccupied Europe and the Middle East, gaining experiences that enabled her to write one of her best-known works, *The Balkan Trilogy*. She had just completed another major success, *The Levant Trilogy*, when she died. Page 335

BERNARD MALAMUD *1914–*

Like many of the characters he created, Bernard Malamud was born into the Jewish immigrant world of Brooklyn, New York. Graduating from The City College of New York, he taught English in the city's evening high schools; he later joined the faculty of Bennington College, in Vermont. With publication of the novel *The Assistant* in 1957, he was quickly recognized as an important delineator of the American immigrant experience. Page 394

W. SOMERSET MAUGHAM *1874–1965*

Orphaned before he was ten, W. Somerset Maugham was brought up in England by a clergyman uncle. He studied medicine for six years but never practised as a doctor, turning instead to the writing that was to bring him international fame. As well as his plays and highly successful novels, such as *Of Human Bondage* and *The Moon and Sixpence*, he wrote many short stories of which he was an acknowledged master. Page 531

HERMAN MELVILLE *1819–1891*

Until fairly recently Herman Melville was the most ignored of America's great writers. Born in New York City of Scottish-Dutch parents, he was one of eight children. After working as a bank clerk, farmer and teacher, he went to sea on a merchantman, and later took part in a whaling cruise. Two accounts of his experiences in the South Seas, *Typee* and *Omoo*, were immensely successful, launching him on a writing career. When, however, his monumental novel, *Moby Dick*, appeared, it was misunderstood and condemned by the critics and ignored by the public, and his fame was eclipsed. Page 507

LIAM O'FLAHERTY *1897–*

Liam O'Flaherty was born on the Aran Islands off the Galway coast, served with the Irish Guards in the First World War and afterwards roamed the globe as deck-hand, porter and clerk. In the civil conflict of 1922 he fought for the Republicans. His novels, such as *The Informer*, speak harshly of the world's violence, but his short stories are touched with poetry. Page 450

JOHN O'HARA *1905–1970*

The eldest of eight children, John O'Hara was born in Pottsville, Pennsylvania. Prevented from going to college by the death of his doctor father, he worked as everything from ship's steward to film critic. In 1934 the success of his first novel, *Appointment in Samarra*, established him as a writer. His novels regularly made the best-seller lists and at least three of them—*Pal Joey*, *Ten North Frederick* and *Butterfield 8*—were made into popular films. Page 50

VANCE PALMER *1885–1959*

Edward Vance Palmer was born in Queensland, where he returned after a time in England at school and then working as a freelance writer. After army service in World War I, he travelled Europe extensively before settling again in Australia. There he became well known both as a writer and radio broadcaster. Page 554

EDGAR ALLAN POE *1809–1849*
One of America's first important writers, Edgar Allan Poe was born in Boston. Orphaned at three, he was reared by foster parents in Richmond, Virginia. Working as an editor, critic, and writer of short stories, he first gained attention in 1833 with his tale "MS. Found in a Bottle." There followed a series of world-renowned short stories, including "The Murders in the Rue Morgue," the first true detective story.   Page 62

R. S. PORTEOUS *1898–1962*
Born in Melbourne, Richard Sydney Porteous led an adventurous life. After service in the cavalry during World War I, he worked first on an Australian cattle ranch and then as skipper of a coastal trading vessel. It was during World War II, while he was in the Merchant Navy, that he began his very successful career as a writer.   Page 77

OLAF RUHEN *1911–*
Before joining the Royal New Zealand Air Force at the outbreak of World War II, Olaf Ruhen had worked principally as a deep sea fisherman and cattle drover. Since the war he has devoted himself to writing, publishing more than thirty books and becoming a foundation member of the Australian Society of Authors.   Page 255

"SAKI" (H. H. Munro) *1870–1916*
As a master of humour as well as the chilling and macabre, H. H. Munro (or "Saki" as he styled himself, after the cup-bearer in *The Rubá'iyát* by Omar Khayyám) has very few peers. Born in Burma but educated in England, he learned the craft of writing first as a reporter, then as a foreign correspondent in Russia and France. What had already become a brilliant career ended tragically with his death in battle during World War I.   Page 216

FRANK STOCKTON *1834–1902*
Frank Stockton's faculty for expressing the quaint turns of his amusing and eccentric mind won him a unique place among American humorists. His short story, "The Lady or the Tiger?" caused a sensation when it was first published, sparking debates throughout the country. It was produced as an operetta in 1888.   Page 87

JAMES THURBER *1894–1961*
A gifted cartoonist before he began to write, James Thurber won an international audience for his special brand of humour. Born in Columbus, Ohio, he attended Ohio State University, then began work as a newspaperman. Both "The Secret Life of Walter Mitty", one of his best-known stories, and *The Male Animal*, a stage hit of 1940 written with Elliott Nugent, were also successful films. There exist nearly a dozen collections of his essays and stories.   Page 303

ELIZABETH TAYLOR *1912–1975*
Elizabeth Taylor began writing at school, churning out countless novels, but she was thirty before anything was published. Her subject matter was almost invariably the English middle classes of whom she wrote with acute perception, coupled with an unusual blend of warmth and astringency.   Page 384

WILLIAM TREVOR *1928–*
William Trevor was born in County Cork, and educated at Trinity College, Dublin. After beginning his career as a sculptor he turned to writing, and is now a member of the Irish Academy of Letters. He has won several important literary prizes and many of his stories, adapted by the author himself, have been highly successful as plays on television. He is married, with two sons, and lives in Devon.   Page 117

H. G. WELLS *1866–1946*

Certainly one of the most prolific writers of modern times, H. G. Wells averaged a book a year for the better part of his lifetime. An honours graduate in science, he developed a reputation as a master of science fiction—*The War of the Worlds, The Shape of Things to Come* and *The Time Machine* are famous examples. He wrote other more realistic novels as well, and for many years no respectable bookcase could be without his encyclopædic *Outline of History*.   Page 24

EUDORA WELTY *1909–*

Most of Eudora Welty's writing has been in the short-story form, but she has also produced three well-received novels, *Delta Wedding; The Ponder Heart*, which was dramatized in 1957, and *Losing Battles*. She was born in Jackson, Mississippi, and educated at the University of Wisconsin. Her writings have been acclaimed for their penetrating evocation of life in her native South.   Page 94

ACKNOWLEDGMENTS

THE YOUNG MAN FROM KALGOORLIE from *The Stories of Flying Officer X*, copyright H. E. Bates, and is reprinted by permission of the estate of H. E. Bates. THE MAGIC SHOP by H. G. Wells, copyright Professor G. P. Wells, is reprinted by permission of Professor G. P. Wells. THE ROCKPILE, copyright © 1965 by James Baldwin, is from *Going to Meet the Man* by James Baldwin. Used by permission of The Dial Press and of the author. THE PIONEER HEP-CAT by John O'Hara, copyright *The Pioneer Hep-Cat* from *Short Story Assembly*, published by Cresset Press 1962, is reprinted by permission of Curtis Brown Ltd., London, on behalf of the estate of John O'Hara. Page 59, line 30: excerpt from "Poor Butterfly", copyright 1916 by Harms, Inc., copyright renewed, all rights reserved, is used by permission of Warner Bros. Music. WINTER NIGHT, copyright 1946 by Kay Boyle, copyright © 1957 by New Directions, is from *Thirty Stories* by Kay Boyle. First published in *The New Yorker*. Used by permission of New Directions Publishing Corporation. JELLICOE by R. S. Porteous, is from *Little Known of These Waters*, published by Dymock's Book Arcade Ltd., Sydney in 1945 and reprinted by permission of the author. THE KEY, copyright 1941, copyright © renewed 1969 by Eudora Welty, is from *A Curtain of Green and Other Stories* by Eudora Welty. Used by permission of Harcourt Brace Jovanovich, Inc., and of Russell & Volkening, Inc. THE ACCIDENT, copyright © 1967 by Mavis Gallant, originally in *The New Yorker*. Reprinted by permission of Georges Borchardt. O FAT WHITE WOMAN, © 1972 William Trevor, is from *The Ballroom of Romance*, published by The Bodley Head Ltd. THE SHORT HAPPY LIFE OF FRANCIS MACOMBER, copyright by Ernest Hemingway, is from *The First Forty-nine Stories* by Ernest Hemingway. Reprinted by permission of the Executors of the Hemingway Estate and Jonathan Cape Ltd. A MOTHER, first published in 1914 © 1967 by the estate of James Joyce, is from *Dubliners*. Reprinted by permission of the Executors of the James Joyce Estate and Jonathan Cape Ltd. THE HAUNTED BOY, copyright © 1955, 1957, 1963 by Carson McCullers, copyright © 1956, 1959, 1963, 1967, 1971 by Floria V. Lasky, Executrix of the estate of Carson McCullers, is from *The Mortgaged Heart* by Carson McCullers. First published in *Mademoiselle*. Used by permission of Houghton Mifflin Company and of The Lantz Office, Inc. THE MOST DANGEROUS GAME, copyright 1924 by Richard Connell, copyright renewed 1952 by Louise Fox Connell, is used by permission of Brandt & Brandt. A DAY IN THE COUNTRY, © 1973 by Dan Jacobson, is from *Inklings* by Dan Jacobson, and is reprinted by permission of the author. WINTER DREAMS, © F. Scott Fitzgerald, is from *The Bodley Head Scott Fitzgerald*. HOOK, copyright 1940, copyright © 1968 by Walter Van Tilburg Clark, is used by permission of International Creative Management. THE DESERT FLOWER by Olaf Ruhen, © 1964, 1967, was first published by *Squire Magazine* and is reprinted by permission of the author. THE REUNION by Margaret Drabble is reprinted by permission of A. D. Peters & Co.